I0822784

HOLY WATER HURTS

A VAMPIRE'S GUIDE TO VAMPIRE HUNTING

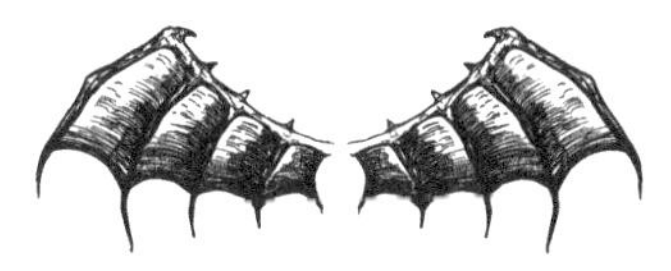

A NOVEL

BY

GABRYÉL GRIMM-GORETEZ

Holy Water Hurts: A Vampire's Guide to Vampire Hunting

A Novel by Gabryél Grimm-Goretez

With illustrations by Michael Batista and Gabryél Grimm-Goretez
Cover by Michael Batista
And formatting by Lorna Reid

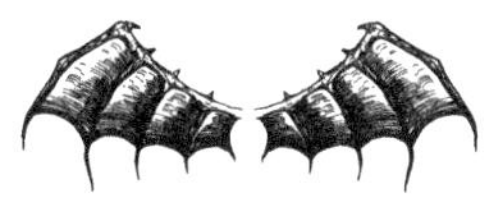

Synopsis

It's 2007, and in the rain-soaked streets of Seattle Washington, Parker is fighting for his life in more ways than one.

Not only is he a starving artist running away from a past that, like him, refuses to stay dead.

But after one bender too many, he now finds himself deep in the underworld of vampire hunting while also battling the same infection he's hell-bent on eradicating.

Parker's grapple with his agonizing reality of turning into the very monsters he hunts proves to be the most terrifying creature he's faced...

That is until a bloodthirsty tycoon promises to make Parker the latest pawn in their undead game.

But Parker -our emo, drug addled, vegan vampire- and his loyal, if not unconventional, chosen family refuses to be shaken.

Together, -a hippie engineering dropout, a second generation vampire researcher, a spunky second generation vampire hunter, and a "reformed" drug dealer- race against all odds to decipher the terms and conditions of this monstrous contract.

As the struggle intensifies, Parker and his friends work to help him reclaim his humanity while battling their own demons as well.

In this thrilling blend of horror, humor, and heartfelt moments Holy Water Hurts: A Vampire's Guide To Vampire Hunting delves deep into the battle of self-acceptance and the eternal struggle of right and wrong in a world where the line between vampire and vampire hunter is all too thin.

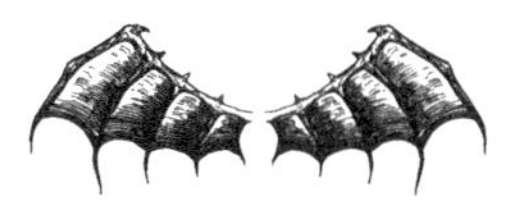

Acknowledgements

Gabryél would like to extend thanks to the following people.

To my incredible and sickeningly intelligent Mom and Dad; this book just wouldn't be the same, nor would it have phrases like "Ad nauseam" without you guys.

My sister, Jennifer; there is no one else in the world I'd rather argue ancient vampire lore with. (P.S. Thank you for threatening to fly to the US exclusively to kill me if I gave up on this manuscript.)

My brothers, Anthony; for always keeping me in comic books. And Michael; for having such a life-impacting emo phase.
And, to my new sister-in-law, Regan; welcome to our strange little Addams family.

My amazing tías, JC and Deon; whose undying support, quite frankly, terrifies me in the best way possible. I am beyond blessed to have you both in my life. Te amo.

Michael Batista and Lorna Reid; thank you so much for lending me your magic for this book.

The three precious souls my family has unfortunately lost before this book was finished; words cannot express how much I miss you, but I know our bond is eternal.

And last but most importantly, to all the misfits and outcasts that the rest of the world has written off, look at what kids like us can do. This one's for you.

Attention!

This is a work of fiction, but it does delve into serious subject matter.
This story includes the following trigger warnings.

- Depression and depictions of other mental illness
- Eating disorders
- Death
- Suicide and self-harm
- Drug and alcohol abuse
- Murder
- Domestic abuse
- Abandonment
- Prostitution
- Terminal illness
- LGBTQIA+ issues
- Depictions of religious extremes
- Depictions of xenophobia
- Outdated terms and language
- Harsh, adult language
- Gore, blood, and other horror themes

Reader discretion is advised.

If you or someone you know is struggling, and needs help please call or text 988 or go to **HelpGuide.org/**find-help to find the number of a crisis line for your specific needs and country in mind.

You are not alone, and you are worth the help.
Take care of yourself.
With love, Gabryél.

My name's Parker Winston and I've been dead for two years, six months, and twenty-seven days…

And *No, Nate!* I don't mean that in a faggy, emo way! Like yeah, I'm dead inside who isn't? But I'm dead on the outside, too.

It all started two years ago; after a rave, I barely remember going to, I passed out or something and some real creep decided to infect me there, and…

Okay, so I don't exactly remember the whole beginning, but hey long story short version; I got really sick after that, I died, but it didn't exactly *take.*

Longer story shorter, I'm a vampire. And unfortunately, I don't mean in the hot homoerotic *Interview With The Vampire* kind, it's more of a *28 Days Later* situation.

And yeah, I know how fucking stupid that sounds, well don't worry, because it gets *stupider… Stupidest? More stupid?*

Anyway, I also hunt vampires, and live with three other vampire hunters, and am currently being hunted by another vampire. Isn't that just… Poetic?

This is the story of how; Parker - *a junkie, artist, vampire.* Nate - *a former-ish drug dealer.* Courtney – *A second-generation hunter.* Aaron - *An engineering school hippie.* Conner - *A second-generation vampire researcher (he swears that's a real thing)* all had the worst fucking year of their lives.

Seattle, WA
September 1, 2007
15:06

PARKER

You come into this world alone, and maybe we're just destined to leave it the same way.

Cold, wet and slimy, terrified of what's next, and alone.

God, that sucks! Conner started us on another one of his "projects", but I can't ever think of shit to write. Okay, no the real problem is that I can't stop thinking of things to write down but then by the time it passes through my drug addled brain and I try and write it down it makes no sense.

There was a knock on the bedroom door, but it was more of a suggestion since Courtney had already poked her head through the crack, "Hey, stop jackin' off, Conner wants you."

"Tell him I'm busy." I groaned, scratching out my sentence with a pen.

She turned her head to look towards Conner's desk, which he could've just yelled at me from, but I figured Courtney was just in the mood to be annoying.

"He's still jacking off," She untangled a strand of her bottle blonde hair from the screw in the door frame.

Con answered, "God, I don't want that mental image, Court."

"Hey, you made me get him." She crossed her arms.

"No, I said 'Hey, let's wait for Parker', you took that upon yourself."

"Hey!" It was easier to just get up and join the conversation than it was to get Courtney to leave, "Come on! You made me write this shit and then you don't let me?" I tossed my notebook on his desk.

Conner squinted at my handwriting, "No, I told you to keep a journal. I genuinely have no idea what *this* is, is this a Linkin Park song?"

"Sorry, I didn't go to college!" I ripped it away from him.

"The most disturbing part is that you did."

"Clown college isn't the same." Nate shrugged from the couch.

"Art school!" I hissed but it turned into a whimper, "What do you guys want?! 'Cause it's already three and if I don't get a xanny nap soon I'm gonna lose it!"

Conner rolled his greenish eyes at me, "I got something, I figured you'd wanna take it."

"Ooh, you're finally gonna let me take *it*, huh?" I jokingly tucked my hair behind my ear, and hopped up onto the desk, "You wanna take it to me here on the desk? In front of everyone? God, that's so hot."

"What's the matter with you?" He smacked at me until I got off his desk, "You're perverted."

"Obviously! That's like saying Courtney's a bitch."

Court put her hand to her chest while her other hand waved at her imaginary tears, "Thank you! It's so nice to be recognized."

Conner and I have been friends since high school, and I've also been trying to hit it since high school, so he should know better than to give me anything I can make an innuendo out of.

I took the two steps from the "living room" to the kitchen of our two square inches of apartment. It was basically a closet with a bathroom and sometimes functioning heater, which I cranked until Con caught me.

"Oh, come on, it was 80° yesterday! You're going to boil us."

I crossed my arms, "Until then current reigning dead trumps! We'll talk about it when you bleed to death."

Courtney rolled her eyes while she pulled off the sweatshirt over her tank top, "Anyone with a comment will be de-nutted."

Con blushed, and his face was almost as red as his hair which was on the border of ginger and a traffic cone.

"Promise?" I cooed.

"I'll keep my comments to the bare minimum," Nate leaned back on the couch squinting his blue eyes at her, "Like God did with your tits."

She laughed, but still knocked him in the nuts anyway.

"Puta!"

"Yup!"

"I'm stealing this." I took her sweatshirt off the couch.

"Go nuts, it's Connie's anyway." She shrugged.

"Ooh, his shirts are so much better, right?"

"Can you guys stop stealing my stuff? Seriously, I haven't been able to find a single pair of socks for weeks." Conner asked.

"Nope!" Court chirped, opening our fridge to take out last night's pizza.

Aaron was super into whatever game he was playing on his ancient artifact of a Game Boy, so I took the chance to tug on one of his long curls when I walked behind him to the other side of the couch.

"Ah!" Courtney threw a balled-up napkin at me, "Apologize to my baby now!"

I stuck my tongue out at her and she nailed me in the back of the head with the TV remote before she gently played with Aaron's hair, "He's sorry."

Court has her favorites… I guess we all kinda do, Aaron's three years younger than us so we're all guilty of babying him, it really doesn't help his case that he's basically an overly-literate 12 year old hippie, and looks the part.

"So are you ever gonna tell me what you got?" I crossed my arms and shivered alone in the chair in the corner.

"I've got a couple of things." Con tapped on his keyboard.

"You got a favorite?"

He shrugged, "Near Cherry Creek, it's a little less open…"

"That's like an hour away." I crossed my arms.

"Yeah, but they've had at least three recorded disappearances in the last month. Aaron's estimating fifteen vamps."

I blew out a breath, "That's pretty good. Got a plan yet, or we just gonna wing it?"

Conner scoffed, "Yes, I have a five-point plan for how to lock up the apartment when we leave, but I figured we could just wing this." He glared at me, "I had a thought,"

"Hey, that's more than Park's ever had." Nate took the opportunity, as he grabbed a slice of pizza from Courtney.

Con leaned back in his swivel chair, "It's in the open on a trail so I can't get my car up there, and we can't use blood around you."

"*Oh, right, I almost forgot.*" I sassed.

Con just rolled his eyes, "We need a decoy; however many are up there it's been a few weeks since they've fed, they're hungry."

"Is this a good idea?" Aaron asked, playing with the stud in his lip.

Conner shrugged, "Maybe not, but we have to get them out of there somehow."

"What's the decoy plan?" Courtney asked, still chewing, "Sit in the grass and try to look juicy?"

"It's a part of a trail, someone could hike up it a bit, the rest of us wouldn't be too far behind."

I shrugged, "That works, I'll do it."

"Mm, that might not work." Conner scrunched his nose.

"What are they gonna do, kill me?"

"That's the point, we need live meat."

"Not it." Nate raised his hand.

"I'll do it." Aaron pushed his glasses up.

Court made a high-pitched squeak before she jumped in, "No, the fuck he will not!"

"Um," Conner wavered under Courtney's glare, "Maybe Court's right, maybe it would be better if I did it."

Aaron tilted his head slightly, completing his puppy dog look, "Why? It's not like I won't be armed, and you said you guys would be right there."

Courtney shot Conner another death glare.

Which Con just shrugged, "It's up to you if you're comfortable…"

"I am. I think?" Aaron squeaked back.

"Fine," Court crossed her arms, "But he's not going in alone."

September 2, 2007
02:35

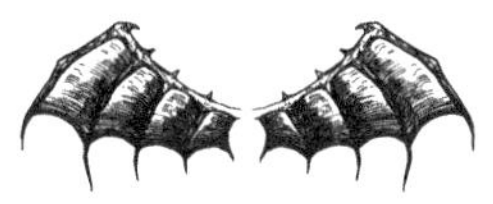

Parker

We waited until dark.

Conner gave us another rundown of our plan, smacking me on the side of my head while he gestured.

"You guys got all that?"

Nate shrugged, "Mas o menos."

"Sure," I added.

"Okay, *confidence inspired*. Let's go."

"Hang on, hang on!" Courtney put her hands out, "In case we don't make it,"

"Oh, my God…" Con mumbled.

"Okay! I say this with nothing but love, you guys are all a buncha fuck faces and I wish I never met you but like in a good way."

"Enlightening as always, thanks."

She blew us a kiss and started up the trail with Aaron.

When they got in their positions so did we.

When Nate went to ask Conner something, I took the chance to climb one of the millions of trees before I got yelled at.

"Great." Conner sighed when he realized I was gone, "Parker! We don't have time for this!"

"Pendejo!" Nate yelled.

It's kinda cute that he has pet names for us.

I looped my legs around a branch and hung upside down, so I was face to face with them, "Wassup?"

"You're going to get stuck," Con started to reprimand me.

"And I'm not gettin' you down again." Nate crossed his arms.

I rolled my eyes, "I'm fine! Besides I have a better advantage point."

"The advantage is being a dumb ass stuck in a tree."

"Hey!"

"Just get down here!" He swatted at me

"Jesus. Yes, Dad." I straightened out and jumped from the trunk, barely landing on my feet and splashed Conner's shoes with mud.

He glared at me, his glare was less intimidating since we were in the sun and his eyes didn't look like a Van Gogh painting, "That's the other thing, the next time you call me Dad or Daddy, you owe me twenty bucks."

"Ooh, prostitution, kinky."

"Get in position." He barked.

"Sir, yes sir." I winked at him and ran by at my top speed before he could yell at me again.

Then I hurled myself up the tree behind Aaron and Courtney.

We didn't have to wait long, a vamp sneaked up behind the tree. It got close before a bullet whizzed by, ripping through its chest with a loud crunch, the vampire disintegrated into ash instantly.

"Nice shot!" Courtney hollered to Conner as she got up and started to go after the few that were starting to trickle in.

I watched for a second as one got closer without seeing me.

The irony of what I do isn't lost on me, and I think about it a lot. Maybe it's some kind of masochistic way of killing the parts of me I don't like? I don't know, though, those were Conner's college educated words.

Other than the obvious and the infection we share, I find it hard to draw similarities between what I am and what we hunt.

The vampires we hunt are like rabid animals, they don't care about anything except their next meal.

They walk around like corpses, most of the time shriveled and bony, the illness decomposing their bodies with them still in it. The only sign of life was in their glowing yellow eyes. And I've never been able to wrap my head around how I could be the same thing.

I had to stop the thought before I spiraled too far away from me, besides I had a job to do.

I decided to target the bigger one of the vampires, he was about twice my size but his eyes were dull, and he had a gaping wound in his side down to bone the skin around it was turning purple, green and black.

I plunged my knife through his heart, it came back out with a squelch and splattered syrupy ash on my clothes.

I couldn't help but feel like I was doing him a favor.

There weren't many and we got through the hunt quickly.

"Okay! Five," Conner yelled once the area was cleared.

“Four!” “Three!” Aaron and Courtney responded as we shuffled into the middle of the field.

“420.” I answered.

“69.” Nate one-upped me, and we high fived.

Conner crossed his arms, “Can you guys ever take this seriously?”

“What?” I shrugged, “We said numbers…”

I trailed off, Conner said something, but I didn’t hear him.

The air around me filled with the scent of something metallic, which quickly turned to a sickly sweet scent like a cherry wine, then I was overwhelmed by the smell of meat and a ball of anxiety dropped in the pit of my stomach.

Blood, I was smelling blood.

“Parker?” Conner said my name, but his voice sounded far away.

My head quieted enough for me to at least think of something.

I fumbled for the flask in my pocket, it was filled with holy water, and I downed as much as I could handle.

“Parker!” All four of them yelled at me.

It felt like drinking boiling vodka. I could feel the searing all the way down to my stomach, but the pain was enough of a distraction for things to settle back to normal.

Conner grabbed the flask from me, “What the hell are you doing?!”

I coughed and soot splattered my hand, I wiped the rest off my mouth with my sleeve as I walked away, “Nate’s bleeding.” I mumbled on my way out.

(＼(•̀w•́)／)

03:01

CONNER

Parker left us standing there wondering who we should be more worried about.

"Are you bleeding?" I asked.

"No," Nate answered.

"Yeah!" Courtney wiped her hand over his bicep and held up her blood-covered fingers, "I'll get the kit."

I tossed her my keys.

I assessed the situation while we waited for her.

Luckily it was just a scratch this time.

I still wrapped it in gauze hoping that it would at least dilute the smell for Parker.

Nate glanced down at his bandaged arm; he gave me a weird look when he saw the band-aid holding together the gauze.

"Hello Kitty? Really?"

"They were fifty cents cheaper, and two thousand dollars cheaper than the ER."

"Fair." Nate readjusted his sleeve.

"Question," Aaron said as he tried to brush the ash out of his hair with his fingers, "Can we get coffee now?" Everyone was very clearly over this hunt.

(＼(•̀w•́)／)

A tired waitress led us to a table through the empty diner.

"Okay," I pulled out my notebook when we sat down.

Parker groaned, "No, not the hunt review!"

"Yes, the hunt debrief! Things must be organized, thoughts, plans, areas, everything."

Parker threw his head back and rolled his eyes.

I checked my watch, "It's 3:22 am September 2nd," I clicked my pen, "How do we feel?"

"Horny," Parker blurted out, being as helpful as always.

"Hungry," Nate added on.

Aaron nodded, "I second that."

"Triple," Courtney gestured with the straw she was chewing on, "Hungry and horny, thanks for asking."

"Fine, we'll do this later." I closed my notebook and nodded towards Parker, "How are you feeling?"

He shifted when he realized we were all looking at him, he tugged the sleeves on his hoodie over his hands, "Fine?"

"*Fine?*"

"Yeah, fine. What do you want me to say?"

I sighed, I already knew how this was going to go, and he wasn't going to be happy.

"You're hungry," I stated carefully.

He scoffed, "I'm not, I'm fine."

"Nate wasn't bleeding that much."

Parker shrugged, "I have a better sense of smell," he gestured to my notebook, "Your science."

"Parker, your eyes changed."

He went to say something, but he stayed quiet for a minute, "I know what you're going to say."

"And I know you're not going to like it, but it's been four months and you're getting sick."

"I'm not getting sick,"

"You passed out yesterday." I said, exasperation in my voice.

"I was drunk!"

I took a deep breath, "I know you don't like the idea of drinking blood," the waitress approaching our table with a coffee pot quickly turned around.

"Nice one." Courtney nudged me.

I sighed, "I understand, but you still need to eat. You're slowing down, you're not healing as fast, and now your eyes are changing. I'm not saying you have to bite someone. We have options."

"You could order a steak." Courtney offered.

"It's not that easy," Parker leaned against the table, his hand supporting his head, "I've been vegan since I was twelve! Any "option" is going to make me hurl. And besides! Who's to say I'll even stop with steak? How long is it until that's not enough and I'm outta control?"

"How long until you're so hungry you're completely out of control?"

He sat back in his side of the booth.

He didn't say anything.

"We're not going to let you do anything, you've never had a problem before."

"Because Courtney duct-taped me to a chair!"

Court played with the wrapper to her straw, "Ooh, and I'll do it again."

"I'm not going to let you starve yourself either, so just think about how you want to go about this."

Parker half smirked, "Is that a threat, Conner Stephens?"

"Wouldn't be the first, won't be the last."

He crossed his arms, "You're so bossy. It's hot. Tongue me now."

I rolled my eyes.

The waitress hovered a few tables away, making sure a normal conversation was happening before she approached, "Hi, what can I get you guys?"

"Uh, question about the double cheeseburger," Nate answered first, "How much meat is that?"

"About half a pound."

"It juicy?"

"I'd say."

"Perfect, lemme get that with bacon. And can it be rare? Like still bleeding when I bite into it rare?"

Parker shot him a look and tried his hardest not to gag.

"Um, sure..."

"And like whatever blood comes outta it on the grill, can you put it in a cup so I can dip my fries in it?"

That was it, Parker had to climb over Aaron and run to the bathroom.

Nate laughed handing the menu back to the girl, "I'm just kidding, gimme a tall stack."

"You're an ass." I reminded him.

He just shrugged.

September 2 2007

08:50

Parker

I don't wake up early, the only reason I'm ever awake before noon is 'cause I haven't been to bed yet.

But today I had a weird dream that kept me up, I can't remember it too well, it was hazy, and I hadn't really been asleep long enough for it to really come to any conclusion.

I was in the middle of the woods, alone, looking for something or maybe someone? I felt lost but I knew where I was, maybe it was because of whatever I was looking for?

Then I was in a library, on top of some guy, which isn't out the question for me, but I was holding a knife to his throat… All of it was far too scrambled to make any sense out of, plus I could feel a headache coming on when I tried to think about it.

I shuffled out of the bedroom and took a shower.

I stared down at the drain, watching as my black hair dye bled into the water.

I was trying to make sense of the dream, but with my drug-addled subconscious who knows what he hell is going on.

"Hey," I nodded to Conner, who was already showered, dressed, and working on his computer.

"Hey," he glanced up at me, he sounded surprised, "You're up early."

"Yeah, had a weird dream." I sat on the armrest of the couch, "Whatcha doin'?"

"Ah, you know, being unemployed." He joked but it fell kind of flat, "Looking for a job, looking for a hunt…"

"Got anything?"

"Mm, Blockbuster's hiring, but if I have to work another customer service job, I'm going to go postal. *Literally.*"

"No, I meant the hunt."

"Oh," he chuckled, "Yeah, right, sorry. I've got a few things to go over, Aaron and Nate have work so I figured we could restock our supplies."

"Cool, what happened to Court?"

He raised his eyebrows with an annoyed look, "Boyfriend's."

"Oh, sorry."

He gave me a weird look, "Why? What did you do?""

"No, I meant about her boyfriend, I know you don't like talking about him."

He shrugged, "Why would I care?"

I crossed my arms, "Seriously?"

"What?"

I laughed, "Dude, you've had a crush on her forever!"

He rolled his eyes, "I'm twenty-five years old, Parker, that's way too old to still be having crushes."

"I still have a crush on Jessica Rabbit!"

"That's because you're basically eight."

"Hey! I'm at least twelve!"

Conner rolled his eyes at me again, "Will you just go get ready?"

I stood up flaring my hands out, "So bossy!"

My back was turned but I knew he was flipping me off.

I went back to the bathroom to carry out my dumbass vampiric check list; three layers of sunscreen and long sleeves so my skin doesn't blister, the darkest pair of sunglasses I could find so my eyes didn't get French fried outta my head. And the smudgy eyeliner was a choice, but also a necessity.

Conner locked up the apartment on our way out.

"We're walking?" I whimpered.

"There's a church two blocks away, besides my car's making a weird noise."

"What's up with it now?"

"Well, if I knew anything about cars, my guess would be that it hates me."

"Fair." I pulled up my hood, "What do we need?"

"The usual, holy water, bullets. Aaron also asked for a few things, extra holy water, empty bottles, seltzer tablets, and this terrifies me the most, a water carbonator?"

I snorted, "What's he up to now?"

Con shrugged, "I try not to ask too many questions, us mere common folk wouldn't understand the answers anyway."

"Coming from the guy that puts the dick in valedictorian."

He rolled his eyes and walked ahead of me but I could hear a chuckle.

We got to the church, the smell of candle wax and polished wood took me back to the time I was in the sixth grade and my mother was begging an elder to "Have the devil release me from his grasp".

"You got it?" Conner got my attention.

"Please, I'm a professional sinner." I winked at him and went to talk to the priest.

It wasn't a total joke, I'd been disappointing my parents' church since I peed on the Bishop at my baby blessing.

"'Scuse me, uh, father?"

The older man turned to look at me, "How may I help you?"

"I was wondering if you were still doing confession?"

"Certainly." He gestured for me to follow him. I took the opportunity while his back was turned to stick my tongue out at Conner.

As I got in the booth the priest said a short prayer that I mumbled along to.

"Please, start whenever you're ready."

"Oof," I leaned back against the wood wall, "Where to start, uh, drugs, drugs, drugs, liquor, one-night stands with men and women, sometimes both, ooh sometimes at the same time. Uh,"

He didn't say anything, but you can always tell when you get a reaction.

"Oh, I stole my friend's weed and told him he smoked it already, I've done that a few times."

"… Well, the bible does speak of redemption and…"

There was a light tapping on the other side of the wall, my signal from Con.

"Yeah, I'm not much of a redemption kinda guy, I'm more a 'learn my lesson by passing out in gutters' guy."

It was quiet for a little bit.

"…Son, I'm not sure I know how to help you."

I may be a horrible person, but I honestly take pride in that. I spent too long being demonized by the church I grew up in to not find pleasure in it.

I shrugged, "Eh, what are you gonna do." I opened the door to the confessional, "Thanks anyway, father."

"Um, I must say we have a very nice "recovery" program here at the church. Let me get you a brochure." He left and I ran to Conner and grabbed him by the arm.

"Hurry up, we gotta go."

He awkwardly shoved the flasks in his pockets, "What did you do?"

"He's trying to get me in rehab, we gotta go!"

We burst out of the church doors without further incident and headed to the store.

Which was boring since Conner insisted on paying for everything we grabbed instead of just walking out, and then, like a fucking chump, made me empty out my pockets and apologize to the manager before we left.

"Now what?" I asked once we were half a block from the store, then unwrapped the candy bar they weren't able to take from me.

"Bu… Where did you get that? They patted you down!"

I shrugged, "They never check the underwear."

"I'm disgusted, but relieved to know you're wearing underwear for once and a little afraid to ask where you found some."

"They're yours." I held the candy bar in front of him, "Want some?"

He cringed, "God, no. Anyway, we need bullets."

I groaned, "Does that mean…"

"Yes," He cut me off, "And do me a favor, stay quiet this time, I don't feel like getting punched today."

"He called me a 'pill head, whore, poser, goth fuck, that had been stuck more times than a pin cushion'!" I whined.

Con hid his laugh, "I know, and just because it was true doesn't make it any better. Just be quiet, okay?"

I crossed my arms, "Air said he could melt silver! Why don't you just let him do it?"

"Because he said he *thought* he could melt silver, and I like living in an apartment building that isn't burned to the ground, besides where are we going to get silver?"

"I could rob my parents' house."

He rolled his eyes.

"Come on, they'll never expect it a fourth time!"

"You know what? I changed my mind, start being quiet now."

I glared at him.

We stopped at a nice shady alley, the kind you could take a nice heroin nap in. I was disappointed it wasn't for anything fun.

A tall guy was waiting for us, Chris. The only other hunter Conner knew and the only one that could get his hands on pure silver bullets for cheap, but he's a major dick. I gotta be honest, I'm kinda into it.

"Stephens, Wilson." He raised an eyebrow at us.

"Win." I corrected him.

"Huh?"

"Winston. Win."

"Oh," He looked me over with a chuckle, "Kinda ironic, right? Just, loser like you, y'know?"

Conner just pat my shoulder, "Sorry, but we've kinda got places to be."

"Uh-huh, sure, $100."

"Wait, last month it was $75."

"Alright alright, fine, I'll drop the price back down," he held the box over Con's head, "If, you set me up with your hot little blonde friend."

"Mm," Conner made a face, "You know, I think Aaron's seeing someone."

"Hilarious. I mean Courtney. The hot piece of ass, or $100."

Con grit his teeth, "Do you have twenty bucks?" He asked me.

"But that's my pill money," I whined.

He shot me a look.

I leaned over Conner to hand Chris the twenty, "Y'know… I'm free."

Conner smacked the back of my head.

We said our goodbyes and Conner kept me from climbing him.

We got back to the apartment and dumped the bags on the kitchen counter.

"Here," Con held out a plastic-wrapped Styrofoam meat tray from one of the bags, "This is yours."

"Nuh-uh,"

"We talked about this Parker; you *have* to eat something."

"… When did you get that?"

"When you were busy trying to stuff a PlayStation in your pants."

"It was an Xbox; I already have a PlayStation in my pants." I winked at him.

"You know what, for that you owe me." He slid the steak across the counter to me.

And it was a standoff.

"Parker," He sighed, "I'm worried about you, just do it for me."

I groaned and wiggled around so he knew I was throwing a fit, "Why do you always play that card?"

"Because the orphan card isn't going to help me right now."

I crossed my arms, "Fine, one condition, I'm getting blasted first."

Conner went to say something, but he stopped himself, "I don't need to know."

"… This feels like a trap."

"It's not a trap, if that's what it's going to take for you to take care of yourself, then I don't need to know about it."

"Fine."

Con's never been a fan of my drug habits, but honestly, at this point, it's just who I am so he deals with it.

I locked myself in the bathroom, took a handful of pills, and did whatever I had left over from the weekend.

The one good thing about being dead already, no more ODs.

(＼(•̀ω•́)／)

09:20

CONNER

Parker staggered out of our bathroom, barely catching himself on the kitchen counter, he was in there for a while, and I was starting to get worried.

"Are you okay?"

"Perfect." He wiped his nose on his sleeve, "Let's get this over with, I snorted like three sleeping pills, so I've got like five minutes before I'm gone."

I wasn't too happy with the situation, but if he wasn't going to argue with me, I wasn't going to complain.

I cut the cellophane on the steak and set it on his lap.

"God, the smell…" He trailed off.

It was an interesting thing to watch, the way everything about him faded when his eyes started to glow yellow.

If I had been a rational person, it would've been terrifying, but it didn't happen often and he wasn't anything like the vampires we hunted, they're animalistic, vicious. The only time I ever saw a slight glimpse of it was when he was hungry and even then, he fought it well.

There was no hesitation as he devoured the steak, the blood flowed down the tattoos on his arms which he licked up.

After a few seconds his eyes flashed to their usual dark brown.

"How do you feel?" I asked.

He leaned his head back against the couch, "… Goodnight."

"I'll take that as 'good'." I pat his knee and threw a blanket over him.

I sat back in my desk chair, at least I'd have a quiet few hours for once to get stuff done.

There's an alert program I had set up on my computer, it scans news reports on its own and saves any deaths that had been reported as "suspicious".

It might have taken me far too long to perfect it, but seeing as most of my process isn't exactly *legal*, everything had to be perfect and undetectable.

From there I would manually scan over what it flagged, if the incident didn't sound human related I would hack into the local police department's online records to determine if what I was looking at was suspicious in the vampire sense.

Which typically leads to some gruesome crime scene photos, but between doing this for nearly a decade and Parker's "art", it takes quite a bit to shake me.

It was fairly easy to determine if what I was looking at had anything to do with vampires, based on autopsy records, manner of death, that sort of thing.

The world isn't exactly privy to everything we had the pleasure of knowing, so I always get to read some outlandish theories as to the causes of death.

The latest being that there was a serial killer cannibal with the MO of ripping their victims' throat out, even though these deaths go back for decades, maybe centuries.

Or that there's a wild animal loose in the city theory, I hear that one a lot and it seems to be the one everyone comes back to once they see teeth marks.

There was nothing new as of this morning, nothing abnormal, I suppose. Living in a strange city like Seattle we were bound for a certain number of abnormal deaths.

(＼(•̀w•́)／)

PARKER

I dug around for my keys realizing I didn't have them so I knocked on the door of our apartment, hoping someone was home. The door swung open under my fist.

I took a step inside, the room was pitch black and my shoe sunk into the carpet making a squelching noise as I took another step and felt around for a light switch. I eventually found it and realized I was in the wrong apartment.

Everything quickly turned into a horror movie as I looked around.

There was blood everywhere, it was completely soaked into the carpet, smeared on the walls, and splattered on the ceiling.

It was like the time I got high and forgot to close my red paint, just way, way grosser.

Against the better judgment I don't have, I followed the bloody trail into the bathroom. I could smell the blood through the door, but it didn't stop me from opening it.

I wish it had, what was on the other side was far worse than the living room. A woman was in the bathtub, the water was red with her blood. Her head was back so I could see the massive hole where her throat should've been.

I know my heart doesn't beat but I felt like it was going a mile a minute, and my head was swimming in a weird way. I knew I was still in the room looking at her, but it almost felt like I was looking at her from farther away through a funhouse mirror.

Her eyes were open and bloodshot, her pupil completely dilated, the color of her eyes looked…red?

I could've sworn for a second she looked at me.

It wasn't until she opened her mouth and blood started pouring out that I realized she did.

She made a gurgling noise that will haunt me forever as she tried to say something but I was too freaked out to process anything else.

All I could do was scream "CONNER!!!!!!!"

September 3, 2007
10:40

Conner

I was minding my own business.

I had slept late so I was getting back to last night's work while Parker was still asleep on the couch, and Aaron was in the shower.

I took the time to make myself a cup of coffee and was just settling into my chair when Parker shot upright with a loud scream, gasping for air.

Needless to say, he startled me, and I flung coffee everywhere.

"Jesus! Why do you always do that?!" I frantically tried to dab the scolding coffee out of my keyboard, "God, you're like if Shelley Duvall was a cuckoo clock!"

Parker looked around as he calmed down, "Sorry," He rubbed the back of his head, "Just a dream, I guess."

"Are you okay?"

"Yeah, I think I'm just getting another migraine…"

Courtney flung open our front door, "Hey, do you know there's like a gaggle of cops downstairs?"

I looked over the top of my computer at her, "What? Why?"

"I just assumed they busted Parker and Nate," She shrugged, "I'm not trying to get got, too!"

"They didn't say anything?" I asked.

She shook her head, "No, they have the entire second floor taped off."

My curiosity outweighed my social anxiety, and I needed to know what was going on.

"Con, don't go down there," Parker followed me, "I can't go to jail again! I haven't been waxed."

I just rolled my eyes and tuned him out.

Courtney was right, there was caution tape starting at the second floor landing and maybe a dozen cops coming in and out of an apartment.

We caught the attention of one of the officers and she made her way over.

"Oh, we're fucked," Parker mumbled, "We're *fucked.*"

I tried to swat him behind me without drawing too much attention.

"Excuse me, do you live here?" The cop asked.

I nodded, "Yes ma'am, the fourth floor…"

"I don't," Courtney cut me off, "I live on the other side of the city."

"Yeah, me too." Parker piled on, "Like way, way over there."

I rolled my eyes and pretended I couldn't hear them, "Can I ask what's going on?"

"We were called about a possible death, can't say more than that. Do you happen to know anything about the people that live in 217?"

I shook my head trying to rack my brain, "Um, I've only ever seen a woman getting mail. She moved in about a year ago, I think. Other than that, nothing."

"Have you heard or seen anything unusual lately?"

"No. Was it a murder?"

"I can't say," She handed me a card, "Thank you, give us a call if you remember anything else."

We trekked back up the stairs

Parker was quiet, he was absentmindedly tracing a black fingernail over a scar on his forearm.

"Stop that," I swatted at his hand getting his attention, "What is it?"

He hesitated for a second, "What happened last night?"

I raised an eyebrow, "You know as much as I do."

"No! After…" He trailed off.

I quickly caught on, "No, Parker, don't even go there, you know you had nothing to do with this."

"How? I don't remember anything from last night."

"That's because you were high out of your mind and were asleep all night. Trust me, we don't even know how or who died or even that it was last night. So just hang on, okay?"

"That's so sad, someone died, in your building…" Court butted into our conversation shaking her head as the thought quickly left it, "Do you guys still have pizza?"

I ushered them back into the apartment, Aaron was out of the shower sitting at the counter tinkering with a few loose screws and a gadget, while Nate was rifling through the cupboards.

"Oh! Hi," Aaron slid off his headphones when he saw me, "Do you have a second?"

"Sure!" Courtney answered for me, "Whatcha workin' on?" She asked the question I was too afraid to ask, mostly because when he was tinkering with something a few weeks ago he short-circuited our VCR and caused a small fire.

"Hydro-projectile." He said, his voice in a higher register raised with excitement.

"Fancy, what's it do?"

"You know how you put a mento in a soda?"

"Uh-huh."

"The ultimate idea is a hand grenade type design with a mechanism and/or chemical rigged to release a steady stream of holy water in the surrounding area, but for now..." He dropped a seltzer tablet into the bottle of carbonated water.

The bottle burst, drenching everything, including the three of us.

Courtney got the brunt of it since Parker decided to use her as a human shield while Nate stayed dry by ducking behind the couch.

Aaron removed the wet strands of hair from his eyes, "It's a work in progress." He then gestured to the water dripping down the wall behind, "Would you say that's about twenty feet?"

I nodded as I used my shirt to dry my face, "I would."

"Cool!" He went to get some towels from the bathroom while I went to change and find something for Courtney to change into.

"High fashion." She joked, pulling her hair out of the gray shirt that said "Byre High School PE" on it and wiggled into a pair of my shorts, "We gotta get you a girlfriend, babe. Or at least a better wardrobe."

I shrugged, she wasn't wrong on either argument.

Aaron was occupied cleaning up his mess, I turned on the TV so the other three would be entertained while I did a few things.

Sometimes I swear I'm a glorified babysitter.

I pulled up some recent police reports hoping that there would be something about what was happening downstairs, but it took hours for anything to come up.

My guess was that it was going to be a long investigation for them.

There wasn't an autopsy yet, just investigator's notes which would be enough for my curiosity.

"I've got something." I had to speak loudly to get their attention.

"On?" Nate asked.

"The situation downstairs,"

"Mm," Nate took a drink from his can, "Toldja, there's a cream for that."

Courtney snorted.

"No! I meant with the cops."

"Cops?" His eyes widened, "Cops! You're telling me now? I've got hella shit in here, man!"

"Don't worry, Parker smoked and snorted it all first." Court joked.

Parker nodded.

I glanced over at Aaron to make sure he still had his headphones in knowing he wouldn't want to hear about it.

"Someone died downstairs,"

Parker sat up, "You have how?"

"Young woman," I scanned the report, "Mid-thirties, she was found..."

"In the bathtub." Parker interrupted me, his eyes wide.

"How did..." It was just going to be one of those days when I didn't get to finish my own thought.

"I had this gross dream last night," he shook his head, "I thought I was in our apartment, but I guess it was just in the building, there was blood everywhere, and this girl... She was just sitting in blood with this huge gash in her neck."

"Mm, this says her larynx was ripped out."

"Jesus," Courtney added.

"So, you were was high as fuck." Nate crossed his arms.

"Usually, my drug dreams are more Alice in Wonderland-y, not so much Nightmare on Elm street-y." Parker shrugged then he paused for a second and stood up, "I wanna go down there. I need to know how much adds, up this can't just be a coincidence!"

"That's hard to argue with, but they're not just going to let you into a crime scene." Court said flippantly.

"Eh, not my first time breaking into a crime scene."

"You're going to get arrested." I warned.

"Again, like it'll be the first time?" He tapped Aaron on the shoulder, "I need a favor."

I felt obligated to follow them, mostly because someone was going to have to get Parker out of trouble. Plus, someone was going to have to tell Aaron what he was getting into.

Courtney and Nate came too, either to see Parker get arrested or out of morbid curiosity. There are some questions I don't need answers to.

Unfortunately, Parker was right, the cops were gone but the second floor was still taped off.

"Um, what are we doing?" Aaron grew suspicious.

"Breaking into a crime scene," I answered before Parker could lie and he shot me a glare.

"What?" Aaron squeaked as his already huge eyes widened under his glasses.

"Not for real," Parker lied, "It sounds like a weird crime scene, vampy maybe. I just need you to pick the lock."

Aaron didn't trust it; I can't blame him. He just continued to stare at Parker.

So, Parker batted his eyes and said "Pretty, pretty please."

"We can just wait until the rest of the reports come in," I said.

"How long's that gonna take?" Parker asked.

"This isn't a good idea," I said instead of answering him.

"Yeah, and if I got paid for bad ideas, I'd have all the money in the world, I know. We need to get in there."

I hated to agree, but I wanted to know, too.

Aaron reluctantly picked the lock for us, as we continued to argue.

Once we were in, I used the sleeve of my sweater to turn on the light, "Don't touch any…" My voice trailed off as the horrific scene set in.

There was blood everywhere, it was hard to fathom that that much blood could be from one person.

Parker covered his nose and mouth with his shirt, he looked nauseous.

"Well, this is gross," Court stated, "What's the 'sitch?"

"Everything's exactly the same as… Hold on." He backed out of the room into the hallway.

"Are you okay?" Aaron asked.

"I'm fine," Parker staggered but stabilized himself enough to sit against the wall.

He let his head fall into his hands.

"Parker?"

He let out a groan before he slumped over.

We all scrambled to make sure he was okay, he came to a few seconds later.

"Are you okay?" I crouched down to his level; something was off but not enough that I could pinpoint it directly.

"I wanna go upstairs." He mumbled.

We gave him a second to get sorted out before Nate and I helped him back up the stairs.

"I'll ask the obvious question," Courtney handed him a glass of water, "What the fuck?"

"Mm," Parker ran his fingers through his hair like he was checking his head for an injury, "I don't know, I just got this really bad pain in my head."

I had to closely study his face before I was able to start closing in on what was odd.

"Can you hand me a flashlight? Second drawer on the left." I gestured to my desk.

Aaron was quick to hand it to me.

Parker flinched when I shined it in his eyes, "Ow."

"Sorry, just look at me."

His chestnut-colored eyes looked darker than usual; under the light I could see why. They were a deep cinnamon-red color.

"Air," I gestured Aaron over for a second opinion.

He took one look at Parker an quickly looked at me for confirmation.

"What?" Parker put his hand over the light, "You guys are freaking me out."

"Your eyes…"

"They're red..." Aaron finished.

(＼(•̀w•́)／)

17:43

Parker

I'd be lying if I said that didn't cause a major panic attack.

"What does that mean?!"

"It means sit your ass down!" Conner yelled over my freak out, "The last thing we need is you passing out and hurting yourself."

I crossed my arms and fell into the couch, "You don't gotta yell..."

He thought about hitting me, I could tell, "It's speculative, let me start there..."

"Spectacular how?"

"*Speculative.*"

"Just tell me what you mean!"

He sighed, "I've never seen it, but my parents had their theories." He got up and shuffled through a few dust-covered books on the bookcase in the small hallway between our bathroom and bedroom. "I've only heard of red eyes in terms with shifters."

"But shifters aren't real." Courtney interrupted, "They're just a hunter's urban legend."

"I agree, and so did my parents." He sat on the coffee table in front of me and flipped through an old journal.

Con's parents died when we were in high school, there were a lot of different opinions on how and why, but I knew them, and they were good people that shouldn't have died... They were hunters, too. Their life's work was studying the illness that caused vampirism.

Other than their work, Con didn't like to talk about them a whole lot anymore.

Conner continued, "But the rumors had to have come from somewhere, obviously the red eyes are possible."

"What do red eyes mean for shifters?" Courtney asked.

Conner scratched the back of his neck with a sigh, "None of this is scientific, and you have to understand that what I'm about to say is completely based on lore from the 19th century, got it?" He made sure I knew he was talking to me.

I nodded.

I was pretty sure I wouldn't understand it anyway.

"Marcheur de la mort," Sometimes I forget he speaks French, but it's hot every time, "Loosely translates to death walker. The red glow to their eyes was believed to be from a malevolent spirit or even the devil that would take over bodies after death. Marcheur de la mort could take over any dead body, I'm assuming that's where the "shifter" portion comes into play. In true vampire fashion, they have superior speed and strength, fed on blood, typically violent when unprovoked. However, in that time there was a lot of provoking..." He mumbled to himself while he thought, "As far as the eyes, they were typically an indication of power, the redder they were the more power they had."

"So, what does that mean for me? Are you saying I'm possessed?" I panicked, "Did that bitch possess me?"

"Calm down, nothing like that," Conner leaned back on his hands, "It's probably nothing. My best guess is that the red color is what they were noticing when their eyes were transitioning between whatever their natural color was and the yellow we're familiar with."

"Did my eyes turn yellow?"

"No, but you controlled yourself really well around all that blood, maybe this is just a weird middle color. You're in the middle, dead but human, your eyes are, too."

I picked the black nail polish off my nail, "I guess that makes sense."

"What about the passing out?" Courtney added, "You said he fed last night, shouldn't he be, oh y'know, not doing that?"

"That could've not been enough, or because it wasn't human...?" Con shrugged.

"You think it had anything to do with the blood?"

I shook my head, "It wasn't about the blood."

"What happened?"

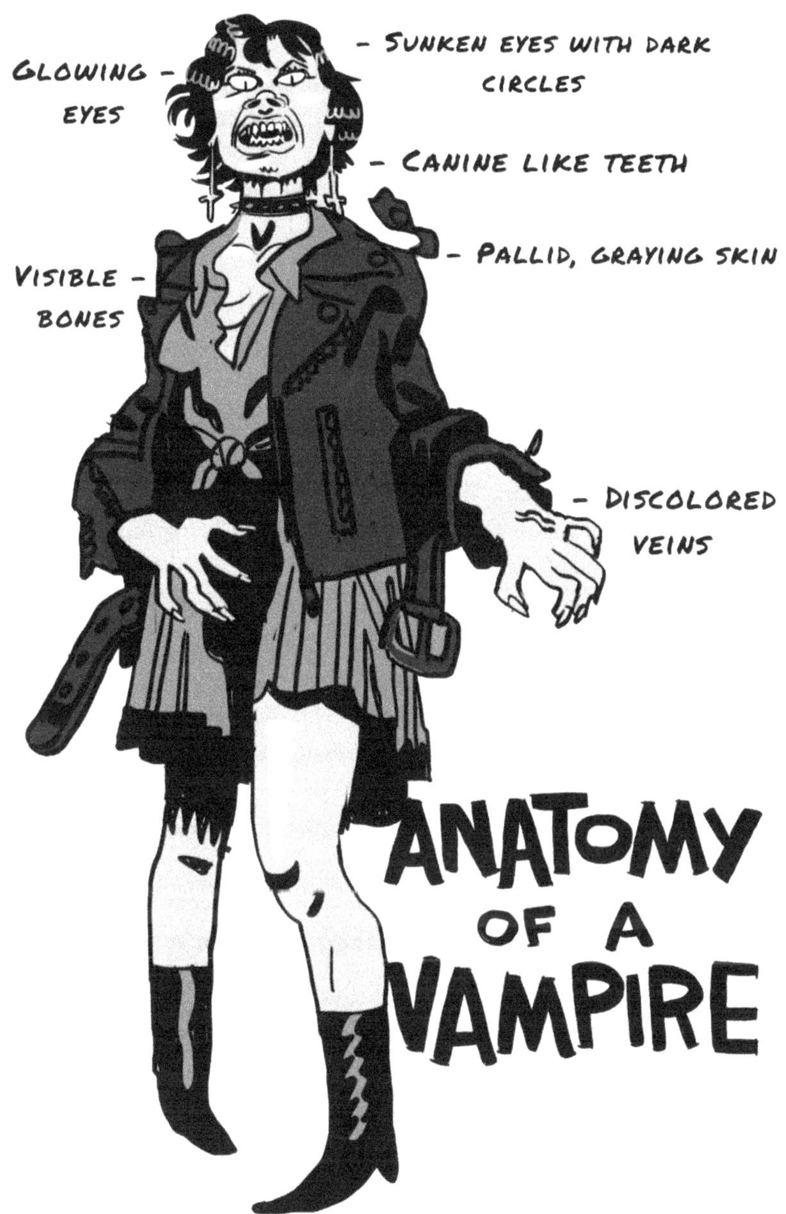

"I don't know, I got this really bad pain in my head, I didn't even know I left the room."

Aaron's ears perked up, "Wait, you said you had a dream, did you have a headache then?"

"… When I woke up, yeah, a little. I guess…"

"What are you thinking?" Conner looked over at Aaron.

Air made a face, "So you know how my grandma was a witch?"

That being the least odd thing he's said in the last three days, we nodded along.

"Um, I don't know how true this is either," he was sure to clarify, "But my grandma was really into the belief of telepathy, telekinesis, auras… And visions."

"Visions?" Courtney asked.

He nodded, his blond curls bounced against his shoulders, "Most of what she believed in could translate to the science of vampires, it could be a lesser-known vampire trick."

Conner nodded, "We can't rule out anything at this point."

"Y'know there's something similar in Spanish," Nate finally added something to the conversation, "Ser jodidamente loco."

Court got an idea and smacked my leg, excited, "Hang on! It's like the swirly eye thingy just red!"

"What?" I had to rub where she smacked, I don't think she knows how hard she hits.

"Can't vampires do like the "woo woo" thing?"

Conner raised his transparent eyebrows, "The woo woo thing?"

"Yeah, y'know how Dracula does this," she pulled her hands up to her face arching her wrists and wiggling her fingers, "The woo woo thing!"

"… I feel like you're mocking me…" Conner paused, "Do you mean like hypnosis?"

She rolled her eyes, "Forgive me if I don't know the technical term, college boy. I just mean he doesn't remember anything from when he was turned,"

"That's drugs, babe," I answered.

"Seriously, if someone gets changed the vampire's gotta do something, right? It's not like someone's just gonna let some rando bite and infect them!"

"Could be," Conner nodded, "Could be that, could be the venom having some effect…" He trailed off scratching at his orange hair, "I'm going to call my grandma tomorrow, maybe she'll be able to overnight some of my parents' books."

I was quiet for a minute, just trying to absorb the day.

Visions, infection, murder. *What even is my life?*

"Okay, well what about tonight?" she asked.

Conner shrugged, "There's not much else, I'll see what I can look up, but you know the internet."

"Okay, executive decision," She stood and pulled me up with her, "It's been a long, blood-soaked day, how 'bout Con lends us his blockbuster card and we'll get some beer."

"Sure, just no more porn."

"Don't be such a baby." She took the card from him and shooed me out the door.

I guess she sensed my head space, but she waited until we were down the stairs, "You talk to Con?"

"Huh?"

"Something's bothering you, just wanna know if you've talked to "dad" about it before I mother you."

I scoffed, "My life would be way less fucked up if you were my mom. Weird, but less fucked up."

She nudged me, "What's goin' on, babe?"

"Does any of this make sense to you?"

"Maybe I'm just too stupid to understand anything Con's saying," I shrugged, "I don't get it. Visions, infectious disease, super strength and speed. I'm dead but I'm conscious. All of this sounds like a bad superhero! It's been two years, when is this shit gonna start making sense?"

"My guess is when this silly little planet gets flung into the sun."

"What?"

"Park, nothing in this world makes sense. It's dirty, it's gritty and it's fucked up. It doesn't make sense for anyone, if it did I would've grown up in Germany and you would be Mormon.

But it doesn't and there's no normal. We may never get the answers we want, you may never know why you're a human vamp and I may never know why my adoptive dad ran off with the first bimbo he saw! It's not about any of that, life is like a jigsaw puzzle, okay? Except instead of just one picture, your little sister mixed up the pieces of three different puzzles and put them all in one box. Does the kitten's face make sense with the dinosaur body? No, but it's about what you make with the pieces you're given.

Luckily you know some people," she pointed at herself and jokingly winked, "That are pretty damn good at puzzles, so just hang on, okay? It'll start coming together, it won't be the picture you want but it'll be beautiful! And probably more understandable."

I stopped in my tracks, "How do you come up with this shit?"

"You get creative when you get kicked outta your country as a baby." She joked.

"You were adopted, that's not being kicked out."

"I disagree!"

We walked for a while the only noise was the crunch of the prematurely fallen leaves under our feet.

Courtney spoke after a while, "Do you remember the first thing you asked me to do?"

"... I asked you to kill me." I mumbled.

She nodded, "Do you remember what I said?"

She didn't give me time to answer, "You have a bright spark, Parker. You have a real reason for being here, we all do, just because you don't know what it is yet isn't a reason to give up. We were all put here for a reason."

It was hard to think of something to say to that, "What's yours?"

"To make Conner's life a living hell, duh." She laughed and opened the door to the video shop for me, "We'll figure it out. Don't fret." She clapped her hand against my back, "Now let's go get some porn!"

September 4 2007
15:50

Conner

After our hundredth viewing of Silence of The Lambs last night we all ended up asleep on the couch.

I woke up early this morning, did my usual routine, and checked for updates on the murder case to no avail. But I had a couple of hunts lying around so Aaron helped me look over them.

While Parker hovered over us.

"What are you guys looking at?" Parker leaned against my back.

I scooted him over, "A place in Bellevue,"

"Any good?"

Aaron shrugged, shuffling the papers around the kitchen counter, "Guesstimating twenty, twenty-five."

"That's it?" Parker crossed his arms, I knew he didn't mean to be that flippant, so I let it go, "I thought we were going bigger."

"We will, we have to work with what's around first."

"But how are we going to get anything from small stuff?"

"We're still observing and it's still a hunt..."

"But we should be going after nests! Getting answers!" He demanded, slamming his fist into his other palm for dramatic effect.

I rolled my eyes, "Be patient."

"I don't know how to do that!" He pouted until I had to shoo him out of the kitchen so Aaron and I could finish what we were doing.

By the time Nate was back from work and we got ahold of Courtney, we were ready.

(＼(•̀w•́)／)

22:00

Conner

"How much longer?" Parker bothered me from the back seat of my car.

I sighed, "It's a sixteen-minute drive, Parker."

"So?"

I would've rolled my eyes, but I was driving, "Three minutes."

Courtney let out a laugh.

"Please don't encourage him."

I was able to drive all the way up against the tree line which would make it easier for us to draw out our targets with the alarm, luckily, we were pretty far out of the way so the noise wouldn't be a problem.

The only problem would be what would happen to my car this time, it didn't help that it was ten years younger than me and hanging on by a thread.

"Don't!" I stopped Courtney once we got out, "Don't slam the door."

She gave me a weird look as she closed the car door softly, "No offense, but why does it matter?"

"Because if you slam the door, it starts knocking."

"What's knocking?" Nate asked.

"I don't know,"

"It's probably your engine," Court said as she tied up her hair, "Probably a combustion issue."

"... I have no idea what any of that means."

She sighed, "You're a waste of testosterone,"

I scoffed, "I could've told you that."

She shook her head, "I'll take a look at it later. C'mon."

I chuckled to myself.

"You... Brought an axe?" Parker asked Aaron, quickly derailing everything else.

Aaron shrugged, "I wanted to test its practicality."

"But it's not silver," Parker ran his finger over the blade.

"I'm pretty sure there isn't anything on earth that can survive its head being chopped off." I chimed in, before moving them along.

We did a quick scout of the area and decided on our standings, we were spaced out a few hundred feet but close enough to still see each other.

I hit the alarm button on my key fob.

There wasn't a wait, the vampires were extremely responsive to the sound since they were further from the city.

There were a few and they were coming in waves.

These ones were plumper and faster than our last hunt, clearly well-fed.

More and more vamps started filtering through the trees until it seemed like there was a steady stream.

I wasn't worried though, this was common, especially in more desolate places.

Courtney got our attention and offered an idea through a hand gesture, Circle. It would mean splitting up be we could cover more ground; I didn't like the idea but since there were more than we were expecting it wasn't a bad idea.

I reluctantly nodded.

Parker was ecstatic about the idea and let his hyperactivity take over, he was already covering a large base with just his knife before the four of us could even move.

There was a hill in front of me, I thought it would be a good vantage point but on the other side had a steep drop into the trees.

I decided to try to quietly walk down the slope, and in true Conner fashion my foot slid out from under me. I slid all the way down through every twig and bush on my way down, making as much noise as possible.

By the time I was down, I had already had a vampire on me, we were face to face, their eyes glowing yellow as their fangs distended. I couldn't reach my gun; all I could do was try to get it off me and that wasn't going well...

Suddenly and loudly a gun went off, splattering the strange liquid across my face and covering the rest of me in dust.

I wasn't expecting the person on the other side of the gun.

Chris was towering over me, his hand extended out towards me.

My ears were ringing, and I didn't know what he was saying but I was guessing he was offering to help me up.

I shook my head as I dusted myself off.

I tried not be bitter or hold a grudge, but this guy just rubbed me the wrong way and it didn't seem like he was overly fond of me either.

The ringing in my ears slowly started to dissipate enough that I was able to hear Courtney yell "Five!" from the top of the hill.

I sighed when I realized Chris was coming with me.

KICK!
BLAM
BLAM

Aaron

"Four," I approached our home base where Courtney was waiting.

"Hey," she gestured for my axe, which she examined closely, "This was a fuckin' kickass idea, kiddo."

I smiled at her, "Thank you!"

She high fived me and kissed my cheek.

I pulled myself up onto the hood of Conner's car while we waited.

"'Sup," Nate made his way over followed by Parker who was running a little too fast and had to use a tree to stop himself.

"Two!" He slammed into the tree, knocking off some leaves as a bird crowed and flew away.

"Where's Con..." Courtney's eyes landed on something, and she rolled her eyes, "Oh, great."

"One," Conner answered walking up the hill, he sounded peeved but it wasn't until I looked over that I understood why.

"Well, if it isn't God's gift to women." Courtney's tone changed drastically to one I was grateful to have never been on the other side of.

"And if it isn't the hottest piece of ass on this side of the Pacific." Chris responded in a way that pissed us all off.

"Classy," she crossed her arms, "Though, I'd expect nothing less from a douche bag like you."

"Hey, nothing wrong with a good douche." Parker tried to joke... I think.

"Wow, come on, babe, take a compliment." Chris missed the point and arrogantly put his arm around Courtney's shoulders, "Though, I wouldn't mind banging that bad attitude outta you."

The four of us all jumped to interject but she put her hand up to stop us.

"Not your "babe", asshat," she dug her elbow into his ribs as she shoved him away, "And it's gonna take more than two inches to change this attitude. Next time you put your hands on me I'll shoot your nut sack off."

"Goddamn, what's with you guys and the hostility? I haven't even done anything." Chris responded.

Conner was mad, genuinely, "What are you doing here?"

"Apparently saving your ass, you're welcome by the way. Other than that, you took my hunt, thought I'd let it slide when I saw you brought the whore."

Nate wasn't having any more of it, "Say one more word, puta."

"What are you gonna do about it, spic?" Chris bowed up.

Conner got between them before anything transpired, "Okay, thanks for whatever you were helping with. Hunt's over, let's just all go home."

Parker was glaring at him, Chris took the opportunity to get two more hits in, "Got something to say, fag? What about *her?*" He said pointedly at Parker and me.

Courtney feigned a laugh, she took a step forward a slugged him across the jaw hard enough to make him stumble back, "Hilarious, say it again, wont'cha?"

"You're a fucking bitch!"

"And don't you forget it."

He finally walked away and we finished packing.

Courtney rubbed my arm, "I'm sorry, baby. You okay?"

I nodded.

"Uh AHEM!" Parker cleared his throat, "He called me a fag!"

Court shrugged, "You are what you eat." she joked.

"WOW! Wow ... Just *wow.*" Parker tried to hide his laugh.

We dropped Courtney off at her apartment and headed home, there were some boxes in front of our door that Conner seemed excited about.

"Are those more of your parents' books?" I asked.

Conner nodded, "I asked my grandma to send their journals and other unpublished stuff. I'm hoping we'll be able to find, well, anything. I'll start going through them tomorrow."

Something fell out of the box as he picked it up.

I grabbed it, "Can I help?"

"If you're willing, that would be awesome." He nodded, smiling.

I handed him the piece of paper from the floor, he gave it a weird look.

It was a business card with a little top hat printed on it, there was something written on it but it was old, torn and stained while the writing was completely faded.

"What is it?" I asked.

"No idea," He tried to squint at it, "My dad had a habit of writing on anything, probably just a note." He put it back in the box and we didn't worry about it.

September 5 2007

12:30

Conner

Aaron and I were up early trying to make sense of my parents' very specific and very different organization methods before we were able to start researching their...well, research.

We tried to condense what we were working on to the coffee table, but it managed to overflow to the kitchen counter.

"Nate! I swear to God if you spill anything!" I threatened as he rummaged through the kitchen.

"Jesus, fine." He just grabbed a pop-tart and a twenty from my wallet by the keys, on his way out.

Parker woke up later, "Whoa," He looked around at everything, "This must be what your guys' brains look like."

He stopped, picking something from the pile on the counter, "What is this?" He held up the business card Aaron had found last night, "What is THIS!?!"

I shrugged, "It was in with my dad's stuff. Why? Does it mean something to you?" I tried to stay calm as I asked.

He took it and stared at it for a few seconds, "... It was in my pocket..."

Aaron looked confused, "No, it was in the box over there."

"No, that night it was..." He seemed dazed.

Aaron looked at me as if I knew what that meant.

"What?" I asked puzzled.

Parker shook his head, "After I got roofied and turned," He thought he clarified, "When I woke up this was in my one of my pockets..."

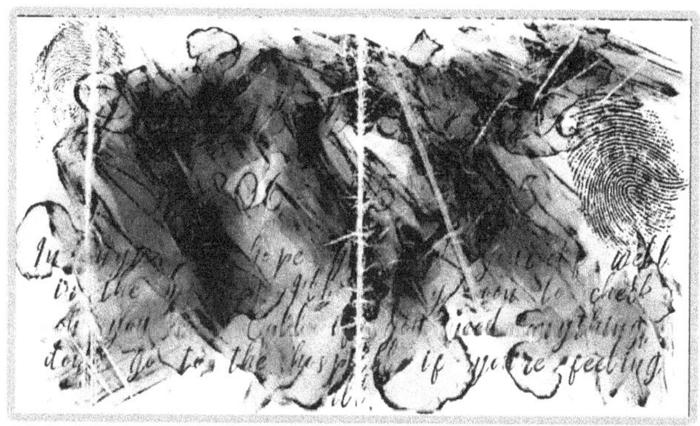

"You never said you found anything!" I exclaimed, losing my patience.

"I didn't think about it! I was fucked up and figured I took it to chop up coke or something, I just threw it away."

I quickly took it from him before he could corrode any more evidence on it with his dirty hands, "What do you remember about it?"

"I think I put my gum in it."

I rolled my eyes at him.

"No! Written! A name, a phone number, anything?"

He shrugged, "There was a number or address or something on it."

I would've choked him, but I didn't have the time or energy to deal with all the issues that would make him like that.

"What do you mean by that?" I had to physically put my hands behind my back.

He pointed out the unintelligible blob of washed-out ink, "There was writing on it, I don't remember what."

I pushed him onto the couch by his shoulders, "Try!"

As he plopped down on the couch, Courtney slammed the door open, "Guys! You're never going to believe this!" I couldn't read the look on her face, shock, fear, relief?

"Wh..." I started.

"Chris is dead!"

"What?" I didn't believe her.

She shook her blonde hair out, "It happened last night, he got stabbed!"

"How do you know this?" I asked.

"His sister called me,"

"Why would his sister call you?" Aaron asked.

Courtney rolled her eyes, "I did her once, not important. She said that they think he got mugged. Serves him right." She scoffed.

"Courtney!" Aaron gasped.

"... Which part?"

I tried to redirect the conversation, "That's kind of "coincidental","

"Yeah, it's called karma! Wouldn't be surprised if it was another chick he was harassing." She got up to get a soda.

"Or Nate," Parker added, "Those to go at it like they're fucking."

Courtney snickered.

"Guys," Aaron said softly, "Somebody still lost their life."

Court sighed, "You're right, babes. We should be nicer." She ran her hands through his hair so she could cover his ears, "We can party later."

Aaron gave her a disappointed look.

Parker went to open his mouth again.

"Hey," I stopped that immediately, "Say something helpful or stop talking."

"You want him to never talk again?" She joked.

"Ideally," I handed her the card hoping she would be able to see something we didn't, "He forgot he had a clue."

"Forgot *and* threw it away," He added, "How the hell did it end up with your shit? That was a long ass time ago."

"Good question."

Courtney handed it back with a shrug, "You know where you got it from?"

"It was in my pocket the next day... Whoever turned me, must be theirs? Or important to them at least?"

I was caught between a sarcastic remark, an eye roll, or pummeling him. So I opted to hit him with the book in my hands, as I rolled my eyes.

Realizing we weren't going to get anywhere with him or the card, we turned our attention back to the journals.

I spent the rest of the day reading nonstop.

Aaron and Courtney took breaks, but I couldn't bring myself to, because I knew I wouldn't be able to stop feeling and thinking. Being surrounded by my parents stuff was harder than I thought it would be.

It's a strange bittersweet feeling reading my parents' journals.

It's not like I've never read anything, both of them were published authors.

I have every single one of their books, but their personal journals were a very different experience.

I hadn't wanted to read them since they died but I couldn't put it off anymore. Helping Parker seemed like a great way to continue their work.

"Hey, look what I found!" Courtney got everyone's attention; she held up the book turned to a page in the middle. There was a polaroid taped to the paper, it was a picture of me as a baby, swaddled tightly in a blue blanket and nestled close in my mother's arms.

"You were so bald!" She squeaked.

I took it from her and stared at it for a minute.

I was sixteen when my parents died, it'll have been a decade next year. That sounds like a long time and sometimes it really feels like it, but I still remember everything about them from the warmth of my mom's hugs to the scent of my dad's cologne. I don't talk about them much, it's too hard to think about, but I'd like to think if they were still here, they would be proud that I took over for them.

In all honesty, hunting is the truest way I feel connected to them.

"The journal's dated '82," Courtney stated, "That's your birth year, right?"

I nodded.

"God, you guys are babies!"

"You were born in '79." Parker piped up.

"Yeah, that was before '82!"

"I was born in 1985." Aaron added.

Courtney's eyes widened, "Stop, I can feel gray hair growing!"

I chuckled to myself to keep my eyes from welling up.

September 5 2007
03:21

PARKER

I tried to help Conner sort through some of the books he had but after I said his mom was hot, I was called "Unhelpful" and "Disgusting" therefore I was banished.

I laid on the bed for a while weighing my options; I could read the book on the nightstand about quantum physics that Aaron left there, gross.

I could go back into the living room and risk getting yelled at by the tiny angry ginger again. Or I could climb down the fire escape and find some kind of trouble to get into.

The fire escape was definitely the funnest option.

I changed out of my pajamas into a more appropriate streetwalker outfit. Meaning short shorts and a black glitter tank top that'd only get covered by my hoodie but at least I'd look hot if I found somewhere warm.

Wandering around our neighborhood for a while I decided to head downtown to see if anything was still open. When nothing was, I cut my losses and headed back home.

I took my time, there was something weirdly calming about walking around a sleeping city.

I saw a few cars closer to the highway but other than that I hadn't seen another person, not until I got a little closer to the apartment.

A woman was walking through the alley I usually took a shortcut through.

I don't know why I followed her, but I got the feeling that I should.

I stayed a few feet behind her staying as quiet as I could. She was wearing a long black coat with her hair flowing down her back, the streetlight illuminated her face for a split second before she stepped into the building.

I slipped through the door before it closed and watched what apartment she went into. Then I slid through that door too.

She turned around, sensing something off.

She jumped when she saw me.

I was quick to cover her mouth before she could scream.

"My apologies, but I have to send a message...May God have mercy on my soul."

Before I could do anything else she headbutted me, I stumbled back and fell to the floor.

"Parker?!" Conner hollered.

I felt carpet under my hands, when I opened my eyes I was surprised to be back in our bedroom, on the floor next to the bed.

"Parker?! You okay?!"

I scrambled out of the bedroom in a panic.

Court gave me a weird look, "Should we ask?"

"I think I killed someone." I blurted.

Con was already over my drama, so he just rolled his eyes, "In your sleep? You've been asleep for twenty minutes."

"No! I..." The sleeve of my shirt caught my attention, I was still in my pajamas... I snapped around to look at the clock on the stove, 3:40.

"... I was asleep?"

"Dude, y'know how you sleep," Nate answered, "Thought you were dead."

I ran my hands through my hair.

"You okay?" Courtney offered.

"I-I guess... Must've just been a dream..."

"What happened?" Aaron put down his book.

"I dunno, I saw that girl..."

Conner turned his attention, "You had another vision?"

I shook my head, "No, no, it...no."

"How are you so sure?" Aaron asked.

"Because that's not normal!" I snapped, I let out an exasperated laugh, "Oh man, I'm going fucking nuts. It's happening."

"Calm down," Con said.

"When has that ever worked for me?!" I yelled.

"When have you ever calmed down?" Nate responded, raising an eyebrow.

"Just sit down," Conner demanded.

I didn't want to; I wanted to keep freaking out but Con wasn't asking.

I sat next to Aaron.

"Freak out if you want, but this is still happening. Also, would you mind telling us what the hell is going on?"

I went to explain my "dream" but before I could even open my mouth there was a knock on the door.

Nate just looked at us all like he was counting in his head, "Who the fuck's that?"

"Probably another noise complaint." Conner sighed as he got up to get it.

There wasn't anyone on the other side of the door, but Conner brought in a vase full of yellow flowers.

"Are those for the neighbor?" Aaron asked.

Conner raised an eyebrow as he scanned the message, "No, they're for us." He handed me the card, it was identical to the one that was in my pocket when I was turned, just newer.

On the back, handwritten was, "Sorry for your loss".

"What. The. Fuck."

(＼(•̀ᴡ•́)／)

03:45

CONNER

"Great, great!" Parker paced in front of the counter, "Visions, cards, and now tulips! This makes sense!"

"They daffodils, dumbass." Courtney corrected him, "My mom used to grow them in our garden in Jersey, she said they're supposed to symbolize rebirth or renewal. Some shit like that." She laughed, "When my sister, Drew, was little she used to call them 'daffodildos'."

Nate snorted.

"... Rebirth?" I asked in an attempt to get the conversation back on track.

Courtney shrugged.

"What does that mean?!" Parker yelled.

Aaron and I exchanged a look.

"Do you want to tell him our theory?" I asked Aaron.

"That's okay, you can do it." Aaron smiled sheepishly.

Parker crossed his arms, "What?"

"We found something that might make sense," I said.

"Uh-huh." Parker nodded while he rotated his hand, indicating I should go on.

"You know how we think vampires have a different way of communicating?" I was careful as I slowly peeled off this bandage, "We have reason to believe vampires share a telepathic connection with the vampire that sired them."

"Are you saying someone's reading my mind? Yeah, that won't send me back to the nut house!" Parker rolled his eyes.

"No, not that kind of telepathy, you know how you can forward an email?" I tried to explain it in Parker terms.

"What the fuck are you saying?" Parker asked, getting annoyed.

Guess I missed the mark. I sighed, trying to think of a relatable way to explain this.

"Think of it like someone writing an email, they decide what it says, you're just receiving it. That would be along the same lines as your "vision".

Aaron stepped in, "And think of the red eyes like the transmitting light on a tower."

Parker shook his head, flinging his black hair into his eyes, "He wants me to see this dead chick, why? What kind of sick message is he trying to send?" He scoffed, "Seriously, like we're not looking for his stupid ass? Why not just say something?"

"It doesn't sound like it would be quite that straightforward. My mom describes it as a more involved process. I'm guessing that's why he would send flowers. It would be an easier way of communicating."

"It would explain your headaches," Aaron added.

"Wait," Courtney crossed her arms, "Why are you so sure it's a 'he'?"

"Court, he's a murderer," I said at the end of my rope.

"So? Women can be murderers, too!" She said exasperated.

"I wasn't saying that, but is that really the hill you want to die on?"

"Most definitely." She smiled evilly.

"Hey, hello!" Parker snapped, "What are we supposed to do now?!"

He wasn't going to like my answer, "We have to wait for him."

Parker screamed into the couch cushion, he took his annoyance out on the cushion, "Fine! Find us some hunts."

I sighed and sat back in my desk chair, "On it."

He stomped out the front door and slammed it hard enough that it made the window to my right rattle.

Aaron hovered over the desk and slid a blue folder in front of me, "I had plans for this place on Sicklemore," he thumbed through the papers and maps and took a pen, "I'm estimating forty-ish, just give me twenty minutes I'll get it down for you to review."

"Don't worry about it,"

He gave me a blank look, his head tilted slightly, "Hmm?"

"It's not a good idea for Parker to be hunting right now, he's..."

"About to snap?" Court offered.

"Gonna jump off a bridge?" Nate added.

"*Distracted.*" I gave them both a look. "We have other things to focus on anyway," I gestured to the massive collection of my parents' work that was taking up our kitchen space, "I'm just going to tell him there isn't anything."

Aaron made a face. He's a self-proclaimed lousy liar, he doesn't even have to be the one telling a lie to give it away.

"It's fine, he won't ask."

He shrugged his narrow shoulders and put the folder back on my desk, Nate stood as Aaron returned to the books.

Nate did a weird stretch as he got up and grabbed something off the coffee table, "Imma go see if Park jumped off the roof yet."

Court raised an eyebrow, "You care?"

"Eh, I want to smoke a blunt, and Con gets weird when I say that."

(＼(•̀w•́)／)

04:13

Nate

Parker was lying flat on his back staring into the dark sky making a weird-ass noise from his throat.

"What the fuck are you doing?"

He pointed to the powerline above the roof, "Talking to the bird... I wish I were a bird."

"... Pretty sure that's a Safeway bag."

He groaned, "Ugh, I'm already a piece of trash!"

"Get up." I kicked him in the ribs with the toe of my shoe.

"Ow!"

"Shut up." I tossed an Altoids tin on his chest, that got him up.

"Oh, yay."

I sat against the barrier and lit my own blunt.

It was quiet for a good twelve seconds before Park had to open his mouth again.

"Do you think I'm nuts?"

"Yup," I blew out some smoke.

"I'm serious!" He whined, "Can I tell you something?"

"Say whatever, I'm not listening."

"I feel like a whore,"

"You are."

"You said you weren't listening!"

"Whatever."

"For real, though. The hits just keep coming, you know? I'm a tired whore!" He declared loudly, "I'm tired and I'm cold and my jaw hurts!"

"You remind me of my brother sometimes,"

"Huh?"

"My little brother, he's a little fucking bitch like you."

"God, thanks." He slumped down to lay back on the roof, "... Maybe my mom was right, my coat's just not cut for this."

"... That some kinda Mormon thing?"

"No," he tangled his fingers in his hair, "When I was a little kid I ran away from home one time and my mom said she knew I'd be back because my coat wasn't thick enough. She said the same thing when I moved out... That was her way of saying I couldn't make it, and she was right."

"Oh, shut up."

"She was! Not even two years later I was back..." He took a long drag off the blunt before he let the smoke pour out of his mouth, "I want to go home, I want to go wherever I can go where I don't have to deal with this, any of it. I want to go where I can lay down and take a nap and not have to worry about where I'm going to get twenty dollars. That's all I've ever wanted since I was twelve, but that place just doesn't exist for me."

"Stop bitching," I rolled my eyes, "Con lets you live with us rent-free; I keep you in free weed and pills, and Air gives you free cheesecake. So, one chick died, people die. So, you hear voices, we all assumed you did anyway. Get it over it 'cause you have that shit."

"... Yeah, I guess... Do you have twenty bucks?"

"If I did you wouldn't get it."

He chuckled.

September 7 2007

21:00

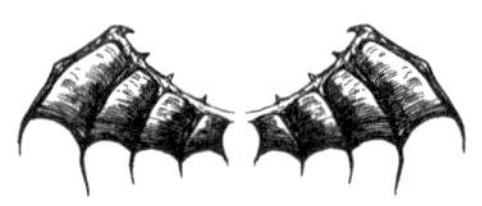

PARKER

It'd been a few days, Con was ignoring me and kept telling me to sit down anytime I asked anything.

"Con..."

"Sit down." He cut me off without even looking up from his book.

"I am!"

"Oh," He glanced up from the dusty relic and shook his head, "Then no."

"I didn't even...! Ugh, you're annoying!"

"Now you know how it feels."

"I was just gonna ask about..."

"No,"

"Conner!" I finally got fed up, "It's been two days! Stop it!" I whined.

"You grew up with siblings, aren't you used to this?"

"No, my sisters used to just hit me! I just wanna ask about a hunt."

"I know, and no."

"WHAT DOES THAT MEAN?!"

"It means no."

"Ugh!" I shoved off the couch, "I'll just go ask Air."

"Sit down." Con barked.

"Aaaah!" I finally screamed.

Conner eventually had to pee so I took the opportunity to steal his keys and leave.

I would've taken his car, but I wanted to drink, and I have a habit of losing cars and Con doesn't find it as funny as Nate does.

I drank what few dollars I had in my pocket, the bar eventually closed which led to me wandering for a while, I didn't mean to, but I was drunk and I couldn't get that poor girl out of my head, every time I closed my eyes I saw her staring back at me.

It was cold out; my hoodie wasn't cutting it. The cold wind bit at my face, it got my attention and I eventually looked up realizing I was walking with no direction. I stopped at two old brick buildings with a dark narrow alley.

A dark alley.

Like my vision.

I walked down it, maybe it would jog something or maybe I would get stabbed, you know win-win.

I ran my hand across the wall as I slowly made my way through, the cracked brick had seen better days and scratched at my fingertips. I stopped when I found a large chunk taken out of one of the bricks, it had a sharp jagged edge.

It wasn't even a second thought, I ran my index finger over it harshly. It snagged my skin leaving a cut, and a stream of black syrupy soot pooled in my hand before the cut quickly sealed itself, I let the liquid run through my fingers where it splattered on the concrete.

I glanced down and noticed other dots on the ground, bigger redder splatters that weren't from me. I followed the trail through the alley to the other side where it stopped.

The streetlight was on the opposite side of the street casting me into the shadows. I looked around, the street was empty, but a shadow caught my eye.

A shadow that set off every alarm in my head.

(＼(•̀ᴡ•́)／)

23:40

Conner

Parker slammed through the front door while I was trying to call him for the twentieth time.

"Where the hell have you been?"

He stood on the tips of his sneakers to stare through the peephole, "Sh sh shush!"

Parker stayed pressed against the door.

"What are you doing?"

"Someone's following me."

"What?"

"*Someone is following me.*" He said slowly.

Aaron put down his book, "Who would be following you?"

Parker pulled away from the door. He got that look, the light bulb went off, here we go, "Top hat,"

"Don't," I shook my head.

"Top hat! He's following me!"

"Why would..."

"He's following me!"

"You're paranoid," Nate added.

"Paranoid?! *Paranoid*! Paranoid was the time I got high and thought there was a yeti in the closet!" He flailed about before gesturing to the flowers on the counter, "He knows where we live!"

"Parker," I made him go sit down, "Calm down."

"I am! And we're gonna die!"

I sighed and whispered "Jesus" under my breath.

He cut me off before I was even able to say anything, "We have to do something, we have to keep hunting."

"I don't think..."

"I don't care!" He grabbed my notebook and folder of maps from my desk and sped off into the bedroom.

I tried to relieve some of the tension in my head by rubbing my temples.

I should've finished my degree.

"You know what's gonna happen," Nate stopped midsentence.

He realized we were all looking at him, "Gotta spell it out?" He pointed towards the bedroom door with his thumb, "Psycho in there's gonna go off on his own and get himself killed... But hey, make our lives easier."

Aaron gave me a concerned look.

I sighed, "You still have that hunt from earlier?"

September 8 2007

22:30

CONNER

Our hunt tonight was simple, Aaron estimated fifteen vamps and he was spot on. We held a basic line while Parker weaved through.

The vampires were average, they responded to us like they were hungry, but I didn't notice any signs of decay.

Incidents were minimal, I wouldn't refer to this as an interesting hunt, and unfortunately neither did Parker.

The hunt took us the standard thirty-two minutes, but Parker insisted on sticking around to check things out.

I agreed that it was worth seeing if there were any clues. After we thoroughly cleared the area Parker took a few steps over the line, it was the addition of literally shaking trees that I felt was too much.

"Stop throwing shit at me!" Parker yelled from the top of a tall tree after Courtney had nailed him in the back of the head with a well-thrown pinecone.

"Here kitty kitty!" She threw a stick next.

I had to stop her from throwing anything else, "Come down here."

He less than gracefully clambered down, "What? I thought I saw something."

"Really?" Aaron voiced our surprise, "What?"

"Something red, glowing. Pretty high up."

Aaron sighed, "That's a cell tower!"

"How am I supposed to know that?!"

I shook my head, "Parker, you're becoming obsessive."

"Duh! You don't do coke unless you're fucking obsessive!"

"Come down or I'm gonna let Court tag you with a rock."

"Ooh!" She started looking around for a viable rock.

"I'm not! We've got to figure something out!"

"We will, but we're not going to get a breakthrough every day."

"But it..."

We both got distracted when Courtney started walking down the path away from the car.

"Where are you going?" I hollered after her.

"The chick's gotta piss and the hens won't stop clucking!"

I had lost my train of thought, so I just got in the car.

(＼(•̀w•́)／)

September 9 2007

00:22

NATE

Park was still bitching when we got back, and Con was trying to get him to stop but I'd started ignoring them before we left the hunt.

Air was asleep on the couch; Courtney was gently laying a shitty blanket across him.

She leaned against the side of the couch, "Hey, what time is it?"

I shrugged, "Dunno, midnight-ish."

She nodded with a huge grin, "Wanna go cause some problems?"

(＼(•̀w•́)／)

00:45

We ended up at her apartment building's parking lot with two bats.

"Who's the target this time?" I asked as she sought out the car she was looking for.

"Leo,"

"Your boyfriend?"

"Not anymore!" She took a key to the door of a shiny red S40 Volvo.

"What'd he do?"

"You know my waitress friend you've been trying to get with?"

"Uh-huh."

"Her."

I stabbed my knife into the front tire, "Bastard."

"Damn straight."

"Next time I see him I'll jump his ass."

"Thanks," She raised one of the bats, "But he's got insurance, and his car warranty expires tomorrow."

I caught the bat before she swung it.

"Hey!"

"Shut up," I lowered my voice, "Someone's watching us."

"Huh? Where?"

I glanced around, "Dunno."

She dropped the bat to her side and crossed her arms, "Then how do you know we're being watched?"

"Seven years of drug dealing and doin' this with you for three."

"Well, you better get your dealer radar checked 'cause I don't see anyone."

"Just go." I nudged her and was close behind.

Conner

Parker didn't even allow a day of rest between annoying me for hunts, luckily Aaron had one he liked, and we had already somewhat planned out.

It was another simple hunt.

The trees were denser in the area, so we split up slightly and kept a similar approach to Parker's constant movement.

The vampires were hungry and more than one was disheveled, but we weren't dealing with many, Aaron estimated twelve and I would say that was about right.

We cleared the area together and still found nothing.

As we were packing up the trunk Aaron got my attention because he was on his own.

He was standing at the top of the hill maybe a hundred feet from the car, staring off.

I didn't think much about it, he does this kind of thing pretty regularly when he's thinking, but I realized he was staring at something instead of off into space.

I let Parker Nate and Courtney finish packing up while I went to check on Aaron.

"Hey, are you okay?" I carefully put my hand on his shoulder, so he knew I was talking to him.

"Hm?" He nodded, "Yes, sorry. I just thought I saw something..."

"What was it?"

He shook his head, "Oh, it doesn't matter."

He started to walk towards the car, but I stopped him.

"Of course it does."

He hesitated for a second, "It was probably a deer, they're up here a lot this time of year." He reasoned, "I don't think it was anything."

September 10 2007

22:20

Conner

Parker wasn't letting up, so Aaron and I were up again scouting more hunts.

He and I were tired, to be fair I think we all were.

Hunting back-to-back isn't typically like us, I like to have some time to get everything done.

Parker wasn't listening and truth be told I didn't say no emphatically, I want answers too.

"What about this one?" Aaron yawned as he pointed out a street name from our list.

I scanned the notes on the page, "Disappearances are low," I typed it into the map on my computer, "Nothing around."

"It's pheasant hunting fields."

"What are you thinking?"

He shrugged, "Maybe five. It would be small."

Parker jumped up from the couch, he didn't even try to pretend he wasn't listening, "Let's take it." He was already scrambling around for his gear.

"We still need a plan." I reminded him.

"For five vamps?" Parker scoffed blowing black strands of hair out of his eyes, "That's one for each of us, I could do that alone."

I tried to talk but Parker cut me off.

"Let's go!" He was already out the door.

"Parker!" I groaned in vain; he was probably already in the parking lot by now.

Courtney tied her hair up, "We better go before he gets lost."

I shook my head, "This isn't how we do things, and he knows that. If he wants to be a pain in the ass..."

She hit my arm, "You don't mean it, besides he's kinda right. Five is easy, a little bang a little pow, and we're eating waffles in fifteen minutes."

"It's just not smart."

Her hands fell on her hips, "What's the biggest hunt you've taken alone?"

"Thirteen, but I was sixteen and stupid."

"It'll be fine," She patted me on the back as she walked by, "Get the stick outta your ass, Connie. Not everything has to be so rigid."

(ヽ(•̀ω•́)ノ)

Parker

It was cold, colder than the usual end of summer nighttime breeze.

It was cold, dark, and humid.

The air felt dense and tasted salty thanks to the nearby coast. If it hadn't been for the trees I would've guessed we were in a serial killer's damp concrete basement.

"Here's the plan," Conner stated. Once those words were said my eyes glazed over.

Five vamps, I could do that with my eyes closed with one knife and no powers.

Once Con was done yapping, I separated from them and sped off the hunting trail.

Conner's car alarm started to blare.

After a few seconds three vampires zapped in my area, they were big, they looked healthy, but I was able to quickly take them out.

Another two popped up, I quickly stabbed them too.

I got back to the guys with a smug look on my face.

"What'd I say!" I threw my hands up as a challenge.

The only response I got was a simple "Move!"

"Huh?"

I didn't get it until Courtney unloaded a few bullets behind me.

There were five more vampires behind me, the guys beat me to the punch and cleared them out.

At that point something... *Shifted.*

The woods became silent, and the trees seemed to move like they were closing in on us, but they morphed into bodies in the dark.

"Nest," Conner tried to say calmly, "We just hit a nest."

In no time they were swarming us.

I got separated since I was further back, I had no less than ten on me at a time and they were persistent.

I could hear gunshots coming from every direction, so I chose a direction and started to fight my way through the crowd.

The vamps were packed back-to-back, snarling and hissing like rabid dogs desperate for anything to grab onto, a few were even taking each other out.

A handful of them were in pieces while others were still put together well, which seemed weird.

The air was filling with a cloud of thick smoke, and it was getting hard to see, I tried to stay low.

I finally made it through to a pocket Conner had cleared out.

"What are we doing?" I covered his back while I waited for an answer.

"See how many you can clear out, if you run into the guys or Court tell them to try to make it up the trail, we'll make a plan there."

"Got it."

I tried to weave through the crowd.

So much for being invisible to them. I thought to myself as they snarled and one chomped at me.

My arms burned from using my knife and my hands down to my elbows were covered in soot.

I saw a gap and sped through; I slammed into something.

"Watch your ass, güero!" Nate yelled above me.

"Sorry!" I popped up off the dirt, "Where's Aaron?"

He took a few shots, "Dunno."

"Court?"

"Dunno."

"Okay, Con's up to the le

ft he said to keep heading to the trail."

"West or north?"

"I dunno. He said up so I guess north."

He rolled his eyes, "Heard."

(＼(•̀w•́)／)

NATE

Park and I split up, figured we'd be able to find the other two easier that way. Parker went deeper into the trees while I tried to keep on the trail.

I denied my gut instinct and followed the gunshots.

Up on the hill, I could see both Courtney and Aaron hundreds of feet away and unaware of each other.

Court was swarmed on her own fighting, while Aaron seemed to be struggling with something, instead of shooting, he had his knife out and was bobbing around.

I didn't think anything of it, I just figured he needed help, so I went to see what was going on.

"Que paso?"

He gestured over his ears, "What?"

"What happened?!"

He shook his head, "My gun jammed!" He yelled back, "I have to re..."

I cut him off "Gimme the knife."

He and I quickly traded weapons.

It happened fast.

I heard a loud, sharp yell coming from where I knew Court had been.

Aaron helped me cut through the vamps, what was behind them I was not prepared for.

Courtney was pinned to the grass by a zombie-looking vamp.

She jabbed him a few times with her knife, a growing splotch of blood saturated her shirt, fast.

Aaron and I ran the fastest either of us had ever ran.

"Court! Hey."

"I'm okay." She was quick to answer, she pushed herself up to her knees.

"Easy,"

"Don't *easy* me," she snapped.

"Lemme see."

I shined the flashlight on her; her arms, and face were scratched up good, but no real damage ‘til I got to her shoulder. There was a massive chunk taken out of the space between her neck and shoulder, and a long deep slash over her throat.

Aaron went pale so I knew what I was looking at was real.

We didn't have another option, so I just scooped her up off the ground.

Aaron kept a clear path for us until we made it to the top of the trail.

Conner

“Hey!” Nate flagged me and Parker down, something was wrong, he was frantic. I’d never seen him like that.

Parker kept running around, killing vampires, while I went to go see what was happening.

“What…” Before I could finish my question the severity of the scene set in.

Courtney was drenched in blood, and so was Nate where she had been pressed against his chest.

“Put her down!” I commanded, and quickly pulled off my jacket.

Nate gently put her down on the grass, and I used my jacket to apply pressure to the wound.

“What happened?”

“I don’t know,” Nate spoke fast and panicked, “She went down, I guess she got bit, I don’t know.”

"Courtney?!"

She was still awake, that was good.

"Can you hear me?"

A cough rattled in her chest as she tried to respond, she took a sharp jagged breath, "I'm fine, I gotta get up..." She tried to move me so she could get up.

“No, no, stay here.” I kept her lying down.

I felt a warm sensation on my hand, her blood was seeping through the fabric.

"Okay, okay," I tried to keep things on track before any of us started to fully panic, we just didn't have the time.

I dug around my pocket until I found my keys, and I threw them to Aaron, "There’s no signal up here. Two miles south, go into town, my phone’s in the glove box. Nate, get Parker’s attention and get Aaron to the car and make sure no other vampires come up this way."

Aaron and Nate stared at me in a panic.

"Now! Go!"

They quickly ran down the trail.

Courtney tried to clear her throat, but it only made blood spurt out of her neck, "I gotta sit up."

"You don't, stay here."

"God, how bad is it?" She tried to feel around but I kept my hands over the hole in the side of her neck.

"It isn't," I had to grit my teeth to hide the lie, "It's not bad, just a scratch. We've seen worse."

Her denim blue eyes bore into mine, and she gave me her signature expression like she was looking into my soul.

She responded with a chuckle that felt so out of place, "Fuck, you're a bad liar."

"We're going to get you help."

She shook her head, "I'm not gonna last that long," Her words flitted with her breath, her voice was barely a whisper now.

I took a hard breath and kept myself calm, "Don't talk like that."

"C'mon, use that big brain." She went into a brief coughing fit, blood bubbled out her lips.

"Courtney,"

"I'm fine. Now pay attention, I need a favor. Actually two, tell my mom I'm okay, I'll be okay now."

"I..."

She stopped me, "Just tell her that."

"Okay."

She gathered enough energy to lift her hand to the silver heart pendant dangling from the chain around her neck, it was now blood-soaked.

She ripped it off and placed it in my hand, "Give it to my sister, don't let them bury it with me, got it? That stays with Drew, I swear to Christ, tell her it's *hers.*"

I nodded, I didn't want her to waste her breath on an explanation.

"Also clear out my apartment before my mom does, you can keep the porn." She joked with a smile despite how labored her breathing was becoming.

"Do me a favor now, just focus on your breathing."

She listened to me for once, but after a while she fought to keep her eyes open.

"Keep your eyes open, please."

She nodded, "Conner?"

"I'm still here."

She squeezed my hand tightly, "I love you."

I chewed the inside of my cheek, "I love you, too."

She let out a heavy sigh…

But she didn't inhale.

"Court," I gently shook her, "Courtney, take a deep breath."

Her eyes didn't flutter, and she didn't respond in any way.

My chest felt tight, but I didn't have time to process anything else.

I could hear Parker and Nate shouting back and forth, and I didn't have a good feeling about it.

I didn't know what to do until Parker yelled louder.

I knew I'd have to come back for her, but the thought made me sick.

"I'm sorry. I'm so sorry, I'll be right back." I told her as I stood.

At the end of the trail, I saw even more vampires than before were coming through.

I got Nate and Parker in a triangle formation, and we tried to get through as many as we could.

Almost as suddenly as they were coming, the vampires suddenly stopped.

I shot the last vampire, and we raced to the top of the trail.

The pit in my stomach grew more than I thought was possible, it almost felt like it could swallow me whole.

And just like that the situation went from terrible to truly hellish.

Courtney was gone, all that was left in her place was the blood-soaked jacket lying in a large blood stain on the grass.

In a panic, we scattered in different directions to find her.

We had maybe five minutes to scour the area before sirens closed in on us.

September 11 2007
01:11

Conner

The police pulled us away, kicking and screaming, to establish the area.

Another officer stood in front of us, patiently waiting for the four of us to stop yelling.

"You have to let us back up there, please." I pleaded.

"We got a call about a cougar attack, no one goes anywhere around here right now." The cop responded, oblivious to our hysterics.

"I'm who called!" Aaron stepped in, he was nearly in tears, "Our friend, she's up there! We have to help!"

"Mountain rangers are on the way, if there's anyone up there, they'll find 'em."

"She can't wait! She'll bleed to death!"

Parker got a look on his face, I grabbed his wrist. That was his "they can't stop me at high speed" look, and that was the last thing we needed.

Parker pulled out of my grip and crossed his arms, he was furious, as was Nate who was busy yelling at another cop further ahead.

Aaron stood at my side, he was anxious and breaking down, while I was trying desperately to stay emotionless, I didn't have time to freak out yet. I could do that when we found her.

"You witnessed the attack?" The officer asked.

"Yes," Aaron and I spoke at the same time.

The officer motioned above my head for someone else, "You need to get checked out, then. You're in shock."

We argued as multiple cops and a few EMTs had to physically move us.

We were each wrapped in an emergency blanket and asked a series of unnecessary medical questions.

Parker flatly refused to answer anything, Nate was answering unhelpfully, and Aaron was curled up in a ball under his blanket hyperventilating.

"Aaron," I carefully pat his back, "You need to breathe," I unearthed him and helped to straighten him out, "You're going to faint,"

That got Nate and Parker's attention and they were quick to help comfort him. Parker got him some water while Nate scooted closer until Aaron was tightly wedged between us.

"Excuse me," A woman's voice penetrated our armor, "Ranger," She gestured to her badge, "I need to ask you some questions."

"I got Air." Nate assured.

"Okay," I was reluctant to answer but I didn't have a choice, "Could we go somewhere else?" I didn't want Aaron to have to re-experience everything.

The ranger gave me a nod and lead me to the other side of an ambulance.

She looked me over, assessing the blood that I was covered in, "Assuming not yours?"

I shook my head.

She grabbed a pad of paper and clicked a pen, "What's your name?"

"Conner,"

"What were you doing up here, Conner?"

I cleared my throat and ran through the note of the area in my head, "We hunt pheasant, we wanted to get a look at the area."

"Why so late at night?"

"We all work late."

"Where do you work?" She quizzed.

"At the college," I said the second it entered my brain.

She was satisfied with that, "Tell me what happened."

I revised everything as quickly as I could, minus the vampires, we didn't need to need a mental evaluation on top of everything else.

"Did you see the cougar?"

"No,"

"Did any of you?"

"What does it matter?" I snapped, "I know my friend got attacked! What does it matter what the cougar looked like."

"And you didn't see where she went?"

"She wasn't in any state to go anywhere."

"Can you describe the injuries?"

A cold chill washed over me and my stomach twisted, "Gaping wound to her shoulder neck area, smaller wound to her throat..." I had to pause, "She was bleeding a lot. Too much."

"And the victim?"

"Courtney,"

"Can you describe Courtney for me?"

I cleared my throat again, forcing the lump away, "She's twenty-eight. Blonde hair, blue eyes, white. Five two, she's wearing a black shirt and blue jeans..."

"Does she have any family?"

"Yeah, her mother and her sister live in Seattle. Rachel and Drew Hart."

She wrote that down.

"... Would it be okay if I tell them?... Before you guys do?"

"Of course, thank you for talking to me."

I took a second to try to get my bearings before I went back to the guys.

Aaron surprised me when I sat back down, he wrapped his arms around me and buried his face in my shoulder, that's when I finally broke down. My chest was tight I considered that I might be having a heart attack.

I couldn't deny it anymore...

I had just watched my best friend die.

(＼(•̀ᴡ•́)／)

04:50

PARKER

We kept asking to help look for Courtney, but we kept getting rejected.

So, we waited hoping they'd find something. We sat there on the rocks for hours. None of us really knew what else to do really.

The dark night clouds were starting to part revealing the rising sun that stung at my skin like I was standing too close to a fire, and that stupid foil blanket wasn't helping, it just caused more of a reflection.

I could deal with the burning for a while, the pain was a helpful distraction from the situation and helped me keep the tears from flowing.

Aaron glanced at me, "Parker," his eyes widened when he noticed how red my skin was turning, he unbuttoned the sweater he had gotten from his car earlier and threw it over my head, "Are you okay?"

I held my hand out from under it to give him a thumbs up.

Conner sighed heavily, "Maybe we should go," he shook his head, "They're not going to let us do anything and we need to go talk to Mrs. Hart."

We reluctantly mumbled our agreement.

(＼(•̀w•́)／)

Aaron

We made a pit stop at the apartment and got cleaned up.

Conner also made sure everyone wore something presentable, and by everyone, I mean mostly Parker who ended up stealing one of my work shirts just to pull one of the hoodies from his collection over it.

We drove to the nice side of town.

Conner parked on the street in front of a row of expensive town houses, the kind made of old brick with a rocking chair on the fancy porch and a few plants, sandwiched so tightly together you wondered if the neighbors could hear everything.

We shuffled along behind Conner, down the sidewalk to a house adorned with lights, cutely painted pots holding beautiful flowers, and a swinging bench.

Conner rang the doorbell.

The door opened after a minute; an older, tall woman stood on the other side. Her long braids were tied up in a neat bun on top of her head. She wore a pink sweater over a long skirt, I remembered Courtney saying something about her mom being a teacher and that's exactly what she looked like.

She looked us all over, her dark brown eyes stopped on Conner.

"It's about Courtney, isn't it?"

I could hear Conner gulp, "I'm so, so sorry."

Mrs. Hart took a breath and stepped back from the door gesturing for us to come in.

The inside was as nice as the porch, homey and comfy. It reminded me of my dad's house before he married my stepmom...

Mrs. Hart offered us a seat on the couch while she paced in front of us, "What happened?"

"We had a hunt late last night; we stumbled into a nest... She was bitten twice."

Mrs. Hart's gasp turned into a quiet sob.

"I'm sorry."

"Don't be," she spoke through her tears, "... I always feared this day would come."

"It happened fast," Conner said in an attempt at reassurance, "She was gone before the ambulance showed up. She didn't suffer and she wasn't scared."

Parker stared at Conner for a second.

"It's okay," Conner nodded, "She knows."

Parker's eyes widened, "... How much?"

"All of it." He confirmed.

"I taught her everything she knows," her voice shook, "Though, now I wish I never did." She balled up her skirt in her hands, "Where is she now? Do I need to call the police?"

We were silent.

She wiped a tear away from her warm cheek, "Conner?"

Conner's voice broke, "We don't know. She disappeared."

"What does that mean?"

"After she..." Conner paused to clear his throat and reset, "I had to go help clear the area, she was gone when we got back."

Mrs. Hart was quiet for a while before she stood up, "I need to call Drew..." she stopped between steps, "I'm sorry, can I get you boys anything?" She shook her head before any of us answered, "I'll put on a pot of coffee, and I have a leftover quiche, I'll put that in the oven, too."

She was adamant about feeding us, she moved us into the kitchen and sat us at a round breakfast table.

"I know one of you is vegetarian, are eggs, okay? If not, I can make you something else."

"It's okay, that's already way more thought than my own mom..." I couldn't tell if Parker was joking or if it was just an oddly placed observation.

She placed ceramic plates in front each of us, the quiche was cheesy and smelled amazing, but my stomach was too twisted up to eat.

Conner and Parker politely picked at their plates while Nate scarfed his down.

"About Courtney..." Mrs. Hart spoke after a while, "You're sure? You're sure she's gone?"

Conner hesitated for a minute.

"I don't need sugar coating, just tell me if we're looking for her or her body."

"Her body... I'm positive."

She squeezed her eyes shut, "... Okay."

"The park service is looking; they've closed off the area so we can't get back in but hopefully they'll do a better job."

She nodded, "I'll get in contact and see what else we can do." She placed a hand on top of Conner's, "I greatly appreciate you coming to tell me, all of you. How are you boys doing?"

She looked to me, a frown present, "You're not eating, sweetheart."

I had hoped Conner would answer for me, but unfortunately, he couldn't read my mind.

"I'm okay..." My throat was raw and my voice hoarse, it had been a while since I had spoken.

"He doesn't talk much anyway." Nate responded.

Mrs. Hart reached over the table to take my hand, "If you need anything, any of you, you call me. We mourn together, okay?"

The front door creaked open, "Mom?!"

"Kitchen, honey." Mrs. Hart answered.

Drew, Courtney's sister, stepped through the kitchen arch way.

She was the opposite of her sister in every way. Way taller than Courtney, her long silky dark brown hair dusted against her angular features and her olive skin. The only thing about her that was similar was her eyes, but even then, they were a very light icy blue unlike Courtney's.

I had met her a few times. Courtney would always make a big deal when she was around.

"I got your message, what's..." Drew paused when she noticed us all there, "... What's going on?"

Mrs. Hart gestured towards the sliding glass door, "Let me fix you a plate first, would you go check on Bowie?"

Bowie turned out to be a large German Shepard mix, he broke past Drew and was in the kitchen, in a matter of seconds he was barking and bound towards Parker who in a flash was up and across the room.

Mrs. Hart grabbed the dog by the collar before he could continue to chase Parker.

"I'm so sorry!" Drew shouted over his barks, "He doesn't usually act that way."

Parker clamored as he climbed on top of the counter.

Animals and kids don't tend to like him, Conner didn't have a theory as to why, but I think it had something to do with dead aura around him.

"Take him upstairs, please."

Drew mumbled a few more apologies as she dragged the dog from the room.

"Sorry, I should've thought of that." Mrs. Hart helped Parker down.

"It's fine... Just not a dog guy."

"Or bird," Nate added, Parker glared.

"It's interesting though, I surely can't tell, if Courtney hadn't told me, that is."

"Either way, thanks for not killing me."

"About that, Drew doesn't know about any of this, vampires or... Hunting, so please just follow my lead."

We all nodded our agreement.

After a few quiet seconds Drew was back.

"Honey," Mrs. Hart stood and guided Drew into her seat, "Courtney is missing."

(＼(•̀w•́)／)

Conner

We stayed for a few minutes longer.

Mrs. Hart calmly led Drew to the couch before she gave us each a hug and walked us out, we offered a last condolence.

Mrs. Hart stopped me before I stepped over the threshold, "Jared Quinn, you know him, correct? Our family from New Jersey?"

I nodded.

Courtney's closest friends from New Jersey, I hadn't met them personally, but I had heard the stories, and I had talked to Jared over the phone before.

They frightened me.

"Good, I need him and everyone else to know what's going on, but my daughter needs me..."

I didn't let her finish the question, "Consider it done."

"Thank you."

She gave me another hug and let me go.

I waited until we were back to the apartment, I lagged behind while the guys went inside.

I dreaded this, but had roles been reversed I would have wanted to hear from him.

It rang a few times, I thought maybe it would go to voicemail.

I *hoped* it would go to voicemail.

"Hello?" A soft slightly musical yet harsh voice picked up.

"Jared? It's Conner Stephens..."

"Conner, hey," There was a hesitation, I wondered if he was annoyed it was me.

"Do you have a minute?"

"Sure," His answers were short and direct.

"I'm afraid I have bad news," I didn't know how to go about it so I just said it, "We had an accident, Courtney's... *Gone.*"

The line was quiet for a long time.
"Jared...?"
"We're on the way."
His side clicked off.

September 15 2007

14:30

Conner

The next few days were silent.

A cloud hung over all of us and pain just flooded the apartment.

None of us spoke about it, either out of pain or shock probably both.

We just waited for the phone to ring to either tell us we could help or that they found her, but neither came.

I wasn't sure what to do, so I did what I always did.

I kept reading, I took notes, I scoped out hunts.

I scoured for a new job; *and I cried at a job interview.*

Needless to say, I kept myself busy.

Parker turned to his usual vices; and we didn't see much of him. He was in and out of the apartment in varying degrees of intoxication.

Aaron spent most of his time zoned out with his cassette player turned up so loud I could hear the music from my desk.

While Nate took it upon himself to cling to Aaron.

Nate waved his hand in front of Aaron's face and gestured to his headphones.

Nate handed him a bowl of something, "You gotta eat, perrito."

Aaron nodded; I don't think he had talked in two days. He leaned forward to put the bowl on the coffee table.

Nate sat next to him with a sigh, "Portland is a three-hour drive, lemme take you to your mom's."

Aaron shook his head.

"Your dad's?" Nate offered, trying desperately to soften his voice, "Please?"

Aaron rubbed his swollen eyes, "I'm okay."
"You're not."
"But I want to be..." Aaron's tiny voice broke.

(＼(•̀w•́)／)

PARKER

The sun was bright, high in the sky drenching all of Seattle in beams of bright gold that the city hadn't seen in what felt like years.

It'd been weirdly sunny for the past few days.

I still find it beautiful, maybe even more now that it has the power to dust me.

I had a reason for being out, I wanted drugs and I had to go out and get them. But now I was absent mindedly walking around.

I cut through the park and took a seat on a painted pastel pink bench, swallowed a handful of pills and looked around.

It was a weekday, not many people were in the park aside from a handful of parents and kids over at the playground. The trees were blowing in the breeze, it was peaceful.

I wanted to feel that peace.

I slid down my hood and took off my sunglasses, holding my face out I let the light wash over me.

The warmth from the sun felt nice on my cold skin for a few seconds before it started to burn.

I sighed and pulled my hoodie back on, Con would kill me if I came back with another sunburn.

I lay back on the bench and watched the clouds.

My head was quiet, but my thoughts were racing at the same time, it had been like that for days.

I groped around my pocket for my cell phone.

Flipping it open I clicked through my contacts on impulse.

My thumb hovered over the call button as I thought.

Thinking's not my friend.

I held my breath as the line rang... And kept ringing.

I sighed, knowing there wouldn't be an answer I waited for the machine.

I cleared my throat and hoped the tears that were now streaming down my cheeks weren't audible.

"Hey mom, it's me... I know we haven't talked in a while and..." I trailed off, my voice breaking, "Look, something really terrible happened and I, I just need to hear you or-or Dad..." I ran my sleeve under my eyes, "Call me back."

I sat up and rested my head on my knees.

I hadn't talked to either of my parents since I moved to Seattle, I think it's probably better for everyone that way. I'm not exactly the best son, and they're not exactly the best parents.

Besides, they're hardcore bible thumpers and I'm a junkie vampire.

I thought about calling my older sister, but I didn't know if she'd answer either, or even if I had her current number.

My siblings and I don't talk either. The younger two hate me and my older sister... It's complicated.

September 18 2007

08:50

Conner

In the past week I haven't slept much, it was too hard to fall asleep.

I was still trying to keep myself busy, but it didn't seem to be enough.

I wasn't finding anything on either front, I was losing my touch.

I needed a break, and it was either realize it or completely shut down.

Despite the massive collection of books Aaron and I had between us, I opted to go the library.

Most of what we have are about vampires, or scientific books anyway, I needed something else for now.

The University had a great library, and regardless of my dropout status, my library card was still good.

I scanned the shelves and grabbed a few things, mostly fiction, it had been a while since I had read for leisure.

I also grabbed a few things for Aaron as well, I thought he could use a distraction, too.

I sat at an empty table and tried to whittle through my selection.

"Conner?"

I heard my name but unless it was followed by yelling or "Parker just!" I tend to believe it's someone else.

"Conner," I looked up when I realized someone was standing next to me.

Drew smiled at me, "Hi,"

"Hi, sorry."

"Hi, do you mind?" She gestured to the chair across from me.

"No, please."

She straightened out her skirt and sat, "I didn't know you went here."

"I don't, well, did. I dropped out a couple years ago..."

"Oh."

I awkwardly cleared my throat, "Veterinary medicine, right?"

"Right, how did you…"

I rushed to answer so I didn't look like a creep, "Courtney told me, she was excited when you got in."

"She likes to brag..."

I nodded, "Especially when it comes to you,"

She raised any eyebrow to challenge me without saying a word.

"I know you graduated high school with honors, you made the Dean's list last year, Drew is short for Andrew, you were named after your uncle, and your favorite color is mint green."

There was a split-second silence, and I worried that I still came across as creepy until she laughed.

"Well, she didn't tell you my favorite flavor of ice cream, so at least there's still *some* mystery." She joked as she tucked her hair behind her ear, "Well, um, I'm actually glad I ran into you, my mom said she was going to call you today, but maybe it's better in person,"

She pulled a paper out of her bag and tried to flatten the creases out against the table, "We're putting together a search party..."

She had hardly finished her thought before I answered.

"We'll be there."

She feigned a smile, "Thank you, we've already had so many people cancel on us already, and the police aren't even answering our phone calls anymore... I'm sorry, I'm rambling," she handed me the paper she was messing with, "All the information is on there, if you have any questions, well you already have my mom's number." Drew shuffled for a pen in her bag, "Let me give you mine."

"Oh, I already have it." I shrugged, "... Courtney gave it to me."

"I should have figured." She let out a small quiet laugh, but it was flat.

The table was quiet for a minute.

Drew was staring at the picture of Courtney on the flyer, while I was searching for the right thing to say.

I finally cleared my throat, "Do you want to get a cup of coffee or something?"

"No, I really should go, I have a class I have to get to."

I nodded.

She stood up, but lingered for a minute, "I know I don't really know you that well, but would it be okay if I asked you for a hug?"

"Yeah, of course."

I didn't realize she was quite a bit taller than me until I hugged her, she didn't tower over me like most people, but had her boots had a thicker sole she probably would have.

"Thank you," she wiped the tears dotting her cheeks, "My sister's right about you, you know?

I awkwardly chuckled, "I hope that's a good thing."

"It's a great thing." She hoisted her bag onto her shoulder, "I'll see you on Monday."

I waited for her to leave before I went to return some of the books to the shelves, when I came back, I noticed she'd left a flyer on the desk.

It was printed on bright orange paper that Courtney would've loved, it had little butterflies on the corners to match the tattoo on her hip, and a picture of her in the middle.

She was smiling, of course she was, there wasn't ever really a time she wasn't.

I couldn't look at it too long, the guilt hurt my stomach, the pain migrated to my chest making it hard to breathe.

I ran my thumb over the picture to remind myself it was just paper.

"... I'm sorry." I whispered to try to control the break in my voice.

MISSING
HAVE YOU SEEN THIS PERSON?

September 22 2007
05:30

Parker

It was early.

So fucking early.

Conner pulled me out of bed and shoved me into a shower.

He let me lay in bed while he got ready if I promised any kind of sobriety, which for once, I didn't mind.

As badly as I didn't want to have to go back to that area, I wanted to be alert when I did.

We drove in silence, and it made the situation worse.

"Can I turn on the air?"

Conner glanced at me in the crooked rearview mirror, "You're hot?"

"No, it's just been a while since anyone talked."

Con shook his head.

"Do you think there are really mountain lions up here?"

Nate just looked at me, "Shut up, Parker."

I crossed my arms and sunk into the seat.

We slowly pulled up to the hunting trail where there was a makeshift parking lot roped off.

We stayed in the car waiting for someone else to be brave enough to get out.

"Is everyone doing, okay?" Conner asked as he set the parking brake.

I was the only one to answer.

"No,"

"Yeah, me either." He took the first step and opened his door while the rest of us slowly fell out.

The area looked so much different in the day, it was sunny again. The light was streaming through the trees which seemed thinner, I felt like I could see everything that was around unlike that night.

It felt like seeing a monster in the dark and turning on the light to see your jacket hanging on the back of your closet.

I shuffled along with the guys, everything felt numb. I wanted to cry but there was nothing left.

There was a small group of people scattered around talking to each other, some I recognized from Courtney's wild parties, but for the most part I didn't know anyone.

Mrs. Hart waved at us as she made her way over, despite everything she had a smile on her face, I guess that's probably where Courtney got it.

We each got a warm hug and a shoulder squeeze.

"Oh, thank you so much for coming. Here," she gestured towards another small group, "I want you to meet my boys."

Four other guys came over.

Mrs. Hart introduced them individually.

"This is Vince,"

Vince was tall, and I don't mean that like how 5'10 to my 5'7 was tall, I mean *he was tall.*

He towered over Nate and his hair didn't help. It was a fluffy afro, the tight curls brushed against the raw umber skin of his neck.

Mrs. Hart went down the line, "Wyatt,"

Wyatt was closer to my height; he seemed like someone I would party with.

His light brown skin was taken over by a sea of black tattoos.

His long straight dark hair was back folded into a half bun.

Mrs. Hart moved down to the two I had to assume we're brothers, they were nearly identical and looked like they were made of porcelain. And that's coming from a vampire.

"Jared," he had piercing emerald green eyes, I didn't realize I was staring at him until Wyatt cleared his throat with a glare.

Jared was more... Feminine.

All his features were somewhat dainty, he was small but tall.

Longish black hair that cut off at his pale jaw.

"And Nicky,"

He looked younger than his brother but had the same careful carvings.

His eyes were a muddier green and his hair was short and blond.

Mrs. Hart patted the brothers on the back, "I'll leave you to it."

There was a solid minute of awkwardness.

Jared cleared his throat, "You're staring at me."

"I'm sketching..." I muttered dreamily.

"What?"

Conner stepped in and swatted at me until I moved, "Sorry, he's an artist."

"Oh, it just sounded weird, I guess." Jared commented.

"No, *it's weird.*" Con shot me a look, "I'm sorry. It's nice to finally meet you. Uh, all things considered, I mean."

I could tell Conner was uncomfortable, there's never been a social situation he was comfortable in, but the uncomfortable-ness was around us.

They already seemed like they hated us.

The silence and the tension paired together nicely, and not being one for either I decided to help.

"You're a hunter?" I asked looking Nicky over. I sort of blurted it out and I really didn't mean it any kind of way, he just seemed really young.

"What about it?" He snapped back.

"But you're like twelve."

"And you're like a vampire." His voice was harsh as he stared through me.

Jared bent to whisper something to his brother.

Yep, they hate us.

A younger girl in a ranger uniform with a large badge that said 'volunteer' bounced over to us just in time.

"Hi, have you gotten checked in yet?" She barely waited for us to answer, "We're set up to send everyone in with a partner, so how about..."

She set up Conner with Aaron, Jared with Nicky. Then she pointed at me and Wyatt.

Wyatt laughed, "Yeah, hell froze over this morning," He looked me over, "No offense."

"Only some taken." I mumbled

Conner elbowed me.

Wyatt yanked Vince to his side, "I'm with him," he nodded at Jared, "He'll take the kid, and the other four can fuck right off for all I care."

They definitely hate us.

(＼(•̀w•́)／)

Conner

The other group of guys left, and the volunteer was quick to leave after Wyatt had yelled at her.

"A'ight," Nate put up his hand, "Not it."

"Not it for what?" I asked.

"I'm not getting stuck with the incredible climbing dumbass again."

"Hey!" Parker protested, "I'm an asset!"

"You're an ass*hole*." Nate chuckled.

Parker crossed his arms, "I wanna go alone anyway."

I rolled my eyes, "Parker, you know how he is."

"It's not about Nate, I think I can cover more ground on my own."

I sighed.

There wasn't any reason to argue he was going to do what he wanted anyway.

"Fine, just not in front of everyone."

"Con, I'm not stupid."

"Debatable."

He glared at me before his silhouette turned into a blur.

So much for not in front of everyone.

"He gets stuck in a tree again, I ain't getting his ass out." Nate shook his head.

"He'll be the rangers' problem."

Aaron finally spoke up, "Do you think we're going to find anything? If her... If *she* is still out here, they would have found her by now, right?" He questioned as his voice pitched higher.

"Who knows what all's up here," Nate shrugged.

I kicked Nate's shoe to get him to stop, "I doubt there will be anything, but it'll make us feel better, don't you think?"

Aaron's blond curls bounced as he nodded.

"Hi, sorry," Drew got our attention as she walked over, "I didn't mean to interrupt. Don't mind me."

"No, you're fine." I assured.

"I'm sure you guys probably have plans to search together, I was wondering if it was okay if I joined one of your pairs? I just wanna talk... Well, I have some questions."

"Um," I glanced at Aaron and Nate, they both gave me a nod before they walked off.

"I think that actually works out."

"Thank you," she took a quick look around, "Parker didn't come?"

"He's... Floating around."

"Well, I'm glad you came."

One park ranger gathered everyone into groups, while another one handed out safety vests, and a third spoke about safety and protocol at the head of the group.

My watch ticked over to six o'clock and they declared the search active.

Everyone broke from the group in pairs and went their separate ways.

"Where should we start?" Drew asked, she was pulling her long dark hair into a hair tie.

I pointed towards the highest hill, where I had last seen Courtney, "East of the hills."

"Is that..." Drew trailed off.

I simply nodded; I didn't want to have to answer.

Drew and I started up the path, there wasn't anything said between us until we were on the hill.

The blood stains were gone, but the grass in that area was noticeably darker.

Drew cleared her throat, "You said east?"

I nodded.

We deviated from the trail and into the forest.

The trees weren't as dense up here, we were still swallowed up by them, but we were able to stomp out a trail and see a clear way through.

"So, what happened that night?" Drew asked cautiously.

I tried to avoid the question, "No one told you?"

"My mom said it was a cougar... I just don't think I believe her."

"Why not?"

"I don't know, she's just been weird about it all, our friends have been, too. It's like they're avoiding something, or not telling me everything."

I shrugged in an attempt to come off casual, but I'm about as smooth as crumpled ball of aluminum foil, "Grief is a strange thing."

"I guess... Why were you guys up here anyway?"

I never thought I would envy Nate, especially his ability to compulsively lie.

"We were looking for a new place to hike..." It would've taken someone I met five seconds ago one look at me to know the thought of me hiking was laughable at best.

"I thought this area was known for pheasant?"

"... It's both..."

"Oh, all of you hike?"

"Well, Aaron likes hiking, Nate's from California so he's never really been in a forest, and Parker likes to paint the scenery..." I tried to reign in my awkward rambling, "So we try to go together."

"That's nice, I can never get my friends hiking. Courtney and I used to go from time to time... Although her idea of hiking was hiding in bushes to scare me as I walked by."

I chuckled, "She threw rocks at us."

Drew smiled, "Sounds about right."

After six hours of wandering around the woods to no avail the search was called off for the day.

It felt completely useless, helpless was more like it.

It was becoming glaringly obvious that there would be nothing anyone would be able to do, and there was nothing more to find.

Drew gave me a hug once we were back at the clearing, "Thank you for letting me infiltrate your group."

"I'm sorry we didn't find anything."

"Maybe it's for the best," She took her hair down, "I'm not sure how I would've handled that. I should go find my brothers; I'll see you later?"

I nodded.

Parker popped up next to me as Drew was walking away.

"You guys find anything?" Parker was a mess; his jeans were covered in dirt, and he had sticks and leaves in his hair.

"No, what the hell happened to you?"

He picked the sticks from his hair, "Me neither, and no one told me pheasants are aggressive!"

I snorted, "You got attacked by a pheasant?"

"Pecked!" He flailed his arms out, "I was PECKED!"

I laughed.

"I probably have rabies now!"

"Not like it's the first time," Nate made his way over with Aaron in tow.

Parker crossed his arms, "You guys find anything?"

"Nah, and hiking is bullshit, by the way,"

I put my hands in my coat pocket, my wristwatch clank against something metallic.

God, I can't believe I almost forgot.

"Hang on," I cut into Nate's complaint, "I'll be right back."

I scanned the area until I found Drew walking towards the "parking lot".

"Drew!" I was able to get her attention before she was too far gone.

I jogged over, well "strangely trotted" is more like it.

I carefully placed the heart pendant in her hand that I had cleaned very thoroughly, "Courtney was adamant you got this."

Drew raised an eyebrow, running her thumb over the smooth silver, "I gave her this a few years ago... Why would she want me to have it?"

"She didn't say."

I didn't realize it was a locket until she opened it, a small gold key fell out into her hand.

"I don't suppose you would know what that's to?"

"I don't, sorry."

She shook her head, "Thank you, I really appreciate it."

I wasn't sure what to say so I nodded.

We were about to part ways before her mom caught up with us.

"Drew, did you tell him about the vigil?"

Drew's hand floated up to cover her mouth, "No, I *completely* forgot, sorry."

"That's alright, baby, it's been a long day." She rubbed Drew's arm, "I want you to go home with the boys, Wyatt said he'll drive your car back to the house. Go on, I need to talk with Conner anyway."

"Okay,"

"I'll see you at home."

Drew walked off and Jared met her halfway.

Mrs. Hart waited until she was out of ear shot before, she spoke.

Mrs. Hart took my hands in hers, "I know this sounds terrible, but I don't want you to waste your time worrying about Courtney,"

"I'm... Sorry?"

She shook her head, "Listen to me. I'm her mother, that's my job. She's gone, unfortunately there's nothing we can do to get her back, and as much as I would like to bring her home to rest, I can't ask you to do that. That's my job, you have your hands full with Parker, she would want you to finish that chapter."

"But she's my best friend."

"And she's my daughter. Don't get me wrong, I appreciate everything you boys have done, but you've done enough now. It's okay to step away, I'm asking you to."

I truly didn't know how to respond.

I slowly took my hands away, "... I'll think about it."

"That's all I ask."

There was a pause.

Mrs. Hart cleared her throat, "We're holding a vigil on Wednesday..."

"We're going." I was quick to answer.

"Of course, that's not what I'm talking about, Conner, I want you to remember her, but I don't want you to obsess over her death, any of you. You're far too young for that, okay?"

I reluctantly nodded.

"Good, it's at eight o'clock. I'm asking that no one wears black, this is a memorial not a funeral." She carefully straightened my jacket, "If you would like to say a few words, I think Courtney would really like that."

Those words really stuck.

Courtney would really like that...

September 23 2007

19:01

PARKER

I got up late, I've been trying to sleep as much as I can, just 'cause it's been an easier escape, and a cheaper one than coke.

I guessed Aaron and Nate had gone back to work since it was just Con.

He was sitting at his desk scribbling something in a notebook. He looked tired and his orange hair looked more like mine, messy and pointing in all directions. It was a wild comparison to his usual neat style.

"Hey, whatcha working on?" I asked as I sat on the arm of the couch.

"Hm?" Con didn't look up from his page.

"You working on a hunt?"

"Why would I be looking at hunts?"

"'Cause weird shit's happening and it's kinda what we do."

He sighed, "Our best friend just died."

"Exactly! Our best friend died! We need to keep hunting!"

"We're not hunting."

"So, you don't want answers now? What about your parents? What about Courtney, for Christ's sake?!"

He shook his head, "Shut up, Parker."

"You think she'd want us to quit?"

"Shut up."

"You think she'd want to die for nothing? She would want us to keep going!"

"How would you know what she wants?!" He snapped, "None of us do, she's dead! As her best friend I can't even say what she'd want."

"Look, just because you wanted to fuck her doesn't mean you cared about her more than the rest of us did!"

He stood up, "Get out,"

I crossed my arms; I knew I was being a dick, but I dug my heels in deeper.

"I mean it, get out before I do something I'll regret."

I grabbed my shoes on the way out, "You're lying to yourself, Con."

I slammed the door before the balled-up paper he threw hit me.

I didn't waste my time feeling bad, I never do.

I'm more of a self-imploder than apologetic.

So naturally I headed to the warehouses in the industrial district of the city.

An old friend introduced me to the scene of drug clubs a few years ago, and it sounded like a good idea tonight.

A dirty abandoned room filled with people, bad music, watered down beer, and any drug imaginable.

Sounded like an appropriate place, besides that's how I cope.

Feelings are gross.

It was still early though, so I'd have to find something else to do for a while.

I climbed up the broken fire escape of one of the crumbling buildings and watched the water on the other side of the pier separated by a chain link fence.

The salty sea air took me back to that last night with Courtney...

Luckily my phone rang with enough time to distract me.

It was my parents' house phone.

I snapped it shut immediately.

Screening works both ways, Mom.

In complete fairness Eva Mendez could've been calling, and I would've ignored it, I just don't feel like talking.

After a while I decided to listen to the voice mail, it could be funny, whatever my parents had to say after ignoring my pleas for help *again.*

This should be good.

"Elmer? It's Mom." I cringed at the sound of my government name, "I got your message, I'm sorry about whatever's going on this time. I put fifty dollars in your bank account I hope that helps," and that's about the extent of my mom's sympathy, "Anyway, I ran into that nice girl you used to go to school with from down the street," *Oh God, no,* "Caitlin something, well she's living in Seattle now. I gave her your number," *Motherfucker.* "You owe that nice girl an apology, Elmer."

I groaned loudly.

Bad news, a betrayal, and my birth name all in one sentence.

Fan-fucking-tastic.

Well, at least I have money now.

After a bit, a few shady people started sneaking into a warehouse.

Those are my Peeps.

It was as dusty, dark and... Musky, as I remembered.

I found a wobbly chair in the back of the warehouse to try to get wasted from whatever was poured in my plastic cup and to watch everyone else.

Usually, I'd be the guy up on tables, dancing, stripping and making a lot of noise, I just didn't feel like it.

I just wanted to be shit faced, I didn't wanna feel anything.

This insanely hot woman walked towards where I was sitting; God she looked like something I'd draw late at night.

She must've seen me drooling 'cause she made her way over and casually sat on my lap.

"Hey,"

"Hi," she ran her hand through my hair, "What's your name?"

"Parker,"

"What's your poison, Parker?"

"Blow."

"You or the drug?" She flirted.

"Either"

She chuckled, "You can't afford me. How much you want?"

"Just a bump."

She rolled her eyes, "A bump, how am I supposed to pay rent with a bump? I'll tell you what, I'll give you a grab bag of pills, too, for twenty-five."

"What are they?"

She shrugged, "Mexican ibuprofen or Oxy, your guess is as good as mine."

I only had a ten and five, but she took it. I wish all drug dealers were like her... Or were her.

She got off me and sat in the chair next to me, "So, what's a bad boy like you doing in a perfectly suitable place like this?"

"Forgetting shit."

"Ex..." She looked me over, trying to guess, "I can't read you, boys or girls?"

I shrugged, "Both."

She chuckled, "Fair enough. Is it an ex-girl slash boyfriend?"

My hand instinctually went to tug down my sleeves, but I didn't get my hoodie when I stormed out, but it was fine because you couldn't see anything in the flashing pink and green lights.

"Kinda, not entirely."

"Self sabotager, huh?"

"... Huh?"

She pointed at the scars on my arms as I took a drink.

So much for the lights.

"Oh... It's a kink." I lied.

"Mm," she sipped her drink and casually hiked up her sleeve revealing her own graveyard of scars, "Mm yeah, me too. Tried to kill myself and everything."

"Sorry..."

"Don't be, it's better now." She said in a tone that I'm used to people preaching at me in.

I kept drinking, "Mm, rehab, religion, or shock therapy? Been through 'em all."

She chuckled, "Buddy, I just sold you coke."

I rolled my eyes, "What's your name?"

"Strawberry,"

I lost my train of thought and scoffed, "Your name's not Strawberry."

"And I'll bet yours isn't Parker."

I crossed my arms, "Fine, what's your preach? Just get it over with, I can't be saved."

She smirked, "Drugs are bad. Crack is wack. That enough of a preach?" she stood, "Next time you need a fix, ask for Strawberry."

I watched her disappear into the crowd before I went to get another drink.

There was a major shift in the huge room as a blood curdling scream came from the bathroom.

Everyone was crowded to see what was happening.

I tried to push through, but it was better that I couldn't, I could already smell the blood.

I was able to get a glimpse from where I was, the door to the men's bathroom was propped open and everything was covered in blood.

Unfortunately, none of that was what caught my attention, there was something written on the mirror in the blood.

191

(ヽ(•̀ω•́)ノ)

20:15

Conner

I tried not to stew in my anger from what Parker said, in all honestly it wasn't even close to the worst thing he's ever said to me.

Besides that, I don't think it was really him I was mad at anymore.

Although when he crashed through the front door, I decided I wasn't talking to him.

"Con, Con," Parker floundered around, "Conner!"

"We're not speaking." I turned the page to my book and ignored him.

It didn't even slow him down.

He opened his mouth, and a swell of words crashed against me before I could decipher any of it.

I slowly put my book down, "What?"

"I speak cocaine," Nate decided to help, "Somethin' 'bout a rave, a strawberry, and a murder?"

Panicked, Parker felt around his pockets, "Here, here," he pulled out a crumpled piece of paper, another card.

"I was at this rave this girl gave me some coke, this guy died and..." He was incoherent again.

"Despacito, Jesus, how much coke did you do?"

"None! Look, *look*."

Aaron and Nate huddled around me as Parker scrambled to flip his phone open and pounded on the keys before he handed it to me.

It was a faraway photo of an industrial bathroom, it was blurry, but I could make out a someone lying on the floor and a pool of blood around them.

"Look at this!" Parker clicked the arrow on his phone, this one was of a mirror and there was a number scrawled onto it in dripping blood.

"191, does that mean anything to anyone?" I asked.

"Well," Aaron fidgeted with the stud in lip, "It's a Sophie Germain prime number. That's about it, but if you round it down to 190 it has a lot more. It's a triangle hexagonal and a centered nonagonal number. Oh! And it's also a truncated square pyramid."

Parker's eyes widened, "What does that mean?"

I shook my head, "It's the kind of math us non-scholarship holders don't understand."

"Sorry," Aaron made a face as he thought, "Hmm, I think 191 is something in mythology, supposedly it means a higher level of consciousness and confidence... But that's all folklore-y, it's probably the truncated square pyramid."

"Maybe it's a date!" Parker blurted out.

"Right," I scratched my forehead, "The ninety first of January."

"Shut up,"

"That was stupid."

"Don't say I'm stupid 'cause you're mad at me."

"I'm not, I'm saying you're stupid because you're stupid."

"You're stupid!"

"Mom, Dad," Nate nudged us both with the TV remote before he gestured to the program.

It was a breaking news story, "Hysteria at local rave".

"Isn't that one of those slutty little emo bands you listen to?" Nate snorted.

Parker ignored him, "Turn it up."

Nate turned it loud enough for us to hear the anchor, "A local man was found dead less than an hour ago at an underground warehouse rave. The victim has yet to be identified, police aren't releasing any information at this time but suspect foul play. This comes weeks after a woman was found murdered in her apartment. As Seattle anticipates a possible serial killer, we speak with..."

Nate turned it back down, "191 is penal code for matricide in California, don't think that helps but gets us away from Qbert over there."

I went through the drawer in my desk and shuffled through endless notes to find a blank paper to scribble down everything we said, including the math wizardry Aaron gave me, though I hoped we wouldn't need it.

Parker stood next to me, he leaned forward on the counter, his palms supporting him, "So where are we on hunting now?" It was the cockiness that made me consider knocking his arm out from under him.

"Don't be a jackass."

He crossed his arms, "Come on, this is staring us in the face."

I rolled my eyes and slammed my notebook shut.

"What are you doing?" Parker huffed.

"I'm going to bed; I told you what I thought, and you don't want to hear it."

"No, you don't want to hear it! This guy isn't gonna go away!"

"And what's another one of us getting killed going to help?! For God's sake, we have to go to memorial tomorrow. Just leave it alone."

"Fine!" He stomped in the other direction towards the front door.

"Where at you going?" Aaron asked.

"Target! Come on, Nate!"

Nate shrugged in response but went with Parker.

(＼(•̀w•́)／)

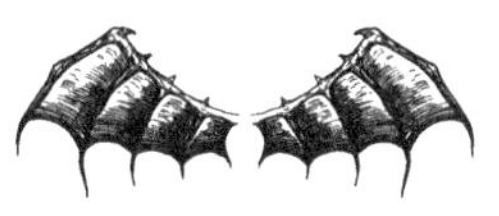

PARKER

I forced Nate along 'cause I hate driving and I wanted to get high without Conner yelling at me, besides Target's a nice place to be while high.

"You wanna talk 'bout it?" Nate asked half-heartedly as he watched me fill my hoodie pocket with gummy worms.

"I'm not a jackass! What about my feelings and..."

"Ugh, why'd I ask? Shut up."

I grumbled, every time I opened my mouth, he told me to shut up.

We took a short cut through the cosmetics, and something caught my eye.

Nate groaned, "Park, stop with the eyeliner, bro, it's getting gay."

"You're gay."

I might be dead but like any living person I have a normal trauma response, getting high and deciding to dye my hair.

And like any sane person, I did both in the gas station bathroom down the street.

The part I fucked up was asking Nate to help me.

It started with "I worked in my aunt's salon one summer" and ended with chemical burns from the bleach.

"Stop moving," Nate held my head down under the sink faucet trying to rinse out my hair.

"This is starting to remind me of something else."

He snorted and slapped me on the ass, "Better?"

"Ah, memories."

He threw a paper towel over my head, "Shut up."

I tried to blot the water out of my hair with the paper towels, but it kept disintegrating in my hands.

I hadn't looked at my hair yet, not until it fell in my face and I thought the color looked a little... *Off.*

So, I looked in the mirror, the places where my hair wasn't singed off from the bleach were dyed the brightest most aggressive shade of neon pink I have ever seen.

"WHAT THE FUCK?!"

"What?"

"Why is my hair fucking pink?!"

"It's red!"

"This is not fucking red!"

"You said get red; I got red!" He shoved the box in my face, "See, fuchsia."

"Fuchsia's pink, you asshole!"

"What?"

"FUCHSIA IS A SHADE OF PINK!!!"

"Hey, look at that, you finally got to use your art degree."

I hit his arm until I felt better, but that never happened.

"So, no head?" He laughed.

"I hate you."

I pouted the entire way back home.

September 24 2007

08:48

Conner

"Good morning," Aaron greeted as he stretched, his glasses were on top of his messy brownish blonde hair, "Did you know Parker's pink?"

I nodded taking a sip from my coffee mug, "I saw that when I got up, I thought he was a stuffed animal."

Aaron chuckled, "If only he slept like one, he keeps kicking me."

"That's better than waking up with Nate... Never mind." I shook the thought out of my head.

Aaron poured himself a cup of coffee and sat on the couch in front of me, "Are you still working on that number?"

"Mmhmm, looking into the death, too."

"What did you find?"

"Twenty-something guy, stabbed twice, throat slit."

"That sounds... Oddly normal."

"It is, just like the woman downstairs. It's just so *normal.*"

"Why would a vampire be killing people with knives? Wouldn't that much blood change them?"

I nodded, "I don't think it's a vampire."

Aaron's head cocked to the side, "You don't think it has to do with us?"

"No, I do. I have a theory, in the lore, what's to say a shifter couldn't possess a live being?"

He nodded, "Okay,"

"It would be one thing to communicate among each other, but... I don't think it would be too far out of reach."

"I thought shifters weren't real."

I shrugged, "It's looking more like they are."

"That would be a huge breakthrough for your research."

"*Our* research. I think you work harder than I do."

He offered me a tiny smile.

It was quiet for a second.

"You know your parents are proud of you, right?" He asked.

I cleared my throat, "If they were still here, I hope they'd be."

"They *are.*" He said softly.

Parker, in a hot pink haze, stumbled through the bedroom door.

He squinted at us with one eye, "Is the Space Needle still there?"

(＼(•̀w•́)／)

19:50

Most of my day was spent vetoing Parker and Nate's inappropriate outfits like I was the fascist principal of a conservative girls' school.

I glanced at my watch, despite having started this feat hours ago, we were about to be late now.

I sighed and grabbed the last two shirts that were left on the hanger, "Put these on and shut up."

Nate held the blue shirt I gave him up to his chest, "This yours?"

I shrugged in exasperation, "Probably why?"

"'Cause this is gonna be a crop top on me, shawty."

"Then pull your belt over it and keep your arms down."

"Do I have to wear pink?" Parker whined.

"Your hair is pink!"

"Exactly! It's too much."

I pinched the bridge of my nose, "Parker, I've seen you go on a date in a sequins tube top."

"Hey, she loved it, okay!"

Nate snorted.

"Just get dressed." I stomped out of the bedroom.

Aaron handed me a half-tied tie for me to slip on while he worked on the other two.

Sometimes I wonder how Aaron and I ended up the parents of the two oldest toddlers in the world.

"A tie?" Parker groaned as I tried to get everyone out the door, "Seriously? Last time I had a tie on I got..."

"Parker! For Christ's sake." I *had* to stop that thought.

"What?" He loosened it, "I was gonna say I went to a boarding school, God."

I glared at him while I unlocked my car doors, "No, you weren't."

"Nah, I wasn't."

I just shook my head and turned the key in the ignition.

I was greeted by a loud sputter.

"No, no, please." Another sputter, "Come on, you gas guzzling..." I grumbled and gave up, letting my head rest against the steering wheel.

"Just say fuck, you weirdo." Parker helped.

"Shut the fuck up."

Aaron cautiously tapped my shoulder, "We can take my car."

(＼(•̀w•́)／)

Aaron's car pulled into a parallel spot next to the curb and we arrived at the park without further incident.

The area was lit up with twinkle lights, they bounced off of the pond's water and illuminated everything in a dazzling rainbow.

There were over two hundred people huddled around with lit candles, there wasn't a black piece of clothing in sight.

Courtney would've loved how colorful everything was.

Bright and colorful, just like her.

When we walked up there was a cloth table with candles to take, next to it a cork board on an easel.

Every inch of the board was covered in photos of Courtney cataloging all the way from when she was a baby to just weeks ago.

Parker took one off the board, he was quiet for a minute, "I wish it were me. Hell, no one would even miss me."

"Don't talk like that," Aaron reprimanded.

"We'd miss you." I assured.

He looked at me, tears in his brown eyes, "Promise?"

Suddenly everything I was mad at him for melted away. It's hard to remember that's his way of processing, especially when he makes you want to strangle him, but I wanted to hug him.

Sometimes I wonder if I'll ever get used to how cold he is.

"Are you still mad at me?" Parker asked when I let go.

"I'm sure I will be later."

He cleared his throat as he put the picture back, "... I've been drawing her a lot... Is that weird?"

"Not any weirder than still having her jacket in my trunk." I offered.

Aaron tucked his hair behind his ears, the lights glistened off of the yellow smiley face shaped earring in his ears, "She left these in our bathroom a little while ago."

Nate crossed his arms, "I can't tell if the three of you are creeps or I'm heartless."

"Heartless." The three of us agreed.

He shrugged and went back to the board, "Whoa," he pointed out another picture.

Courtney was wearing a purple dress, red lipstick, she had a purple corsage on her wrist, and of course a pair of converses.

Her hair was done and curled into a formal style. Her arms were crossed, and her expression seemed annoyed but she still had a hint of a smile.

"She looks like an actual chick there." Nate said in amazement.

"I think that was prom." I speculated.

"It was." The four of us jumped at the addition of a new voice to our conversation.

It took a second for us to realize Jared was standing behind us.

"Hi," he gave us an odd look, but quickly moved past it, "Mrs. Hart asked us to get you."

"... Us?" Aaron asked.

Jared turned to his side before rolling his verdant eyes, "How long has he... Never mind." He just gestured for us to follow him.

Jared glanced out of the corner of his eye at Parker as we walked, "Your hair's different... You look like Starfire."

"... Thanks?"

"You're welcome."

Jared led us through the crowd, everyone's heads were quietly bowed in prayer while our sneakers squeaked against the wet sidewalk.

Everyone was staring at us.

I considered jumping into the lake and sinking to the bottom.

We stopped next to the rest of the guys from New Jersey, all except for Nicky. Vince offered us a friendly wave while Wyatt offered the slightest nod.

Jared bent to say something to Wyatt who looked confused.

"I'm nice." Wyatt crossed his arms.

"That is so extremely off the mark it's hilarious." Vince added.

"Whatever, I can be nice," Wyatt turned his head to look at Parker and paused, "I'm gonna go get a drink..."

Jared patted his friend on the back as he walked away.

We stood there silently with the crowd.

I struggled to see over the person in front of me, but from the side I could see Mrs. Hart at the front addressing the crowd.

"Good evening, it's been such a beautiful night so far. I would like to thank each and every one of you for coming out here with us, it's incredible to see all the lives my daughter has touched in her short time. I know it would mean the world to her..."

I could picture Courtney's reaction to all these people; it would be a short laugh followed by, "Wow, don't any of these people have anything better to do?" But I think even she would be surprised by the turn out.

Mrs. Hart continued speaking, "Though we couldn't honor her in the traditional sense, I'm glad we're able to do something she would like. With tonight's ceremony, our family has decided that as well as going to the search to bring Courtney home, that the use of the funds everyone has graciously donated will also commemorate a place for us to mourn until then." Mrs. Hart gestured over to a bench sitting beneath a giant willow tree on the other side of the lake, "The city and the park have agreed to foster us until we can have a proper burial for her. Now, along with that I've asked close friends of the family, Jared and Conner, to say a few things about Courtney."

The second I heard my name I started to sweat.

With everything that happened in the last twelve hours anything that wasn't involved got dumped out of my head to make room.

Aaron leaned in over my shoulder, "Are you okay?"

"No,"

Before I could say anything else Jared was nudging me along.

He must have thought I was such an idiot, and everybody was about to learn what a complete asshole I am.

Luckily Jared took over instantly, he went first.

I listened while I tried to think of something.

Jared spoke softly in a way that almost sounded musical; I wondered if that was his natural voice when he wasn't stressed.

He was calm, he seemed so gentle and completely different from the guy that spent the last four years striking fear into me through the stories Courtney would tell me.

"I met Courtney in 1991, her mother was my fifth-grade teacher. Courtney was in the sixth grade, but that didn't stop her from making friends with everyone in her mom's class. She's been one of my best friends since then.

I never understood why she was friends with someone like me, I've always been a quiet, solemn person, and I'm not much fun. So, I asked her once why she sought me out.

I remember the way she hugged me, a big grin on her face, 'Everyone deserves a friend'

That's the kind of person Courtney was. There wasn't a person she didn't know, and she made sure no one ever felt alone. It's a talent I envy and one I hope to instill in my little brother." He sighed as he flipped his page over, "Courtney was a lot of things. A sister, a daughter, a girlfriend, a best friend, a fighter, and one of the brightest lights this earth has ever had. Things are dim without her, but I know she wouldn't want us to notice, she would want us to do everything we could do to keep her spark alive." He raised his hand in a slight wave, "Thank you."

Jared stepped out of the way and tried to hand me the microphone, but I was too enthralled with what he had said.

It took a minute for me to notice.

"Um," the microphone felt wrong in my sweaty hands.

I tried to clear my throat and the speaker's feedback deafened me.

Off to a great start.

"Um, I didn't actually prepare anything that nice but um... My name's Conner... I met Courtney my first few days in Seattle, she stole my wallet," I awkwardly blurted that out but everyone seemed to think it was a joke, so I kept going, "She then bought me a coffee with my credit card and returned my wallet and gave me a lecture about being an easy target." I took a breath and tried to corral the many things I wanted to say, "That was the first of many things she taught me... When I moved out here, I had just lost both of my parents," I cleared my throat, "I didn't know what I was doing or where I was going, and I was scared. I was in a brand-new city and I was completely alone, but there was Courtney, who was willing to walk with me, she made everything seem less... *Daunting.* She believed in me when I didn't believe in myself, she taught me how to. Even as I stand here today, I hold that with me, I hold on to her blind belief." I chuckled hoping to hide the break in my voice, "I guess that's why I didn't write anything, if I had she probably would've ripped it to shreds and shoved me up here. Through the years she's been my courage to do things I never thought I could, like dropping out of college and breaking up with a girl that was willing to take me for everything..." My vision blurred as my eyes watered, "I wish someone would've told me sooner that this life is ours to do with it what we wanted, but I'm overjoyed and unbelievable fortunate that it was her..." I cleared my throat one last time, "I think that's it... Thank you."

(＼(•̀w•́)／)

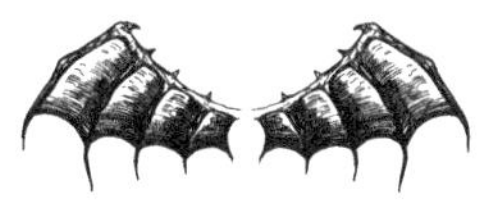

PARKER

I tried to listen to what was being said, I really did, but hyperactivity might as well be my middle name.

Wyatt was standing right next to me; his arms were crossed, and I could see every inch of skin was tattooed.

"Dude," I spoke without any thought, "How many tattoos do you have?"

Wyatt gave me an annoyed look, "None," he turned his sight back to Conner and Jared, "Stop talking."

Nate snorted next to me, "I like him."

I shoved my hands in my pockets while I pouted.

My head started to do the whirly thing, either from withdrawal or vampiric reasons I didn't know, so I parted from our groups and sat in the grass a few feet back.

Instead of going back to whoever was talking something else caught my eye.

A little girl was staring at me from over her mom's shoulder.

I was getting used to kids staring at me weirdly, usually I'd try to make them laugh and it would end with crying, I'm guessing it has something to do with the "dead aura" Aaron keeps mentioning.

She ran over to me the second her mom put her down.

"Hi!"

"Hi,"

"I like your hair."

"Thanks! I like your dress; you look very pretty."

"You look pretty, too."

Honestly, I was about to burst into a puddle of tears. Instead, I handed her the small flower I'd plucked out of the ground and was playing with.

"Thank you," she swayed back and forth, "He says he's sorry about your friend."

"I, huh?"

"He heard about it," the light caught the side of her face, her big red eyes bore into me sending a shocking chill through my body, "He's sorry, but he can fix it."

I caught myself from falling over, "What?"

Her mother rushed over and grabbed her by the hand, "Chelsea! What did I say about wandering off?"

I scrambled to my feet, "W-wait..."

She was tugged away by her mom before I could finish processing.

Conner

After a short moment of silence, Mrs. Hart dismissed the crowd of hundreds.

She gave Jared and I a hug, "That was beautiful, thank you both so much."

"It was an honor." Jared responded.

"Yes, thank you for asking us to do it." I added.

She smiled at us for a second, "It's getting late, I wouldn't be a mother if I didn't send you home, especially you," She rubbed Jared's shoulder, "You have a long flight tomorrow."

Jared nodded, "I know, and I should probably find my brother before then,"

Jared stood over me, I thought he was going for a hug but stopped short and I was locked into an awkward handshake, "It was nice to finally see you, tell your friends we said 'bye'."

"Same here and tell Wyatt that I'm sorry about Parker."

Jared chuckled; he walked off with Mrs. Hart.

I scanned the area for somewhere to collect myself for a few minutes before I went to look for the guys.

The new bench caught my eye, so I made my way over.

It was made out of a thick, pale wood and beautifully caved, it had a few painted orange butterflies scattered across its surfaces.

"Dedicated to Courtney W. Hart, A beautiful soul that has left us far too early, you were a hero in life and in death."

I could hear the fallen leaves behind me crunch.

"It's pretty, huh?" Drew's soft voice came from next to me.

"It's beautiful," I cleared my throat to get rid of the lump.

"Mom wanted to do hearts, I felt like it was a little on the nose." She offered a warm smile as I sat, "You look nice."

I tried my best to return the smile, "So do you."

The light sway of the large tree and the bubbling of the pond filled the quiet space.

Drew spoke up, "Your speech was great, by the way."

"Thanks."

"... I was supposed to speak tonight, but" she shrugged, "I finally stopped crying maybe five minutes ago."

I nodded my sympathy.

"I should probably go; my mom is waiting for me."

"Me too, hopefully the guys haven't left without me. Is it okay if I walk with you?"

"That'd be great."

We were halfway through the park before anything else was said.

Drew adjusted her coat, "Are you doing anything Saturday?"

"I shouldn't be, why?"

She shrugged, "I was wondering if that offer for a cup of coffee still stands? It'd be nice to get out of the house for a while."

"... Yeah, sure. Of course."

(ヽ(•̀w•́)ノ)

NATE

Leaning against the side of Aaron's car I watched Parker frantically look for us.

Aaron felt bad, "I'm going to go get him."

I put my arm in front of Air, "Hang on, he'll figure it out."

He won't, but I was entertained, and he was leaving me alone.

One of Court's guys from Jersey was a few cars over, he caught my eye 'cause he had a pack of cigarettes.

"Hey!" I forgot his name, but I got his attention and waved him over.

"Hey, Wyatt." Aaron greeted him.

Wyatt shrugged, annoyed, "What?"

"Lemme bum one?"

"If you got a light," he gestured with the cigarette between his fingers, "That fucker took mine."

I nudged Aaron 'til he gave me his Zippo.

Wyatt was surprised, "You smoke?"

It was fair, I might as well have borrowed a two hundred buck, all silver, engraved lighter from a toddler.

"He's more of an arson kinda guy." I flicked the flame on and let Wyatt light his cigarette first.

"Mm, Is that what your deal is?"

Aaron shrugged.

"What's his?" He nodded towards Parker who was jogging over.

"Coke, but mostly that's just him."

Park looked "frazzled" when he got to us, "Con's not here? Where is he?"

"I saw him walking with Drew." Aaron helped.

"Did you see anything weird?" Parker blathered on.

"God, you're like a coke weasel. I dunno, weird how?"

"I'm not high!" Parker looked over his shoulder at Wyatt, "Just *weird?!*"

Wyatt was just enjoying the show.

"'Sides you, right now?" I asked, "Nah, no weird."

I'm guessing by his weasel like movement, he didn't like that answer.

"Alright, alright, alright, alright." Parker ran his hands through his neon hair, "I'll wait for Con."

The little blonde kid stomped over next, his arms crossed. He ignored us and went for Wyatt, "Can we go?"

"Where's Jer?"

"Yelling at me, can we leave?"

"Sorry, kid, your brother's got my keys."

"And your balls." He mumbled.

Wyatt rolled his eyes.

"You're welcome to hang out with us." Aaron offered.

"Right, that's at the top of my list. I don't 'hang' with murderers."

"What's that supposed to mean?" Parker stepped in.

Wyatt grabbed the kid by his arm, "Nick, for once, just shut your mouth."

Nicky didn't take that advice, "It means, *she* was always fine when she hunted with us,"

"And there he goes." Wyatt mumbled to himself, stomping out his cigarette.

"Besides, you're a killer yourself." Nicky shot at Parker.

Parker scoffed, "What are you? Seven? You don't know shit."

"I know that I've been doing this for three years and I've never had a problem."

"Give it another two, shit happens. Could've happened to any of us." Wyatt popped off.

"But it didn't, it happened when she hunted with one of *them*,"

"Cut your shit," Wyatt warned, "If one of them doesn't hit you, I'm gonna."

"You didn't even care about her, did you? She was just another blood pack to you."

Parker rolled his eyes.

"I understand. You're upset, we all are," Aaron went to put his hand on Nicky to keep them apart.

He shoved Aaron back, "Don't touch me."

Parker got the look that usually got us bounced out of bars.

I grabbed him out of the air and held him back.

"Don't you ever put your fucking hands on him!" Parker hissed.

I'm pretty strong, but even I can't fuck with vamp strength.

Even in Parker's compact form.

"You hit him; your ass is goin' to jail." I warned Park.

Nicky put his arms out in a taunt.

Parker weaseled outta my grip like the little motherfucker he is.

Parker tackled the kid, but Nicky got a good hit in.

I sized up Wyatt. I waited to see what he was gonna do, 'cause I wasn't gonna let Parker get his ass kicked.

I didn't have to find out, 'cause Conner, Vince and Jared ran over from wherever they were.

It took the five of us to separate them, Conner and I drug Parker back while Jared held his brother up by the back of his jacket.

"What the fuck is going on over here?" Jared and Conner said almost at the exact same time.

Parker and Nicky yelled back and forth at each other.

"Enough!" Jared and Con did it again and just stared at each other in shock and annoyance.

Conner cleared his throat, "Go ahead."

Jared looked over at us for an explanation.

Wyatt crossed his arms, "Avril Lavine over there's right, Nick was talkin' shit."

"He tackled me." Nicky argued.

"He punched me in the face!" Parker added.

"Seriously?" Jared dropped the kid, "You hit him? Are you serious? Is this really how you want to honor our sister? Y'know what?" Jared gestured for Parker, "Go ahead, tear each other to shreds. There's only one person that'd care if you did, and she's not here."

Everyone went silent.

Jared crossed his arms, "That's what I thought. Go get in the car."

Nicky hesitated.

"Now," Jared growled making everyone jump.

Wyatt and Vince quickly got Nicky to move.

Jared shook his head, "I'm so sorry. Are you okay?" He asked Parker.

Parker shrugged it off, "I'm fine, he just shoved Aaron..."

"I'm sorry,"

"Don't be," Aaron spoke up, "I shouldn't have tried to touch him, that's on me."

"No, it's not. *It's on him.* He's just been so aggravating lately..." He shook his head again, "He had no reason to be an asshole to any of you. I'm really, *genuinely*, sorry about this. I'm gonna lay into him for this one."

Parker scratched the back of his neck, "Uh, I kinda don't have the ability to feel guilt anymore," He tried to joke, "But I know he's a kid, it wasn't cool of me either."

Jared chuckled, "Thanks, but you probably would've done me a favor if you kicked his ass. Now, I've got to deal with him." He paused for a second, "All things considered, it was nice to see you all, and if you guys need anything, seriously, anything. You have my number." He offered us an awkward wave as he walked off.

We all got in the car, no one said anything.

"So," Conner cleared his throat, "You'll apologize for tackling someone, but when I get a concussion from getting hit in the *head* with a *shoe*, suddenly you don't know what's going on?"

"I saw a little girl with red eyes," Parker blurted.

Con turned around in the passenger seat, "Huh?"

"*I saw a little girl with red eyes.*"

"No, I heard you. What are you talking about?"

"*A six-year-old* came up to me and her *eyes were red!*" Parker emphasized by pulling his eyelids down, "She said, 'He heard about our friend' and 'He was sorry but he could fix it'."

"You're sure about that?"

Parker crossed his arms, "What's that mean?"

"You're not the most reliable source."

"I'm not high! I know what I saw!"

Parker crossed his arms, "I'm not high."

"Well, we were late because you had to go smoke a joint."

"I *was* high, seeing your dead best friend's whole life in photos at her memorial kinda sobers you up!"

I shrugged, "Can vouch for that."

"Why didn't you say anything sooner?" Aaron asked at a stoplight.

"'Cause New Jersey's own Paris Hilton attacked me!"

"What else happened?"

"Nothing," Parker sighed, "Her mom came and got her, I couldn't even say anything."

"There's your theory." Aaron added.

Conner nodded, "There it is."

September 25 2007

03:33

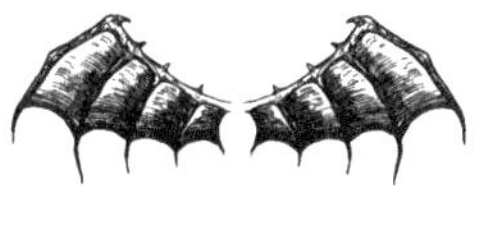

Parker

Everyone went to bed hours ago, but I was still awake, sitting on the cold bathroom tile.

I couldn't sleep, everything was haunting me every time I closed my eyes.

The little girl with the red eyes was at the front of my mind. God, she seemed so young, way too young to be messed with.

Conner and Aaron seemed excited at the idea, but it made me want to throw up.

No one had an idea what the message could've meant.

Conner suggested we sleep on it, maybe we could see clearer with fresh eyes...

"He's sorry..." The words of the small girl echoed in my head, "He can fix it."

'He can fix it'... What does that mean?

'He's sorry', he's not sorry, but he will be.

If we could ever figure out what any of this means, well, he will be sorry when I rip his heart out of his chest myself.

The crowding thoughts faded when my hand started to feel wet.

I'd forgotten what I was doing again.

Sitting on the cold bathroom tile, I was running a razor across my wrist.

At one point in my life, I had an entire kit devoted to this, but Conner found it and threw it out a few weeks ago.

These days I was restricted to what I could get in the bathroom without anyone noticing.

The repeated movement, the sting from the cut, and watching the wound seal itself closed again was strangely relaxing to me.

I figured it had to do with years I'd been doing it, but in terms of instant relief, it was better than any drug I'd ever taken.

I was desperate for the control it gave me.

Black muck was pouring down my wrist onto my hand, I'd cut too deep, and it was taking its sweet time healing.

"Son of a bitch..." I mumbled, I crumpled up some toilet paper and held it closed.

It felt fine, good actually, but I knew Conner was gonna have my ass if he found the "bloody" paper or noticed the new scar.

I don't think I'd ever get used to the syrupy black ooze.

Unlike blood it was weirdly cold, instead of soaking into the toilet paper it would stick and glop up, wounds didn't gush they dripped like tar, and rather than smelling like metal it smelled like death.

And God, does that smell stick when you're hunting.

Finally, the oozing stopped, the wound tapered shut until it was closed completely.

I took a deep breath and gave in; I felt slightly better so I tried another handful of sleeping pills and burrowed into the bed comforter next to Aaron.

Hopefully, if I was lucky, I'd fall asleep.

September 26 2007

12:40

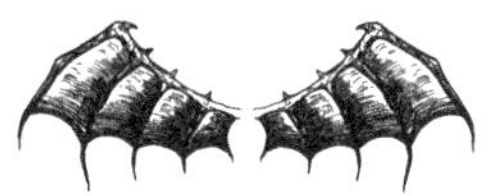

PARKER

I have a habit of sleeping through days, Con said it's a side effect of not eating but I called it peace.

I could avoid things, and it was less permanent than death... A real one, I mean.

I was still asleep when I got a sharp throbbing pain in my head, it hurt so bad that I thought Aaron had kicked me in his sleep again.

I got dizzy and started to see stars; my sight narrowed until it went black.

It happened in a flash; I was back in the apartment downstairs.

I held a terrified woman to my chest; my hand covered her mouth while I held a large shiny knife in the other.

She saw the moment to headbutt me and got out of my grip.

She ran for a drawer in the kitchen, she was scrambling for something, I didn't realize what until there was a loud bang.

A gunshot.

The bullet pierced my side, but I couldn't feel pain, yet I just felt pressure, a lot of pressure.

I held my hand over the wound before I steadied myself on the wall, "You've made a *grave* mistake."

I squeezed my eyes shut until the pain in my head subsided.

When I opened them, I was back in bed in my apartment.

Nate stood over me, trying to wake me up.

"What?" I snapped at him.

"Con just left and Air's at work," he held a blunt in front of me, "Thought you'd want some."

"Weed or something else?"

"Light up, we'll see."

(＼(•̀w•́)／)

12:50

Conner

Drew had told me to meet her at a small coffee shop between our apartment and Mrs. Hart's house.

The soft pitter-patter of the rain outside coupled with the airy music playing over the speaker system and the sound of distant chatter from the other customers set a relaxing atmosphere, one that I hoped would help with the awkwardness I felt from Drew picking the only coffee shop in the entire world I had ever worked at and quit from.

I sat in the far corner from the door, so I had to stand up when Drew arrived.

"Hi, sorry I'm..." Drew draped her coat over the back of her chair as she glanced at the clock on the opposing wall, "... I'm not late."

"No," I chuckled to myself, "I'm always way too early... Unless I'm with Parker."

"I'm the same," she slid into the seat across from me, "My mom drilled that into me as a kid."

"How is your mom doing?"

"She's doing good... Strangely good, I don't know how she does it. I feel like I'm falling apart at the smallest things, and she's..." Drew shook her head, "I'm sorry, I'm rambling."

"No, you're fine. I'm a rambler, I tend to just go on and on. Like a few weeks ago, I was at a bar, and I spent twenty minutes just talking, I have no idea where it comes from, I just keep going, and going..."

She laughed when I finally stopped.

I chuckled but shook my head, "That was a dumb joke."

"No, I needed a laugh." She played with the sleeve of her sweater, "Thanks for coming with me, by the way... A lot of my friends, they just don't really get it."

I nodded, "Of course."

There was a lull.

Drew was playing with her necklace, I noticed it was the same one Courtney made me promise to give to her.

"Did you figure out what that key was to?" My question caught Drew off guard.

"Hm?"

"In the locket." I pointed to the pendant.

"Oh," she twirled the chain around her finger, "No, I mean yes... We started cleaning out her apartment, I found a box under her bed. I know that's what the key's for, but I can't bring myself to open it."

"That's understandable."

Drew paused for a second, "I'm sorry, I know I asked you to come so we could talk and I thought I wanted to, but I just can't talk about her right now."

"No, I get that. Trust me."

"Thanks... I like your necklace, that's a cool pattern. Oh, and it matches your ring."

I ran my thumb over the engraving of the silver ring on my right hand, "Thanks, they were my parents'."

"They're gorgeous. What does it say?"

"It's French, they were both from Montreal and native French speakers. I was actually born in Canada."

"It's cool that you know that; I was adopted. I don't know anything about my birth parents. Like at least Courtney knew she was from Germany."

"You don't know anything?"

She shook her head, "Well, I know they were Native American, that's about it. My mom was always adamant about teaching us about the cultures and countries we came from."

"That's awesome."

She nodded, "Are your parents still in Canada?"

"Um, no... They're dead."

Drew's hands flew over her mouth, her icy eyes were huge, "I'm so sorry."

I couldn't help but laugh, "It's fine, really."

"Ah, I can't believe I forgot something like that. I remember Courtney telling me that too, and... God, I'm not doing a very good job at not talking about her."

"Drew," I tried to pat her hand in a comforting way but I think it just came off awkward, "It's okay, everything is overwhelming, I get it."

She tried to shake the thought from her head, her long dark hair dusted the table when she did, "Do you want to show me a picture of your boyfriend so I can call him ugly, too?" She joked.

"I, uh? Boyfriend?"

Her eyes widened, "... You're not gay either, are you?"

I chuckled, "No,"

"Wow, *wow*. Okay, I'm just going to stop talking now. I'm sorry."

"Don't be, I get that a lot. I think I was probably meant to be gay, just no one told me," I joked back.

Blushing she tried to hide her face behind her hand, "So you're..."

"If straight is a thing, I'm that." I smiled to try to put her at ease, but as I'm usually the one sticking my foot in my mouth, I don't think it was that helpful.

She smiled back and apologized again, "Are you seeing someone?"

I shook my head, "No, it's been a few years."

"You don't have a girlfriend?" She sounded surprised.

I shrunk in the seat slightly, "Is that weird? The last girl I was with was three years ago, we were together a year," evidently it was now my turn to embarrass myself as I had to keep talking, "I thought we would get married, but she was, well she wasn't horrible, but she wasn't great for me. Courtney talked me into breaking up with her and..." I sheepishly laughed when I realized I was over sharing, "See told you I'm a rambler."

"No, no, it's not weird. I just find it hard to believe, you're so sweet and kind."

I felt my face start to get hot, unfortunately I can't take a compliment, and my face makes it apparent immediately.

"I'm not that..."

She cut me off, "You dropped everything to come get a coffee with me because I was having a hard time, who else would do that? I get why you were Courtney's best friend."

(＼(•̀w•́)ノ)

23:15

Aaron

I had a long night; Saturdays were usually the busiest for the restaurant I worked at.

It was exhausting, but at least the tips were okay.

I finished my side work and chose a booth to collapse into while I counted my tips.

I wasn't really paying much attention to what I was doing, in my head I was already on my way home, in my car with a Pearl Jam tape in the player.

Halfway through the cash the paper between my fingertips shifted to a much different texture, it was far thicker than a bill.

I forced myself to zone back into what I was doing.

I glanced down at a piece of cardstock in my hand, a metallic black top hat was printed onto the card.

On the back, in red ink, was my full name in perfect cursive,

Aaron J. Henson

Below my name was an underlined number, *191*.

I don't think I drove home very safely after that.

(＼(•̀w•́)／)

Conner

I had reserved myself to the thought of a relaxing evening, I had a nice time talking with Drew, and since my head hurt from everything I was working on, getting a break sounded nice, and it was, until my computer started chiming.

Then Parker and Nate were arguing over something.

"Guys," I tossed a balled-up paper at them.

"Sorry," Parker said in an annoying voice and tossed the paper back.

I thought about knocking their heads together until something caught my eye, "What happened to your neck?"

Nate had a couple of marks across his neck, he's not exactly a stranger to mysterious injuries.

He shrugged it off, "From a girl I met few nights ago."

"Uh huh," Parker had his arms crossed and raised his eyebrows in a challenge, "She a biter?"

"Worse than the fucking vamps."

I must have missed something, because Nate rolled his eyes and shoved Parker across the couch, "Cállate. Why the fuck you so close to me?"

Parker just smirked before he turned his attention to me, "Whatcha doing?"

"I found a more detailed report of the woman downstairs,"

"You think we missed something?"

"We might have, the report says they found a revolver. Smith and Wesson, .380..." I shook my head, "That gun holds six bullets, one was missing. The five remaining," I raised my eyebrows, "Silver."

"You're kidding."

"Nope, and," I turned my computer screen around to show Parker a picture of one of the white walls, it had a black smudge that almost looked like a handprint.

"She hit him." He said what I was thinking out loud, "I saw it."

"Obviously, it didn't stop him, but she knew enough to use silver."

Parker shook his head, "Why? What's this guy getting at?"

"Maybe he wanted to put the number on the mirror in a more obvious place, he probably didn't have time after he was hit. So, he tried again at the warehouse party."

"But why? And why that number?"

"I'm still working on that. Could be an area code, zip code, cipher, a red herring." I sighed, my head was starting to spin from the millions of things it could be, "It could mean anything, or nothing."

"And the other vic? He a hunter too?"

"I don't have anything that says he was."

Parker leaned against my desk, "He's going after hunters, Chris, our neighbor..."

"Nuh uh," Nate interjected, "Chris seemed like a favor."

He threw out his arms, "What the fuck was the favor?"

He sat on the couch with a defeated grunt.

At that time Aaron opened the front door, he had a weird look on his face but he seemed calm.

Nate's eyes widened when he saw him, "Que paso?"

"Um, I'm trying to not freak the fuck out, but" Aaron responded, his voice was at a pitch that was making the neighborhood dogs bark.

He handed me a top hat card; this one had his name on it along with the same number from the bathroom.

I inspected it while Parker and Nate huddled around to do the same.

Aaron tried to lower his voice back into human range, "What do you think this means?"

Parker talked over me, "It means he's coming after hunters and you're next."

Nate took the opportunity to smack Parker in the back of the head.

"Ow! What? It's obvious! He killed Courtney, and we're next, we're all next!

"What're you on about?" Nate crossed his arms.

"He said he could "fix it"! How do you fix it? How do you fix dead?! What, she just disappeared? No! She either got up or he took her! And one of these days we're going to find her out here, mindless and rotting away just like the rest of them!"

I shook my head, "Parker, I saw her take her last breath."

"So what?! I took mine three years ago!"

Nate slammed his hand into Parker's shoulder, "Calm down, or I'm gonna calm you down, okay?" He glanced over Parker's head at Aaron, he looked like he was about to be sick.

Parker crossed his arms, "Two weeks,"

"Two weeks, what?" I asked.

"Give me two weeks to get this figured out and handled, after that I want you to put a silver bullet through my heart and each of you get out of this, got it?"

"Parker, none of this is your fault."

"It sure as fuck seems like it."

September 27 2007

10:30

Conner

It was a long night of trying to get everyone to calm down.

Aaron was dressed for work; a cautious look was on his face as he hovered at the kitchen counter while I was eating.

"I have to go to work..." He stood perfectly still.

"Are you okay?"

"I don't know."

I shook my head, "You *are* okay, Parker's paranoid. If this guy is coming after us, he's not going to do anything in broad daylight in public,"

Aaron took a deep breath and nodded. "You're right."

"Besides, you're a good hunter, you would know what to do."

"I have my switchblade."

"Good. Do you have your phone?"

He gave me a confused nod before he handed it to me.

I plugged it into my computer, "I have a tracker, it's a little crude at the moment, but I think it'll make everyone feel better."

I handed it back to him once it was done downloading, "Do you want me to come to work with you?"

He shook his head, his hair dusted his shoulders, "No, I'm okay." He chirped.

14:00

Aaron

I had the lunch shift at work today.

I didn't mind it much, I almost preferred it with everything going on, but I was still cautious.

I kept turning to look over my shoulder and, to my relief, I wasn't met with anything.

They ended up cutting me from work early since it wasn't that busy, which, again, was a relief.

I tried desperately to keep the panic out of my head, but it still crept up on me every so often. So, I forced myself to have a calm, relaxing drive home.

The weather was nice today, slightly overcast with a refreshing autumn chill. The trees were gorgeous, a blurry mix of oranges, reds and yellows as I drove by.

I tried to keep my head clear for most of the day, and forced my drive back home to be as calm and relaxing as I could.

I put a CD into my car's radio without even looking at it, I didn't recognize the album for a minute, the songs didn't seem cohesive... Until they did.

Courtney had made me a mix tape last year for my birthday, she purposely only put songs that came out the year I was born on it.

It was a really nice present, and I liked every song on it, but it hit a little close to home today.

I let one song play before I turned it off and opted to drive in silence for a block or two.

I had an idea, but it required that I turn around and make a quick stop at Yankee Candle.

I knocked on the apartment door just to make sure no one new had moved in before I picked the lock.

That would have been embarrassing.

No one responded, so I proceeded to pick the lock.

The entire apartment was desolate, Courtney's couch, her stereo, her CDs, her tv, her movies, and the wall of pictures she had next to her bedroom door, everything was completely taken down.

It was bare with no signs of life.

It was really sad, but I tried to block it out while I set up the four candles I bought in the north, west, south and east corners of the apartment.

I sat in the middle of them all, I crossed my legs under myself and tried to meditate.

There are a few things about me the guys might not exactly know about, like my interest in Paganism and witchcraft is a little more than something I like to read about.

Courtney was the only one that knew the full story, most people think I'm insane when I tell them I see ghosts. I mean, I guess that's perfectly normal reaction, but not Courtney. I don't know why she believed me, no one ever did, but she was always supportive over anything I did. I'm not trying to lie to the guys about it, I just know it would freak them out if they knew, so I decided to keep it to myself.

I took a deep breath, "I call upon the spirits, my guides, and the universe to protect me. I call upon the spirits, my guides, and the universe to direct me. I call upon the spirits to ask about my friend, Courtney."

It was quiet, so I tried again, "I call upon the spirits to ask about the happenings of my friend, Courtney."

After forty-five minutes and getting almost no activity, I let my shoulders slump forward with a sigh.

"Courtney, please," I gripped the hunk of quartz I held tighter, "I don't know where you are, but I just need to talk to you for a minute."

"Please?"

This hardly ever works, but as a last resort it sounded like a good idea.

After another five minutes, I gave up and laid back on the hardwood floor.

"Courtney," I sighed, "I know you're not around, but I'm going to talk like you are anyway and hope you can hear me."

I sat back up and moved my hair over my shoulder, "I miss you so much... I really hope you're happy wherever you are and that they're taking good care of you." I forced myself to chuckle or else I was going to start crying, "I know you wouldn't ever need anyone to take care of you, but you know what I mean... I really do miss you; I didn't think I could miss someone this much... I just wanted to tell you thank you, thank you for everything you've ever done for me, for all your support, and for being the older sister I never knew I needed..." My voice broke, "I'm really sorry about what happened to you. I'm sorry we couldn't help you more, I hope you know we're trying." I wiped the tears running down my cheek, "I hope you know how much we all love you."

(＼(•̀w•́)／)

"Hey," Nate was sitting on the couch when I got home.

"Holy shit," He shot up when he saw that I was crying, "What happened? Are you hurt?" He looked me over to make sure I was okay.

I just shook my head.

"What happened?"

"...I can't find her." I choked out before I started crying harder.

"I can't understand you."

He didn't really know what to do so he just held onto me tightly and pet my hair for a minute.

I couldn't calm down, and I think it kinda freaked him out.

"Hey," He patted my shoulder, "Where's your phone? Do you wanna call your dad?"

I just nodded.

September 28 2007

08:08

Aaron

I had fallen asleep on the couch while I was still on the phone with my dad, after nights of not sleeping even our lumpy couch felt like memory foam.

I woke up while Conner was making coffee.

I slid my glasses off to rub my eyes, "Morning..."

"Morning, sorry I was trying to be quiet." He stopped what he was doing to come sit by me and gave me his undivided attention... It was intimidating, I don't like being the center of attention.

"Nate said you were upset when you got home, are you okay? Did something happen?"

"No, I just..." I fidgeted with my lip ring as I avoided eye contact, "I think I just had a panic attack."

"Are you okay now?"

I hesitated but nodded.

Conner patted my shoulder as he stood, "If you have a second, I want you to take a look at something." He handed me a hiking trail map.

I stared at it, "Is... Is this where we were?"

He nodded, "Does something seem weird to you?" He hinted as he sat on the couch.

I pushed my glasses up with the back my hand, "There aren't any buildings... Caves?"

Conner shook his head, "No caves."

"No animal dens?"

"None big enough for the number of vampires we were dealing with."

"It wasn't a nest?"

He took a sip from his mug, "I've been digging, looking for anything that could be a nest. There's no way."

"Where did they all come from?"

"I don't know, but hundreds of people searched that area, not one vampire surfaces?" He put his mug down, "We didn't wander into a nest, this was an attack." He poked at the paper with two fingers to emphasize his point.

"What are you saying?"

He sighed, "I hate to admit it, but I think Parker might be right. Whatever this is about, it isn't just about Parker, it's about all of us."

I rubbed the fabric of the couch cushion between my fingers, "... It wasn't my fault?"

"Aaron," he looked up at me, "No, of course it wasn't. It wasn't anyone's fault, I'm the one that left her there."

I shook my head; my eyes were starting to burn again.

(＼(•̀w•́)／)

11:05

Conner

Aaron and I spoke for a while longer, I felt bad, had I known he blamed himself... It just wasn't fair. He's the one that kept her alive longer, I'm the reason she's missing.

I tried to explain that, but I don't know how much got through, Aaron seemed like he wanted the conversation to be over and went to get ready for work.

I wish I could fix it for him...

Well, if I'm wishing for things, it would be that none of this happened.

"Hey," Parker shuffled out of the room, his hoodie was up over his head and his hands were stuffed in his pockets.

The dark circles under his eyes seemed deeper, and his skin paler, "Do you have the AC on?"

I sighed and wrote a note to myself about that, "It's been broken for six months."

"This apartment is a demon away from a hellhole."

"Well, we already have you."

He hissed his response, yet still had the audacity to sit next to me on the couch. He pulled his legs up under himself and wiggled closer until he was pressed against me.

"What are you doing?"

"You're warm." He moved my arm until it was over his shoulders.

"Parker!"

"What?" He poked at my laptop screen, "What's this? Hunt?"

I sighed and just let him stay there, moving him was going to require some holy water and something to wedge between us and I didn't have the time.

"I'm just looking into something; I don't know what it is yet. But you'll be happy to know I'm about to finally say what you've been waiting to hear for ten years,"

He sat up, a smirk on his face, "You're finally gonna fuck me?"

"Okay!" I shoved him off me, "That is a *hard no,* and it's always going to be a no. I meant, you were right."

"Oh, bummer. But hey I was right about something?!"

"Might, I said 'might'."

"No, you didn't. What was I right about?"

"Whatever all of this is about," I gestured vaguely around, "It involves all of us. I looked over the hunting area, there's no way it was a nest."

He shot to his feet, "I told you I wasn't paranoid!"

"Technically, Nate called you paranoid. And I didn't say you we're wrong, we just needed the proof."

Parker crossed his arms, "This is why you don't have a girlfriend; you can't be wrong."

"Bite me. Anyway..."

He wasn't done, then again, when is he?

"So, if I'm right, that means he's coming after Aaron..."

"I didn't say that."

"Whatever, what if he is? We have to be prepared. They already got to him once while he was at work. We gotta do something,"

I feel the need to emphasize the next thing I said was completely sarcastic, "What are we going to do? Follow him everywhere?"

A light bulb went over Parker's head.

"No," I tried to interrupt his thought, "Parker, I was being facetious, that was a joke!"

"No no, that'll work."

"No, it won't. You can't follow him around waiting for something to happen."

"Why not?"

"I need a reason?! It's a total invasion of privacy, for starters."

"Not like I'm gonna follow him to the bathroom."

"Parker," I sighed, "He still needs and deserves space!"

"Eh, he'll never know I'm there."

"Your hair's bright pink, Park."

He rolled his eyes, "Vamp speed, he'll never know."

"Okay, now you're being paranoid."

"How am I being paranoid?"

I just stared at him for a second, "... You want to stalk Aaron." I said slowly.

"It's not stalking, it's just watching him, from a far, to make..."

"That's the definition of stalking!"

He crossed his arms, "We already lost one friend, Con."

"I get that, but Aaron's a big boy, he can take care of himself, he knows what to do."

"Courtney didn't?"

"She got ambushed."

"Whatever, I'm not letting it happen again."

I sighed, I'm fully aware I can't talk him out of anything, "I'm not gonna fight you, just know I don't think it's a good idea."

(＼(•̀w•́)／)

17:45

Parker

Against Conner's advice, and probably better judgment, I decided go through with watching Aaron.

I followed him to work, watching him from a blind spot in the corner of the building, I freaked out most of his co-workers, and almost got kicked out, but he didn't ever notice me.

I broke into his car while he was adding up his tips and hid under his backseat.

Aaron drove a couple blocks before his phone started to ring, he let it go for a while before he sighed and pulled over at a coffee shop to answer it, "Hi Mom."

In the amount of time, I've known him, he hasn't really talked about his parents much, I mean, we got the gist, and I knew he was on good terms with them, but something seemed off, maybe it was because they didn't know about hunting, I don't know.

"No, no. I talked to Dad. Because there's no reason to." He sighed again, "I know. It's been seven years, Mom. Yes, I promise. I'll try. Mom... I gotta go, I'm driving. Bye, I love you." He hung up, tucking his hair behind his ear, I could feel the stress coming off him.

After a minute of sitting in silence, he felt around the backseat for his book, his hand nearly brushed my hair.

I just stayed silent, scooting it closer to his hand.

He got out and went into the coffee shop.

I scrambled to get out of the car while he was gone and shimmied my way into a bush where I got a good view of Aaron through the window.

The fact that I hadn't been arrested yet was kinda impressive.

Aaron came back out a few minutes later, sipping whatever he bought, and sat a couple hundred feet in front of the bush I claimed.

It didn't take long for him to zone out into his book, he absent-mindedly flicked his lighter open and closed while he read.

'God, he's gonna light this place on fire.'

I'm pretty sure he wasn't aware he did it most of the time, like Conner's bizarro pen tapping/clicking thing.

After a while, I noticed the pretty hot waitress checking him out.

She approached him, after she watched him for a minute like a creep, "Excuse me?" She set his food down in front of him.

Aaron glanced up, "Oh, hi."

"Hi, I got a break coming up, can I get a cigarette from you?"

He gave her a weird look, kinda disgusted, but overall, just missing the message, "I don't smoke." He went back to his book and ignored her.

I don't think I've ever facepalmed so hard in my life, I wanted to throw a rock at him, I would've, if I had one, best I could've done was a handful of those red wood chip things that always end up in your shoes.

He sat there for half an hour, he ate half a sandwich, reading and being completely oblivious to how stupid he is.

I took the opportunity to break back into his car when he went back inside to pay the bill.

I fully meant to stay there, and make sure he didn't know what was going on, but I got bored and decided scaring the shit out of him sounded like a better idea.

"Oh, my God! Aaron!" I sat up screaming.

I scared the shit out of him, making him swerve, and scream back.

I laughed, "It's just me, chill."

"Oh, my God! Why would you do that?!" He yelled at me, well, it was more of a squeak.

"Sorry, sorry." I tried to stop laughing, I couldn't help it.

"What are you doing?!"

I shrugged, "Got bored."

"You almost totaled my car." He glared at me through the rearview mirror, "How long have you been back there?"

"Uh, just back here? Fifteen minutes."

He pulled over so he could turn around in his seat, "What does "just back here" mean?"

I scratched the back of my head, "Kinda been following you for like hours."

He blinked a couple of times, "What do you mean "kinda"?"

"I mean, one hundred percent." I got out to get in on the passenger side, I can't believe he didn't ditch me.

"Why are you such a freak?"

I shrugged, "It suits me."

He let it go for a while, or tried to, "So... For *hours*... You stalked me?"

"It wasn't stalking! But look, if a chick ever asks you for a cigarette, you find her one, you know what? Just keep a pack on you all the time."

"But I don't smoke..." He got this look on his face, he finally got it, "Oh... She was hitting on me?"

I hit his shoulder, "There ya go."

He shook his head, "How was I supposed to know that?"

"What? Did you want her to just say, "hey, goldilocks, I'm hitting on you"?"

"Well..." He shrugged, "Yeah, I guess so."

"Aaron, you know I love you, but you're so stupid."

I think he started questioning why he's friends with me, because he just went dead silent, and slowly turned up the radio.

He turned it back off after a few seconds, "Why are you stalking me anyway?"

I didn't answer, I opted to slide in whatever CD he had on the floor, unfortunately I'm the only one distracted by that.

Aaron turned it back off, "Parker, seriously, you're starting to freak me out."

I sighed, "After you got that card I apparently got "paranoid", and I wanted to make sure you were safe."

"That's nice, but why didn't you just say something?"

"I didn't want to freak you out."

"So, hiding in my car, and almost getting me in an accident?"

"... I never said it was bulletproof, Air." I gasped at my own genius, "Or accident proof"

He shook his head with a chuckle but his smile wavered, "... You think I'm next?"

"I don't know, but I'm here to make sure you're not."

The rest of the drive was dead silent, can't say I blame him, I'm the fucking angel of death.

"I'm sorry, Air." I finally broke the silence when we got out at the apartment.

"For what?"

I shrugged, "Dunno, feel like this is kinda my fault."

"I didn't even know you when I started hunting, I made that decision, I do every time, I know what could happen, it's just," He shrugged, "Might as well go down swinging, right?"

I gave him a huge hug, "I love you, dude."

He awkwardly patted my back.

"... You don't have to say it back, it's fine..." I tried to break the tension.

He laughed, "Love you too."

"I swear to God, I'm not gonna let anything..." I trailed off, I got a pain in my head that was so bad that it made me unable to talk for a second.

"Parker?"

I tried to steady myself against the car.

My body completely shut down and I felt myself collapse, but I couldn't tell you if I hit the concrete or not.

I totally blacked so if it was a vision, I wasn't getting anything.

I came to a few seconds later to Aaron standing over me, two Aarons, actually.

"Are you okay? You hit your head."

I blinked until they merged into one, "I'm fine, my head just hurts."

"You hit it pretty hard. Do you know where you are? What's going on?"

I nodded, "I'm fine, Air. I think it's just; I don't know." I lied, "It's probably just vision shit." I pulled my sleeve back down, not that it mattered, my left forearm was already burning.

"What did you see?"

"Nothing."

"Then how do you know it was a vision?"

I ignored the question.

"You're sure you're okay?"

I nodded, "I need to get outta the sun."

He carefully helped me up.

I refused his help to the door, but realized I wasn't gonna make it up the stairs based on how fast the rest of the room was spinning.

I stumbled into the wall, knocking over and breaking the potted plant next to the door.

Aaron caught me by my waist, "Are you..."

"I'm fine!" I semi snapped, I wasn't annoyed with him asking, it was the situation, I hate feeling helpless. It reminds me of a time I hate thinking about.

I forced myself upstairs, white knuckling the handrail the entire time.

Aaron unlocked the door, and I barely made it to the couch before I fell.

Conner glanced up from his computer, "Are you okay?"

"He doesn't like that question," Aaron answered, "And, no, not really."

"I'm fine!" I yelled, muffled by the couch cushion.

"What's wrong?" Conner knelt in front of me.

"Nothing, I'm fine." I rolled over onto my back, resting my arm over my eyes, hoping to make the room stop.

"He passed out and knocked himself stupid," Aaron undermined me again, "He barely made it up here."

"I made it."

I could hear the eye roll, didn't know who it belonged to, but I knew it happened.

"So, you're dizzy?" Conner asked.

"No, no," I sat up to prove my point, "I'm okay. Look,"

That time, I remember hitting the floor.

Conner and Aaron helped me back up onto the couch.

"What is wrong with you?!" Conner pulled my sleeve down in the process, he glared at the new scar on my forearm, "What's this from?"

"I fell." I pulled my arm back from him.

Conner sighed, "I won't lecture you about it right now, when did you do it?"

"I don't know, the other night."

"Let me see."

I hesitated but let him look at my arm.

"Is it still healing?"

"No, it's closed."

"Doesn't mean it's healed," he looked it over, "Bruising is still there,"

"Ow!" I pulled away when he pressed on it.

"It's tender?"

"Yuh." I rolled my eyes.

"Well, it's been almost a month since you fed."

"Can you not say 'fed'?"

"It's not a vision, you're just hungry."

"I'm not hungry."

"You're weak from being hungry, you can't go this long without eating."

I crossed my arms, "You get one lecture a day, it can either be 'feeding' or cutting."

"I'll take feeding, Aaron can have cutting,"

Aaron gave him a thumbs up.

"I've gone longer without blood. I'm fine."

"That doesn't matter, you're going to start getting sick, and..."

I cut him off, "And I'll start rotting, yeah yeah, so what?"

Conner crossed his arms back at me, "This building has a strict no rotting flesh policy."

I hate blood, I hate meat, and I absolutely hate eating it, but the thought of my skin turning black and falling off... Yeah, that one was winning out.

"Fine."

September 29, 2007
15:35

Parker

As much as I hate it, I'll admit, I don't actually know what it's like to drink blood.

I know what the lead-up felt like; an anxious dread in the pit of my stomach as I was tied to a desk chair, the pain of my gums being sliced open to accommodate my fangs while the smell of dead meat and blood flooded around me, and the overwhelming frenzy I could feel take over when Conner held a raw beef flank in front of me.

The loss of control was terrible, it's like being in the back car of a train barreling toward a cliff. There's absolutely nothing I could do, I couldn't even be sure all that was going to happen, but I knew something awful would.

It's the most helpless feeling in the world, it's like dissociating to the umpteenth degree, to a point where you feel like you don't even exist anymore because you don't. It's just your body and your conscious clawing and biting to grab control of anything.

After a while I would start to gain back my body, it started with the small stuff, really focusing on my body parts amongst the blackout.

I had to get control of my fingers before my hands, my hands before my arms, and so on. Eventually, I could force myself through the blackout.

When I came to, I was still tied down, I fought against the rope before I remembered where I was.

My hands were bloody, my face was sticky, and my mouth tasted like meat.

"Parker?" Conner checked on me.

I let my head fall back against the headrest and shut my eyes for a second, "I gotta get this off of me."

Nate grabbed a towel and started to wipe up the blood while Aaron tried to cut me free as fast as he could.

"Ain't your first time in this situation, huh?" Nate joked as he gave me a smack on the side of my face.

"Shut up." I squeezed my eyes shut.

Had I not felt like I was gonna hurl my guts out, I would've laughed.

I rubbed the rope burns on my arms while Conner bent to get close to my face and looked into my eyes.

"Brown, good."

"Give me a kiss to wash away the blood taste?" I joked... *Partly.*

"And annoying, check." He scribbled in his notebook, "How do you feel?"

I held my finger up, "Gimme a sec or a beer."

Conner crossed his arms, "Yeah, I'll get right on it."

"Seriously, I'm about to puke and I refuse to do it sober."

"You already took six pills." Nate ratted me out.

I glared at him when I was given a glass of water.

Conner shook his head as he leaned against the back of the couch, "How are you feeling?"

My headache was gone, but I wasn't about to admit that I felt better and prove him right.

"Does it matter?"

"Yes, that wasn't a lot of blood, I'm worried the virus is going to burn through it too quickly..."

"In that case, I feel fine."

Con clicked his pen while he thought, "I don't know if animal blood is cutting it anymore..."

"Don't," I stopped him before he finished his thought.

"How do you know what I was going to say?" He crossed his arms, "I'm not saying you have to go out and bite a stranger."

"Right, I'll just drink from one of you," I said sarcastically.

He raised his eyebrows with a shrug.

I laughed, "You've gotta be fucking me!"

"We all have clean blood," Con paused once he locked eyes with Nate, "I think... It would be a good option."

"It's not an option at all!"

Aaron raised his hand before he interjected, "Couldn't we get it from a blood bank?"

Conner nodded, "Theoretically, yes. But it would be better if it were fresh from the vein, warm would be..."

"Stop," I held back a gag, "God,"

"What if it made you feel better?"

"What if I don't stop? What if whoever I bite gets sick, and we end up right back here?! What then?!"

Con went to say something, but I shook my head.
"I don't wanna talk about this anymore, I gotta lay down."
Conner sighed as I walked away, "He never listens."

Conner

To refer to Parker as frustrating would be the nicest thing I could say about him. I probably would've spent the rest of the day arguing with him, but Aaron had asked me to go to work with him so that got me out of it.

I started to pack up my desk while Aaron got changed.

"Do you have somewhere I can use my laptop?"

"Mm, we have *something...*" Aaron buttoned his shirt, "Wi something, I forgot."

"Wi-Fi, it's new, I think." I shoved a few things into my bag, "I'll figure it out."

He gave me a thumbs up, then we were out the door.

Aaron pulled out of the parking lot as he asked; "Are you planning on working at the restaurant?"

I nodded, "I'll see what I can get done, maybe have a cup of coffee..."

Aaron shook his head, "You don't want to drink the coffee there. I'm the last person that cleaned the machine and that was three months ago."

"... Noted, do you mind if we stop, then?"

"I would advise it."

We stopped at a coffee shop that was only a few blocks away from the restaurant he worked at.

As we stood in line Aaron tapped my arm before he gestured over his shoulder, "Isn't that Drew?"

It caught me off guard to see her there. She had a pastry box and was on her way out, so she just offered us a little smile and a wave.

I didn't think much about it, so I ordered our coffee, and we went to the restaurant.

I got set up in a booth in the corner of the dining room so I was out of the way but could still keep an eye on Aaron and all his tables.

I laid out the few things I brought across the table, most of them were loose notes that I would have to try to remember what they meant.

I scanned through a folder; it was a few different cipher keys that I thought might be able to crack the card's code.

As I was working on the seventh or eighth cipher I got distracted.

"Conner?"

I looked up once I heard my name, Drew stood behind my booth with a surprised smile on her face, "Hi,"

"Uh, hi," I raised an eyebrow, "Are you following me?"

She chuckled with a slight head tilt, "Mm, no, I think you're following me." She joked back.

I ended up awkwardly staring at her as I tried to decide if this was just some wild coincidence.

"... Are you okay?" Drew asked, getting my attention.

"Oh, sorry." I realized everything I had scattered on the table and tried to quickly put it away, "Sorry, sit."

"Thanks," she slid into the other side of the booth, "Are you eating alone?"

"No, Aaron works here, I was just coming to hang out."

"Gotcha, funny. My mom sent me to come get dinner, and breakfast for tomorrow." She set the pastry box on the table and gestured to my stack of papers, "What are you working on?"

"Um... I, well, I've been kind of writing something for a while now."

"Oh, really? Like a novel?"

"... Kind of."

"Wow, what's it about?"

"Um," I picked at my napkin while I tried to think of something, but I was at my lying quota for the day, "Vampires, kind of a, um, modern take."

"That sounds interesting, I'd love to read it."

I chuckled, I leaned forward with my elbows on the table, "If I ever finish it, you'll be the first to know."

She reached over to put her hand on mine, "I look forward to it."

Things were quiet for a minute.

Drew holding my hand seemed to put my brain on the fritz and I found myself without anything to say, it got worse when she smiled at me.

Her smile reminded me of Courtney's, and her frosty blue eyes bore into me just like her sister's did.

I cleared my throat, "How has school been?"

Drew nodded, "Fine, my professors have all been very understanding."

"Are you still staying with your mom?"

"Mmhmm, yeah, I don't think she's ready to be alone yet... Or, at least, I'm not. I've never had such a hard time sleeping."

"It's a weird side effect, right? I don't think I slept for three years after my parents died."

She played with the ring on my middle finger, I took note of that because it was pure silver, it proved I was once again overthinking a normal conversation. I was being ridiculous; what did I even think she was?

She shook her head, "Yeah, I've never lost someone before..."

This time the silence wasn't awkward, but I felt bad.

I held her hand back in an attempt to comfort her.

"Conner... I have a question for you..."

Before she could say anything, else Aaron approached the table with a take-out bag, "Hi, Drew. You were picking up, right?"

"Yes, thank you." She gave Aaron a hug before he disappeared back into the kitchen.

"What were you going to ask?" I stood so I could walk her out.

"You know what? Don't worry about it, I'll ask you when I run into you next." She joked.

I leaned forward to grab the bag for her, but she caught me off guard.

Drew brushed her nose against mine as she kissed me softly.

(＼(•̀w•́)／)

September 30, 2007

00:00

PARKER

It was getting late, and I was the only one awake.

I was stuck thinking about, God, everything. But it had been the conversation earlier about blood that made me feel antsy.

I tried my best to open the bedroom window without waking anyone up and climbed down the fire escape.

Usually, when I couldn't sleep, I'd go up to the roof, but I felt like I needed more of a distraction, so I went for a walk.

It was cold enough to make my hands numb, and wet enough to make my hair stand up in every direction. But let's be honest, at any given point, I look like a pink hedgehog.

I kept walking until I got to the church at the end of the street.

I hate churches, and I don't go in one unless I get to lie to a priest, but I noticed the lights were on and the door was unlocked.

I slid my hands back into my hoodie pocket, I pressed the handle of my knife into my hand to make sure it was there.

"Hello?" I called out in true horror movie fashion.

There was no response other than the floorboards creaking loudly despite me standing in place.

"The door was open..." I hollered into the empty, dark hallway.

"The doors are always open."

The voice sent a jolt through my body, I caught myself from falling over as I tried to turn around, "Jesus fucking Christ!"

An old priest stood behind me with an offended expression.

"Uh... Amen?" I offered.

"Can I help you, young man?" He sidestepped me to get to the altar covered in candles.

"... Why am I here?" I didn't realize I had asked that until the priest answered.

"Why are any of us? Purpose, fate, or pure luck. Many people struggle with that question,"

"No, I mean literally it doesn't seem like I end up in places by luck anymore."

He bent to light a few of the candles.

My grip on my knife tightened.

"Well, why do you think you're here, son?"

I picked the blade with my thumb; it burned my skin.

"Divine intervention?"

Before I knew what I was doing the knife was pressed against the priest's throat.

"You don't have to do this; take anything you want."

"You don't understand," I maneuvered so I was in his ear, "I want your soul."

The knife sliced through the throat like a butter knife through a steak.

I could feel the blade saw against his windpipe before he dropped to the floor, gurgling, and spouting blood everywhere.

I watched as he died in agony, a long minute before the guttural sputtering stopped.

I stood over the body, staring into the blank eyes before I knelt.

"Consider yourself lucky." I ran my tongue across the bloodied side of the knife.

The blood tasted far different than anything I'd experienced before.

It was sweet, bodied, and musky like an old wine.

It was delicious and I was starving, but I wanted something else.

I took the knife and created a large wound under his chest big enough to fit my hand through.

I felt around the squelching wound, breaking any bone that was in my way, and I carved out the man's heart.

Blood dripped down my arms as I held the vessel in my hands, I was quick, eager.

It was like biting through the juiciest plum in existence. I couldn't believe how incredible it was.

The front door creaked open revealing another younger man also in a priest's outfit, "Oh, my..." He took in everything surrounding him before he looked at me, "You shouldn't be here."

I've never felt rage like that before. I was boiling as I cornered the man and plunged my knife into him over and over until he was ripped apart.

I had never understood the word "Wrath" so clearly, so... Literally.

I got up and went through the dark hall, dragging the blade across the wall.

I heard myself humming a tune as I turned into the bathroom. I stood in front of the mirror covered in blood; my eyes were glowing an almost neon yellow.

Yet I ignored it, and I kept humming as I slid my bloody hand over the mirror's smooth surface.

(＼(•̀w•́)／)

I bolted upright out of bed with a panicked yell.

Aaron rolled over to smack me with a pillow, while Conner threw balled-up socks at me, and I heard Nate mumble half asleep "Shut the fuck up, Park."

I took a deep breath as I stared down at my clean hands, if I had a heartbeat, it would be racing right about now.

Why? Why! Just, why?

I settled into the bed and tried to catch my breath, but when that never happened, I forced myself up and into the bathroom.

I sat on the tile and glanced at the razor on the edge of the counter.

That wasn't going to be enough this time.

I scooted closer to the toilet before I jammed my fingers down my throat.

I made myself puke until I wasn't throwing up blood anymore.

For the first time since all of this started, I felt clean.

(＼(•̀w•́)／)

10:20

CONNER

Parker was passed out on the couch when the rest of us got up, I wish I could've thought that was odd.

We each went about our business, and I watched Aaron try to take a seat on the couch without waking up Parker, who jumped awake anyway and scared Aaron.

"Ah!" Aaron caught his coffee before it spilled.

Parker scanned the room before he landed on the VCR clock.

He pressed his palms into his eyes with a sigh.

He looked horrible, the normal purple circles under his eyes were black, and he looked practically transparent, had I looked close enough I'm sure I could've seen his veins through his skin.

"What the hell happened to you?" Nate asked glancing from the TV over to Parker.

Parker mumbled his response, "I ate the heart out of a priest's chest."

Nate clicked the TV off and tossed the remote onto the coffee table, "A'ight, I'm listening."

I closed my laptop, that definitely got my attention as well, "What?"

Parker shook his head, "Forgot the context,"

"How do you forget the context?" Aaron turned to give Parker a stern look.

"It's been a long night, okay?!" Parker tried to prop himself up against the couch cushion, "I had another vision last night,"

I held a pen ready for his next word, but it never came. Instead, his eyes rolled back into his head, and he slumped over.

"Parker!" Aaron held him up.

"Hey," I gently pat the side of his face, "Parker,"

Nate clicked his tongue, "Con, that ain't how you slap someone awake."

I rolled my eyes as I put my hand back against Parker's cheek, I couldn't have been right the first time.

I moved his hoodie out of the way, "His bite, touch it." I instructed Aaron.

Aaron gently put the back of his hand to Parker's neck before his eyes widened, "He's burning up."

"I thought so,"

"What happened?"

"I don't know,"

Parker came to but I held him by his shoulder just in case.

"Are you okay?" Aaron asked.

He leaned forward, anchoring his weight on his knees, "I'm fine."

"You're..."

He cut me off and brushed my hands away from him, "Fine, really." He sat back and pulled his hoodie around himself, "Withdrawal, it's been a few hours. Can we focus on the vision?"

I wasn't content with that answer, but I wasn't going to get a true one no matter how hard I pushed.

So, I reluctantly returned to my job as a scribe.

"You mean, the church down the street?" Aaron asked once Parker was done talking.

"I think, I don't know it was within walking distance."

Nate shrugged, "Been watching the news all morning, ain't heard anything like that."

Aaron gave him a skeptical look, "Why have you been watching the news?"

"New female anchor, huge..."

"Okay," I felt the need to interject before he finished that thought, "If it's that grotesque the cops probably don't want it in the media yet, I'll do a deep dive into their reports and see what I can find."

Parker nodded, he slowly steadied himself as he stood, "Great, I'm gonna go take twenty Xanax and take a nap."

"You shouldn't do that while you're this sick."

"What? Like it's gonna kill me?"

(＼(•̀ᴡ•́)／)

14:40

I must have searched through every police database in every county adjacent to Seattle and with nothing coming back I realized I needed some space and some fresh air.

Besides, I had a million other things pounding through my head.

I drove halfway across town to the park just to sit in front of Courtney's plaque.

"Hey, friend," I dusted the dirt and shards of grass off the granite next to the bench, "Sorry, I didn't bring you flowers or anything, but to be fair the one time I tried to give you flowers you beat me with them." I chuckled at that memory before I shook my head, "I must be going insane, I'm talking to a piece of marble... You know, last night I prayed to a God I don't think exists?" I sighed, "I haven't done that in a long time."

I drummed my fingers against the bench before I took a seat, "Something about you has always had me screwed up, though..."

"Hey stranger," For a brief second, I thought I heard Courtney's voice.

I whipped my head around to see Drew standing a few feet away with a beautiful bouquet.

I responded with an awkward wave.

Seeing Drew today sent my heart into an episode and my head into a tailspin, I could barely comprehend whatever it was that happened yesterday evening.

I watched as she bent to put the flowers into the pond.

I must have had a strange expression on my face.

"It's for the fish," Drew clarified as she straightened, "Courtney didn't like flowers, but I read somewhere the fish eat them..."

She stood on the edge of the pond without moving for a few seconds.

"... Do you want to sit?"

"Um, sure." She walked over quickly and sat swiftly without saying another word.

I can only explain the next few minutes as abrasively uncomfortable.

We both sat there, searching the area desperately for something else to focus on until one of us finally got up the courage to say something

"I'm sorry." We both spoke at the same time.

"Why are you sorry?" We did it again.

I shook my head, "Sorry, go ahead."

Drew held her face in her hands for a moment, "Ugh, I'm so sorry. I know you were just trying to be nice to me and... I don't even have the slightest idea what I was thinking! Look, I get it if you hate me and never want to see me again but just know that I am sorry, I misread everything."

I chuckled; the sound surprised me too.

"I don't hate you."

She softened slightly, "You don't?"

"No, do you hate me?"

"Of course not." She went to put her hand on my shoulder but hesitated before ultimately deciding against it, "I... I'm sorry."

"I am, too."

There was a long pause.

Drew stared down at the grass, her cheeks reddened, "It's such a bad time. You were just so nice to me and... Damn, when my sister's right, *she's right*."

"What do you mean by that?"

She shook her head, "She tried to set me up with you on multiple occasions, swore up and down that I would like you and... She was right, I should've listened to her sooner. This is just awful, *awful* timing and now I made a mess out of everything..."

I put my hand over hers and when she looked at me, I took the opportunity to kiss her.

I don't know what came over me, sometimes it seems I'd rather shoot myself in the foot than be the person to take action.

Yet here I was, on the bench dedicated to my dead best friend, kissing her sister...

Drew pulled away after a few seconds, she searched my eyes, "What are we doing?"

"I don't know."

The only thing I did know is that if Courtney were still here, I would have been running for my life.

(＼(•̀w•́)／)

15:50

Aaron

I was trying my hardest to read my book, but Parker was sitting next to me whining.

I sighed and put my book down, "What?"

While my arms were out of the way he wormed across me and curled up on my lap like a dog.

"I need attention."

"There a time you don't?" Nate sparked.

"I'm a little too high and I need love and affection, asshole!"

I gently pat Parker's shoulder and left him be, I could live with this if it made him feel better.

As soon as Conner stepped through the door to our apartment Nate's ears perked up and he spun around to look at him.

"You got laid!"

Conner tossed his keys into the bowl by the door, "What?"

"You got a look to ya."

He rolled his eyes, "You're wrong."

"I'm never wrong." Nate challenged.

"That's true," Parker piped up from under my book, "It's like his sixth sense."

"You couldn't possibly know that, and if you could, you would know I didn't get laid."

"Then where were you?" Parker asked.

"I need some fresh air; I went to the park."

"My guy! In the park?!"

"I did not have sex in the park!" Conner tried to defend himself, but his face quickly grew redder as he realized what he said.

"Then what happened?" Nate raised an eyebrow.

Con shrugged, "I ran into Drew, we talked for a bit."

"And?"

"*And* I walked her home. It was scandalous, I'm sure there will be headlines about it tomorrow."

"Did you hold her hand?" Parker asked.

"Oh, my God! What is this sixth grade?" Conner shook his head on his way to the bedroom, "Why am I even entertaining this?"

Nate crossed his arms, "You're overbearing."

"Me?!" Parker sat up knocking the book out of my hands.

The bedroom door slowly opened, ending their bickering as Conner stood in the frame.

Conner sighed, "I kissed Drew."

Parker made an unholy screeching noise as he shot up and dragged Conner back into the room, "What happened?!"

"I don't know!" Conner gestured around, "I don't know, you know I've been spending time with her, she unexpectedly kissed me last night. It caught me off guard and I thought it was strange, but I didn't say anything and today she was saying how she really likes me..."

"Do you like her?" Parker asked.

"I don't know,"

"How do you not know?"

"She's sweet, she's a really nice girl, it's just..."

"Just what?"

"Sometimes... She just really reminds me of Courtney."

Nate groaned, "Con, what kinda Alabama, backwoods shit are you doing?"

"No, that's what I thought! Well, not my thought *exactly*,... Maybe I only like her because I can't have Courtney."

Parker clicked his tongue, "I know whatcha mean, I used to feel the exact same way about Beyoncé and Solange."

Nate laughed, "Except for Con has a real shot with Drew, fuckin' pendejo."

"Hey! I could've had a shot!"

"Bro, you wouldn't have a shot with another corpse."

"That's not what your..."

Nate launched one of the books on the table at him, "Shut up!"

"Conner!"

Conner pressed his fingers into his temples, "For God's sake, you guys."

I took the book from Parker before he could throw it back at him.

"Children! You guys are children!" Conner sat in his desk chair with an exasperated sigh.

"Can I ask a question?" I spoke, "Do you want to see where things go with Drew?"

Con went to answer but he hesitated.

"For just a second don't think about Courtney, just Drew."

He nodded, "She's really great, but I don't want to screw her over."

"Are you planning on screwing her over?"

"Of course not! But what if the only reason I like her is because of Courtney?"

"What if you don't like her, period? How is that any different than just going on a date and deciding she's not for you?"

"I just feel like I'm being an asshole."

Nate decided to help, "Bein' an asshole is fucking her, her sister, and her aunt," He crossed his arms when we all looked at him, "What? Her aunt was still doable! It's not like I fucked her mom, too... Wait, yeah, no, I didn't. That's someone else."

"Besides she's a lot different than Court in a lotta ways too." Parker piled on.

"I know, they look way different..."

"No, I meant Drew's nice."

Conner fought a chuckle, "Yeah... I can't help wondering what Courtney would think of this."

"Oh, don't wonder, she'd kick you 'til you stopped moving. But she'd want you to move on, too."

Conner played with his phone, flipping it open and shut, "Well, you make it sound so appealing."

"Perrito's right," Nate said, "Just ask Drew out."

Parker nodded, "Like now."

"Now? I just saw her."

"Exactly she'll know she's fresh in your head!"

"I don't know, I'm gonna blow it."

"You're not gonna blow it!"

"You know she already likes you," Nate assured me.

Conner took a deep breath, "Fine... I refuse to say you guys are right, but Aaron is."

I smiled.

Parker waited for Con to close the bedroom door, "He's gonna blow it."

October 1, 2007
09:53

PARKER

"Morning," Conner chirped from behind his computer screen.

"Good morning," I answered as I reached the top shelf of the cabinet on my tiptoes.

Conner glanced up when he heard my voice, "Oh, I thought you were Aaron."

"What, I don't get a 'good morning?'"

"You're not usually awake during the morning, and when you are, you're annoying."

"Hey, that's not fair! I'm usually drunk or high still." I opened my pop tart while I leaned against his desk.

Con let out a sigh and dusted the crumbs off his notebook, "Right, and this morning's chipper disposition is brought to me by...?"

"Sobriety,"

"Uh-huh, and I'm not a ginger."

I crossed my arms, "I'm serious.

He looked up at me in shock.

"What, do I gotta pee in a cup? God, why don't you ever believe me?"

"Why would I?"

I dropped my arms to my sides, "Mean, but fair point. But I feel good."

It wasn't a total lie, I felt like I was in control for once, like that sword hanging over my head that was going to drop and kill somebody at any moment was lessened, it was still there but I had a hand on it instead of it being held by a piece of thread. But when it came to how I felt physically... It was like I was hit by a truck covered in smallpox.

"Well, you look like shit." Conner's eyebrows rose.

"Thanks." I was quick to change the subject before he read too much more into it, "How'd it go when you called Drew?"

He nodded while scanning his computer screen, "Fine, we're going to a... Double massacre in a church."

"Interesting first date choice, Con."

He shook his head, "Sorry, we're going to dinner. I found a double massacre at a church, one with throat and chest contusions, one stabbed... That can't be right, a hundred and seven times?"

I choked on the lump in my throat, "No, that sounds right."

I sat as gently as I could on the couch, I was starting to feel dizzy just from the thought of it.

"Do you know how hard it would be to stab someone even twenty times? Especially a vampire, that would override the exhaustion factor but the amount of blood that would produce..."

"Con!" I leaned back before I passed out.

"Sorry,"

My phone went off, giving me a distraction while Con read through the rest of the report.

I checked it once the dizziness went away, "Hey, you remember that girl I dated sophomore year?"

"You mean the one you got arrested? Umm, Caitlin Garcia, right?"

"Why does everyone keep harping on that?! It wasn't my fault! ... *Totally*."

Con shook his head, "What about her?"

"Her parents still live next door to my parents, I guess she moved out to Seattle from somewhere else and my mom gave her my number."

"Why?"

"'Cause," I cleared my throat and lowered my register to try sounding 'holy', "The only way one can receive forgiveness for their sins is to make amends."

Conner shrugged, "Well if there's a list of people that deserve an apology from you, she's definitely amongst the top,"

"Whose side are you on?"

"I'm right below her, by the way."

"You're too busy being right below Drew!"

He threw a balled-up paper at me, "Don't talk about my..." He caught himself and quickly turned bright red.

"Your what?" I taunted, "Your Freudian slip?"

"I was going to call her my friend, and I will give you twenty dollars if you can tell me what that means." He rolled his eyes.

"Yeah huh, it means you're Freud-ing her!"

"Shut up,"

My phone chimed again, "She's texting me."

"Drew?"

"My god, you're *obsessed!*" I teased.

"We were just talking about, never mind. Why do I talk to you?"

I laughed as I read the text, "She wants to meet up."

"Seriously?"

"She says I owe her a drink."

Con scoffed, "So she can poison you?"

"Come on, it wasn't that bad."

"You were both arrested! Are you really thinking about it?"

I shrugged, "What's the worst that could happen?"

"Someone finds your body in a ditch somewhere."

"Been there, done that." I punched a text into my phone, "But, seriously, you go out with Drew, I'll get some drinks. Oh, but we're gonna need a sitter for Aaron and Nate."

(＼(•̀ω•́)／)

20:45

I ignored Conner's sarcastic warnings and decided to meet up with my ex, I mean what was the worst that could happen?

I hadn't seen her in over ten years, how mad could she still be?

Besides, our few texts back and forth had been alright.

"Parker Winston," Caitlin stood when she saw me walk towards the bar, "Wow, I hoped I'd never see you again."

I laughed but part of me thought it wasn't a joke.

"I thought you'd be dead by now, or at least taller."

"Yeah, me too," I smirked at the irony, "How've you been?"

She rolled her greenish brown eyes at me, "Save it, buy me a drink, and maybe we'll talk."

She left me at the bar and sashayed over to a booth in the corner.

I stared at her while I was waiting for our drinks.

She was hotter than I'd remembered, she was like the pin-up girls I would draw before I started stealing porn. Curvy, with long caramel hair that complimented her hot deep bronze skin.

She wore a tight pink dress with a "better than you" pout and a bitchy glare.

It was hot.

Caitlin frowned when I put the bottle in front of her, "Beer?"

"Were you expecting champagne, Ms. Hilton?" I said sarcastically into my bottle.

She rolled her eyes again and flagged down a waitress.

"You look great, by the way."

CAITLIN

She crossed her arms when she caught me staring at her boobs, "And you look like you just woke up."

"You'd know what I look like in the morning."

There was a pause as her glass of wine was dropped off.

"I don't know what you think this is about, but you're wrong."

"No, I know exactly what this is about." I crossed my arms, "You're new in town, I'm the only person you know, you're hard up and I'm a great bang. Easy as that."

She scoffed, "First of all, you're a pig, and second, as if! You know, I did this as a favor to your mom, she said her loser son was in the gutter again," she scoffed, "And to think I gave you the benefit of doubt, maybe you'd changed after all these years, but you're still the same pathetic, self-centered, junkie bastard that you've always been!"

I laughed into my bottle.

"What?" She emphasized the 'T' as she snapped.

"And you're the loser that ran away with me."

"You used me!"

"Hey! I got you out of that shit hole town, didn't I?!"

She huffed and fell back against the booth, "You're an asshole."

"You're a bitch."

There was a long pause.

"I've always wondered; why me, Parker? Huh?"

"You were easy."

She slapped the shit out of me as she stood, she stomped off only a couple of feet before she turned to look at me.

"Get up." she demanded.

"What?"

"Get. Up." She said through clenched teeth, "I'll show you who's easy."

Caitlin dragged me outside and shoved me into the back of a car.

I went to send a text to Con "I think I'm being kidnapped." But before I hit send, Caitlin was all over me.

If I had a dollar for every bad decision, I made in the backseat of a car I'd have enough money to fund my original backseat bad decision.

(＼(•̀w•́)／)

Conner

Drew picked the restaurant, it was nice, romantic with candlelight and velvet seats. I was glad I didn't let Parker pick my wardrobe like he insisted.

Drew wasn't there yet so I took the time to take a deep breath and reminded myself that I was allowed to feel anyway I wanted to about this evening. I was allowed to enjoy this, and I was allowed to feel like it was a bad date too.

"This was a normal first date, not just dinner out with the woman of my dreams' sister..." I mumbled to myself and shook my head, "No, that's good. You should lead with that."

Drew showed up shortly after I was done reprimanding myself.

"Hi,"

"Hi." She hugged me and her icy blue eyes flitted over me as she took a step back.

I adjusted my shirt self-consciously, "What's wrong?"

"No, you're fine, I just," she tilted her head, "What color are your eyes?"

"Oh, I, um, one's blue one's green."

"You have heterochromia? How did I not notice, they're beautiful."

I felt my face grow hot the longer she stared into my eyes, "You're beautiful."

Not awkward at all.

"This is a nice restaurant." I stated as I pulled her chair out from the table.

"Yeah, my professor recommended it, actually."

"Oh, really?"

She nodded, "Do you want a drink?" she offered.

"Sure."

She ordered a fancy IPA; I panicked and did the same.

I got into my own head and from there it was awkward. Neither of us could find anything to talk about.

"... How was class today?"

Drew played with the straw in her water glass, "I didn't have any classes today... How was work?"

I cautiously took a drink from the Belgian glass and shook my head, "Unemployed."

"Right." She cringed before she started to laugh, "This is awkward, right?"

"Excruciatingly." I adjusted the napkin on my lap, so I didn't have to make eye contact.

"What's wrong with us?"

"I know what my problem is,"

She raised an eyebrow encouraging me.

"I'm waiting for someone from your family to round the corner and stab me."

She chuckled, "Well, the two people I can think of doing that are back in New Jersey and one's watching over me....so yeah, I'd watch my step if I were you."

She made me laugh and that loosened me up a bit, I could tell it did her as well.

Drew put her menu down, she leaned forward on the table and spoke with a lowered voice, "I know I picked this place and... Well, who am I kidding? There's a pub a few doors down, do you want to go get a cheeseburger and a normal person beer?"

I let out a sheepish laugh, "You would be saving yourself from a date with the world's most awkward person."

She smiled, "Come on."

"After you."

I followed her out of the restaurant, and said "Thank you, by the way."

She responded "Please, I'm saving myself the embarrassment of having to order something French in front of you." She flashed a smile that would have made me sweat if I hadn't bathed in antiperspirant before I left the apartment.

"So," Drew slid her hand into mine as we walked across the street, "How was your day of unemployment?"

"Mm," I chuckled, testing the feeling of her hand in mine. "Well, I got to watch my other unemployed friend stick a fork in the toaster to retrieve a pop tart,"

"Parker?"

"Yep, great guess, and then I had to drive him around for a half an hour while he tried to figure out where his date was."

"Oh, he had a date tonight too?"

"I would call it more of an aggravated, yet justified, assault. At least, that's what I think the judge would call it."

A waitress offered us a seat at the bar while we waited.

"Do you know the person he went out with."

"Yes, but even if I didn't, anyone would have the to right to assault Parker."

"Fair enough," She laughed into her beer bottle, "Well, either way, I'd much rather be out with you."

"I'm at least reasonable, a credible date, maybe."

"Credible?"

"Mmhmm, a night with me is very believable, an evening you will more than likely forget."

"Don't talk like that," She leaned into me pressing a soft vanilla scented kiss to my lips.

She smiled as she wiped her lipstick smear from my mouth, "That's something I won't be able to forget."

"Quel soulagement! Tu me fais tourner la tête."

"What does that mean?"

"I have no idea, just kiss me again."

Drew laughed and put her arms around me, "Oui."

(\(•̀w•́)/)

23:00

Tonight was far better than what my anxiety was predicting, we spent the rest of the meal laughing, talking and stealing each other's fries.

Drew was amazing, and I wondered why I never let Courtney get us together... Oh, right, Courtney...

She kept crossing my mind all night, and the amount of times Drew reminded me of her was haunting. I tried desperately not to think about it, especially as Drew was kissing me good night.

Nate frowned at his watch as I walked through the door.

"You're early,"

I placed my keys in the bowl and my coat on the hook, I sighed, "Whatever you were doing, could you not do it on the furniture?"

"Nah, I already did that in the shower,"

I cringed at the information.

"Seriously, why're you home early? Date sucked?"

"I was gone for three hours! No, it was great."

"Then why aren't you under her right now?"

"Jesus," I rolled my eyes, "Because some of us have dignity."

At that exact second Parker slammed through the door, "Guess who got fucked in a Mercedes!"

"And then there's Parker." I mumbled to myself.

"!Mi chico¡" Nate hit him on the back, "Usually you gotta get on your knees to get in a car like that."

"Oh, dontcha worry, I was on my knees."

"Caitlin wasn't mad?" I was surprised, I thought he would come home with a drink thrown in his face.

"No, she was pissed, she slapped me and everything."

"She slapped you?!" Aaron asked his eyebrows knit in concern.

"Uh huh, we fought for like fifteen minutes and then had the craziest, hottest 'I hate you' sex in her car. It was awesome." Parker got a beer from the fridge, taking a drink from the can, he sat on the couch and looked up at me, "Why are you home? Date sucked?"

I crossed my arms, "No, it was great. You guys are just easy."

Nate and Parker just shrugged.

"Are you seeing her again?" Aaron asked me, trying to move past Parker's traumatizing admission.

I nodded, "Yeah, we're going to have lunch between her classes."

"That's where she's gonna...?" Nate made a gesture that I would require counseling and puppets to describe.

"You're sick."

Nate shrugged.

"I'm seeing Caitlin tomorrow night, too," Parker added, "And she'd bringing a friend, she already said no to a three way so..."

"Down." Nate answered before the question was out of Parker's mouth.

I shook my head, "You're both sick."

October 2, 2007

20:45

Nate

Parker gave a mumbled introduction to me and his new friends before he dipped out into a booth in the corner with his girl.

"I'm Pepper, by the way." The other girl laughed, "Cate's not one for introducing people."

"Noticed. Nate."

"Hi, Nate."

We sat, I ordered a beer and only half listened as she droned on.

I watched as Parker tried to swallow his date. I thought about flicking a bottle cap at him, the longer I watched the more pissed I got.

I was already bored.

"Nate?" Pepper crossed her arms.

"What?"

She chuckled and dug through her bag, "You smoke?"

"I quit."

"Bummer," she held a cigarette between her dark lips, "You mind?" She gestured outside.

"No," I followed her out and watched as she lit up.

I motioned for it and took a long drag.

"I thought you said you quit."

"Eh, gotta die from something, right? 'Sides hot girls and cigarettes are kinda my kryptonite."

She laughed, "Oh, you are into girls?"

"What's that mean?" I took another hit before I gave it back to her.

"Based on how you were watching your boy in there, I thought you were jealous."

I scoffed, "Nah, he wishes."

"Mm, right." she let the smoke pour out of her mouth, "Make me believe it." She winked.

I kissed her and we ended up making out on the sidewalk.

She put a hand on my chest, "Don't start something you can't finish." She warned.

"Aw, come on."

"Sorry, babe," she straightened my jacket and nodded towards the door, "I'm not as easy as your friend."

Parker appeared next to me, "Hey,"

I glared at him.

"I better go find Caitlin. Here," Pepper put a cigarette behind my ear, "For the drive home."

"You ready?" Park asked when she left.

"I should beat the shit outta you, cockblock. For fucks sake, how're you and Con gettin' nailed and I'm not?"

"Shit sorry, but I got enough for us both."

"Bathroom?"

"Booth." He winked.

"Uh-huh, you got lipstick on your neck, jackass."

"Don't be like that! I'll make it up to you, 'kay?" Parker slid his hand into my back pocket.

I smacked him til he moved, "Get off me!"

He laughed his stupid laugh and winked at me again.

I went to get my keys outta my pocket.

I rolled my eye when I felt the piece of paper, "Alright, how'd you do that?"

Parker stood at my truck's door, "Do what?"

I held the card between my fingers.

It was the same card that the three of them'd been obsessed with.

On the back was my name and a number.

Nathaniel E. Tucker-Mendez

520

"Shut the fuck up!" He snatched it from me.

Without saying anything he was a bat outta hell, I leaned on the horn to get his attention, but he was gone.

Jackass.

(＼(•̀ᴡ•́)／)

21:15

Aaron

I was minding my own business, sitting at the small counter separating the kitchen from the living room.

I had my headphones in so other than the loud drum beat in my ears I couldn't hear anything as I brainstormed an elaborate mechanism for my latest project.

Had it been a tap on my shoulder or just about anything else, I wouldn't have thought much of it.

But Conner was in the other room and from what I could tell I was alone.

The energy in the room shifted, I felt something brush past me quickly.

A cold rush of air nipped at the side of my face, most people assume ghosts are cold, but they aren't. This was something different, and it sent a pang of anxiety through me.

I would like to preface this again by saying *I was minding my own business.*

As a hand slammed down on my shoulder I spun around.

My fist made contact with something cold.

"Fuck! Aaron!" Parker stumbled away from me.

"Oh, my God!" The anxious pit in my stomach was quickly replaced with guilt, "You scared me!"

I ripped my headphones out and threw them on the counter, I ran to his side.

"No shit!" Parker's hands cradled his nose, "Jesus Christ, you hit like a biker!"

"I'm so fucking sorry!" I wailed.

"What the hell is going on?" Conner flipped his phone shut as he came to check out the yelling.

"Aaron just broke my nose!" Parker shook his head and lowered his hands, "It bad?"

I glanced over at Conner before I reacted, he was staring and that was the only thing I had the capability of doing as well.

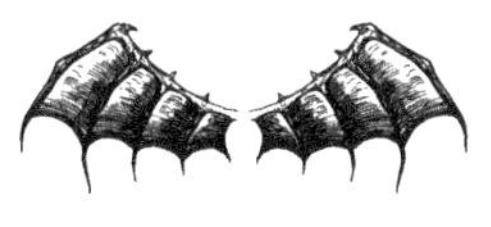

PARKER

Based on the way Conner and Aaron looked at me, my nose had to be some kind of gory mess.

"It's broken, isn't it?" I asked.

As far as punches to the face I've suffered it was a good one, but it didn't feel broken.

I looked around for a mirror or something, grabbing the half-charred toaster next to the stove.

My reflection was the same, my nose was fine.

It took me a minute to notice what they were staring at.

I wiped the syrup dripping from my nose.

It was...

Crimson.

"What the fuck?"

Conner didn't say anything else; he grabbed a paper towel off the counter and blotted at my nose.

"Ow!" I whimpered.

Con analyzed the red blotch on the towel, he held it to the light.

"Is it blood?" Aaron asked.

Conner shook his head, "That would be literally impossible."

"Then what is it?"

"I don't know," Con grabbed a container from the cabinet and put the paper towel in it, "I still have my professor's number from when I was a lab assistant, I'll ask if we can use the lab."

Aaron's gray eyes lit up, "Awesome."

"Not awesome! What if I'm dying or something?"

Conner sighed, "Do you think we can postpone this freak out for at least twenty-four hours?"

I crossed my arms, "Fine, freak out number two then?" I threw the card Nate found on the counter.

Aaron picked it up and looked it over, "It's the same handwriting as mine,"

"Are you sure?" Conner asked.

Air nodded, "Yeah, oh, but the number's different. 520, untouchable, idoneal number... Aaron mumbled some other math-y stuff under his breath that I purposely ignored so I didn't have to try to write it down later.

"One nine one, five-twenty..." Conner played with the silver pendant on his neck.

"Phone number?" Aaron suggested.

"191 isn't an area code, and it's one number off."

"520 is Arizona."

"Maybe," He wrote it down.

Aaron tilted his head, "Where is Nate?"

I suddenly remembered leaving him on the sidewalk, "... Oh, *fuck*!"

I ran out of the building; I got as far as the parking lot where I was almost rundown by Nate's nondescript truck.

Nate slammed the door as he got out, he was yelling in Spanish, but I knew I was in trouble.

So, I scrambled to put as many locked doors between us as I could... It didn't help that he had a key.

Nate shoved me back into the counter when he caught up, "Skank!"

"Hurtful!" I shielded my face as he kept smacking at me.

"Guys!" Conner wedged himself between us, clearly already annoyed with our idiocy.

He brought his laptop over and scrolled a webpage, "520 was on the mirror in the church report. I must have missed it the first time."

My eyes were glued to the blood image, and I thought I might puke, "How do you miss that?"

"Well, the mangled, heartless corpse distracted me." Con shot back.

My stomach turned at the thought of that image, there it was.

I shoved past Aaron so I could puke in the trash.

"The squeamish vampire," Nate mocked.

My head may have been in a trash can, but I could still flip him off.

"It's not just him," Conner added, "I felt like I needed to hold a baby or something after that."

I took a minute to get it back together.

I held myself against the wall and Aaron was nice enough to give me a glass of water.

"So, what's our plan?" I carefully sipped my water.

"I'll talk to my professor on Monday," Con ran his thumb over the card as he thought, "In the meantime, I'll look more into the cards... I looked into the logo, there must be thousands of businesses that use a top hat as their logo." He sighed.

"And the blood thing?"

"I think you should eat again, maybe it has something to do with that blood."

I groaned.

"You're getting sick again, obviously last time wasn't enough."

"But shouldn't everything stay the same, then? You know, like fasting for a blood test?"

He saw straight through me, "Nice try, no. I'm wondering if it has something to do with your feeding..."

I gagged.

"Sorry. It did come from your nose, maybe you aspirated it or something, we should do everything the same as it was today."

"And what are we gonna do about Nate and Air?" I tried to dodge the topic.

Con crossed his arms, "You're eating."

I groaned louder this time and dragged my feet on my way to the bedroom, "This apartment is a prison!"

October 4 2007

10:35

PARKER

Nate assaulted me awake and hit me with a pillow until I got annoyed.

"What?!" I refused to get out of the blanket that was over my head.

"Con wants you up," He smacked me on the ass as hard as he could, "C'mon."

"Ow!"

He laughed while walking out.

When I got out of bed I was ambushed.

Nate shoved me and held me down into a chair while Aaron tied me up.

"I like where this is going," I tried to ignore what Conner was doing.

"Enjoy it while it lasts because you're gonna hate the next part."

"Why? You outta lube?"

Conner gave me a horrified look once he finally got it.

I laughed.

"Did you have to kidnap me?"

"Would you have sat down without an argument?"

"Fair enough."

"Besides, this needs to be done fast. I need to get to the lab; we can only use it for an hour."

Even though I joked, I panicked.

The smell of blood, that sticky, rusty smell became noticeable, and then unbearable.

Conner held a piece of raw meat in front of my face.

It was gone before I could even tell what it was.

I clawed desperately for control over my own body, by the time I won out, Aaron was carefully cutting me out, but I panicked.

My chest tightened and I felt a deep swirling pit in my stomach.

My hands were splotched in blood, and I couldn't convince myself I was okay.

Conner tried to ask if I was alright, but his voice was far away.

I stumbled to my feet once I was out of the tape, I slammed through the bedroom door

My hands shook as I shuffled through the dresser's drawers, behind the clothes in the closet, under the bed and all my usual hiding places.

The bedroom door opened as tears stung my eyes, I felt like crying, throwing up, passing out, and dying at the same time.

Nate leaned against the wall, "Con flushed your dope again,"

"No shit." I collapsed onto the bed, the blood on my hands stuck to the bed sheets as I tried to quiet the rush of anxiety in my head.

Nate watched me from the doorway, he dropped his arms to his sides with a sigh, "Fine, you tell Con I'll kick your ass."

He tossed a small baggie of white rectangle pills on the bed next to me.

I didn't even count how many there were, I just needed this feeling to stop.

The cloud of impending doom started to disappear just knowing I'd be high soon.

I stood and held Nate by his face and gave him a sloppy wet kiss on the mouth, "I love you."

He put a hand on my chest, he was annoyed, "Save it, junkie."

(＼(•̀w•́)／)

12:01

CONNER

Parker locked himself in the bathroom for fifteen minutes, I was sure it was just to spite me since we were on a schedule.

Eventually he came out and I got him to shuffle along.

Aaron helped write a list of hypotheses as I drove, and Parker slipped in and out of consciousness.

I knew he was high, it would be better to wait and yell at him while he was strung out. He still wouldn't listen, but it was more fun for me.

Once we got to the university's lab Aaron wasted no time getting comfortable, meanwhile I gave direct instructions to... Nobody.

Nate and Parker were already ignoring me and touching everything they could get their hands on.

The first crash I heard sent me into convulsions.

Parker had taken the liberty of trying on a lab coat before I had to drag them away like disobedient toddlers. I made them sit at the desk where I had moved away anything they could break or steal.

Aaron appeared next to me, "Everything's ready," he chirped and produced a large syringe, "We just need a sample."

I looked at Parker who shuddered.

"No way, I don't do needles."

"So, your tattoos?" I asked sarcastically.

"I magic marker them every morning," he matched my attitude.

I rolled my eyes, "Nate?"

"Mine are blueberry scented."

"The syringe, Nate."

"What do you want me to do?" Nate crossed his arms, "Oh, I get it. The Puerto Rician knows how to hit a vein."

I rolled my eyes again, at this rate I was going to get a headache, "You used to take care of you grandma."

"Yeah, and I've done this a hundred times, just check yourself, güero." He took the syringe from Aaron.

Parker let out a whimper, "Of all the people I trust to do this, he's the last."

Nate snapped a glove over his hand in a dramatic flourish, "What? You die I just move outta state again."

Nate rolled the sleeve of Parker's shirt and tied an elastic around his bicep.

"Ready? We'll go on 'three'." Nate assured as he jabbed the needle into the crease of Parker's arm with no warning.

"Ow!! You didn't even...!"

He flicked Parker on the forehead, "Shush. Stop squirming."

Nate carefully drew the plunger back; a thick sludge slowly filled the tube.

I nodded to let Nate know that was enough and took it from there.

The substance looked like molasses, it was viscous and dark like pitch, but I was surprised to see it was slightly tinted red when I held it up to the light.

I dropped a few dots onto a microscope slide.

I was only able to take a few good glances at it before I was startled by a loud thud followed by an "Oh fuck" from Nate.

I didn't need to ask what happened, Parker had crumpled and was face down on the desk.

"What did you do?"

"Why's it always me?" Nate tried to prop Parker up.

I gave him a sideways glance, there wasn't any time for a sarcastic remark.

Parker came to fast. He held himself up on the counter, he somehow looked worse than he did an hour ago before he fed.

The ever-present dark circles under his eyes were almost black, his face was sunken, whiter than usual, and he shook.

I was surprised to see him like this, there was no reason he should be this sick.

He just fed, he should have gotten at the very least, one week of relatively fine health, but he looked the way he did if he had gone months without feeding. Like the virus was running rampant, rampaging free inside of him.

"Parker?" I held my breath waiting for a response.

"I don't know what happened." His speech was slurred.

"It's alright, stay sitting." I eased him back into the chair, his usual icy skin felt feverish.

He complied.

I thought he was going to say something, but he stopped short and opened his mouth again.

A small stream of red blood escaped the corner of his mouth.

I watched as Parker's eyes flickered between gold and brown like a broken television set.

Aaron quickly maneuvered through the lab to get a towel and a glass of water, "What's going on?"

"I think I might have figured it out... I'll explain it when we get home, right now we need to get this cleaned up and get him home. Nate, stay with him, don't drop him this time!"

Aaron and I scrubbed any trace of us being there as well as anything the virus could've contaminated.

Parker was cognizant by the time we were in the car; he wasn't exactly coherent, but I don't think I could blame that on whatever was happening.

I peeked in the rearview mirror.

Parker had his head on Nate's shoulder, his eyes were closed but his expression was contorted with pain, "You said you'd call..." He mumbled.

He muttered a few more things but I couldn't hear what they were, all I caught was "Trav" and I didn't know what that meant.

Parker let out a laugh, "Fuck you."

Aaron twisted around in the passenger seat to check on him, "I think he's delirious." He observed.

"Or coked out." Nate offered.

We got to the apartment's parking lot and Parker was talking about stuff I could understand now.

"My head's killing me." He could stand but he was still wobbly, so Nate helped him walk.

"God, why's the sun gotta be so bright?" Park let out a small hiss, I tried to adjust his hoodie to cover most of his face.

As quickly as the episode was brought on, it seemed to be phasing out at the same speed.

When we reached the entrance Drew was sitting on the steps of our building.

Drew stood and gave us a meek wave, "Hi,"

"Hi... Did we have plans?" I was surprised to see her but it's not unlike me to forget, especially with everything going on.

She went to answer me, but Nate cut her off in his usual vexed tone, "You mind? He's heavier than he looks."

Parker glared at him.

"I'll be right up." I gave Aaron my keys.

I thought Drew was waiting for them to leave to say anything, but they had turned the corner and were probably halfway up the stairs now.

She had a weird expression I couldn't pin down; she wasn't sad or hurt...

"Are you okay?"

She held up the rectangular wooden chest that was next to her on the step, "Do you know what this is?"

I hadn't seen it before, "No?"

She unlocked it and shoved a VHS tape into my hands, "This?"

"Um," I started to think she was pulling a joke on me, but her exasperation said differently, "Drew, what's going on?"

"It's a tape, Conner! A tape!" She shook her hair out, I could finally pinpoint her expression now, disbelief, "Her dying wish was to give me a tape! I don't get it, my sister's always been bizarre but I..."

I felt my hands go numb, I had a good idea what was on that tape, but I had to know for sure.

I swallowed and tried to ask as normal as I could, "What's on it?"

"It's Courtney," She let out a short laugh, "She's talking about vampires! Of all things! A hundred and sixty minutes, she's just blabbering on and on! What is this just her last prank or something?"

I searched desperately for the right answer, maybe I could take a play out of Parker's book and act dumb.

"What makes you think I would know?"

"At the end she says I need to talk to you or Jared. So what? Ha ha, she got me?" She crossed her arms.

Thanks, Courtney.

"What did Jared say?"

"He's not picking up the phone," She shrugged, "His girlfriend says he's not there; I think he's dodging me."

And thank you too, Jared.

"... I think maybe you should talk to your mom."

"She's being weird, she's *been* weird." Drew shook her head, "This isn't funny, Conner, just tell me what's going on."

"I don't know what to tell you,"

"That my sister needed some serious help?" She offered.

I sighed.

I couldn't tell her; I promised her mom that. But there was clearly a reason Courtney wanted her to know, it was her last wish.

"I think you should come inside."

"What?"

"I can explain what's going on, but it's a lot and... Just not out here."

She laughed, "So, what? Are you saying it's true?"

I put my hand on her arm to guide her into the building, "Come inside, please?"

"Oh, my God, is there something in the water?" She shrugged my hand off, "God, you must be insane!"

"Drew, give me fifteen minutes, I can... We can explain everything."

"We? Oh, lord, my boyfriend's a serial killer."

"No, no, I meant the guys and I."

Drew kept shaking her head, her long dark hair whipped around, "No, this is too weird, I can't believe this."

"Five minutes, okay?" I took her hand, and she seemed to soften slightly.

"Five minutes... But I get to keep my organs."

I chuckled and opened the door, "Deal. I just want you to talk to Parker,"

She had one foot over the threshold, "Why Parker?"

I hesitated, "He's... *One*."

She turned to face me and when I didn't laugh, she started running.

She was a lot faster than her fuzzy boots led me to believe, she was already half way down the side walk.

"Drew!"

I followed behind, mostly to make sure she was okay, but it only made her run faster.

After half a block Drew finally stopped running.

She didn't even break a sweat, but I was panting.

"I'm sorry!" Drew yelled across the street, "I don't know why I did that!"

"It's fine, just come back!"

"Um, no thank you. I'm okay here!"

"Okay, stay there. I'm going to call your mom to come get you."

"Wait!" She shook her head, "No, no. It's okay."

She stayed on the other side of the street, unyielding.

"Are you sure?"

"Yeah... I'd rather you kill me than talk to my mother."

"I'm not going to kill you."

"Do you promise?"

I wasn't sure where the sudden anxiety of being killed came from, but I complied, "On my parents graves."

She crossed the street and walked back to the building with me.

"... That's something a serial killer would say, by the way."

Drew hesitantly followed me inside. I'm not sure what kind of torture chamber she was expecting, but it clearly wasn't our "humble" apartment.

"Your place is nice..." She offered.

"It's a hole." Parker answered from where he was lying on the couch.

"Ignore him," I took her coat, "But he's not wrong."

"Hi," Aaron got up to greet Drew, "Can I give you a hug?"

She nodded and it seemed to settle her slightly until he swatted at something over her head.

"Aaron," I guided his hands, which had started to hover around Drew, back to his sides, "She's already nervous, she doesn't need her aura cleansed."

"Oh," he tilted his head, "Are you sure?"

I nodded.

"Okay." He went and sat down.

Nate took a brief break from his snack search to look over at Drew, "What's she doin' here anyway?"

"She... Has some questions about vampires."

Aaron's eyebrows rose behind his glasses, "I thought she didn't know."

"She didn't. Evidently, Courtney took it upon herself to make a video telling her."

Parker honked out a laugh from his spot, "Mrs. Hart's gonna kill you."

"Thanks, I hadn't thought of that!"

"What's my mom have to do with this?" Drew was still weary.

"Your mom asked us to leave you out of this world."

"The vampire world?" She spoke slowly as if she was addressing a child... Or a crazy person.

I gestured for her to sit in the saggy brown armchair next to the front door and hoped she wouldn't take it as an incentive to run away again.

I sat on the arm of the couch as I thought of the best way to approach this, "I know this sounds unbelievable,"

"I was starting to worry you didn't know." She tucked a long strand of hair behind her ear.

"That's not lost on me, but" I took her hand in mine, "Courtney fought to make sure I gave that to you, it was important to her for you to know this. Don't you think, maybe, there's some weight to it?"

She stared down at my hand, she ran her thumb over my ring as she thought, "For a minute, let's say this is real, I'm not having some kind of break or meltdown..."

"I know what it's like to be where you're sitting," Parker interjected, he was nice for once, so I let him continue, "As much as you wanna assume you smoked something bad, believe it, there's actually wilder shit out there."

"Really?"

"Yeah, like the virus, there's the blood, the zombie-ness, and..."

"Okay," I stopped him, "You're not helping anymore."

Parker's eyes widened, "I was helping? Hey, good for me."

Drew shook her head, "I'm not following."

I took it from there, "When I say vampires, I don't mean like Dracula, it's... More of an infection, a disease."

"It's like AIDs," Parker jumped back in.

I shielded my eyes with my head bowed in disappointment, "Thank you, Parker."

"AIDs with a touch of rabies, maybe a little madcow disease and a bad bath salts trip."

"You're a mad cow." Nate mocked from the kitchen with a full mouth.

"Your mom..." Parker was shut up by Nate who winged him in the back of the head with a Chips Ahoy.

I shook my head, "I'm sorry about them."

Drew didn't seem to notice, "What are vampires like, then?"

"Well, Parker's comment wasn't entirely baseless. It's kind of like rabies, well in most cases, it causes its host to become violent, but I think that's more about the hunger it causes."

"Like zombies."

"Kind of,"

"Mm," Parker nodded his head solemnly, "*Zompire.*"

I chose to ignore him.

Drew arched one of her dark eyebrows, "And zombies?"

"Not real."

"Right, that would just be crazy." She nodded as she thought, "So the whole thing about fangs and blood...?"

"True, they don't have blood, so their bodies crave it to help fight off the virus, if they don't feed the virus decays them from the inside out."

Parker and Drew gave me the same disgusted look.

"How... How do you get it?" Drew asked cautiously.

"It spreads through a bite. Vampires tend to bite to slow down their prey, that's enough time for the virus to be transferred and start the incubation period in its new host. From there usually they'll feed on the victim once they're done fighting, and if you don't die from blood loss first, the virus takes over. You get really sick, if you don't die from shock now you have a short window to feed before the virus kills you itself."

Drew looked me over. She reminded me of Courtney the way her eyes seemed to bore into me to see something no one else saw.

"... Is that what happened to my sister?"

The room was so quiet I could hear the neighbors two floors below.

"I don't think that's..."

She cut me off and repeated in a sharper tone, "Is that what happened to Courtney?"

"No," I gulped.

"I want to know."

I looked at each one of the guys, but they all had the same deer in the headlights look I was feeling.

"Was she infected?" Drew's voice was harsh as she shoved herself up out of the chair, "Answer me!"

I hesitated, "She didn't have enough time to be infected."

Drew sunk back down into the chair, her fire was gone, and her voice was barely a whisper, "God."

"I'm sorry."

"What was she doing around *that*?"

"Well, that's kind of our job, we hunt them."

"Of course, you do." She let out a pained laugh, "Shouldn't the government do that? You know National Guard or something?"

"It's an incredibly well-kept secret, from what I know, the government doesn't even suspect that they're around."

"Why do you guys know?"

"My parents were hunters; they dedicated their careers to researching vampires."

She looked over at Nate who shrugged.

"I bullshitted my way into the info, chica."

Aaron offered a shy smile when she glanced at him, "My grandma was a wiccan, she believed in lots of stuff."

She landed on Parker, "And you?"

Parker looked to me for approval for once.

I nodded.

Parker sat up against the other armrest, "I didn't know about it until I got 'sick'."

"You're..."

He pursed his lips to the side with a shrug.

"I don't get it."

"Parker's an anomaly... In a lot of ways." I added.

Drew paused for a second as she studied him, "... Can I ask what that's like?"

Parker shrugged again, "I don't remember how it happened, but I remember being really sick, that's why I called Conner. Other than that, it's not that different. I mean, I bleed this weird soot stuff, and I don't have to breathe."

He raised eyebrows, "You wanna hear something funny? I've been vegan since I was fifteen."

Nate scoffed, "He goes down on a cheesecake twice a month."

"Hey, that's not meat! And meat's murder, dude."

"Bro, you've smoked crack before."

"Not true! But I swallowed a crack rock once."

I felt the need to apologize for them again.

"I have a question," Drew interrupted their... 'Disagreement'.

Parker nodded.

"Do you have any powers?"

Parker waved his hand in a so-so motion, "I can run really fast, pretty strong... Lately I've had visions?"

"Visions of what?"

Parker picked at the already chipped paint on his nails, "Mostly people dying."

"Did you see Courtney die?"

He shook his head, "Nah, we wouldn't be sitting here if I had."

Drew got to her feet; she was quiet as she paced the carpet in the living room to the tile in the kitchen.

I cleared my throat, "I know it's a lot to process..."

"How do people not know about this?"

"There's no one to tell, no one survives to speak about it." I answered.

"But how long has this been going on?"

"I have no idea. Forever, as far as I can tell."

Something had occurred to her; she didn't say anything but instead dug for her phone and pointed it at Parker.

Parker cringed at the flash, "Ow, what's that for?"

"I want to know if you have a reflection."

"Uh yeah!"

"I don't know!" She shut her phone and tossed it back in her bag, "What about garlic?"

"Vampires have a stronger sense of smell," I replied, "You know how onions and garlic burn your eyes while you're cutting them?"

She nodded.

"I imagine it's like that just worse."

"Okay, what about holy water?" She kept firing off questions, "Sunlight? Crucifixes? Are you allowed to enter people's houses? What about stakes?

Parker kept up easily, "Sunlight burns, just a way worse sunburn really,"

"Lack of red blood cells makes you more susceptible to sunburns." I clarified.

"Holy water is a bitch,"

"Purified water kills the virus" I continued, "I have yet to figure out what churches do to it differently."

"Also," Parker kept up with her questions, "Crucifixes annoy me but that's more about growing up religious, nothing to do with vamps. According to the cops, I'm not allowed to enter houses uninvited anymore, but who's gonna stop me? And stakes, uh Con?"

I shook my head, "No, it could stab him but it wouldn't kill him."

"How do you kill them?"

"Silver, best option is to their heart."

"Why silver?"

Aaron answered that one, "It's one of the purest metals on earth, it's strong and durable, and it conducts energy really well. Platinum would be the best, but no one makes platinum bullets."

"Anti-bacterial properties kill the virus." I added.

Drew paused as she moved her hair over her shoulder, "... I think my brain is overloading."

"It's okay, it's a lot," I reassured, "There's no way anyone can absorb all of this in one afternoon."

"Afternoon," Her eyes widened as she repeated, "What time is it?"

I glanced at my watch, "Three forty."

"Damn it, my class got out half an hour ago. My mom's going to kill me."

"Hang on," I had to stop her from blowing through the door, "Can I at least take you home?"

"Aw, that's sweet, but no," She slung her bag over her shoulder, "I like you and I would really like for my mother to not kill you brutally."

I forced a mangled chuckle out, "Fair enough."

I waited for her to finish saying goodbye to the guys before I insisted on walking her to her car.

"Are you doing okay?" I asked, knowing full well Parker was pressed against our door the second I closed it.

"I think so... I just got a lot more than I bargained for with you, huh?"

I chuckled, "You're the first woman to say that."

"Stop," she nudged me with her elbow as we walked down the stairs, "Besides I'll take vampire hunter over some of my other boyfriends."

I smiled at her.

"What?" She stopped at the glass door of the ground floor.

"Are you saying I'm one of your boyfriends?"

She laughed to herself, "If you expect a non-awkward answer you'll have to wait until some of my brain power isn't on vampires."

"Okay, well, in the spirit of being awkward, can I kiss you?"

"Only if I can call you at three in the morning with vampire questions." She joked.

"I'll be waiting by the phone all night."

"You're sweet," she brushed my hair away as I leaned towards her.

We kissed briefly.

I didn't want to let her go but I didn't want to be in any hotter water with her mom than I already was.

(＼(•̀w•́)／)

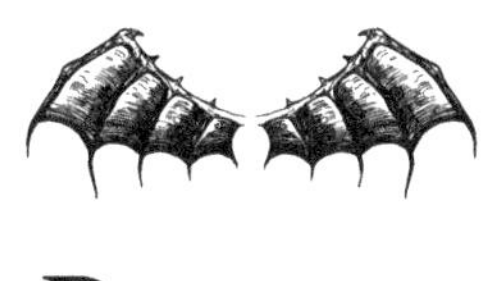

Parker

When Conner got back upstairs, I was lying across the couch on my stomach with my hands under my chin while I dreamily swung my legs, "Did you kiss her?"

Con rolled his eyes, "Get over yourself,"

"Is Drew doing okay?" Aaron's more polite than me... And Nate, he didn't even say anything.

"I think so, she's just still trying to process it all."

"Yeah," I sat upright, "It's crazy, I was up for like three nights processing it."

"'Cause you processed it with coke." Nate stated.

Conner ignored that side of the conversation and scribbled on a notebook page, "How are you feeling now?"

He didn't look up from his scribbles, so I didn't realize he was talking to me.

"Parker?"

"Huh?"

He mumbled something about me under his breath, "I asked how you were feeling."

"Oh, way better than earlier, I think I'm over it."

"We can thank the healing for that," He sat in front of me on the coffee table with a flashlight that he shone in my eyes, "All brown," He reported to Aaron who was quick to write it down.

Conner put his hand to my forehead, I pulled away when the silver of his ring singed my skin.

He gave me a weird look.

"Ring."

"Crap, sorry." He went back to reporting, "He's cold again."

"What are you thinking?" Aaron asked, "Did you end up seeing anything on the slide?"

Con took the notebook from him and flipped through a few pages, "I have a theory, the "Sludge" is the virus in its purest form..."

"Is that the scientific name?" I cut him off.

"For lack of a better term, yes," he glared at me.

"*Anyway,* I've seen that stuff under a microscope, and it doesn't look like what I saw today. Yours, it's docile."

"What does that mean?"

"Usually that 'sludge'," He air-quoted, "Is reactive, it's looking for something to drain nutrients from, yours wasn't. Interestingly enough, I saw what I thought were blood cells, but to be fair I only looked for a few seconds."

Aaron made a face, "Is that possible?"

"Saying zero is impossible and one is a chance... I would say 00000.01%." Conner scratched his forehead.

"What are you saying?" I asked.

"I don't know how this is possible at all, but I'm suspecting that you have normal, human blood mixed in with all that sludge."

I blinked a few times waiting for that to settle.

"But I've been bleeding soot and 'sludge' for years."

"It must not be a lot, but I guess it's enough."

"Enough for what?"

"Enough to keep you alive, enough to keep you human," Con shrugged, "It's why you're not mindless, it's what's keeping you Parker."

My stomach twisted.

This was it; this was the answer I'd been waiting for almost three years, but I felt like I had more questions still, yet my head felt empty at the same time.

"The good news is, there might be a chance we could counter the virus." Aaron added.

"How?" I was so excited to ask I barely let him finish.

"Could we do a blood transfusion?" He asked Conner more than me, "Maybe that could flush it out?"

"I would have to..."

Conner didn't get to finish his thought.

"I wanna try," I cut in.

"It's just a hypothesis," Conner tried to curb me, "It's not promised, and it's definitely not proven."

"I don't care, I wanna try. I would try anything, you know that, and you said if that's what we have to do, we would try everything."

Con reluctantly nodded, "Okay, but you have to give me some time, if we're going to do anything it still has to be done correctly."

I shot up off the couch, grabbing Aaron and Conner in each arm I squeezed them and kissed them both, "Fuck yeah!"

"Don't get too excited," Conner warned, "We don't know what could happen."

October 8 2007

05:34

PARKER

It had been a few days of Conner trying to get me to calm down, but I was on edge.

I mean, come on! You can't drop a bomb on me like that and expect me to be a normal person about it.

I was getting restless, and I needed something to do with myself.

It was late, but I didn't care.

I started by sitting on the roof, but that wasn't enough.

Going for a walk seemed like a normal request even though the city was asleep. It seemed like this was almost becoming routine for me at this point.

A few things stirred in my head as I walked, the main emotion I landed on was guilt.

I felt so awful being happy when a lot of other people weren't so lucky to be given an opportunity of being fixed... One of them being my best friend.

I hadn't been paying attention to where I was walking or for how long, but the sun was rising now, stabbing at my uncovered skin.

I don't usually leave the apartment without a hoodie, but I hadn't been thinking about it when I left.

I had to find somewhere to duck out for a few minutes so I could figure out my next move.

I was only a few feet away from a huge ornate looking building. It looked like it had seen better days, so I was guessing it was abandoned.

I got a weird vibe from it, but I'm not one for great decisions so I climbed the concrete stairs up to the huge wooden doors anyway.

The dark doors had large fancy, golden doorknobs.

It was a long shot, but I tried it anyway.

It was open.

The doors led into this gigantic open lobby, there was a desk to the left, a huge ass chandelier that looked like it was seconds from falling and impaling someone.

In the middle of the room sat a piano that probably didn't work anymore.

The place was old, everything was covered in a thick layer of dust, and the decor seemed to date it.

It was creepy, the quietness sent a shiver down my spine.

Everything was so eerie down to the wooden moth-bally scent.

I rounded a corner, half expecting to see a set of blonde twins waiting for me.

Hopefully I don't get 86'd by an axe murder, that'd be some shit.

To be fair, I've always had the energy of the girl that dies first in a horror movie.

The floor creaked with every step I took.

I went through the entire ground floor. I don't know what I expected to find, maybe something expensive I could pawn for my next craving, but most of the rooms were locked or completely empty.

There was one door left in the very far back of the hallway, it was alone, away from all the other rooms on the floor.

I ignored the little voice that screamed at me not to go down that hallway.

It was unlocked.

It was a hotel suite, and it was huge. The main room was at least twice the size of our entire apartment, but like all the other rooms it was empty.

The curiosity killed me, so I went into the bedroom.

Of course, that door was locked.

I searched around for something I could jimmy the lock with like I had made Aaron show me.

I finally found a paperclip lying around.

The door opened into a pitch-black room.

I desperately felt around for a light switch and the florescent lights finally flickered on.

Three stripped hospital beds lined the middle wall that had a blacked-out window. The walls were bare with what looked like cleaned up smudges on the white paint.

In the other corner of the room was a desk covered in papers.

I shuffled through the papers trying to make sense of this room or the building, but I couldn't understand the fancy writing. I think it was in another language.

Eventually I uncovered an envelope, this writing was in English.

It had an address line that wasn't in America, but I made a point of remembering the name.

Chuck Young.

A pounding in my head slowed me down, and I got the overwhelming feeling that I needed to get out of there.

I ran out of the room, tripping on the rug in the hall.

I stabled myself enough to realize the room was spinning.

I kept my hand against the wall trying to get to the door.

Everything slowly shut down until I was on the floor, I stayed conscious long enough to swear to God I heard the piano.

(＼(•̀w•́)／)

When I came to, I was back in our apartment, laying on the couch.

Aaron was sitting at the counter, Conner at his desk, and Nate was in the chair next to the couch, on his laptop, either on Myspace or illegal porn.

"Mornin', Ms. Bubblegum." Nate joked.

I didn't even notice his comment.

I glanced around the room.

"You good?"

"What time is it?"

"Uh, like, five, I think. Why?"

My head wasn't hurting anymore, small victory.

"When did I get back?"

"Are you okay?" Conner asked while Nate gave me a skeptical look.

I shook my head, it took too long to register, "Yeah, I think I had a vision."

"What was it?"

Conner's pen managed to keep up with me as I word-puked details all over the place.

"So, you're insane." Nate said once I was done talking, "I knew you'd be the first to break."

"Really? The vision's what you have a problem with? Vampires are cool, but that's what you draw the line at?"

"What was the name?" Con spoke over us.

"Charles? Chuck, Chuck Young, I think."

Con nodded, "Give me an hour."

Nate hit my shoulder, "Give him an hour and let's go get blasted."

"Deal."

"Hang on," Aaron's ears perked up, "You're not worried about what the card means?"

"Lotta people've tried to kill me," Nate shrugged on his jacket, "Perro no one's done it yet."

Nate made a point of ditching me the second we stepped through the bar, I guess he was still bitter about last time.

It was fine though, I'm not a stranger to getting drunk alone.

So, I sat at the bar, took two shots and watched him chatting up a group of girls.

Jackass.

I got distracted fast, though, a woman sat a few stools down from me and I couldn't stop staring at her.

She sat at the bar with the elegance of a starlet walking the red carpet, her long hair traced intricate coils around her face and down her shoulders.

She was gorgeous, like a mix of the old Hollywood actress from the movies my dad used to make me watch and a Victoria's Secret angel, or maybe like a painting but that was mostly because of her features.

Cat like eyes set in her blemish free olive complexion, perfectly lined red lips, and carefully arched eyebrows, it was like an artist had spent hours drawing her.

My eyes trailed down her body, she wore a tight black business-y skirt and a suit jacket that didn't seem to have anything under it.

In my head that jacket was long gone.

I didn't think she noticed me, God why would she ever even glance at someone who was a mere mortal next to her? But she winked at me and motioned me over with one finger.

I would've crawled if I had to.

I smirked, taking the stool next to her, "Hi,"

Her deep brown eyes looked me over before she answered, "Hello,"

I nodded towards the bartender, "What are you drinking?"

"Martini, dirty, two olives." She answered directly.

"I like it dirty, too," I winked while I tried to get the bartender's attention, "I'm Parker, by the way."

She smiled and held her hand out in a way I'd imagine a princess would, "It's a pleasure, Parker."

We got our drinks, and I kept talking as long as she let me.

"So, are you a model or something?"

"Pardon me?"

"You're just so gorgeous,"

She snorted as she was taking a drink of her cocktail, she grabbed a napkin to blot at her red lips, "Excuse me, but does that really work for you?"

"You tell me,"

"It doesn't."

I shrugged, "Worth a shot,"

"You should save your breath."

"Fair, you have a pen?"

She thought about it for a second before she dug through her bag to give me a pen.

I started to sketch on the napkin in front of me, "What's your name?"

"You can call me Donna."

"So what'cha do for a living?"

"Human resources, of sorts,"

"Gotcha, I went to art school,"

"So, you're an artist?

I shrugged, "I'd say starving artist, I dropped out anyway."

"I wouldn't know your work, then?"

"Just this," I finished the rose and dainty flowers I was drawing, wrote my number down and slid the napkin toward her, "I'd hold onto it, it'll only be worth as much as the napkin 'til after I'm dead." I joked.

"I could arrange that if you like." She tilted her head and let a sliver of a smile slip.

"Eh, get back to me later in the month."

She analyzed the piece,

"Interesting, but it needs something. May I?"

"Please," I gave her back the pen.

I was confused when she flipped the napkin over.

With a few swift movements she drew a top hat before handing it back to me.

"What's the matter, darling?" She looked up at me when I didn't say anything, "Oh, were you not expecting a woman?"

I couldn't talk.

I couldn't even tell what I felt, rage? Hatred? Sadness? Excitement?

"That's okay. I don't normally look like this, I just needed to get your attention. Seems as though you and your friends needed some help opening your eyes."

I had a million questions clawing to get out at once, but all I could ask was...

"Why?"

"You'll need to be more specific," She used a toothpick to spear an olive in her drink.

"Who are you? Why are you doing all of this?! Why? Why me?"

She tapped her long pointy nails on the counter, "What was it you told that girl? You were easy," She echoed.

"... What?"

"I've been watching you for a long time, Parker. Long before you were even what you are now, even before your 'little accident'."

"You... Know about that...?"

"Do you mean your old life, or Travis?"

My blood, whatever's left of it, boiled.

I wanted to stomp off, throw my usual tantrum. I didn't want to hear any more of it, but I knew I'd regret leaving.

"Fuck you," I grit my teeth.

She smirked, obviously happy with my reaction, "I'm the one who sired you, Parker. I'm inside your head, I know everything. From where you hide your 'stash' from Conner to the awful things you like doing to that girl from your hometown." She leaned into me, she held a finger under my chin and lifted my head until our eyes met, "I own you, dear." She caressed my cheek.

It took everything I had to not snap and put my hands on her there, Con would be pissed about another bail call. So, I hissed.

"But I'm not here out of the goodness of my own heart,"

"Then what do you want?"

"I'm here to offer you a deal;"

I watched her through slitted eyes.

She was careful to not move or express in anyway as if to not tip me off to her master plan.

"You're far more powerful than you think you are, it isn't as cut and dry as your friend would have you think." She paused "There is more to us, much more. I need the help; you have the power. " Another pause, as if to gage my reaction, "You help me with my plan, and you'll be compensated handsomely." She finished with a smile.

"And what's the plan?" I asked, trying to calm down.

"Patience is a virtue, you know?"

"Mm, this is starting to sound a little Hitler slash master race-y, just so you know."

Her eyes narrowed, "This has nothing to do with a master race and everything to do with those who have wronged us. You and I, the millions like us, we can't live in this world. A world of hunters, we need protection and rebirth. We deserve salvation and you can help with that. I thought you would want to, you of all people know what it's like to be an outsider."

"And if I don't? Cause let's face it I'm no one's savior."

"This is an offer, Parker," She took a drink from her martini, "Just know that no is not an answer I'm willing to accept."

I crossed my arms, "So?"

"*So,*" She blinked once and her eyes glowed a shade of red I've never seen, "I'll do everything in my power to get a yes from you, should you continue to say no I have methods to change your mind, is that understood?"

I chuckled to myself, "Shove it up your ass, toots."

She let out a scoff, "For once in your life don't be so flippant," She slid another card in front of me, "You have a lot to think about, I will leave you with it and I'll be in contact soon. Besides, you should retrieve your little toy before one of my girls misplaces her thirst."

I glanced over to check on Nate and by the time I looked back she was already walking away.

On instinct I went to look at her ass as she walked away but that pissed me off even more.

DONNA

October 8 2007

18:08

Conner

The front door opened, producing Parker who was dragging Nate by the wrist.

"You ditched me first, jackass." Nate rolled his eyes.

"I *ditched* you 'cause you wouldn't..."

"Shut up," Nate pulled out of Parker's grip.

"Whatever!" Parker retaliated, crossing his arms he flopped down onto the sofa.

Parker glanced at me, realizing they weren't the only ones in the room, he shot to his feet, "Motherfucker!"

He pat around his pockets as he bounced around the room like Scooby Doo discovering a clue.

Parker spoke in quick jumbled sentences as he shoved something into my hand, "I met her! I met *her*!"

I smoothed the soft paper out in my hand, I was surprised. "You saw Top Hat?"

"Talked to," Parker ran his hands through his hair, he was much more animatedly freaked out now, "I actually spoke to her."

Aaron stumbled over the kitchen stool as he hurriedly pulled his headphones out, "What happened?"

"This woman just sat next to me! And all of a sudden she drew this and started talking like The Godfather and..." Parker shook his head trying to get his thoughts to align, "She said she wants me for some kind of Nazi sounding bullshit!"

We all stared at him.

"What does that mean?" I asked more to myself knowing that Parker probably didn't have the answer.

"What did you say?" Aaron added.

"I told her to shove it!" Parker flicked his hair out of his eyes, "What was I supposed to say?"

"You could've asked questions," I clarified.

He shook his head as he started to pace the floor behind the couch, "She made it clear she wasn't going to answer my questions, she wouldn't even tell me her name!"

I looked back at the napkin, "So what is 'Sotos'?"

He grabbed it from me, "She wrote on it?"

"You didn't notice that?" I scoffed.

"No, I was a little busy shitting myself!"

"What did she look like?" Aaron asked.

"God, like a goddess, I don't... She said something weird about it, like 'I don't always look like this' or something. She looked like a normal person to me."

"Was she possessing someone?"

"I don't think so, no, she did this thing with her eyes. She made them change to red, like she did it all time, no problem."

"That sounds shapeshifter-y," Aaron said, eyes wide.

"It does," I concurred, taking a note as I spoke.

"So what?" Parker's hands were tangled in his hair, "What now?"

"I'll see what I can find, I mean Sotos isn't so common, how hard could it be?"

Parker groaned, "I need to be much higher for this shit."

October 9 2007

07:36

CONNER

I'm in the small classification of people that if I were to say the phrase "as sure as the ground beneath my feet", a giant sink hole would open up and swallow me.

That fact was obvious after I had been so sure last night the finding the name Sotos would be easy.

"Good... Morning...?" Aaron tested as he had walked in on me knocking my head against my desk.

I kept my head on the desk, I was too tired to hold my own head up, "Good morning."

"I take it you aren't having any luck?" He sat on the edge of the couch's armrest.

"None, zilch, rien. I'm being flooded by variations of 'Sotos', and Donna is a frustratingly common name so I'm completely blind here."

"What about the other name?"

"Chuck Young? God, there have to be at least two million just in the Pacific Northwest."

"That many?"

"And not one drawing a line to each other," I sat up right and extended my arms out, "I'm stumped."

Aaron offered me a sympathetic pat on my shoulder.

Soon after, Parker shuffled through the kitchen.

"Morning," he mumbled.

"You're awake?" I was surprised.

Parker rifled through the kitchen drawers, "Couldn't sleep, got the shakes..."

"Well, good luck, I flushed all your stuff."

He sighed slamming a draw shut with his hip leaning against the counter, "You're real mean, you know that?"

"I know, I'm a horrible person." I rolled my eyes.

"What am I supposed to do?" he whimpered.

"Maybe have a cup of coffee like a normal person?"

He crossed his arms, "Coffee's no better than Adderall, y'know?"

"Good, maybe you'll be helpful for once."

He just glared at me, but he quickly forgot why.

"You got anything?"

"Very little. Nothing on the names, nothing on the logo, but the numbers on the cards." I flipped through my notebook, "If you break up it up 19 15 20, it's S O T, which must be Sotos, and I'm willing to bet we can expect more cards,"

"She said she'd be in contact."

I sighed, I hated to say it and he hated to hear it.

"We just might have to wait until she is."

Parker looked like he wanted to scream, but instead he stood up and stomped into the bedroom.

(\(•̀w•́)/)

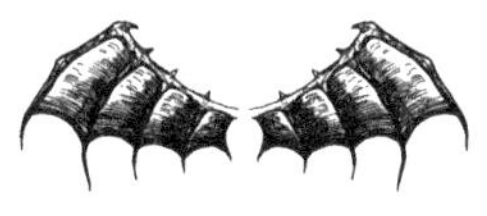

PARKER

It wasn't even an acceptable hour yet and my day already sucked hard.

Conner couldn't get anything, and last night's encounter kept me up. Well, parts of it did.

I let myself fall back onto the mattress on the floor.

Once I landed, Nate hit me in my kidney.

"Ow!"

"The fuck, man?"

"Sorry, I thought you were awake."

"I'm not." He kicked me as he rolled over.

"You sure?" I laid across him and kissed his neck, "What do I gotta do to get a joint?"

He shoved me off, "Lárguese, aquí no pinta nada, pendjo. Fuck, que te la pique un pollo."

"Huh?"

"Shut up, lemme go back to sleep."

"Done,"

"Top drawer, papers are in the back."

"Con doesn't flush your shit?"

"Shush."

"Thanks!"

He threw a nearby shoe at me.

I got what I needed before another shoe came my way and climbed up the fire escape.

Con always throws a fit when his stuff smells like weed.

The roof's kind of become my safe space... It has been a while.

I was only wearing an old t-shirt and a pair of pajama pants I stole, but I couldn't feel the cold.

One thing was on my mind, and I couldn't shake it.

"I know about your little 'accident',"

"I know about your old life,"

"*I know about Travis.*"

My hands shook as I tried to light my joint.

I couldn't tell what the problem was anymore, withdrawal? Lack of sleep? Trauma response? Who knows?

I took a few deep breaths, letting the smoke blanket me until the wind quickly took it away.

"Travis," I held my head in my hands, "God."

I hadn't thought about him in... Well, minutes now.

I tried desperately to shove all of those memories down, bury them in an ocean of liquor and pills, and I'd been doing an okay job until now.

"Hey," Nate threw his leg over the railing and pulled himself up, "Con said I gotta come make sure you don't jump."

He threw a blanket over me and asked for a puff.

I didn't say anything for a while, Nate seemed to be enjoying the quiet until he noticed the tears on my cheek.

"Oh, God, are you crying? Jesus Christ." Nate's not one for emotions but he still moved closer to me and put his arm around my shoulders.

"¿Que paso?"

"She knew about Travis." I sniffed.

"Shit, man."

"I don't... She said she knew everything... You're the only one I've ever told."

"You should tell Con about this, man, I don't think I'm qualified for this shit."

I shook my head, "I can't tell Con about this."

"You tried to kill yourself, Park,"

"Exactly."

Nate sighed, he rubbed my side, and I put my head against his shoulder.

"It's gonna be okay."

October 16 2007

11:11

Parker

It had been a week with no progress.

We were all on edge, but I was going on a hundred and twenty hours with no sleep.

Every time, the second I'd start falling asleep, the nightmares would start.

They were all the same, I was in a car, going way too fast.

The endings were different though.

Sometimes I'd end up wrapped around a tree, sometimes in a river.

I could get out and I would be screaming for help into the nothingness of the night, or I'd be watching as EMTs zipped closed a body bag while my mother sobbed.

I couldn't take it anymore, my stomach panged with guilt, and that's not a good feeling for me.

I flicked my phone open and stared at the names on my screen.

The very last name, all the way at the bottom, mocked me.

I put an X by it so I wouldn't have to see it ever.

Why I kept the number was beyond me. I guess I saw it as a link to my old life.

A link to normalness, a link to life before death.

My thumb hovered over the call button.

I couldn't believe I actually thought of it, in a bit of a panic and as a way to punish myself for going there, I went back to the top of the list and hit the button this time.

"Hello?"

"Hi, Mom,"

"Hello? Who is this?"

This was already an awful idea.

"Who else calls y..." I sighed, "Parker, Mom."

"Oh, hi son. What do you need?"

"No, I was..."

She sighed, "Do you need money? What are you using it on?"

"No, I don't need money," I fell back on the bed, "I was just checking in."

There was a long pause, I thought she hung up.

"Mom?"

"I'm here,"

"How's the family?"

"We're doing good."

"How's Jeb-Jeb?"

"Dead,"

"Oh... *Great*," I picked at the blanket under me, "Were you gonna tell me, or?"

"You hated that cat,"

"Nuh uh, Ellysha hated him 'cause he ate three of her beanie babies, the rare ones, too."

I heard my mom chuckle, I hadn't heard that in a long time, "I can't believe you remember that."

"Why not?"

She didn't answer and I just moved past it.

"How's Dad?"

"He's great, the church hired his team for an expansion, so we've been able to spend more time there,"

I didn't think that was possible, my parents practically lived at the church when I was in high school.

"Elijah's been really getting involved too. He's really enjoying Sunday school, and..."

My mom kept talking, but I sort of zoned out.

My little brother's name made me happy; I hadn't seen him in so long.

He was the youngest of us, and the only other boy.

I was sixteen by the time he was born and at the peak of my delinquency, as my dad put it.

I didn't spend a lot of time with him while I was still at home, but he was still my little brother.

My sisters were older by the time I left, but he was still a baby, so I felt totally guilty about leaving him. I didn't want him to end up like me, but what could I do with how fucked up I've always been?

I wondered if he even remembered me.

"How's Elijah?"

"He asked about you a few weeks ago."

I felt my chest grow warm, "Really?"

"Mmhmm, he asked if I thought you were still alive."

And with that my heart was ripped apart.

"Can I talk to him?"

"He's at school right now,"

"I can call back."

"I don't think that's such a good idea,"

"But, Mom, he's..."

"He's still so young, Elmer, he's impressionable..."

"What do you think I'm going to do to him?"

There was another pause on the line.

"I'll tell him you called,"

"Thanks." I said flatly.

"I have to go, we'll talk soon?"

"I guess."

"I love you, Elmer."

"I know."

I never had to wonder if my mother loved her son, though I did question whether or not she loved me.

I hung up.

I sat there and stared at the wall for a minute before I went to go annoy Conner.

"Hey," I sat on his desk, "Can I borrow five bucks?"

"What do you need it for?"

I shrugged, I felt weirdly defensive, "Pills, what else?"

"For five dollars?"

"Why do you care?"

Con sighed but he gave me a bill, "I wish you'd talk to me."

I went to a convenience store down the street with a sign that said, "We sell stamps!".

I spent the cash on a card with a cutesy little lion on it, one of those bubble mailers, a candy bar, and a couple of stamps.

"You have a pen I can borrow?" I asked the clerk as she rang me up.

There was no one else behind me so I used the counter to write on while the clerk awkwardly watched me.

"Hey Eli, I'm thinking about you.

I miss you.

Ask mom if we can talk soon, I love you.

Your brother, Parker."

I slipped the package into a mailbox on my way back to the apartment.

I wondered if my brother would get it, or if my mom would throw it out before he saw it.

(＼(•̀w•́)／)

Conner

I was sitting on Drew's bed while she was cleaning her room at her mom's house.

"I just think it's silly," She weighed a trinket in her hand as she dusted the dresser, "What's more ridiculous? A vampire causing disease, or a horse that's evolved a horn and magically abilities?"

"No," I laughed, "You're totally right."

"I am, huh! Well, who's to say they don't? The same people that say vampires aren't real. What else? I mean what else do we not even know about? Like what's in Area 51?"

"Old military aircrafts,"

She turned around with a raised eyebrow.

I shrugged, "... It was one of the first things I hacked into."

Drew put her hands on her hips and shook her head, "Conner Stephens, you are an enigma."

"Mm, I'm more of an unclassified document. But you, Andrew Hart, are exquisite."

She was surprised, "You know my full name?"

"Of course, I do. I also know you were named after your mom's brother."

She shook her head with a smile, "Is there anything my sister didn't tell you?"

"Unfortunately, no, every thought she ever had was thrusted onto me."

She giggled, "Yep, me too."

Drew's smile slowly slipped as she stood there, for a second her eyes searched the wall behind me, "Is this weird?"

"I guess it is,"

"But is it *too weird*?" She sat on the bed next to me.

"Does it bother you?"

She stared into my eyes, she reached up and moved a strand of my hair back into place, "No, I like you."

"I like you, too."

I kissed her.

Drew glanced at the clock next to her bed when we parted.

"I have to go put in the roast for dinner,"

I nodded and followed her down the stairs.

"Are you staying?"

"What kind of mood has your mom been in?"

She thought for a second, "How 'bout I just send some with you?"

"Deal."

She went to get the ingredients, so I checked my phone.

I had a text from Aaron.

- Did you talk to Parker?

- Not yet.

- :-/

He and I were both understandably concerned about the blood transfusion theory, especially since neither of us knew what we were doing.

"Hey, Drew?"

"Hmm?" She looked up from what she was doing.

"What do you know about blood transfusions?"

She blinked at me a couple of times, "I'm in veterinarian medicine, Conner."

"It's still medicine, and Parker is just barely above eating kibble out of a bowl on the floor."

Drew laughed, "Okay, what do you want to know?"

(＼(•̀w•́)／)

When I got back home, Parker seemed pretty down, but it was hard to tell the difference between his "artistic flare" or if something was bothering him.

"Hey," I got his attention before he went back into his cave, "We wanted to talk to you about the blood transfusions,"

He sat back down, "What about it?"

"Just if,"

He cut Aaron off, "I want to do it."

"Okay," I tried to interject, "But if,"

"I want to do it, there's no "if" about it." He cut me off.

"Okay, but I'm not totally sure it's going to work, there isn't anything about it and it's just a hypothesis."

"I don't care," Parker shrugged as he stood, "How're we ever gonna know? It works or it kills me, either way we'll have an answer."

"... I guess we just have to figure out how to get blood."

"What? Like I've never broken into a hospital before?" Parker scoffed.

October 18 2007

02:03

Conner

After an entire day of hypothesizing how one actually gets blood.

We decided, much to Parker and Nate's excitement, breaking into the hospital was our best bet.

Please don't ask me, I am very tired.

Before anything got underway, we had to wait for Parker, who insisted on taking a shower before we left, and then he also had to straighten his hair, because, and I quote, "If we get caught I wanna look hot in my mugshot."

I had to stop talking to him after that. Besides, by the time Parker was finally done it was two o'clock in the morning.

Aaron stopped me as we were about to leave, "Just checking, we're really doing this?"

"I guess so,"

He shrugged while he adjusted his beanie, "Okey-dokey."

I wish we could all have his demeanor.

We took Aaron's car, as it was newer and less descript than the fossil I liked to call a car.

He drove around until I was able to scope out an area that the hospital's security cameras didn't reach.

"Okay," I turned around in my seat, so I was able to face everyone, "Plan, there's an employee entrance in the back of the west side of the building. The hospital's blood bank is in the basement. There's a nurses' station a few feet from the stairs. It shouldn't be a problem if we time it correctly. Parker you can move the fastest, Nate and I can keep a look out, Aaron you stay out here in case we need to leave *fast.*"

Aaron frowned, "I'm the getaway driver?"

"Oh, sorry, I just assumed you wouldn't want..."

"I'll stay," Nate leaned back in his seat, "Full disclosure, I'm high anyway."

"Even fuller disclosure," Parker chimed in, "I took a handful of what I'm now thinking were uppers, I can see colors."

I put my hand to my head and tried to massage out the headache I was getting.

Aaron tilted his head, "Can't you always see colors?"

"Can we focus?" I begged, "Is this something you can do or not?"

"Easy peasey!" Parker looked out of the window for a second before he looked back at me, "What were we talking about?"

I sighed, "This is going to be a nightmare."

Aaron jimmied the lock to the back door, as we went through the hallway it led us to a janitor's closet and a break room.

I started looking around for a misplaced key to one of the lockers, or if luck was on my side, an ID badge.

"Hey guys," Parker said with a laugh that concerned me, he was pulling a lab coat over his hoodie, "Dr. Wilson, close enough. I'm a doctor."

"That's a terrifying thought," I semi joked.

Aaron quieted his snicker.

"Look there's a whole bunch," Parker was still going through the hanging coats on the wall, "Hey, there's a Dr. Lecter, need."

I kept looking while Aaron was popping lockers open and closed with ease.

Show off.

Parker came over and draped a coat over each of us, "Doctor," He nodded at me and then Aaron, "Doctor."

I rolled my eyes, "Can you stop screwing around? Help us look,"

"What are we looking for?"

"An ID badge, we're going to need it to get into the freezers."

"... Would it be laminated?"

"Yes,"

"Does it look like this?" Parker pulled a badge from the pocket of the coat he was wearing.

Aaron and I exchanged a look and savored this moment, none of us will ever be this lucky again.

"Alright, let's go steal some blood."

I gave Parker the list of things he needed to grab, and gave the two of them a simple direction, don't get caught.

I hung around with Aaron for a second to watch Parker dart down the stairs so I knew he was clear.

"I'll be back," I assured Aaron; he gave me a double thumbs up.

I followed the signs on the wall upstairs to one of the supply rooms.

"Saline. Saline. Saline..." I mumbled to myself while I searched the shelves, "Needles. Syringe. Ha, IV tubes."

I grabbed a few extras of everything just in case.

As I was about to walk out the door swung open and I was standing face to face, well, my face to his chest with a security guard.

Aaron

Conner's plan was concise, but not so much when it came to what I should be doing...

I was frazzled, but I needed to learn to do some of the not-so kosher stuff.

It seemed like there was more of it these days, or maybe it was Courtney's absence that made it seem like that.

Either way, "The job's gotta get done." as she we would put.

So, I tried my best to ignore my conscious and my "puppy dog" demeanor.

Besides, it wasn't too long ago that I would've called this a fun night.

After a minute collecting myself, I decided if anyone needed a distraction it was Conner. After all he couldn't zip around at eighty miles an hour like Parker.

The second I stepped onto the next floor a nurse intercepted me.

She was equally shocked to see me as I was to see her.

"Ma'am!" Ah, here we go, "Visiting hours are over, what are you doing here?"

I ignored the "ma'am" comment and added some distress to my voice, it was easy since she had scared the crap out of me.

"I'm sorry! No, I know. I just fell asleep in my uncle's room. I didn't realize how late it was and now I can't figure out where I am." I spoke fast.

"That's okay," She tried to assure me, "This is the second floor, the elevator is down the hall, take a left, you can't miss it."

"Thank you!" I was already running down the hall.

I got past the corner and started stalking around for Conner.

(＼(•̀w•́)／)

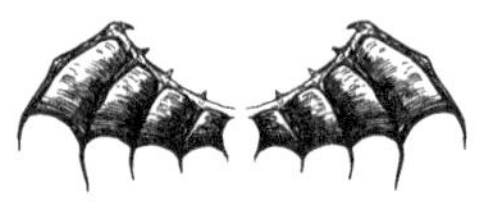

Parker

I hate hospitals, all their blank white walls, the smell of bleach, the flickering florescent lights, and the dead bodies.

God, the dead bodies.

That one wasn't lost on me since I was in the basement, every door I opened I expected a corpse to be on the other side.

Christ, I couldn't even see the morgue, bodies aside I'd see one of those metal tables and start imagining myself on it under the microscope of a doctor like some kinda bug.

"I hate it here, I hate it here, I hate it, I hate it, I hate it." I mumbled to myself, pulling my shirt over my nose as I kicked open another door.

Nope.

There was one door left, and it took an ID card like Con said.

I should start listening...

Nah.

The freezers were even more bland and sterile than the rest of the hospital, and the smell of industrial cleaner was suffocating.

Everything was packaged and vacuum sealed, but I could still smell *everything.*

I kept my shirt over my nose, didn't breathe, grabbed what I was there for and got the hell out.

(\(•̀w•́)/)

CONNER

I just stared up at this security guard like a deer in headlights.

My brain totally shut down, it was like my head was on dial-up and someone was using the phone at the same time.

"What are you doing in here?" The guard asked.

"Um..." I shoved whatever was in my hand into the pocket of the lab coat Parker put on me, I had an idea. Not a good one, but it was an idea.

"I'm a doctor...?"

"You're a doctor," The guard crossed his arms over his broad chest, "Aren't you a little young?"

"I'm twenty-five," I raised an eyebrow, "And I have patients, so..."

I tried to squeeze by, but he blocked me.

"Look," I sighed, realizing I was going to just screw myself more, "I get that you're just doing your job, but so am I. Okay? I'm up in the NICU and I have a two-day old waiting for me. Now, I *assure* you I am a medical professional! If you don't believe me, I can bring in whatever you need me to later, but right now this baby is my top priority!" Jesus, my hands were shaking so bad, yelling at this huge man was terrifying.

I'm going straight to hell but thank God for Courtney making me watch General Hospital.

He went to say something but was interrupted.

"Excuse me? Excuse me, hi!" Aaron ran over.

The guard gave him a weird look, "What are you doing in here?"

"I got a call about my uncle," Aaron's voice hitch, "They told me I had to come down here and, I..."

"Kid, I'm busy..."

Aaron let out an impressive sob, "I can't find him, is he dead? They won't..."

"Kid,"

"He can't be dead!" Aaron continued to sob.

I was caught up in Aaron's act, but I had to take my opportunity.

I ran, I ran fast until I slammed into the backseat of the car.

Nate adjusted the review mirror to look at me, "'Sup?"

(＼(•̀w•́)／)

20:00

After our late-night adventure in misdemeanor crime, I still had some research to do... That is after I woke up on the couch sandwiched between Aaron and Nate with Parker asleep across our laps.

We had a few hours to wake up, and I had some time to get my notes ready before Drew arrived.

I was quick to answer the door before Parker or Nate could get to her.

"Hi," Drew took a step into the apartment.

"Hi," she brought out a smile from me, "How was school?"

"It was fine, thanks." She greeted each of the guys.

Parker hung off the back of the couch, "Ooh, Drew's here!" He sang.

I flicked him on the forehead as I walked by, "She's here to help you, dumbass."

"Aw, that's so nice. Wait, with what?"

"We talked about this," I rolled my eyes, "She's in medical school, she knows what she's doing."

"Veterinarian," Drew added as she set her bag on the counter, "To clarify,"

"But you've done this stuff before," I tried to reassure her.

"Yes, but more on dogs and never on people."

"That's fine," Nate chimed in, "Just muzzle him, and kick him if he starts to hump your leg."

Parker crossed his arms with an audible "Humph!"

"Conner," Drew nodded me over to the other side of the counter.

"Are you sure about this?" She kept her voice low, "I'm not sure I'm the best person to handle this."

"It will be okay, besides the only other option is one of the three of us."

She unconsciously glanced at Nate, "... Okay,"

For a second, I forgot where we were and gave her a quick kiss, which was interrupted by childish cheers and whoops.

I was shocked by Aaron's participation.

"You too?"

He shrugged with a laugh.

I rolled my eyes, "Sorry, Drew."

We got Parker set up and tied down to the desk chair, I didn't think it was necessary, but he insisted.

I couldn't believe he could still smell the blood through the insulated bag. He said it was fainter than it had been in the hospital, but he was still worried about turning aggressive, especially around someone who wasn't familiar with it.

"Little pinch," Drew warned as she was inserting the IV.

Parker cringed, pulling his usual flair for the dramatic he screamed, "Ow! Ow! Ow!"

Drew jumped, "Oh my god, I'm so sorry! Are you okay?"

He laughed before I hit him on the back of the head.

I feel like I should establish that we're all idiotic and this should *not* be tried at home.

(╲(•̀ᴡ•́)╱)

20:15

Once everything was started and Drew made me promise everything was going to be okay, she went home, and I kept an eye on everything.

"How are you feeling?" I asked.

Parker wiggled against the duct tape, "I feel like I was lied to about how long this was gonna take."

"It's been fifteen minutes,"

"Can't you like speed it up or something?" He whined.

"If we do it too fast your veins will burst."

"... And that's a bad thing? They don't, like, grow back?"

I stared at him for a solid second, the disheartening part was that I didn't think he was kidding.

I tried multiple times to get back to my journal and notes just to be interrupted by Parker's constant whining.

"*Coooooooon!*" He moaned for the hundredth time in twenty minutes.

"Oh. My. God."

I grabbed a knife as I pushed off the desk.

"Chill! I just wanted the remote!"

"Shut up," I started sawing at the tape holding him down

"Wait, what are you doing?"

"Giving you your freedom, and me my sanity." I pulled the duct tape off his sleeve, "If something were going to happen it would have by now."

"That a direct quote from your last girlfriend?"

Nate made his presence known with a loud "HA!" From the couch.

I crossed my arms, "Do I need this?"

(＼(•̀w•́)／)

21:30

Parker was more relaxed, having the option to move around kept him from driving me to homicide.

He had made himself comfortable on the couch, propped up against Nate who had nodded off a while ago.

"Hey Con,"

"Yeah?"

I looked over to see Parker poking at the tube in his arm, "This hurts."

"Well, stop poking at it."

He grumbled something under his breath. He was now playing with the bag of blood like it was a water snake toy.

"Parker!"

"What?"

I went over and took it from him, "You have to keep this elevated,"

"I thought if I squeezed it, it'd go faster."

"I've seen you fall out of trees; I know you know how gravity works. Keep it up,"

That wouldn't be the last time I would have to yell at him about the bag.

(＼(•̀w•́)／)

23:00

Towards the last twenty minutes of the transfusion, Parker drastically calmed down, he was quiet and sitting still.

An extremely rare occurrence.

Out of genuine concern, I checked on him, "How are you doing?"

"Fine. Tired." He had his head back against the couch.

I nodded, and checked everything else, "It's probably going to take a while for your body to get adjusted."

"Figured."

"You have about fifteen minutes left, are you going to be okay?"

"Don't have a choice, right?" He sunk deeper into the couch.

I'd be lying if I said he didn't look like crap, I just hoped it was temporary, and he'd bounce back quickly.

"Con," Parker got my attention after I had gone back to research, "Gimme the blanket off the bed."

"You want the comforter?"

He already had his hood pulled over half his face, and his sleeves covering his hands. I didn't really think much of it until I handed it to him and noticed how bad his hands were shaking.

"Are you okay?"

"Just really fucking cold in here..."

It wasn't, if anything, it was a little stuffy.

I pressed the back of my hand against his forehead.

I tried to hide my concern, and shook Nate awake.

"Does Parker feel hot to you?"

"Holy shit, man." Nate pulled away from him, obliterating my plan to keep him calm.

"Does anything else feel wrong?"

Parker shook his head, "No...?"

"Then let's just keep an eye on it, okay?"

Parker complied and burrowed into the blanket.

After a few minutes of quietly watching TV, Parker popped up and staggered over to the trash can in the kitchen.

"Are you okay?" Aaron got up to check on him while Nate and I rushed over.

Parker could only answer by shaking his head. He tried to stand up, but halfway through, decided he was better on the ground.

"Can you tell me what's wrong?"

"The room's spinning." He rested his head on his knee.

Blood started to drip from his nose.

He gagged as more blood trickled from his mouth, then it ran from his eyes.

"Oh, God,"

We were all freaked out, but Parker took it to a theatrical level.

"This is it," he held himself off the ground on his hands and knees, he watched as the blood dripped into the carpet, "This is the rapture."

The good news is that there was blood, I guess, but something was very wrong.

I handed Parker a tissue while we tried to get him up, "Aaron, can you come get this out of his arm, please."

Parker started slipping in and out of consciousness while Aaron was taking out the IV.

"Parker," I lightly shook him, "Stay with us."

"What the fuck?" he asked slowly and slurred.

"I don't know yet, just hang in there, okay?"

I moved for a second to grab my notes.

Parker staggered to his feet; his eyes were a glowing yellow with a vibrancy I've only seen a handful of times.

He zeroed in on me.

He leaned forward like he was about to pounce, but his eyes shut, and his body gave out under him.

Aaron barely moved fast enough to catch him before he hit the coffee table.

"Parker." I tried to shake him, "Parker."

There was no response, other than a slight twitch before he started seizing.

Oh shit. Fuck. shit...

Aaron and Nate looked at me for an answer I didn't have. So, I tried to mask my panic, kicked the coffee table further back, and drug Parker off the couch.

"Hold his head." I instructed Aaron and turned to Nate, "Holy water, just in case."

We all had to stand there, completely powerless until he stopped.

"Parker!" I tried one last time to shake him before I unzipped his hoodie and checked for a pulse, breathing, or any kind of movement.

I don't know what I was expecting to find, especially since he did neither of those in the best of times.

The entire room was completely silent.

"Is..." Aaron finally spoke, his voice shaking, "I-is he... Dead?"

I realized both were staring at me.

"... I don't know."

I had to swallow my panic and try to figure out what happened.

Parker was still on the floor; we hadn't wanted to move him just in case.

It had seemed like his bleeding had stopped, but there was still a pool of blood next to him from his nose and mouth.

"Now what?" Nate asked.

"I don't know." I knelt back down at Parkers side. I'm not exactly sure what I was looking for.

His fever was still so high that I could feel how hot he was with my hand hovering over him.

His sleeve had moved at some point during everything. Something had caught my eye, I thought it was a tattoo until I remembered he didn't have tattoos that far down on his wrist.

I pulled his sleeve the rest of the way off.

"Holy shit!" Nate said, leaning over my shoulder.

From Parker's IV site to his shoulder his veins looked like he had black tar running through them.

"Is that the sludge?" Aaron asked.

"I would say yeah, but...." I gestured to the fresh blood stain on our carpet.

"I have a way to find out." I didn't like the way Nate said that, and I liked it even less when he came back with a knife from the kitchen.

"What are you doing?"

"Got a better idea?" He picked up Parker's arm and hit Parker in the face with his own hand before cutting him.

Parker's blood came out the same red color as it went in.

Nate glanced at me.

I still had no answer.

Nate decided since he had Parker in a prone position it was time for him to do his own experiment. Which consisted of him slapping the crap out of Parker and yelling expletives in his face.

"Nate."

"What?" He stopped to look at me. "Oh, you already try that?"

I just shook my head and pushed him out of the way so I could continue to look over Parker.

I saw nothing else out of the ordinary.

Just as I had bent down to check his eyes, Parker took a sharp, dramatic breath and jumped to sit up right.

Not only scaring the crap out of me, but also head butting me in the process.

Nate was too busy laughing his ass off to check on either of us.

Parker gave me a confused look for holding my head. "What's going on?" he asked.

"Undetermined." I answered while shaking my head.

"Are you okay?" Aaron helped me up.

"I'm fine,"

"I was talking to Parker."

"Oh,"

Parker shrugged, "I guess." He looked each of us up and down, "...Who are you people?"

He laughed as he watched the panic set in.

"Okay, I'm just fucking around."

"That's not funny!" Aaron squeaked.

Parker tried to stand up but had to catch himself on the couch.

"Are you okay?" I helped him sit down.

"Stop asking that!" he pushed his hair out of his face, "What happened?"

"You had some kind of adverse reaction to the blood, I haven't quite pinpointed down why yet, but I'm thinking the virus is attacking it."

"Ugh, would that be why I feel like shit?"

"We need to keep a really close eye on you, what are you feeling now?"

"I'm tired," he wiped the sweat from his forehead with his sleeve, "I just wanna go to sleep..."

"Don't!" We all yelled at him.

"Okay, damn... I don't know, it just feels like I got run over by a bus carrying smallpox."

"So, it's the virus?" Aaron raised an eyebrow.

"It's sounding like it," I clicked my pen while I thought, "Go get comfortable, you look like shit."

"Thanks, Con."

"Oh, and one other thing, nobody tells Drew about this."

October 21 2007

09:00

Conner

It seemed like the virus was attacking the new blood we had put into Parker.

Which means, for all intents and purposes; this was a good way to keep the virus busy.

For the next few days Parker was sick, he had a fever and complained about pains in his muscles and headaches. He would get a bloody nose occasionally, and he would shake uncontrollably.

It was all typical of the virus, as if it were in its very late stages, it was almost as if the virus was working backwards.

It was interesting.

I kept a close eye on him and documented it closely

He started to feel better in a matter of a day or two, he started to complain about being cold, and he was cold to the touch again. Nothing seemed much different from how it was, nothing improved but also nothing worsened.

I questioned if it did anything really, other than making him sick for a few days.

I considered pulling the plug on the operation, our first attempt was traumatic for us all, but Parker insisted that we continue.

I was able to convince him that his system needed at least a few weeks to recover, and Aaron Nate and I deserved at least half of that.

I know he was worried that this was our last hope, but I didn't see the point in making him sick when the same thing could be accomplished with a flank of beef.

I digress...

October 23 2007

23:45

PARKER

Con had me on strict bed rest for a solid week, disappointingly it was nothing like it sounded.

Con'd eventually let up and let me move to the couch, but everyone kept a close eye on me, and they were all ruthless dictators.

Especially Aaron, who would resort to reading whatever he had in his hands as loudly as he could 'til I'd do what he wanted, and more often than not it was something stupid like calculus.

I was feeling better, but no one would hear it.

It was funny, being cared about for once was nice, but at the same time I don't do so good with restrictions. Which is why whenever someone wasn't yelling at me; I'd bolt for the door.

My phone kept going off, I knew it was Conner yelling at me. I figured I could at least tell him I wasn't dead.

- Where are you now?!!

This isn't funny!!

Aaron is DISTRESSED!!!!!

CALL ME

I rolled my eyes and just texted him back.

- I'm fine don't worry about it

- I'm worried about it

- Dude I'm fine swear

- Are you drinking?

Oh, right. The good ol' sobriety plan Conner put me on while I was sick, it didn't last an hour.

-Course not

I typed with a blunt between my fingers.

- Whatever. Get home before 2 or the chain will be on

- Yes dad

It didn't take a rocket scientist to figure out where I ended up; Caitlin called, we got a couple drinks, screwed around, and shared a blunt in her bed.

We'd been keeping our distance, things were strictly physical, we hadn't even spoken much, other than a few arguments over things that happened a million years ago, but that just kept it hot.

So, when she started asking questions it started getting awkward.

"What happened to no questions asked?" I dodged whatever she asked.

She rolled her eyes, "You know what that meant,"

"I thought it was a blanket rule,"

"Parker, I just asked what you were doing for work."

"Yeah, but that's not what you meant,"

"What?"

"You start by asking me what I do, then you'll ask me if I'm seeing someone, then you're asking me what all this means." I gestured around vaguely.

"Don't flatter yourself, I was just making small talk." She pat me on the chest before she got up.

Caitlin was in the bathroom for a few minutes before she came back out and pointed at me with her toothbrush, "So are you seeing someone?"

I gestured to prove my point, "What do you care?"

"You're the one that brought it up! That's suspicious," She crossed her arms, "So?"

"Christ,"

"If you're screwing around on your girlfriend, I gotta know,"

"Why?"

"That's the decent thing to do, if you're making me the side chick."

"Yeah, I guess you'd know about side chick rules."

She spun around to grab something off the counter and launched it at me.

I ducked out of the way, so it hit the headboard, "Jesus Christ!"

"It's a tube of toothpaste," She rolled her eyes, "Answer the question, or it'll be a bath candle."

"No, you crazy bitch!"

"Not now?!"

"Not ever! Jesus, get over yourself."

"Oh... So, like, *never*?"

I crossed my arms, "I'm not answering that."

"Of course, you aren't, you have the emotional capacity of a plastic dinosaur."

"No, I'm not answering it 'cause you're nuts... Wait, like a dinosaur toy or like one of those huge bone replica things in a museum?"

"Oh, my God, you're such a freak! You know that, right?"

"You threatened to throw a candle at me!"

"Get over yourself," She shot back as she came over and grabbed the toothpaste.

By the time Caitlin was back we were both over it and making out again.

She put her hand on my chest and pushed me away for a second, "In all seriousness, you're not going to answer my question?"

"You asked me, like, twenty questions."

"Parker, we haven't seen each other in like ten years, I'd like to know at least a little about the guy I'm hooking up with, you don't?"

"I'm more of a 'don't ask, don't tell' kind of guy."

She rolled her eyes, "Why do I bother?" She scooted towards the other side of the bed, "Can you get yourself home, or do you want me to call you a cab?"

I scoffed, "You're kicking me out?"

"Why wouldn't I?"

I crossed my arms and fell against the bed now that I wasn't getting my way, "Fine, what do you want."

"What do you do for money?"

"Well," I scratched the back of my head, "Every few months I sell a couple of paintings at this flea market downtown,"

She nodded.

"Problem is they stopped doing that market like two years ago, but my plan is that hopefully someday I'll die, and all my art will sell for millions."

“Right,” She chuckled, "And if that doesn't work?"

"The plan is exactly the same, just without the money."

She laughed.

"Some dream, huh?"

"Why don't you just go get a job?"

I looked up at her, "Are your parents still rich?"

She raised an eyebrow.

"Okay, let me explain this, there's this thing called 'being poor'..." I pulled my sleeves back to show off my tattoos, “And unemployable!”

"Your parents are rich too; we went to the same prep school!" She rolled her eyes, "And you do realize I have a job, right? That I work?"

"Yeah? What do you do?"

"I'm in real estate,"

"Mm," I ran my thumb over my eyebrows, my memory was foggy at best, "Didn't your dad own a real estate company?"

She crossed her arms, "... That doesn't matter."

I laughed holding up a finger, "No, no, no, it so does!"

"Hey, I could get any job I wanted to, I have an MBA."

"Yeah, who paid for it?"

"Who paid for your associates in finger painting?"

"Nobody, I dropped out!"

She tilted her head at me, "Do you think you're one upping me?"

"... Yeah? Kinda, I dunno! What were we even talking about?"

"But seriously why don't you work?"

"It's not that simple,"

"Why not?" She kept picking.

"'Cause I'm not like you and everyone else," that just got blurted out from annoyance, but I knew I fucked up.

"What does that mean?"

"Nothing, forget it."

"No, tell me."

"I just meant, it's not as easy for guys like me."

"'Cause guys like you are...?"

"God, do you let anything fucking go?"

I pressed my palms into my eyes and tried to figure a way out of this.

"Look," I sighed, "I don't want to get into it, but I got really sick and now... Things are just really different."

"Sick... *How*?"

I glared at her.

"Well! You can't have sex with a girl and then tell her you're sick!"

I shook my head, "It's nothing you gotta worry about, something to do with my blood."

"Oh, my God, is it AIDS?!"

I rolled my eyes, "*Oh, my God*, do you ever shut up? No! It's not AIDS."

"That's what you would say so you'd keep getting laid." She dramatically slapped her hand on her forehead, "Am I going die?"

I rolled my eyes as I thought this must be what Conner must feel like when he talks to me.

"Never mind, I should probably go..."

I went to get up, but she kept talking so I reluctantly sat back down.

"Well, hang on, is it serious?"

"Yeah, but not *that* serious."

She nodded, I think she meant it in a compassionate way, "I didn't wanna say anything, but you look sick,"

"Thanks,"

"I kind of assumed you were on drugs, though."

"Mm, baby, save the dirty talk."

"Sorry! I don't know what to say..."

"Nothing is an option," ...Or so Conner had told me regularly.

"My mom had said you moved back to Byre for a while, was that why?"

I paused, I played with a loose thread from the comforter while I thought. The answer to that one might've been worse than the vampire disease.

Only one other person knew the full story, but that was because I could blackmail Nate and mostly 'cause he didn't care.

"No, that was before I got sick,"

"What happened?"

I wondered if this is how everybody else felt when I asked a ton of questions.

"... Car *accident*,"

"That bad?"

"Eh," I felt around for my pants somewhere on the floor, "I broke my leg in three places, a few bruised and broken ribs, and had a pretty bad concussion."

"Wow..."

I nodded and pulled another blunt out of the front pocket of my jeans, "Are you almost done?"

"Fine, I'll leave you alone."

She took the blunt from me, and lit it before she took a few puffs and gave it back, "Just one thing,"

"Jesus Christ," I rolled my eyes.

She hit my chest, "I was just going to tell you that there's this party, and I'm supposed to invite as many people as I can,"

I made a face.

"Relax, it's not a date or anything, we probably won't even see each other, God willing." She smirked, "But seriously, it's a huge party, the guy is an investor, so my company is just trying to make a good impression."

"You mean your dad's company?"

She glared at me, "Anyway, there's free booze, I thought you'd be interested. You can bring whoever you want, just do me a favor and don't wear anything you own."

"Oh awesome, finally somewhere I can go naked!"

October 24 2007

19:45

PARKER

Conner spent most of the day yelling at me for "sneaking out".

"Con," I grabbed him by his shoulders to get the ranting to stop, "I get that you're worried about it 'cause you've been yelling for like an hour, but you know you're not my dad, right? I mean, you can always be my daddy, but..."

I went to play with his hair, but he swatted at me.

"Why do you always have to make everything weird?"

I laughed.

"What if something had happened to you?"

"A boy can dream."

He smacked my arm.

I shrugged and plopped down on the couch, "I feel fine,"

"You always say that." He rolled his bluey green eyes at me.

Nate was sitting next to me and took the opportunity to dig his knuckles into my side.

"Ow! What?"

"Dontcha got somethin' to share?" Nate widened his denim eyes to prove his point.

I crossed my arms and buckled down.

In all honesty, I was feeling okay, it really seemed like whatever had happened was a fluke, but Conner wasn't having it.

Meanwhile with what Nate was getting at, I'd suppressed that for almost five years, what was a lifetime, really?

"It would just make me, and I think everyone else, feel better if you took things easier for a little while."

"You wouldn't let me out of bed for a week!"

"That's not what I meant,"

"Then what?"

Conner sighed and took his usual "serious talk" seat on the coffee table, "You're using a lot again."

I rolled my eyes, "Is that really what this is about?"

"I noticed it when we lost Courtney, but it's getting out of control now and the last thing we need on top of everything else is you overdosing."

"Oh, my God, it's not that serious! You know, I'm starting to really get sick of you controlling my life."

"How am I controlling your life?"

"You don't let me do anything! You tell me when to eat for God's sake!" I popped up to emphasize my point, "You tell me when I'm sick, when I should take it easy. When I'm drinking or using too much. Jesus Christ, I'm not your science experiment!"

"That's not fair, you don't know half of the stuff that happens to you. You would've killed yourself a long time ago without me."

"Yeah, well, I wish I would have!" I blurted.

The look of annoyance on Conner's face quickly turned to one of concern, so did Nate's.

"Don't look at me like that!" I snapped.

"Parker..." Conner tried.

"Don't," I stepped over his legs, "Don't, I'm done with this."

He went to grab me, but I was out of his grip and slamming the door behind me before he could even stand.

This was exactly why I didn't want to tell Conner what happened in the few years we didn't talk, I couldn't relive it, but I couldn't deal with his or Aaron's disappointment either.

I wandered around the block for a while 'til I started to get drenched from the rain.

As a last resort I texted Caitlin and asked about the party she was talking about.

I had nothing better to do and I couldn't go back to the apartment, so if nothing else I could get high in the bathroom.

She texted me the address to the penthouse of a real swanky apartment building uptown.

The place was packed from the wall feature made of marble to the luxury balcony overlooking all of Seattle with well-dressed guests and catered wait staff.

This already sucked.

I told myself it'd be fine to just get a drink and maybe I could lift a few watches on my way out.

I shoved through the room of monopoly men and supermodels glaring at me like the tiny cockroach I am.

To be fair, I'll always get off on the fact that my existence alone was enough to piss off one-percenters.

I made my way over to the bar.

This tall dark and handsome stud-muffin of a guy in button up vest was tending the bar.

He was tall, his short black hair was slicked back away from his soft olive skin.

He was a cigarette and a white cat away from being a bond villain.

"What can I get you?" He flashed a perfect smile that nearly blinded me.

I choked on my words, even his voice was bond villain-esque, it had a tinge of *something* I couldn't place.

I was so into it.

"Uh... Rum and coke..."

He turned to reach for the shelf, "Is Diplomatico alright?"

"Are you fucking nuts?"

He chuckled to himself, "It's all I have, but it is an open bar."

I nodded.

I watched him pour my drink while I silently begged whatever entity oversaw giving out tickets to Pound Town that this motherfucker was into dudes.

He wiped up something on the bar before he poured another glass, "Do you mind if I join you?"

He didn't say anything else, only offering a semi smile when I glanced up at him.

I felt like I needed to say something, "Pretty good gig when they let you drink, though I'm sure people have a hard time saying 'no' to you."

"You could say that"

"Hell, I'd let you do anything you wanted." I let my eyes glid over him.

He chuckled and bent at the waist so he could lean on the bar and be eye level with me.

His deep brown eyes scanned me.

I suddenly felt self-conscious, "What?"

"What's the matter, darling?" He faked a frown, "You don't recognize me?"

My heart fell through my stomach as I searched his face.

The same olive skin, the perfect features...

I tried to pull away, but the barstool wiggled under me.

He caught me before I fell.

I swatted him off me, "Don't touch me!"

He raised a black, perfectly arched eyebrow at me, "Next time I'll let you fall, then?"

"Yeah, you'd love that, huh? You sick freak."

He chuckled, "I wasn't the one picturing us in a... Should I say, 'comprising' position, now, was I?"

My face burned; this must be what embarrassment felt like.

I stuttered for something to say, I was guarded.

He stopped me, his glass a few inches from his perfect lips, "Parker, whatever you seem to think this is, it's not," he took a drink before setting it back on the bar, "Please sit down. Enjoy your drink, enjoy yourself. This is for you after all."

"What?"

"I told you I would be in contact," he gestured around the posh room, "Did you not expect some persuasion?"

"... But Caitlin invited me," I mumbled to myself.

"And who do you think invited her?"

"She's not..."

"No, no she's not one of mine, purely coincidental. But she is friends with a few of my girls."

"Leave her alone."

"Rest assured I mean no harm to your little girlfriend,"

"She's not my girlfriend! Jesus, what do want? Why am I here?"

"I thought that was clear," he uncapped the bottle and topped off my drink, "You had an idea of what this was, I'm simply showing you what it truly is."

"You mean your cult?"

He clenched his jaw, the tinge to his voice thickened up to an accent but only when he said, "*Boorish*," he cleared his throat and it disappeared, "But call it what you must,"

I shot back what was in my glass and tapped it, so he'd refill it.

He shook his head, "That is meant to be sipped..."

"I don't sip."

I watched closely as he refilled it.

"What is it you want, Parker?"

"What?"

"Answer the question, anything you could have, what is it that you want?"

I rolled my eyes; I didn't know what he meant.

"A million dollars, a pound of coke, and three hookers."

"I could have each of those wishes met in this room in five minutes."

I rolled my eyes again, "Sure, you could."

I honestly thought it was a bluff until a Ken doll sat next to me and winked, "Hey, tiger."

I shot a glare up at the man in the vest, "You're a freak, I'm out." I shoved off the bar.

"Parker, sit back down." He commanded.

I spun on my heels, "Give me a good reason,"

He stepped out from behind the bar, "I would like to introduce you to some people,"

It wasn't an offer or even a question.

Before I knew it his arm was slung around my shoulder. The smell of high-end cologne, expensive fabric, and top shelf whiskey surrounded me as he drug me across the room.

There were so many people, and everyone seemed so important.

I even recognized a few of them, though I didn't know where from.

Top Hat stopped when we came across another man in a suit. He was smaller than Top Hat, small and round, he was a money bag away from being a New Yorker comic character.

"Mr. And Mrs. Beverly," he flashed another flawless smile, "So great to see you here, I'm glad you could make it."

Top Hat took the hand of the woman that was with the man, "Mrs. Beverly you look ravishing, it's always a pleasure, my dear."

"Only because you make it one..." I think she went to say his name, but Top Hat slightly twitched his eyebrow, and she stopped there.

I should've punched him in the kidney when I had the chance.

"We were surprised to see your invitation," The man spoke, "What's the occasion?"

"Oh, you know me," he waved his slender hand before placing it on my shoulder, "Always trying to make a deal."

They shared a snooty laugh that our whole apartment couldn't afford.

"However, I was hoping to introduce you. This is my good friend. Parker, you know Mayor Beverly, and this is his wife, Amber."

I rolled my eyes as I shook their hands.

"Of course, I do." I mumbled sarcastically, "In fact we had a luncheon last week."

Top Hat glared at me.

"Oh, by the way, Mayor, I had a thought for you," I added.

The mayor nodded, "Of course, it's always nice to hear from the voters."

"Ew no, I don't vote, but seriously legalize weed already."

Top Hat cleared his throat as he stepped back in, "I hope you don't mind, but there are many people I have to introduce Parker to."

He tugged me away to the other side of the room until we came across a gorgeous woman in a designer dress.

"Véra," he smiled, "Bonsoir! Comment ça va?"

"Bonjour, beau, fantastique! Que puis-je faire pour vous?"

Somehow when Conner spoke French it was never this obnoxious.

I wished he was here; he'd know what to do or at least get a kick out of all of this.

"This is Véra, she is one of the Pacific Northwest's most avid art collectors, she is also a curator for numerous galleries."

"Oui," She held her hand out to me bent at the wrist, "It's an honor."

"… For me or you?" I reluctantly took her hand in a weird handshake.

"You know which," She giggled, "My friend tells me you're an artist? Tell me about your art,"

What he was doing wasn't lost on me, so I decided to have some fun with it.

"A little gore, a little porno." I shrugged, "It's like a Francisco de Goya feel, but I like to do some blow and whatever happens, happens. Dicks, tits and ass, you know how it is."

Top Hat was shocked, he had to bend down to be able to whisper to me, "Are you insane?"

"No," I crossed my arms, "I do coke, I feel like you're not listening."

"Véra, would you give us a minute?"

She waved her hand and sashayed into the crowd.

He went to say something, but I just talked louder.

"I know what you're getting at and it's not gonna work, bucko!"

He glared down at me but quickly dropped the look, "What are you implying?"

"I know you're trying to buy me, I'm not for sale."

"Not anymore, I take it?"

"Look, ass hat,"

"Parker," He demanded in a low dominating voice that made me wanna roll my eyes... And maybe moan a little.

"Perhaps we should continue this discussion in my office."

I crossed my arms, "Right, like I'm doing that."

"I do enjoy a challenge," He walked by me, looping his arm over my shoulders, "However I know you have questions, and I've always had the answers. You can make your own decision."

He started to walk away.

I was pissed, but I had to follow.

He led me through a small hall where I stopped with my hand on the door and told him "I'll scream 'rape' as loud as I can to all of those important people out there if you don't give me answers here."

I don't think this overly composed asshole had ever gaped at someone in shock before, but he got himself together quickly, smirking as he responded.

"No one would come to your rescue or even be overly surprised if that's what you're hoping for, the people in this apartment are far worse than what you're even imagining I am." He continued down the hallway.

I tried to hold in the snort that escaped me anyway, as I figured I had no choice but to follow.

We entered an elegant office at the end of the hall, after I came through, he made a show of leaving the door wide open.

"Would you like to sit and have a drink so we can have a civilized conversation?" Top Hat almost purred in a way.

"I don't even know if you have a name, dude."

"Allow me to rectify that," he wrapped his hand around mine in a firm handshake, "Donatello Sotos, your sire." He smiled so I was able to see his fangs as his eyes blinked from an almost black brown to bloodred.

I'm sure that was supposed to scare me instead I saw an opportunity, "How do I do that? And I'm not really into 'sire', I can work with 'daddy' though." I snarked trying to get under his skin.

For the first time since I'd been around this asshole, I was a little afraid as he glared at me, visibly trying to regain his composure.

I decided I should either sit quietly or make a run for it.

I chose to sit, thinking my vampire speed was okay but his was probably better, plus he kinda seemed like a predator that would enjoy chasing me.

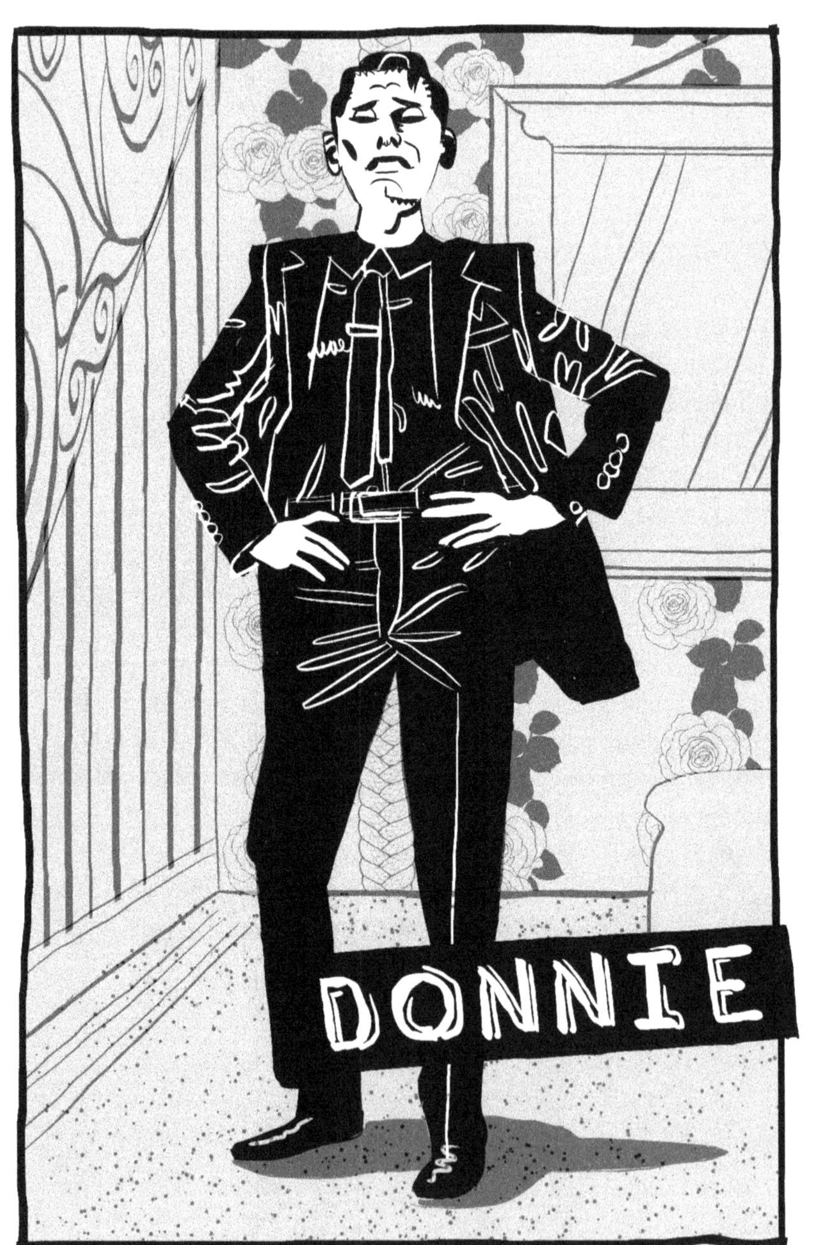
DONNIE

He walked over to the drink cart and started pouring liquor into glasses as he spoke, "I must ask, how is it possible you still associate with and consider yourself a hunter when it's very clear what you are?" He shook his head as he handed me a glass filled with amber liquid, "Is it a form of self-hatred? Are you trying to obliterate who and what you are when you attack your own kind?"

I looked at him, I'm sure my confusion was written all over my face.

"That's a lot of pretty words to ask me if I hate myself," I scoffed, "Thought that was pretty obvious to literally everybody, I mean have you looked at me? As to why I hunt with my 'hunter friends', someone has to do it." I shrugged. "I'm really about as deep as a blob of paint on the Styrofoam plate I use as a pallet. I don't have reasons for doing shit, I just do."

"What about why maim and scar yourself? You have no reason for that?"

"Mm, you're gonna have to be more specific. The tats or piercings?" I dodged the question.

He took it in stride, "So there was no reason as to why you drove your car into a tree at a hundred and fifty miles an hour?"

I shrugged, "Just feel like doing it. Works with sex, works with drugs, if it's there and I feel like it. I do it! Again, not super deep." I hoped my voice wasn't shaking as I tried to act unconcerned.

Top Hat... or Donatello just stared at me. "Parker, Parker, Parker you forget I already know the answers to all these things. I know your accident was about running away from heartache, I know that's why you're sleeping with your little friend."

"Then why ask?"

"I was curious if you would be honest with me."

"Well, I guess you got your answer, huh?" I didn't feel anyway about it, if he truly knew everything about me, he knew I was a liar.

I leaned back in my chair and kicked my muddy converse up on his desk, "So that mean if I'm lying to you, you're going be less than honest with me? 'Cause I could just leave now both of us keep our secrets..."

"What would it benefit me to lie to you, Elmer?"

I flinched at my name.

He continued in an almost whisper "As it doesn't benefit you to lie to me."

"Fine," I finished my drink and put my glass on the edge of his desk, "My turn,"

He waved his hand, indicating that I should continue, while he slid a coaster under my glass.

"Why'd it take you so long to talk to me?"

"I had to be sure you were equipped to handle something of this magnitude, I also had to make preparations for you."

"What's that mean?"

"You'll find out."

"Comforting, really. How old are you?"

"Older than you think."

"How long have you been...?"

He cut me off, "Longer,"

"Where are you from?"

"Nowhere important."

I crossed my arms, "So, how many are in your cult?"

"It's not a cult," he clarified before he answered, "And thanks to your friends, the number dwindles daily."

"Are all of them your vamp jizz or am I just lucky?"

He raised an eyebrow but moved past it, "There are a few, however no others like you."

"How's it work? You just sit around and flip through everyone's heads like cable?"

"You're the only one I feel it necessary to keep an eye on." He kept up a bored monotone.

I took that as a challenge.

"So, I'm your only problem? No wonder you have such a hard on for me."

A flash of anger, now we're getting somewhere.

"Parker, do you truly not have anything intelligent to ask me?" Back to bored.

I crossed my arms, "Few nights ago, how, or I guess, why did you show up as a woman?"

"Did it not get your attention?"

I shrugged, "You just really good at drag?"

"It's a morphing trick, something you'll learn some day."

"Uh huh, what are you then? You just kinda like a Ken doll down there?" I admit I was past getting information and was just trying to annoy him at this point.

He looked at me disgusted, at least he wasn't bored anymore.

"That seems awfully disrespectful. Especially for someone with friends like yours, is this line of questioning something you would allow for Aaron?" He cocked an eyebrow, "I would think you of all people would be more *sensitive.* Those in glass houses, and such."

My hands clenched, who the fuck did he think he was bringing my best friend into it like he knew anything?

I needed to calm down, who knew when or if I'd ever get this chance again.

Every petty part of me wanted to shove everything off his desk, but I just sat down.

"You said I'm different... The vamps in your, whatever, they're not... Awake?"

"That wasn't what I was referring to, but to answer your question; not all of them, no. The handful of vampires I house, only two are fully conscious as we are, the rest are vicious, but we're working on it."

"How?"

"Regular feedings, medical and psychological intervention. We've tried the usual, antibiotics, homeopathic medicines..."

He stopped when he realized I was making a face, his lips tugged at the corners in a kinda sarcastic smile, "Did you think Conner and Aaron were the only ones interested in vampire science? It's an illness, Parker, we're not monsters. You, of all people, should understand that."

"Why am I like this?"

"That is the million-dollar question, is it not? I can't say for sure what makes the few coherent, but I have my theories as to why you are, you are something special." He smiled in a Cheshire Cat kind of way; it sent a chill through me.

"Uh... Huh?"

He answered quick, and blunter than I was expecting, "Strigoi,"

"... Street koi?"

"*Strigoi,"* He said in a heavier accent before he sighed and rolled his eyes, "What I was expecting, I'll never know. I believe Conner calls them *shifters*?"

My hands went numb.

I tried to play it off with a laugh, "What?"

"The vampire hunter's idea of an urban legend." He quoted, "The rumors of shapeshifting creatures, with mind bending abilities, 'deplorable behavior', and incredible power. 'Ghoulish and insatiable'... Strigoi, Parker, this is what you are. Your visions, your dreams... You have an untapped wealth of power," he chuckled, "And you are completely oblivious to it."

"Wait... Y-you're not the one doing the vision shit?"

"Charmed, alas, no. Your visions are all your own."

"Do you..."

"On occasion, more when I was younger, but never with the frequency nor accuracy as yours."

"And you're, whatever, too?"

He nodded, "In all my years, I have not come across another."

I ran my nail over a scar on my arm, this was all way too much to process... God, I would've killed for something sharp.

I want Conner.

"I... No, I don't get it. So what? You want my 'power' for your cult?"

"No, I want to make you what you are. I want to help you harness that power. Everything is an exchange, Parker. I save your life, you help me keep my community safe, I teach you all the things you can do, and you pay back to the community with it. It doesn't stop there, anything you could possibly want, it's all yours. Quid pro quo."

That was all too good to be true.

He kept talking but I was only a quarter listening, the other quarter was still trying to figure out how to pronounce strigoi, and the half was wondering what he meant by that...

"... Since you can't control the simplicity of your fangs, I anticipate it will require a lot of training to..."

I held my hands out in front of me, "Back up, you just said you saved my life?"

He gave one nod, "Precisely, I did say that."

I scoffed, "You think you saved my life?!"

"As I brought you back from death, yes."

"What are you talking about?"

He scanned me, staring into my eyes for a solid minute, "You don't remember being changed,"

"Did you just read my mind?" I can't believe that was an actual question I just asked.

"But you remember the actual progression, interesting."

"Stop that! Tell me what you're talking about?!"

"The night you were turned," He acted like he had answered something, "I've watched over you, long before you were a vampire, Parker, like a guardian angel and you should consider yourself blessed that I was there that night."

"Blessed, *stalked*," I shrugged, "Matter of opinion, I'm sure."

"It was for your own good, and it truly was a miracle I was there. You spent the day in a Xanax haze, soon that wore off and you were begging strangers for cash just to get the shaking to stop. Eventually you relied on your 'personal skills' to supplement your addiction. Despite all the drinks your patrons had offered you, it still wasn't enough. You swallowed a few more pills to get you to a bar's bathroom where you could use the counter and white powder to heal yourself. Once you were escorted from the bar you decided to head to the shelter to sleep it off and reembark on the same mission the next day. Only you never made it, it was cold out and you were starting to get tired, so tired that you had to sit. Leaned against an alley wall, swaddled in a thin jacket that provided no protection against the snow, you struggled to find your breath, gasping for sharp shuddering breaths. While, unbeknownst to you, your capillaries were beginning to burst from the strain you had put on your heart. The drop in your temperature was no help, as your heart seized. You lay there, on the concrete cold and alone, convulsing until the blood supply to your brain had stopped. Your last breath nothing more than fog in the frozen night. Yes, it was a blessing I was there."

I was quiet.

Nothing would come out of my mouth.

Since I was fourteen years old, I wanted to die, knowing it had actually happened...

"I, I don't believe you..." I stuttered out.

He tried to smile in a comforting way, but it came off as condescending, "You do believe me, that's the problem, isn't it?"

"Why?" I gulped, "Why, why did you save me? Why *would* you save me?"

"You lived a cold, lonely life. I wasn't willing to let you die the same way. I chose you, Parker, because you know what it's like to be lost, to be confused, to be broken and shattered, you understand it. You need me as much as I need you, you cannot survive in this world, not in the human world. You were never meant to."

I took a jagged breath; I hadn't realized I was holding until the noise startled me.

"But I don't want this, I don't, I can't..." I trailed off.

My shocked sadness started to turn into a boiling rage, "I never asked for this, I don't want this! I don't want to be like this!" I stomped as I stood up, bringing all my 5 foot 6 inches as close to him as I dared and growled "Who the fuck do you think you are, God?" I thought it was impressive until I realized even as he sat, I still was pretty much eye to eye with him.

He must have realized the same thing because he smirked as he pushed me out of his space, "Others in your shoes have been more grateful."

"That's their fucking problem! You don't get to just play God!"

"Since I created you, I'm not surprised you made that parallel, and just so you know I do reserve the authority to destroy what I create, I would watch my step if I were you."

"Then do it! What, that's supposed to scare me?! I thought you already knew all that stuff; shouldn't you know I'm not afraid to die? I want to die for God's sake!"

He looked at me with what I could only describe as annoyance as he slumped against his desk, "I am fully aware how flippant you are with your mortality, Parker. It sure would be a shame for Conner, Aaron and Nate to suffer the same fate as Courtney."

He did fucking NOT!!!

I was up and grabbing at him before my brain caught up.

In the next second, I was being held back by two security guards as Donatello straightened his cuff links and walked out of his office without so much as a backwards glance.

(＼(•̀w•́)／)

22:00

Nate

Con sighed and tried to get our attention, "Has anyone heard from Parker?"

I shrugged.

Aaron shook his head while he played with his earbud.

"He's not answering my calls, can one of you try calling him?"

"How come?" Aaron asked as he got up to find his phone.

Con shrugged, "I've gathered he feels like I'm being suffocating,"

"Thought you were lettin' him cool off." I added.

"I am," Con played with the antenna on his phone, "I don't know he's been gone for a while, usually after he storms off, he stumbles his way home or texts by now."

"Hang on, I think it's in the room."

I waited for Aaron to be out of ear shot, "You think Park's gonna kill himself or something?"

Conner whipped around to look at me, "I didn't 'til now, why would you say that?"

"What?" I shrugged, "Two weeks ago he said he was gonna load himself full of silver."

Con went back to his phone, "Jesus Christ, Nate."

The door intercom buzzed.

Conner relaxed at the sound of Parker's voice.

"Hey, I forgot my keys."

I hopped between Con and the com, "Where's your phone?"

"What?"

"Where's your phone, jackass?"

"In my pocket? Just let me in."

"Why aren't you answering it?"

"Nate,"

"Lo siento, no hablo Ingles."

"Nate, let me in!"

"Con's been trying to call you for an hour,"

"Yeah, and I'm outside! Open the door!"

"Nah,"

"Nate! I'm gonna buzz Mrs. Miller!"

"Do not buzz Mrs. Miller! She'll call the cops on us again." Con shoved me out of the way and buzzed him in.

Parker barreled through the front door like the fucking Cool Aid man and into Conner.

Con stumbled back but Park held onto him in a bear hug.

Aaron walked out of the room, with a confused look on his face.

Park sped over and wrapped him up next.

"What's going on?" Conner asked, "You're worrying me."

Parker tried to come for me, but I held my arm out, "We good."

"Long night, I went to this party and Top Hat, I mean Donatello, I mean..." He was talking so fast I could barely keep up and I'm used to his coked-up nonsense.

Like an hour and a promise of a cheesecake later, Con managed to get Parker to calm down and tell us the whole story.

"Hang on," I hit Park in the back of the head.

"Ow! Why!"

"You go to a party without me, and follow some guy? You're lucky your ass didn't get kidnapped."

Conner moved past it, clicking his pen, "What was that word you said he used?"

"God, I dunno," Parker rubbed the back of his head, "Stroganoff?"

Con rolled his eyes, "You think he said you were a Russian beef and noodle dish?"

"I dunno! It's been a long night, okay?!"

"Strigoi," Aaron offered pushing up his glasses, "Romanian lore, I think, I don't know much about it."

"That's more than stroganoff over here." Con nodded while he wrote, "You saw him, you spoke with him, we have his whole name, you still don't remember him?"

Park shook his head, "I don't remember him, I don't remember the story he told me..."

"You don't remember the night at all?"

He picked at his nails, his face went all serious, "I kinda, I mean, I remember passing out somewhere and it was cold. But, come on, that could've been last week! All I really remember is waking up a few days later in a motel room so sick I thought someone had stolen my organs."

"But he didn't look familiar?"

"Trust me, I'd recognize this guy."

"Do you think that was his 'final form'?" Aaron air quoted.

Parker shrugged, "Seemed like that's what he wanted me to think, but who knows."

I swirled my can around, "What'd he look like?"

"Like Bela Lugosi and James Dean birthed one of those dudes that hangs around Abercrombie without a shirt on."

"So, like the exact opposite of Con?"

I finally got a chuckle outta Park, and a glare from Con.

"Was he older, then?" Aaron asked.

"Nuh-uh, he didn't look any older than us, but there was this like..."

"Je ne sais quoi," Conner offered.

"Yeah!"

I rolled my eyes, "Queer,"

"Hang on!" Aaron snapped his fingers before he scampered off to look for something.

Conner smoothed his orange hair back, "I just don't get it, if he's going to give you his name as simple as that, what was with all the cards?"

"Arrogance?" Parker scoffed.

Aaron was back, shuffling through a newspaper, "I can't believe I didn't make this connection sooner. There's this guy I was reading about; nobody knows who he is really, only that he goes by Donatello. He's kind of turned into a local legend, in the last few months he's poured a lot of money into the city. Just a couple of weeks ago, there was this book shop across from my restaurant that I like to go to, it was going out of business until someone donated two hundred and fifty thousand dollars."

Parker clicked his tongue, "This can't be the same guy."

"Yeah, maybe it's the turtle." I drank the rest of my beer.

The three of them stared at me.

"... Donatello, ninja turtles? Heroes in a half-shell?" When no one responded I got up to get another beer, "Goddamn, I'm wasted on all of you, man."

"Donatello was always my favorite..." Aaron said softly.

"Aha!"

They went back to talking and I focused on my beer and wondered how many nods I could get away with before I got called out. I figured anything they were gonna say was over my head anyways.

Aaron was piecing stuff together with the newspaper, "It just says 'he'd rather remain anonymous'."

"I'm sure he does." Parker spat.

"I'm not sure we're working with a real name here, but" Conner shrugged, "If he's making big donations like this, I'm bound to find something."

"I might be able to dig more up on these donations, while you do that."

Con nodded, "That's a good idea."

The three of them stood up.

Aaron tilted his head at Parker, "Where are you going?"

Park held his arms out while he stretched, "Smoke a bowl and go to bed, I don't wanna deal with this shit anymore."

October 25 2007

10:45

CONNER

Parker grumbled out of the bedroom and slumped next to me on the couch.

"Hey, I wasn't expecting to see you before noon,"

"Mm," he put his head against my shoulder and bonked into me like a cat seeking attention, "I couldn't sleep much last night, everything that creep said just wormed its way into my dreams, you know, I actually had a dream I was a vampire rabbit being chased by a rottweiler. What do you think that means?"

"That you need to stop smoking weed before bed?"

"Maybe I need to stick to pills."

He watched me hit at a few keys on my laptop before he asked.

"What are you working on?"

"Aaron was able to dig up a few things, I was looking at the donation records to see..."

"How come this isn't plugged into your radar thingy?"

"Huh?"

"Whatever you do to keep it rolling for hunts? Whatever you have it plugged into?"

"I unplugged it for now, I figured with everything else we're working on, hunting was pretty low on that list."

He scooted away from me, "So what? We're not hunting anymore?"

"I didn't say that, I think," I shook my head, "You know what? Maybe we should discuss this as a group, 'cause you and I just end up arguing."

"Fine,"

After a few seconds of sulking, he put his head back on my shoulder and tangled his arms around mine.

I let him, if it made him feel better, and prevented another argument, I was game... As long as he kept his hands to himself.

"Were you able to find anything?"

"A few things, Aaron and Nate went to get food so I was just waiting for everyone to get back."

Parker nodded.

He sat there in total silence while I worked, it was borderline eerie.

A quiet Parker is not something I've encountered many times.

"Oye, putas," Nate's voice boomed through the apartment, "Look what we found."

"Hi,"

Drew's voice made me spin around in my seat, "Hi! What are you doing here?"

"Well, I don't have class today, so I was wondering maybe there was a vampire lore class?" She offered a cute smile.

"Oh, baby, class is always in session for you." Nate intervened.

"Puke," Aaron verbalized my thought exactly.

"Of course," I stood to greet her, "I wish you would've called first; we've got a few things we've been working on, I don't know how educational it will be."

"That's okay, I'd love to help if I can."

"Um,"

Parker didn't even try to pretend he wasn't listening, "I don't care, she can stay,"

I shook my head, "Alright, but tell me if you get too bored, okay?"

"Will do." Parker answered.

Drew giggled, "Don't worry about me."

"I'm sorry we didn't get you anything," Aaron apologized as he set a few paper bags on the coffee table, "If you want, you can share my taquitos with me."

"That's sweet, but I'm okay, thank you."

"Hang on, you didn't get me anything?" Parker pouted.

"They don't got vegan, güero."

"So, you seriously didn't get me anything, though?!" He whined.

"You don't eat!"

"But I like to!"

Nate mumbled something else in Spanish, "Fine, you can have my other taco, but you can shut up and pick the cheese off. Don't say I never did nothing for you."

"What's in it?"

"Carne asado,"

"Is that meat?"

Nate glanced up at me before he straightened out, "Nah, it's like that wack soy shit you order, you'll like it."

I kicked Nate under the table.

He winked.

"May I ask something?" Drew picked at some tortilla chips, "How did you all get into hunting?"

Parker shrugged, he was already halfway through his borrowed taco, "Didn't really have a choice with these guys, but once I figured it out, I got into it."

"How does that work with your veganism?"

"They're not living beings."

"Fair enough."

"I was kinda stand-offish to the killing part of it, too," Aaron agreed, "But there's no way to help them so all we can do is make sure they don't hurt others."

Drew nodded, "Is that why you started?"

"In a way, my grandmother was a green witch, she believed in a lot of things, and she used to tell me stories about all kinds of creatures. When I got older, I wanted to do some research because I didn't know what was real and what was just my grandma being her. When I stumbled upon some vampires, I quickly realized I wasn't going to get many answers when it was either them or me. When I met Conner, though, is when I really got into the hunting side of it."

"Your grandma sounds fun."

Aaron tilted his head halfway with a chuckle, "She was colorful."

"I only started when I moved in with these nerds," Nate said through his mouthful of burrito, "Con and Air were talking about something secretive," He shrugged, "I'm nosy, so acted like I knew what was up 'til I was in the middle of it."

I rolled my eyes, "He's joking,"

Nate shook his head, "Dead ass,"

"You said your dad..." Aaron trailed off.

"He coulda, I dunno! I don't even know who that fucker is!"

The room dissolved into laughs as we finished eating.

"What about you?" Drew asked me.

I raised an eyebrow, "My parents,"

"No, I know that I just meant how did you decide to start doing it?"

I cleared my throat, "Well, it was a few months after they died... I had locked myself in the basement trying to make sense of their deaths, and it was just a natural progression. Someone had to finish their life's work."

"But do you want to do it? What do you think you would be doing if they were still around?"

I took a second, no one's ever asked me that before, I must enjoy it or else I wouldn't be hunting... Right?

"According to recent lore," Parker spoke back up, "I'd be dead in a ditch somewhere."

"I'd probably still be in school," Aaron answered.

Nate shrugged, "Back in Oakland, either selling drugs or making fucking tamales, who knows?"

"I... Have no idea."

I really didn't, I often wondered what life would be like if my parents were still around, but I never wondered what my life would be like without hunting.

I forced myself to take a deep breath and decided that it was a crisis for another day, we had work to do.

Nate and Parker very reluctantly cleared the table while Aaron and I got our things in order.

"I wanted to look at the donations first, if that's okay?" Aaron pushed his glasses up while he sorted through his notebook.

"For sure,"

"I was able to find four, I think, just in the past year."

"Four, what?" Parker hurried back to sit with us.

"Donations under the 'Donatello' moniker; there was the one for the bookstore I told you about,"

I nodded, "I wasn't able to find anything on that one, it was done completely anonymously. The owners said it was a direct donation."

"Mm, I have one for Seattle's homeless housing project,"

"Again, direct donation."

"Okay, school library fund. That's a federal one, there has to be something on that?"

"There's a last name, Sotos. The address is fake, and..." I clicked a few more things before I sighed, "Bank account has been closed."

"Son of a bitch, I thought for sure we'd find something through that!"

"How much money is he putting into this?" Parker asked.

"Um, collectively, a little more than four million." Aaron answered.

"Jesus Christ!"

"I did find one article, 'Seattle's richest unknown man'," I leaned back, "It's about as helpful as you would imagine."

"What happened when you looked up his name?" Drew chimed in.

"As far as the state of Washington's records are concerned, there is no Donatello Sotos. There are no birth certificates, no parking tickets, no tax records. I'm not sure how that's even possible, it's 2007 everyone's everything is everywhere!"

"Big brother is always watching," Aaron agreed.

"Please don't get Nate started on that again."

"This is bullshit," Parker shoved himself up, "So he's this great, fantastic guy that saves the community and donates to bookstores, but he's a serial murderer and he runs a cult!"

"Well," I shrugged, "To be fair, we don't know it's a cult."

"Whose side are you on?" Parker snapped.

"Sorry," I rolled my eyes, "Donatello Sotos is very clearly not a real name, so who's to say these donations are?"

"Apparently Seattle,"

"No, I meant, he's trying to spin a narrative here, why?"

"I don't know but he was trying to prove a point last night, too. He had all these important people around, clearly he thinks he's important." Parker plopped back down between me and Aaron.

"I have four million that says he is," Aaron added, "He'll slip up somewhere, it's human nature."

"Yeah, but he's not human." Parker mumbled.

I sighed, "We need to take a break, did you want to see what I found about strigoi?"

Parker glumly nodded.

"Alright, I read most of this at three in the morning while wearing Aaron's glasses, half of it was in another language, bear with me here." I got up to get my notebook and paced around while I scanned through what I had scribbled, "It's a little like the death-walker theory, 'eyes glow red from the possession of a malevolent spirit'. These spirits are 'thought to possess the dead and mostly animals, but does not exclude humans, depending on the strigoi'..."

"The little girl," Parker blurted, "The one from Courtney's memorial, so what? He was possessing her?"

"It's one listed power,"

"That's disgusting."

I kept reading, "Another version of this is telepathy and projection."

"Dream manipulation would be a part of that, right?" Aaron asked, "That could be your visions and dreams."

"It sounds like that would be your doing, though."

"Huh?"

"'Projection is used to see through another's eyes,'" I pointed out.

"But how would I be doing it? I didn't even know it was a thing until three seconds ago?"

Aaron shrugged, "He did say you were more powerful than you thought."

"Uh-uh," Parker was up and shaking his hands out, "Don't like that, don't like it."

"I don't blame you, but unfortunately, there's more."

He made a dry heaving noise and leaned against the back of the couch, "Tell me,"

"They can shape shift to an extent, it's called skin shifting, they can change to look like other people, but not animals or objects. Nor can they replicate 'non-organic features'... Like tattoos and scars, I guess. According to this lore, all of these take a lot of practice, and some don't even become prominent until the subject is 'around' for a while."

Parker didn't say anything for a while.

"... Are you okay?" Aaron finally asked after a minute or two.

"I don't like this." Parker mumbled into his shoulder

"I'm sorry," I wasn't sure what else to say, "But at least we know, it's a step closer to finding a cure."

"About that," He stood upright, "I want to do the transfusion thing again."

"Why? It almost killed you."

"Yeah, but it did something! What else do we have?"

I pinched the bridge of my nose, "I'm sick of arguing with you,"

"Perfect," he clapped his hands together, "Then, before that we can take a hunt."

It amazes me how he can just flip a switch and go back to being arrogant, but I knew I should give him a small break, he's had to process a lot.

"Fine, we can talk about hunting, but we're a group so we have to decide together."

Parker crossed his arms.

"Aaron, Nate, how do you guys feel about getting back into hunting? I think it's too soon; we still have things to figure out and there's so much up in the air."

"But we still have a job to do," Parker argued, "Court wouldn't want us on standby, she'd want us out there making sure what happened to her doesn't happen to anyone else."

"Our emotions are high, when we're not thinking clearly, we make more mistakes and something awful could happen again."

"Something awful is gonna happen with or without us, it already is! This prick's gonna keep killing people, we gotta get under his skin somehow."

Aaron tucked his hair behind his ears, "Sorry Con, I think I'm with Parker on this one. Courtney would want us out there, I want to be out there for her."

"Okay," I sat, if I was being unreasonable, I wanted to hear it, "Nate?"

Nate shrugged, "I hear ya, but maybe Con's onto somethin'. We're more likely to fuck something up."

Drew raised her hand, for a brief few minutes I forgot she was here.

"I don't want to step on any toes, but since it's my sister and all?" She offered a sheepish smile as she moved her hair over her shoulders, "When we were kids, our mom used to have this huge garden in our backyard, Courtney and I used to love to just be outside with her... Granted most of the time Courtney didn't do anything, but it was still something we all did together. Lately I've been helping my mom garden again, and I don't know... It doesn't bring her back, and it certainly doesn't make me miss her any less, but it's nice to have something to do that still makes me feel close to her."

Drew stated "You guys are really good at what you do, and it sounds like you really do enjoy it. It might be good for you guys to get back into it, maybe it will make you feel close to her again, maybe it can be healing. That being said, you should most definitely take your time, and maybe change a few things so you're safer." She shrugged, "It's just something to think about."

I clicked my pen while I thought.

I got what she meant, hunting definitely helped me feel close to my parents.

"Alright... But things are going to have to be different, and we're going to have to do more planning, and be safer..."

"Whatever," Parker cut me off, "I'll go out there in bubble wrap if you want, but Drew's right we have to get back out there."

I looked over to Nate who shrugged his opinion, "Fair, I'm on board if you are."

I nodded, "I'll look around, see what's going on. We'll keep an open dialog."

In a flash of pink and faded black, Parker's arms were around my waist, and I was a couple inches off the ground.

"Thanks, I don't like being mad at you."

He kissed me on the mouth before I could demand to be put down.

"PARKER!!! My mouth was open!"

"I know, you taste like salsa. I liked it!"

I squirmed until he let go.

He made a beeline for Drew, "Also thanks for listening to..."

"Hey!" I stopped him before he could do anything repulsive, "Don't touch her."

Drew got away with just a hug.

"Well, I have to admit, I do have a slight ulterior motive," She admitted with a slight smile, "I want to hunt."

It was so quiet we could hear the neighbors TV.

My first instinct came out of my mouth before anything else could, "No,"

To be fair that was my second and third instinct, too.

"I thought you would react like that. I'll listen to your argument, but my sister can't be your sole reason for saying no."

Aaron was already up and trying to escape the before I asked, "Can you guys give us a minute?"

Drew stopped him, and motioned for him to sit back down, "No, no, I want their opinions, too. You're a team, right?"

God, I knew that was going to bite me on the ass, but I didn't think it would be like this.

"... Okay," I gave Parker and Nate a look, hoping they would realize it was a plea for silence, but I already knew that was going to be blown right out of the water.

"Uh, Drew, you have to understand we've been doing this for a few years now, there's a lot of training and..."

"Not really," Nate chimed in.

Here we go.

"I mean, what kinda training do we got?"

"... We know how to properly use guns."

Aaron's hand raised.

I wasn't going to acknowledge it, but Drew did.

"Go ahead,"

"I didn't know how to shoot a gun before I started..." Aaron answered quietly.

"Uh-uh, me neither," Parker added, "Con taught me."

Drew shrugged, "I know how to shoot a gun, my mom taught me when I was a kid, she was adamant about it."

"I... Didn't know that." I searched my brain erratically, "Would you be okay with having to kill things?"

"I want to be vet, I'm well aware that sometimes things have to die so they don't suffer."

"Damn, we didn't even have to say anything that time." Nate laughed.

"Quiet!" I snapped, "What about your mom? What would she say if she knew you were wanting to hunt?"

"She wouldn't want me to, but I'm asking you, I'm not asking her."

"It isn't a good idea."

"Why?"

"Because, Courtney! Jeez, you're just going to push me until I say yes like..." It took me far too long to realize what I did, "You always do this and..."

Once again, the room was silent.

"See!" She shifted back on her heels, arms crossed, "You can't even separate me from my sister, can you?"

I didn't know what to say so I didn't say anything.

Her demeanor shifted from proving her point to realizing something, "Oh, wow," She shook her head, "Wow, this all makes so much sense now."

I didn't like the way she looked at me.

"Drew,"

"Mm-mm, no. No thanks." She grabbed her bag and slammed the door.

I wanted to go after her, but all three of the guys stopped me so I just fell on the couch.

"How bad did I just fuck up?"

Nate rubbed my shoulders, "You just nuked Switzerland, bro."

October 28 2007

15:00

Conner

It was a take "two Xanax and a cup of Irish coffee" last couple of days, but as I'm a glutton for punishment, and not Parker, I was going it alone.

Just a boy and his crippling anxiety against the world.

Parker's phone had gone off, and by instinct, I checked mine.

"Oh, my God, dude," Nate rolled his eyes, "She's gonna call, chill."

"She's not going to call, she hates me."

Parker sucked the air through his teeth, "Yeah, probably,"

"Thanks,"

"Well, have you called her?"

"Six times, she's sending me to voicemail."

"Hold up, you called her six times?" Nate raised his eyebrows in concern.

"How many times am I supposed to call her?"

"None!" Parker and Nate answered at the same time.

"Look," Parker was up and leaning over my shoulder, "Sorry about your girlfriend and all, super sad, but like what are we doing about hunting?"

"Thank you for your sympathy," I rolled my eyes, "But I haven't had a minute!"

He crossed his arms and went to sit back down, "You're so grumpy,"

"I don't want to talk about hunting!"

Aaron took one of his headphones out, "Are we talking about hunting?"

I leaned forward and let my head slam against my desk.

"I've been thinking about it, and maybe it might be good to have Drew around. We're used to a certain number of hands, she'll still be new but if she wants to do it and can shoot..."

"Maybe Air's got a point," Nate said, "We're kinda used to five on a team."

I sat upright, "I don't care if we're used to fifty, it's not a good idea."

"Maybe not, but she's still safer with us than by herself." Aaron reasoned.

I mumbled to myself as I got up.

"Where are you going?"

"I gotta go talk to Drew!"

I spent the entire drive thinking of what I was going to say, but once Drew answered the door and her icy blue eyes looked me over, I lost what smidge of nerve I had.

"What do you want?" She stared at me as I tried to string together a sentence.

"I'm sorry,"

"I don't care."

"... I didn't expect you to."

"Good," she stared at me for a minute waiting for me to say something else.

"Can we talk?"

"I don't feel like talking, Conner."

"That's fair, but I'm the one that needs to do the talking."

She sighed, "Fine,"

She stepped out instead of inviting me in, she gestured to the wire bench on the patio.

It was cold and uncomfortable, but so was the situation.

I offered her my jacket, but she didn't want it.

"I wasn't completely honest with you, and I'm sorry."

"Okay, about which part? That you weren't honest about being a normal guy? Or vampires? That you think I'm incapable of hunting, or that you wanted my sister and settled for me?"

"I didn't say that,"

"No, you didn't have to,"

My thoughts were swarming, but I could only imagine how she felt.

"Drew, I promise it's not like that."

She shook her hair out of her face.

"It isn't, I..." It was hard to admit, especially to Courtney's sister of all people, never mind my "girlfriend".

"I had an idol worship crush on Courtney, yes, I'm not going to lie to you about that, but... You're so much more than your sister, you're not her and I never saw you as her."

"Then why did you call me Courtney?"

"I mean, you do remind me of her, you're both stubborn..." I decided to stop there before I dug a deeper hole, "Drew, I had this stupid kid crush on Courtney, I knew she didn't like me, I knew it'd never be anything. The way I feel about you is so different, I really care about you, more than I thought I could, and more than I ever have for somebody, and that's saying something! My last girlfriend, I thought I was going to marry... I'm rambling..."

"Why didn't you tell me?"

"Well, because I didn't want you to feel like this."

"Ironically,"

"Yeah," I cleared my throat, "I get it, if you never wanna see me again, I do, but I need you to know I didn't play you. I care and that's the whole problem with you hunting. I don't, I can't lose another person I care about, it's selfish..."

"It's not selfish," She finally said, "I understand, but my sister's gone, Conner. I need something, even if it's as silly as trying to hunt, I need a piece of my sister back. I know you know how that is, you said it yourself you wouldn't be a hunter if your parents were still alive."

I let go a deep sigh, watching as the cold wind took my warm breath, "I do, and if you're sure this is something you have to do... I'd be honored if it were with me."

She played with the ends of her hair, it hurt that she wouldn't look at me, "I have to think about it."

It was a quiet, cold couple of minutes.

I finally got up the courage to ask, "Should I leave?"

Though I knew the answer.

"I think you should."

I nodded, "Thanks for listening."

She nodded back as she stood, I watched as she took a couple of steps to the door.

She paused, turning the knob, she went to say something, but she stopped herself, "Bye, Conner."

"Bye."

(＼(•̀w•́)／)

Nate

We were waiting for the latest on the Conner fuck up scandal, there's a betting pool on whether Con could pull it off. Aaron hopefully and stupidly put up forty bucks.

I was looming over the back of the couch spying on Parker, mostly 'cause I know it annoys him.

"What're you doin'?"

He punched at the keys on his phone, "Nothing,"

"Who are you textin'?

He glared at me, "No one, why?"

"Nate!" He yelled and swatted at me when I grabbed his phone.

"Caitlin?" I raised an eyebrow

I was kinda surprised, but mostly relieved that's all he was texting.

"She was at the party last night," He pulled it outta my hand, "I needed to make sure she was okay."

"Oh, so you're checking in now?" I mocked, crossing my arms.

He rolled his muddy eyes at me, "It's not like that, if something would've happened to her that's on me."

"Uh-huh, sure." I joked.

He gave me that annoying ass smirk he does, "What's wrong? You jealous?"

"Nah, it's just so unlike you to care about someone else."

He gave me a finger and went back to his phone.

Conner walked through the door before I could keep annoying Parker.

Aaron's ears perked up, "How did it go?"

"Well, I'm home and unharmed," Conner shrugged, tossing his keys on the counter.

"Aw, so no makeup sex?" I frowned.

Con rolled his eyes, "Why do I tell you guys anything?"

"'Cause some of us are supportive!" Aaron shot a glare at me, "Is she gonna be hunting with us?"

"She said she'll get back to me, but," Con sighed, he collapsed on the couch next to Park's feet, "I don't think I'll ever hear from her again."

"So we doing the hunting thing?" Parker double-checked.

"You're relentless,"

"I'm just checking!"

Con pinched the bridge of his nose, "Fine, since you brought it up, I think it would be in everyone's best interest for you to feed before we hunt."

"Why does that matter?"

"Aside from you not hunting hungry? Parker, you were so sick and you refused to eat anything,"

"And I was fine."

"You survived, but you weren't fine! There's no way your body's going to make it through a hunt..." he dropped his hands to his side, annoyed, "God, I'm sick of having this argument with you! And quite frankly, I'm having a pretty shit day, so you're doing it!"

Con stormed off into the bedroom without saying another word.

"Don't yell at me!" Parker yelled back, crossing his arms, "It turns me on."

After a while, Con came back into the room just to grab his shit and tell us to leave him alone.

Parker clicked his tongue, "The 'I just got dumped' depression jerk off. Poor guy."

"I can still hear you!" Conner yelled through the door, “Shut up!"

Aaron got up to come read in the living room, “He's probably looking for a hunt." He completely missed the joke.

Park was still texting, so I turned on the TV and flipped to the channel with the hot weather girl, which reminded me of something... Well, two things.

"Perrito?"

"Hmm?" Aaron didn't look up from his book.

"What're you doing for your birthday?"

"Oh," he played with the edges of the page, "I guess it's that time of year again..."

"Three days, perrito."

He didn't want to talk about it.

He never cared about his birthday, but Courtney always made a point to go all out for everyone's birthday.

It worried me how he was gonna deal without her.

I tried to be soft, but I wasn't good at it.

Concern came off as condescending, caring sounded sarcastic.

"Mine's in four days," Park said when Aaron went silent.

"Don't care,"

Parker pouted.

Aaron shrugged, "You know how I am, I'd rather put my energy into Halloween."

"So what'd you wanna do then?"

He didn't answer.

"Didja wanna go back to Portland? I'd go with you," I shrugged, "It could be like a thing."

"We could all go!" Park added, "I like Portland, they're freaks there."

Aaron shook his head, "No... I don't really wanna go home right now. Maybe we should just focus on hunting and the whole Donatello thing."

I crossed my arms, "Mirar, we're celebrating your birthday so tell me what you want, or we're gonna end up at a strip club."

"Ooh!" Parker's eyes widened.

Aaron gulped when he realized we weren't kidding, "... I like waffles."

"Got it."

"I know a place where we can eat waffles off of strippers!" Parker suggested.

"Just the waffles will be fine." Aaron shrunk.

October 29 2007

17:00

Conner

I should've known better than to ask for peace and quiet while I worked, it would've been more realistic for me to ask for a million dollars.

Between Nate's snide comments hurled at the game that was blaring on the TV, Parker's drunken finger painting with his headphones as loud as they could go, and Aaron trying desperately to talk on the phone, the million dollars was looking much more practical.

To add to the noise, my computer beeped at me.

It was a Seattle Times article that one of my programs flagged.

The headline read; "Second body found in Tacoma hiking trail"

It was from earlier this month, but I clicked through it anyway.

"A second body has reportedly been found in Swan Creek early this morning. This comes as the shockwaves of the first body still ripple through the port city.

Back in August the body of the missing Tacoma hiker, Sam O'Reilly, was found along the Swan Creek hiking trails where he had disappeared earlier that week.

The second body has not been publicly identified; police do not suspect the two victims to be connected but have not made an official statement yet."

I scanned the rest of the article, but I knew I was better off getting my information from the police reports.

A few keystrokes and I had the same information, uncensored.

Swan Creek - Sam O'Reilly,

Swan Creek - Unidentified Victim 2

Reported missing: August 15 2007 20:00 - Found: August 18 2007 05:30 (See missing person's report.)

Victim was reported missing by his fiance when he couldn't be located after an early morning hike.

Body was discovered by trail rangers approximately a hundred and twenty feet north of the creek.

Male, 6'2", twenty-eight, brown hair, brown eyes, Caucasian.

Victim was identified as Sam O'Reilly, who has been missing since mid-August.

The body showed early stages of decomp but no other disturbances.

Victim had no obvious signs of trauma other than an apparent animal bite under the left bicep.

Bite has not been identified.

ME listed the cause of death as blood loss from the brachial artery, and manner of death as accidental.

Found: October 3, 2007, 07:40

It is not known if the victim has been reported missing, a found person's report has been filed. (This report will be updated with more information as it is learned.)

The body was discovered by unrelated hikers, five miles from Worcestershire at the mouth of the creek.

Female, approximately 5'7", age is believed to be around 19 - 30, brown hair, green eyes, race is undetermined.

Due to dramatic animal interference, the victim has not been identified. (Awaiting DNA and dental records.)

```
Victim had numerous animal bites, much of the tissue
and muscle were missing as a result, the liver, heart,
and both kidneys were also missing.

Body was left semi-skeletonized, torso and upper body
had the most trauma.

Other than this initial interference, body appeared to
be in the very early stages of decomp.

ME has listed the cause of death as unknown but noted
large lacerations to the throat as a possible cause.
Manner of death was listed as undetermined.
```

Oh, to be a fly on the wall, I wondered what non-hunters told themselves to be able to sleep at night.

"You're making the face," Parker popped up, his headphones followed but his iPod hit the floor, "Whatcha got?"

"Two bodies in Tacoma looks like feeding grounds for a small nest." I clicked through the pictures quickly; the crime scene wasn't helpful and there was no reason to see the victims. I knew what I was looking at, and besides I had already been traumatized this week by a sketch Parker was pitching.

I continued, "It will be a simple hunt, though. They're getting desperate."

"What makes you say that?" Aaron asked.

"Winter is coming, and fewer people are around. They've cannibalized a body; their food supply is already becoming scarce."

Parker dry heaved loudly.

"They'll be easy to draw out," Nate added, making a gun motion with his fingers, "Easy to pick off."

"Exactly,"

"But it's in Tacoma." Parker groaned.

"So? We've crossed state lines before."

"Yeah, but *Tacoma*," He clicked his tongue, "They're down there thinking they're all better than us with their weird-ass glass."

I blinked a few times waiting for that to make sense, "Nate, what's he been taking?"

"Do you want it or not, pendejo?"

"Want!"

"Then shut up!"

I just shook my head, "We're going to have to hurry up, we need supplies and getting them during Halloween is going to be impossible, not to mention hunting."

Parker crossed his arms, "I might be a ditz, but come on I can tell the difference between Count Chocula and a real vamp."

Sometimes I wonder if there is anything behind those brown eyes at all.

"I'm more worried about the people that are outside hearing gunshots."

"Quick question," Aaron raised his pencil to not be intrusive, "What are we going to do about silver without, you know, Chris..."

Nate shrugged, "Knew his supplier. Price'll be higher but wouldn't be my first time shakin' someone down."

October 31 2007

11:20

Nate

It was still morning, but the real little brats were already running around with their parents.

Aaron was getting a kick outta seeing all their costumes but seeing as I'd been slammed into by three baby Flashes, I was over it.

He's been quiet most of the morning, it wasn't anything outta his norm, but I was paranoid and just glad to see him smiling. It'd been a while.

I shoved my hands into my pockets, it was freezing and damp which was bullshit 'cause I knew right now in Oakland it was 75° and sunny.

"What's on Con's list?"

"The usual, I'm thinking the holy water might be a little easier to get today, though."

"Yeah, the freaks are out." I pointed out a guy dressed like Parker, all black and heavy makeup.

Aaron snorted.

"Told the guy to meet us over..." I got cut off when I got blindsided by a little blonde girl.

"Hey!" I had to catch myself awkwardly before I crushed the kid, "Mucho ojo!"

Air picked the girl up and put her back on her feet, "You okay?"

"Thanks!" She dusted off her costume and ran off to her mom.

It was lost on me how nice he is, maybe it's something they taught in Portland schools. It sure as hell didn't make it down to Oakland.

"Whose side you on?" I hit his shoulder with the back of my hand.

"Supergirl's,"

I crossed my arms.

"What? She has laser eyes, you know!"

I kept an eye out for rogue mini superheroes the rest of the way.

We ducked behind a guns and ammo shop to meet our guy.

He was the typical guy you'd expect to run one of those shops, "You the guys that called about the silver?"

Aaron gave a thumbs up and I cringed, kid's clearly never been a part of a drug deal before.

"Yeah, how much you got?"

"You said two boxes, I've got two."

"How much?"

"How much is Chris charging you?"

"Five bucks,"

The guy laughed, "Worth a shot, chico. Two fifty."

"Lemme see,"

He flicked one of the bullets.

I caught it and held it up to the light before giving it to Aaron to look at, he had a better chance of knowing if it was real.

"Chris was giving me seventy-five,"

"That's 'cause his ass didn't have to make 'em."

"Got one seventy-five on me."

Aaron nodded, letting me know they were real.

"Fine," He handed me the boxes once I gave him the cash, "You mind me asking what you boys do with 'em?"

"Jewelry," I shrugged, "Got a few clients that like the aesthetic of bullet necklaces and shit, must be the emo craze."

"Yeah, I got one of those at home. Don't know what it's all about, but it keeps my daughter happy."

"Thanks,"

He pulled open the back door, "Pleasure."

I shoved the boxes in Air's backpack, and we were out.

"I thought you would say maybe because they're untraceable."

"Huh?"

"... The bullets?"

I smacked the backpack, "Why don't you talk?"

We were half a block from the church when Air pointed out a little shop shoved between two other buildings.

"Do you mind if I pop in real quick? I can meet you back at the church if you want?"

"Nah, it's cool, I'll come in."

I didn't know what it was, but the place smelled like Parker after what he called a 'burn and paint', whatever the fuck that was.

There were a shit ton of glass jars with a bunch of herbs in them, and a few thousand candles covered every surface.

"... What the hell is this place?"

"It's for like herbs and holistic stuff,"

"Bro, that's like witch shit."

"It's not witch shit," He took a bottle off the shelf with a laugh, "This helps with my allergies."

"Oh,"

He grabbed a few other things and dropped them at the register.

The hippiest girl I've ever seen outside of a photo from Woodstock checked him out, "$45.60 please."

I gave the girl the last fifty I had.

He gave me a weird look, "What are you doing?"

I shrugged, "Air, it's your birthday, and unless you want another bag of beef jerky for a present, let me."

Aaron mirrored my shrug, "I like beef jerky."

Stevie Nicks handed him the receipt, "Have a blessed All Hollow's Eve."

Air smiled back.

"'Blessed'?"

He shrugged.

We hit up the church, I was kinda surprised to see no sorta decorations or anything Halloween.

Hell, all of Seattle had been Halloween-ified out the ass for the last three weeks.

I was glad I brought Aaron; Park would've never stopped complaining... Or trying to grope me with a plastic skeleton arm.

"You want the priest or the water?"

I turned around when Air didn't answer.

He was still a few feet behind me, petting a muddy and matted black cat that made its home under the fence post.

"Dude, what the fuck? That's a whole street cat!"

"No, he's not," the cat stretched out to meet his hand, "He's fat and friendly, he must be the church's cat."

"Still, you don't know where he's been, probably has fleas or mange, or some shit."

He shrugged, straightening out, "That's the same thing I told Conner when you moved in."

"Ha, hilarious."

I waved him into the church.

He pretended to look around while I went to find the priest.

The priest saw me but didn't really want to acknowledge me.

"Hey," I made a show of walking over, making sure I had Air covered.

The priest took a look at me, he sighed when he was done analyzing, "Let me guess, you're here for holy water?"

"Huh?"

Between this and dealing, I've heard and said some shit, but this is what threw me?

"For some kind of ceremony or party? We don't do that."

"Nah, looking for a job."

He looked me over again, landing on the tattoos trailing up my arm, "Is that so? I'm sorry to tell you, but we're not hiring. There is a 'gentlemen's club' down the street, perhaps they are."

Accurate, but *damn*.

I crossed my arms, "Aren't y'all about no judgment and shit?"

He didn't like that.

Hell, wouldn't be the first time I was kicked outta a church.

Aaron was up on me like a ghost out of nowhere before I said anything else, "Hey, ready?"

My first instinct was to swing, but if I hit a child, I'd have to step out in front of a bus, "Christ."

The priest glared at me.

Eh, I said what I said.

Air gave the fat, friendly cat a goodbye pat, and we made our way through the beginning of the rain.

Oakland would never do me like this.

I faked fumbling the keys in my pocket, hitting the buzzer to our apartment with my elbow to let Con and Park know we were on the way up.

"Happy birthday, Aaron!" Parker screamed when Aaron opened the door.

Parker blew a noise maker, causing Conner to roll his eyes.

"Why did I let you get those?"

Parker responded by blowing it again, this time in Con's face.

"Happy birthday," Con yelled over the honks.

"Thank you!" Aaron yelled back.

They'd put up a Halloween-colored banner above the door, and thanks to their "height restrictions", I walked like Frankenstein's monster through a spiderweb.

"Guys," I tacked it up higher, "Either hit puberty or get a stool."

Park honked at me.

"I'll shove that up your ass."

"Anytime, anywhere, anyway." He sluttily licked the tip of the noise maker and gave me a wink.

Con knocked him on the back of the head, "Can you stop being disgusting for five minutes?"

"Probably not."

Conner rolled his eyes again before just focusing on Aaron, "We know you don't like presents, but"

He slid a bag across the counter.

It wasn't much, a cassette tape for his ancient Walkman, a box of waffles, and a bag of beef jerky.

"Ah, how did you know I wanted beef jerky?!" He squeaked.

20:45

Aaron

The guys were making it a point to make my birthday special. I knew they were worried about me, and I appreciated it, but I've never really liked the attention my birthday brings. I'd rather pay attention to the holiday anyway.

We didn't have many kids in the building, but I still tried to hand out candy where I could, and when they were sure we wouldn't get any more trick or treaters the guys insisted on taking me out.

I tried to refuse but they insisted.

"It won't be crazy," Conner promised, "We won't go to a bar, we know you don't like to drink."

Parker scoffed, "What do you mean no bar?!"

"Aaron doesn't like to drink." Con reiterated.

"But we do! How else are we supposed to celebrate a birthday without getting shit-faced?"

"By doing whatever Aaron wants to do, seeing as it's *his* birthday."

I was on the couch, already in my properly festive skeleton pajama pants, rereading I Am Legend for my eighth Halloween straight.

If only fourteen-year-old me would've known the irony of the tradition he had started.

I shook my head, "I'm perfectly happy here."

Conner exchanged a look with Nate.

Nate crossed his arms, "Perrito, put on some pants. Pendejo, shut up."

Parker and I both whimpered.

"We'll get you waffles, and I'll bring a flask."

Parker examined his black and orange painted nails, "Two flasks, both tequila."

Nate shrugged, "Yeah, whatever."

"Sold." He popped up.

Once I realized no wasn't an option, I complied. Especially when waffles were mentioned.

We ended up at a restaurant a few streets over, they offered cake and donut waffles as well as bottomless screwdrivers, so Parker and I were both satisfied with the decision.

The dining room was filled with tired parents and their sugar-crazed little ghouls and goblins.

My mind was wandering, I wondered what Courtney would've come up with for her party this year.

Halloween was her favorite holiday too, and with my and Parker's birthdays, she would turn it into a huge party, complete with two different cakes and way more presents than were necessary.

Last year she rigged Parker's cake to ooze a strawberry jam blood, which made him gag for no less than half an hour, but he loved it. Mine was jack-o-lantern shaped and spewed Skittles when I cut into it.

"Parker!" Conner yelled, getting my attention.

"What?" Parker's mouth was full, even though we hadn't gotten our food yet.

Conner crossed his arms and glared at him.

"It was two pills! It's not like I'm snorting coke in the bathroom, unclench."

"Can you at least try to stay sober enough to celebrate with us?"

"This is me celebrating, besides! If I don't start drinking and popping pills now I'll wake up sober tomorrow, and if I'm sober at any point on my birthday I'll have to jump off the Aurora bridge."

"You're not funny,"

"And I'm not joking." He picked his glass up, clinking it against Conner's, "Cheers."

Con gave me an apologetic look.

We were all pretty used to Parker's habits, but we could only argue with him so much.

The table was relatively quiet while we ate. I could tell we were all thinking about Courtney, but no one wanted to be the one who brought it up.

Eventually, Nate brought up last night's football game, he and I went back and forth while Conner tried to nod along.

I asked if we could hurry home, and I said I had to call my mom back.

Luckily they didn't ask too many questions, though had they, I don't know how I would've told them I was planning on summoning a legion of the dead.

Once we got home I disappeared to the building's basement.

I had to clear a small corner, and after fighting a gang of spiders for the territory I was able to set up my altar.

A few weeks ago, I borrowed a book about seances and spiritual summoning from the library. This was the kind of stuff my grandma considered dark magic, so she didn't teach me much about it.

I scattered my herbs and lit my candles.

I took a moment to clear my mind and meditate, the incantation was in Latin, so I would need all the focus I had.

"Aaron," A voice broke my concentration before I could finish my protection spell.

I slowly opened one eye.

Dr. Stephens, Conner's mother, stood over me in her other-worldly form.

She wasn't transparent or pale like movies liked to imagine. Sometimes I had a hard time differentiating the living from the dead, especially with Dr. Stephens, if I didn't know better and it weren't for the feeling I got in the pit of my stomach, I could easily mistake her for a real, living, breathing person.

I was used to seeing her, though. She liked to hang around Conner a lot, and so did his dad. She and I would chat from time to time when I wasn't at risk of looking insane.

She was always really kind, and she liked to know how all of us were doing, not just her son.

I sighed, and let my shoulders fall forward, "Hi,"

"Hi," She stepped into the circle, extinguishing the flames with the simple movement, "What are you doing down here?"

"... I'm performing a seance,"

"I can see that," Her honey hair swayed as she took a seat on the floor with me, "This is about Courtney, I assume?"

"Dr. Stephens, I..."

"Celeste," She corrected me, "Talk to me, tell me what's going on."

"I need answers already, I need to know where she is. I tried to do this the safe way and I was ignored, so now I'm out of options."

"I understand, trust me I do, but your grandmother asked me to come talk to you,"

"Why doesn't she come talk to me herself?"

"I guess she thinks you'll listen to me more than her 'royal kookiness'." She smiled at the joke I had told her a few weeks ago, "But Effie is worried about the way you're using your talents, and quite frankly, so am I. I completely understand where you're coming from, but Aaron, you are a smart boy. You know what you're doing, tonight of all nights, it isn't safe."

"But I need to know, I need answers."

"I know, this really sucks, and I hate to say it, but sometimes we don't always get answers."

"Can you just tell me if Courtney..." I grit my teeth, hoping the lump in my throat would fade, "Tell me if she's on your side?"

Celeste sighed heavily, "Aaron, you know I can't answer that."

"Why not?"

"For the same reason, I can't tell you what's in the afterlife, mon lapin. I'm very sorry, but my hands are tied."

"What am I supposed to do then?"

She put her hand on top of mine, "Breathe, let go. Everything you need to know; you'll learn soon enough. I know that doesn't help right now but believe me. I wish someone would've told me that when I was alive, if they had I'd be able to hug you right now." She offered me a sad smile and gave me a second before she spoke again, "Everything you feel is valid, I don't want you to think it isn't, but you're going to drive yourself crazy. You need to take all of that, all of your pain, your anxiety and anger, and use it. Turn it into something special for yourself, for Courtney, for everyone who loves you. Let that pain give you strength and use it in all that you do. If you take that with you into your hunting, into your research, and your investigation, soon enough you will have every answer you need."

"Yes, ma'am."

She stood, signaling for me to stand with her, "You already have everything you need, remember that."

I nodded.

"Now clean this up before somebody gets hurt, also give my son a hug for me."

I nodded again.

"And one other thing," she smiled at me, "Happy birthday, Aaron."

November 1 2007

10:40

PARKER

My dreams lately had been nuts, the kind of shit I would've expected from my acid days, they would've gotten any psychologist off.

They'd start simple, being chased or falling, and they'd end in a bloody mess.

Most of them happened so fast I couldn't even remember them when I woke up.

But last night was the eeriest because I didn't have a dream at all.

I woke up feeling like something was hanging over me, but it was hard to tell if that was coming from the dreams, or the anxiety of my birthday, or maybe it was because Nate chose to wake me up by sticking his finger in my ear.

I started swinging, but nothing landed, "What the hell?!"

He dropped my phone on the bed next to me, "Been ringing for an hour, your mom."

I groaned, squinting at the screen I immediately flipped it closed, "What, it's not bad enough it's my birthday?"

Nate chuckled.

I realized the call duration was still on the screen, "You've been talking to my mom for ten minutes?"

"What? I've seen pics, she's hot."

I rolled back over, and burrowed under the blanket, "Con's mom was way hotter."

"Speaking of," He nudged me, "Con told me to get you up."

I whined, "Why? Nothing good's gonna come outta today anyway."

He pulled me out of bed, letting me fall to the carpet, "Get up, puta."

"You're so mean!"

He shrugged, walking out of the room.

I crawled around the room trying to find something warm to wear.

My plan to stay blasted from last night all the way through today was great in theory, but I just ended up waking up with a headache.

I'd moved my stash after Conner flushed everything, but I still needed to stock up.

I dry swallowed the few pills I had left and hoped for the best, if the guys really loved me they'd get me a powder keg of coke for my gift.

I mean it was the least they could do for making me function today, especially since Aaron had the nerve to turn 22 when I was going on 25. It was disrespectful!

"Happy Birthday!" Aaron squeaked as I shuffled outta the room.

"What's so happy about it?

"Stop being such an emo ass bitch." Nate flung a waffle fresh out of the toaster at my head.

"No!" Aaron tried and failed to grab it out of the air, "Not his birthday waffles!"

I curled up into a ball on the couch while they argued.

"Why am I up?" I asked Conner who was just trying to eat his cereal.

Con shrugged "Wasn't my idea," he nodded to Aaron who was over my shoulder. He held a pastry box in front of me, it was a cheesecake from his work with "Happy Birthday" spelled out in waffle pieces.

"I didn't have a lot of room, but basic geometry..."

He barely had enough time to put it down before I jumped on him.

My birthdays sucked, they've always sucked. As far back as I can remember my mom could always find a way to ruin something. I couldn't go back and thank Courtney for always trying to make the day special, so I wasn't gonna let the same happen with the guys.

Except I didn't know how to form it into words, so I just ended up sobbing over the cake.

Once I got it together, they gave me gifts, a new sketch pad, and a few other things and I was back to crying.

"What happened?" Aaron tried to whisper.

"He's not used to people caring," Conner whispered back.

"Idiot," Nate did not whisper.

"Sorry, I was an unloved child!"

"Well get over it! You're twenty-five!"

"No!"

"I'll call your mom back,"

"Okay," I ran my sleeves over my face, "I'm fine, you psycho!"

"You're the freak crying over paper."

There was a knock at the door, but Nate and I already chose violence.

"I'm sorry you can't process proper emotions." I pointedly directed at Nate.

"Neither can you, last week your eyeliner broke, and you screamed like your dick fell off."

"It was worse than my dick falling off! I spent $25 on that pencil!"

"Wow, now I hope your dick falls off."

"You first!"

"That sucks 'cause the only time you're not yappin' is when it's..."

"Guys!" Conner yelled over Nate; he was holding a vase full of flowers.

My stomach sank, and the room got deafeningly quiet.

I could practically hear the screeching of the horror movie violins. The flowers were white lilies with these tiny blue star-shaped flowers, undoubtedly another message, I didn't understand.

I snatched the card out of them and read it out loud. "Happy Birthday, Elmer. -Donnie"

I crumpled up the card and slammed it into the trash, "Get me a hunt now." I growled at no one in particular as I violently cut into my cheesecake.

November 2, 2007

15:05

Conner

Parker was exceedingly on edge.

To say he was fuming would not be an overstatement. Not that I could blame him, but I was still worried. Especially since it didn't appear as though he had slept at all last night.

He was quiet and I knew that was never a good sign.

We spent the rest of the day yesterday planning our hunt.

So, Aaron and I had a few things to cover this morning.

Aaron was helping me restock the trunk of my car, it had been a while since we had done it properly.

"I had an idea a few days ago," Aaron said while he was sliding bullets into cartridges, "I need to find a quick way to evaporate water, I think if I could make a compact heating coil..." He continued for a while longer, but I didn't have the slightest idea what he was talking about, sometimes he's too smart for his own good.

My mind was drifting, so he didn't have my full attention. I was thinking about giving Drew a call, to let her know we were going on a hunt.

Lately just thinking her name was enough to fill me with anxiety and guilt.

"I don't know, I'm worried that it might start a grass fire. What do you think?" Aaron asked, bringing me back.

"I think that all I can hope for is that when you become a mad scientist, you'll let me be your Igor."

He chuckled, "Someone has to keep the death ray warm."

He was joking, but it wasn't funny, given the very real death ray threat he made when he failed his final a few years back.

I closed the trunk. "Will you do me a favor and see where Parker and Nate are at? I need to make a phone call really quick."

"Sure!"

I watched him make his way to the front doors and tried to think about what I would say to Drew. I had made a promise, both to Drew and to myself, that I'd leave her be, so I had. Unlike Parker who was pressing me to practically stalk her.

When I finally hit the call button, I felt a bit of relief that was quickly squashed when I was instantly sent to voicemail.

I still wasn't sure what I wanted to say but that didn't stop me.

"Hey, it's Conner..."

"She knows that that's why she's screening you." I thought.

I cleared my throat, "Anyway we have a hunt down in Tacoma, the invitation is still open if you're interested… We'll be leaving around eleven tonight..." I paused, I thought I was done talking, but much to my surprise, I was still going. "I know you're sick of hearing from me, and I don't blame you for not speaking to me, but I'd like to know that you are safe, and doing ok." I hesitated for a second, "I'm sorry." I snapped my phone closed before I made a bigger ass of myself.

If she called back or not, I hoped she would know I was genuine.

When I got back upstairs Parker's silent, solemn demeanor had been replaced by his regular annoying one.

"Aaron said you were calling Drew. What'd she say?" he spoke so fast that Aaron didn't have time to deny the accusation.

"Don't worry about it," I said to a horrified Aaron who was in the process of smacking Parker.

I shook my head at them.

"She didn't pick up, huh?" Park asked.

"It's none of your business, for once please just let it go, Parker."

"Nuh-uh! Not when you're bitching to me, besides we tell each other everything, like that one girl I..."

I held my hand up so he'd stop, "Whatever horrible thing you are about to trudge up, can we just bypass it for once? We have stuff to do, you know?"

"What? Car's packed, you made our game plan all night."

I made my way to the fridge while he complained.

"What more do you want from me?"

I held up the package with raw steak in it.

Parker responded with a gag "Get away from me."

"You said if I got a hunt, you'd feed."

"I lied!" He smirked

"Most verbal contracts are binding in the state of Washington, I have two witnesses, I could sue."

"Go ahead! I have 36 cents in my bank and a half a joint in my shoe."

Nate crossed his arms over his chest "My weed, pero whatever."

As Nate distracted him I tried closing the distance between Parker and me.

"Con, I swear to God," Parker zeroed in on me.

"You don't believe in God."

"Christ, everything's an argument since Drew dumped you!"

I rolled my eyes, "Fine if you're not going to take care of yourself like you promised, then the hunt's off." I started back towards the fridge.

"You can't do that!" Parker wailed.

"It's my hunt, I can do whatever I want."

He stood in front of me, waiting for me to give in. When I didn't, he wailed and stomped around. "Fine! fine, fine, fine! God, I hate it here!"

After a full-blown five-minute temper tantrum Parker finally complied.

From the second the cellophane on the steak was cut I paid very close attention to Parker. He turned quickly, telling me he was hungrier than he had let on. We were prepared for this with a second steak.

What we weren't prepared for was Parker devouring both steaks faster than we could track, I'm not sure how he didn't choke.

This just confirmed that he had been starving himself to me.

I kept waiting for something new, a complication from the blood transfusion but everything was normal. Of course I was glad, I just wasn't expecting it.

Parker came to in his usual haze, "Everyone still alive?"

I squatted down to look into his eyes. Normal.

"All but you." Nate joked

"How are you feeling?" I asked.

"Think I'm still coming around."

"Take your time." Aaron offered him a glass of water which he gulped down.

(＼(•̀w•́)／)

22:00

Parker was like a relentless cuckoo clock as soon as the sun went down he was ready to go so we had to be too. Needless to say by the time we were ready to go we were all relieved.

Parker was still prattling on. "Why don't you shut up?" Nate smacked him in the back of the head as he passed him on the stairs.

"He doesn't know how..." I answered, I was quickly stunned silent when we walked out and I saw Drew sitting against the hood of my car. I was stuck in place so Parker decided to take the reins.

"Hey, sexy." He went over and helped her down. "Great night to slay the damned, huh?"

Nate elbowed me in the side, and I watched as she hugged Parker and then Aaron when she went to hug Nate he responded with a fist bump.

"He's not a hugger." Aaron clarified.

"Not a hugger, not a kisser, not big on foreplay." Nate shrugged.

I rolled my eyes and mustered up an awkward, "Hey,"

She looked me over, and I started to sweat.

"Hi," She handled me with a certain air of aloofness I couldn't blame.

I cleared my throat, "I wasn't expecting you to come..."

She played with the ends of her braid before tossing it over her shoulder, "Then why did you call me?"

"I just mean... I'm glad you did; I was hoping you would."

"So, did you change your mind?"

I paused and took the time to try to form a coherent sentence since I seemed to have a habit of sticking my foot in my mouth.

To be fair, no, I hadn't changed my mind. I didn't think her hunting was a good idea, but I was also relieved that if she had to do it, I would be around for it.

Parker popped up over her shoulder before I could make a mess of things, "We're good to go!"

I rolled my eyes and just shuffled along because I knew he wouldn't let us finish the conversation, but I was glad I dodged the question.

Once we were in the car no one spoke a word, it was just five minutes of Parker uninterrupted, screeching along to the screaming on the radio.

I let it go until his voice caused a pain behind my left eye and I had the urge to drive us into the truck in front of me.

"Hey!" Parker protested when I turned it off, "I was listening to that!"

"I know, the entire state of Washington knows, and trust me, I'm doing them a favor."

Aaron snickered in the seat next to him.

"That's rude." Parker crossed his arms.

"Not wrong, though." Nate added.

Aaron selflessly offered his headphones, though our peace only lasted the length of a song.

Parker leaned forward on the console between Drew and me, "I have a question,"

"No, you don't." I cut him off and tried to push him back into his seat with my elbow.

"Oh, but I do!" He sang.

I shot him a look in the rearview mirror to set a boundary that he just blew right past.

"You guys fuck yet?"

"Parker!" My grip tightened on the wheel.

Nate scoffed and hit Parker's shoulder, "Why you think he's been such a little bitch? Someone finally took his virginity." he pushed Parker out of the way so he could wedge himself between us, "So, what's it? You pop his cherry?"

"They're idiots, you don't..."

She surprised us all by talking over me, "Why, Nate, you need someone to take yours?"

I laughed.

Nate smiled, "Mira, amor..."

"Stop," I warned him before he started.

No one should have to endure the horrendous things Nate says under the guise of Spanish.

Drew turned in her seat to face him, with a cocked eyebrow and a smirk, "Yo no soy tu amor, no soy tu nada, y no su chica. Mi nombre es Drew, me llames así, bien?"

I could only imagine the look on Nate's face, based on Aaron and Parker's reaction I could tell it was good.

"Que?" He was dumbfounded.

"Problema?"

"Uh, tengo miedo... Pero, me gustas." He clapped his hands on my shoulders, "Marry this one, or I will."

Drew started laughing and so did the rest of the car.

"I'm after Nate on that list, okay?" Aaron joked.

"Brother husbands!" Parker gasped, "I wanna be your guys' brother husband... Wait, do brother husbands get to fuck?"

"And, just like that, I'm out. Sorry, Drew." Aaron remarked.

Parker huffed, "Anyway, how was it? My crits' pretty outdated, but when we did it..."

"What are you even talking about?" I rolled my eyes.

"Oh, you don't remember?" He ran his fingers through my hair and ad-libbed by licking my neck.

"What the hell is wrong with you?!" With one hand on the wheel, I flailed around until I hit him somewhere and kept hitting.

"OW!!!" Yet he kept laughing.

"Is this always how your hunts are?" Drew tried to hold back a laugh.

"No," Aaron answered, "Usually it's Nate that hits him."

"The next time you even touch the console, you're going in the trunk."

"God, you're so touchy."

"You licked my neck!"

"I know, it was magical, huh!"

"Shut up!"

"Is that why you dumped him? He's so unromantic, I get it." He pouted.

"I didn't dump him..." Drew spoke so softly that I wondered if it just slipped out.

I glanced at her, but it didn't help decipher anything.

"It's okay," Parker reassured her, "If the pumpkin spice latte was more milk than spice, you can tell us."

"Please don't ruin pumpkin spice lattes for me." Aaron pleaded.

"Parker, leave her alone."

"Why? I don't get what you're so bent outta shape about! I was gonna tell you about this girl I'm banging."

"No one wants to hear that."

Nate shrugged, "I'd listen."

"I'm putting my headphones in!" Aaron yelled before their atrocities reached his ears.

I quickly turned the radio back on to drown him out.

A long root canal without novocaine would've been less grotesque and appalling.

"So," Drew tucked a loose strand of hair behind her ear and tried to think of a way to ask her question nicely, "Is this how it always was with my sister, or is this just for me?"

"Oh, no. You don't want to know what they talked about with her, nothing she ever said was fit for human consumption."

She chuckled, "You wouldn't want to know the details I got as her sister."

"I don't doubt that."

By now we were on the highway.

The streetlights were on, but thanks to the foliage, the streets were still dark and the rain wasn't helping. Luckily, only a handful of drivers shared the road.

"How are we going to see in this?" Drew gestured out to the windshield.

"I'll drive us up as far as I can, we can use the headlights, plus we use the alarm to draw them out."

"They come out in this?" She sounded surprised.

"Believe it or not they come out more, especially in the winter. With fewer people hiking the trails, their food supply is lower."

"So, they'll bite at anything," She shook her head, "No pun intended."

"Right,"

"I get the whole 'undead' dead thing, but just out in the woods, how do they survive?"

"A lot of them don't. They're pack animals and if they don't have a pack to help out, especially with a nest and hunting," I shrugged, "They don't stand much of a chance."

"What are their nests like?"

"The ones in the woods typically stick to caves and dens, usually close to hiking trails or campsites. In more populated areas like Seattle, they like abandoned buildings, but they mostly just look for warmth."

She didn't say anything for a minute, when I glanced over at her, her eyes were wide.

"Are there a lot of them in the city?"

I loosened my grip on the steering wheel while I thought for a second.

I was on the fence; I didn't want to scare her any more than she already was.

"Um, I mean, in the city, they have a little more potential, warm abandoned buildings, they're closer to a supply and have their choice of people. Besides, I hate to say it but they blend in, a lot of times they get written off as junkies."

"I'm not a junkie!" Parker yelled over the radio.

I rolled my eyes and turned the knob on the radio, "I wasn't talking about you, relax."

"No, that's so unfair!"

"Why? You're a junkie." Nate pointed out.

"First of all, that's a slur. Second, I'm not a junkie!"

"That's not a slur, f..."

"Nate!" I quickly intervened before I had to pull over, "Guys, we're ten minutes out, can you cut it out until then?"

Drew was laughing.

"Kiss me and make it better?" Parker leaned over Aaron to get in Nate's face, who put his palm against Parker's face to push him back into his seat.

I rolled my eyes again.

We made it to the trail without a physical fight, but Parker was still making a point by trying to annoy Nate.

He even took it upon himself to wrap his arms around Nate's waist while we were standing around.

"Perrito," Nate gestured to our arsenal lying on the trunk of my car, "Gimme that knife."

"Oh yeah, are you finally gonna prick me, baby?"

"Parker," I snapped my fingers to get his attention, and Nate took the opportunity to shove him off.

"Can we get on with this, please? Preferably before Nate presses charges and the rest of us have to get a lobotomy."

Parker crossed his arms with a pout.

"Anyway, we have a few things..." I leaned against the front fender of my car so I could skim my notes in the headlights, "The lake is off limits, they found both bodies over there so I'm guessing their nest is in that direction. Not an active crime scene, but we still don't want to leave anything behind."

"Like bullet casings?" Drew asked.

"That too, but more than likely gum or cigarettes." I glanced up at Nate.

"What?"

I glared so he got the point.

He scoffed and spat his gum into his hand before sticking it to one of my rear tires before joining Parker's pity party.

"We have approximately ninety minutes before this drizzle becomes a downpour, we should be out of here in thirty, but just in case. Aaron's estimating three to six, right?"

"I'm thinking closer to five or seven," Aaron clarified as he tucked his blond hair up into his beanie, "They'll really like this weather, but they've fed recently so they'll only send a couple."

Drew politely raised her hand to ask, "How can you tell?"

"Based on the time frame of the attacks, state of the bodies..." Aaron shrugged, "They were brutally cannibalized and missing organs, so there's either a lot of them or they're getting nothing up here."

"Gross, but interesting."

I went back to my notes, but Aaron held his hand up before I continued.

I laughed to myself, "You guys don't have to do that."

"I just wanted to make a suggestion," Aaron made an awkward gesture to Drew's hair, "Can I?"

"Sure," She nodded.

He took her long dark hair that was in a neat braid and twisted it around itself until it was out of the way.

"Vamps are a little like cats," he clarified, "If they can get it, you'll regret it. You can ask Parker about his belly button piercing later." He joked.

Drew let out a nervous laugh, "Good point."

"One other thing," Parker butted back in and made his way over, "Not only a hazard but '85 called and she wants her bangles back." He went to take them off her wrist, but recoiled back the second he touched them, "Fuck!"

"Pure silver," Drew simplified.

"No joke!" Parker shook out his hand.

I snorted, "When you're done with that, can you do a quick survey before we start?"

He was confused, but raised his eyebrow defiantly, "Why? We do that after."

"We just talked about it."

His expression changed to a blank, confused one.

"Last night?"

He responded with a blink.

I sighed, I don't know why I bothered.

"As a part of our new safety rules," I tried but he still wasn't following, "Just, can you scope out the area and make sure we're not close to a nest or walking into anything?"

"Oh, that's a good idea." Parker sped off.

"Wow," Drew watched in amazement as he turned into a blur, "How fast can he go?"

THE BOOK OF MORMON
Another Testament of Jesus Christ
HOLY WATER

Aaron answered, "Last time we measured it, it was somewhere over a hundred miles an hour."

Parker looped back around to where we were waiting, a few twigs and leaves poking out of the hot pink mess on his head.

"Nothing weird. Scared the hell out of a couple of raccoons, though."

"Good, thanks." I tossed my notebook into the passenger window of my car, "I'm guessing they'll be coming up from the southwest. We'll stick to a mostly V formation and keep Drew on the inside. Parker, stay close and out of the trees, keep behind us. Under no circumstances do we split up. In case there's an emergency, run off the trail and get to higher ground but avoid the trees. Any questions?"

Drew shook her head.

Nate clicked a clip into my extra S&W Parabellum and held it for Drew to take, "Safety on the side, cock once and you're good. You got fifteen rounds 'fore you gotta reload." He gave her two more clips, "Aim, point, squeeze, keep your elbow..."

"Thank you, but don't worry, my mom has had me shooting since I was eight."

"Respect," He nudged her with his arm, before giving an arrogant nod, "Six."

"Everyone ready?"

I got two "Readys", a thumbs up from Nate and a wink from Parker so I hit the alarm in my key fob.

For a minute or two it was just the sound of the alarm, echoing off into the wilderness for miles.

But eventually, shadows started to seep out from the dense trees.

A pit of anxiety opened up in my stomach from the familiar image.

I tried to swallow the lump in my throat and push the panic attack to the back of my brain, I didn't have the time right now.

The vamps seemed to stick to the trees for a minute to watch us, but there was one that got curious and decided to get closer slowly.

He wasn't even two hundred yards out before the first shot rang out and hit him square in the chest blasting a cloud of soot out into the air.

I followed the sound of the shot and glanced over at Nate who shook his head and nodded to Drew.

Damn, that's something Courtney could have mentioned. I thought.

Following the loud noise a few more vampires spilled through, though these came out with more of a purpose and faster than the first.

I watched Drew for a second as she took another shot, she fired and killed it like she had done this a million times over.

Parker zeroed in on a few trailing closely on the edge of the tree line, he crisscrossed between the trees to get their attention and bring them closer.

Parker ran around to stab one through the back, while Aaron and Nate each shot off around.

Two final stragglers crept down from further up the trail.

Nate and I must've seen them at the same time but had different ideas.

"Eleven and eight!" He yelled out to Parker.

"Hold!" I called out, eliciting varying looks from my partners.

I hadn't gotten a second to survey how any of the others looked, I just wanted to make sure everything was kosher.

Once they got closer, I could tell they were hungry, they had the typical sunken features with small wounds where I'm guessing the virus was trying to manifest into blisters.

It was what I was expecting and hoping to see so I gave Parker a thumbs up and he finished the job. He then went through and double-checked for more vamps. I tried to keep an eye on him in case he ran into any issues while Nate, Aaron, and Drew went to turn off the car alarm and start cleaning up.

I didn't think anything of it until Aaron ran up to my side with so much concern on his face that made my heart pound.

Poor Aaron didn't even have the opportunity to say anything before I panicked, "What happened?"

"I don't know, Drew's having a panic attack."

I took a second to breathe, "That I can handle."

"Just hurry, I made the mistake of leaving her with Nate."

That made me move faster.

Drew was sitting in the backseat sideways, so her legs were still out of the car, she leaned forward with her elbows on her knees while she tried to catch her breath.

Nate was "supporting" her by keeping a hand on her shoulder with no effort whatsoever. He patted her on top of her head, "Here your boyfriend's here."

I crouched down even though we were finally the same height with her sitting, "Are you okay?"

"I don't know."

"You're fine, I know this is incredibly overwhelming..."

I was hesitant to touch her, I didn't want to overwhelm her anymore. She leaned forward to put her head on my shoulder, so I wrapped my arms around her.

I felt useless when she started to sob.

All I could do was hold her and say, "It's okay, we'll be okay."

"It's cold out here," Aaron said in a normal conversational tone, "Can you feel how cold it is? It feels like the rain is getting heavier,"

I glanced over at him, but before I could ask, he just mouthed "Trust me."

"Are you getting wet?" He asked her.

She shook her head.

"Are you cold?"

"You can have my jacket." I offered.

She shook her head again, "I'm fine..."

"You are fine," he repeated to remind her, "I have some water, I think it might be a good idea for you to drink some."

She took a breath and nodded, I slowly let her go and Aaron gave her his water bottle.

"I left it in the trunk, so it's at least nice and cold, but it also smells like the trunk."

She let out a tiny laugh, "It's alright."

I stood upright, but I kept an arm around her, and she leaned into my side.

"You're okay," I repeated.

She nodded as she took a few good sips of water.

Drew calmed down a lot, but unfortunately, this was at the same time Parker sped over to us.

"Found nothing," He leaned against Nate and nodded at Drew, "Hey, how was your first hunt?" He asked with an oblivious and stupid smile on his face.

Nate hit him upside his head.

Surprisingly, Drew laughed, "Great, I never want to do that again."

I chuckled with her.

"I'm so sorry..."

Aaron stopped her, "You have nothing to apologize for."

She took another deep breath and wiped the tears from her cheeks, "I guess it just hit me all at once, they're just... They're so much more human than I was expecting, they're someone's kids, someone's siblings... How do you guys deal with that?"

"That's generous," Parker answered.

I shook my head, "Don't."

"No, really. They *were* people, but they're not anymore, they're nowhere near what they used to be and it's no way to "live". Trust me, you're doing them a favor by putting them outta their misery."

I sighed, "I hate to agree with Parker, but that's part of the reason we do it. We can't save them, but we can save the people they're killing, and that has to be something."

There was a long silence.

Drew sniffled, "Can we go?"

"Of course." I squeezed her arm before I walked around the car.

Aaron went to sit with her while I made sure everything was cleaned up.

It was a fairly clean hunt, and thanks to the rain the ash didn't spread too much, but I still felt the need to wipe my hands and face, at the very least. So I took the rag out of my glove box, cleaned my hands, and tossed it to Parker whose hands were caked black with soot.

"Do you ever get used to the smell?" Drew asked once we were driving back down the trail.

"No," The four of us unconsciously answered at the same time.

I drove around for a while until I found the only open place, a small cafe that had just opened for the morning.

It took a second for me to realize I had, it was starting to become muscle memory.

"It's kind of a routine to stop after a hunt... Do you want me to take you home?"

Drew undid her braid and shook out her hair, "That's okay, I could use a cup of coffee."

Parker opened my glovebox and pulled out a flask, "You're welcome to make it Irish."

"When did you put that in there?" I reprimanded.

He took a swig, "I have 'em in more places than you'd think."

I stained against my seat belt to try to get it from him, but he tossed it to Nate.

"Whiskey?" Nate asked before sniffing it.

"Gin,"

"The hell's the matter with you? You can take that shit." Nate handed it to me while giving Parker a disgusted look.

I promptly poured it out onto the pavement.

"Killjoy," Parker made a point to slam the car door as he got out.

"He's technically a buzz kill." Aaron corrected.

Parker offered a middle finger, heading into the cafe without us.

We caught up and arranged ourselves into a booth and ordered a pot of coffee, while Parker took the time to find an item in the menu with the most sugar.

It ended up being a milkshake with three shots of espresso in it.

"That's not vegan..." Aaron mumbled in an attempt to save us all.

"Nuh uh, Con took my booze now I get whatever I want."

"But it's dairy..."

"And a lot of caffeine. It's also a half hour back to Seattle," I started my lecture, but Parker just spoke louder.

"I'm not gonna puke in your car!" He rolled his eyes before sticking his hand in his pocket, he gestured to Drew's water since she was the only one who had asked for one, "Can I have a drink?"

She nodded.

He quickly tossed something in his mouth and took a drink.

"Seriously?" I sighed.

"Oh, shit you're right, that was so rude." He held up another pill between his fingers to show Drew, "Do you want one?"

I think Drew was too tired to process his idiocy.

I hit his arm.

"Ow, what? You're mad when I don't share and you're mad when I do?!"

"That's more about eating the entire box of Captain Crunch and less about playing pill roulette."

"Tomato, potato. Besides, I know this one's Columbian xanny."

"Put it away before the waiter calls the cops!" I yelled in a hushed tone.

"Relax, it's fine!" He popped it in his mouth, too.

Nate was far more amused than I was.

"One of these days I'm gonna tell you we're going to get ice cream and I'm taking you to a clinic."

"And until that day, I will stay blasted higher than that one Elton John song." He winked at me.

Aaron glanced at him from behind his mug, he finished his sip of coffee and asked, "And The House Fell Down?"

"What? No, Rocket Man, dummy."

Aaron just shook his head and went back to his coffee.

While we waited for our food, I took the opportunity to page through my hunt log, which elicited an audible groan from the guys the second they saw it.

"Grow up," I ignored them and continued to look for a blank page.

"Hunting was grosser than you thought?" Nate nodded to get Drew's attention, "Well, your boyfriend's more annoying than you thought, too."

"It's just a report I like to keep," I clicked my pen, "Who's first?"

Aaron finished gulping down his coffee, "Nothing notable, but I did see a opossum, that was cool."

"Aw," Drew cooed.

Parker tore off a piece of pancake and stuffed it in his mouth, "It's weirding me out that you say the 'O' in opossum."

"We're in North America, you're supposed to say the 'O'."

"I've literally never heard anyone say the 'O'."

"Everyone in Portland says the 'O'."

"He's right," Drew said as she pulled apart the pastry in front of her, "Opossums and possums are two different animals."

"Okay but like no one's ever like 'Oh, you know, O as in opossum'."

"My dad says that all the time," Aaron added.

"I don't," Parker crossed his arms, "Call him right now."

"Guys," I had to fight for their attention, and once I got it Nate immediately derailed it.

"Y'all ever had opossum meat?"

I knew we wouldn't get back on track after that one, so I just wrote "Argument of opossum ensued. Normal hunt, report will be summarized."

I clicked my pen and closed my notebook while I tried to process the conversation, "Are you trying to tell me you've eaten opossum?"

Nate shrugged, "Man, can't be sure what my grandma put chili on."

"I, nope, I've got nothing to say to that."

But Parker did, "Have you ever had veal?"

Nate straightened out to cock his head at Parker, "No, you trust funded little bitch. I never skied or went to a prep school, either."

"Hey, what'd I do? It was just a question, Con went to a prep school, too!"

"I was on scholarship." I quipped.

Parker glared at me before he launched off on a rant.

Despite the chaos, I noticed Drew was quiet.

I lowered my voice to not draw more attention to it, "Are you doing okay?"

"Hmm? Oh, yeah." She hesitated for a second before gesturing to my side of the booth, "Do you mind? I think I just need some fresh air."

"Yeah, sure, of course." I did an awkward little shuffle to get out of her way.

"Can we talk?" She asked so quietly as she stepped past me that I wasn't even sure she said anything.

I didn't think it would be good, what else could she tell me?

I followed her out into the pitch-black parking lot, the fog clung to the only streetlight so the only illumination we had was from the cafe behind us.

It got worse than that, though, seeing as Washington could easily be mistaken for a tundra.

Our breath was visible, and the wind pierced through my jacket and the sweatshirt I had under it, yet I still went to pull it off unconsciously.

Drew stopped me, "I'm okay," she pulled her coat shut to emphasize.

"Right, sorry, I guess I'm just used to Parker..."

The "thunk" of the rain hitting the awning above us was the only sound for miles.

Drew studied my face; it was the first time she had looked me in the eye over the last couple of days. It made me nervous.

"... My mom thinks I'm being too harsh on you."

I cleared my throat, "Really? I thought she was strongly anti-Conner."

"You'd be surprised."

At a total loss of what to do, I sat on the curb. Which immediately soaked through my jeans, yet I stayed there.

"I was talking to my sister-in-law, um, Jared's wife..."

She trailed off and for some reason, I felt the need to say something.

"I didn't know he was married."

"Mmhm, they eloped a little while after they left here..." She went to sit next to me, but I quickly stopped her.

"Don't, I'm sitting in a puddle. It was here when I sat, by the way, I didn't make the puddle."

She laughed at my rambling, "And you're just going to stay there?"

I shrugged, "Well, it felt rude to stand up while you were talking."

"You're such a gentleman," she joked as she offered her hand to help me up.

I let her pull me to my feet and tried to wipe some of the rainwater off my ass, "Anyway, your sister-in-law?"

She shook her head, "I really don't know where I was going with that, I'm just trying to figure out a way to apologize."

"For what?"

"Ignoring you, screening your calls," she shrugged, "Being a bitch."

I scoffed, "Please, I've had a woman clip me with her car, you are not a bitch."

She cracked a half smile, "That was Courtney, wasn't it?"

"Yeah, but it was my fault. I should've known Bon Jovi is an untouchable topic."

She snickered.

Drew paused, she reached her hand out but hesitated before picking something off of my coat, "I overreacted, and I'm sorry."

"You didn't, and you don't have anything to apologize for. I should be sorry, I'm the one who overreacted, and I underestimated you immensely. Then I called you another woman's name, I've seen other guys get shot for that."

She chuckled, "Lemme guess, Nate?"

"Two for two, I'm impressed."

"I get it, though, I act a lot like my sister. Especially when I think I'm being challenged."

"That's not a bad thing, you guys are both driven and strong, but you're your own person and I'm so sorry if I ever made you feel like you weren't."

"Everything between us," she wouldn't look at me again, "Was that just 'cause I remind you of her?"

"At first, I was worried about that, but if I'm being honest I've never felt the way I do about you... I know that's cheesy, sorry."

"Me either, and I like that you're honest, even if it's cheesy."

The moment called for it, but that didn't stop my anxiety from screaming "This is a bad idea" when I moved her hair behind her ear and leaned in to press a kiss to her strawberry-glossed lips.

She kissed me back and I started to feel like less of an idiot.

Our moment was over as fast as it started once the door behind us opened and cheers erupted.

Parker scrambled to get his phone out of his pocket and snapped photos of us like he was with NatGeo.

"Get a life." I swatted at the camera.

Aaron tried desperately to corral him and Nate, "We'll be in the car, take your time!"

Drew laughed, "We should probably get going. I take it we're okay?"

"Of course we are."

She smiled and bent to put her arm around my waist and her head on my shoulder while we walked to the car.

"So, a crush on my sister, huh?" She joked.

I couldn't help but smile, "I'm never gonna live that one down, am I?"

"We'll see."

November 3 2007

05:00

PARKER

We split off the second Conner unlocked the apartment door.

Nate hit the mattress on the floor and fell asleep in his shoes.

Aaron took the time to go through his nightly routine even though it was 5 AM.

Conner flipped through TV channels and tried to stay awake so he could threaten us if anyone woke up Drew who was already out on the other side of the couch.

Meanwhile, I was hurling my guts out before curling up on the cold, cracked tile of the bathroom.

It felt so good to be back on a hunt, but I still felt so out of control and the thought of blood in my stomach wasn't helping.

I never felt back in control, but I just had nothing left.

I squeezed my eyes shut and begged for the pounding in my skull to stop, which only got worse when my phone on the counter started vibrating.

I didn't have to sit up to know it was my mom, she'd been calling on and off since my birthday.

Moving just enough to reach my arm over the sink I felt about 'til I grabbed my phone and sent the call to voicemail just for it to start ringing again fifteen minutes later.

I was so tired.

"Yeah?" I gave in, sat up, and answered it, and hoped I didn't sound too out of it.

"Hello, good morning. How are you? That's how someone should answer the phone, especially when it's your mother."

Here we go.

"It's five in the morning."

"And God has blessed us with another beautiful day."

I groaned.

"Why haven't you been answering my calls?" My mom's tone was always harsh, but she was bitter today.

It never occurred to me she would feel any way about me not answering her calls, I mean, she never calls me.

"Because that's what a good son would do, Mom. What do you want?"

"I wanted to tell you happy birthday, but I guess you were too busy to talk to me."

Unconsciously, I was feeling around under the sink until I found the small box I hid under there, "Well, you know, Satan doesn't worship himself."

"You're not funny, Elmer!"

"Disagree." I ran my fingers over the lip of the tampon box I used to hide my razors in, it was the only stash Conner hadn't found yet.

"Anyway, I did want to talk to you."

And just like that the blade in my hand felt like a warm, fuzzy, teddy bear.

I made my first cut while she was talking, I didn't want to hear what she had to say anyway. It was just a scratch, and it sealed back up immediately.

The second cut stung and that's all I was really looking for.

"Did you hear me?"

"No, you're cutting out." I giggled at my morbid joke.

I just didn't care anymore. Nothing mattered when I got to this place.

"I asked if you sent Elijah something in the mail."

I don't know why that caught me off guard, but it stopped my cut.

"I, uh... Well, yeah, I was thinking about him."

"You don't need to do that."

I made a hard quick slice across my forearm and watched it mend like a line drawn in sand.

"What? Think of him?"

"No, you're confusing him."

The accusation was so uncalled for I didn't even know what it meant.

"He hardly remembers you, you're just a name to him at this point, to your sisters, too. They have no big brother; you can't just step into the role whenever you feel guilty."

I lost track of what I was doing, it felt like I got punched in the stomach.

"But I'm trying to do better."

"Are you? Are you really? Are you working? Are you living on your own? Are you sober?"

I could barely speak, "I've been selling a few things..."

"That isn't a job, Elmer! You're always asking me and your father for money. Where is it going? You don't do anything, you don't drive, you don't cook, Lord knows if you even take care of yourself. The last time I saw you, you weighed ninety pounds. All you do is use drugs and drink and spend your time with sinful women. You do all these things, why? To stray further from your family? From our Heavenly Father?" Her voice shook and I heard her sigh, "You're broken, my son, you are shattered, and one day you're going to have to answer for your sins. I spend hours praying that God will be merciful on you, but is that even what you want?"

I gritted my teeth and tried to ignore the tears streaming down my face, "I get it, Mom."

"I don't think you do, Elmer. This isn't right, this isn't..."

"I get it!" I screamed, "I get it! I'm a loser, and I'm a junkie, and I'm a piece of shit son, and I'm going to rot alone in Hell, I get it!" My voice broke and I started to sob, "I just want to talk to my brother."

"What would you even say to him? When he asks why you're not here, what would you tell him?"

"All I want is to tell him I love him, that's all."

"I'll pass it on. Goodbye."

"Mom, wait, please..."

She hung up while I was still pleading, while I was collapsing.

It made me wonder if she did the same thing when I was a baby if she'd just leave the room when I was wailing for her. She's always been this way, even six years ago when I had tried to kill myself and wrapped my car around a tree. It was my sister's lap I had to curl up and cry on because my mother was too upset to see me.

Then when she did come to see me, the first thing she did was kick Ellysha out of the room.

I still remember the way my mom wouldn't even look at me, she held my hand, but she didn't say a word until it was time for her to leave. Then when I begged her to stay, she pressed a kiss to my forehead and dried the tears in my cheeks.

"You aren't my baby boy anymore, Elmer, after what you've done, you have to answer for your sins as a man now."

It was just another notch on the endless tally of disappointing my family.

(＼(•̀ω•́)／)

08:00

NATE

The only reason I was up was 'cause Aaron tripped over me when he got up and 'cause I was a hungry.

"Morning," Con was up and already dressed, he was trying to act like he was reading but he was clearly watching Parker aggressively scratching something into his sketchbook.

"Hey," I swung open the fridge and gave the carton of milk a swirl before taking the gamble, "Where's your girl?"

"Bathroom. Would you get a glass?"

I ignored his question and put it back in the fridge, "Damn, you sure your relationship's solid enough for her to be in that hole?"

"I did a rat check before I let her go in there. Let's just hope she doesn't turn on any of the taps." He scoffed, "Speaking of, I'm going to take her to class. Do me a favor?" He gestured to Parker, "He's not talking, but I'm pretty sure he's been listening to the same song for an hour?"

I blew a breath out as I bent to lean on the couch, "What're we talking? Metallica or Muse?"

"I think it's Fall Out Boy."

"Fuck," I sighed but clapped Conner on the back, "I got 'im."

"Thanks."

"Good morning," Drew smiled at me, she went to put her hair behind her ear, "Hang on, my earrings."

She left again and I took the opportunity to bug Con.

"She's a good girl," I sat on the couch and tried to angle so I could see what Park was drawing but I couldn't tell what the hell it was.

"She is." Con tried to hide his little smile.

I didn't really care, I was glad he was happy, and it wasn't with one of those psycho bitches, but I still wanted to give him shit.

"Yeah, so you better take her somewhere nicer than your shit ass Corolla 'fore you ask her to blow you, huh?"

He cringed before he started turning redder than the cinnamon bear mold he came outta.

Drew was back before he could ask what was wrong with me, and was eager to get her outta the apartment so I couldn't say anything else.

Parker took his headphones out the minute the door latched, "Did Conner leave?"

"Yeah," I gave him a look, "You not talking to him or something?"

"No? I'm high as fuck, and I don't need another lecture." He giggled like a middle schooler; he tried to pull his zipped hood off without unzipping it and got stuck.

I laughed at the struggle 'til I realized he was serious, and then I laughed harder.

"Nate!" He whimpered.

"Come here," I grabbed his arm and pulled him over so I could yank the zipper, "Pendejo."

"Thanks," He laughed and sat on my lap, "Would you believe I'm stuck in my pants, too?"

I rolled my eyes and smacked his stomach.

"Seriously, though, wanna make out?"

He put his arms around my neck, and I saw something huge on his forearm.

It took me a second to figure it out, at first it looked like scribbles from a hyperactive toddler on his arm, but I realized it was carved into his skin.

I grabbed his arm and moved his sleeve more, from his elbow down to his left hand was covered in long cuts.

Most of them were still scabbed while a few were healed but raw.

"What the hell did you do?"

"Stop! Don't." He pulled out of my grip, he got up, and scrambled back for his hoodie.

"What happened?"

"Nothing, don't worry about it." He put his hood back on and pulled the sleeves over his hands.

I grabbed him by the waistband of his pajama pants before he could walk away, "What happened?'

He went from panic to rage real fast, "What do you think happened?! I'm a junkie and a cutter, what the fuck do you want from me?! Let go!"

"Park,"

"Let go!"

I only let go 'cause I knew I wouldn't get it outta him, Conner was always better at that anyway, I just had to keep the idiot from hurting himself.

He stomped off and slammed the bedroom door, but he forgot what he was mad about and stumbled back into the living room.

He started on the other side of the couch but somehow ended up lying across my lap.

"You done pouting?"

"I'm not pouting,"

I rolled my eyes, I wasn't gonna play this game.

"There's a good game on tonight."

"I hate baseball."

"Baseball's over."

"Whatever, boo sports."

I ignored him, "Seattle's damn near undefeated, Air said if Oakland could pull it off he'd give up on the 'hawks and join me on the dark side. It'll be rough though, we ain't got no O line and a quarterback that gives away balls quicker than you take 'em. Seriously, the shovel pass will be the end of our season, and they can't ever run that damn ball, besides this asshole only throws clean to the other team. Plus he's always hurt. The defense's always fouling..."

Parker finally broke, "My mom thinks I'm an asshole."

I shrugged, "She's right."

"That's the problem!"

"Dude, you need to get outta here," I smacked him in the chest, "Let's go for a walk."

"We're out of weed."

I shrugged.

He frowned, "You can't go for a walk without weed, we'd just be walking like a bunch of nerds."

"Whatever, just go put on pants I can't see your dick in, nerd."

He kept pouting but got up and went to change.

I gave the same offer to Aaron who only agreed if he could bring his book, the fucking nerd.

Parker bitched and moaned the entire walk.

"What's wrong?" Aaron was nicer and wasn't ignoring him like I was.

"I don't like walking and I don't like sobering up!" He whined.

"But it's such a nice day," Aaron tried, "The sun's finally out for once."

"I know, it hurts."

"Oh, right, sorry..."

Parker kept bitching, I kept ignoring him and tried to keep Aaron from walking into traffic since he refused to put the damn book down, but I managed to get him to the park alive.

"Isn't it kinda cold for the ducks to still be out?" Aaron ditched us the second he saw the pond.

Parker took a look around then shrugged, "Cool, went outside, can we go?"

God, they're like toddlers.

I grabbed him by the back of his neck and steered him to the back of the park and over to Courtney's memorial bench.

I tried to make a point to stop by when I thought about her, typically it was on my lunch break to smoke a cigarette, it didn't make me feel any better but I figured it'd be a good place to stop after our first hunt since we lost her.

I made Parker sit down.

I grabbed the carton outta my pocket and grabbed a cigarette, I lit it and took a hit before I offered it to Parker.

"I thought you quit."

I rolled my eyes and got comfortable on the bench, "You gonna ride my dick, or do you want a cigarette."

He took it, "You usually let me do both."

I went to put my arm on the back of the bench and smacked the back of his head in the process.

He finally shut his mouth, and I got a second of peace.

'Til there was some loud static coming from the plaza, a loud voice boomed across the park. Some holy roller on a soapbox.

I just ignored it 'til Parker popped up and started running over there. Hell, if he was gonna get his ass whooped by a nun, I wasn't gonna miss it.

"God designed a life of devotion and purity. Every day we stray from His design," No one else was listening to this bullshit but Parker, and he was in a mood.

"It's not just that we stray, but we surround ourselves with those who refuse the divine path."

Parker made a point to get the lady's attention and crossed his arms in a challenge.

"The sinners will be the ones to end this world, they bring the attention of Satan and his demons with their actions. It's the alcoholics and the drug addicts, they bring glutton. The homosexuals bring lust..."

"Wanna add Mexican on there and check every bigot box?" Parker yelled over the megaphone and threw a nod over to me.

"Puerto Rican," I tapped the ash off my cigarette.

Park was far from done, "Your god preaches love and acceptance, but kids are killing themselves every single day because people like you love to leave the acceptance out, don't you? You would rather spread hate than admit that people can live differently. Tell me, all the shit that you preach, would you be okay if "God" took *your* child for their sins? If your son were gay, could you sleep at night if someone took his life for being gay? Would that be okay with you? Because that's what you're saying, you're preaching that you would be fine if a person of blood and flesh were murdered right in front of you if it meant justifying your religion. Honest to God, do you think that's really what He would ask of his children?"

The sister was stunned silent, and so was I. I'd never seen Parker so... Coherent? Especially when it came to religion, he'd usually get mad, scream something about wanting to be a smote, and then storm out.

I was proud of him 'til he decided he needed to emphasize his point by sticking his tongue down my throat, "Now, if you'll excuse me, Imma let this fine Puerto Rican bend me over and pound me hard." He snapped the gum he took from my mouth for effect, "Hail Satan."

I grabbed him by the arm and yanked him away so I could beat the shit out of him somewhere else.

Aaron had a shit-eating smirk plastered across his face, "That was a lovely kiss, fellas."

"Shut up," I slightly shoved Aaron but punched Parker's arm, "You owe me breakfast now, slut."

Parker put his arm around my waist and put his head on my shoulder, "You're such an easy whore."

I glared at him, and he slid his hand into my back pocket.

We stopped at the first restaurant we saw on the back to the apartment since Park was bitching about walking again.

It was a standard diner; I didn't think anything of it 'til I saw one of the waitresses outta the corner of my eye.

She was small and had overly blonde hair so I had to do a double take.

She was a few tables over but walked over when she saw me looking at her.

She slid into the booth across from me and next to Parker without saying a word.

Up close, she looked nothing like Courtney close up, her skin was darker, and her eyes were this weird orange.

I casually slid my hand into my front pocket where I usually kept a knife.

"Don't do anything stupid," She warned.

"What are you?" Parker asked defensively.

"Well, my name's Hayley, if that's what you're asking. Don't bother remembering it though, 'cause it's fake." She put something on the table in front of Parker, "Parker Winston, consider yourself served."

She looked at us like we were stupid when we didn't say anything or laugh, "It's a joke... Anyway, I'm here 'cause we have an enemy in common.'

She was annoyed when we didn't respond again.

"Good old Donnie boy?"

Parker must've gone for his knife 'cause she rolled her eyes.

"Dude, don't blow this. Don't you think if I wanted you dead you'd be empty blood bags by now? Look, we're contracted under Donnie, so I'm trying to do you a favor right now, got it?"

Parker put both his hands on the table.

"Good boy,"

"What do you mean 'contracted'?" He asked.

She didn't answer, she pulled a napkin out from Parker's hand and started to write on it, "Have your little ginger pal run this against immigration, he'll get everything you guys need. One more thing," she dropped an old dusty leather-bound book on the table, I lost my concentration trying to figure out where she hid it, "This doesn't belong to him either."

"Why are you helping us?"

"Let's just say the boss doesn't like the way he's fucking her anymore, and that prick's got it coming. By the way," she stood back up, "Ol' Don ain't gonna be too thrilled about this, so do us all a favor. Don't fuck it up."

(＼(•̀w•́)／)

11:15

Conner

I sent a quick text to Nate to check in on things, he said he had the Parker situation handled and when I asked what he meant by "handled" he told me it was better if I didn't know. I really did not like that answer, but knowing Nate, he was probably right.

So, I sent a text to Aaron who was able to confirm everyone was still alive and found my comfort in that.

I went ahead and sat with Drew through her lecture, once that was over, she insisted on making me a proper breakfast and wouldn't take no for an answer.

Drew unlocked the front door to her mother's house and led me into the kitchen.

"Hmm," She paused as she was pulling a few things from the cabinet when she saw a huge potting plant of tiny, brilliant orange flowers sitting on the kitchen island, she put the few things she had on the counter and looked at the label on the side of the pot, "New Jerseyan Butterfly weed." She shrugged, "Would you mind moving those to the breakfast table?"

"Sure. Not something you were expecting?" I chuckled.

"No, but my mom's been talking about starting a garden with her students, might be what it's for."

It was almost as tall as my torso and a lot heavier than I was expecting. I noticed a plastic card holder poking out of the dirt, I didn't need to look at it for my stomach to sink.

I dropped it on the table and snatched the card out of the flowers.

"Conner?" I must've had a look on my face because she sounded worried.

I glared at the black top hat before turning it over in my hand, but what I saw only pissed me off more.

In perfect cursive was "Andrew Hart, welcome to the club. 1519"

"What's wrong?" Drew slowly approached me.

"Get in the car." I spat without thinking of anything else.

"What?"

"We have to get out of here. Call your mom, tell her not to come home."

"Conner, you're scaring me."'

"Good," In one hand I took her arm and grabbed her bag with my other.

I kept my head on a swivel as I got her back out to my car and locked the doors until I got to the driver's side.

"What's going on?"

I handed her the card as I tore down the street, "It's a warning. I'm guessing he's not liking that we're hunting again."

"Who? What are you talking about?"

"Parker's siree, Donatello. We usually get one of those cards before something bad happens."

"Like what?"

"We got one before Courtney died."

She went quiet and scanned the card, "Got it."

"We can keep you safe..."

"Don't worry about it, I'll rip that bastard's heart out myself,"

I called Nate on the drive.

"'Sup?" He answered.

"Are you guys home?"

"Yeah, and we got a situation."

"How bad?"

He must have heard it in my voice, "It can wait, everything good on that side?"

"Unsure, can the three of you meet us in the parking lot?"

"How far out?"

"Five."

"Got it." He hung up.

As I pulled into the lot, I caught a flash of pink from the corner of my eye as Parker ran along the car.

Nate and Aaron were waiting in Nate's truck.

"What's up?" Parker asked when I opened my door.

"Donnie sent a card to Drew."

Parker immediately lit up angrily, "Oh, Hell no."

Aaron opened Drew's door for her, and we all escorted her up to the apartment.

"Are you okay?" Aaron asked.

Drew nodded her response; she hadn't said another word. But she wasn't afraid, she was pissed, and it was rolling off her.

"Now what?" Parker crossed his arms.

"Well, it's going to depend on what Drew w..."

She answered before I could finish asking, "I want to kill him myself."

"I thought you were done with hunting,"

"This isn't hunting, this is settling a score."

Parker smirked, "Love it, let's go."

I grabbed him as he stepped in front of me, "Where are you going to go? We know nothing, we have nothing."

Parker crossed his arms, "What like that's something new?"

"Actually," Aaron spoke up.

The three of them exchanged a look that worried me, especially since it was followed by silence.

Knowing them it could've been anything from "We spilled salsa on the carpet" to "Oops, we started a government coop."

"For God's sake, what is it?" I asked nervously, "Parker, what'd you do?"

"Why do you always assume it was me?"

"'Cause when is it ever not?"

He pouted.

"Not this time," Aaron went around the counter and slid an old, weathered leather-bound book across the tile.

I gave it a look over before I flipped open the cover, "Property of Dr. Scott Stephens" was pressed into the inside of the leather.

I had a memory of giving this to my dad as a Father's Day gift, but I couldn't remember the last time I saw it, I just assumed it had been on a shelf somewhere.

"Where did you find this?"

"Believe it or not," Parker crossed his arms, "One of Donnie's vamps caught up to us."

"Well," Aaron pushed his glasses up his nose, "She made it very clear she was not one of Donnie's."

"Hang on, you guys spoke to another vampire? She was like you?"

"Kinda sorta." Parker took a seat on one of the mismatched stools, "She was human-y but her eyes were a really weird color,"

I accidentally cut him off, "What color?"

"Huh? Oh, like red but kind of yellow-ish."

"... You mean orange?"

"Yeah, I guess it would be orange."

I blew out a sigh.

"I asked about it and she got kinda defensive and said, 'Well, we can't all be shifters'."

"Huh..." I thought about it for a second.

"How do you think they're doing that?" Aaron asked what I was thinking.

I shrugged, "Well, if her eyes were kind of red maybe she was possessed, or we know diluting the virus is a possibility..."

"Is there a way there are more like me?" Parker blurted.

I took a second to think about what I was going to say, "I don't want to give you false hope, but who knows what Donatello has been able to come up with." Aaron nodded his agreement, "We know he has the cash."

Parker shifted; he didn't like that answer.

Unconsciously, I thumbed through the pages of the journal.

"So this other vampire, she gave this to you?"

Parker nodded, "Yeah, she said it didn't belong to Donnie. She was returning it."

I looked through a few of the pages, I wondered how I had missed that it was gone, but then I saw a date on one of the pages "January 2001". I realized I hadn't missed it because I was busy pretending it didn't exist.

"Everything okay?" Aaron asked when I didn't say anything else.

"Fine," I slammed the book closed, "It's my dad's"

"Seriously?" Parker went to grab it, but I put my hand on top of it before he could move it.

"Don't."

"What?"

I picked it up, took it over to my desk, and dropped it in the drawer, "You're not reading it."

Parker gave me a weird look, I could tell he was trying to think of how to tread carefully for once, "Why not?"

"It's my dad's journal from the month he died," I started again, "If anyone is going to read it, it has to be me."

It was quiet for a second.

Drew put her hand on my shoulder, "That's fair."

"Why the hell would Donnie want that?" Parker crossed his arms.

I sighed, "Who knows, maybe my parents were onto something with the virus... I don't know."

After a while, Aaron cleared his throat loudly.

Parker gave him an oblivious look.

"There's more," Aaron nudged.

Parker sat up straight, "There is?"

The usual sparkle in Aaron's eye faded with annoyance, "The napkin?"

"Oh, shit." Parker shot off the stool and patted around his pockets to look for something that Nate pulled out of his own pocket with ease and handed to me.

It was a thirteen-digit number written on a napkin with absolutely nothing else.

"What is it?"

Parker shrugged, "She said to run through immigration?"

"Thought it looked like an alien number," Nate added.

"Any idea from where?" I offered the napkin to him.

He took another look at it, "Uh uh, Dominican's is SDO."

Parker narrowed his eyes at him, "I thought you were Puerto Rican."

Nate ignored him and gave me the napkin again.

"Mmhmm, I know MTL but I have no idea where BHC is."

Parker raised an eyebrow at us, "I always forget you guys are aliens."

Aaron was the only one who responded, he cracked open a Red Bull while he added his thoughts, "Me too, but more of the Hitchhiker's kind and less earthly."

"Okay, um, is there anything else Parker's forgetting?" I moved past it.

He shook his head taking a long drink from his can, "Nope, that's all this time."

I let go of the napkin and watched it sway down from my hand onto my desk, "Drew, I think it'll be a good idea for you to stay here for a while, just until we know what Donatello's next move is."

Drew perched on the arm of the couch, opposite my desk, she knit her dark brows together "What about my mom?"

"She'll be okay," I tried to reassure her.

"Donnie's really only focused on me." Parker agreed.

"He was in her house. Besides, my mom's not going to be satisfied with that, she's going to want to know *everything*."

"We can talk to her."

She scoffed, "Rachel Hart, my mother, you've met her, yeah? I appreciate it, Conner, I do, but what am I supposed to tell her? "A crazy vampire that killed your daughter is now hunting the only daughter you have left". Sure, that won't give her a heart attack."

"We can work this out, we'll tell her what she needs to know,"

"And when I tell her what she needs to know I'll go to 'Mom Jail'." She crossed her arms, "And then you'll go to 'Mom Jail', we can reason with her, but it won't matter! It won't matter that I'm twenty-five years old, and it definitely won't matter that you're not even her child! She will lock down on our asses like Alcatraz!"

"Yeah," Nate rubbed the back of his neck, "I got one of those, pretty sure they breed 'em exclusively in Oakland. Y'all won't get shit done for weeks."

Drew pressed her palms to her eyes and sighed before she got up, "I'll see what I can do, but when she busts down your door and drags me away by my hair, don't say I didn't warn you."

She went and called from the bedroom for the illusion of privacy, and we politely pretended not to hear the conversation.

She wasn't even gone for a full five minutes before she came back and fell on the couch in defeat.

"How did it go?" If I didn't know Aaron, I would've thought he was being sarcastic.

"So my mom just threatened to send me to go live with my father in Indiana." Drew said with a laugh, "But she said she was comfortable with me 'being out' as long as it was with one of you or her."

Parker sat next to her and put his arm around her to hug her, "For what it's worth, I'm sorry."

"For what?"

"Dragging you into this, all of you, really. You guys don't deserve all this shit."

Drew hugged him back, "Welp, we're already in it now, so we might as well get to work."

(\\(•̀w•́)/)

15:00

Parker

"Parker!" Conner finally snapped, he rolled up a legal pad and swatted at me until I climbed off his desk, "For the last time, this is a federal database! I'm not going to crack it in an hour, and your breath on my neck is not helping!"

I glanced over my shoulder to look at the clock on the VCR, "It's been two hours,"

He glared at me.

I crossed my arms and sat on the couch annoyed, "Come on! It took you five minutes to get into Courtney's dad's bank!"

Drew looked up from the book she was reading, "Huh?"

"Shh," Con shot another glare at me when Drew wasn't paying attention.

I watched him pretty closely. That way when he had something I would be the first to know.

Conner stood up and I scrambled to get up at the same time.

"What? What do you need?"

He gave me a weird look as he stretched his arms over his head, "I was just going to get a snack..."

I zipped around the counter in the kitchen and grabbed the pack off gummi worms Aaron had in front of them.

"Hey!" He yelled at me as I shoved the package into Conner's hands.

"Sit down, keep doing your thing."

Conner looked both confused and bothered by my response.

"What? You want something else? I'll get it "

"What's happening?" He looked more concerned.

"I'm helping," I scoffed as if it wasn't obvious, "You keep doing your little hacker thing, I got the rest."

"Well, stop it," he gestured to his laptop with one hand while he went to get another cup of coffee and returned Aaron's worms, "I have most of this automated anyway. I just have to keep an eye on it."

"Got it." I sat in his chair and kicked my feet up on the desk, "What am I watching for?"

Conner shook his head, "If it makes you feel better, by all means, but right now it's filtering through every single immigration request in the United States from 1977 to now trying to find a match to that number, so you better get comfy."

I took a pen off the desk and twirled it around my fingers, "Why '77?"

"You said he couldn't be any older than 30, right?"

I shrugged, "I guess."

"What do you mean you 'guess'?"

"Well, I didn't card him! He looks like a kid but, I don't know, he talks old."

"How do you talk old?" Nate popped off, "Four score and seven years ago." he added his best "old timey" voice, but it came off more Keanu Reeves' Jonathan Harker than anything close to Abraham Lincoln.

"No, more... Pretentious,"

"Oh, like Con."

Conner crossed his arms, "Was that necessary?"

"I guess it would make sense if he's not American. Could just be a real light accent?" I shrugged again.

"I'm sorry if this is a stupid question," Drew spoke up, "But vampires really don't age?"

"There are no stupid questions," he made his way back to the desk and double checked that I didn't fuck with anything, "But the best answer would be I don't know. The virus definitely seems to age them when they're not fed, but since it keeps them alive against most other things when they are, it would be a strong hypothesis to say that they don't age."

"So could it be a safe assumption that maybe he's a lot older than he looks?"

I shifted to look up at Con with a wide, semi scared, smile on my face.

He shook his head; he wheeled me and the chair out of his way.

"I'll add another few decades, it should only add to the search by a few days." He said sarcastically while he typed, "While we're at it, can you dig through your smooth peanut butter brain and make absolutely sure you're not forgetting anything else?"

Aaron spun around on the kitchen stool and pointed at me with the pencil in his hand when he got an idea, "Why haven't you drawn him yet? It'll probably jog your memory better."

It was a good idea, so I ran through the apartment trying to remember I put the sketchpad they'd given me not even three days ago... Damn, it might be time to stop smoking weed.

I finally found it, made a pit stop to kiss Aaron on the cheek, flung myself on the couch, and started sketching.

When Conner was done typing, he shuffled through the few books he and Aaron had collected on the coffee table.

"You're not going to read your dad's journal?" Drew was surprised.

Con took a second to answer, "I have a few other things to catch up on, and I'd rather give that my full attention."

"Fair enough," She leaned against him when he sat next to her. "So can I keep asking more dumb questions?"

He laughed to himself, "Of course."

"Great. So, if vampires aren't "supernatural", why does religion work against them?"

"It doesn't, that's a Parker trait, not a vampire one."

"But I saw holy water boil through their flesh."

"Oh, got it. That doesn't have to do with religion, it's a conduit like silver is."

"Mmhm," Aaron jumped in, "It's all about the energy, it's purified, and they soak pure silver crucifixes in it."

"So do crucifixes work?"

I took a second from my sketch to stick out my tongue and flash the black cross stud I had pierced through it, "Nope, all this is good for is saying I eat pussy for the Lord." I jokingly added the sign of the cross over my chest.

"If religion truly has nothing to do with it, why don't you make the water yourself?"

The room was dead silent until a literal pen dropped.

Poor Aaron looked like he wanted to yell, so he did. A lot.

"Are you fucking kidding me?!" he squeaked so loud; it sounded like someone stepped on a dog, "We could've been doing that this whole damn time! I could've been putting crystals and sage and..!"

"Aaron!" Nate yelled over his whistle tone, "¡Callate! Son of a bitch, you're gonna set off the neighborhood dogs again!"

Aaron crossed his arms and sat back down. "I just need everyone to know that we only have 2.5 IQ points put together."

"Everyone already knows, look at Parker. You don't gotta scream it."

I flung my eraser at Nate, he caught it and hit me in the head with it.

"Dumbass."

"Leave him alone, if this is on anyone it's Conner."

Conner raised his arms in a shrug, "I never thought about how my parents got holy water, okay? I just knew they used it. But, Air, this does fix our morality issue."

Aaron rolled his ghostly blue eyes at us, "Poor Drew is in danger of losing brain cells by being in our vicinity."

Drew giggled, "Sorry, I can't help but feel like I'm a little bit responsible for this."

"It's not your fault, I fear we're depriving some facility their control group. I mean, seriously..." He held up his notebook before tossing it back on the counter, "We haven't even been able to crack this code for months and it's his last name." He crossed his arms and leaned against the counter, totally smug... Until he realized what he said, and his eyes widened, "Holy fuck, I just figured out his code!"

I was up and by Aaron's side in less than half a second, "What is it?"

"It spells out S-O-T-O-S, that's his last name, right?"

"That's how he introduced himself, yeah."

Conner was on Aaron's other shoulder, "What would the point of sending these cards spelling out his name if he was just going to give it to you anyway?"

"You mean, other than to be a massive prick?" I crossed my arms.

"To keep us busy?" Aaron suggested.

"I'm sure that was a big factor, but can I?" Con shook his head and took the notebook, "This is a guy who is used to things being a certain way, and you are a guy who has never followed any kind of rhyme or reason whatsoever."

I shrugged, "So?"

"So, he's getting frustrated. That's a good thing, he's slipping, he'll slip some more," he gestured to his laptop, "And we're not, so we'll have everything we need before he knows we have it."

For some reason I didn't find Conner's confidence comforting. I was worried we were finally gonna get something good, and then the rug would be ripped out from under us again.

I took a deep breath and tried desperately to calm my anxiety, "I need a blunt."

Con made Nate go with me "just in case", so we opted to hot box in Nate's run-down old truck.

He ran the engine so we didn't get hypothermia, and so he could blare a No Doubt CD.

After a couple of songs, he turned down the stereo.

He let the smoke pour out of his mouth, "I'm gonna regret asking this, but why so quiet?"

I shook my head and took the blunt from him, "I'm getting sick of this shit already. I want this to all just go away, I don't wanna have to deal with any of it anymore. For once in my miserable little life, I just wanna feel good."

It was a serious statement, but I got uncomfortable with the realness, so I scooted over the console between the seats and sat on his lap.

"So, what do you say, Sailor? You wanna make me feel good tonight, baby?"

He rolled his eyes at me, "Shut up."

I moved so I was only a few inches from his face, "Make me."

Unlike earlier today, he leaned into me and met my mouth.

I'd forgotten how soft his lips were and was still surprised every time, even more when I'd try to sluttily eat his face, he was still so smooth.

Okay, so... Nate and I may have been hooking up on and off through the last couple of months.

It started when we got a little too high and started making out as a joke. Then the joke turned into a handy and we decided we were into it and kept it casual.

And yeah, I know I never wrote anything here about it, but he made it clear he didn't want anyone to know about it. I knew he was having some issues coming to terms with some of it. And since I didn't care either way, I planned on glossing over it... No pun intended.

But there was something about tonight.

Something was different.

He started kissing my neck so I put my head on his shoulder.

"For someone who's not into dudes, you sure are into this." I teased.

"Shut up."

God, that thought took me somewhere else that I was too high to follow. To be fair, I'd said that to more men than I'd care to admit.

I was starting to get the giggles, and it didn't help that he was running his fingers down my ribs where I was ticklish.

"Trav, stop." I laughed.

His hand quickly went from my side to my chest so he could push me away.

"What?"

"Huh?"

"What'd you say?"

It took me way too long to process what I just did.

So, when he went to ask again, I quickly swooped forward and kissed him before he got the words out.

I knew Nate was as high as I was, but just to be safe, I went down on him hoping that would be the part he remembered.

The irony of Artificial Sweetener blaring in my ears wasn't lost on me.

November 4 2007

08:40

PARKER

Nothing more came from the night, well, other than Nate I mean.

I crashed early on, and ended up waking up at 3 AM from a dream I couldn't remember.

That seemed to be happening more, and to be honest it unnerved me more than creepy ass dreams I was getting.

No one else was up, which was rare. But I just popped a couple of pills, and turned my iPod on super loud so that way I didn't have to be alone with my thoughts.

I picked up where I left off with my drawing of Donatello, I really needed something to focus on and it was the only thing I had.

Luckily once I started drawing I was able to zone out pretty hard. I barely noticed Con had started setting up for the day.

I took one of my headphones out when I realized he was talking to me.

"Have you been up long?"

"Uh, what time is it?"

"A quarter to nine."

"Oh, nah. Only six hours."

If he had visible eyebrows I think they would've touched, "Is everything okay?"

I knew it'd be a lot quicker and easier for everyone involved if I lied, "Yeah, I took three Adderall instead of Ambien. I gotta stop with that shit, though, there's no high and it just makes me wanna do something."

He snorted, "You know that's what it does for people that need it, right? It's supposed to do that."

"So should I take more?"

"No," he sighed as he sank down into his chair.

"Anything yet?"

Conner scanned the computer screen before shaking his head, “Nope, but it's at 63%.”

His optimism only made it worse. The closer it got the further away it felt and my anxiety had already peaked.

I tried hopelessly to go back to my drawing ‘cause I knew Con wasn't gonna let me chug a bottle of tequila first thing in the morning. Buzzkill.

I shoved my headphones back in until Nate got up a little later.

I got his attention as he shuffled out of the room. Winking at him, I stuck my tongue in my cheek.

He just rolled his groggy eyes at me.

“Drew make it home?” Nate took a cereal box off the fridge and dug around in it with his hand.

Conner nodded while he typed, “Yeah, her mom came and picked her up while you guys were still outside,”

I don't know what Nate heard that I didn't, but he stood up straight and gave me a weird look that took me a minute to register as panic. I don't think I've ever seen Nate panicked before.

"Uh..." I played with the edge of my sketchpad, “... Did you walk her out?”

“No,” Con laughed, somehow missing the daggers Nate was glaring at me, “Actually, her mom walked up here with a loaded .44 mag."

Nate's entire mood shifted, like he was never worried he let out a whistle, "Damn, her mom still single?"

I snickered, "Hey, if you married Drew he could be your father in law."

Conner pressed his lips into a thin line, "You know, I think she would vindicate that break up."

Nate gestured at Con with the box of cereal in his hand, "That there's why you get called pretentious."

All of a sudden the front door lock switched open and we all snapped around in a panic.

Aaron opened the door, his hair was tied up loosely at his neck, and he was wearing real sneakers.

His eyes widened when he realized we were all staring at him, he carefully put the tray of coffees he was holding on the counter and tried to untangle his headphones out of his hair, "... Good morning?"

"Bro, I didn't even know you left." Nate shook his head, "You're lucky my gun's still in Con's trunk."

"Me either," Con sighed relieved it was just Aaron, "I thought you were in the shower. Where were you?"

"I had a panic attack, went for a run," He shrugged, "I'm sorry, I told Parker I was leaving."

Conner and Nate looked at me for confirmation.

I scrunched up my face and squinted, "... I kinda remember that."

Aaron just shook his head and handed us each one of the cups he brought back.

"I don't think Parker needs anymore caffeine," Conner stated.

"Oh, his is hot chocolate."

I widened my eyes with pure love, "Marshmallows?"

"Strawberry mallows." He corrected me.

I took a long sip, "We're making out later."

He awkwardly patted the top of my head, "No, we're not." He caught a glimpse of my sketch, "Can I look?"

"Sure, it's not colored yet, but it's pretty much done."

Aaron pushed up his glasses, "Oh... 'Kay."

Nate leaned over Aaron and let out a laugh, "Dude, you've told us you're into some pretty weird shit, but what the hell's wrong with you?"

"What?" I tried to bat my eyelashes innocently.

"Why's he in panties?"

Conner turned his full focus to his computer, "I don't want to know."

"Because!" I grabbed my sketchpad back, "It's a contrast pin-up piece! Every time I've ever seen him he's been in a three piece suit... Well, except for one time."

"What do you mean?" Aaron cautiously raised an eyebrow.

"Well, when he first showed up, he was in some pretty elaborate drag, or I guess he'd shape shifted to get my attention or whatever."

I flicked to the next page where I drew his female side in a more dominatrix style.

Aaron's hand flew to cover his mouth.

Nate laughed again, then sucked in a breath, "God, you're one sick puppy, y'know that? Can I get a copy of that?"

"They're well done..." Aaron tried to be subjective, "I just really feel like her nipples follow me when I move..."

"Well, what do you want?" I asked, "He's pretty androgynous, but when he's a chick, y'know, tig ol' bitties."

Con pinched the bridge of his nose, "I can't look at this all day. For the sake of posterity, can you help me out here?"

I rolled my eyes and clicked my tongue at him, "Censorship kills art, *man*."

The computer chimed and Conner sighed, "Thank Christ."

"You got something?" I stumbled over myself and my markers to get up.

"Hang on," he scanned the computer.

"What is it?!" I practically screamed.

"Careful, he doesn't edge well." Nate thought he was funny 'til he realized what he said and then he wouldn't look at me.

Con ignored us as usual, "Give me a second some of this is redacted."

I zipped around him to read over his shoulder.

"Here we go," He clicked on some things, and it took him to another page with what looked like an ancient black and white picture.

Con enlarged the photo for me, "Is this our guy?"

I was practically vibrating.

Donatello's face was seared into my brain by pure hate alone, I didn't even need to look at it longer than a second to know it was him.

He hardly looked any different.

His jet-black hair was cropped even shorter than it was now, and greased back slick, he wore a shirt with matching tie and one of those old-school Army hats that kinda looked like a Dorito.

The only thing that was different from now was how sick he looked. His cheeks were hollow, and his eyes were sunken, he looked like he was dying in front of the camera.

Hell, he probably was.

Part of me felt a little bad for him.

"Where's this from?"

Conner backed out and scanned the document, he read so much faster, I couldn't even keep up.

"US Army enlistment document, looks like it's from 1943." He scanned a little more, "There's a lot less here than I was expecting... Jamais Lucian, does that sound familiar to you?"

"Not a syllable." I shook my head.

"Born 1924 "Tulcea", Romania." Con gestured.

"Why the air quotes?"

"I don't know Tulcea is in quotations." He kept going through, "Family "not applicable"... Huh, he was enlisted and discharged in the same year."

He grabbed a pen, "Corporal Lucian retired at Corporal status with highest honors for his services. Then assigned to Sergeant Reinfrank to be escorted to the US for asylum."

"What's that mean?"

Conner kept reading but still answered my question, "Usually someone seeks asylum if they're being persecuted, it's kind of like a refugee. Which makes sense seeing as he was a non-white person in Romania during World War II, but what "services" could he have served in a few months?"

I could see the page slider on the document was already at the bottom and that scared me, "Is that it?"

"I see a record of him becoming an American citizen, a loan for some land looks like in... Nevada, a couple of car titles and that kind of thing. After that he pretty much falls off the face of the earth, then out of nowhere he pops up again in 1967 with a marriage license but filed for divorce in 1972. That's all of it."

"Who did he marry?"

"Dorothy... Hold on, I'll come back to her and Reinfrank later." Con did something else and a bunch of what looked like gibberish to me came up.

Then another black and white photo popped up on the screen, this one looked like a mug shot but the kid in the picture looked entirely different to the one from earlier.

"Is that Don, er, Jamais?"

Conner nodded.

This picture took all the air out of my lungs.

He looked like he was just a kid.

His face, which was so gaunt in the last picture, was plump and round in this one, framed by chin length dark curls. His wide eyes were shades lighter than what I was used to seeing in Donatello. Even his skin seemed darker and less ashen. He wore a striped jumpsuit that had two upside down triangles pinned to his chest above a number, the one on top was dark and the one below it was a lighter color with an "R" in it.

I didn't need to read German to know what the plaque he was holding in his chained hands meant.

The poor kid looked so terrified that it made me want to cry.

I tried to swallow the lump in my throat, "How old is he here?"

Conner pointed at the time stamp, "This says 1940 so..."

"He would've been sixteen." Aaron answered.

"Jesus Christ." I genuinely felt sick to my stomach, "I gotta sit down."

I sat on the arm of the couch.

Aaron gently put his hand on my back, "Are you okay?"

I shook my head, "No, no, in no way am I okay. He's just a teenager, for fuck's sake! I thought we were dealing with Charles Manson or like Jack the Ripper, but he's a kid! God, no wonder he looks so fucking young."

I let myself fall backwards onto the cushions of the couch.

"That was almost seventy years ago." Aaron tried to rationalize, but it was like trying to band aid a severed artery.

This was too far.

(＼(•̀w•́)／)

20:00

I was pretty much incapable of doing anything other than imagining the kinda hell Jamais had gone through.

Conner went to the library to print a copy of the file, and I immediately took the photos.

I was getting obsessive, but I just couldn't believe the child staring back at me was the same person that had made my life a living hell.

Aaron pointed out the double upside-down triangles on Jamais' shirt, he told me the dark one was probably brown meaning he was Roma, and the light one was pink and meant they flagged him as gay. Aaron seemed pretty sure that combo would've been an almost immediate death sentence.

I was curious why they didn't kill him, but more than anything, it just fucked me up.

Staring between his concentration camp mugshot, his Army portrait, and my sketch…

It made me think of all the "Cautionary tales" of Satan I was told as a kid.

Jamais and Donatello had a stunning resemblance to those stories.

He was a normal kid, probably at one point, he was a good son. But something changed him, it moved him to disobedience which drove him to sin and ultimately turned him into a monster.

If it could happen to an angel, why couldn't it happen to anyone else?

After all, he was just like you or...

He was just like me.

F
31661

My trance was broken when Conner snapped his fingers excitedly, "Alright so! Dorothy Lucian was a dead-end, both figuratively and literally. She died a while ago, but all she had was the usual. Property, parking tickets, yadda. She had nothing, but Charles Reinfrank sure does."

"What?" I dumped all of my art shit on the coffee table and sat on Con's lap.

He grumbled to himself but showed me what he had.

"Born November 30th, 1922, Las Vegas Nevada, to Abigail and Clyde Reinfrank. Both of whom are dead. He has a sister, Ava, also dead.

Looks like he joined the Army right out of high school in 1940. He was stationed in Poland for a year before being sent to Romania where he spent the rest of his military career."

Conner pulled up another photo.

This guy was night and day from Jamais. The only thing that was similar was the military uniform, but he had a lot of pins and bars on his jacket.

His skin was really light, and so was his hair. His hair was cropped close and slicked back behind the same hat. His features were a lot softer compared to how angular Jamais' are.

Charles looked really young, too. His eyes kind of reminded me of Aaron's, big with a lot of sparkle behind them, he was smiling in his picture despite whatever horrors I'm sure followed it.

"In 1943 he was moved over to the reserves, and with-in the same month filed to be a sponsor for the immigration of one Jamais Lucian.

He bought a pretty decent sized property in Nevada..." Conner raised a transparent eyebrow, "Jamais was also on the deed. In 1945, when his father died, Charles also inherited a cafe, Jamais was also added onto that deed as well."

I crossed my arms, "Next you're gonna tell me they adopted a daughter named Claudia! God, does this get any gayer?"

"From there it's just the normal stuff. In 1970 he sold the cafe turned bar," Con's forehead wrinkled, "It says he died six months after that."

"Really?"

"What was the COD?" Aaron asked.

"Undetermined." Conner rolled his eyes, "Conveniently, he had a son, Charles Jr. who there was absolutely no record of until his will."

"Anything on him?"

Con scoffed, "Of course. He virtually has no record; it says he was born August 5th, 1952. No mother listed, just Charles. He also enlisted into the Army in 1970 and was stationed in Vietnam." Con pulled up his enlistment photo, "Strong family resemblance.

It was practically the same picture except this one was in color and his uniform got an upgrade.

I snorted, "Glad I don't look that much like my dad. So he's a vamp?"

"Must be, doesn't look like he's aged much from his own..." Conner paused, "Oh, he went MIA in '73."

I crossed my arms, "Vietnam didn't have enough f..."

Con cut me off, "He was killed in a bombing, they never recovered his body."

"... Now I feel like an asshole."

"Well, you are," He kept scanning the screen, "Doesn't look like even a vampire could survive that blast. I'm willing to bet that's also where Jamais dropped off and Donatello picked up."

I tangled my hands in my hair, and tried to take a deep breath, "Now what?"

Conner clicked his pen on the desk, "We wait a few days, see if Donatello makes a move, if not we know pushing his buttons is as easy as hunting. We can do a couple, maybe we can shake something loose."

I nodded, "I like that."

He wrote a few quick notes, "I'll keep a closer eye on anything that looks like nest activity, too. There's no way we'll be able to clear one, but at least we'll know where they are."

I turned so I could kiss him on the cheek, "I love you."

He dumped me off his lap and onto the floor, "Get out of here!"

November 5 2007

03:45

PARKER

I didn't want to go to sleep, I didn't wanna be alone with my thoughts the way trying to go to sleep would make me, but Conner dumped my Adderall down the sink like the little bitch he is.

So I had the TV up half as loud as it could go, I got half way through the second tape of Buffy The Vampire slayer Aaron had before my eyes started to glaze over. But Conner was able to help with that. He came out and beat me senseless with his pillow after Willow let out a particularly blood curdling scream.

He took the remote, turned the TV down, and threw it back at me, "Turn it up again and you'll need a Colorectal surgeon!"

"Jokes on you, I don't know what that is!"

"I'm sure you don't! Just be quiet!" Con stomped back into the bedroom.

I sighed and stared at the ceiling for a minute. There were two ways I knew would be a surefire way to keep myself distracted, unfortunately, when I woke Nate up he told me to go to hell, my booty-text to Caitlin was met with the bummer response of "WTF?!", and thanks to Conner I was out of pills.

There was this place on the other side of Montlake Bridge that I knew I could get drugs and sex from, and if I played my cards right, maybe a little cash.

I flipped my phone screen open to check the time, from what I remembered, I had a good two hours before they closed and everyone there was sure to milk those last few minutes for all they could get.

I left the TV on and clumped up the blanket in case any of the guys got up while I was gone they'd hopefully think I was asleep.

I thought about hijacking Nate's truck, but other than the thought of driving making me wanna hurl, I thought I'd be faster if I ran. Besides, it's not like anyone would see me.

Pretty much everything was closed, and every building had its lights off, except for one rundown, seedy little shit hole.

I stared at the rusty barred door for a minute. I hadn't been to this damn bar in probably five years, but it looked the same.

I'd swore to myself I wouldn't come back down here unless it was necessary. But hell with my week/month/year/life, it was necessary.

When I opened the door the smell of cheap cigarettes and even cheaper cologne suffocated me.

Very dim red lights fought to illuminate above the bar, while the few ceiling lights that actually had bulbs struggled to light the rest of the room.

The radio was turned up loud enough to drown out the other conversations in the nearly bedroom sized room.

I sat on one of the torn leather stools at the bar while I gauged everyone else in the room.

There were only a handful of other people there. The bartender who didn't want to have anything to do with the place, the guy passed out in a corner booth, two girls who were counting cash and chatting in the back of the room, a table full of people who were dead silent and another who seemed to be having the night of their lives.

One of the guys at the silent table looked me over and motioned for me to join them, but I couldn't. The memories this place brought back were nearly paralyzing.

"Fred, can I get a rum and coke please, baby?" A soft voice behind me spoke to the bartender.

When I turned around a guy who I could only describe as a young boy was standing behind me.

For a minute, I thought I was projecting the kid thing onto him until he sat next to me, he didn't even look old enough to be sitting at a bar.

He was small, too, and that's coming from me. He was a few inches shorter and probably a good fifteen pounds lighter than what Nate likes to call my "crackhead frame".

Despite the freezing temperature outside, he was wearing short shorts and a mesh tank top.

I felt like I was looking through a crystal ball into my past.

The amount of dots I was connecting at the moment were incredibly uncanny.

He looked me over, and relaxed once I passed his scan, "Hey girl, don't think I've seen you before. You working tonight?" He didn't wait for me to answer, "Gotta warn you, you picked a slow night. But the guy eyeing you from the booth's good for at least a meal. Real gentle, too."

I took a deep breath and held it for a second. In almost seven years it never set in until now, but to be fair I was never on this side of it... Or sober.

This was really the kinda shit I did? And all the guys I let touch me could actually stomach it?

He reminded me so much of myself before all of this vampire bullshit, God he could've been my brother... And that thought right there was the straw that broke this whore's back.

"How old are you?" I accidentally snapped at him.

He tensed up again, "Are you a cop? You have to tell me if I ask."

I scoffed at the thought, "Yeah, dude, cops look like me."

He blinked once.

"I'm not a cop! What's your name?"

He hesitated, "Trevor,"

"Parker," I tried to keep my voice even, but I couldn't keep shit together, "What the hell are you doing out here? Fuck, what are you, twenty?"

"Next December…" He mumbled.

I blew out the breath I was holding, "What is it? Coke? Pills?"

"Look, I'm not…"

I grabbed his wrist before he could get up, "I get it, I get it more than anyone."

His eyes widened and I let go.

"Sorry," I murmured, "Look, I'm not crazy, I swear,"

He didn't believe me, I didn't believe me either.

"I'm not, okay? I've done… I do this shit, okay? I know! At first it was just to pay my rent, then the guys started giving me drugs, and the next thing I knew…" I stopped my rant once I realized it started, "What is it? Why are you doing this?"

He seemed to soften a little, but kept his edge and didn't answer.

"I've been out here seven years, how long you been doing this?"

He gulped, "Six months." His voice was barely a whisper, "I don't use, but my boyfriend… He thought I could make at least enough to keep our lights on."

"He hitting you yet?"

He only nodded once.

I grabbed him by the shoulders.

"Look at me," I grabbed the couple of twenties I swiped from the guys' wallets on my way out and shoved it into the kid's pocket, "Get out. Get out while you can, before it starts, trust me. Don't circle the drain, there's no way out. Am I scaring you?"

"A little…"

“Good!” I slid out of my hoodie and threw it over him, “Get as far away from here as you fucking can, got it? Dump your boyfriend and don't ever look back.”

He searched my face and just nodded, “I don't wanna be doing this.”

“You don't have to, get out now.”

He nodded again and I drug him to the door.

I kept my hands on his shoulders until I got him through the doorway, “If I ever see you in this shit hole again…”

Poor kid was so confused but Christ I hoped I was getting through.

“Just don't come back, ever.”

“... Thank you.”

I watched him leave before I cut my losses and figured out how to get back to the apartment before the sun started to rise.

As I was headed out, I heard a scream come from the backroom, no one else reacted so I felt like I had to check it out.

The door to the tiny office was unlocked, and in the chair behind the desk was a fresh body. The girl's neck was at a really strange angle, and it was obvious when I got closer that she wasn't breathing.

"Back away," when I turned around the bartender was in the door frame pointing a shotgun at my chest.

I opened my mouth to defend myself, but a louder voice spoke over me.

"We had a deal."

I glanced around the room, I knew I didn't answer, but I was for sure the only one in any condition to speak.

"This wasn't the deal,"

"No, but it does send a message, wouldn't you say?" The voice talking started to sound familiar, "An eye for an eye, and all that. You kill one of mine, I kill one of yours."

Donatello... But why can't I see him? I thought.

"I didn't kill anyone," The bartender held his stance.

I felt something burning in the palm of my hand, so I tossed it at the bartender's feet. Tiny silver pellets fell and bounced off the hardwood floor.

"Then I fear you may have taken the silver bullet part of the cocktail too seriously."

When I looked down at the burn in my hand the sleeve of my hoodie was replaced with a cuffed white dress shirt sleeve.

"Fuck."

I pressed my eyes shut and hoped to wake up, but nope.

"What are you gonna do?"

"I'm in the business of second chances, Fred, but it appears you are running out of them."

"What do you want? Anything."

I stood up straight, and smoothed out the blood-stained shirt, "Well, if we were being fair, in this instance I feel we're more "eye for a kidney liver and lung". So, how else can we even that score? I'm open to suggestions."

"I can get you two new girls."

I scoffed, "For you to kill them as well? No, not even."

"A quarter of a million dollars,"

I felt myself laugh, "You underestimate my worth, besides I do not do this for the money."

The bartender gulped, "What is it you want?"

"Hm," I licked the blood from my fingers, "Your heart would suffice."

"Please..." He pleaded as I took a few steps closer.

The distance between me and the bartender closed, my hand was on his throat and he was pinned to the wall.

"Fret not, I work fast."

I was screaming and fighting to do anything I could to let him go but it was like my body just ignored it and was overrode.

There was nothing I could do.

I tried to shut my eyes again, but I could still feel the crunch of the man's windpipe under the pressure of my hand.

I tried to let go, but my grip wouldn't give.

I knew logically I wasn't going to be able to stop it, I knew it was a dream or connection, vision, whatever. There was nothing I could do and it was hell.

I didn't think it could get much worse until I felt something warm and wet down to my forearm. When I opened my eyes my hands were shoved up an incision in the bartender's chest cavity.

I could've puked.

The poor guy's insides squelched while I groped around, my fingers finally hit something solid, and I struggled to get a grip on his heart.

There was no thought, no hesitation, as soon as it was out of his chest my teeth tore through the spongy cartilage.

Blood cascaded down my chin.

As quickly as it started, it was over.

I wiped the blood on my hands on my black slacks and stood to open the back door out into the alley.

The voice spoke out to no one, "Clean this up, drain them, strip them for parts and bring them back with us. We could very much use the supply.",

I stepped into the bathroom.

Watching as the water from the tap ran red from the blood on my hands, I dipped to wash the blood from my face too.

I dried my hands and unrolled my sleeves, realizing the scars and tattoos on my arms vanished.

When I straightened out Donatello stared back at me from the mirror.

His nearly black brown eyes searched the reflection.

He leaned in closer against the sink.

He closed his eyes for a second and when they were open, they were scarlet red, "Breaker, breaker. Let's hope this thing is on." A smirk broke across his face like there was a single fucking thing funny about any of this, "I believe it's due time we followed up on our previous conversation. What do you say, Parker?"

He paused for effect.

The fucking douche.

"In two nights, the seventh of November, 9:20. Right here. I won't request you come alone, I'm well aware of how you are, so your little friends may come, however, I do not think you need me to tell you that would be a bad idea. Also, perhaps this time we can forgo the tantrum?" He raised one sharp eyebrow, "Goodbye."

15:00

Aaron

"He just looks tired, Celeste."

"No, he looks tired," Dr. Celeste gestured to me, "I know our son, and he looks stressed."

"He probably is, hon, that's 75% of the DNA that makes up a Stephens," Dr. Scott tried to rationalize, "He has your nose and my anxiety."

My eyes had glazed over half an hour ago when Conner's parents had started bickering.

His mom and dad had been taking turns hovering, it was a lot more than usual, but they were zeroed in on Conner and weren't chatting with me much so I wasn't sure why the sudden concern.

Either way, I kept one headphone out while I took apart our toaster.

"He's going to make himself sick," Celeste continued, "Ugh, this is so hard! I just want to hold him."

Scott put a hand on his wife's shoulder, "I know, I hate to see him like this. He was always such a happy kid."

"This is all our fault."

I pretended to take a phone call so as to not tip Conner and Nate off to my crazy.

"Hi, is there something you guys need help with?"

My acting must have been somewhat decent because Celeste shushed Scott.

I chuckled to myself, "I'm talking to you."

Silence.

"Doctor, I'm talking to you." I widened my eyes until they realized I meant them.

"Oh, right, of course."

"I've noticed you guys are around a lot lately,"

"I'm so sorry, we don't mean to impose..." Scott trailed off.

"No, no, I just meant, is everything okay? You both seem worried."

"I'm sure everything's fine, mother's intuition." Celeste offered a preoccupied smile.

I nodded, "It's about the journal, isn't it?"

"Somewhat,"

I knew I had to beat around the bush quite a bit, ghosts were awfully selective about what they could say, "Do you know anything about how it went missing?"

Scott shook his head, "I wish my mother would've had enough sense not to send it to Conner,"

"Don't be mad at her, look," Celeste gestured to our overflowing bookcase in between the bathroom and bedroom, "I have to imagine this is some of his doing too, how could either of them know?"

"Do either of you happen to know how it was taken?" I tried to get their attention again without tipping off Nate, who I could tell was already half listening.

"Oh, about Donatello?" Celeste raised her hand and waved it off so casually, "I'm not surprised, it seems like something he'd do."

"You know about him?" I tilted my head and played coy to mask my shock, my real feelings would've blown my entire cover.

"No more than you," Scott answered with a shrug, "We know he's been sniffing around; we try our best to keep you boys safe."

"I appreciate that, but you don't have any information on him for me?"

"I'm afraid not, no."

I pressed my lips together, "Okay, is there something about the journal, then?"

There was a hesitation and a lingering look between them.

It took a while for Celeste to answer, "Unfortunately, you'll find out soon."

"Is it something you need my help with?"

"That's alright, Mon chéri, you help us enough." She offered a smile, but I could feel the sadness rolling off her, "Though, if I'm not intruding too much, I think I'm going to hang out for a little bit. I think Conner needs to know we're around."

Typically, when the doctors would hang out there was an air of playfulness, Scott was always smiling and Celeste was always laughing. I had never seen them this serious and I was worried, but it was clear it wasn't any of my business.

"Of course,"

"Also," Scott hesitated for a second, "However you have to, can you just let him know all of this, everything, it was always all for him."

Celeste put her hands on her husband's shoulder, "He knows, honey. He knows the truth, if he ever doubts it Aaron knows, too."

"I'm always here for him, he knows that." I reiterated.

They both gave me a nod and then went to stand vigil on either side of their son.

I clacked my phone shut and watched them for a second.

Though my brain didn't have much time to process or even guess what was going on with all of this until my thoughts were scared off by Parker jumping upright out of a dead sleep screaming.

"Calm down, calm down." Conner was already up and trying to sooth him, "It's just me."

Meanwhile Nate clicked his tongue and threw the TV remote at Parker, "The fuck's wrong with you?"

"Sorry, sorry..." Parker mumbled as he ran his fingers through his hair, "Was I asleep?"

"You have been since last night."

"I've been here all night?"

"Yeah, of course." Conner gestured to the TV over his shoulder, "I had to come turn Legally Blonde off around midnight."

"... It wasn't Buffy?"

Conner looked to me for an explanation I didn't have, "Are you okay?"

"I think?" Parker pressed his shaking hands to his eyes, "God, is there any way to know if your brain's a liquid?"

"No need, yours has always been tequila." Nate scoffed.

Conner moved Parker's hands away from his face and tipped his head up to get a better look at his eyes in the light.

"If you're gonna kiss me, will you gimme some tongue?"

Conner immediately dropped his face, "Your eyes are slightly red, a little cinnamon-y."

"Yeah, that felt like a vision."

"What happened?"

Parker shook his head and blew out a breath, "Gross, disgusting shit, I must've caught him feeding."

"Okay, what else?"

"There wasn't anything else, just bodies and blood. Y'know, I'm getting real tired of these shit ass snuff films, you jackass!" Parker lashed out into the nothingness of our ceiling.

"Shh, the neighbors don't need another reason to call the cops on us."

Conner hit his leg with the back of his hand, "You didn't see anything? Signs, buildings? Anything I can track?"

Parker shook his head again, "No, nope, nothing."

"Why lie?" Scott tried to ask under his breath.

"I think it's just a reflex at this point." His wife answered.

"That's just great..."

He and Parker went back and forth for a minute, but Celeste made a point to get my attention.

"Aaron, I've been thinking," She made her way over to sit on the stool in front of me, "It seems like there's "visions" are coming in when he's the most relaxed, correct? A while ago you had told me you felt like it was easier to communicate with us when your head was clear, and for you that's tinkering or meditating, at least that's when I notice I'm interrupting you the most. There has to be a way like that to fine tune this."

"That's a good idea." I responded out loud without even thinking, I hadn't noticed until the guys each gave me a weird look.

"What? Brainwashing?" Parker judged me harshly.

"What? No, I was just thinking to myself, that your visions really seem to come when you're relaxed. There has to be a way to better control that."

Celeste gave me a thumbs up.

"I agree," Parker popped up off the couch, "I'm gonna go snort six Oxys, let's see what comes through then, huh?"

"Hang on," Conner put his arm out to stop Parker, "Before we go straight to pills, can we at least listen to what Aaron has to say?"

Parker crossed his arms but sat back down.

I stood and joined them a few feet away in the living room, "I just think there has to be a way to tap into this, a kind of concentration, like meditation, yoga, running..."

"It would make sense; I was reading something... Have you guys ever heard of something called Folie à deux?"

Celeste clapped her hands together, "Mon puce, that's so smart."

Conner didn't miss a beat, "The exact translation, madness of two, or shared psychosis. Since we know a sire and their offspring are tethered, it would make sense that you're tuning into that. Meditating might be a way to connect the line directly."

Parker blinked a couple of times, "You lost me at concentration."

"Okay, well, what clears your head?" I asked.

He shrugged, "Oxy, sex."

"Have you ever tried meditating?"

"No, but I'm a big fan of medication."
Conner sighed, "Stop with the drugs, it's not going to happen!"
"Just sayin'," Nate butted in, "I would pay to watch Park meditate."
Parker smirked, "Fifty bucks, a hundred if you want me all night."

November 6 2007
17:40

CONNER

Aaron deserved a presidential medal of honor for his attempt to teach Parker to meditate.

Aaron was so calm and persistent, and Parker was the exact opposite to the umpteenth degree.

They were sitting on the floor with their legs crossed, Aaron sat loose and comfortable while Parker was ridged, he looked like he had the same stick up his ass that he always accused me of having.

Oh, how the mighty fall.

"In," Aaron instructed as he inhaled sharply, "Three, two, one, and out."

"This is stupid," Parker sang on his exhale.

"It's not, it helps."

"No, it is. Watch," Parker held his breath for a solid three minutes to prove his point, "I feel literally no different either way."

"The point is to give your brain something to focus on, you know kind of like how you can't pat your head and rub your belly at the same time. Try again. Back straight, eyes closed. Deep breath in..."

I have to give Parker credit; he really did try... For about fifteen seconds.

He popped one eye open, "Yeah no, what else you got?"

"Okay, hang on."

Aaron went to the fridge and came back a moment later and, for reasons I cannot even begin to rationalize, placed a raw egg in Parker's hands.

Parker stared at it for a second completely bemused, before he held it above his head, "O holy egg, bestow upon thine thy worldly knowledge!"

"No," Aaron, with the patience of a Saint, guided Parker's hands back in front of him, "Focus on the egg."

"How... Why do I have to focus on the egg?"

"It's an exercise, how does the egg feel in your hands?"

"... Eggy?"

I have no idea how Aaron didn't crack it against Parker's head.

"It doesn't feel cold?"

"Yeah, I guess."

"Smooth?"

"Uh huh, chalky?"

"And?"

I often wonder what leads Parker down the path to the decisions he makes or better yet what makes him deviate from said paths, and oh I don't know for instance, squeezing a raw egg between his hands until it implodes all over the carpet.

"Parker!" I yelled.

"Oops,"

I glared at him until he grabbed a towel from the kitchen and feigned blotting it out of the carpet.

"Maybe it's time for a break." Aaron chuckled sheepishly as he helped pick eggshells out of the carpet fibers.

"I'm never getting this deposit back..." I muttered to myself as I traced back my place in my dad's journal.

Parker's shenanigans provided a pretty good distraction and since I was dragging my feet as much as I could on reading it, I welcomed any escape. I don't know why, but from the second Parker handed it to me yesterday I was filled with an unrelenting dread. I couldn't pinpoint it, yeah, it's always hard to read either of my parents' work, but it's all that I have left of them, and it's become somewhat comforting, but this journal... Seeing the date, reliving that day... It hurt just as much as it did eight years ago.

I squinted at the clock on the VCR, I wondered if my grandma was busy and if there was any way she wouldn't question why I made the three-hour drive down just to watch reruns of Cheers with her.

Scanning the first few pages, I took a deep breath and thought maybe it would be better to dive in than to wade.

I flipped through to the middle of the book where the last entry was.

My dad wrote vaguely about the long week they had, how my mom was spending time organizing their basement lab while my dad was working on refining their research and putting it together for their last book.

He was also proud of their last hunt, and boasted about his joy for hunting, then about his love for his family.

He spent a few paragraphs talking about my mom but there were pages about me, saying how lucky he felt to be a father, how grateful he was for the son he was given, and how amazed he was to watch me grow into the smart young man I was.

A coldness washed over me as I read the last page.

"I love you, Conner, more than you could ever imagine. You are my purpose and everything I have ever done has always been for you. I know you'll have a lot of questions, and that life won't be easy, but I know with your valiant heart that nothing will be able to stop you.

Luc de Clapiers, Marquis de Vauvenargues has a great quote, "In order to achieve great things, we must live as though we're never going to die." I hope I've been a good example and taught you that well.

And in the words of your mother; Une vie honorable est une vie éternelle.

I love you, my son.

Allow nothing to hold you back, and live until you can't anymore.

Love, Dad."

It wasn't until then that I realized what I was reading wasn't much of a journal at all, but more of a suicide letter.

My hands went numb, and I felt myself grow pallid.

"Are you okay?" Aaron was right in front of me, but he sounded miles away.

I didn't know what was happening, but all I knew was I had to get away.

I stumbled down the stairs of our building the best I could, my chest was tight, and I was unsteady.

I collapsed dramatically to my knees on the concrete walkway in front of the building's doors.

Suddenly Parker was beside me, he pulled me up by my arm until I was on my feet and slung his arm around my waist when my knees threatened to give out again.

"Jesus Christ, what happened to you? Are you okay?"

"No, not at all."

He carefully sat me on the front step out of the rain.

"What happened?"

I finally looked up at him and scanned his face, he was confused but not panicked and that settled me slightly.

"They knew."

"Huh?"

"My dad and mom, they knew."
"Knew what?"
"They knew they were going to die."

(＼(•̀w•́)／)

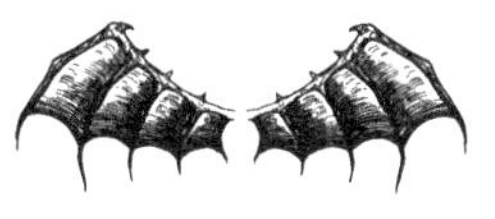

PARKER

I got Conner a little calmed down and back inside, but he was soaking wet and shivering from the rain. He looked like an orange tabby someone abandoned in a box in the middle of the sidewalk. I just wanted to sit on his lap and smother him with love and support.

I hadn't seen Conner like this since his parents' funeral.

God, I don't know how he ever came back from that.

Even when we lost Courtney, he seemed to keep a level head, he never lost it like I did. I knew it was killing him like it was all of us, but I'm not sure I ever saw him cry. Even now with this discovery, he withdrew, and he was quiet, but he didn't cry.

I walked into the bedroom as casually as I could and stood at the door.

I got Aaron's attention and waved him over.

Nate ignored me until he knew I knew he was being an asshole.

He rolled his eyes, "What?"

"Come here." I mouthed.

"Why?"

"Just come here."

"Why?"

"Nate!" I stomped and he finally got off his ass.

I gestured wildly until they got in a circle.

"Is Conner okay?" Aaron lowered his voice, reading the situation.

"He thinks he found his dad's suicide note."

"What?" Nate finally joined our concern.

"Why does..."

"Guys," Conner interrupted us by yelling through the wall, "First off, I can hear you. Second, you don't have to huddle, I'm fine."

We tripped over each other to get out of the room.

"How could you possibly be fine?" Aaron asked.

"My mom and dad have been gone for almost a decade; I've come to terms with it. This just wasn't something I was expecting."

Aaron's eyebrows were practically touching, "You really think it's a suicide note?"

He shrugged, "You guys are welcome to read it."

I took the journal he offered, Aaron and Nate read it over my shoulder.

I'd seen my fair share of suicide notes, Con wasn't wrong in assuming that's what it was.

"Why would he..." Aaron's question trailed off.

Conner shrugged again, "I don't know... Fuck," He shrugged again, and we got nervous since he never says fuck, "Maybe everyone was right, maybe my dad did just snap."

"Nah, nuh uh," I threw the journal back on his desk, "I knew them, I don't care what anyone else says Dr. Scott Stephens was an incredible man, he loved you and he loved your mom so much. He would've never done this."

"Did he ever seem suicidal?" Nate tried to show sympathy, but it just looked like he had to pee.

Conner was quiet so I answered, "No! He and Este were so happy, they'd just celebrated their 25th wedding anniversary, for Christ's sake! It was this huge deal that they did up in Canada with all their families, I was even invited. And every time I was at your house, they were so loving, they couldn't keep their hands to themselves, and they looked at you like you were the second coming of Jesus. I'm telling you; it makes no sense that Scott would ever just *snap*."

Conner sighed, "Their deaths were classified as murder/suicide because my mother's throat was slashed and my father had what they thought was a gunshot wound to his chest. I always thought it was a hunt gone wrong, but maybe if it looks like a duck and it quacks like a duck..."

"Your dad would've never ever killed your mom or slashed her throat."

"Yeah, but vampires don't slash and shoot, they bite and rip."

Aaron shook his head, and his blond curls went flying, "No, I agree with Parker. We've all heard and seen weirder things."

Nate shrugged his agreement, "Hell, saw a vamp chew through his arm once."

Aaron tilted his head, "Are you thinking of that hiker in Utah?"

"What hiker?"

I waved my hands in front of my chest to clear the conversation, "Look, we know one vamp that slashes and shoots."

Conner let himself sink into the couch, "This was eight years ago, we weren't even on his radar, why would Donatello have killed my parents?"

A light bulb practically went off over my head and electrocuted me, but for once I kept my mouth shut.

I didn't appreciate Donnie's thinly hidden threat, but I didn't want the guys to go with me either way. So, I kept it to myself 'cause I knew not one of them was above following me.

"What? Like it's outta his level of serial killer crazy?" I crossed my arms.

"Well," Aaron played with the silver stud in his lip while he thought, "He's made several references to having "watched over" you for a while, who knows how long that's been."

"And think about it!" I added, "Who are the only people that would've protected me from him?"

Con sighed, "So what? They got too close?"

"Mm, I don't think that it could ever be that simple," Aaron's eyebrows rose, "People like Donnie, they have standards. Y'know, honor among thieves? There's a calculation to it."

"I agree with that, yeah, no, I don't know what he's doing but he's not killing randomly, I know that much..." I shrugged, "He offered me a deal, he sees himself as some kinda broker."

Nate held up his thumb and counted, "They were loaded, educated, half decent kid, Celeste was hot as fuck." Nate raised his eyebrows at Con, "What else could he've offered?"

"My mom was great at reading people, she would've had nothing to do with the guy, and my dad would've stood by her."

"Well, maybe it was..."

"Guys," Conner cut me off as he leaned forward to put his head in his hands, "I can't do this, not now. Can we just..."

I zipped to be by his side, but all I could do was sit next to him and put my hand on his back, "Whatever you need."

"No matter what, we're always here for you." Aaron added.

"Stole my co-worker's full Blockbuster punch card." Nate was quick to change the subject and offer the bare minimum of support, "For the one on 2nd and Cherry? You'd haveta go, though, I'm not allowed in there."

I squinted at him with curiosity, "One time I fucked a girl in the back room, and they still didn't ban me!"

Conner lifted his head to give us a disgusted look, "This isn't a competition!"

"I got banned from the bodega shop down my parents' old street when I was eight." Aaron chimed in.

"What the hell is happening?" Con rubbed his eyes.

November 7 2007

05:46

Aaron

"Aaron," my name was barely a whisper I heard when I rolled over in my sleep.

"Aaron," this time it was slightly louder, but it wasn't enough to wake me up until I felt a hand on my arm shake me awake.

"Huh?" I mumbled, assuming it was Parker checking to see if I was coherent enough to rat him out for pill popping.

"Aaron, I need your help." It didn't sound anything like Parker, and when I rolled over he was asleep next to me.

I had to lean over Parker to feel around for my glasses on the nightstand, when I slid them on is when I finally saw Conner's dad standing at the edge of the bed closest to the door.

"I need your help," He repeated.

I gave him a groggy nod but nestled further under the comforter.

"Aaron?"

"I'm listening..." I closed my eyes until I felt his hand on my shoulder.

"Okay, sorry." I carefully crawled over Parker and quietly closed the bedroom door behind me.

Scott popped up next to me.

"Hi,"

"Hi, I'm sorry to wake you up..."

There was a long pause.

"What did you need?"

He ran a hand along his blond quaffed hair, "I didn't kill my wife,"

"I know."

"I," He paused at my answer, "You do?"

"Of course, I do,"

He straightened out, "Well, I had a whole speech prepared..."

I tried not to laugh, "You're welcome to still give it if you want, but," I gestured to the bookshelf where Conner kept all of their books, "I'd like to think I know you and Celeste by now, if not from firsthand interaction or through Conner, then sheer observation."

He chuckled, "That's exactly what Este thought you would say."

"I've talked to Conner about it, I think right now he's just trying to process."

He nodded, stroking his beard while he thought, "That's what I'm worried about; I know my son, he's a man of science and a lot like his mother, he needs hard proof and facts. I'm worried he's accepting this as the truth because the "proof" has been misinterpreted."

"Mmhmm, I don't think he'll accept that I got the truth from you either." I thought about it for a second, but my sleepy brain wasn't keeping up, "You could write it down and I could slip it in one of the journals."

Scott hid his chuckle, "As good of a plan as that is, I don't remember what happened."

That wasn't the first time I heard that, but it was the first time I heard it from someone who's been dead as long as him.

"Really?"

He shook his head, "I think I was sick, that's what Este told me..."

"You were shot."

His eyes widened in surprise, "See, I feel like I'd remember that."

"Does Celeste remember?"

He thought about it for a second, "I'll be right back."

He blipped out of the apartment and in seconds he was back with his wife by his side.

"Good morning," she offered a warm, chirpy greeting, "It's morning, yes?"

"It is..." I whimpered as I shuffled over to the coffee machine, "Just give me a second."

They waited for me to make a cup of coffee, get comfy on the couch, and come to terms with the ridiculous terms of my life.

I took an extra long sip from my mug before I raised my hand, "Okay, I'm ready. Celeste, do you know how Scott died?"

"Of course,"

"Oh, perfect, it's not usually that easy."

"I shot him point blank through his heart."

"See, more along those lines," I sighed and dropped my head.

Scott gave her a rightfully offended look, "Why would you do that?"

She shrugged, "We were going to die anyway, it seemed like the most merciful way for everyone."

"What do you mean by that?"

"We were sick," she said matter-of-factly, like it was what everyone knew.

"Okay, I'm gonna need a little more clarification on this. What are you talking about?"

"We were running an experiment, Scott ended up getting bit on a hunt a week or two before we died, it wasn't bad but in a couple of days he was getting really sick. While I was caring for him," she sighed and shook her head, "I was heartbroken and wasn't taking the precautions I should've, and I ended up infected by his blood. After a long, long discussion, we decided we wanted to die a hunter's death, not a vampire's. At the time, we thought we were saving Conner the grief."

I tried to swallow the lump in my throat, "He didn't know you were sick?"

Celeste shook her head, "It all happened so fast, Scott didn't want his last memories of us to be us sick, I didn't either. We thought it would be better for him if it were sudden, than to see us turn into animals."

I could've cried, I still remember how scary it was when we learned my dad was sick even though it was caught early. I made a mental note to call him later.

"None of this was recorded?"

She shook her head again, "This all happened in a manner of days, and I didn't expect it all to get so twisted up."

Scott held her and the room was silent.

After a while I spoke again, "I'm sorry, what about the slit to your throat?"

"What? Nothing happened to my throat."

"Conner seemed to think your throat was slit,"

"No, I shot myself in the chest, as well." She played with a short strand of hair behind her ear, "It was harder to hit my own heart than I thought... But no, nothing happened to my throat."

There was another long silence, that was strange, but I really didn't know what to say.

My brain was sore, and my heart was broken.

I combed my fingers through the ends of my hair as I thought.

"I don't know how I'm supposed to tell Conner all of this." I mumbled to myself.

"I know it's a lot to ask," Scott's eyebrows knitted.

"No no, of course I'll tell him what really happened! I just, I don't know… I'm not sure what the best approach would be."

I mistook their silence for reservation and hadn't noticed Conner had shuffled out of the bedroom, but he also didn't notice I was seemingly talking to myself.

Conner looked like he hadn't slept, and since I could hear him tossing and turning all night it was a fair assumption.

His eyes were dull and even though he looked at me it seemed like he saw through me.

I offered a quiet "Good morning, "

He seemed surprised when I said, "Oh, hi, good morning..."

"I know you're not doing great, but is there anything I can do?"

He poured himself a cup of coffee and was quiet for a second while he got the milk, "No, I'm, I'll be okay. Really, I just need to clear my head." He chuckled but it was a lazy attempt to assure me, "You know days like today I kind of miss the abuse of Starbucks? At least it was something to do."

"I guess you didn't hear back from that assistant position?" I tried to keep the conversation going.

He shook his head and took a long sip from his mug, "Or the bartender, or the waiter, or the cashier. Funny story, I applied to stock while I was there, and they told me I was too short." He pressed his lips into a thin line.

I pat his shoulder, "Sorry."

"Do you wanna go job hunting today? I have the day off, if we go down to the college..."

"That's okay, I appreciate it. But I talked to my grandma last night, I think I'm gonna head down there for a few hours."

"Why wouldn't you stay the day?"

"It's a long drive, and my radio cut out last week..." He trailed off.

I could tell he didn't want me to worry so he didn't say it was because he didn't want to be alone.

"Like I said, I have the day off," I shrugged, "Can I come?"

He seemed relieved, "I'd really appreciate it, but I don't want to drag you around either."

"No, it's fine. I like your grandma, and besides, I like long car rides. I'm like a dog that way."

He broke into a small smile, "Thank you."

I gave him a hug.

Scott waited for Conner to go to the bathroom before he spoke again, "If you're going down to Byre you could talk to the police. Sheriff Shadi, he was a good friend. He'll have the information."

I nodded and wrote down the name on a scrap of paper.

"Thank you."

Celeste added something in French that I didn't understand, but assumed to mean "Thank you".

(＼(•̀w•́)／)

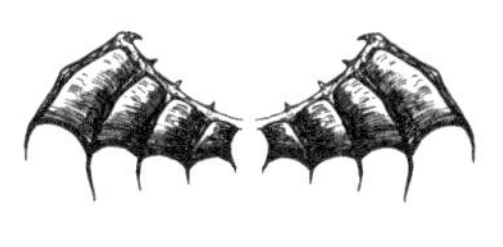

Parker

Conner woke us up to tell us he and Aaron were leaving, and once the door latched all Nate had to do was raise his eyebrow. I was on him like one of those overly horny monkeys at the zoo.

We made out, took a shower, and ended up in bed. It sounded weird, but we'd never been in a bed together.

While Nate was lying next to me, smoking his cigarette, I cuddled up under his arm and against his bare chest.

"What're you doing?" He responded in a judgy tone.

"I'm cold, you're warm."

He scoffed, "Whatever."

"Why you always gotta be like that?"

"Like what?"

I rolled my eyes, and air quoted the shit he'd say, "'Cuddling's chick shit', 'eye contact is too intimate', 'anal's fucking gay', *'I'm not gay'*."

"I'm not."

"Bisexual, whatever."

He scoffed, "I'm not confused, I know what I like."

"Cock and balls?"

"I'm, okay, serious, how many times I gotta tell ya? I'm just not into dudes."

I felt the defensiveness crash onto me like a wave, "Then why are you fucking around with me?"

"'Cause it's just..."

"Easy. Yeah, I know. I'm just easy." I mumbled and rolled off him.

He groaned, "What?"

"Nothing," I crossed my arms.

"Oh, my God. Stop being such a little bitch, what?"

I stayed quiet.

I don't know why my feelings were hurt.

Typically, I didn't care what anyone did to me as long as I liked it and, Hell, Nate was right, all this was about was a convenient fuck.

But suddenly it took me back to sobbing my eyes out in my car, driving a hundred and fifty miles per hour.

The brutal crunch of metal brought me back to the right reality.

"I don't know, okay? I just got flashed back to Travis for a sec..." I lowered my voice and hoped he didn't hear me, "When he dumped me, he wouldn't stop telling me how he was never really into guys that I was easier to fuck around with and just..."

"Jesus, Park..."

"It's not about you. We set up our ground rules weeks ago, that's on me. Sorry."

Nate's dark curls swayed when he shook his head, "The guy's a piece of shit, why're you still so hung up on him?"

When I didn't answer he pushed me until I was sitting up and he had enough room to get up.

As he pulled on his shirt he added onto the question.

"Look, something's been nagging at me, why am I the only one who knows about this jackass?"

I shrugged, "I dunno..."

His eyes searched me, between him and the creepy way Courtney's eyes could always cut through me, I had to wonder if people with blue eyes had X-Ray vision or something.

I crossed my arms back at him, "Why won't you tell anyone you're bisexual?"

"That's different." He snapped.

"How?"

"One's not true, and the other's you not being able to get over a shitbag that got you hooked on heroin!"

"He got me off of it!"

"He hung you out so bad you tried to kill yourself."

"You don't think you're bisexual?!" I tried to fight back, tears bit at my eyes, no matter how hard I tried to not cry, "Your tongue was just in my mouth! We're fucking for Christ's sake!"

"Parker," he wasn't annoyed anymore, he just said my name softly and it made me start sobbing.

"You're a fucking hypocrite!"

"He turned you out like a whore,"

"Go to hell!"

It was dead silent except for my sobs.

"Park,"

"Fuck you!"

He sighed and put his hands on my shoulders, "Alright, whatever, I'm sorry. Stop fucking crying."

He was annoyed when I couldn't just turn it off.

"C'mon," he pulled me into a hug.

I sobbed into his chest.

"You want me to call Con?"

He held me until I calmed down, not that I gave him a choice.

"I gotta go to work, but they're used to me blowin' 'em off. If you're not..."

I shook my head, "Nah, stop. I'm fine."

"... You sure?"

"Withdrawals," I wiped my face and searched for another excuse, "I'm gonna take a few pills and take a nap. Besides, I told Caitlin we could meet up later so... I'm fine."

After the hook up and my meltdown, it was incredible I remembered I needed to set an alibi.

"You're still seeing that girl from high school?"

I picked at the lint on the blanket, I didn't wanna look him in the face anymore, "On and off."

"Nice. You gonna need a ride?"

I forced my tears into a smirk, "Nah, I think she's got it handled."

"Attaboy."

Neither of us said anything else as Nate got ready for work and I rolled a blunt.

As he pulled on his shoes he looked me in the eye, his question couldn't have been further outta the blue, "You ever think 'bout getting sober?"

"Sure," I didn't think he was serious, so I opted to make a joke, "I hear you sober up once you die."

He seemed bummed at the answer but gave me a smirk back and just pat me on the shoulder, "See ya."

"No kiss goodbye?" I bat my eyes at him.

He flipped me off and walked out the door.

(＼(•̀w•́)／)

09:50

I didn't wanna think about Travis or Nate anymore, so I switched my brain back over to Donatello.

I decided really early on I was gonna take my sweet ass time getting over there.

I needed some of the time to get my questions together for the asshole, but I wanted to make a point by showing up late. I figured it'd piss him off, and maybe it'll give me some of my power back too.

I retouched my hair to the blinding florescent pink Nate had fucked me over with a few months back. Funny thing, as pissed as I was at the time, I couldn't believe I hadn't dyed it this color before.

It was starting to grow on me.

Anyway, after I washed it out. For the first time ever, I let my hair air dry completely before straightening it.

Made sure my guy-liner was up to a level Billie Joe Armstrong would've been proud of.

Hell, I even de-wrinkled my jeans.

Just before I left, I dug one of Aaron's empty Monster cans out of the trash and filled it with holy water.

This time I came armed.

I added two knives, one down my pants and in my shoe. Then Con's Smith in my waistband, all my questions written on the palm of my hand, and a picture of Scott and Celeste Stephens.

I was going to get real answers one way or another.

According to the clock on the bus's dashboard, I was an hour late.

I was shocked when I got down to the bar and nothing looked off. No cops, no crime scene tape. Just a sign that said "knock", which I immediately ignored and tried the handle anyway, it was locked.

A huge bouncer opened it and looked down at me, "There was a sign,"

"I don't take orders well, big boy."

He pulled me into the bar and shoved me against the wall.

"I like where this is going,"

He spread my legs with his foot.

"Big guy like you, I'm willing to bet you'll need them spread further than that. I can put my ankle behind my ears, y'know?"

I kept provoking, but he ignored me while he patted me down.

He tossed the gun onto one of the tables, then the knife down the front of my pants. He gave me a stern look.

"What? It's no fun if it doesn't hurt a little."

The guy was too thorough, he took my shoes and socks off.

Hell, it was more than Seattle PD ever did.

It was at least worth a shot.

He pulled me off the wall and handed me back my Monster can.

I took a swig to sell the lie, it stung my mouth and down my throat like a cheap tequila. I kinda liked it.

"He's clear." The guy, finally, spoke to what I thought was an empty room.

"Good, I'll let the boss know." A familiar little twink stepped out from behind the bar.

It took me a second to place him, but when I did my blood started to boil.

"Remember me?"

The child whore from the other night, he swapped his hot pants and mesh top for a button up collar and blazer.

His messy hair was neatly combed back, and now that the bar was lit, I could tell what I wrote off as "druggy signs". The sunken eyes, pale lips, bone skinny, were all because he was sick, too.

"You weren't real?" I hissed.

"None of us were," He gestured to a booth in the corner, the bartender whose heart I felt Donatello rip out raised his beer as a sort of salute.

I wanted to scream, but I swallowed it and just followed him to the back office.

Never mind the crime scene status I last saw it in, the room was spotless.

The kid made me sit in a velvet chair in front of the big oak desk.

"Anything I can get for you? I'm supposed to make you as comfortable as possible." Even with the offer, he still looked at me like I was a piece of chewed gum stuck to the bottom of his designer loafers.

I scoffed as I crossed my arms, "My sixty bucks would be great."

He smirked, pulling a wad of cash out of his inside jacket pocket.

He handed me a hundred-dollar bill, "I know you could use it."

I tried to lunge at him, but a strong slender hand shoved me back into my seat.

Donnie was standing next to me; he trailed his hand off my shoulder as he made his way to the desk chair.

He was so tall it only took him two steps to close the space.

He sat down and the kid stepped outta the room like he was ordered to, despite not a single word being spoken.

"You're late," Donatello finally spoke.

"Better late than never. Besides, I'm always late, thought you knew everything about me." I put my Monster can on the desk and kicked my feet up for effect.

But I was too short to actually reach the desk, and my ass slid out from under me. I grabbed the side of the desk before I hit the floor.

Donnie watched me with a raised eyebrow, he was amused but he didn't show it, "Are you alright?"

"Bite me." I shot to my feet and dusted the concrete off my black hoodie, "What do you want?"

He crossed his legs, lacing his fingers and he placed his hands on his knee, "I understand you have been doing some research."

"So what? You've been stalking me for years."

"I suppose fair is fair."

He didn't say another word, just leaned comfortably into his chair.

After a minute of silence he sighed, "I'm offering you the floor, Parker. I'm assuming you have more questions?"

I had millions, but the first one that came out surprised even me.

"What happened to Conner's parents?"

The only way I knew Donnie was surprised was by the way he raised his eyebrows, "I was expecting something more along the lines of "what was it like to live in a concentration camp?" but I suppose we all process differently." He chuckled at his own joke, "Now, what about Conner's parents?"

I grabbed the picture of Conner's parents at what I assumed was a work function since they were both wearing lab coats and holding champagne flutes.

Donatello took the picture and nodded once, "Dr. Celeste D. Stephens, PhD. And Dr. Scott R. Stephens, MD. What do you want to know?"

"You knew them?"

"Of course, they were the most leading in vampire research... And not only because they were the only two."

I gnawed on my cheek, trying to keep myself from jumping the gun.

"What happened to them?"

He shook his head, and gave me back the photo, "It was a real shame. Is it not incredible how so many lives can be completely demolished with two tiny bullets?"

I grit my teeth, "Is that how you killed them?"

Genuine shock took over his face, I didn't know he could feel real emotions, "Pardon me?"

"Why did you kill them?"

"What makes you so certain I did?"

"You knew them,"

"That's quite the leap; you should go into law enforcement."

"What happened to them, then?"

He shrugged, the movement looked so unnatural coming from him, "How am I to know? I only read about it in the papers."

"But you said you knew them."

"I did, I knew them before the incident, but I haven't the slightest idea what happened."

"Bullshit."

He waved his hand, "You're never going to believe what I say, so let's "cut the bullshit"?" He air quoted, "I met them, mm... The dates are fuzzy, but I met them early on in their research, so I offered them a deal..."

I cut him off, "Lemme guess, their souls for your cult?"

He didn't even acknowledge my statement, "The deal was they continued their research, they kept me up to date, and in turn I funded the whole thing. Anything they needed, test tubes, microscopes, DNA samples, tuition for their son's private school."

"You're so full of shit! Conner earned that scholarship."

"I'm sure he did, I give around scholarships pretty regularly, but the schools get to decide who receives them."

He was right, I didn't believe him.

I tried to take a shot, "Was your husband okay with you orphan-ing kids?"

He leaned forward on the desk with his chin on his hand, "I believe the word you're looking for is "orphanize", and once again, I did not kill the Stephenses."

"It's pronounced "Stephens-i"," I smart-assed with a glare.

I crossed my arms and kept probing, "So Charles didn't care that you're a killer? Or a war criminal?"

He couldn't have been less impressed.

"Oh, I get it. He was a serial killer, too, huh? That's probably where you learned it. What? You were trying to impress him but the only thing that got him off was torturing someone?"

Donnie looked me over, stopping when he met my eyes, "You could not be further from the mark."

"Huh?"

He didn't break eye contact when he sat up right, "I don't believe I know what you're referring to. Can you repeat that question?"

I opened my mouth to answer but totally blanked.

He smirked when he realized I forgot.

"How the fuck did you do that?!" I demanded.

"Excuse me?" His eyes changed to brown when he blinked, but I couldn't remember what color they were before.

"You just Men In Blacked me!

He shrugged, "Apologies, but I don't know what that is."

Pissed, appalled and violated, I only let it go 'cause I wanted more answers, and partly 'cause I know I have the memory of a goldfish cracker.

"What about Courtney?"

He shook his head, "Should I know something?"

"Courtney Hart, you asshole!" I slammed one of her bright orange missing person's flyers that'd been crumpled in my pocket for the last four months, "She's been missing since August! Every fucking person in Seattle knows her face at this point, where is she?!"

I was standing over him, screaming, but he didn't even blink.

"I am aware of the situation," He gently put his hand on my chest, and I was back in my chair, "But I have no more information."

"Then why did that girl say you could fix it?"

"Pardon?"

"Courtney's memorial at Belltown Cottage Park," I tried, "This tiny kid came up to me with the freaky red eye thing and told me that you could fix it!"

"I'm afraid you misunderstood," his expression softened like he really meant it, "I meant I could fix everything else, but I'm sorry, I cannot bring back your friend."

"What happened to her?!" I roared from my chest.

"I apologize, I don't know."

When he didn't give me more of an answer, I grabbed the crystal decanter off the desk and whipped it at the wall as hard as I could, sending shards all over the office.

"Parker, please," He calmly stood up, his voice was so even, if I didn't know him, I would've mistaken it for concern.

He took a few steps towards me with his hands up like he was approaching a rabid dog, he put his hands on my shoulders and quickly spun me around, he held me close to his chest before I could keep lashing out.

"I'm aware my offices are extremely satisfying for you to destroy, but I need you to stop. A moment is all I'm asking for; we need to talk."

"About what?" My rage caused tears to flood my eyes, and that only pissed me off more, "About why're you doing all this?! Tell me! Tell me why you drug me down here! Tell me why you faked the vision! For the fuck's sake tell me what you want from me!"

He carefully guided me back to my chair, "This is going to sound callus, but it was a test..."

"For what? That you're an asshole?! Well, guess what! It's conclusive!"

He shook his head, trying to hide his chuckle as he sat on the desk in front of me, "You remind me so much of myself."

I rolled my eyes 'cause I doubted I could roll his without some kind of backlash

"I'm being quite serious. That black and white thinking, right and wrong... I was the same way. When I was a child, I thought I was going to do better, I thought I could change the world. Then when I was fifteen Nazis stormed my village," he tilted his head pointedly, "Eighteen when they stripped me of my humanity. You're going through the same metamorphosis, except you do it to yourself. You sabotage the part of you that wants better, and you feed the part of you that craves eradication. I can see it in you every day; it's the warmth in your chest when you cut yourself just right, the pride you take when you can tear someone down with just a few words, the titillation of feeling a vampire dissolve to dust under your own hand." He narrowed his eyes like he was zeroing in on something, "That's what it's really all about, is it not?" He laughed, leaning back on his desk, "That is exactly what it is. You pretend you don't like it, but the killing, it gives you a rush, right? Almost like an orgasm?"

"What the fuck?!" I threw back at him, "You're sick."

"You don't have to admit it to me because you are just like me." He bent to be in my face, "A perfect, little, killing machine."

I knew the only thing I could control right now was me, so I snorted.

"Bitch, I've never been perfect at shit!" I laughed, "And I'll never be anything like you."

He let something slip, suddenly the look in his eyes was different, the way he was standing shifted. It was like he finally relaxed.

"I was in a concentration camp. Eighteen months. They did everything to me, electrocution, waterboarding. They'd slice us open with a scalpel, rub it with dirt, let it fester, let it rot, then they'd lob off the limb without anesthetic. They'd let you get better, just so they could do it again. They beat me until the brink of death, I saw a light, I saw my mother, she told me I could go with her, that I could be free. When I followed her, I felt a lightning bolt in my chest, and when I opened my eyes to look for my mother a Nazi was standing over me with a scalpel. Does that sound familiar?"

In the blink of an eye, I was on the concrete floor of my high school's gym locker room.

Four players from the football team stood over me, a hail of fists and shoes beating down on me while I tried desperately to protect my head, but eventually it was too much, I passed out. And when I did, I was on my knees in front of Donnie's desk.

"Our stories aren't too different, you know? Except you were saved by someone who wanted better for you, and I was saved by a sadist that just wanted to watch me die and injected me with one too many illnesses. But that hope you hold onto?" He laughed, "That is exactly what will lead you down my path. Hope will only get you killed, Parker." The accent I wasn't even sure he had thickened, "I hoped I would get out of that camp in one piece, I hoped I would see my family again, I hoped I could live a normal life. Do you know what that hope brought me? It brought me pain and anguish each time it was ripped out of my dirty, bloody and broken hands! Every! Time! It just pushed me closer to death. It has taken decades for it to be beaten into me, there is no line between salvation and destruction. There is no black and white, no good or evil. There is only survival."

There was a long run of silence.

Thinking I wasn't getting the point, he added to it,

I dug my fingernails into the palm of my hand.

He was right.

Motherfucker, he was so right.

"My only bit of advice for you," He loosened his tie and tilted his head back to reveal a scar the size of a nickel under his chin.

He made a gun with his first finger and thumb, pressing it into the scar, "Make your peace with it or shoot it through your heart instead, because sooner or later you will have to make a decision."

"You're full of shit, I don't believe a word you say."

"You don't have to believe anything I say, you don't have to believe in anything I do. After all, who is Jesus Christ to an atheist." he pulled a cigarette seemingly outta thin air, and I jumped when he struck the match to light it, "But can you not see it? I am not Donatello Sotos, I am not even Jamais Lucian. I am you and you are me. Everything always comes full circle, and one day we will see who's correct," He blew out a mouthful of smoke and looked me dead in my eyes as he took another long drag, "And for all that it's worth, I hope to God I am wrong."

11:00

Aaron

We were more than halfway to Byre, and Conner still hadn't said a word about his parents, but not from lack of speaking. He spent a good twenty minutes venting about Parker's "idiosyncrasies", which I think we all need to do from time to time.

But he was surprisingly cheerful right now, I hoped it was genuine, but I was worried it was just a front.

Flipping through my tape collection, Conner held up one of them, "Britney Spears? You know you can't let Parker in your car, he practically moves in."

I chuckled, "That's mine, actually."

He raised an eyebrow, "Sorry, amongst Slipknot and Against Me! It looked out of place."

"It is, but it doesn't make her any less of a cultural icon... Or tabloid phenomenon, damn, I really do hope she's okay."

Conner shrugged before putting it back in the box, "She'll be fine, she did nothing. I've seen Parker have bigger meltdowns in Fred Meyer's ice cream aisle."

I snickered.

Pulling off the exit ramp, a few miles ahead a small green rectangle on the side of the road declared "Welcome to Byre Washington! Population 4,587."

The bottom half of the sign was covered in indiscernible graffiti that Conner scoffed at.

"Parker's work," he clarified, "To this day I still have no idea what that's supposed to be."

"Jeez, they still haven't fixed it?"

"Of course not, nothing ever changes here." Conner pointed out an old building, it looked like a structure from biblical times, especially since it was held together completely by hope.

"That building's been abandoned since I was a little kid, I ended up clearing a small nest out of it right before I graduated."

"By yourself?"

"It was only maybe six or seven, in hindsight it was idiotic, but..." he shrugged.

"Hey, I'm not looking to analyze my teenage actions either."

The town was a lot more spread out than Conner and Parker lead on, the space between the buildings was shocking to me as a city kid.

Old colonial-looking houses turned into small businesses or tiny offices made up almost all of the town. The road wound down the hillside overlooking the ocean, thanks to the heavy fog rolling off the shore and the lack of bustle in the middle of the day reminded me of something out of an Edgar Allan Poe story.

Conner nodded to a house turned bakery we drove by, "Every Sunday for the past two decades, my grandma has bought macaroons from there. I bet you I could walk in there right now and the husband and wife that own it would be bickering."

The next street over Conner gestured for me to stop. The house he picked out was a real home this time.

It was practically a mini mansion perched atop the hill.

"The Winston's," he pointed out one of the huge picture windows, a large dining table was on the other side. A sewing machine sat on top, "Mrs. Winston must be home. Based on the time of year, I'm guessing she's starting her Christmas Eve pajamas."

I raised an eyebrow, "How do you know that?"

"Nothing changes here," he repeated, "It's weirdly comforting, sometimes I miss the repetition of it all."

"Have you ever thought of moving back?"

"No." He was fast to answer, and his energy shifted.

I wasn't sure what happened.

We passed a few stop signs until he spoke, "I guess that's also the worst thing about it here, everyone knows me. Everyone knew my parents," he shifted his head, "I'm always going to be the kid whose parents killed themselves."

"I'm so sorry."

He only shrugged.

I felt like an asshole, even more so when I noticed the cemetery coming up on the left side.

While I contemplated speeding through, Conner's voice made me jump.

"Can you pull over here?"

My heart ached for him, "Are you sure?"

He stared out the window, scanning the headstones, "I wanna see them..."

I pulled through the gate and parked.

"Is it okay if I come with you?"

Conner seemed surprised when I asked, "Of course."

I followed him down the sidewalk.

I've never liked cemeteries, normal creep factor aside, with the things I could see, it was like walking into a room with a capacity of 300 with 500 people in it, all of them begging for impossible favors.

Typically, the amount of energy felt suffocating, and I wanted to leave the minute I was within a thousand yards, but today everything was quiet.

There were still a lot of ghosts around, but instead of trying to get my attention or popping up in my face, they stayed back and watched us move through from a distance.

I wasn't sure what was happening until I realized Scott was walking by Conner's side, Celeste trailed behind with me. Every now and then she would nod at someone, I assumed as a thank you for their respect.

The cemetery itself was actually beautiful. The lot of land was big, but there weren't millions of headstones, only a few scattered around.

Two gigantic oak trees shaded the far side of the cemetery from the road just across the fence, while wildflowers bordered around closely to the same fence.

It was a lovely touch, but I was sad to think of how depressingly poetic it would be in a few weeks when the temperature dipped, and all the flowers died.

All of the graves were clean, and a majority of them were decorated with flowers, photos of loved ones, notes, stuffed animals... I noticed a common theme of yellow flowers.

Conner stopped abruptly at a double marbled headstone with "Stephens" elegantly carved into it, and underneath were their names, birth and death dates, as well as their wedding date which I thought was cute.

"C'est cela l'amour, tout donner, tout sacrifier sans espoir de retour." Was carved into the base.

Celeste's was on the right, her side had quite a few candles, and a bouquet of the same yellow flowers.

Scott's on the left, however, had nothing.

Conner sighed, he took the chrysanthemums off his mother's grave and placed them on another abandoned looking grave nearby.

“Toussaint,” He knelt and swept the petals away, "It's kinda like the French Catholic version of Dia De Los Muertos… Byre was settled by the French who didn't want to go to Canada, so it's a big deal here.”

“But your parents were atheists.” I nodded.

He chuckled to himself, "And Mom detested chrysanthemums.”

"In all fairness, I was allergic." Celeste defended with a laugh.

He split the candles between the graves.

I knelt with him and offered the lighter I kept in my pocket as something to fidget with.

"Thank you," he lit the candles and gave it back, then he picked up two little ceramic doves that sat on both of their graves.

The only thing on Scott's.

Conner dusted them and placed them back.

“My grandma must've left these.”

“Is she big on tchotchkes?”

“No, I just mean… My grandma and I are the only people who leave him anything. The rest of the town, they'll leave stuff for my mom, pay their respects. Even at their funerals, everyone was there for my mom and just whispered about Dad…” He sighed, staring at the clouds above us. I could tell he was trying to avoid crying.

I don't think I've ever seen him cry...

“I never understood why everyone thought he was such a monster, I mean, what the hell did they know? He was my dad, and for Christ's sake, he was my hero. You know how when you're a little kid you think your parents are invincible, they can do anything, and they know everything?" His voice broke so he paused to clear his throat, "It sounds stupid, but I never lost that. I've never, ever thought of them in any way other than as these super humans. Then I read that letter, and... What if I was wrong? What if I missed something like that? What if for the past decade, I've been betraying my mom?"

He dipped his head, resting against the stone.

I scooted over so I could pull him into a hug, “It's okay.”

Celeste squatted down to our level, she put her hand against the side of his tear streamed face, "There isn't a single way on this earth that you could ever betray me, ma puce."

Scott held his shoulder, "There's no salvation in guilt. Life is already the hardest thing you can face, don't make it harder on yourself."

I had started crying with Conner, I wanted to take a page out of Parker's book and just smoother him until he felt better.

Conner only allowed himself a few minutes to pull himself together. He stood up and dried his face with his hands, he seemed annoyed, but I wasn't sure why.

He placed a silver loop, just like his necklace, on each of their headstones.

Patting the marble, he sniffled, "God, I'm way too old to be so naïve,"

"Or too young to be so cynical." I offered.

Conner was quiet for a minute before he rubbed his hands together and placed them in his pockets, "We can go, it's getting really cold."

I had to assume that was because Celeste had looped her arm around his and placed a kiss on his cheek.

It was gut-wrenching to watch his parents escort him out of the graveyard.

I blasted the heater as high as my car would allow.

"Thank you,"

I shrugged as I pulled out of the empty parking lot, "It'll take a minute for the engine to warm up, but..."

He patted my shoulder in that "bless your heart" sort of way, "I meant coming with me, keeping me grounded," He shrugged, "Being my friend, I don't know. I just, I know we all joke around a lot, but I really hope you know you're my best friend."

I shook my head, "You don't have to worry about that, we all do what we can for each other, we're like brothers that way."

He smiled at me, but he looked like he wanted to cry again.

Celeste let me in on why, "Ever since he could talk, he's always made it very clear he wanted a little brother."

Conner gave me a really weird, concerned look when I started bawling my eyes out.

"Are you okay?"

"No! I love you and now I'm ruining a perfectly nice bonding moment!"

He couldn't hide his chuckle, "What are you talking about?"

In the rearview mirror, Scott gave me a corny, enthusiastic double thumbs up that reminded me so much of his son.

I sighed, and used the road as an excuse to not look at Conner as I told him, "I know this is kind of invasive, and I don't want you to think I was snooping in any way, but I knew it was bothering you and I just..."

"Aaron," He saved us both from my rambling, "What's going on?"

I forced myself to blurt out the words, "I called the Sheriff of Byre about your parents' case."

It was quiet, and I was afraid to look over at him.

When I finally got the courage, I was surprised that he wasn't mad, just confused.

"Okay, and?"

"... Well, he sent me a copy of their autopsy reports," I bluffed and tightened my grip on the wheel.

I was already awful at lying but with the guys it was so much worse.

Since he didn't call me out, I continued, "Scott had what the ME thought looked like maybe a healed over coyote bite on his left wrist, and the "slash" to Celeste's neck wasn't actually a wound, it was where blood had pooled from her nose and eyes..."

"They were infected?" Conner asked so softly that I wasn't sure if it was a question.

"That was my inclination."

There wasn't another word spoken until I pulled up to the sidewalk of his grandmother's house.

He ran his thumb across the pendant at his neck as he thought, "I remember that morning, when they left for their "hunt". They woke me up before they left, they always did. My mom gave me a hug and told me she loved me, so did my dad, nothing was off. The only thing different was that my dad gave me this," He held the pendant still, then thought about it a minute more, "Dad sat on my bed for a while, usually he and mom would want to get on the road pretty quick, but I don't know, my dad seemed groggy. I mean it was four in the morning, I just..." Something must have occurred to him, "My dad had the flu the week before, I remember that! My mom wouldn't let me around him; she was worried I'd catch it and miss school."

He pulled the car door open without even undoing his seatbelt, "I gotta talk to my grandma."

(＼(•̀ᴡ•́)／)

15:00

PARKER

I'd made it back to the apartment on my own.

Donnie didn't really seem to care if I stuck around or not so I just left and had been back for a while.

I thought I was processing everything fine, until I grabbed this stupid ass journal and started writing this bullshit.

That's when everything crashed in on me.

I didn't like the way it was sitting, so I did what I usually do and got high.

Except for this time, it only made it worse.

I couldn't tell you what happened, what the panic attack was even about, all I knew was I couldn't breathe. It didn't matter how many times I told myself I didn't need to breathe. "You're a monster, you don't need air to survive!!!" I yelled.

I fished my phone out of my pocket, I had no fucking clue who I was going to call. I didn't wanna bother Conner. One, 'cause he had enough going on, and two, I knew he was going to jump my shit for walking into the lion's den alone.

That was also why I couldn't call Nate or Aaron.

My mom would try and have me committed again, and my sister would probably just assume I was tripping and hang up on me.

By the time I had thought all this out I had already dialed without noticing.

My breath hitched while I waited to see who answered.

"Hello?" The feminine voice was familiar, but when I couldn't place it as my sisters' or my mom's, my brain took over and filled in the blank itself.

My chest fell, "Courtney?"

"I'm sorry?"

"Courtney?!" This time I screamed into the phone.

"Honey," her voice softened, "It's Drew. Are you okay?"

Any feeling I had left in my limbs drained away.

"Parker?" She said my name when I didn't answer, "Parker, are you okay?"

I ran my fingers through my hair, I picked at strands in an attempt to keep myself from crying, "I don't know."

"Are you with Conner?"

"Uh uh,"

"Are you with anyone?"

"No,"

"Where are you?"

"I, uh, I'm at home."

"Stay there. I'm coming to get you, okay?"

Half an hour later I was sitting on Mrs. Hart's couch, Drew practically swaddled me in a nice fluffy blanket and gave me a cold glass of Sunny-D and two oreos.

I felt like a toddler and had to wonder if this is what loving mothers did.

"What happened? What's going on?" She sat next to me and carefully rubbed my shoulder.

I gulped down the glass.

I didn't think I said a word since she picked me up, but now I wanted to talk about everything.

"In the summer of 2001 my parents gave me money to go to school in Seattle that I immediately blew partying, which ironically is both what I was on and what I had to do to keep doing it."

She blinked at me once trying to process what I was saying, "Are you okay?"

I laughed hysterically at my own before just stopping without warning, "I'm on a lotta coke right now."

"Okay? Is there anything I can do for that?"

"Mm, I can tell you what you shouldn't do. You shouldn't go to the shit side of Northgate to spray paint your shitty art in the alley. You also shouldn't go into one of the shitty bars to get a shitty beer, and let the guitarist of the shittiest band you ever heard pull you up on stage and then fuck you in his shitty van."

I hadn't even noticed I was crying until Drew was nice enough to wipe the tears dripping down my face, "I loved him so much."

"Do you want to tell me what happened?"

Poor thing had no idea the flood gate she just opened.

"He was great! He was so sweet, and funny, and tall, and hot, and God, super kinky. He was 23 when I was 18 so he'd buy me liquor and drugs and shit, I mean what more could a guy ask for?"

"Sounds like a great guy."

I couldn't tell if she was being sarcastic or not, but I still felt defensive.

"He was! Whenever they'd play a show, he'd skim forty bucks and buy me all kinds of art supplies, when they'd go sell CDs he'd sell my art. One time, he almost killed this guy for tryna pull some shit while I was passed out..." I clutched one of the couch pillows to my chest and melted into Drew, "He knew I was a whore, and he didn't care, Hell he protected me! He took care of me; he loved me like nobody else ever has!"

"Then what happened?"

"I don't know! He just turned on me..." I trailed off.

My face must've told the whole story.

"He was hitting you?"

"I mean, we both did. We fought a lot, beat the shit out of each other, then we'd fuck and it'd all be good again. Y'know, I think it got worse when we got off heroin? His friend got sick from the needles," I shrugged, "Then he didn't wanna do it anymore. He'd get real mean when he was sobering up, though... He gave me a black eye once for dropping a bong. I was always doing something. Fuck, I can't do shit right and he'd always tell me I was unlovable 'cause of it. I mean, he was right."

Drew slammed her arm into my shoulder, then felt bad when it hurt and hugged me, "Stop it. None of that's true!"

"But it is, not even my family cares about me."

"They're stupid, then. They don't know what they're missing."

I scoffed, "You sound like your sister."

"My sister loved you," she squeezed my shoulders, "And I do, too. So do the boys."

I buried my head in her shoulder, "If just one person told me that three years ago, I probably wouldn't know you. I wouldn't have died in an alley and got vampire gang banged back to life and into this bullshit. Fuck!" I shoved myself off the couch, "All of this shit, every single fucking thing could've been avoided if I didn't hate my own fucking guts!"

"Hey, none of that! If you hate it so fucking much than change it!" I wasn't expecting her to yell at me like that, "All of this is absolutely awful and I'm so, so sorry you're going through it. But you have to do something about it, you can't always be a victim and at some point, you have to be a fighter."

I snorted, "That's the same thing Courtney yelled at me when I begged her to put a silver bullet in my heart."

"You're not the only one she's screamed it at. Let me tell you a secret," she made me sit back down with her, "Everyone hates themselves, but it doesn't matter! What matters is how much you love your family!"

I scoffed, "My family's been done with me since I got kicked out of boarding school, imagine what they'd do when they found out I've been taking dicks like ibuprofen."

"That's not what I mean. I mean, Conner and Aaron and Nate and Courtney, you love them, right? You'd do anything for them?"

I nodded.

"Then forget everything else, change that voice that tells you you're not good enough to sound like them telling you how much they love you."

I could tell what I said next wasn't the correct response.

"If something happened to me, you'd take care of Conner, right? Aaron and Nate, too?"

Her expression was the exact one I was dreading, the shock, concern, anger, and panic, "Parker..."

I shook my head, "I don't need the speech, just... Yes, or no?"

"Of course, I would," she moved her arm that was resting on my shoulder so she could grab my face in her hand and forced me to meet her eyes, "But nothing's going to happen to you, right?" She demanded.

I nodded my head slightly. Knowing that was the only acceptable response.

I had one more question I needed to ask.

"... Will you not tell Conner about this?"

She went to talk but I stopped her to clarify, "I'm going to, I just... I need to do it in my own time."

She nodded, "I get that, but if he asks, I'm not going to lie to him."

"Thanks."

She used a tissue to wipe off the eyeliner running down my face, "There's this movie playing, it's about Rembrandt, I think. You like art, do you wanna go see that?"

I made a face, "Nah, but can we go see that little rat chef?"

"Oh, honey, I don't know if anyone's still playing that movie."

"... What movie?"

She went to ask, but the front door unlocked.

Her mom stepped in; she looked surprised to see me.

"Hi, Parker. What's going on?"

"Nate and I are fucking." I blurted.

Drew shook her head and stood up, "I'm going to make some tea."

Mrs. Hart stared at me, confused, for a really long time.

I felt like I needed to fill the silence.

"Do you have a cigarette?"

November 8 2007

09:45

Conner

My grandma insisted on having us stay overnight since snow was starting to dust the coast.

She was so excited to see me, I felt really guilty until she smacked me on the hand with a spoon and told me to cut it out while we were making breakfast.

I had asked her last night about Dad.

She said she remembered my mom saying he had the flu, and that she seemed dead on her feet trying to take care of him.

As strange as it sounded, I could practically feel the relief pump through my heart.

God, it wasn't anything I'd wish on my worst enemy but knowing that it wasn't a choice they made to leave me, but that they still got to go out on their terms, fighting like hunters.

It was a weird surge of pride, but I still felt like a bad son for doubting my dad.

Aaron was right, though, they would've only cared that I knew the truth.

I just wish they would've told me.

I spent most of the drive back to Seattle with my nose in my notebook. Aaron probably thought I was a freak for not saying absolutely anything about, well, anything.

I leaned forward to turn down the radio until I heard the song playing.

Castles Made Of Sand by The Jimi Hendrix Experience.

"Are you okay?" Aaron asked when I froze.

"Yeah," I shook my head, "Sorry, just, my mom always played this song..."

"Oh, really?" He glanced at me through the side of his glasses, so he didn't have to look away from the road.

"She loved Jimi Hendrix," I smiled at the memory that washed over me, "She always joked that if she hadn't met my dad when she did, she was going to run off and be one of Jimi's groupies and that they were going to fall madly in love." I rolled my eyes.

Aaron chuckled, "What would your dad say?"

"Oh, all he'd have to do was bring up Stevie Nicks. Then the wheels to a ridiculous joke argument were off. Which would only end when my dad would agree he'd also leave my mom to be with Jimi, and my mom subsequently would say she'd leave Dad for Stevie." I laughed.

Aaron clicked on the blinker to merge onto the highway, "You know, you don't really talk about them a lot? Outside of their work, I mean. What were they like?"

"My dad was a lot of fun, you and him would've been best friends. He was kinda quiet, but once you were alone with him, he'd get goofy, he always had a joke or something smart to say... My mom would pretend to be the serious one, but she was just as silly as he was. You wouldn't guess it by their work, but they really just couldn't take anything seriously. Even when they'd fight about something serious it'd dissolve into nonsense and giggles. They were ridiculously happy," I shook my head, "I know that sounds extremely rose-tinted glasses of me, but it's true. They were just filled with so much love, even with Parker, they only got to know him for a few years, but they treated him the same way they treated me. I never really understood why they didn't have another kid, but they seemed happy just putting that love into me and everything around them..."

"That's my mom, last time I was in Portland I told her she needed to have another kid."

"What did she say?"

"That she thought it would be too hard to have kids twenty-two years apart."

I chuckled, "Fair enough."

We used the rest of the drive to swap our childhood war stories.

I hadn't realized that I'd spent so long trying to run from the pain of losing my parents that I never had time to just think of them. To think of the way things were.

I miss them so much.

And I owed Aaron a lot for that.

(＼(•̀w•́)／)

12:00

We didn't hit the city's limits until a little before noon, and when we did I made a point to stop and get something to eat since Aaron did all the driving, and pretty much everything else.

When we walked into the apartment I hesitated.

It was a coin toss on what we'd walk in on after Nate and Parker had been left alone for 24 hours.

I anticipated some kind of tequila fueled raccoon fight club.

Nate was passed out on the couch with a bong balancing on his chest, meanwhile Parker was stripped down to his boxers snorting a line of coke off our kitchen counter.

"Are you kidding me?!"

"Oh, hey!" Parker tipped his head back, "You're back! Welcome back!"

"Are you serious?!"

Aaron shrugged as he slung his backpack over his shoulder on his way to the bedroom, "Hey, I was expecting the ramen incident of '05, part two."

"The ramen incident of '05 was part two," I recalled as I grabbed the dust buster and vacuumed our counter.

"Woah! Hey!" Parker whimpered.

"Don't! And for Christ's sake, go take a shower. You smell like an ashtray someone mistook for a shot glass and tried to clean with Axe body spray and Old Spice." I snatched the bong off Nate's chest, waking him up, "And what'd I say about smoking in the apartment?"

"What?" Parker whined, "I didn't fall asleep with a lit joint this time! God, you never appreciate the little things."

Nate sat up and patted around the couch, he opted to blatantly ignore me and lit a cigarette right in front of me.

My brain could have exploded.

"I thought you were quitting," I crossed my arms.

"I am. Down to one in the morning, one at night."

"It's noon."

He squinted at the time on the VHS player before he shrugged.

"Guess who I talked to," Parker jabbered.

Nate pointed his cigarette at him when he had his guess ready, "Pete Wentz, he's finally suing you for crimes against emos everywhere."

"Nuh uh! Fuck him! I was emo first!"

"You're eating up too much of LA's coke supply and Steven Tyler's pissed." Nate kept going, "Elton John..."

"Stop guessing!" Parker hissed.

"Parker!" I had to clap at the syllables in his name to get his attention.

"What!"

"Who did you talk to?"

"Oh, Donnie," Parker snapped his fingers until Nate let him have a puff off his cigarette, "I need more blood."

It was hard to follow the train of thought when it had no tracks.

"Is there more to that?"

"I wanna do another blood transfusion!" He defended like it was perfectly discernible the first time, "The blood's making me more human, right? I need more *human*."

"The last time almost killed you." I don't know why I tried to reason with him, I could barely get through to him while he was sober.

"Then let it! If those are the options, let it kill me."

I shook my head, "Can we talk about this later when you're..."

"What, sane?!"

"I was going to say sober, but six of one..."

He ran his hands through his hair, "Argh! I can't do this!"

He stomped off into the bedroom, after a few minutes I heard the window slam and assumed he was going to pout up on the roof.

It was a completely normal response.

"Any idea what that was about?" I asked Nate.

Nate shrugged, "He's been popping pills and drinking since you left, I dunno what got up his ass."

"He said he talked to Donatello?"

Nate shook his head, "Didn't say anything to me."

I sighed.

He'd sober up eventually and maybe then I could decipher what was going on with him.

Until then I narrowed my sights on Nate, who had a bunch of small bruises down his chest.

"What happened to you?"

He shrugged again.

I went and opened our only other window and hoped the smell of cigarettes and weed would dissipate before I got sick, and Nate and Parker called me a narc.

Meanwhile, I let my grandma know we made it back safe and checked in on Drew. Based on her urgency to call, I guessed she was getting cabin fever from "Mom Jail" by now.

"Hi," I answered, stepping out into the hallway before Nate could act up.

"Hi, how was Byre?"

"Cold, how's "Mom Jail"?"

"Just lovely," She sarcastically sweetened up her voice, "Hoping to get paroled any day now. Just so you know, these calls are known to be subject to monitoring."

"Unacceptable, I'll contact an attorney right away."

"Thanks," She giggled, "Is Parker doing any better today?"

"Um, well, he's currently on the roof half-naked so, I'd say the same as ever. Why do you ask?"

"We were hanging out for a while last night; I got the feeling he was having a hard time with something..."

"Mm, did he say what?"

"Oh, he said a lot. I managed to talk him down and he seemed a lot better when he left, but he wouldn't say what triggered it and he didn't wanna answer his phone when I called this morning."

"To be fair, he doesn't usually wake up until three o'clock." Something crossed my brain, "Hey, he was talking about doing another blood transfusion, I was curious, does your school give you access to the lab machines?"

"Mmhmm, just last week we had a midterm on biological analysis."

"Great, I'd like to look at a few more things before we almost kill him again."

"You know, I would really prefer you do that, too. And yeah, I could definitely sneak you in, but I do have to warn you, they do have a very strict beautiful assistant policy," She flirted.

"Well, that's perfect. Not to brag, but in high school I was voted "Class of '01's Prettiest Assistant". It was a tough competition, you should've seen the swimsuit category."

She laughed, "I'll check with my professor, but you better bring that swimsuit just in case."

"Yes ma'am."

(＼(•̀ω•́)／)

NATE

I was only half listening to whatever nerdy shit Conner and Aaron were talking about, mostly 'cause I was laughing at Parker's dumbass trying to plead with me through text message.

Parker: help

↳ - Nah

P: The door locked

P: :(

P: STOP IGNORING ME

↳ Come back the way you went

P: Can't

P: Scary cat's back

P: I'm cold

P: Pls I'm burning

↳ That's what you get

P: >:(

"Have you heard a word I said?" Conner started lecturing, "Why are you laughing?"

"Park's dumbass is locked out on the roof again."

Con sighed, "Well, can you go get him? This would all be a lot more helpful with him here."

I raised an eyebrow, "You think he's gonna help something?"

"I heard it as soon as I said," He rolled his eyes, "I just want to know what's going on with Donatello, and if he wants to take a hunt."

I sighed and took my damn time.

I stood in front of the roof door when I unlocked it so his little punk ass couldn't blow past me.

"Sweet baby Jesus," He ran across the roof, and tried to climb under my sweatshirt.

I tried to push him off, but he moved around like a spider and just clung to me. I had to peel him off like a squirrel outta a car grill.

I stopped him before he could open our door, "We gotta talk."

"You should've come up sooner, I had to burn our last blunt to stay warm." He joked.

"I'm serious,"

He smirked, biting his bottom lip, "Uh huh, I'm listening."

He stretched up to try to kiss me and was really confused when I put my hand on his chest to stop him, "What?"

"I talked to Drew."

That didn't connect the dots for him, he just pointed at the door, "Okay, is she over?"

"She called me last night, dumbass."

He kept playing dumb, "Why would she call you?"

"'Cause you were trippin' balls, talking 'bout killing yourself and I was the only one in town."

He crossed his arms and shrugged, "So what? I do that like once a week."

"Was it about Travis?"

He wouldn't look at me and I knew I was in the right vein.

"This is sick, I'm not doing this shit anymore."

He shook his head, "What are you talking about?"

"You don't see what you're doing, jackass?" I scoffed, "You're so fuckin' quick to point out I'm hiding shit from myself, look in the fuckin' mirror."

He looked shocked and a little hurt and that's when I realized this was a bigger deal than I thought it was.

"You put all this shit on me like I'm the one that did it."

He shifted defensively, "What are you saying?"

"That I ain't gonna let you turn me into Travis."

"You're a son of a bitch."

"Nah, I'm a hypocrite, remember?"

He shoved past me, slamming the door before I could step in.

"Hey," Conner stopped him before he went to the room to throw his tantrum, "Did Nate fill you in?"

"Oh, you wouldn't believe what he's filled in." He shot a condescending glare over his shoulder at me.

November 11 2007

07:45

PARKER

"Hey," Someone shook me awake.

When I opened my eyes, Caitlin was standing beside me, fixing her earrings, "Get up, I gotta go to work."

I was in her fancy ass bedroom, with no memory of how I even ended up on this side of town.

She slipped on her heels, "And based on the fact that I still can't find my favorite solitaire diamond necklace, I'm not letting you stay here alone again." She started to make the bed around me, "Get up."

My head was pounding, "You have to work on a Saturday?"

"It's Monday," She fixed the button on her blouse.

"What happened to Saturday?"

"You drank, smoked, and snorted it." She straightened out and crossed her arms, "You're a real class act, you know that?"

I folded my arms under my head, "I try."

She smacked my chest.

"Ow! You're serious?"

"Yes, asshole! You come here all "my best friend is missing, feel sorry for me", and you can't even remember we spent the weekend together?!"

"No, I... Obviously," I rubbed my eyes, "It's just really early..."

"Where did we have dinner last night?"

I looked her over for any guess, "Uh, somewhere over in Fremont."

She smacked at me a few more times, "We haven't left this bedroom all weekend, you dickhead!"

"Oh, I fucked up." I groaned.

Another smack.

"Okay, okay! I'm sorry! Let me make it up to you," I moved the blanket next to me, so she'd lay back down, "Jog my memory, baby."

She leaned down into me like she was gonna kiss me, but was just reaching over to fix the blanket, "Not a chance."

"Oh, come on," I got up, grabbed her hands and pulled her over so I could put a mark on her neck and kissed up to her jaw, "Anything you want, babe, I'm your bitch."

"Mm," She leaned into me, "Anything?"

"God, yeah."

"Perfect," She grabbed me by the jaw, leaving me with a hot as fuck kiss before she pushed me off, "Get the hell out of here."

"What?" I whined.

"I told you, I gotta go."

"You're a real tease."

"And you're easy."

I scoffed, "Like you're the first to tell me that."

She tossed me my shoes while I wiggled into my jeans, "If you get out now, we can talk about drinks and maybe just a taste of what you missed."

"Mm, yes, mistress." I purred.

She threw my hoodie over my head, "Out."

(＼(•̀w•́)／)

"Where the hell have you been?!" Conner was already yelling before I even had that door open.

"I honestly couldn't tell you."

"Well, thanks for gracing us with your presence." He crossed his arms.

I shrugged it off, "What's the problem?"

He looked about ready to jump me, "Where do you want to start? Never mind the "crazed vampire" after you," he air quoted, "But I told you we had a hunt, told you we wanted to go ASAP, and you just disappeared for two days?"

"I didn't mean to disappear, sorry."

He pinched the bridge of his nose and sighed, "It's east, over by Tolt-Macdonald. It should be pretty quick; I just want to get some samples of soot to run against your blood."

"Yum," I tossed my shoes over by the door, "Wake me up when you're ready to go."

"Hey," Conner stopped me before I got to the bedroom, "I don't gotta remind you we need you sober for this, right?"

"I got it, Officer." I saluted him.

And he flipped me off.

Nate was getting up as I was about to throw myself on the bed.

He looked me over and blew me off without a word.
“You said it had to be like this.” I reminded him.
He still didn't say anything and that pissed me off more.
“Go to hell.”

November 12 2007

03:00

Conner

I didn't know what was going on, but Aaron was the only one willing to listen to anything I had to say.

Parker was clearly agitated about having to be sober after his weekend bender, and I wasn't sure what Nate's problem was, but they found every situation to be at each other's throats.

They fought over the way stuff was put in the trunk, over the radio volume, and even over whether or not it was raining.

I just hoped they'd punch each other out eventually.

"How many are we even looking at?" Parker asked obstinately.

"Probably four, six," Aaron shrugged.

"Cheap ass hunt." Parker mumbled.

"Puta, stop bitching!" Nate snapped, "Holy shit, man."

They were getting exhausting.

"Not everything's about you," Parker snapped, "Piece of..."

"Enough!" I yelled at them and made a mental note to put a can of pennies in the glovebox for this exact situation, "Do I have to separate you two?"

"We will turn this car around!" Aaron was joking, but he was as fed up as I was.

"I didn't do shit." Nate crossed his arms.

"Yeah, you're right. It's me, it's always me! Right?!"

I brake checked at the light to get their attention, "Shut up! Both of you, if you can't stop just stay quiet!"

"Good luck with that." Nate scoffed.

"Don't." I sneered before Parker could pop off, "Just stop."

Thankfully, they finally listened.

Everything moving forward was dead silent.

"I'm definitely only expecting a few," I spoke while I checked my gun, "But stranger things have happened, it's a big area so stay close. Parker," I gave him a small vial, "If you can, get me a sample. Sludge would be great, but if ash is all you can get, then that'll have to be good. While he does that, let's make sure we cover him." I glanced pointedly at Nate who shrugged innocently.

"Alright, ready?"

I waited for all three confirmation nods before hitting the alarm button.

It took a while, and we still didn't end up with as many vamps as I was expecting.

Only three trickled out.

Not surprising, it happens sometimes.

What I was surprised by was that the few that showed up seemed almost uninterested. They were well-fed and seemed in pretty fair shape.

Before I made any further observations or clicked the safety off on my gun for that matter, Parker ditched us.

Flanking left, going completely against every spoken and unspoken rule we ever made, and snuck up on the first one.

"What the fuck is he doing?" Nate asked, sporting the same annoyed look I'm sure I had on my face.

I tried to grab Aaron as he ran after Parker.

"Just cover 'em." I ordered, knowing we couldn't stop Parker, and Aaron would follow him over a cliff.

Not that Parker seemed to need our cover, or Aaron's help for that matter.

He stabbed the next through the back, before slamming the third to the ground.

The third one had to be at least three times Parker's size, but that didn't stop him from throwing his body against it and straddling it to subdue it.

He stabbed his blade through the chest but didn't stop there.

Parker got this really strange look; one I'd never seen before.

He kept stabbing, over and over again, putting all of his force into it.

I lost count after fifteen, which is when I finally interjected.

"Parker!"

He still wouldn't stop, and I had to physically restrain him and pull him off of the body.

"What the fuck you doing?" Nate yelled at him; he made a point to step in front of Aaron to block them from each other.

"Hunting." Parker responded as he flicked his blood, soot, and rain-soaked hair out of his face.

"We had a plan." I reminded him.

"I improvised." He shrugged, out of breath.

"We don't "improvise"." I tried to get through to him.

Nate nudged Aaron and softly reminded him "We don't improvise, perrito."

"There were three of 'em." He rolled his eyes.

"You could have gotten yourself killed!"

"There. Were. Three." He said again slowly as he threw my vial back at me, before he started back to the car.

"No, we're going to talk about this." I said as I caught up to him.

"What's to talk about?" He asked coldly.

Nate patted me on the shoulder, as he had his other arm around a dazed looking Aaron, silently telling me to let it go.

I wasn't thrilled Nate had to be the voice of reason, but he was right, now wasn't the time.

It would be better to talk to him when we had all calmed down.

So, we cut our losses...or wins, I guess.

(＼(•̀w•́)／)

05:00

"Stop fucking moping." Nate threw a sugar packet at Parker who had been pouting since we walked into the restaurant.

"Leave me alone." Parker flicked the sugar packet back at him.

"Not until you stop being a little emo shit."

"So...You're never gonna leave me alone." Parker grumbled.

Nate kept throwing packets at him, and my sleep deprived brain decided it would be a good idea to help.

"Stop!" Aaron exclaimed, fishing a packet out of his cup of coffee, "My coffee and I have done nothing to deserve this disrespect!"

"Sorry, Air" Nate and I forfeited the sugar packet war... For the time being.

"Why're you being so bitchy anyway?" Nate asked Parker as he shoveled food in his mouth, "Wake up on the wrong side of someone else's bed?"

"Oh, you wanna talk about someone else's bed, whore?"

Nate scoffed, "You wanna talk about whores?"

"Hey, hey," I wedged myself between the animosity, "What's going on with you two?"

"Mind your business." They both barked at me.

"And you really wanna know why I'm so bitchy?" Parker dramatically threw his fork on the table, "I'm sick of being manipulated by assholes!"

"I'm manipulating you now?" Nate crossed his arms.

"You, Donnie."

"Which is it? I'm Donnie or I'm..."

"SHUT UP!" Parker screamed, slamming his hands against the table, "Not every fucking thing is about you! I'm tired, okay?! Fuck! It's not just that! I'm sick of looking at you all and wondering if that's the last time I'm gonna see you, just cause you're going to work or whatever!"

He rested his head on his crossed arms on the table, "I'm sick of getting more questions! I'm sick of not knowing what happened to Courtney or Con's parents!"

I took a drink of water, having tuned out his tantrum, it took a second for my brain to catch up. "Wait, what do you mean?"

"He gives us nothing!"

"Yeah, but why would you think he knows anything about my parents?"

“Huh?”

“What about my parents?”

Parker got weirdly silent, "...I asked him about them..." he almost whispered.

"What? When? Did he say something about them?"

He stayed quiet for what felt like an hour.

"Parker?"

He tried running a hand through his stiff hair, "I think he had something to do with, y'know… He said they had a deal."

I felt the blood drain from my face, "What?"

"I don't know, he said he was “helping” with their research. I didn't buy it, and…”

“And you failed to mention it?"

"I forgot?" he shrugged.

"You forgot. This has been eating away at me for a week, and you forgot?!"

"It's been a long couple of days."

I snapped, "You don't forget something like that!"

"Con it's not like I was trying to keep it from you, I just didn't think it was important at..."

"You didn't think it was important?!"

Nate grabbed my shoulder; I hadn't even noticed I got up.

I scoffed, "Why am I surprised?"

"What's that supposed to mean?"

"Of course you didn't think it was important! It wasn't about you! God, forbid you take a damn second to "remember" something about someone besides yourself!" I screamed.

"Con..."

I threw my napkin on the table and stormed off.

"See?" I heard Nate say as I left, "Nothing good ever happens at The Waffle House."

(＼(•̀w•́)／)

05:00

Parker

Conner wasn't talking to me, not that I blamed him.

How could I be that fucking selfish?

He wouldn't let me help with anything, but still didn't say anything, just glared at me whenever I tried to touch anything.

I wondered if I could manage to piss off Aaron within the week, too.

Randomly, while Con was writing his report, he clicked his pen at me, "What kind of deal?"

"What?"

"What kind of deal did he have with my parents?"

I shrugged, "He said he was helping with funding, all he wanted was what they knew, but I didn't buy it."

"You said that," he put down his pen, and leaned back in his chair, "That was it?"

I nodded, "Swear to God, I wasn't trying to hide or lie..."

He shook his head, "Stop. I don't care."

"I'm sorry."

"I don't care." He repeated, getting up he dug through his duffle bag and pulled out a little first aid kit.

He sat next to me on the couch and pulled on a set of latex gloves, "Take off your hoodie, let's get this over with."

He was already pissed so I let the joke go, but I didn't really know what else to say.

Conner tied off my arm and carefully searched for my veins for a while until he finally found one in my hand he could use.

Even though he was mad, he didn't try to hurt me. I hoped that was some kind of sign.

"Are we okay?"

He ignored me and we just watched the little vial fill with what looked like thick black cherry jam.

I could smell it through the glass, which was incredibly sickening, especially since it smelled like rot.

Conner raised an eyebrow, "Does it smell like blood?"

I shook my head, "Maybe if you left it out in the sun."

"Noted," he wrote on the label.

I saw him think about putting a band-aid on my hand, but the puncture was already healed enough that he couldn't find where he poked.

He carefully put the vial back in his bag with the kit, and that was it.

He didn't even talk to me when he told Nate and Aaron he was leaving.

God, I felt like such a prick.

(＼(•̀w•́)／)

15:00

Aaron and Nate both had to go to work, and I kept myself pretty loaded, so I didn't have to be alone with the shittiest person in history. *Me.*

I took a few sleeping pills, and I actually remembered falling asleep, but I know it was on my side of the bed, and not in a dimly lit dungeon.

I was laying on the concrete floor, the only light source was from a single light bulb hanging from a ceiling that my short ass considered low.

"Ah, you're awake." Donatello's voice echoed off the wood paneling walls.

His expensive, probably designer shoes thundered down the stairs. It was loud, but he walked calmly.

He had to duck to fit into the small room, his perfectly slicked back hair dusted the ceiling.

"How are you?" He asked with an amused smile that begged to be punched off his face.

"Fan-fucking-tastic! Nice dungeon you got here, by the way." I stood up, brushing off the back of my pants and tried to ignore the fact that I could stand up completely straight without touching the ceiling.

"Oh, no, this dark little hole is all you." He took a seat on the bottom step, for once not looking quite so prim and proper.

"What are you talking about?" I stayed standing, it felt nice to tower over him for a change.

He raised an eyebrow, "This is your dream, Parker. I'm here by invitation only." He held his arms out, "You summoned me here."

"I, wait, this is a dream?"

"Obviously." He gestured to the tiny slit in the wall that was supposed to be a window. At first glance, I thought it was raining, until I looked closer and realized something purple was leaking from the ground and drizzled up into the clouds.

"What the fuck is that?"

"I assumed you were using before bed." Donatello laughed, the sound was bizarre coming from him, "But, if I had to guess, I would have to say, it is a metaphor your sick little mind cooked up, hmm?" He winked at me, instantly filling me with rage.

"Don't wink at me!"

He kept talking, waving me off, "Ah, yes, a beautiful cliche." He gestured towards his chest, "Dark and moody inside." He then gestured towards my hair, "And colorful and strange on the outside."

He tapped his chin while he looked around, exaggerating all of his movements, "This room... It signifies how you feel trapped, caged, looking out through a tiny window to the free life you used to lead. Colorful, extreme, chaotic, fun... Now you're just stuck, tied to the chaos. Watching as your friends live normal lives. Oh, poor little Parker, just watching and waiting for the other shoe to drop." He batted at the light bulb making it sway, he looked like a housecat in a fine Italian suit, "Although I'm fairly certain you didn't summon me to analyze your fucked up dreams." He put both his hands under his chin in an almost playful motion, "So what can I do you for?"

"Go to Hell."

He pretended to be hurt, "But the upside down rain is so much more fun. Do you think you could dream me up a drink? Scotch on the rocks, with a twist. Perhaps with one of those cute little umbrellas you are so fond of."

There was a crazy loud clap of thunder before I even said anything.

"You could have just said no. You are always so emotional, Parker." He tsked.

I glared at him.

"Well, how about a cigarette?"

"Trust me, if I could control this you wouldn't be here."

"Or would you have me tie you to this banister, and beg to call me Daddy?" He smirked with an annoying little laugh, "Apologies for the disappointment, but you aren't quite my type."

I think what pissed me off the most was knowing that under any other circumstances I would've bedded him by now.

"Bite me."

"I already have, but you would like it more if I did it again, wouldn't you?"

I stepped over to him.

I wanted to hit him, shove him, stab him, anything that would've hurt. But my next move was outta left field, even to me.

I leaned into him so I could put my knee on the stair he was sitting on and sat on his lap.

He looked me over with a raised eyebrow and a little bit of a laugh, "This is beyond self-destructive, at this point, even for you."

"I'm not your type, right?" I ran my fingers through his perfect hair just to fuck it up, "Why not? Worried everyone'll find out about your little boyfriend?"

He chuckled, "That string isn't attached to anything, unlike you I am very comfortable with my attraction to women and men... As well as everyone else."

"I'm comfortable." I scoffed, "You don't make a cash flow by getting plowed and bowed like I have and not be comfortable!"

"So, you are "out of the attic", then? Is that the expression?"

I couldn't have rolled my eyes harder, this must be what Con feels like, "Closet. And fucking obviously! I talk about it all the time!"

"Yes, but have you ever used the words "I'm bisexual"?"

I clenched my teeth.

"If you are as proud as you say you are, why won't you admit to it?"

I shoved him and got up.

"Oh, come on, I thought we were getting somewhere." He teased, puffing out his bottom lip in a pout.

"If you were the last fucking person in the entire universe, I'd be hetero pretty fast."

"Oh, don't lie to me." He stood up gracefully and stepped into me.

I made it a point not to budge.

He bent down, closer to my height and traced his finger over my throat, "You want me, I can read it all over you, and that just drives you mad. It speaks volumes about your psyche."

"Freudian?" I rolled my eyes, "All that's bullshit."

"It is science. You are only attracted to me for what I represent, you are only attracted to the side of me you pretend to hate. The side of me that reminds me of yourself, now that is what true hatred looks like." He leaned further down to whisper in my ear, "That is why you are obsessed with being dominated, you think you deserve it. Well, that and because your parents never showed you any praise as a child, that is why you also like older men, correct? Your father never paid attention to you? Aw," he held my jaw in the palm of his hand, "You think you are incapable of being loved, that is quite cute." He let go and patted my shoulders, "That is okay, though, you don't need love, you are a classic narcissist either way." He finally took a few steps away from me and playfully walked the small room

"Isn't that a little pot calling the kettle unlovable?" I crossed my arms.

He scoffed, "Why do you think I know this? I have had to learn most of these things, as opposed to you, they come so naturally. For instance, the way you seek out and only keep your relationships based on necessity..."

"What do you mean?" I bit the bait like an idiot.

"Well, you came back to Conner because you knew he would be able to solve this, right?"

"Yeah, but not..."

"Nate gives you whatever you want, sex, drugs, cash, with really no questions so long as you do the same."

"It's not like..."

"It's not like how you keep Aaron sympathetic towards you because you think he is the only person who will put his morals before your relationship and put a bullet through you?"

I defeatedly folded to sit on the stairs as our roles went back to how they were supposed to be.

"You know everything about them, but how much do they really know about you? You won't tell them you're bisexual, nor about Travis. Ooh, or about your suicide attempt," he clicked his tongue, "That is a big one. I would be willing to bet they do not even know that you were homeless for six months, do they know you had to die to get away from it? Do they know that I had to pull you out of the gutter like a drowned rat?"

He shook his head, "You have been lying to your friends this entire time, they have no idea who you are, and quite frankly, neither do you. Not really, no. You are still in denial about what you did to that poor vampire tonight."

"Enough!" I shot to my feet and up onto the fourth step, so we were an even height, "What about you, asshat?! Huh?! You hide behind your suits, you change your name to run from the past, you're a permanent teenager playing "Grown Up"! You're no better!"

"That is the exact point, Parker, we are the same. Simply meant to be."

"What about Charlie, huh?" I crossed my arms, "Was he the same? Thought he was something he wasn't?"

It was like I slapped him across the face.

I was thrilled when he tensed.

"That's what got him killed, isn't it? Thought he was some Rambo badass and went running into those flames..."

"Quiet!" He snapped, he quickly tried to recompose himself by clearing his throat and straightening his jacket, there was a pissed off glint in his eye that reminded me of a shark. "People in glass houses shouldn't cast stones. You really should stay in your lane, boy!"

"You threw the first one, motherfucker. And why would I start now?" I snarked, knowing I had his attitude compromised, I kept pushing. "I'm smarter than you think."

He scoffed, "Sure."

"Seriously," I hopped down from the steps, "Don't you want to know what happened to dear old lover boy?"

He tilted his head, "Excuse me?"

"You heard me." I bluffed, "C'mon, you know it takes a little more than a war to put us down."

He laughed, taking a couple steps closer until he stood over me. "Listen to me very closely, Parker. I invented this little game you seem to think you have mastered. You are never going to know anything more than I want you to know. I will always be thousands of steps ahead of you, little boy. You will never win this game no matter how many centuries it lasts."

He bent to get in my face. "You had the right idea when you jerked your steering wheel."

"Or did your little boy toy when he disappeared?"

He slammed his hands into my chest, shoving me as hard as he could into the banister so I jolted myself awake.

Punk ass bitch.

(＼(•̀ᴡ•́)／)

CONNER

I was sitting in the university's lab with Drew, angrily scratching my hypothesis notes.

"Hey," Drew spun my stool around so I would be facing her, she smiled at me, and I melted into her beautiful crystal eyes, "You're so quiet, is everything okay?"

"Sorry, it's been a weird couple of days."

She stopped me before I could go back to my notes, she put her arms around my neck and ran her fingers through the ends of my hair, "Do you want to talk some more?"

"That's okay," I shook my head, "I feel like I'm always dumping my life on you."

"Stop it, it's not dumping it's venting, and you let me do the same."

I sighed, "I'm still mad at Parker, but I'm a little worried about him."

She nodded sympathetically.

"I have no idea why, but he and Nate are just at each other constantly."

"... Like, sexually?"

"What? No, I mean they've been fighting a lot?"

"Oh..." She played with one of the microscope slides, "That sounds unlike them,"

"I know, Nate doesn't squabble. He'll either yell for twenty minutes, or punch somebody, but either way he gets over it fast." I shrugged, "I don't know what's going on with them, neither of them will talk about it. But what bothers me the most is Parker still won't tell me what Donatello wanted this last time, and I really don't like how he disappeared this weekend... I mean it's nothing out of the ordinary, but usually he, at least, will text me and let me know he's not in a ditch somewhere."

"You don't think he's thinking of joining..." Drew wouldn't even finish the thought.

"No, no, of course not, it's just. He's using a lot more than normal. I can't help but wonder if the two things are correlated, and I'm just worried he's going to do something stupid." I shook my head, "Okay, well more stupid than the hunt last night. I'm just worried he's going to keep doing stupid shit and get himself in a situation I'm not going to be able to get him out of. Like three years ago, after we graduated high school, he went off the deep end. When I went back to Byre for winter break no one had heard from him in six months, his mom could only tell me he was somewhere in Seattle. I hadn't seen him, I never heard from him, then just out of nowhere he was knocking on my door begging for forgiveness because he thought he was dying. It was so weird, four years we spent every single day together and then out of nowhere," I shrugged, "Nothing."

"You've never asked him about it?"

"That's the problem, I have multiple times. He dodges the question, he jokes that he doesn't remember, or he changes the subject. He's never answered me, and as absolutely insane as he drives me, he's my best friend... I'm afraid for it to happen again."

"Maybe we should throw an intervention,"

I snorted, "Why not? We haven't had one this year yet."

"I think he just needs a little support,"

"Yeah, I think he forgets. I know his parents really messed with his perception of... Well, everything." I sighed, "I don't know, I'm being self-centered, I'm still mad."

She rubbed my arm, "That's okay, you're allowed to be. I'm sure he needs some time to settle, too."

I leaned forward putting my head on her shoulder, "Where have you been all my life?"

She giggled, kissing the side of my cheek, "New Jersey."

I didn't know what it was about her, but she just had a way of calming all my anxieties.

She's so comforting.

"Okay," she tipped my head up and pressed a kiss to my lips, "Let's get back to work, I have another class in half an hour."

I chuckled, tucking a strand of her long dark hair behind her ear, "You wanna see something freaky?"

"Always." She smiled.

I shook a little bit of ash from the vial onto a slide and slid it under the microscope.

"Is that... Vampire death ash?" She made a face.

I hadn't had a second to properly acknowledge the morbidity of it all.

"Well... It's disgusting, but in theory, the virus in its purest form."

"I kinda wanna see that." She twisted her hair and held it over her shoulder to lean over the microscope.

"Why do they just turn to ash like that?"

"Has something to do with the rapid decomp, it just ravages the cells, you can see it. There's nothing left but it."

"... Is it safe to be messing with this stuff?"

"Well, I've been covered in the stuff before, so it should be fine." I, unfortunately, thought out loud.

She sat up to look at me to see if I was serious, and when she realized I was she decided to move past it.

"What does Parker's blood look like?"

"That's the strange thing," I smeared a bit of the paste like blood onto another slide and switched them, "It looks how I would expect the virus to look in an active state, but it almost seems slower? And since the blood transfusion the mutation of the cells has slowed significantly."

"That's good, it means it's working, then. Hmm..." She readjusted the scope a couple of times.

"Did you see something?"

"Well, the ash version is what happens when it mutates all of the cells in the blood, right?"

"Right,"

She motioned for me to look, "It's really subtle, but this one, it looks like it's actively consuming the cells."

I looked through the microscope again, she was right. It was like a tiny, microscopic version of Pac-Man.

Drew tapped the ash vial with her blue polished fingernail, "This is a virus," Then gestured to the microscope, "That's a parasite."

"Can a virus mutate into a parasite?"

She shrugged, "This one sure can."

I grabbed her face and kissed her, "You are incredible!"

I was already on the other side of the lab by the time I remembered she drove.

(＼(•̀w•́)／)

For a brief moment, my excitement overwhelmed how mad I was at Parker, but my anger quickly spiked when I spoke to him.

"Hey, hey!" I tripped over myself trying to get through the door at the same rate my brain was running, "Drew found something!"

Parker was laying on the couch, his eyes half-mast, he was unimpressed as he picked at the black nail polish flaking off of his fingers, "Oh, you talking to me again?"

"It's about the blood I took earlier..." I paused, expecting him to shoot up to his feet, ask me something, or show any kind of excitement whatsoever.

When he didn't, I asked, "You're not going to say anything?"

He just shrugged.

I went to explain it to him, but his apathy was like an ice cube down my back.

I tried to read the room, look around for any context as to what was causing this reaction, a pill bottle or powder on the coffee table. All I came up with was his sketchpad sitting on the couch next to him, he had ripped up and crumpled a couple of pages.

"What's going on?" I went to move the papers so I could sit next to him, but he grabbed them out of my hand before I could glance at them.

"Don't," He shook his head, "Don't worry about it, it's fine."

"What's fine? Or what's wrong? What's going on with you?"

He thought about it for a minute, his hand instinctively tugged his sleeve down, "There's nothing to worry about, just my usual selfish asshole attitude, nothing to it."

"Stop it. I'm starting to get worried about you..."

"I'm trying to tell you that you don't have to," He finally looked up at me, his gaze was cold, "You don't have to pretend to care about me anymore. Really, I get it."

That really came out of nowhere, and I was so confused.

"What are you talking about?"

"I know you don't trust me; you made that clear last night..."

"Of course I trust you. Sometimes I just don't know what's going through your head."

"Neither do I! You shouldn't trust me! I don't trust me!"

"That's what I'm worried about, you're slipping. I've never seen you like this."

"That's because you don't know me..."

"I think the problem is that you don't trust *me*. You never let me in, not like you used to. Hell, it's been four years, Parker, you still won't tell me why you fell off the radar."

He set his jaw, "It doesn't matter, I'm just a science experiment, right?"

I didn't know what I did to set him off, but I couldn't lie, my feelings were starting to get hurt.

"*I thought we were best friends...*" I mumbled under my breath.

"Yeah, me too."

It was quiet for a really long time until he stood up.

I followed him into the bedroom, where he pulled a spare duffel bag out of the closet and started shoving random crap into it.

I sighed, "Where are you going?"

He shook his head, "I should've never come back. I'm sorry."

Words couldn't comprehend the hurt I felt. I don't think he's ever realized that, other than my grandma, he was the last connection I had to any of my past. And in six words, he so easily severed it.

I should've never come back.

For all those years he was gone, the second he stepped through my door and I hugged him, it all disappeared. Anything that happened between graduation and then just didn't matter, yet here he was throwing it in my face so that I let it go.

I sat on the bed and took a deep breath, trying desperately to not let it fester.

I know Parker, he'll take a few days to get over whatever this is, he'll come back when he's out of money and we'll be okay.

That's how it always works.

At least that's how I hoped it worked this time.

November 17 2007

06:45

PARKER

I think it probably would've hurt less if Conner literally gutted me.

What the fuck did he mean we were best friends?

Jesus Christ my life practically revolved around the guy, at this point we were an old dog and B&B away from being life partners!

I don't know, but I couldn't look at him, I couldn't deal with that shit.

So, I coped the only way I knew how, a five day bender.

I just wanted to block everything out and act like nothing was wrong.

My friends didn't hate my guts, my best friend wasn't missing, I didn't have a crazed war criminal psychologically torturing me. No, none of that was happening, I was just high as fuck, dancing on tables to songs I was too drunk to remember the words to, letting random dudes take advantage of me for more drugs, but mostly for fun. And making out in weird places with any girl that would let me.

By the time I came to I was face down on a plush rug with someone pouring cold water on my neck.

I woke up swatting around, "What the fuck?"

Caitlin was standing over me in a skimpy light pink nightgown holding a bottle of VOSS water, "Thank God, I thought you were dead."

I tried to wipe myself dry with the collar of my T-shirt but that was wet, too, "So you're pouring seventy-dollar water on me?"

She was in the middle of a sip, so she shrugged.

Twisting the lid back on the bottle, she set it on the dresser before taking a seat on the bed.

She looked like a blow-up Barbie doll, her makeup was done to match her nighty and her hair was pulled back into a sleek ponytail. I doubted she was partying with me last night, but I was positive she'd risk me choking on my own puke to finish stuffing her bra just to spite me. It worked, though instead of making me feel bad about myself I was just trying to figure out how much I could see through the lace.

She crossed her arms over her chest when she caught me staring.

"You look hot,"

"You look," Her honey eyes scanned me, "Strung-out."

"And you're so into it," I jokingly bit my lip and wiggled my eyebrows at her.

She rolled her eyes, "What the hell are you doing here, Parker?"

"I could tell you what I wanna be doing here."

"I'm serious," She snapped, "You're not allowed to show up here in the middle of the night, begging me to have sex with you, and then pass out on my rug when I say no!"

"Well, if we didn't have sex, how'd I pass out on your rug?"

She didn't think I was funny and threw a little white pillow at my head. *I'm assuming that's why they're called throw pillows.*

"Ugh, you're infuriating!" She shoved herself up off the bed and paced over to bathroom door before spinning around on her heels, she pointed at me in a way that made me stagger to get to my feet out of fear, "You come over here, you make all these promises to get me into bed, and then you just disappear for weeks! Who does that?"

I shrugged, "What do you want from me?"

"I want you to stop treating me like I'm just some kind of sex toy you can put in a drawer and forget about! I'm a woman, and a pretty high-quality one, goddamn it! And you're going to start treating me like it, or you can drop my number!"

"Stop yelling at me! You're confusing me!"

"What's confusing, you idiot?!"

"You know that's a kink I have!"

"Oh, Jesus Christ!" She put her hand to her forehead in annoyance, "I hate you; you know that?"

I shrugged and flopped onto her bed, "I'm completely fucked up! I don't know what you want me to tell you!"

She sighed and reluctantly sat next to me, "Son of a bitch, I think we're both fucked up."

"I thought you were a high-quality woman."

"I was until I fell for a high-quality moron."

"Oh, you're seeing someone?"

"Parker,"

"What?"

"Dear God, you're so stupid." She sighed again, "Sixteen-year-old me is gonna be so disappointed in me for saying this out loud, but... I like you, and I really wanna know where this could go."

I thought she was joking so I laughed, "Yeah, sure. Next Thursday, Canlis at eight."

"I love that place,"

The way she smiled took me back to high school, she smiled the same way when I told her we could get away from our families.

I felt like such a jackass.

So, I leaned into her and tried to kiss her softly, "Let's do it."

Hell, I could choke down one fancy dinner so she could realize, like everyone else, that I'm far from worth it.

07:30

Conner

I tried to push everything with Parker to the back of my mind and went ahead with the parasite investigation with Drew. Knowing, or I guess hoping, Parker would come back around once he sobered up in whatever ditch he found himself in this time.

"Conner," Drew pressed her soft lips to my cheek, "Baby,"

I hadn't realized I fell asleep, I thought we were still watching a movie, but the sun shining in through the curtains and my watch said differently.

"Good morning. My mom's making breakfast, but fair warning, it could be a trap."

"I heard that, Andrew!" Mrs. Hart yelled from the kitchen.

Drew let her smile drop, "Save yourself," she joked.

I let her go into the kitchen first, just to be safe.

Mrs. Hart looked me over, her eyes narrowing, "Did you sleep here?"

Drew rolled her eyes, "Mom, you walked past him on the couch."

"You slept on the couch all night?" Mrs. Hart probed.

"Yes, Mom." Drew her fingers combed through my hair in an attempt to rid me of my bed, or couch, head.

"So, there was no hanky-panky?"

Drew rolled her eyes.

"Sweetheart, we went over this when we had the talk, if you're old enough to be having sex you're old enough to talk about sex."

I could feel my face growing hot red, which only made Drew giggle.

"Mom, stop torturing him." Drew glanced down at her phone on the counter when it rang, "It's my professor, I'll be right back. Mom, be nice, please?"

Mrs. Hart waved her off, and placed a mug in front of me, glaring at me until I took it.

"We aren't having sex," I felt the need to blurt out, "We wouldn't do that... In the house, I mean, it's not like we haven't, it would just be disrespectful to do it in your house. We usually go to her apartment," I scratched the back of my neck, knowing what I was doing but not knowing how to stop it, "She's thinking about getting out of her lease, has she told you that, yet or...?"

"Conner," She held her hand out so I would stop talking, "Not what I'm worried about, I was just screwing with Drew,"

"Oh,"

She leaned on the counter, so she towered over me a little less, but it didn't make her any less intimidating.

"You told me my daughter was done with hunting,"

"... She told me she was."

Mrs. Hart walked past me, placing her hand on my shoulder, she said, "Follow me,"

She slid open the back door and did as I was told.

Leading me through the garden, Mrs. Hart stopped at an old, gnarled shed, and undid the tamper-proof padlock.

"If you tell Drew what's locked out here, you will be locked out here too, understood?"

"Yes, ma'am."

She creaked open the old door with a shove.

Steel gun safes lined the back wall while the opposite wall held a giant corkboard, every crime scene photo and newspaper article about Courtney's disappearance was neatly pinned to the board with corresponding color-coded notes.

Mrs. Hart gave me a second to get acquainted with the info before she asked, "Do you like this "Donatello" for it?"

I nodded, "Parker does, I was trying to see what else we found, but it's all a little too coincidental."

"Drew wants to kill him,"

I scratched the back of my neck and hoped that it wasn't my fault.

"She might've mentioned that..."

"What do you have on this guy?"

"I'll bring you copies of everything; we could really use the help."

She nodded, "I promise I won't step on any toes..."

It felt wrong cutting her off, "It's your daughter, step away."

She offered me a half smile, "I'm glad Drew has you. Don't screw it up again and stay out of her apartment."

I chuckled sheepishly, "Yes, ma'am."

I somehow managed to get back to the kitchen unscathed.

Drew was excitedly waiting for me, "My professor took a look at the parasite, I told her we found it on Bowie," She bent to pat the dog lounging under the table who was just happy to be involved, "She wants to see how it responds and breaks down to different triggers, she'll let me know what she thinks about treatment!"

"That's amazing!" I went to kiss her but hesitated when I felt her mom's eyes on me, so I opted for her cheek instead, "Parker's gonna be..."

It hit me after I said it.

Screw him.

(＼(•̀ᴡ•́)／)

09:00

I dropped Drew off at her class and went back home.

When I unlocked the door, Nate was hanging out of the window trying to light a cigarette in the rain, while Aaron was quietly tinkering on something.

"Hi," Aaron took a headphone out to greet me.

"Hi, morning. Parker here?"

He shook his head, "I'm starting to get a little worried,"

"Why?" Nate finally got his cigarette lit, "He's bottoming out, probably in more ways than one, he loves that."

Aaron promptly ignored him, "Do you think we need to be worried?"

I scratched at the underwhelming stubble on my cheek, but Nate chimed back in before I could answer.

"He took a bag," Nate took a long breath from his cigarette and let the smoke puff out while he spoke, "Maybe we got lucky and he's finally Vancouver's problem."

"What's been going on with you two?" Aaron asked Nate.

"Mind your own shoes, eh, jackwagon."

"What?"

"Aprende Espanol, gringos culos," He dropped his cigarette, and the scales of karma balanced, "Motherfucker!" He glared at us before he retreated to the bedroom, "Jodete! Shut up!"

Aaron and I tried to keep our laughs quiet.

"Whatever it is," Aaron said, circling back to the Parker and Nate drama, "I'm not a fan."

"Me either, it's fishy."

Aaron enthusiastically nodded his agreement, "It's sketchy."

"I don't know," I shrugged, "It's hard to worry about Parker when he reacts like this to everything, but I just can't shake the feeling he's going to do something stupid."

"Stupid, how?"

"I wish I knew," I sighed and leaned back on the counter, when my hand slid into the empty space between the coffee maker and the refrigerator, I couldn't help but notice the scrap parts Aaron was working with, "What happened to our toaster?"

22:06

Aaron

Since Nate wasn't talking and Conner's level of concern wasn't as high as mine, I decided to take matters into my own hands.

Conner was out with Drew, but I knew all of his passwords in case there was a fed situation, and he needed me to wipe it.

So, I abused my authorization and used it to track Parker's phone to a rave over in the warehouse district.

I never understood the appeal, I mean I'm not a stranger to that side of life, Parker had dragged me to more than a few. But between the lights, the weed smoke, and music, it was like walking into a migraine.

I stuck out in the scene of neons and glitter like a smudge of beige.

Most of the people I passed on the way in gave me a strange look, it made me nervous until a very tall blonde drag queen in six-inch heels and a glow in the dark boa peeked over her shutter glasses at me, she winked at me letting me know she clocked me and blew me a kiss.

It was probably the only time someone outing me made me a shred more comfortable.

She made her way over and shouted over the music, "Isn't it past your bedtime, little boy?" She joked.

I tossed my hair over my shoulder to joke back, "Oh, Mother, that's what triple shot espresso lattes are for."

She squealed, "Okay, baby boy! What are we drinking? I'm guessing you're like a black diamond martini guy, but I basically got beer and light beer."

"Oh, that's fine, I don't drink, thanks."

"You don't drink?" She frowned, "No no no, honey, that just won't do,"

I chuckled, "It's okay, I'm just here to pick up my friend."

"Who's your friend?"

"Pink hair, lots of piercings, there's a good chance he's been naked at least once by now or cried."

"Ah, you mean Aimless Winehouse, yeah! Been hitting on my girls all night!"

I couldn't help laughing at the nickname, Nate would've loved that one, "Do you know..."

Before I could finish asking, she whistled at a deafening volume and waved someone over above my head.

Parker was by my side, completely appalled to see me, "What the hell are you doing here?" He said in a judge-y tone that made me feel even more out of place.

I crossed my arms, "You can spy on me, but I can't stalk you?"

"Ooh!"

Parker glared at the queen over my shoulder, who just rolled her eyes, "So touchy. Call me, cutie." She waved at me as she sashayed to the other side of the room.

"What're you doing?" Parker snapped at me.

"We were worried about you,"

He crossed his arms, "You were worried, so stop caring like everyone else and get outta here before you get hurt."

"Don't be like that, please, you know we care."

He didn't want to hear me out, so he just walked away.

But I followed him, "Parker,"

"Leave me alone!"

He practically ran away from me; I tried grabbing at him just for him to turn around and shove me back.

He knew he didn't mean to shove me that hard, but I fell back on my ass.

"Hey," a guy standing by who thought we were fighting, grabbed Parker by the shoulders.

Parker spun around on his heels slamming the guy into the wall with his hand against his throat.

He must've been at least three times Parker's size.

Parker dropped him in the blink of an eye, realizing what he was doing, but by then they had cut the music and brought the lights back on.

Parker had this look of fear and pain that only got worse when he noticed all the eyes on him.

"Parker!" I tried to get through to him, but he had already bolted.

(＼(•̀w•́)／)

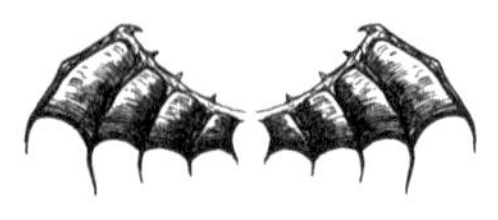

PARKER

I couldn't think clearly, and it wasn't bad enough that I was tripping balls.

I wasn't positive about what just happened, happened.

All I knew was I didn't like it; I didn't want it to happen again.

Then the realization that I could've really hurt someone, really hurt Aaron, crashed over me like a ten-foot wave.

I collapsed against the side of a building and crawled until I was hidden in the alley.

I brought my knees to my chest, crossing my arms, I hid my face.

I wanted to cry, but the fear was caught in my throat too badly.

So, I just sat there for God knows how long.

"Parker," I heard someone say my name, but I was too broken up to identify it.

"Parker," I felt a gentle hand on my shoulder, and mustered up enough courage to lift my head.

I was gutted when it wasn't Conner, God he could've fixed all this right there.

Instead, Donatello stood over me.

"Please, not now." I mumbled, "Just go away."

He unbuttoned his suit jacket and risked his slacks to kneel down and put the coat around me.

The act of care felt so foreign I didn't believe it happened.

I didn't want to look at him, so I kept my head down and hoped he'd leave.

But I felt him sit next to me, I couldn't imagine the guy sitting on a dirty alley floor.

"I know," His voice was so soft it didn't even sound like him, "I have been through this too many times. You need to take your time, but this is not the place to do it."

When I didn't respond for a few minutes, he sighed.

"There is a motel just across that street, can I please take you there?"

I still didn't answer.

"Alright, question answered."

He grabbed me by the wrist and effortlessly pulled me to my feet and bent to wrap his arm around my waist keeping me steady.

I was far too out of it and weak to fight and just reluctantly shuffled along.

November 18 2007

06:00

PARKER

I was asleep when a light turned on in my face.

I refused to accept it and squeezed my eyes shut tighter, if I did, I could pretend all of this was just a bad, beyond fucked up, nightmare.

Donnie said my name somewhere close to my head, "Wake up."

"Uh-uh,"

"Parker, wake up, the maid found your stash and called the police."

I sat up and squinted at him, the blackout curtains kept the room dark with just one lamp on, but my head still made it feel like the sun was in the room with me.

"What?"

He chuckled, "Gotcha,"

I squinted until my eyes adjusted and the black blob in front of me turned into Donatello. He was in an all-black suit with a black trench coat, complete with a pair of blackout sunglasses that screamed "JFK's been assassinated and all I got were these nerdy ass glasses."

"I was really banking on you being a bad trip." I threw myself back on the mattress and put a pillow over my head.

"Hmm, I suppose there's no way I can prove I'm not, is there?"

"Uh uh," I threw the blanket over my head too, "Don't do that, I'm too hungover and it's too early for that shit."

"I'm sorry, I can't hear you under all that."

"Go away."

"Pardon?"

I took the pillow off but left the blanket, "Fuck off!"

"Quite the pathetic little cabbage, we are." He chuckled, his laugh was a low rumble in his chest which was far less serial killer-y when I couldn't see his eyes.

I finally got some quiet for a solid minute, then I guess he thought I fell back asleep.

"I'm still here,"

"Why?" I whined.

"I had the suspicion you were about to do something stupid."

"Yeah? Where were you three weeks ago when I cut my own hair?"

"I'm more of a guardian angel, in retrospect."

"Angels aren't real."

"You didn't believe in vampires either, tell me how that worked for you. Now, get up, Parker."

"Eat me, Jamias."

"Juh-may-us," He corrected me, "And I went by James, but if you're wanting to revisit original names, I'm happy to entertain that, Elmer."

"Look," I whipped the blanket off my face, practically blinding myself, "Either kill me or get the fuck out."

"Here, sit up." He handed me a glass of water and put two pills in my hand.

"Cyanide?"

"No, it will help you feel better," he offered me a tissue from the box on the nightstand, "It should also help with the nosebleeds."

I didn't realize I was bleeding until a drop dripped from my nose onto the bed.

A blackish smudge on the bleached white sheets.

Poetic.

He sighed, "You are so depressing, it's just blood." He yanked me out of the bed and pointed to the chair angled in the corner, "Go."

I didn't have anything left to fight with, so I just did what he told me.

I was still in my pleather short shorts and wrapped in his jacket, I was practically swimming in the fabric, but it was warm and soft.

Last night started to play on a loop, I felt so out of control. Especially when I grabbed that guy, that wasn't me, that wasn't what I wanted... I started to realize a lot of my life was like that lately.

All I did was stuff I didn't want to do.

I didn't wanna be fighting with Nate, I didn't wanna be a dick to Conner.

Why am I always doing this shit? And how long is it until it escalates past last night?

How long until I can't control it anymore?

My stomach churned at the thought.

If I could do this emotionally to them, what else was I capable of?

I could've killed Aaron last night, for Christ's sake.

Fuck.

Maybe it was better for everyone if I didn't come back.

I just wanted to cut, or throw up, maybe go back to sleep, anything I could actually control.

"Oh, mercy..." Donnie interrupted my pity party, he kept talking, but I couldn't understand him.

I figured I was either having a stroke or he switched to a different language.

He shook his head with a sigh, "Parker, you are a strigoi, a powerful one at that. Yet you keep letting the cruelness of the mortal world get to you."

"God, tell me there's another planet somewhere, anywhere."

"Maybe not another planet, but there is another world right here in front of you. Parker, you aren't met for this world. Can you honestly tell me you've ever felt like you belonged? Look at you for God's sake, you stick out like a sore thumb, you always have."

My throat burned as my eyes filled with tears.

"The life you think you should lead; it isn't meant for you. It's hardly meant for anyone, but someone like you, you are very far from that mark. You don't belong here, and you never will. If you think you are ever going to change that, you are severely mistaken. You might as well save yourself the time and agony."

I buried my face in the sleeves of the jacket and tried to keep my sobs silent.

I would've given anything to stop this pain. Both mine and the pain I inflict.

"Parker," he gently put his hand on my shoulder, "I think it's time I showed you what our community looks like. I told you last time, you can't live between these worlds, it's time you made a choice. Is it your friends or you?"

I sniffled and nodded, "I don't wanna hurt anyone anymore..."

"I know."

(＼(•̀w•́)／)

Donatello made me get cleaned up and had me follow him out to the street.

Standing in my ripped-up fishnet, wrapped in a jacket I would have to sell a kidney to afford, an all-black Phantom Rolls-Royce pulled up to the sidewalk.

Donnie opened the door for me and gave me a strange look when I didn't move, "Is something the matter?"

"No, just feeling so Vivian Ward, right now."

"I'm sorry?"

"Pretty Woman?"

He patted me on the shoulder before sliding into the car, "I'm sure you are a very pretty woman."

I snickered to myself and finally slid in, "You're serious about this? This is actually your car?"

"It was a gift," he answered like it was a sweater someone knitted for him.

He leaned forward moving the partition, "Good morning, Mr. McClain."

"Good morning, sir, are we going to the hotel?"

"Yes, thank you."

I ran my fingers over the stitches in the leather, "I've never been in a car this nice, not upright, at least."

"You don't have to share every thought you have; you know?"

I shrugged and stared out the tinted window.

I had too many things circling my brain that I couldn't even keep track of what I was feeling from minute to minute.

But the overwhelming emotion seemed to be sadness.

We had been driving for a few minutes, but Donnie hadn't said another word. I assumed he was just as confused that I agreed to this as I was, but everything was too scattered for me to even wonder what I was doing.

I couldn't stand the silence, and asked pretty much out of nowhere, "Why did you go by James?"

"Excuse me?"

"Your name, why'd you drop the cool part of it?"

"It was a different time," He shrugged, "People were less accepting than they are now, and a lot of people were not pleased with a European soldier dodging the war in their country. I couldn't change my skin, so it was easier to change my name."

"Oh... That... That was a lot deeper than I expected, I just didn't wanna be like my dad..."

This time I gave into the silence and watched as the buildings and trees passed by, using the time to beat myself because I knew my dad didn't want me to be anything like him either. I was the worst yardstick you could be held against.

God, even I was getting sick of myself.

My sulking was forced to a stop with the car. When I zoned back in, we were in front of a building that was beyond worn out.

The bricks crumbled, the windows were duct taped to prevent further shattering of the spider webbed glass, and scaffolding seemed to be holding up the higher floors.

It was like the building version of Weekend At Bernie's.

"Thank you, McClain." Donnie leaned into me to open the car door and motioned for me to get out.

“This is the community?!" I stumbled out of the car.

Donatello elegantly stepped out, "Indeed,” He walked up the cracked and decomposing steps like we weren't looking at the same building.

The only thing that wasn't falling apart was the taped over seal on the door, the kind they use on condemned places.

"We don’t use these doors often." He clarified, using the key in his hand to slit through the tape.

It took most of his effort to get the ancient door to budge.

It opened into a fancy foyer, devoid of any decay, with another door Donnie had to unlock.

The foyer led into the most ornate, lux lobby I had ever seen.

There was a crystal chandelier over an all-black grand piano, for Christ's sake!

It was something outta Elton John's dreamhouse.

H EL
O

But then it started to sink in, the chandelier... The piano... I'd seen this before, and it was eerie. Like that deja vu feeling you get in an airport or train station you've never been in before.

Donnie must've thought I was impressed 'cause he got more smug, but I was more surprised to see a few people just hanging out, drinking and chatting like it was a regular hotel.

"... Are they all…?" I trailed off.

He bent down closer to me to lower his voice, "Are they vampires?"

"Yeah," I whispered back.

"Yes," He said in a normal tone as he straightened back out, "And they are aware they're vampires, you don't have to whisper."

I watched a couple of them that were closer, sitting on one of the expensive red couches.

It was a guy and a girl, sipping white wine and chatting.

"I found it inspirational,"

"Did you?" The guy leaned back on the rest of his arm, "I thought it was boring."

"You think every movie without an explosion is boring!" She laughed.

If it weren't for their eyes, I probably wouldn't have known better.

They looked normal, healthy, all that was different was their eyes were a vivid red.

"They're like me?" I asked Donnie.

"More or less, they aren't able to always keep up on their own," he dipped to my height so I could see his eyes were a similar red, "That is where I try to help."

That made me feel gross, "You're controlling them?"

"No, not necessarily. Some just need a little help keeping things... 'Tamped down'." He air quoted, "We believe the virus just responds to each brain differently, some need more help than others, and some are, unfortunately, beyond help."

"How do you help them?"

"Hypnosis is the most helpful, but it's draining for me, especially since I'm the only one that can do it. We have had to rely fairly heavily on drugs in the past."

"Like X, or like heroin?"

He tilted his head slightly at me, "Mostly antipsychotics. Our doctor has noticed it helps with the violent outbursts."

"You have a doctor here?"

"And multiple nurses," He gave me a look like it was obvious, "I wouldn't expect to even guess anything about modern medicine, back in my day everything was treated with a heroin pill and a cigarette."

"That's my health plan." I joked as a reflex.

It felt so fucking weird when he laughed at my joke.

"We even have a dentist," he flashed a smile, his perfect human teeth quickly covered by the dog like fangs I was used to, "You would be surprised by the amount of those that don't want to keep their primal teeth, though, I'm one to talk," he smiled again, this time it was only his top canines that were elongated, "I prefer more of a traditional fang."

My brain was trying to process faster than it ever had, but I still couldn't keep up, "So, like, vampire doctors..."

"No," he cut me off, letting me know it was a stupid question before I started, "Most of our medical staff volunteer their time, but I try to compensate them reasonably."

"And they're just fine knowing about vampires? What if they told someone? Like the government or whatever?"

"It's more complicated than that, and there's far more paperwork, but put simply, there's an agreement."

"What kind?"

"Well, we are considered a charity,"

"So, fraud?"

"It's not fraud; we are a genuine charity. We house, clothe, feed, and provide medical help to those that have nowhere else to go, especially to the sick."

"That... Doesn't sound right."

"Contrary to popular belief, I'm not the monster you think I am. If there were a place like this for me when I needed it, well, we wouldn't be having this conversation. Imagine how much it could have helped you." He shook his head, "Too many people just need a place to go, and I'm just trying to help."

"How many people are here?"

"I believe fifteen, but we're losing people every day. Between the virus itself and hunters, it's quite difficult to keep up."

"And none of them are like me?"

"As far as consciousness? There are a few that don't need help, yes."

"Are they what we are... Spaghetti-os, or whatever?"

"Strigoi," he corrected, but I knew I could never make the same sounds he was; he said it effortlessly with the perfect accent flair.

Even when I said it in my head, it sounded so disappointingly American.

"Is that a Romanian thing? Is that why it sounds so Dracula when you say it?"

He glared down his nose at me, "Bela Lugosi had a Hungarian accent, mine is properly Romanian... But, yes, strigoi is a Romanian word. To answer your original question; not all of them are strigoi."

"So, what are they?" I pointed to the couple on the couch.

"Mullo," He waved his hand for me to follow him across the massive room, "There are many types, mullo would be considered standard issue, they are what you would be used to seeing when it comes to vampires, the rabid beasts you hunt."

I was overcome with a wave of nausea, "Are you telling me they know what's going on?"

He shook his head, "Not without help, no, if there is no immediate interjection the virus eats through their cognitive abilities before anything else. I hate to admit it, but the ones you kill, yes, you are very much doing them a favor."

I sighed, letting out the breath I was holding, "What else is there?"

"Strigoi, of course, and dhampirs. Strigoi are *la crème de la crème.* We possess the same speed, strength, heightened senses as well as the hyper-healing as the mullo, with a few other unique perks; shapeshifting for one. Telepathy, better connections with our offspring,"

"Don't say offspring." I mumbled.

"In addition, we all have our strong suits."

"What does that mean?"

"Some of us develop... Almost a sixth sense, if you will. For instance, I'm capable of easily weeding out the gene within each vampire. I suspect yours might be clairvoyance."

I scoffed, "Clairvoyance?"

"Well, you are the one with visions of the future, are you not?"

I shook my head, "Wait, hang on, genes? What genes?"

"Strigoi and dhampir are a specific gene that you are born with, it lies dormant until the virus is introduced. If you have a strigoi gene, you get a strigoi. Dhampirs make dhampirs. If you have no gene, which most people do not, you get a mullo."

"That's... Frustratingly straight forward."

"Like you would not believe."

"So, what's a dhampir?"

"Well, if you had stopped asking so many questions, I would have told you in the correct order." It was hard to tell when he was joking, his voice never changed tones, and his expression stayed neutral just with a very slight tip to the corners of his mouth I read as a smirk, "They're typically what happens when vampires breed with humans, it's extremely rare. Although, unlike strigoi, I have reason to believe dhampirs can be... Artificially created."

Something clicked in my brain.

I really didn't think I was capable of figuring shit out like that, that was more Conner's thing.

"That's why I still have blood?"

Donatello nodded, "Correct, if you dilute the virus enough, there is something else to attack other than your brain, causing more cognitively aware vampires. However, without the entire nervous system being taken over by the virus to replenish itself completely, the survival rate is almost non-existent. So far, you are the only trial that has survived."

I tried to laugh off the sinking feeling I got in my stomach, but my throat tightened, and it came out more of strangled *hmph.*

Donnie didn't seem to like the sound, and gave me a look of what I assumed was confusion, "What is it?"

"Nothing, just," I ignored the lounge chair a few feet away 'cause I didn't think my legs would carry me that far, and just crumbled 'til I was on the floor, "Do you have any idea how many times I've tried to kill myself?" I ran my fingers through my hair and tugged at the ends, so they were in my face, I didn't wanna be looked at, "Every night since I was twelve, I've prayed to God and begged to just let me go to sleep and never wake up again and... And now you're telling me, when my prayers were finally answered... I defied all odds."

Nothing was said between us for a long time, and no one else seemed to notice the exchange.

I tried to pull my shit together, and cleared my throat, "Why? Why me? Please, just answer me, honestly."

Don offered me his hand to help me up, "I've never lied to you about that, Parker. There is so much more to you, you are far more powerful than you think you are. The world needs you, they might not know it yet, but I do, and I need you too."

I let him pull me to my feet and tried to act like that meant something. Like I didn't feel like I was just being conned.

"Come along, you need a break, and I have more to show you."

I followed him down an endless hall of doors that just oozed the same creepiness from the never-ending hallway in my vision months ago.

"What're all these rooms?"

"Mostly empty banquet halls, one is a library, I am working on getting..."

Thanks to my impulsive thoughts, my hand ended up on the doorknob.

"Oh, I can't advise you to open that door,"

Which meant I, of course, had to yank the door open.

A mop fell out of the door and scared the shit out of me, so naturally I flung myself to the other side of the hallway like a cat, I think I even hissed a little.

Donnie laughed.

"You're an asshole."

"Curiosity killed the vampire," He moved me along further down the hall to one of those ancient looking cage elevators.

He pulled the door open and stepped on effortlessly and gave me a look when I didn't follow, "What? Oh, do not tell me you have a fear of mops and elevators."

I tried not to feel some type of way about it, but the fact that I tripped getting on just pissed me off.

He chuckled quietly.

The outside of the building seemed smaller, but the buttons panel proved there were fifteen floors, thirteen above ground and two below.

"A lot bigger on the inside," I mumbled mostly to myself.

"Yes, much smaller than what will be necessary, but it's a good start."

"Why are there two basements?"

"Industrial freezers and a quarantine ward,"

I didn't want to think about what was down there, but before I could block it out, he hit the -2 button.

"... Which one are we going to?"

"Quarantine ward," He checked his watch, "Dr. Andrés should be on site, I would like for her to examine you."

"No," I crossed my arms over my chest as it filled with new anxieties, "I'm fine."

"I would like for her to determine that," he dipped to look at my face closer in the dim light of the elevator, "If I had to guess, you won't be much longer. When was the last time you fed?"

Just the word "fed" made me nauseous. So, I ignored his question and refused to move when the elevator bounced on the last floor.

He didn't really notice my protest, he just moved around me to open the door and guided me by my shoulder to a set of huge metal industrial doors. Multiple signs hung on and around the door, but I was more focused on five deadbolts that kept it closed to read the signs.

Donnie knocked once, waiting a second before knocking again.

I couldn't hear any response from the other side.

He used a massive keyring to unlock the door, which, surprise surprise, led to another door, this one was chain link with just a padlock.

"Seriously?" I was unimpressed and kinda annoyed, the whole thing was starting to feel a little perp walk-y, especially since he had to lead me down the hall because the concrete walls were too narrow for us to walk side by side.

Then there was the high-pitched buzz from the overhead lights which made my brain feel like it was going to leak out of my ears at any minute.

There were three vaulted doors at the end of the hall, one on the right, left, and center.

I waited for him to spin around and announce, "Behind one of these doors is a brand-new car!"

Instead he just boring-ly unlocked the middle door.

I drug my feet so I could scan the room, the concrete walls were painted over white, the lights seemed to be cranked up to "sunbeam", while a handful of beds and curtains lined the far wall like an emergency room, which only turned my stomach more and cranked my fight-or-flight to eleven.

It seemed like forever since I saw anyone else, so I was kinda surprised to see an older lady crouched over one of the counters.

"Good morning, Mr. Sotos," she got up from her stool and what she was doing, taking off her surgical mask as she made her way across the room, "You must be Parker." She offered me a comforting smile that totally threw me for a loop.

"He is," Donnie replied when I didn't, "I do apologize for calling on you so early in the morning,"

"That's alright!" She beamed, "I wanted to check some of our samples as well. A few hiccups, but things seem to be moving forward as expected."

I didn't like how vague that was.

He nodded once, the only way he acknowledged her statement, "Enzo should have filled you in over the phone. I am very interested in seeing how things have been progressing in him," it took me a minute to figure out he was talking about me, "Despite his years, he seems quite ill."

"Hmm, okay," she stepped to the counter shuffling a few papers before grabbing a clipboard, "Were you thinking of a full lab draw with a genetic mockup as well?"

"No, we can forgo the genetic testing, but I would like you to have a look at his labs. I understand he has been supplementing with blood transfusions."

Her eyebrows raised behind her glasses as she wrote, "Interesting. I'd really like to see that, too." She got as close to me as she could without touching me and scanned me really closely, "I see what you're saying. I need a weight, and we can get him into a bed. I'd like to do a physical exam, if you think it's necessary?"

"I agree." Donnie answered like I wasn't standing right there.

She gestured to a manual scale towards the middle of the room, and they moved along like I didn't have a say in any of this.

I dug my heels in again and wouldn't move.

"Come along," he called me over like he was trying to get a stray dog out of the road.

For a second, I thought his eyes flashed but it happened so fast that I wasn't sure until I caught myself shuffling forward.

"Stop doing that." I snapped.

"Then stop acting like a spoiled child." He put his hand in the middle of my back and forced me along.

Sensing if I pushed it further, he'd pick me up and put me on the scale himself, I saved my dignity and stepped on it myself.

"That can't be right..." The doctor mumbled under her breath as she tapped the scales around, "Do you know you're almost forty pounds underweight?"

Wow, that took me back a little. I really hadn't realized I'd lost that much weight, but I guess it made sense. It's not like I was doing anything good for my body.

Donnie gave me the same look I'm used to seeing from Conner when I start going through withdrawals, that "This is a wakeup call, moron" look. But it didn't have the same bite to it from Donnie, if anything his disappointment kinda made me feel like I was doing the right thing.

"That does not surprise me," Without warning he lifted the jacket and my shirt away from my body in a swift motion, "He is practically skeletal."

"This is definitely not alright." She examined my ribcage, poking at me with the cold metal tip of her pen.

I jumped away and swatted Donatello so he'd let go, "I get it, okay?" I wrapped myself back up, the air felt like ice against my skin, "Jesus Christ, I've had anal that's less invasive, you know?"

To make it worse, she held a thermometer to my mouth.

I split a dirty look between them, and warned, "I'll bite."

“That is not the threat you think it is, not here.” He smirked, making a point of letting her take his temperature.

"The heater's usually on full blast down here," I didn't know what that had to do with anything until the thermometer beeped, “Eighty degrees,” She nodded, “Exactly room temperature.”

She turned back to me.

"Nuh-uh, not after it's been in his whore mouth."

She took it as a challenge and put it under my arm before I could protest again.

I was pissed that I hadn't thought of it first.

"Come on, this has to be like a HIPAA violation, or whatever."

"That is not what HIPAA is, but valiant effort. I am surprised you knew the word."

"Besides," The doctor added.

But I talked over her, "Oh, great, you're chiming in."

She ignored me, "Based on your weight alone, I could deem you unfit to make your own medical decisions."

"Gee, thanks."

She smiled at me checking the thermometer, "Eighty-three. I would consider that a fever for a post-mortem. Have you had any other symptoms?"

"He has been somewhat faint." Donatello answered before I could. It made me think of when I was a kid, and my mom would take me to the doctor.

"He seems to get queasy regularly."

"Is that always, or just today?

"I would say it's normal for him,"

They continued like I was nowhere around.

"Given his level of emaciation, I'm willing to bet that's from malnutrition. You mentioned blood transfusions, is he eating meat and blood with that as well? Or is that a supplement?"

"Well, that there is the hook, Dr. Andrés, he's a vegetarian and flatly refuses.'"

"Vegan." I scoffed to make myself known.

The doctor looked concerned, "When was the last time you've consumed blood or meat?"

I shrugged. I wasn't just trying to be difficult this time I really couldn't remember.

But Donnie sure seemed to, "Nearly a month,"

She looked at me like I was going to keel over at any minute, "The fact that the virus hasn't completely ravaged your body and killed you yet is astonishing." She used her pen to scratch her head, "I hypothesize that may be in part to the blood transfusions." She thought for a second, "I'm hesitant to check his blood, any amount of blood loss could be fatal in his condition."

He sucked a sharp breath in between his teeth as he thought, "Yes, I suppose we should avoid killing him if we can."

"Aw, how lovely! You must be sweet on me." I used a thick posh British accent to mock him, but weirdly enough it came out more Australian.

"I don't suppose sarcasm is a treatable symptom?" He gestured to a bed in the far corner of the room before crossing his arms, "Go have a seat and allow the grown-ups a moment to chat."

I only agreed because I wanted to use the time of them actively ignoring me to do some snooping.

Hell, with all this medical equipment, I could either find some good pills or something good to sell for pills.

Neither of them seemed to notice, or at least care, that I made a beeline for the cabinets on the other side of the room.

There wasn't anything in the cabinets or drawers, just a bunch of medical junk. I did swipe an empty IV bag though, mostly because I was curious if I could blow it up like a Capri Sun pouch.

I was quickly losing my will to give a fuck, and my boredom was creeping in. Which led me to the panic of what I was doing there in the first place.

I scanned the blank walls for something to look at, but they just reminded me of the barrenness of a hospital wasteland, and it brought up too many flashbacks.

Maybe it was just my imagination, but the lights seemed dimmer on this side of the room. The beds ran out maybe fifty feet away.

Aside from the cabinets, I was the only thing over here...

I was just grateful that something else got my attention, even if it was in the form of the doorknob behind me jiggling, and it scared the hell out of me.

I wasn't totally sure I saw it move, but Donnie and the doctor had lost interest in me, so I had no one to ask.

I stepped up on my tiptoes to try to reach the 6x6 window on the door.

Whatever was on the other side of the glass was pitch black, and all I could see was my own eyes staring back at me.

Just when I was about to write it off, I swore I heard a thud followed by a muted scream.

It was so faint, I didn't know if it was real or maybe just the ancient building above us crumbling, so I pressed my ear against the cold steel door.

"Let me out of here!"

That I was sure I heard.

"Get me out!"

I popped back up and got startled when I saw a face on the other side of the window.

A girl pounded on the glass; she was screaming but it was barely audible.

"Help me! Please! You've gotta get me out of here!"

"Hang on, hang on!" I was panicking while I tried to leverage the locked door.

I saw the fire extinguisher mounted on the wall and I couldn't figure out why 'cause I wasn't gonna be able to break that lock.

I pounded on the door to get her attention, "Get away from the window!"

When I couldn't see her anymore, I threw the extinguisher through the window and pulled myself up to reach my arm through.

"Parker!" Donnie called my name across the room.

My fingers just barely reached the knob on the other side, but there wasn't a lock.

Before Donnie could get to me, I realized there was an arm hinge above the door.

That I could reach and was able to wrap my hand around it and squeezed it until it popped.

The door flung open and sent me down to the cracked and stained concrete.

The girl ran for the open door, she made it halfway before something switched.

In a second, she was feet away from me and then on top of me snarling.

Her eyes dripped with so much blood I couldn't even tell what color they were underneath.

When she went to bite me, her teeth were still flat and humany, but blood poured out of her open mouth.

I clenched my eyes shut, expecting any amount of pain to hit me but it never did.

A gunshot echoed off the concrete, effectively deafening me.

I opened my eyes just in time to see a wave of blood, sludge, and soot collapse on me.

Donatello was standing over me, he said something, but my ears rang too loudly for me to hear him, but I was also too busy gagging to answer him either way.

He kept talking as he took apart the gun in his hand and dumped the handful of silver bullets into his jacket pocket.

I was able to make out him yelling, "And why the hell was that door not bolted?!"

I didn't hear the answer, but he was clearly not happy with it, "That is an excuse! You know we allow humans down here! God above us, if she killed the doctor! Then what? She was in a three-week quarantine on day four! You know that is of the highest risk!" He snapped his head to the other side of the room; it wasn't until then I realized there were more people in the room.

He tucked the gun into the inside pocket of his jacket, straightened out his sleeves, and tried to reign in his anger, "Turn off that damned alarm, tell everyone it was an accidental trip in the wiring or whatever. What?" He turned his head again so I couldn't hear any more of that.

Out of nowhere he grabbed my arm and pulled me out of the puddle of bodily fluid I'd just accepted as my place now.

He snapped his fingers in front of my face to get my attention, "Hello? A verbal confirmation would be nice."

"What?"

Annoyed, he just shook his head, "If you can speak, I will just assume you are fine."

I knew Donatello had taken me somewhere, but I'd zoned out and wasn't entirely sure how I got into a different room and was now sitting on a $100,000 bed.

I felt something drape over me.

"Try not to drip on the silk, it is an expensive import."

He dipped down to be in my view, "Are you alright?"

I made a point of leaning back on my sticky, blood drenched hands, especially on the fluffy white fabric at the foot of the bed, "What do you think?"

He pressed his lips together to hide his smirk, "I do apologize for this disaster. However, in my defense I did not expect you to smash a quarantine window, although I suppose with your overloaded hero complex, I should have suspected." He handed me a damp washcloth to wipe my face.

I could only imagine I looked like a clown on bath salts.

"What kinda place is this that I'm not supposed to help a girl screaming for her life?!"

"The kind where the girl is baiting you like a cat with a mouse. Though I know from past experience you would probably be very interested in that."

"Go to Hell."

"I will have you know I saved your life, well," he rolled his hand in a forward gesture, "Again. But, if you are going to stay here, we will have to discuss these kamikaze missions you throw yourself into."

"Or you could y'know, not lock people in dark, desolate corners!"

"And what would you have me do with them? It is for their own safety, turning is not as streamlined as it was for you. It can be a violently volatile process; it was for her own safety she was in there. She could have killed you, or herself. You have to learn to adapt to the unpredictability, that is something I have been trying to teach you since the very first day, but unfortunately your head is much too thick."

I might as well have been talking to my mom.

There was a knock on the door before I could continue my temper tantrum.

Donatello recognized the knock like the freak he is, "Enzo, come."

I half expected Frankenstein's monster to crash through the door and was a little disappointed when it was just a normal guy.

"Good morning, sir." He came to an abrupt pause barely a foot away from Donnie, who made no effort to introduce us.

"What is it?" Donnie seemed annoyed with the guy's lingering.

"I arranged for your driver to take Dr. Andrés home,"

"Good," Donnie pressed his middle finger to the center of his forehead where his eyebrows furrowed, "Hopefully that will keep her from filing a lawsuit. I cannot even begin to fathom the kind of begging it will take for her to return, however. What is the situation for the quarantine room?"

"Already being fixed, and I've made inquiries about adding a second bolt on the outside as well as adding plexiglass to the window."

"Great. How have our residents reacted?"

"Relatively unbothered. Thankfully, most of our residents had already turned in for the night, most of them didn't even notice the alarm."

"Excellent." Donnie paused before gesturing to me, "Could you bring him a change of clothes? He is starting to look like one of those sad oil spill ducks."

"Sure, anything in particular?"

"Something less... It has been a long day, and I'm at a loss for words, just bring him something that doesn't make him look like a common street whore."

"Can I just take a shower?" I interrupted.

Donnie looked down his nose at me, "Since when do you ask permission for anything?" He raised his hand to wave me off, "The door on the left of the closet. Take what you need."

I took that to mean I was dismissed; besides I couldn't care less about anything other than getting the now congealing blood off of me.

There was silence while I shuffled to the bathroom.

"Is there more?" I heard Donnie ask before I closed the door, so I listened for a second.

"There's the matter about the on post quarantine guard."

"Yes, and where was he this morning?"

"He said he thought it was fine 'cause you were there with the doctor."

It was quiet, but I knew Donnie was doing that scowl.

"... Would you like me to find a time for you to talk with him?"

"Ugh, must I? Fire him, kill him. Either way, I don't care at this moment."

I don't know why but it finally clicked that I was alone for once finally.

I looked around the room for literally anything that could be used as a weapon, but the asshole didn't even have a razor.

My heart started pounding, I wasn't sure why, I didn't feel scared but my fight or flight was definitely triggered.

Could've been the fact that I was literally trapped in my arch nemesis's bathroom, or it could've been the fact that I was still soaked in someone else's cold blood that was starting to dry and glue my clothes down to my skin, or it could've been the fact that I was just now starting to think like a normal fucking person! Take your pick!

There was a huge window over the ornate bathtub that was roughly me sized.

Hey, it seemed like a great idea until I climbed over the tub, unlatched the window, and was staring at a thirteen-floor drop.

The door swung open, and Donnie gave me the most vexed look, "Parker,"

My leg was hanging outta the window while I straddled the ledge, but I tried to play it cool, "Oh, hi."

"What are you doing?"

"Uh," my still blood-soaked hand slid off of the window frame, causing sharp metallic taste in the back of my mouth, "Pretty sure having a panic attack."

"You are aware you are free to leave at any time? I will even allow you to use the door."

"Yeah, I didn't realize we were so high up." I glanced down at the sidewalk below the window. It was like the hallway of a horror movie, how it seemed to get further and further the longer the main character looked at it.

I mean, it's not like it would kill me...

Right?

Donnie snapped his fingers to get my attention and grabbed for my hands before I slipped and accidentally flung myself out of the window.

"What is it with you and windows today?"

"I find them comforting!" I sassed back.

"Oh, this is safe?" He motioned like he was going to shove me forward and then laughed when I screamed.

"I am kidding! Joke, joke, joke!" He wrapped his arm around my waist, before I could jump on my own, "Lord, you are jumpy... No pun intended." He laughed again.

He helped me back down, and I felt like a child getting pacified out of a tree by his father.

"You're such an asshole!"

"Oh, calm down. Like I would allow anything to happen to you. You are safer with me than you are with yourself. Clearly!"

"Oh, oh! I'm sorry! I just watched you blow a woman's brains out and am currently covered in her brains! Sorry I panicked!"

He was trying so hard not to laugh at me, so he pulled me out of the bathroom by my hand and sat me back on the bed.

"This is the gray I have been trying to explain to you."

"What? Brain matter?"

"No, Parker," he sighed, "When I look at you, I see the same kid I used to be. I just wanted to help and do the right thing so badly that it got me thrown into another man's war. There is no good and bad, there is only gray, and you must learn to make it work for you. Look at what I'm doing here. Everyone here is here because it benefits them, and I allow them to be here because it benefits me. The deck is stacked, it always has been, and it always will be. That is why people like us must worm in where we can, climb the ladder and disrupt the system. Do you see what I'm saying?"

"No,"

"The girl downstairs," he let out a breath much heavier than a sigh and pushed himself off the dresser he leaned against, "We had a deal. Her mother has leukemia and can't afford treatment. She was going to come work with us and I, in turn, was going to cover her mother's medical bills. But now... Tomorrow I have to go down to her mother's and hope a measly check will help cushion the blow of having to tell her that her daughter will never be coming home. I have to live with that because that is the only thing I can do."

It was right there.

Right in that moment the lesson of everything, the meaning of life, the way to purge pain.

It hit me over the head like a crowbar.

The only way out was in.

I clenched my jaw.

"Okay."

He tipped his head to the side, "What is it?"

The only way I could clean up this mess I made.

The only way I could even out all the trouble I caused.

I could do it right here, right now.

"I'll join."

He looked at me like I lit his designer bedspread on fire, I was with him, I couldn't believe the words coming out of my own mouth.

"What was that?"

"I'll join your community, but I've got conditions of my own."

He regained his composure and hid his excitement, "Name your price."

"Conner, Aaron, and Nate. I want them outta this, all of it, you have to promise anything that ever happens to them won't be vampire related."

He nodded once, "I can do better, full safety detail. Personal vampire bodyguards, I can keep them safe for an eternity. Same thing I have done for you. Obviously, they would have to leave well enough alone and couldn't kill or maim my vampires."

"Right, and I want the same for my family."

He raised an eyebrow, "The family that disowned you?"

"Don't question it, just do it."

He raised a hand, "I was just clarifying."

"And everything you know and have on Conner's parents, you gotta give it to him."

"It wouldn't be anything lengthy, but I could do that. Given, should he continue their research I want to remain in the loop."

"Would you leave them alone?"

He stared at me for a second, waiting for me to add more to that.

"You can't recruit them, you can't fuck with them, you can't turn them."

"Naturally."

"And you have to find Courtney,"

"You do understand that I'm a miracle worker, I'm not a genie."

"You'll figure it out." I crossed my arms.

"Fair enough. Is there anything else, master?" He smirked.

My life for their freedom. That was as clean a deal I could make.

"The only way the deal's off is if I leave, right?"

"Yes, should you decide to leave the deal would be voided from that day forward."

I nodded and held my hand out, "Gimme two days, I'm yours."

He eagerly shook my hand, "It has been a pleasure working with you."

He smiled wide.

Like a lion ready to pounce, and I was the lamb that just freely offered up his life on a silver platter.

November 19 2007
19:00

PARKER

Refusing to stay at Donnie's freakshow hotel, I made him take me back to the motel. I figured he'd leave me alone there, but when the door to my room flung open, I realized I was wrong.

I didn't bother to look up from the mirror I propped up on the desk to do my makeup.

"Oh my, so you are aware of how to get cleaned up." He snarked, obviously annoyed I wouldn't pay attention to him.

"Don't get too hard up, I just stole some make up."

"And what possessed this?"

I picked at the rip in my jeans, Donnie had made his minion get me a change of clothes yesterday, and I wasted no time in turning them into something I would actually wear by stealing a pair of scissors from the front desk.

"Nothing, I've just been thinking..."

He offered an answer where I trailed off, "I don't blame you; I wish I could have said goodbye to my old life, I would give anything to... You should savor it."

It felt weird to have his support, but I guess since I finally said yes to him, he didn't hate me anymore.

"Mmhmm..." I focused on the pad of cycshadow in my hand and swirled the brush back and forth on it.

I didn't want to think about it, but I couldn't stop imagining the guys' faces if I told them.

God, I couldn't do that, that couldn't be my last memories of them.

"I take it it's not your friends? Interesting," he took a seat on the foot of the bed, crossing his knees, "Must be Travis, that's..."

"A stupid idea, I know."

"You need closure," he defended me, "You need an answer. I understand that, and I wish you the best."

His approval left a bitter taste in the back of my mouth, but I needed a favor, so I just swallowed it.

"Look, you have a lot of access to city shit and I was wondering..."

He stood and quickly pulled his hand out of his coat pocket, one of his signature cards pressed between his first and middle finger.

"Are you serious?"

He placed it on the desk when I didn't take it.

"I had a sneaking suspicion that it might be where you were headed. I had my assistant find him. You're welcome."

I rolled my eyes, "Thanks."

(＼(•̀w•́)／)

I played with the cord of my headphones as I watched the rain pour down the bus window.

I'd had the same song on shuffle for the past half hour, but hadn't realized it 'cause I couldn't hear the music over my thoughts.

Well, really just the one thought but it was on a constant loop like the song.

“What the hell are you doing?”

The last time I saw the guy we beat the shit out of each other, and he was screaming in my face about how I never meant anything to him.

I must've been stupid to be willing to go talk to him, but God I must be sick to actually be excited about it.

I could practically hear Conner lecturing me already, there was a good reason I never told him about Travis, but I knew Nate's threats weren't empty and he'd sell me out at any minute.

Then it occurred to me I wouldn't be there for Con's reaction.

I thought I'd be relieved by that, but it stung more than I expected. To be fair, I was starting to miss Con's smug, little face.

Part of me wanted to wash my hands of all this bullshit and just go back like nothing happened, but I knew they weren't safe with me there.

This was what was best for everyone.

Besides, I doubted that the three of them missed me.

Everyone's always said how they need a break or they gotta get away from me, now was their chance.

The bus got to my stop, and I thanked whatever God I pretended to believe in that I didn't have to be alone with my thoughts anymore.

The building was on the other side of skid row and made our apartment look like Donatello's hotel, except they had a working elevator, and I guessed the fire alarms weren't just decoys.

I stared at the chipped and scratched door in front of me.

3C.

I could still back out. I thought.

But then I sighed when I thought about it, or him.

His muddy eyes that turned green when he laughed, his crooked smile, his overly bleached hair that smelled like cigarettes and vanilla, or the way he'd softly kiss the bruises he put on me once I'd say I was sorry.

He'd always say we were Kurt and Courtney but fuck maybe we were Sid and Nancy.

What the hell was I going to say to him? Scream at him and call him an asshole? Or crumble and beg him to take me back?

God, I wished I spent my time thinking about this instead of licking crushed Xanax off the motel's bathroom counter.

"Can I help you?" Someone asked behind me, making the decision for me.

I snapped around to see Travis standing there. He looked so different, his long blond hair was cut close and dark, the piercings in his lip were just two pin pricks, and a wrinkled work shirt covered the shitty tattoos on his arms.

He looked at me like he saw a ghost, I guess he probably thought he did.

"Parker?"

I raised my hand in an awkward wave.

He smiled and I knew I was fucked, "What the hell are you doing here? I thought you were dead!"

I chewed on my bottom lip to keep from smiling, "Right back at ya."

"God," he stared at me for a solid minute before shaking his head, "What the hell are you doing here?"

My heart dropped, I thought he was annoyed, 'til he laughed and I realized he was... Excited?

He fumbled his keys, "Come on, come in,"

He opened the door and let me step into the apartment first.

I tried so hard to act natural, but my heart was pounding, and my hands shook like crazy.

I shrugged, and mumbled, "I wanted to see you."

He was surprised, "Really? Why?"

I didn't know how to answer, so I didn't.

"Sorry, just, after everything I'm kinda surprised you'd ever wanna see me again."

I stood there staring at him, God I probably looked like the most strung out, pathetic, puppy under the bridge.

"... So, how'd you find where I live?" he said with that crooked smile that lit my soul on fire, "Friends in high places?"

"More like enemies in bomb shelter basements." I played with the zipper of my hoodie.

He chuckled and nodded to the couch in the corner of the room, "Get you something to drink?"

He snorted, opening the fridge, "I got Fred Meyer brand root beer, or tap water."

"Root beer? Gross, they just let you outta the psych ward, or something?"

"Mm, close," He got me a glass of water from the sink before he sat on the other side of the couch, "King County Correctional,"

"Jesus, are you serious?"

He leaned back against the arm of the couch so he could face me. He was making a point of trying to seem smaller and giving me some space.

I was on the fence; I didn't want him to touch me, but it was like I came all this way and he was still so far away.

"Yep. Few months after you left, we did a bar show. I got outta pocket, ended up punching a cop, they found coke on me." He shrugged before letting out a small, embarrassed chuckle, "I had this whole David Lee Roth thing goin', you would've loved it."

"Bummed I missed it."

"Yeah..."

It was really quiet for a minute.

He cleared his throat, "Anyway, I got out last November... Thirty-two months," he paused, "Honestly, I spent all of it thinking about you."

What the fuck was wrong with me? That shouldn't have made me feel all warm and fuzzy.

I picked at the seam in my sleeve until I undid a stitch to focus on instead.

When I didn't say anything, he moved on.

"So... What've you been up to? You still doing art?"

"Mm, yeah, still making art that no one buys. The band still together?"

"Nah," he chuckled, "Lewis knocked up his girl, they got a place in Tacoma, and Torrey moved to San Diego, he's doing music out there now."

I nodded, "You guys still talk?"

He tilted his head from side to side in a kinda more-or-less gesture, "A little. They had enough of me, too."

There was another silence 'til he just blurted.

"I'm sorry I never got ahold of you. Kinda figured you hated me."

"I wish I could." Slipped out, and I kicked myself for letting it.

"After a few weeks I realized you weren't coming back. Torrey told me to leave you alone, but I couldn't... When I called your folks' place, your sister picked up, told me you were in an accident and said never call back. I assumed the worst..."

"You... Called?"

He shook his head at himself, "Only sixty, seventy times."

I pulled at the thread some more just so I didn't have to look him in the eye, "When I left, you said you didn't care what happened to me."

"I never meant it,"

My anger finally won over.

"Then why the hell did you scream it in my face after you threw me through the fucking coffee table?!"

"'Cause I wish I did,"

I scoffed and shoved myself off the couch, "Jesus, this was a bad idea. Drive your car off a bridge, asshole."

I went to storm off, but he grabbed my arm, in the split second I flinched and brought up my other hand, either to hit him back or to block his shot I hadn't decided yet.

He let me go immediately, "Fuck, I'm sorry, I'm sorry," he scooted further back and tried to seem like less of a threat, "I'm sorry. I'm so fucking sorry, Parker. Everything I did, now and back then, I'm sorry. None of it was right."

I was pissed and it felt so good.

All of that rage burned through me like a warm fireplace in a snowstorm

I wanted to hit him; I wanted to tell him how much a piece of shit he was.

Hell, I wanted to do anything to make him feel the way he made me feel.

Then, as fast as it sparked up, it was gone.

The snow caved in and smothered the fire.

I wanted to hold onto it for as long as I could, but my insides were so twisted around I couldn't feel anything other than nausea.

I sank back down onto the couch because I didn't know what else to do.

Travis looked genuinely amazed that I was still here.

"I loved you." I snapped, "And for some fucked up reason I still do! No matter what I do! Fucking other guys, or girls, pills, coke, liquor, weed, for fuck's sake! Not even death could numb me from you!"

"I get it,"

"No, the fuck you don't!"

"I do," he softened so much, keeping himself scrunched into the couch even though I was standing over him yelling, "I went through the same thing. You leaving nearly killed me, I OD'd twice."

"Good." I angerly wiped the tears off my face, “I hope it hurt.”

"I went to jail; I pushed everyone out of my life. All of it because I couldn't have you. It took getting sober for me to realize how twisted I truly was." He shook his head, "You loved me so much, I knew I didn't deserve you and I was fucking terrified you were going to leave me. Just you remembering the name of the bar I had a show at scared me shitless."

My hand instinctively went to the scar above my eyebrow that documented that fight forever.

"I thought I could control you, when I realized that was stupid. You were already packing your shit."

"You wanna know something fucked up?" I fell back on the couch, "I wasn't leaving you."

"What do you mean?"

I scoffed, "Trav, it was my brother's birthday. I thought it'd be easier to sneak out than to fight with you. It was a Friday; I figured you'd smoke through the weekend and not even notice I'd left 'til I came back."

That rocked him, he leaned forward with his hands on his knees while he tried to process what I said.

"I'm so fucking sorry."

"Yeah, me too."

"Jesus Christ... I thought you were leaving me." He kept shaking his head in disbelief, "I was so sure, and... And God, this is going to sound so fucked up, but I wanted you to. I finally realized how shitty I was, and you needed to get away from me... I said all that shit hoping you'd hate me," He shrugged, "Go back to school, or home, I just hoped you’d go anywhere away from me."

"I didn't want to."

"Why? I was so awful to you. I was a fucking monster."

I held my hands over my cheeks and hoped he didn't notice my tears, "I loved you anyway."

I don't know what I was expecting, but it wasn't him looking me dead in the eye and with all seriousness saying, "I'm sorry, Parker."

He went to touch my shoulder, but caught himself, "All the shit I did, all the shit I've said, I'm sorry. I wish I could go back; I wish I could undo it. I never meant any of it, you were too good for me and I..." he trailed off when I rolled my eyes, "What?"

"You don't have to lie."

"I'm not,"

"Come on, you were a monster, but I was a piece of shit. Every time you said it, you were right." I shrugged, "And every time you hit me, I deserved it."

"You don't honestly believe that..." He trailed off.

I ignored him, "It's not like I didn't hit you back, we fought like dogs."

"I broke your collarbone,"

"And I broke your pretty boy nose, what's your point?"

"Hey, come on," He hesitated, but could tell I was too broken down to see him as a threat now, so he gently wrapped his hand around my jaw and moved my head, so I'd look at him. He was so gentle with me, which was nothing like him, but I didn't really care, I craved his command like the bottom I am.

Maybe Donnie was onto something.

Travis' eyes searched mine, he sighed, "I loved you, but I didn't know how to, it wasn't you."

My eyes burned as I teared up, "I still love you."

He ran his fingers through my hair, along my scalp and down my neck. The way only he could.

"I always come back to you, y'know? You're the one thing I can't kick."

"Kiss me,"

He seemed surprised I asked, like we weren't both thinking about it.

I pulled him closer by his shirt, pressing my mouth to his familiar lips was like climbing into bed after a long day.

He kissed me back, his hands cupping the sides of my face.

I don't think I've ever felt comfort like this before, he just felt like home.

I thought I was taking things too far by laying back and pulling him on top of me, until he started kissing down my throat.

It was so hot, but after I popped a few of the buttons on his shirt he stopped and sat back on his side of the couch.

"Goddamn," He laughed while shaking his head again, "What the hell is it about you?"

I wanted to say something smart-assed, like I was too good for him, or that he missed his chance. But my tongue was just in the guy's mouth, who the fuck was I kidding?

Travis cleared his throat, crossed his legs and tried to continue the conversation like nothing happened.

"So, I take it you're not seeing anyone?"

I shook my head, "Are you?"

"No,"

"Then what's your problem?!"

"*What's my problem?*"

"Yeah! You're just gonna dry hump a guy and leave him high, dry, and hard?"

He blushed a little and let out a more awkward laugh this time, "Sorry, if I overstepped, I didn't wanna..."

"I do! Fuck me."

Another slightly awkward laugh, when I didn't laugh back, he gave me a look, "You're serious?"

"Hey, it was a long bus ride over here."

He chewed on his bottom lip, thinking before he spoke, but it was so sexy I couldn't resist.

When I kissed him again, he scooted me over and onto his lap.

"You've always been so straight to the point."

"Shut up." I threw my hoodie and shirt across the couch and pulled him closer by wrapping my arms around his neck.

Travis laughed.

"Not what a guy wants when his shirt's off."

"No, nah," he kissed square in the middle of my chest and up my neck, "I can't believe your nipples are still pierced."

"You said you liked 'em!"

"It was a dare! I didn't think you'd actually go through with it!"

"Wait till you see what else I got pierced since then." I winked.

He chuckled, "You still got your tongue pierced?"

I stuck my tongue out and rolled the barbell in it.

"Good boy," he pat my face then let his warm hands find their way to my hips, then he paused for a second, "You're freezing. Let me turn on the..."

"Jesus, stop talking, dude."

He tipped my chin up with his finger. Staring into my eyes he asked with a smile, "You sure 'bout this?"

Hell, if this was my last night as a free man...

(＼(•̀ᴡ•́)／)

To be fair, just seeing Travis again made me so happy, but having him on top of me turned the unholy fucking godly.

He could've done absolutely anything to me and I would've loved it, but something was... Different.

Something was missing from the nostalgia, then it dawned on me; *he cared.*

Back then when we'd have sex, sometimes it just felt like he was using me. And I guess Donnie was right, that's why I was really here, that's what I was really craving.

God, how much more broken could I possibly be? Who wants that?

Travis had his arm around me, playing with my hair, he pressed another kiss to my mouth, "You good? You got quiet all of a sudden."

"Sorry," I forced a giggle and hoped he didn't ask what I was thinking about.

He sat up, leaning over me to pull a cigarette and a lighter out of the side table drawer.

"You still smoke?" He asked.

"Meh," I put my head on his chest, "Got anything better?"

He blew the smoke in my face with a smirk, an old inside joke I couldn't believe he remembered.

I grabbed his face and kissed him. I had to practically choke back the words I love you.

"Seriously, you don't got a joint or something?"

He chuckled, "I toldja, I'm sober."

"You were serious about that?"

"Mm, unfortunately, especially 'cause I miss doing coke off your ass."

I jokingly gasped, "Did you just call me flat? After all that?"

He laughed, "I've missed this, y'know..."

I put my forehead against his and said all sappy, "I've been missing you to death."

"I'm glad you're here." He kissed me.

I collapsed against him and laid on his chest while he rubbed my back.

After a while he said my name softly, "Parker?"

"Hmm?"

"I don't wanna ruin this, but I gotta ask... Why are you really here?"

What was left of my blood ran cold.

How the fuck was I supposed to answer that?

I wanted to be honest, pour my heart out to him, but the truth sounded more made up than any lie I could've said.

I cleared my throat, I kept my head pressed to his chest so I didn't have to look him in the eye, "Well, uh, I found out I'm really sick, and I don't... I don't know what's coming next for me."

When he didn't say anything for a while I felt like I needed to put space between us in case he had as bad of a reaction as Caitlin did.

I scooted over back to my side of the bed; he was just looking at me.

"... It from the drugs?"

I shook my head.

He searched my face, his eyes softened, and I could finally breathe, "I'm sorry."

I cleared my throat again to break the silence, "I just wanted to see you again before shit went sideways."

"Jesus, you sound like Robbie."

The words hung in the air.

Robbie was a really good friend of Travis' when we were together.

He was a great guy; he got HIV from heroin but never wanted to do anything about it. He was the reason Travis made me quit.

Robbie never wanted to be treated like he was sick, so he never acted like it, even refusing to go to the hospital when he really should have.

I helped Travis take care of him for a few months when he got too sick to do anything.

It still kills me thinking about how I found him...

"Is it that bad?" Travis interrupted my flash back, "I mean is it..."

I knew what he meant, so I just nodded once.

"There's no meds, or chemo? There's no treatment?"

"I'm too far gone."

Travis blew out a deep sigh.

All he could say was, "Jesus Christ."

Thinking about it, seeing it so linear...

I choked on my tears.

Travis felt bad for me, but I doubted that he'd really care when I was gone. Hell, I doubted anyone would.

He reached over, running his fingers through my hair again, "Is there anything I can do? Is there like appointments I can take you to, or like..."

I cut him off, "Will you just hold me for a while?"

I couldn't believe the request even though it came from me.

He leaned into me, pressing a soft kiss on my lips as he wrapped his arms around me.

I nuzzled against his chest.

God, it felt so good.

I felt so safe. So loved.

It was all I had ever wanted.

I could've died there, and I would've died happy.

A happy ending to a sad, miserable life.

How poetic.

(＼(•̀w•́)／)

November 20 2007

08:27

PARKER

Travis and I spent a good part of the night having sex, until we finally passed out around 2 or 3AM.

I fell asleep with his arms around me, and when I woke up to roll over, he was practically suffocating me. He made it a point to hold me all night, so I thought it was weird when I woke up and he wasn't there.

"Trav?" I called out.

When I didn't get an answer, I pulled on a shirt off the floor and shuffled out into the kitchen.

A piece of paper was duct taped to the fridge.

"Went out for a surprise.

Be back in 20.

Don't take your tight ass anywhere.

- Trav"

I went to toss it on the counter and heard a loud thud from the bathroom.

Rushing to the bathroom door in his bedroom, the pit in my stomach was impossible to ignore.

"Hey?" I knocked, "Trav, I thought I heard something?"

When he didn't answer I opened the door, or tried to, but it was jammed.

Using my shoulder, I got it to budge enough for me to squeeze through.

Then I realized the door wasn't stuck, Travis was in a heap he had collapsed against the door.

From there everything gets blurry.

"Travis? Hey. Hey!" No matter how loud I yelled or how hard I smacked him across the face, he didn't respond.

My hands went numb as adrenaline washed any thoughts out of my brain.

He made the most horrifying gurgling noise I've ever heard, for a split second I was relieved to know he was breathing, until I saw the foam pooling out of his mouth. At the same time I finally saw the belt around his bicep and the needle that fell in front of him.

"No... No!"

I struggled to sit him up, every time I put him against the bath he'd slump over.

He kept slipping in and out of consciousness, when he'd come to he'd start panicking again, 'causing the rattle in his chest to speed up.

His panic only fueled mine, and I had no idea what to do. I'd seen too many overdoses to know how bad this was.

I held him back up and made sure he hunched forward to help the choking.

I knew I had to go get help, but I didn't want to leave him, I couldn't.

"Hey, okay, I'm... I don't know where my phone is," I wiped the sweat off his forehead, "I'll be right back, okay?"

When I went to stand he struggled to reach my arm and held onto me so I didn't leave.

"It's okay, I'll be right back." My voice broke.

His grip wouldn't loosen, he didn't say anything. He was choking too badly to, but he looked me in the eye for what felt like twenty minutes before his eyes fluttered shut.

"No!"

I scrambled to get him on his back, slamming my hands against his chest. I tried desperately to remember how to do CPR from what I'd seen on ER.

Under my hands, I could feel his shallow breathing stop.

"*Travis!*" I screamed bloody murder, "Travis! Please!"

I knew he was gone; I think my body knew it before I did because I just collapsed next to him.

"Please," I mumbled, I pressed my forehead to his chest, "Please, don't leave me like this. Please. It's not supposed to end like this. It's not supposed to be you..."

I don't know how long I was there. Just on the cold tile, holding Travis' corpse and sobbing.

I guessed the neighbors finally heard me screaming 'cause I could hear sirens approaching, and I was only able to get it together enough to know how bad this was going to look.

I clenched my eyes shut and tried to take a deep breath.

"Baby," I muttered between my tears, "I-I... I gotta go." I choked out, "I've got... I'm sorry."

Cupping his cheeks, I gave him one last kiss, "I love you, Trav. I love you so much. I'm sorry."

As gently as I could, I placed him back on the tile.

On my way out I had one last coherent thought to swipe his belt and needle.

He doesn't need to be remembered that way. I told myself as I tripped down every stair and fell through the building's front doors.

I got down the block before I lost complete control.

I couldn't feel any part of my body, I couldn't even keep myself upright.

But someone caught me, and I was being supported by them.

Part of me hoped it wasn't a cop, while the other half knew by the silk that brushed against my face.

God, if there was a single person in the world I didn't want to see right now, but I was just so glad someone else was here.

If he was there, I could pretend this was just some awful nightmare.

"Tell me this isn't real..." I muffled, burying my face into Donatello's chest, "Please, please."

He wrapped one arm around my waist to keep me upright and put the other on the back of my head in an attempt to comfort me.

"Tell me it isn't real!" I wailed.

"I am afraid so... I'm sorry."

(＼(•̀w•́)／)

Aaron

I got up this morning and tried to just brush off the other night.

I felt so guilty, and I wasn't even sure why.

Okay, maybe I invaded Parker's privacy a little, but I was worried!

Although, I suppose the path to Hell Is paved with good intentions.

No matter how hard I tried to convince myself I didn't do anything wrong, Parker's face popped back up in my mind. He looked so... Hurt, scared, lost.

I wish I would've just hugged him and told him it was going to be okay.

Hell, I wish I knew why this was nagging at me so badly.

I made myself get out of bed and tried to keep my mind busy. When meditation and making coffee didn't help, I turned to books.

"That's a good book," Celeste seemed more ramble-y than usual and it added to my anxiety, "Scott loved it so much he made me read it. It's been a while, though. Before Conner... Hmm, that must've been while we were in college."

She stopped when I stood up fast.

I need a drink. I thought to myself but quickly shook the thought out of my head and grabbed my shoes.

Instead, I went for a run so that way when I talked to my mom later this week, I could tell her I was literally running away from my anxiety.

I decided it was probably time to head back when the second side of my tape ran out, and while I could still recognize where I was.

When I got back to the building I paused on the front steps and held down the speed dial on my phone.

I sighed when it went straight to voicemail.

Staring down at my sneakers I tried to think of what I was going to say while I waited for the beep.

"Hey, hi... I'm sorry about last night, I should've given you your space. I'm sorry. I'll leave you alone, I just wanted to tell you that it's going to be okay. I want to help, but I don't think I really know how... Sorry, this is a lot to leave on voicemail, just call me back, okay? Let me know if you need anything."

I then scared the shit out of Conner when I let myself back into the apartment.

"Jesus," He jumped forward, trying to contain his cornflake spill to the countertop, "This isn't going to become a thing, is it?"

"Jogging?"

Conner chuckled when he realized it was his own observations he should blame, "Can't you leave a note, or something?"

I suppressed a laugh, "Sorry."

Nate walked through the room, he nodded once to acknowledge Conner as he tried to fix the collar on his shirt, then his eyes locked in on me and a smirk broke out across his face, "¡Mujeriego!"

Conner was as confused as I was, especially when Nate clapped me on the back.

"I'm so proud of you."

"Huh?"

"Y'know our boy stumbled in here the other night quarter to midnight, smelling like tequila, and covered in stripper dust? ¿Dímelo?" He tucked his tongue in his cheek, "Oh, right." He realized something then made a V with his first and middle finger while sticking his tongue out.

Conner smacked his shoulder, "What's the matter with you, jeez."

"What?"

Conner thankfully changed the topic, "Doesn't your work open at nine?"

Nate just shrugged, "Yeah?"

"And they don't need a receptionist until," Conner turned over his watch, "11:25?"

Nate shrugged again, "I'm always late, what're they gonna do? Fire me?"

"That's exact- Yes! They're going to fire you."

"I'll fake a limp," he brushed it off, "So who's she? She hot?"

I saw an opportunity and decided to pull what Courtney had always told me about bargaining, "I'll tell you, but you gotta tell me something."

Nate chuckled, "Pull her hair, they love that."

I rolled my eyes, "Not that."

"Then what?"

"What's been going on with you and Parker?"

Everything about him completely shifted, all of a sudden, he wasn't playing coy anymore, he completely shut down, "Don't worry 'bout it, huh?"

"You keep saying that."

"'Cause it ain't nothing, drop it."

"No, you're starting to freak me. You know something, is he going to do something stupid?"

He scoffed, "It's Parker,"

"Come on,"

He just rolled his eyes at me and grabbed his jacket off the hook by the door.

"Nathaniel,"

His eyes snapped to me in response, but quickly narrowed, "Don't government name me, perrito."

"What the hell is going on?" Conner asked.

Nate's only response was to slam the door on the way out.

I looked over at Conner who shared my confusion and concern.

I followed Nate down the stairs, and he wasn't happy about it

We got down to his truck, he leaned against the driver's door, fishing a cigarette from behind his ear and out of his hair.

I waited for him to say something, but he just made a "what do you want?" gesture while he lit his cigarette, giving me an annoyed look without a word.

I crossed my arms in a challenge that got us nowhere.

"You told Conner you were quitting."

"Told Court I would a week 'fore she died, too," He took a deep breath before taking another hit, "Also told my mom I wasn't selling dope."

I made a motion for the cigarette.

He let me take it and then tucked his hands into his jeans' pocket, "Fine, toss it. I'm just as bad as Parker."

I shifted the cigarette between my fingers and watched the embers burn, "Earlier I told you I'd tell you something if you told me something, right?"

I put it to my mouth.

Nate rolled his eyes, "C'mon, got the point, perrito."

I took a long drag, and he looked at me like I suddenly had sprouted another head.

"I used to smoke in high school," I dropped it to the pavement and stomped it out with my sneaker.

He just chuckled, "You'd think after years with me you'd be a better liar."

"I'm not lying. I had bad anxiety, well, worse than I do now. I smoked like a chimney; my mom hated it. I used to smoke pot too, but that was harder to hide."

It took him a minute to actually believe me, he softened when he finally came around, "You stop when your dad got sick?"

"You know, every part of me wishes I had but no, I didn't stop until... I quit when I moved out here."

There was a pause before Nate sighed.

"Look, I moved out here, cuz I got a mess in Oakland waiting for me, okay? My friend got all this shit and fucked this guy over. This crazy motherfucker showed up ate half my burger and killed a fucking guy. When the boss showed up, told me to get his wife outta there, I did and I ain't never been back. I got no idea what's waiting for me."

"Hm, that's unfortunate," I crossed my arms, "It was even more unfortunate when it happened to John Travolta in Pulp Fiction!"

"Goddamn it."

"What's wrong with you?"

"I don't know..." He hesitated, then tried to play it off by rubbing his eyes so he didn't have to look at me when he asked, "How'dja know you were, y'know?"

At first, I didn't know what he meant, then I was taken back by the question, "Jewish?"

Any sincerity dropped off his face and was quickly replaced by sarcasm, "Yeah, dude, yeah. I wanna know when you figured it out, tonto!" he shook his head and pulled open the door of his truck.

"Come on,"

"Just drop it, okay?"

"Nate..."

He'd already slammed the door and threw the truck into reverse.

I shook my head, "I'm so confused."

(＼(•̀ω•́)／)

NATE

Half down the block, I kinda expected to take a turn and see Aaron's car behind me but he finally got the hint.

I made it to work, but I was pissed now.

Sitting in my truck, I pounded Parker's number into my keyboard.

When it went straight to voicemail, I wanted to roll the window down and whip the phone across the parking garage.

The voicemail beeped and I lashed out.

"You're being an asshole, you cunt. You made this fucking mess, you gotta come clean it up, fucking coward."

(＼(•̀ω•́)／)

15:30

Conner

It had been a hell of a week, and if memory served me right, it was only Wednesday.

I guess I didn't realize how connected I was to Parker in the fact that not knowing if he was okay made me a nervous wreck.

I just couldn't shake the feeling that something bad was going to happen, and it was going to be massive.

The raging black hole of anxiety in my chest never settled, it grew worse every time I tried to call Parker, and it went straight to voicemail.

Drew, being the incredible person she is, made it a point to drag me out of the apartment when Aaron and Nate went to work.

She drug me to get a haircut, go grocery shopping, simple things that felt like daunting mountains right now.

We sat in her car for a few minutes after the barber.

Drew ran her fingers through my hair, analyzing my haircut, "There's what my mom calls "an acceptable young man." She joked.

I fidgeted with my phone between my hands.

She kissed my cheek when I didn't respond, "Lovey, a watched phone never rings."

"I know," I sighed, "I've already called him three times today. Screw it."

I flicked my phone open and hit redial, I didn't care if I was being a nuisance anymore.

"He's still not picking up?"

I shook my head, and let it ring through to his voicemail.

I was annoyed that he didn't pick up, but my anxiety quickly overtook it.

"Hey, it's me. I don't know what you're doing, and I don't care, okay? I'm not mad anymore, whatever's going on can we just forget about it? It's gone, just come home. Just let me know you're okay." I paused for a second, "I love you, Parker. We're gonna be fine. Call me back."

Drew kissed my cheek again, "Everything's going to be okay."

"I hope so."

November 21 2007

12:08

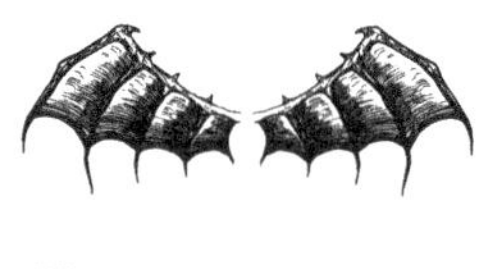

PARKER

I didn't know what it was, if it was a trauma response, how strung out I was, or if it was drinking the shit ass mini bar, but I cried until I finally passed out and slept through the rest of yesterday. But my dreams were haunted by Travis.

By his panic, his fear...

It all just twisted the knife deeper into my heart.

I was starting to wake up when I felt a weight shift at the foot of the bed.

I threw the blanket over my head, so I didn't have to see Donatello, I was sick of his stupid, pretty face.

The bed moved like he bounced on it.

"Go to Hell." I hissed.

"Oh, c'mon! That's a little harsh to say to a dead girl."

The voice was so clear and so familiar I thought I was having a stroke for a second.

When I ripped the blanket off my head Courtney was standing by the side of the bead, hovering over me so her hair brushed against my face.

"Hiya."

I floundered trying to sit up and nearly headed butted her.

"What the fuck!" I grabbed at her shoulders, shaking her a little too hard outta my own disbelief.

"Jesus Christ," She eased my grip off her biceps.

I sat on the bed while the rest of the room swirled around us, "Oh, God, I'm way too fucking high for this."

"You're telling me," She crossed her arms with a chuckle.

She looked... Fine, like nothing ever happened, her eyes were bright, her hair was freshly straightened, I couldn't believe it.

"Okay, I know it's been a while since you've seen a woman, but come on, close your mouth." She joked, "Aren't you gonna say something?"

I couldn't say anything, nothing was willing to come out, all I was able to do was tackle her.

"Park!" She stumbled back under my weight, "What're you doin'?"

I pulled back slightly, squishing her face in my hands, "How? W-what happened? How? Are you okay?"

"I'm fine." She laughed as she moved my hands away from her face.

I was so fucking happy, okay but happy didn't cut it. I was relieved, amazed, and about fifteen other things I don't have words for.

"Are you real?" I whispered.

She shrugged, "Ish."

I scanned her, for the past few months any time I thought of her I could only picture her covered in her own blood, "What do you mean…ish?"

"Think like a 'Ghost Of Christmas Pasts' sitch, oh. Oh! Wait, no I'm Clarence!" She clapped her hands together, "Anyway, continue."

"Wait, w-what does that mean?"

"It's A Wonderful Life? Babe," Her expression softened when she realized I wasn't following, "I'm dead."

The words stuck like another knife to my chest.

I shook my head, "No, no, that's okay, it's okay! Conner, Con thinks he's figured it out, you'll be okay, we'll both be okay."

"No, I don't mean dead like you, honey, I mean for real."

"But" I stifled a laugh before it could come out as a sob. I poked at her arm and shook her again, "You're here, you're in front of me, you're, that's impossible! You're still here, Aaron said it. He knows it, I know it."

I felt like I was going to throw up and pass out at the same time.

"I don't wanna tell you this," She sighed, "I'm not real... I mean, I am, I'm here I'm with you. But I'm just visiting."

"I don't, I don't understand..."

She shrugged, "I'm Freddy Krueger-ing it. I don't get the whole rigmarole either, but I just needed to talk to you."

I got really cold, and then I felt like I was disconnected from my own body. I didn't know what to do, or what to say, I didn't even know what I was feeling.

"... This is a vision..."

"I guess."

I mean, we had to assume she was dead, but I never believed it, not completely. The confirmation just hurt so badly.

I tried to just swallow the pain, move forward and listen to what someone else had to say for the first time in my life.

"What happened to you? Did, where's your body? Did Donatello kill you?"

She shook her head, her blonde hair feathering out behind her, "I don't know what you're talking about."

"How you died? What happened? Who did it?"

"No one," Her blue eyes searched me for an answer, "I mean, I don't really remember it."

"None of it?"

It was so traumatic I could remember every second of it unprompted, how could she not?

"I kinda remember laying in the grass and..." She trailed off and shook her head again, trying to clear the fog in her brain, "Not important now, okay? Stop worrying about that, we need to talk."

"About what, then?"

"I know what you're doing," she whispered.

"Huh?"

"Stringing Donnie along, getting him to agree to leave the guys alone, letting him think you're going to join..."

I sighed, running my thumb over the scars on my wrist, "... That's what's best for everyone," I squeezed my eyes closed, "Please don't try to talk me out of it."

"I'm not gonna," she said bluntly, "I think it's a good idea."

My eyes shot back open, I expected her to be screaming at me by now, "... Really?"

"Well, no, I mean... You're right, there's only one way he's gonna leave everyone alone." She hesitated for a second, but it turned into a long pause as she scanned my face, her eyes probed into me as she thought.

"Listen to me, okay?" Something changed, something shifted, and she was suddenly on edge, "I'm supposed to give you a message, and I'm supposed to tell you about how much this life has to offer and blah blah blah. I know you're hurting; I can feel it rolling off you, but listen to me..."

"I know, I know." I rolled my eyes, "I know the whole spiel, I've heard it a million times. My mind's made up, Court."

She grabbed me by my shoulders so hard I thought her fingers would leave bruises, "It can't be. Look at me!" Her eyes widened to emphasize her next words, "There are somethings you can't escape from, you've been barely sliding by your whole life, eventually there's going to be something you can slide out of. I don't wanna see you suffer."

"Huh?"

"You can't spend your whole life giving in, sometimes the answer is running away, do you get me?"

I blinked a few times. I felt like I was trying to do a connect-the-dots of a Picasso painting.

When I didn't answer she tried again, "All your life you've been letting shit hit you like a train, when do you finally get off the fucking track?"

"... You're fine with this? You're fine with me doing this?"

"No, but" She sighed, she looked so heart-broken, "What's the alternative? This is a losing battle, and you know it, it's only going to get so much worse! You don't want anyone involved, but if you get... Look at it this way, you have two options and they both end bloody."

I scoffed, "So what am I supposed to do? Beg a God I don't believe in?"

She took a deep breath before she looked back into my eyes, "Would you rather be killed when the bombs drop, or in the war that comes after them?"

"Yeah..." I tried to swallow around the lump forming in my throat.

"No more pain, no more mourning, no more suffering, that's all you want, right?"

"That sounds amazing." I dipped my head, but held onto her hand, afraid she was just going to vanish again.

I felt her other hand on my face, "Look at me," this time the words lacked their bite, she was trying to be gentle with me.

When I looked up at her, her eyes had that same intense twinkle that I was missing so badly.

"It's time! You've been doing this for too long. You deserve better."

"But... Do I really?" my voice broke, "I'm kind of a bag of dicks."

"Oh. for sure. But you are the most sensitive, caring, outgoing bag of dicks I've ever met, and you deserve some peace."

I put my head on her shoulder, she felt cold.

"... What about Conner? A-and Aaron? And Nate."

"They'll be okay."

"How do you know?"

There was a slight hesitation before she chuckled, "I'm dead, remember? I know who's gonna win the Superbowl, I even know what the year 2020's gonna look like for Christ's sake."

I lifted my head to give her a curious look.

She shook her head with a shrug, "Some kinda Apocalypse over toilet paper, it's no good, but headphones don't have wires anymore so that's pretty cool I guess."

It was quiet for a minute.

"I want this to be over." I practically whispered; my throat was killing me from all the crying I've done over the past week.

"You have that power." She put her hand on my chest, "You know what to do."

I glanced down at her hand, which was right over my heart.

I nodded.

She stood and I hugged her as tight as I could, "I miss you so fucking much."

"I know, babe. I miss you too." She hugged me back

"Don't leave me again."

"I'm sorry, I have a feeling we'll see each other soon, okay?"

"Please don't..."

She tightened her grip on me and dropped her voice to a whisper I could barely make out, "Don't trust him."

November 22 2007

19:35

PARKER

I hadn't slept since my "encounter with the other side".

I spent the rest of the night thinking about… Well, everything, my night with Travis, how I left things with Conner and Nate. I even thought about the last time I spoke to my mom. Then it dawned on me I couldn't remember the last time I talked to my dad.

It was just a slip'n'slide of all my life's fuck ups from there.

The last twenty-four years of guilt suffocated me.

I wish I could say I was grappling with the decision to execute my plan, but that guilt solidified it for me, it's what was best for everyone, truly.

Besides, I knew since I was fifteen that this was going to be how it went, I'd never even get into the 27 Club, I would always end up another failed artist in the statistics. Then when I got infected, I knew this was the only answer to that problem.

I didn't care though, as long as everyone else was happier and safer, I'd happily climb on that cross.

The Jesus of broken dreams and lost hope everywhere...

God, where's Nate to call me an emo piece of shit when you need him?

I crawled out from the motel bed and forced myself outside.

I zoned out on the walk, ditching my hoodie. I let the sun burn into my skin and savored the pain.

Courtney's words echoed in my head, "Die with the bombs or in the war?"

A drug out, blood soaked, battle, and a body riddled with shrapnel and pain. Or just a thing in the sky, a bright light and then a vast field of nothingness.

It would all be over.

No more pain.

No more suffering.

That sounded nice, and I hoped death would be that comforting.

"Hi..." I crouched down on the grass when I got to the park, awkwardly talking to the bench in front of me.

"You're making me feel like an idiot," I mumbled, playing with the wet blades of grass between my fingers.

"You are an idiot." I could imagine Courtney laughing at me.

"I'm sitting in a park, talking to a piece of metal. You're not even buried under it..." I trailed off, "This is stupid, but I just, I need someone to talk to... God help me,"

I glanced at the clock overlooking the plaza, "I've been sober for eight hours, I've slept on it... Shouldn't I be more, I don't know, more hesitant? I mean, I've spent longer weighing my options on what shade of black nail polish to steal last week, but this... Why is this such an easy decision?"

I sighed and pulled a piece of grass up and shredded it over and over, "Shouldn't I be worried about what happens after? Shouldn't I be scared? God, Travis looked so scared..."

I shook that thought out of my head, "Shouldn't I care? Or feel something? Anything? ... I guess I do, but I just feel... Relieved. I don't know. The only thing I'm worried about's the guys, y'know? I know you said they'd be fine but what if they're mad? What if they hate me? But I guess that doesn't really matter, does it? ... I dunno, I don't want Conner to have to be the one that tells my mom I'm dead, I don't want Aaron to be the one that has to claim my body when my mom won't, I don't want Nate to think it's 'cause of him..."

Even when the tears began to run down my face, I hadn't noticed I was crying, "I don't want them to mourn me, or think that they could've changed something. I don't want them to hate me. Even though everyone else does, including me, but I can't have them hate me..."

I leaned forward and rested my head against the front of the bench to cry in peace.

"Parker?" There was a woman's voice behind me.

I jumped, but then I whipped around excitedly when I heard the tone.

Drew stood over me with an umbrella and some flowers, I felt my face fall.

"Sorry, I didn't mean to scare you."

"No, it's fine, just... Thought you were someone else..." I mumbled.

"Mm, I've been getting that a lot. Mind if I join you?"

"Yeah, sorry." I got up and tried to get the grass off my jeans, "I was just gonna..."

She stopped me and nodded towards the bench, "I'd appreciate it if you stayed, I don't like being here alone." She placed her flowers on the plaque, then took a seat on the bench.

"Con's not with you?"

"No, I'm coming from my last class." She shook her head and patted the bench next to her.

I felt like it was easier to just sit than to fight it.

Based on her insistence, I wasn't expecting it to be so quiet.

After a while she finally said, "Seems like waste."

"Huh?"

"The flowers," She shrugged, "Courtney hated flowers, but I don't exactly know where I would get a bouquet of gas station sandwiches." She joked.

"They're pretty." I felt the need to say something and that was all that came out.

"Thanks, I've been getting into gardening with my mom... Maybe that's why it seems like a waste, but I read somewhere that the ducks will eat them… Courtney would've just stomped them to death."

I tried to laugh but it came out more of a cough, "Sounds like her."

"Where there is chaos there is beauty." Drew chuckled, "I'm pretty sure those were her first words."

"I miss her like hell."

"Me too." She nodded, "I miss the way she made everything seem like it wasn't a big deal."

"Tell me about it..."

There was another long silence.

"How are you do..."

I cut her off, "Please don't ask."

"Conner mentioned..."

"I'm sure he's mentioned a lot about me."

"He's just worried about you, we all are. I've been wanting to talk since our last chat."

"Drew, please stop."

"I'm worried..."

"Don't," I snapped. I immediately felt bad about it, but I couldn't deal with the probing, "I'm sorry, I'm just..."

"You look like shit," She finished for me, "You haven't been sleeping, have you? I'm sure you're still not eating."

I shook my head, and just ignored it, "Can I ask you for a favor?"

Her arms were crossed, she was getting annoyed with me, "It depends on the favor."

"Stop worrying about me, all of you." I stood up and dug through my pocket for the crumpled-up papers I shoved in there this morning, "Give these to your boyfriend."

Her icy eyes scanned me and bore through my soul just like her sister's.

"One other thing?"

She nodded.

"Take care of Conner... Please?"

"Of course I will." She grabbed my hand as she took the ball of papers, "Do me a favor now, take care of yourself."

I nodded and pulled my hand away, "Planning on it."

(＼(•̀w•́)／)

CONNER

I could tell today was going to be a long day.

My computer kept freezing, when I finally gave up on it to make a cup of coffee I dropped and shattered the pot while it was full, by the time I got it cleaned up and went to go buy another one, my car wouldn't turn over and when it finally did my radio was stuck on the bluegrass station.

All before noon.

Not that I've ever been on the good side of luck. Today was just odder than usual, and I clearly wasn't the only one noticing it.

"Hey," I nodded to Nate as I tossed my keys in the bowl on the side table by the door... Which somehow tipped over and shattered into a million pieces right at my feet.

I sighed, and bent to pick up what I could, "Where's Aaron?"

"Bathroom." Nate shrugged, "He's been in there for five minutes."

I raised an eyebrow, dumping the remnants of our key bowl into the trash, "Bold words from a man that spends two hours in there every morning."

Nate gave me a serious look, "He's talking to himself, man."

"He always talks to himself."

Nate rolled his eyes, "He's having a conversation, bro."

"He's probably on the phone."

"Nope," He held up Aaron's Sidekick, "He's lost it, dude."

"I'm sure he's fine."

I went and lightly knocked on the bathroom door, but before I could even touch it the door flung open and Aaron blew past me.

"Are you okay?"

"Yes, no! Just..." He didn't say anything else; he just hurriedly put on his jacket and fumbled his keys.

"Where are you going?" Nate asked.

He didn't really answer, he sort of yelped incoherently on his way out of the front door.

Nate and I followed him.

"Aaron, what's going on?" I tried to catch up, "What happened?"

"I don't know!" He accidentally yelled, "I-I don't... We have to find him!"

"What?" Nate tried.

"Parker!" Aaron kept yelling.

I couldn't figure out where his panic was coming from but that didn't stop it from fueling the pit of anxiety in my stomach.

"Okay, but we have no idea where he is, so we need to go figure..." I put my hands on his shoulders and tried to rationalize the situation, but before I could even start my thought, divine intervention knocked me over the head in the form of my phone ringing.

I gestured for Nate to step in while I checked the screen to see Drew's name flashing.

I flipped it open, "Drew, I'm going to have to call..."

She spoke fast, I could barely differentiate between the words she was saying.

"I know you said you were giving him time, but I bumped into him at the cemetery, and we talked, and he asked me to give you this note and I know I shouldn't have read it but I just got this feeling, and it's a suicide letter and I didn't know what else to do!"

"What?"

"Parker! I think he's going to kill himself!"

"Okay, where are you?"

"I followed him into this motel downtown, the bitch at the front desk won't let me back, but I saw what room he went into. What should I do?"

I sighed, "You're amazing. We'll be right there, okay? Try to stay calm. We're on the way."

(＼(•̀w•́)／)

After breaking possibly every traffic law known to the State of Washington, I managed to get us to the run-down motel Drew texted me the address to.

"Thank God!" The second we were in the door Drew flagged us down, she gestured down the hall and placed herself in front of the annoyed desk clerk, "First-floor second door on the left."

Aaron gave us a quick nod and was down the hallway.

"Hey!" The guy behind the desk tried to step in, "She can't go back there!"

"He's a dude, and shut up, puta." Nate rolled his eyes throwing a twenty on the desk, "That fucker better still be alive 'cause that's twenty on the six hundred he owes me." Nate grumbled trailing behind Aaron.

"Are you okay?" I asked Drew as we followed behind.

Her blue eyes widened, "No idea."

Aaron was already working on the lock, he got it quickly, but the door clunk against the chain lock.

Nate moved Aaron out of the way before he threw his shoulder into the door, popping off the chain and swinging the door open.

We stumbled over each other trying to get through the door.

Parker was slumped over, propped up against the bed's headboard.

A puddle of viciously black blood pooled under him on the cheap bedspread, my eyes were too busy trailing up the large vertical cut that spanned his left forearm before I saw it.

Drew let out a horrified scream.

Parker's hunting knife, his favorite thing he's ever owned, made of solid pure silver, was plunged into his chest down to the hilt. Blood pulsed out of the wound in weak, inconsistent waves.

I couldn't handle the gruesome scene, but I couldn't force myself to look away.

"Parker!" I couldn't tell which one of us was yelling anymore.

I ran over to the side of the bed; his headphones were blasting and his IPod was in the pool of blood.

"Parker! Hey!" I ripped out his headphones and tried patting his face.

To my surprise, he moved away from my hand.

"He's alive!"

All of us took a collective sigh of relief.

"Parker!" I kept patting his face until he moved again, "Hey, wake up!"

"Five minutes." He slurred back to me.

"No, no, stay awake."

Everything felt so warped.

My heart was pounding loudly in my eyes, and the back of my mouth tasted like copper.

I couldn't wrap my head around anything that was happening, but Aaron and Nate were looking at me for our next move.

Drew, however, didn't miss a step.

She stepped between me and the wall, "If I help, do you think we can move him to the floor?"

"I, um, yeah." I nodded.

"Okay," she nodded and commanded the scene over my shoulder, "Aaron, I need you to see if the front desk has a first aid kit. Nate, see if you can find a maid's cart. I need towels, scissors, and any miniatures you can find, a lot of...everything."

Neither said a word but were both out the door immediately.

Quickly, I helped Drew gently move him to the carpet.

"What are you doing?" I finally regained my voice.

She shrugged as she tied her hair up and out of the way, "I guess we're going to find out."

She knelt by his side, "I need you to hold his head and try not to move him."

Cradling Parker's head, I scanned him closely.

It was like I had never noticed how *small* he was before, it sounded strange, but it was as if he was an endangered baby bird in my hands.

He seemed so vulnerable, so helpless.

All I wanted to do was fix it and protect him, but I had no idea how.

Seeing him like this, I felt like I had a matching knife in my heart.

Drew had her head on the unobstructed side of Parker's chest, listening.

Drew shot upright, "Oh, thank God! It didn't pierce his heart."

Parker's eyes fluttered open slightly, he looked at me for a second, his eyes dark and dull, before they rolled back into his skull.

Nate and Aaron slammed into each other on their way back.

"All they had was medical tape." Aaron offered.

"That's perfect, thank you." Drew wrapped one of the towels around the wound on his arm, it was only then did I realize I could see the muscle through the blood.

"Keep pressure on that." She instructed as she took the scissors from Nate, carefully cutting off Parker's blood-soaked tee shirt.

The six-inch blade was angled just under his ribcage and was stabbed through the tissue deep, I had to imagine only missing his mark by mere centimeters.

Black blood flowed out in a steady river now.

Drew paused, assessing the wound itself, "Silver burns, right?"

I nodded.

"How much? If I pull this out, do you think it would cauterize the wound?"

I tried to think, but my brain was like a computer on dial up, all I could think of was the hiss silver would make when I'd stab through a vampire.

I swallowed hard, "Y-yes, it should, yes."

"Alrighty," She poured two miniature vodkas over the wound and took another towel to cushion around the knife, "Parker, can you hear me?"

Parker moved slightly at the sound of her voice.

"I'm going to need you to hold your breath when I tell you too, alright?"

He tried to nod but was far too out of it.

I kept the pressure on his forearm, but used my free hand to wipe the hair, blood and soot out of his face, then I squeezed his shoulder, so he at least knew I was there.

Drew took a deep breath, if she was nervous, she didn't show it, "Okay, ready? Deep breath."

When Parker's breath hitched, she steadied her hand and slowly pulled the knife out.

The sizzle and smell of burning flesh filled the small room.

Parker convulsed slightly, coughing up blood as he did.

"Turn him on his side," Drew instructed.

I did as I was told.

Drew took Parker's left arm from me, I hadn't realized how deep that was either until I realized I was looking at muscle and that was flayed too, she carefully ran the blunt side of the knife against the wound to seal that too.

"Why, shouldn't he, why isn't the super healing thing working?" Aaron stammered out, visibly shaking

I shrugged, "I-I don't know. He hasn't eaten in months; he's lost a lot of blood..." I looked at the dark syrupy soot that covered my hands.

I've never been a squeamish person, but a thousand years of grizzly crime scene photos couldn't prepare me for watching it stream out of my best friend and soak through me.

I felt violently ill.

"He's... He's gonna be fine..." Nate's voice wavered and I couldn't tell if that was a question or a statement.

"He will be," Drew reassured, wiping her hands on a towel as she stood up.

"What do we do now?" I asked as I straightened myself out.

She sighed heavily, "In a perfect world he would go to the ICU. They'd give him a transfusion and put him on a morphine drip, but something tells me he's not feeling much anyway." She gestured vaguely to the white powder dusting the motel nightstand, "For now we just have to wait until he wakes up."

"Will he?" Aaron asked.

"He will, he's resilient." She assured me.

"Stubborn, more like." I ran my hands against my jeans in an effort to remove some of the gore, "God, I can't believe he did this."

"How..." Aaron's voice caught, "How do we know he did this, and it wasn't..." He pulled a strand of his hair in front of his face.

"If it was anyone else, they wouldn't have missed." Nate stated coldly.

Drew gave me her towel and tried to help me clean up, "We spoke for a little bit, he seemed really down... Enough for me to get suspicious."

"You said he gave you a note?" I asked, "What did it say? Do you still have it?"

She nodded and produced five pages crumpled together from her coat pocket.

She tried to straighten them out and desperately tried to wipe off the blood that dotted through.

I tried to read it, but the more I did my eyes blurred with rage and I couldn't make the scrambled letters make sense.

I scanned as much as I could before crumpling it back up, "He did it, I'm sure."

"How?" Aaron asked with a bite of hope in his voice.

I crammed the papers into my pocket, each one was a personal apology and a half assed excuse.

Biting my lip to keep my tears in, I answered, "It's his handwriting, he explained it. He said if the knife didn't kill him," my voice caught, "That he'd hoped that he drained enough blood to turn him so we would *have* to put him down."

Aaron tried to blink away his tears, "Why? Why would he do this?"

"Why does he do anything?" Nate shrugged.

"It doesn't matter right now," Drew interjected, "For now just focus on the fact that he'll be okay. That's all we can do."

I nodded, putting my arm around her waist, "Thank you doesn't seem like it's enough, but..."

"Thank you." Nate, Aaron, and I said at the same time.

Drew forced a smile, "It's okay, he's my friend too."

"Now what?" Aaron tried his damnedest, but the tears leaking out of his eyes betrayed him.

I shook my head, using my forearm to wipe my own tears, "Take my car, I know you have to work, I got this."

Aaron shook his head, "I'm not leaving."

"Can I at least take you home?" Drew offered.

He shook his head.

"Air, go home, Nate and I are just going to clean this up."

"I can clean." He whispered.

"Yeah, perrito, maybe..."

"No!" Aaron snapped, "I'm not going... I'm exactly where I need to be."

Nate and I exchanged a look.

"Okay, but if you..."

"I won't," He cut me off as he walked over and sat in the chair catty-corner to the bed.

"Drew, would you mind sitting with him?"

She nodded and followed Aaron.

Nate helped me strip the bed and get Parker back on it so he could at least have a somewhat comfortable place to wake up.

The rest was a matter of trying to explain the yelling and coming up with a reasonable explanation as to why we were going to clean the room ourselves to the motel clerk. Luckily the place was shady enough that not a lot of questions were asked.

Drew, Aaron, and I scrubbed the entire room, carpet to ceiling, while Nate "took care" of what was left of Parker's drugs. I didn't ask.

"Should I be alarmed that you guys know how to get blood out of carpet so easily?" Drew tried to joke.

"Mm," I forced a chuckle, "New Year's 2004, Parker got drunk and jumped through our glass top coffee table,"

"I fell trying to help him up." Aaron finished.

While we finished cleaning up Nate conveniently and selflessly offered to go pick up some food, at this point, we had been there for at least three hours, and I was too tired to yell at him so I complied.

(＼(•̀w•́)／)

22:00

By the time Nate got back with far too many Chinese food boxes, and a pint of blood from our freezer, Parker still wasn't awake, but the room was the cleanest in motel history.

Drew got Parker started on a blood IV immediately, when she finished that we all sat on the floor, quietly picking at our food with plastic forks.

The trauma was too much to ignore, but it was all we could do to keep ourselves together.

The room was so goddamn quiet.

Aaron put his food down taking a deep breath, he ran his hands over his face before he broke the silence, "My uncle killed himself."

The room was even quieter as we all tried to think of an appropriate thing to say.

"It was while he was living with us, shot himself in the head like it was nothing."

"Jesus," Nate mumbled.

"I am so sorry." Drew offered her deepest sympathies.

"You never told us that," I added, softly.

"I know," Aaron picked at the carpet beneath him, "It was a long time ago, before I started high school... I don't like to talk about it..." His voice caught, "But he was like the closest thing I had to an older brother, and I was so lost and fucked up for so long, and then I met you guys..." He took a sharp breath, "I can't lose you guys too, it's hard enough without Courtney."

"Come here." I scooted over to comfort Aaron.

He slid off his glasses and buried his face in my shoulder.

"We're not going anywhere."

"Ever." Nate leaned over to put his chin on Aaron's head but kept his eggroll just in case.

Aaron let out a tiny squeak that had a hint of a chuckle, "Can you stop eating?"

"No."

"You're getting crumbs in his hair." I interjected.

"They'll brush out." Nate waved me off.

"You know," Drew took Aaron's hand, "I'm sure Parker can hear you if you wanted to go talk to him."

"I think that's a good idea." I patted Aaron's back.

Aaron sat upright, he slid his glasses back on with a nod, "Yeah, yeah, I want to sit with him."

Drew sighed as we all watched Aaron take a cautious seat on the bed with Parker.

"I am so sorry about all of this." She said, hushed.

I shook my head, lowering my voice, "Don't be, I honestly don't know what we would've done without you."

She sat next to me, rubbing my shoulder, "It's just so terrible."

Nate shrugged, shoveling rice into his mouth, "Well, that's Park."

Drew tilted her head, "Has he done something like this before?"

"Unfortunately," I nodded, "In middle school, before we met, he drank floor cleaner."

"So, it's not the first time?" Drew asked.

"It ain't even the second time," Nate snarked.

My attention quickly snapped over to him, "What?"

Nate shrugged like he realized he blurted out something he shouldn't have, then his demeanor shifted in a way I wasn't familiar with being aimed towards me, "Nothin', somethin' else."

"Well, what are you talking about?"

He rolled his eyes like I was the one lying, "Dunno, don't remember."

"Okay, so," I crossed my arms, "Is that what you want to stick to, or do you want to try again?"

He feigned a shocked look, I didn't buy it so he rolled his eyes again, "Fine. We're smoking weed a while back, mentioned a few years ago he drove his car into a tree."

I felt like pieces to the puzzle were finally falling into place, but not enough to make a discernible image.

"I don't, when? Why?"

Nate shrugged again, "Didn't ask, said it was a bad break up."

"Why would you lie about that?"

"Park asked me not to say anything," Nate gestured to the bed with his fork, "Wish I did."

"Why does it matter?"

"Beats the hell outta me."

I narrowed my eyes on him.

He sarcastically motioned an X over his heart with the plasticware.

Drew sighed, putting her head on my shoulder, "I need to call my mom, she's going to lose her mind."

I just nodded and put my arm around her.

"I'm sure she's going to want to talk to you." She chuckled to herself as she stood up, "I'll be right back."

"I'll come with you." I hit Nate's knee as I got up I mouthed "Watch them."

"Whatever."

(＼(•̀ w •́)／)

23:17

Nate

"Watch them."

I rolled my eyes, sitting against the wall behind me.

"Nah, man. Thought I'd snort what was left of Parker's blow and let him sort it out." I thought to myself

I blew the air out of my lungs, wishing I hadn't tossed my cigarettes when Air freaked me the fuck out.

What a fucking mess.

Sitting on a musky ass old carpet, eleven o'clock on a Wednesday night 'cause my friend tried to gouge his own heart out.

Yeah, sounds 'bout right.

It wasn't 'til now that everything started setting in.

Maybe I'm too dense but none of it made any fucking sense.

Everyone was sad, but I was just pissed to hell.

I didn't get it.

I shook my head to get myself to stop thinking and tried to focus on Aaron, he needed me, no matter how confused or pissed off I am.

I tilted my head so I could see both of them.

Parker was still gone, he looked dead.

Hell, I'd seen the guy passed out more times than I could count but this was... This was just so weird.

Aaron sat by his side, careful not to disturb him. Like ninety pounds of Aaron was going to bother him.

It took me a while to realize Aaron was talking.

"He was a dick and he's sorry." Aaron quietly muttered, I could barely hear him.

I chuckled to myself; there's a fifty-fifty chance he was talking about me.

"But he was glad you were there. He loved seeing you..."

I watched them for a minute, the way Aaron was petting Park's hair was kinda adorable, it's very... *Aaron.*

"I'm sorry we were fighting," Aaron played with the faded tips of Parker's hair, "But we're brothers, I guess we're bound to fight sometimes... I just need you to know you are very loved, not just us but a lot of people. Just because we don't talk to people or we haven't seen them in a while, it doesn't change." Aaron took a deep breath, "Whatever you and your family think about each other, I know they're thinking about you, watching out for you... We all are. I'm so sorry you felt like we didn't care or that we weren't here." Air sniffled, "I'm sorry that this is where it had to go, but I know you'll be okay. You have to be, I love you." He bent forward and carefully put his forehead to Parker's, he said something, but his curls were in the way.

I should call my mom... Probably my brother... Meh, maybe later.

I pretended to still be eating when he decided to come back.

Aaron sat next to me with a sigh, he used the sleeves of his UDub pullover to dry his eyes.

I didn't know what to say, so I just went with my gut, "Wanna eggroll?"

He smiled but shook his head.

"You good?"

He shrugged, "I've had better days."

"Mm." I shrugged back.

It was quiet for awhile

"The deal with your uncle," I dug a hole in the middle of the rice just so I had something else to do, "I'm sorry."

"Thanks, but it was a long time ago."

"It still sucks... You could've told us."

He nodded tucking a strand of hair behind his ear, "I know, but I don't like to think about that point in time, it's one of... Many things I'm working on coming to terms with."

"Eh, I get it, we all got things like that. I don't like talking 'bout my dad."

He nodded again.

"But y'know you should, you don't wanna end up like me."

Hey, I got a small chuckle.

"When'd it happen?"

"2000, right before my fifteenth birthday."

"Mm. That why you don't like your birthday?"

He tilted his head like he didn't get the question, "No, I just like Halloween more."

I laughed, "Course you do."

November 23 2007

01:10

Aaron

It was late.

Drew was asleep across Conner's lap while Conner dozed off with his elbow propping up his head against the couch armrest.

Nate fell asleep in the corner of the room against the wall, his arms were crossed.

I was lying on the other side of the bed, across from Parker like always.

I felt weird watching him, but I couldn't sleep.

I was so worried, so anxious, and the voices inside and outside of my head could not be quieted.

I sat upright, taking a look around the room at everyone sleeping... And everyone who was watching over them.

Conner's mom, Nate's grandfather, Drew's great-grandmother, and Travis.

He was new to me, but it was nice to meet him. He seemed nice enough, and I could tell he really cared about Parker. I thought it was a little weird. I hadn't ever heard about him or from him before, but I was too dazed to ask any questions.

I just wished Courtney was there, she would've fixed it all immediately... Or maybe if she was here, it wouldn't have gotten to this point.

"They'll be okay," Celeste reassured me, "I'll keep an eye on everyone." She offered that warm, comforting smile that Conner had inherited.

I nodded once before carefully getting off the bed and quietly closed the door behind me.

I made my way to the front desk, "Hi, can I get a few extra blankets?"

The new clerk nodded before disappearing into the back room.

The pyramid of miniature liquors on the counter behind the desk caught my eye.

"Is this enough?" The clerk snapped me back to reality.

"Hmm? Oh yes, thank you."

He gestured to the pyramid, "Do you need more for your room?"

I hesitated, "No, just the blankets. Thank you." I scurried back to the room.

Everyone was still asleep.

I sighed.

Five years, Aaron... Five years. Don't do this, not now.

I distributed the blankets, trying my best to not wake anybody up.

The last blanket I used as a shield and buried myself under it at the foot of the bed.

Hopefully by the time the sun came up everything would feel okay again.

04:00

CONNER

Drew snuggled in closer against my stomach.

I had been wavering in and out of the weird purgatory of sleep for the past few hours.

My body begged for sleep, but I couldn't allow it. I knew I needed to be awake.

I tried to lean my head back, too tired to hold up my neck, but I was quickly trying to be pulled back asleep.

I sat upright, as much as I could without disrupting Drew.

I took a deep breath as I combed my fingers through her silky hair.

She kept nestling closer to me, it was so comforting.

I could only imagine how screwed I would've been if she wasn't here, her being here felt like the only glimmer of hope my bad luck had ever seen.

Noticing the blanket that had been pushed between her and the couch cushion I pulled it across her while I wondered where it came from.

Pressing a kiss to the side of her head I could reach, I scanned the room to check on everyone else.

I couldn't help stifling a laugh when I saw the vaguely Aaron-shaped ball with the blanket over his head. I just hoped he remembered to take his glasses off this time before we had to have another hair cutting incident.

I came back to Parker.

My worry still hadn't settled.

I knew he was having a rough time since we lost Courtney, we all were, but I didn't think it would get this bad.

I should've known better.

Short of getting up to lay on top of him, there wasn't anything else I could do, so I just watched him for a while.

He'd started to stir in his sleep, and I got more worried.

He turned his head towards me, his eyes fluttered as he fought to open them, then blinked a couple of times before his eyes focused on me.

"Hey."

"Hey," I couldn't hide the surprise in my voice.

"Why are you here?" He half squinted at me.

"I was worried about you, we all were."

"We? Is that why he's here?"

"What?"

He started coughing, he tried to sit up but was too weak.

"Drew," I lightly shook her awake so I could help him.

She shot upright, swatting her hair out of her face, "What? What happened?"

"He's awake."

"Thank Christ." She got up, practically hip checking me out of her way.

I got everyone else up while she tended to him.

"How are you feeling?"

Parker tried to pull away from her, "What?"

Aaron woke up and instantly latched on to Parker.

"He's awake? Good," Nate stood up, "I'm gonna fucking kill him!"

"Nate!" I stepped in front of him.

He calmed down after he accidentally hit me in the back of the head.

"What the hell is going on?" Parker asked, trying to remove Aaron.

That just riled Nate up more, "What the fuck do you think is going on?"

I put my arm out to block him, "Stop, you're not helping."

"I'm not helping?!"

"Jesus, I thought you'd guys be nicer to me here."

Nate practically jumped over me.

I grabbed him before he could get his hands on Parker, instead, he just punched a hole in the wall.

"Nate!"

"What?!"

I corralled him towards the door, "Go outside!"

"But..."

"Now!"

Nate slammed the door on his way out.

Parker let out a cough that rattled his chest, "What the fuck?"

"We'll get there." I sighed.

"How are you feeling?" Drew asked.

"Does it matter?"

"No, we're all going to kick your ass either way," I answered.

Parker nodded before he put his head against the headboard, "I get it, this is the punishment, right? You guys are mad at me, I have to atone or whatever."

I crossed my arms, "That would be nice."

"Well, it's not going to happen," He coughed, "I spent my entire life atoning for what other people wanted from me. I'm gonna rest."

Drew and I exchanged a confused look.

"You're not dead, you stupid fucking dumbass!" Nate yelled through the door.

I threw one of Aaron's shoes at the door.

"Ow!"

"Shut up or get lost!"

"You're not dead," Drew reiterated nicely.

Parker sat back upright giving us each a confused look.

He laughed, "No, no. No." He slowly realized we were serious, "No!" He tried to move his arm, but it caught on the IV in his vein, "No, no, no, no!" He tried clawing at it but Aaron was able to hold him down as I ran over to help him.

"No, get off me! I don't want this!"

"Parker, you need to calm down." Drew interjected.

"I don't give a fuck! Let me go!"

"Don't yell at her." I barked.

Parker fought against us for a few seconds before he was out of energy.

"Please," his voice broke as tears ran down his face, "I-I don't want to be here, I can't do this anymore, please..." He gulped, "Please just let me go, leave me be, you don't have to deal with me anymore. I won't be a problem."

"You know we aren't going to do that." I sighed.

"You aren't a problem." Aaron added, "You can't leave us, we need you."

"You need me gone," He whimpered, "I just fuck everything up, I know that."

"That's not true!"

"It is! I'm just going to keep ruining your lives! This is the only way. Please."

Aaron and I let go, opting to sit on either side of him.

"Where are you getting this?"

"She told me!"

"Who?" Aaron asked.

"Courtney."

The room went so quiet you could hear the rats in the wall.

Nate slowly opened the door, "Did... He?"

I shook my head, "Parker, what are you talking about?"

The four of us all held our breath waiting for his answer.

"I... I..." Parker's hand kept going to the new scar on his chest, "I talked to her. I, she was, it was Court..." He clarified.

"How?" Aaron asked.

"When?" I interjected.

"Last night," Parker shook his head, "The day before, I-I can't remember... She was here or at home?" He ran his hand through his hair, "I don't know."

"Parker," I put my hand on his shoulder as a touchstone, "Look at me."

His usually vibrant brown eyes were hazy and lackluster, that signature Parker glint was gone.

"Focus, what are you trying to say?"

"I don't know..."

"Do you know where you are?" Drew stepped in for me.

Parker slowly shook his head.

"Do you know what happened?"

His hand was back on his chest, "I thought so, but I dunno..."

Drew wiped the tears that snuck up on her, "He's in shock," She took a deep breath trying to stabilize her speech, "And the drugs aren't helping, I'd be surprised if he wasn't overdosing too."

"What do we do?"

"Keep him awake and warm. There isn't much else to do."

"Can we take him home?"

"Medically, no. But if I had my way, he would be in a hospital..." Drew tucked her hair behind her ear, as she shook her head, "I... I don't see why not, I guess it would probably be best for him to be somewhere familiar."

"I wanna go home." Parker mumbled.

"Alright," I went and helped him up, "Let's go."

Nate helped hold him up on the other side.

I glanced at Nate, "Can I trust you?"

He shrugged, "We'll find out."

"Hang on," Aaron hurried over, he put his sweater over Parker's shoulders, "I can take him." Aaron lowered his voice as he shifted his eyes over my shoulder, "I think maybe she needs your help more."

Drew was sitting back on the chair; her hair was in front of her face.

She was silent but it was obvious she couldn't hold it together anymore.

"Thanks." I let Aaron take over.

I sat with her, wrapping my arm around her while I watched the guys shuffle out of the door.

"I am so sorry." I whispered.

That broke the dam, she started sobbing.

I just sat there and held her as tight and as close to me as I possibly could.

I wasn't sure what else to do.

All of this was completely my fault, she didn't need to be here.

Maybe her mom was right, and I should've just left her alone.

"Drew," I moved her hair, "Let me take you home, to your mom's?"

She shook her head, wiping her face dry and she cleared her throat, "I'm fine, I am."

"It's okay if you aren't..."

She wouldn't entertain it, she was already up and pulling her coat back on like nothing happened, "Let's go, Parker needs us with him."

I kissed her cheek when I got up and held her for a second longer, "Okay."

(＼(•̀w•́)／)

14:00

Parker hadn't said a word since we got back. It was like a weird alternate universe where I wanted to beg him to say anything.

Drew worked hard to keep him comfortable, I helped her build a Parker nest on the couch where we could all keep an eye on him.

While Nate and Aaron made it a big deal to put on one of Parker's favorite movies, so he'd stay awake with us, the irony was that Aaron and Nate fell asleep before the previews ended.

Parker was awake, but he might as well have been asleep. Aside from the silence, he was almost completely unresponsive to everything, until I tried to sit with him.

He still didn't say anything, but he made it clear he didn't want anything to do with any of us.

And I tried my hardest to understand where he was coming from and not take it personally, but I couldn't have felt more rejected.

My thoughts swirled around at a dizzying rate, but Drew interrupted my attempts to follow.

Forcing a smile, she set an old, chipped mug on the desk next to me

"Oh... Thank you, you didn't have to do that."

She shrugged, "I needed something to do, I was going to do your dishes but... Your kitchen is immaculate." She chuckled.

"Yeah," I sighed, "I couldn't sleep last night, you should see our bathroom." I took a drink of the coffee, "Um... Did you use the kitchen sink or the bathroom sink for the water?"

She gave me a weird look, "Kitchen, why?"

"You didn't drink it, did you?"

"No? You're scaring me."

I shook my head, "The water in that tap is more rust than water at this point. But I really appreciate the thought." I kissed her cheek as I got up to wash the mug.

"Oh no." She kind of laughed.

"I think we have some orange juice, maybe ginger ale if you want anything. Or um maybe some left over pizza if you're hungry? I think it's a little old, though..." I dried the mug before putting it back in the cabinet, "Sorry, we don't get too many guests."

"That's okay. What are you working on?" She nodded towards my computer.

"Just surveying,"

"Surveying?"

"Yeah, anything weird, anything... Vampire-y..."

She knit her eyebrows, "You're looking for a hunt?"

"Not necessarily, I'm just trying to keep an eye on things... It feels like the only thing I can do right now."

"He's going to be okay." I couldn't tell if she was reassuring me or herself.

"How long is he going to be like this?"

"I wish I knew."

Nate had woken up and was giving us a weird look, I knew a weird comment was coming so I just ignored him.

"That my shirt?" He nodded at Drew.

"Oh, right," She gestured, "I needed a change after... Sorry, I thought it was Conner's."

"I didn't have one that fit over her..." I awkwardly stumbled on my words once I realized what I was saying, and ended up making an even more awkward gesture towards my chest.

Drew shook her head, "I'll wash it and get it back to you."

Nate raised an eyebrow, "... Like in a machine?"

I nodded, "Some people wash their clothes, Nate."

Drew gave me a concerned look.

"I washed that one, I promise."

November 26 2007

20:20

Parker

Those first few days I didn't do anything but sleep or pretend to be asleep whenever one of the guys or Drew would check on me.

It was easier, and I didn't wanna deal with it... When had I ever dealt with any of the awful shit I've done? This isn't anything new.

I kept having weird dreams. They were blurred, I couldn't tell if they were the same day or just the week.

The first dream I had was about Travis.

Specifically, that time he drug me out to California with his band.

We blew all our money on gas and cheap 7-11 beer, so we had to sleep in the back of that old run-down panel van right in the middle of Lagoona beach.

We'd been arguing all day, so I decided to get the last word and stole his pack of cigarettes.

He must've chased me around the beach for a half hour, we eventually forgot what we were fighting about and he finally tackled me off a pier and into the water, laughing the whole time.

We made out as the waves crashed round us, then fucked in the back of the van.

He'd jokingly laid on top of me, pinning me to the van floor, but then fell asleep there.

I didn't mind, though, I savored the moment, the sound of the water lapping the sand, the smell of sea air gasoline and spilled beer that filled the van, the feeling of Travis' warm body pressed against mine, even the taste of the salty ocean water on his skin.

I closed my eyes for a second, taking it all in.

When I thought of Travis this is what I wanted to remember forever.

But that hope was quickly dashed when I opened my eyes.

I was back in Travis' bathroom, with him wriggling on the cracked tile.

"Please..." I sunk to my knees by his side, pressing my head to his chest. I just wanted him to hold me, "I can't do this again, please."

I squeezed my eyes shut, I didn't want to open them again, I wanted to stay there 'cause I didn't want to know what else was waiting for me.

I felt his body disappear from under me, I could hear the wind blowing trees and an owl hooting.

Reluctantly, I opened my eyes.

I was still kneeling, just now in the wet grass beside Courtney instead of Travis.

Tears stung at my eyes as my heart got ripped to shreds.

Blood soaked through Courtney's Iron Maiden T-shirt as Conner was trying desperately to hold her together, no matter how grizzly the sight was though she was laughing.

"You're going to be okay," Conner repeated softly.

"I'm not scared," she smiled, "I'm not. I'm..." she was cut off when she had to take a deep breath. She opened her mouth to say "Fine," but no words came out, blood bubbled past her lips into a stream.

I couldn't tear myself away as I watched that supernova of light behind her eyes dim out until it was gone completely.

I yelled as loud as I could.

It echoed, bouncing off the trees in a vibration and the scene quickly changed around me.

The cold, wet forest turned into a warm, cozy cottage.

I could recognize it from the smell of burnt wood alone, I spent months trying to get that smell out of my hair.

Travis' laugh pulled me back into the scene, he was sitting in one of the log frame chairs next to the bed we had brought out from the bedroom into the den for Robbie, so he felt less lonely.

When we were in the hospital, he begged us to take him to his family's cabin, he didn't want to die in "a barren wasteland"... I'd like to blame him for my fear of hospitals.

Robbie looked like hell; we'd only been taking care of him for a few weeks but his decline was so fast it made all of our heads spin.

He was laughing with Travis, he made a motion with his frail arms like he was holding a shotgun, "You nearly took out my gramps for a squirrel."

"I thought it was a turkey!" Trav joked.

"Turkeys don't climb trees, numbnuts." There was a laugh followed by a deep cough.

Travis got really quiet, and Robbie rolled his eyes.

"Nah, come on, don't gimme that look."

"I'm just worried about you,"

"Why? I'm dying, nothing left to worry about."

"You're hilarious,"

"Yep, I'm a real riot."

Travis sniffed and Robbie rolled his eyes again.

"Oh, get over yourself, you pansy ass!" Robbie thought he was really funny, "Come on, don't be sad, we knew this was coming."

"Doesn't make it any better." Trav never cried, I think this was the first and the last time I ever saw it happen.

"Stop, I'm serious." Robbie used all his strength to stretch a smile across his skeletal face, "This is a good thing! Where I'm going, they don't got hospital machines, no more drugs that just make me sicker, and I ain't gonna be hurting no more. I'm glad I'm going. This is gonna be good for me, Trav."

"What about me?"

Robbie scoffed, "You got a hot twinkie hanging off you constantly and the two of you bang every groupie that comes within a 100-foot radius. You'll be fine. Plus, you guys' are 'bout to go on the road, you don't need to be worrying about me. Just save me a ticket at call, 'kay?"

Travis tried to laugh between sobs, "Deal, but you gotta come, okay?"

"I'm there, I'm there." Robbie shut his eyes, he was visibly drained by the few minutes long conversation, "Wouldja shut off the lights? It's like the frickin' sun's in here."

"No worries." Travis patted him on the shoulder, "Get some rest."

"Trav," he stopped him before he left the room, "In case I don't see you tomorrow... I'll see you at your first show. July 7th, Olympia, right?"

Travis nodded once, "I'll see you at the show."

I closed my eyes again in an attempt to keep myself from crying.

Not even twelve hours later, I'd find Robbie slumped over against the kitchen cabinets.

Something dripped against my cheek, I opened my eyes assuming I couldn't stop the tears, but I was staring up at the sky as rain poured down.

I was back in Byre; I could tell by the sting of the salt in the air and the thick fog rolling in from the water.

"What a shame," One of the girls from our school said to another girl.

"I know. I heard they couldn't find enough of her skull to puzzle it together."

A third girl gasped, "Is that why the caskets are closed?"

When I finally realized where I was, I took off running trying to find Conner.

He was sitting next to his grandma between his mom and dad's caskets.

He was wearing a black jacket his grandma had to have tailored, and his round cheeks were flushed and wet. He looked so small next to the giant oak boxes.

He looked like a little kid; I'd never looked back on the moment from the perspective of knowing he was a little kid.

The replay crushed me as much as it did when it happened.

I grabbed Conner, pulling him close to me and as tight as I could.

"I'm so sorry."

We stayed like that for what felt like hours, both of us bawling our eyes out.

At first, I thought I was crying for him, then I realized I was crying for me. When they died, so did any love from a parental figure I ever got.

"Stop it!" My little sister's yell ripped through the memory.

In a second, I was standing in the backyard of my parents' house.

"You're not even digging!" My little sister kept yelling at me as she ripped the shovel from my hands.

In her defense, I was sobbing too hard, and I hadn't even broken the dirt yet.

That night a coyote had jumped the fence, Winnie put up a good fight, but he was old.

My dad had made it my job to deal with it so my little sisters didn't have to see the horror scene, but I wasn't even fourteen yet and I was more squeamish back then than I was now.

The entire thing traumatized me.

To everyone else he was just a dog, but he was my only friend, and since my older sister had left for college, he was the only person in the house that understood me or actually loved me.

My dad came out when he heard my sister yelling, "What's going on out here?"

"Fuddy won't dig the hole!" My sister sold me out the second he stepped outside.

He looked at me, the understanding he had for my sister vanished the second he saw me crying.

He clicked his tongue, "Libbey, go help your mother inside."

Kneeling down, he waited for Elizabeth to shut the door, "I told you to dig a grave for that dog, didn't I?"

"I don't wanna bury him."

"Stop crying, Elmer," My dad's voice was cut and dry, the voice he used when he was sick of me picking on my sisters, "This is men's work and it's time you learn to do it."

"I know how to dig a hole!" I snapped and my dad responded with a quick slap to my wrist.

"He's just a dog. What did Bishop Paul say about it?"

He waited for me to answer, but I refused to.

"Our souls aren't equally yoked." He answered his own question, and repeated, "It's just a dog."

"That's not true!" I spat.

My dad stood, putting his hand on my shoulder, "Bury the dog, Elmer. When you're done, we're going down to the church, you owe an apology to the Bishop."

My dream was cut there, but I remember my mom having my dad lock the door. I never dug the hole, I stubbornly sat out there until it started to get dark, but my dad finally caved when it started to rain heavily.

This time the overwhelming smell of burnt candle wax, frankincense, and oak wood was what triggered the next dream.

In the blink of an eye, I was standing by my mom's side reaching up to hold her hand.

My mom was wearing a long black dress, my mom never wore black, she always said it wasn't a color the living should wear...

Which meant this must've been my grandfather's funeral.

I don't remember how old I was at this funeral, but I was young enough to not fully understand what was going on.

All I knew was everyone around me was incredibly emotional, and I took that as something to be afraid of, so I clung to my mom.

It also didn't help that my older sister had been telling me about ghosts and zombies all week just to scare me shitless.

The closer we got to the casket the more I cried and tugged at my mom.

She picked me up and shushed me as she dabbed at my face with a tissue, "Be quiet."

I don't remember anything about my grandpa, I was really little when he died and I didn't know much about him then, but I knew what I was looking at in the casket was not my grandpa.

It was some waxy, stitch faced, subhuman and the feeling radiating from the casket was terrifying.

I screamed and continued to cry loudly.

"No, no, calm down." My mom demanded under her breath.

My mom's always been quick to be annoyed, but she was even quicker to embarrass, "This isn't the place, people are watching."

She smacked me on the back between my shoulders to get my attention, she was careful to not actually hit me.

When I wouldn't stop, she turned to hiss at my dad, "Get ahold of your son."

He took me into his arms away from her.

My dad was so... Calm, untouched.

He acted like it wasn't his father lying dead in the casket right in front of him.

My father patted my back in a more comforting way than my mom did, "Quiet, boy. There'll be plenty of time for this later, but you can't be so hysterical around others."

I buried my face into the side of his neck so I didn't have to see any more and so they'd leave me alone.

Soon I felt a hand on my shoulder shake me, "Did you hear me?"

I lifted my head when I didn't recognize the voice.

I was sitting at the breakfast table in Conner's parents' kitchen.

His mom, Celeste, sat in the chair in front of me, her face was serious.

I couldn't help staring at her though, I was happy to see her, and just happy to see someone who wasn't dying.

"Parker?"

I shook my head to try to focus my thoughts, "Yes ma'am?"

She sighed, she put her hand to the side of my face, gentle, caring, loving.

Celeste was always the mother I wish I had, she made it all seem easy, I didn't understand my mom couldn't be like her or why my dad couldn't be like Scott.

She smiled at me but it was small and sad, "You look like Hell."

"I feel like I've been through Hell. Oh, Jesus, is that what this is? Is that why you're here?"

She shook her head, "No, no, you're not dead. I just wanted to chat."

I barely had time to put my arms up before Celeste leaned forward to hug me.

I put my head against her shoulder and just let her hold me.

"Everything's going to be okay."

If my mom would've ever just once said those words to me... I think things could've been way different.

Celeste brushed my hair out of my eyes when we parted, "Do you understand what's going on? Why you're having these dreams?

"Is it a reverse It's A Wonderful Life?"

She didn't think I was funny, "Parker, I love you and I love that you can find humor in anything, but it's time to get real. What do you think this means?"

I shook my head and choked on the words, "I'm branded by death... Everything that loves me dies, and everything I love kills me."

"You're close, you're really close..." she paused, "Parker, do you really think after all this time it's been the booze and pills you've been hooked on? It's death, it's the decay, it's the suffering. This whole time you've been addicted to pain. And I don't blame you, as a child you learned it was easier to accept it than to fight it, but no one ever told you you can fight it. I think somewhere you know that. Somewhere you know it's not because of Donatello's intervention you've made it this far from death."

"But I keep running back towards it like a dog chasing a car."

She held my shoulders for comfort, "Why do you want to end your life?"

"I can't do this anymore," my voice shook, "I'm not a fighter, not anymore. And I thought this could be my last chance to throw one last punch... I wanted to die like you. A hunter's death. A righteous, debtless death."

"Oh, Parker," She sighed, "Can't you see what you're dealing with is so different? When I made that decision... Scott was already gone, if I thought there was any way to make it better I would have, neither of us were ready to leave you or Conner but it's what we had to do to keep everyone safe."

"That's what I was doing!"

"No, it isn't, and you know that. You know the only way to the protection your craving for the boys is through the source itself."

"... Me?"

"Donatello, mon cheri." She pat my hand, "I know you think that you're not a fighter. First of all, you're wrong, but if you weren't that's okay. You don't have to be a fighter, you just have to be a lover,"

I laughed so I wouldn't cry, "I've never heard you sound so... *Flower power.*"

"I'll have you know I met Scott at a Vietnam War protest," she smacked my arm lightly with a smirk, "You're full of love, and I know it hurts because it just makes you feel things so deeply but it's a good thing, there isn't enough of that in the world."

Her jaw tightened and she looked like she might cry, "I'm disappointed, Parker. You've always been a good kid, I know you have it in you to be a good man, but you have to do better. Someday very soon there's going to be a reason for you to be better, but you can't afford to wait for that day, you've been living on borrowed time so now it's time to make the most of it. Listen to me when I tell you what you felt on that beach, it's real. What you had with Travis before he passed it's real. Go back there, life is full of that so chase it."

I shook my head, "I can't do this anymore; besides it's better for everyone if I'm..."

She slammed her hand on the table to get my attention, it worked, and I jumped back.

"You stop that right there! Don't you say that! Parker, when I left this earth, I was so terrified of leaving my boy, but as I've watched the two of you grow up as men, I couldn't be gladder that I left him with you. I don't know what would've happened if you weren't there when Scott and I passed. You've saved Conner's life more times than you know. And Aaron's. Oh, and Nate's! Look at all the things you've helped him learn about himself. You aren't a burden! Parker, can't you see that you're their protector? You think if you were out of the picture Donatello would have just left them alone? You know better than to trust that man, if you weren't in the picture he would've taken my son long before I was even aware of him, that, I know. You are not the problem."

My eyes hurt and my throat burned from how much crying I'd been doing.

I didn't know how to respond, and all I was able to choke out was "Can I have a hug?"

She held me tight and pressed a kiss to my forehead when she let go, "If you can't do it for you, do it for me, do it for your boys, do it for whoever comes next." Her grip tightened on my shoulders, "Your work isn't done here, there's more, so much more to come. You can do this."

She wiped my tears gently with the back of her hand, "Before you wake up, I think there's someone you should speak with."

When I looked up, I noticed someone was suddenly standing behind her with his hand on the back of her chair, and how long he was standing there I have no idea.

He was a total stranger to me, he was tall despite how hunched he stood, he was a broad guy but really skinny. Short sandy blond hair hung in his eyes; I couldn't tell how old he was, but he looked young.

His hand made mine look like a little kid's when he held it out for a handshake, "I'm Cypress, you know my nephew.'

When I gave him a confused look he gave me a half smile.

"Aaron," He settled into the chair in the corner, and I got the sense he wasn't gonna pummel me, so I tried to unclench.

"We should talk,"

November 27 2007
12:45

Conner

Parker regained his cognitive function over the next few days, he still wasn't talking much just enough to lash out over... Seemingly everything.

Drew said she thought he was physically healing well, and from my own observations I agreed, but it did nothing to quiet my mind.

He didn't want to talk, but I sure did, and the longer he brushed me off the madder I got.

I think the shock was starting to wear off so the gravity of what he'd really done had set in and I was pissed. I tried not to be, and I felt guilty about it, but this felt like the ultimate disrespect.

Maybe Parker was right when he said I didn't know him as well as I thought...

I wished none of this was happening.

I wished he hadn't disappeared three years ago.

I wished I had made more of an effort back then.

I wished he would've just talked to me.

I wished Courtney was here...

"Hey, hey," Drew put her hand on the top of my notebook to get my attention, once my pen was off the page she closed the book, "I don't like the look on your face."

I shook my head and mumbled, "Sorry,"

"Nothing to be sorry for," she lifted her hand to fix my hair, "You need to take a break from worrying for a while. Why don't you and Nate go drop in on Aaron at work? Go get lunch, I'll stay with Parker."

I shook my head, "Thanks but... He's going through withdrawal, he's being nasty."

She smirked, a little laugh to herself, "I grew up in New Jersey and I used to play hockey, you'd be surprised at the level of nastiness I can put up with."

I gave her a peck when I stood, "I'd bet that's why you ended up with a bad boy like me."

"Oh, definitely." She interlaced her fingers with mine and pulled me over onto the couch with her.

She had me lay down so she could lay her head on my chest.

I wrapped my arms around her and held her close.

The weight of the world was replaced by the weight of Drew, and it was so much more comfortable, comforting even.

I couldn't figure out what it was about her that was so calming, but I could've fallen asleep like this and slept through the night.

She crossed her arms on top of my chest and used her hands to prop up her chin, she didn't say anything for a while, just watched me.

I took the time to wander through the icy tundra of her eyes.

She kissed me and I closed my eyes, sinking further into the moment.

But of course, the moment was quickly stomped out when Nate walked in.

"Don't let me stop ya," he clicked his tongue, "Not one to pass on free porn."

When Drew was up, I quickly turned our blanket into a weapon.

Luckily Nate's hazing didn't last long, mostly because Aaron walked through the front door with his work tie balled up in his hand and an expression on his face that was similar to the one he had that time I wouldn't let him bring in that sick pigeon.

Nate nodded at him, "Thought you were workin' today."

"So did I! My manager grabbed me before I clocked in and told me I was being let go." He crumpled into the chair beside the couch.

Drew shook her head, "Why would they fire you?"

Aaron pulled his hair out from behind his back and sunk further into the chair, "With all the craziness going on, I just forgot. Evidently, I missed three shifts!"

"But did you tell them why? It's not like you just didn't feel like going in." Drew defended.

Aaron popped up and was on his feet, "What am I supposed to tell them? My terminally vampiric friend went on a weeklong bender, tried to kill himself, I had to aid in his resurrection, I haven't slept in a week, and crying in the shower is my new and only hobby!"

"... Maybe not that exactly."

"Ugh! I need a drink..." He was back in the chair, he pulled his knees up to rest his forehead against, "When she fired me, I was so overwhelmed I couldn't deal with it so I just kinda left, thank God I made it to my car before I started crying."

A hush went over the room as we all tried to figure out how to give him his space but also be supportive.

Out of the corner of my eye, I saw Parker using the doorway to the bedroom to hold himself up right.

He cleared his throat to get our attention, "Am I interrupting?"

"You're fine," I tested the waters, "You need help?"

Parker shook his head, and carefully made his way over, it was obvious he was still hurting.

He made it to the couch, took quick stock of Aaron, and tried to pat his shoulder.

"You okay?"

Aaron looked at him with the fury of a rabid raccoon.

I think we all wanted to give him that look.

When he sat back, he realized we were all looking at him with varying annoyance.

I tried not to be, but I was guarded, he'd been so mean and snappy with us.

"How are you feeling?" Drew volunteered, despite most of his anger being placed squarely on her.

Parker's hand instinctively went to the pain in his chest, "Everything hurts, my head's pounding, I'm pouring sweat, and I can't stop shaking, so I guess..." He caught himself and checked his attitude, "Alive."

The room went dead silent as we all watched him, waiting for the other shoe to fall.

"What do you want?" Nate snapped, his arms crossed, "Huh? Whatever it is this time you can shove it up your ass."

"Nate," I uttered under my breath to get his attention.

Parker tensed, when he finally spoke his voice shook, "I owe you guys an apology."

Nate made a noise that I have no other way to describe other than "?!", rushed over to the side window and ripped the curtain open, "Nah, no pigs. Someone should call Donnie, though, ask if his region of Hell froze over!"

"Stop it." I tried to manage Nate.

"You don't owe us an apology," Aaron spoke softly as he picked the lint off of the chair's arm, "But an explanation would be nice."

Parker was trying to wipe his tears without any of us noticing that he was crying. He nodded, but didn't say anything else.

Nate was annoyed and took the opportunity to shift gears, "Talk to your boss," he tapped Aaron's shoe when he wasn't listening, "You want, I'll go down there with ya. They can't fire you for this shit, Hell, sue 'em."

Aaron shook his head, "I don't wanna talk about work right now."

Parker picked at his nails, "... You guys want me to leave?"

"No, of course not! Why would we? Stay!" The answer was so obvious we all expected someone else to say it, but all our pleas fell silent.

Parker sighed as he stood, "I get it."

I grabbed his hand before he walked away.

I didn't know what to say, there was no right thing to say but plenty of wrong things.

I pulled him back over and down onto the couch, "I'm sorry. Sit down, what's on your mind?"

He wouldn't look at any of us, he seemed weirdly embarrassed but tried to mask it for his next statement, "I wanna call a reverse intervention. I'm calling it a re-vention."

"A... Prevention?" Drew tilted her head, "Never mind, sorry. Private moment, not here, sorry." She pressed a kiss to my cheek and grabbed her coat.

"No, no," Parker popped up and leaned over the back of the couch to stop her, "Stay, stay. I-I, I'm sorry. I've been a real asshole to you, I'm sorry... It's not your fault, and I..." He paused and blew out a breath when his voice caught, "Thank you. You saved me, thank you for that and, Jesus Christ, for everything."

Drew shuffled over to give him an awkward hug over the couch, "I understand, I really do. You aren't as alone as you think you are."

When she let go, he folded in on himself, he didn't want us to know he was crying, but his shoulders shook uncontrollably.

Drew did her best to comfort him, when she couldn't I felt like I had to step in.

I put my hand on his back, so he knew I was there.

He fell forward onto my chest, and muffled something into my shirt.

"Huh?"

He repeated it, but it was chopped apart by sobs.

My heart ached, it felt like the first aid we applied by saving Parker had been ripped apart.

"I can't understand you,"

"I'm sorry!" He yelled as he sat upright, "I'm sorry! I wanna tell you and I wanna explain but... I-I can't, I can't do this... You all hate me and I just, I can't handle it, I can't."

It killed me to know that he thought that we hated him, what was I doing so wrong?

"We don't hate you," I sat next to him on the couch.

"Why not? Everyone else does, my mom, my dad, my sisters... Myself."

"I'm not them. Look at me,"

His tearful eyes reluctantly followed alone up my face and into my eyes.

This moment took me back to cradling his head in the motel room as he lay bleeding, dying. He was so vulnerable, and I still felt like I held his life in my hands. But staring into his eyes now, that memory faded, then was replaced by millions at once; every hunt we've ever been on, every stupid story, every inside joke, every fight, losing Courtney, losing my parents, my first day of high school. Every second of time played out right in front of my eyes.

"I love you, Parker," I pulled him into as tight of a hug as I could, "You're my best friend, you're my brother. Nothing can take that from us, nothing could make me hate you."

For a second, I wasn't sure if he heard me, but his sobs turned to a strangled laugh, "You're a real Nicholas Sparks son of a bitch."

Through my own tears I shared the same strangled laugh.

We rested our heads against each other.

For one second, since we lost Courtney, just for a second, I felt like everything would be okay.

"Fuck it," I heard Aaron cry out, when I looked up, he was climbing over the coffee table, then he wedged himself between me and Parker, "Me too, goddamn it. I'M A LITTLE BROTHER!"

I couldn't help laughing, "Yeah, of course."

Parker buried his face in Aaron's blond curls.

Drew gave me a look, as if testing the waters before she raced around the couch and stooped down to join our huddle.

I tried to use the same look on Nate, extending an invite without saying anything.

His arms were crossed, he was doing his best to keep his aloof demeanor, but I could see it in his eyes, he didn't want us to know it but he was hurting just as bad as we were.

Nate put his hand on top of Parker's head as a show of solidarity, "Yeah, ditto. Whatever, shut up."

Parker took the opportunity to latch onto his arm and licked him from fingertip to wrist before Nate could pull away from him.

"What the fuck is wrong with you?!" Nate yelled.

Tears were streaming down Parker's face, but he was laughing hysterically,

"I never learned to process love properly and this is all so fucking uncomfortable!"

We were all laughing, whether because it was funny, from lack of sleep, or because we were all raw and exposed nerves, that I couldn't tell you.

After a few seconds Parker dried his face, he shook his hair out of his eyes, "I'm okay, I'm fine." He cleared his throat, "I have to tell you something, though. Since the day I showed up on your doorstep, I made a pact with myself, when all of this was said and done, when we finally got rid of Donatello. I promised I'd kill myself, I didn't wanna live like this. I didn't wanna run the chance..." He trailed off for a second, "And I thought this was it. I thought I finally did it."

PARKER

I told them everything, well, mostly everything.

I told them about how afraid I was that I was going to kill someone, I told them about Donnie's monkey-circus-hotel-of-sin, about the loophole deal I made with him, the conversation I had with Courtney, Travis dying in my arms... Except I left out his name and called him a her, then I told them the rest, even down to the crude way I tried to drain the leftover blood in my body.

All of it was met with silence, I didn't know what I expected, but I couldn't deal with the quiet. It gave me too much time to come up with awful ideas, like the fear that Conner was going to instantly revoke everything he just said.

Drew was holding my hand, she made it a point to hold my hand through everything I said, so I tried to ignore my own demons and focus on that show of support... Then I got sidetracked when I noticed her hand was bigger than mine.

I know Con's hands are bigger than mine, but are her's bigger than Conner's? I couldn't tell, he was shredding a tissue in his hand as he thought over what I said.

Oh, right. That's what I should be focusing on... Focus, you miserable bastard.

Conner cleared his throat, "I don't want to come off as insensitive, but why do you think you being dead would get Donnie off of our trail?"

"Because he's obsessed with me, think about it. If it wasn't for him, I'd be a normal person dead, and everything would be fine. Courtney would still be here, so would all the innocent people he's killed to get my attention... That, all of that, all of their blood is on my hands. I'm not supposed to be alive; they are..." I sighed, "If my mom were here, I'm sure she'd say their souls are paying my debt in Hell. They'll be a placeholder as long as my soul is walking free."

Con leaned forward, his eyes searching me, "You don't honestly believe that, do you?" He chuckled like he didn't believe me but not 'cause he found it funny, "This is the woman that told us we'd go to Hell if we didn't repent for cheating on our math homework. She's crazy."

In a weird way that made me feel a little better.

"I just, I feel like that debt's still owed, maybe not to Hell but to Courtney, to the other people."

Drew shook her head with a chuckle, but it was a real chuckle though, "Have you stopped to think about what Courtney would think of that?"

When I didn't answer Drew continued, "She'd tell you to get your butt up and grab her a beer, then she'd sarcastically do that gesture from I Dream Of Jeannie and say your debt was resolved. You don't have to worry about her, every day you get up and fight, every day you live for her. You're already doing everything she'd want you to do."

I took a few minutes as that really sunk in.

I thought of Courtney in the motel with me, she would've smacked me if I'd told her how guilty I felt over her.

"I have a question," Aaron spoke so softly I don't know if I would've heard him if Nate didn't say the same thing.

"I do, too." Nate's arms were crossed, and he was looking at me from the chair, his eyes probed me.

"When you say you spoke to Courtney," Aaron continued.

"I lost track of how many sleeping pills I took," I shook my head, "She just seemed so real. I dunno, I sound crazy."

"No, no you don't..." Aaron trailed off.

Nate held his hand up sarcastically, he kept his eyes locked in on mine, "Who's the ex?"

He was so smug, I wondered if he'd ever come around, if we'd ever be okay...

Drew squeezed my hand, "Take your time."

"I don't know if I've ever really said this out loud before... I know it's gonna come as a real shocker to you guys, but..." I don't know why, but I got nervous, and the words got stuck in my throat.

I could only think of the worst-case scenario and that was what would happen if I told my parents, but I was safe here, hell they already knew!

"I'm bisexual." I ripped off the band aid, and as I expected no one batted an eye.

Conner actually shrugged, making it a point to be nonplussed, or I guess overly-plussed, "And I'm left-handed. We know, and we support it."

Aaron's hand went up and he had a smirk I didn't remember him asking to borrow.

"Yeah, Air?" Con nodded to him.

"I was born a girl," He joked.

I laughed, "Thanks, guys."

"Anytime!" Aaron grinned, clearly proud of himself.

I tried to take their love and hold onto it as tightly as I could, but it was quickly swallowed by anxiety when I realized it was time to tell them about Travis.

Conner said they supported me, but I was terrified it would vanish when they heard the whole story.

The truth was dirtier, grosser, uglier than any lie I've ever told.

God, they already thought so lowly of me, what else did I have to lose?

I spilled my guts and bared my naked soul like a whore begging for redemption from Christ himself.

It couldn't have been quieter, and it felt like all the air had been sucked outta the room.

Conner had stood up a while ago and was pacing in front of his desk. Now he'd stopped and propped himself up with his hands on the desk.

I was waiting for him to say something, anything. I would've done anything for him to just say one word right now.

After a wordless eternal two minutes he looked at me, his eyes cut through me, "If you were with him for a year and it took nine months for you to be on your own again," he crossed his arms and I felt like the lowest level of scum on earth, "Why didn't I hear from you for three years?"

I was chewing on my nails, the chalky polish chips stuck to my throat, and it felt even tighter, "Right,"

I didn't answer.

Conner's arms fell to his sides, "Since the day you showed up at my door I've been asking you the same question, where the hell have you been?!"

His voice rose and my stomach sank.

I scratched at my eyebrow so I could hold my hand in front of my face and not have to make eye contact as I admitted, "I was whoring for coke, okay?! I wasted all the money my mom gave me and I was staying in a homeless shelter. Are you happy now?"

"Why wouldn't you tell me that?"

"Why would I? That shit's embarrassing."

"Parker," He shook his head and sighed, "... I don't know what to say."

"You can say it, you can say you told me so. I know you're thinking it, you might as well. I sure as shit thought it."

He grabbed me by the shirt, part of me hoped he'd hit me. If he did, the pain would be over quick, and the guilt would wash away with it.

He never hit me, though, he pulled me up and into his arms, he hugged me close, "I have nothing to say other than I'm sorry. I wish I could've done something else, so you felt safer to tell me about all of this."

I shook my head, "It wasn't about feeling safe it was just... I didn't want you to be disappointed in me. You're the only person that's ever been, I dunno, I guess appointed in me."

"That's not fair, you didn't even give me the opportunity."

"But I already knew you were gonna be pissed that we didn't keep in touch."

"That wasn't your decision to make, that was mine."

"I know..."

"And it was yesterday, too. The people in this room don't care, Parker! I would take a bullet for you, even if you're the one pulling the trigger."

"We all would." Aaron added.

Nate rolled his eyes, but he nodded.

This felt...

Weird...

I'm not used to people fighting for me, against or with me, yeah. But...

I didn't know how to respond, so I just cried into my sleeve.

"We've danced around this enough," Con carefully walked me back over to the couch and had me sit while he thought, "Why? Why did you do this? Why did you want to kill yourself?"

I shook my head, "Honestly, what the fuck do I have to live for?"

"Us?" Conner offered.

"Yeah, but for how long? Until you guys get sick of me like everyone else does or until I get you killed like I got Courtney killed?"

"Don't go there."

"Why not? It's true! If it weren't for me, she'd still be here! Donnie would leave everyone alone! And that's all I want!"

"Parker,"

"Seriously! If this were a movie people'd be like "Eh! Why doesn't he just kill himself the guy leaves them alone", it's over, BOOM! Roll the credits."

"Parker, you're not thinking straight, this isn't a movie."

"Yeah," Nate chimed in, "If someone was stupid enough to make a story about us it'd probably be a real shitty version of Interview With The Vampire."

Conner threw the roll of toilet paper I was using as tissue at Nate, "Will you shut up? You're not helping."

"I was supposed to be helping?"

"Not now!" Con snapped, "Parker, that isn't the case. We all knew what we were signing up for when we started hunting, none of this has anything to do with you, do you understand me?"

"But..."

"No buts, there are none, what I'm telling you is true!"

I tried to swallow the lump in my throat.

At this point, Conner was just repeating the same words his mom had drilled into me in my dreams. It was slightly eerie.

"No matter what, we're always gonna be okay. Just like we were when we came back into each other's lives, right? Things will never be so bad that we can't recover from them."

I nodded but I wished I could crawl inside his sweatshirt and curl into a little ball on his chest and just live there. I don't know if I've ever felt that safe from someone. I thought I felt it was Travis, but Celeste made it very clear to me it wasn't the same thing as what I was feeling now. Probably because unlike then, I was safe now.

Aaron

Parker tried desperately to get his emotions in check, he seemed embarrassed or maybe scared that he was crying so much.

I wanted to help, but I didn't know how.

He seemed to be asking for space, so I tried to give it to him while also trying to be close by if he needed me to.

"Ugh!" He tried to shake his body like a dog getting water off their fur, "Okay, I'm fine I'm fine. Anyone else wanna say something? Wanna make it like an Alcoholics Anonymous thing? Anyone? Feeling weird and vulnerable right now."

My hand went up really before I could think about it, I realized it was a response from the AA joke but by the time I realized it I was in too deep.

I couldn't tell them this, not now, not after everything Parker just went through.

I couldn't tell them I've been lying to their faces for the last four years, not after we all just criticized Parker for doing the same thing.

Jesus what kind of asshole was I?!

Who does this kind of thing? Who digs such a deep hole for themselves that the only way out is when your friend tries to commit suicide and makes a really niche joke?

How the hell was I going to do this?

Everyone was staring at me, my hands started to sweat, and my forehead ran cold.

Here comes the panic attack.

"Aaron?" Conner said my name and waved his hand in front of my face as if he thought I had just spaced out, "Did you have something you wanted to add?"

"Well, um..." I had two options in front of me, admit and hoped they took the same route of kindness and support that they did with Parker, or I could clam up and continue living a lie.

"I guess... In the spirit of being honest..."

You guys should know I'm a horrible, terrible person! I thought.

Nate snapped his fingers, that made me jump, "¡Dilo! C'mon, we're not getting renewed for a second frickin' season here, perrito. Spit it out."

Conner shot him another look.

Nate crossed his arms mumbling not-so to himself.

"Go ahead, what were you..." I accidentally cut off Conner.

I'd committed, and ended up blurting out, "I see dead people!"

... Not what I thought I was going to say, but I guess it was a start.

Nate clicked his tongue, "Someone page Dr. Crowe."

I shrugged and tried to let the comment roll off my back, I tried so hard, "No, no, go ahead. I'm crazy, I'm off my meds, I've heard it all before."

"Aaron, sweetheart," Drew put her hand on my arm, her voice was soft and sweet, non-judgmental, "What are you talking about?"

I took a deep breath and tried again, "You guys know how my grandma was... Eccentric? She ran a mystic shop and read tarot and cleared curses," I clarified for Drew's sake, then shook my head when I realized I was just blathering, "My grandma was a witch, my uncle was a psychic, and I'm..." I shrugged, hearing how absolutely certifiable I sounded.

"A medium?" Drew offered.

I shrugged again, "In a way, I guess. I-I don't actively practice it, though. It just sorta happens."

"So, ghosts, right?" Parker leaned forward to see me around Conner, he made a face trying to decide if I was joking or not, "Like, you see ghosts?"

At that moment, Celeste felt it was a good time to give me a very supportive double thumbs up.

"Holy shit!" Parker was up, but still a little unsteady, "You see one right now?"

"Well, um," I tried to take stock of everyone around without being too obvious, "Right now? Two."

Parker laughed, but he wasn't laughing at me, he seemed weirdly excited, and it made it so painfully prominent how quiet Nate and Conner were.

"Who?" Parker pressed, "Who's here? Is it just anyone? Can you like see *see* them? What's it look like?"

"They just look like peo..."

"Yeah, yeah," He cut me off, wanting to change his question, "Who do you see?"

"Uh,"

"You can tell them," Celeste was behind her son now, resting her arms on the back of the couch, "It's okay."

I cleared my throat and figured I would start with the guy in the corner, I didn't know him personally, he usually kept to himself when he was around. He wasn't around consistently like Celeste and Scott were, but he was around more since the incident with Parker.

"There's a tall guy, kind of skinny, long dreads, short beard, with snakebites," I gestured to my bicep to indicate his hair.

I didn't have to describe him any further before Parker's excitement shifted "Robbie?"

The apparition smirked when Parker finally put a name to him, "Hey shawty, toldja I'd haunt your bitch ass."

"He says he told you he'd haunt you,"

Parker laughed despite the tears welling in his eyes, "I bet he's pissed right now."

"One word for it," Robbie crossed his arms and folded into a seat on our coffee table, "Not as mad as when you OD'd but yea, pretty pissed. Don't fret, though, already tore Trav a brand-new asshole."

I relayed the message and Parker's ears perked up, "Trav? Travis, is Travis, is he here?" He stumbled over his question.

"No, just Robbie and..."

I looked over at Conner to gauge how he was going to react to this. He was hard to read, he had a quizzical expression, but I couldn't tell if it was plain skepticism or straight denial.

Nate's look was one of pure denial, he thought I was joking.

Suddenly it was six years earlier, and I felt as alone as I did back then, but the cat was already out and there wasn't anything I could do now but be honest.

"I'm sorry," I didn't know what I was apologizing for, but it seemed like the right thing to do, "Conner, your mom is here, too."

He was... Perplexed was a good word for it, but before he could say anything Nate stepped in.

"Nah, man, don't go there." He seemed to have a more defensive attitude over Conner, which kind of confused me. I wasn't sure what he thought I was going to do.

But Celeste got my attention again when she clicked her tongue, "Don't pay any mind to him about this, this is the four-year-old that argued with me about the practicality of the tooth fairy."

I chuckled to myself at the thought of a baby Conner holding one of his notorious PowerPoint presentations, "You didn't believe in the tooth fairy as a kid?"

I didn't realize how strange that would come across without context until

Conner made a face, but he's used to my oddities, so he shrugged and said, "It didn't help my mom woke me up every time she tried to put money under my pillow."

Celeste laughed at the memory, "I bopped him on the head a few times, and I didn't want him to get scared."

"She's right, plus it's rude to not apologize for a head 'bop'." I joked back with her.

Conner had been fiddling with the pendant around his neck all day, but at that moment his hand froze. His mouth opened to ask a question, but he stopped short.

I held my breath, worried I crossed a line.

Wordless Conner was up, he made his way to the cabinet, grabbed the bottle of cheap tequila, and took a swig from the bottle.

Drew made it a point to grab my attention, "I believe you,"

"I do," Parker shrugged, "Fuck, I dunno that I've even thought about Robbie in the last three years."

Robbie popped back off with a laugh, "Try to forget me now, stupid."

"So," Drew leaned forward on her elbows so she could face us all, "I've been on a lot of weird rabbit holes through lore and religion on account of my heritage, also with everything I've learned in the past few months, and really I feel like the common ground is that everyone one believes in ghosts."

"No, no, no," Conner made his way back over, "I'm not saying I don't believe you..." he clarified, but paused while he thought, "Just... Can you run that past me again?"

"Mi amor, mi raison d'etre." Celeste nodded, indicating she wanted me to say it for her.

I sighed, "I'm going to go butcher that,"

"The inscription on his necklace," she pointed, "My reason for being, mi raison d'etre."

She said it slower this time and I tried my best to follow along.

Con blinked a couple of times while he shook his head, "I-I just have so many questions, what is that like? What does she look like? What does she have to say? I'm... My mom?"

"Your dad's around a lot too, your mom just happens to be here now."

He let out a small soft chuckle.

The room was quiet and I felt strangely self-conscious.

"I know it's weird, and I'm sorry if I overstepped..."

"Why are you sorry?" Parker asked, he kinda scoffed, "I'm a goddamn vampire for shit's sake."

"My Grandmother was a practicing witch, and my mom still thought I was crazy." I shrugged, "I don't know, my mom eventually came around but it's ruined other relationships, God, it's ruined lives... My first serious girlfriend couldn't get far enough away from me when I told her."

Nate raised an eyebrow, "What girlfriend?"

"I met her my senior year, we moved out here together to go to University of Washington, I've told you guys about her."

"Hmm," Nate nodded along, "Kinda thought you made that up, like Park and his girl from high school."

Parker just rolled his eyes.

I couldn't believe how easy this conversation was going, this was so... Different.

My mom's always accepted everything about me, so has my dad but they never really understood, no one did. I don't know why it didn't occur to me sooner, maybe it was just hidden too far behind guilt and shame from all the others it's scared off, but these were my kindred spirits.

"So," Nate was less protective now but I could tell he was still very apprehensive, "What about Court?"

Based on the way everyone snapped to look at me, that was the question everyone wanted to ask.

I hated that the only way I could answer it was with another shrug, "I don't know what it is, I haven't seen her, not once. I've tried everything, even down to a seance."

Parker's eyes widened, "Do you think I saw her ghost?"

"... I'm not sure, it's hard to tell when you're that out of it."

Nate, never one to let a room be silent, sat forward with a sort of smirk, "All this time you've been a fucking witch?!"

"I'm not a witch, I just happen..."

Nate crossed his arms, clearly amused with himself, "That summons demons, curandero!"

"I don't summon demons! It was one seance that I didn't even..."

"Burn the witch!" He shouted loud enough to get the neighbor downstairs to bat at our floor with a broom.

We all dissolved into laughter, and suddenly things weren't as serious.

I hoped we could keep this energy, even with more bombshells in their way.

"Can I ask," Conner tested the water, and I was so eager they had questions, "How did you discover this, or when did it start?"

I tucked my hair behind my ears and tried to think, "I always have, I honestly can't remember a time ghosts weren't around. I've learned to put up more boundaries and rules as I got older, but when I was younger," I shook my head, bouncing my hair right back into my face, "It was a lot, it was nonstop and relentless, and then my uncle ended up taking his life over his own inability to cope... it's, it's just a strange thing to live with."

Parker knocked his knee into mine, "You're preaching to the choir here."

"I guess I am," I was playing with a strand of my hair now, looping the curl around my finger. I was feeling brave, and I realized if anyone could understand my past it was them, it was Parker specifically.

I took a deep breath, "My life was complete chaos for a long time, I had all of these crazy voices haunting me 24/7, my uncle died, my parents got divorced, I was bullied relentless in school, my dad got sick, and then I was starting to figure out that maybe I wasn't supposed to be a girl..." I shrugged to try to keep it casual, "I wanted it to stop, I just needed it all to stop, so I drank, a lot..."

I didn't want to look up, I could feel all their eyes on me and no matter how bad I wished the couch would just swallow me whole.

Parker scoffed, "Bring those stones into the glass house, or whatever, what the fuck are you talking about?

I wasn't sure I knew what he was trying to say so I shrugged, "Unfortunately, I'm not as innocent as you all think I am. I used to be a terrible person. I was a horrible daughter, I hated my mom, I fought with my dad nonstop, I slept with every lesbian in my school and half of the girls that said they weren't, I drank, I smoked, I stole, I set fire to my neighbor's shed... That one was a complete accident, though."

"... We'll circle back to that, when you say you drank," he shook his head, this was really catching him up, "What're we talking? Everyone drinks underage, even Con."

Conner just shrugged.

"Okay," I took another deep breath and realized I couldn't dance around it anymore, "By the time I was sixteen I was a full-blown alcoholic, my mom practically threw me into rehab when I was seventeen. I got it together, met my girlfriend, graduated, moved out here, started college, my girlfriend broke up with me, and that's when Con ran me over."

Drew's head snapped to look at her boyfriend.

"I did *not* run him over," Con was quick to jump in, "I did kinda tap him in the parking lot, however."

"Wait," Parker spoke up, "You've been sober since you were seventeen?"

I nodded.

"Why the fuck wouldn't you tell us that?!" Nate was pissed now.

"We would've stopped dragging you around to bars constantly!" Parker added.

"That's exactly why!" Aaron gestured, "Everyone finds out and gets really weird about it. You guys are the only people that see me as a person instead of my past mistakes, my parents can't even do that! Every time my mom calls me; she says hi and then asks me how long I've been sober now."

"You're our friend," Conner reiterated, "We've all done stuff we aren't proud of, that doesn't define us, how we handle it does, all of us." He looked at Parker, "And the fact that you got cleaned up and went to school and are doing so amazing speaks for itself."

"We're proud of you." Nate took my shoulders in his hands and literally shook me.

"Thank you, and I'd like to think I've changed more than just my gender since then, but I've been trying to run from my past for years, and to be honest, it's catching up to me... Actually, I think it double backed on me," I gathered my hair on top of my head to give my hands something to do, "And with everything awful going on I just..." I practically choked on my words, too ashamed to say them out loud, "I want to drink, I catch myself thinking fuck, I could use a drink right now." I let go of my hair and it fell in curtains around me, "I don't need you guys to worry about me, I really do have everything under control, but... I just need you guys to know about it."

Nate was still standing beside me, he patted me fast on the back until I straightened out so he could wrap his arms around me.

"We got you, perrito."

"Both of you." Conner added.

"Sure, whatever."

"I love you guys." Parker said what I couldn't.

I tried to blink away the tears collecting.

I felt Conner's hand on my back.

"That's nice, shut up." Nate couldn't hide his chuckle with me so close. He let me go after a while, but he whispered to me before he pulled away, "I ever see you with a drink, it'll be the last time anyone sees you, a'ight?"

(＼(•̀w•́)／)

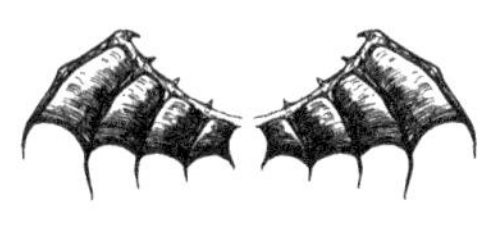

Parker

"Okay," Conner was up and stretching out his back, "I need a burger for emotional support at this point," he tried to joke but I could tell our drama was weighing on him.

Nate shrugged, "Could eat,"

"That honestly sounds fantastic." Drew agreed.

They all kinda looked at me as if to gauge how I was feeling but I didn't care I just wanted outta the apartment.

I was feeling better, but still like shit. Every part of my body ached, and I barely breathed 'cause my chest hurt so badly.

Aaron wanted to do whatever he could, so I let him help me go and get changed.

I couldn't help staring at myself in the mirror when I pulled my shirt off.

I couldn't get past the new scar on my chest.

I was so high, so drunk, so sleep deprived, but I remembered every excruciating minute of it.

Yet, I'm still standing...

Aaron gave me a weird look.

"Yeah yeah, I know..." I mumbled, pulling in a different shirt, "I'm ready."

"No, it's just. No make up?"

I shrugged, shoving my hands into my hoodie pocket, "You guys don't wanna wait on me."

He smiled at me, probably the first time any of us had smiled in days, "Of course we do."

I gotta hand it to the guys, they know me well... Too well, maybe.

We spent three hours sitting at a diner and joking around about everything and laughing at nothing like what we were just going through was nothing.

We just kept moving.

November 28 2007

11:00

PARKER

I was lying face down half on the floor half on the floor-mattress, half sick and half wallowing in self-pity.

My body ached, I was exhausted, and my brain throbbed to the beat of Crank That as my phone rang nonstop.

Nate laughed when he walked into the room, "Hold up lemme send in our chalk outline guy."

I opened one eye to look at him, the room was so bright, "Please tell me you have some pills."

"'Bout that," he pressed lips together.

"No!" I popped up onto my hands and knees, scurrying over to latch on to Nate's leg, "Please, God! Help me! This is fucking hell!"

"Con doesn't want you doin' drugs, and I dunno that it's a good idea to have that shit 'round Air."

"It's not doing drugs it's pills! And they're not gonna be around long."

He made a face.

"Please," I whimpered, "I haven't slept in two days, I've been shaking so bad all of my muscles hurt, I feel like I have bugs *everywhere*." I used his body to pull myself up and then clung to him like a monkey, "I'm going fucking nuts!"

"Yeah, I know." He tried to pry me off, but I wasn't budging.

"Get off."

"Gimme an Ambien."

He took two steps and fell forward, dead weight, onto the bed.

I think he thought it was going to hurt, and I'd let go but in a weird way his weight on top of me felt nice, like being swaddled.

I stayed latched onto him 'til he groaned and told me to scoot over, then I wiggled until I was pressed against his chest.

I just wanted to be held.

I think that's all I've ever wanted.

God, that sounds so fruitily emo.

Nate cleared his throat when it got a little too quiet, "I'm sorry, by the way... 'Bout Travis."

"Sorry you didn't get to kill him?" I tried to laugh; I was sick of being serious and pretty sure cried out for the next century.

"Look, I know I'm bad at the whole sincerity shit, but I mean it."

"I know you do."

It was quiet except for my phone's nonstop ringing.

"Jesus fucking Christ," Nate stood up to get but I grabbed at him.

"No! If you really don't want bad shit to happen to me don't answer it!"

He snorted, "It your mom?"

"Worse, Caitlin. I told her I'd take her out and I kinda sorta stood her up and, y'know, tried to kill myself so she's... Yeah."

He sat back against the headboard, "Damn, I can't imagine why she'd be upset 'bout that."

"Yeah, I feel a little bad about it."

He laughed, "Only a little?"

"Well, she reamed me over the phone pretty good already, not in the fun way though."

"You talk to your family yet?"

"Uh-uh, I tried my sister, but she said she'd call me later this week... I dunno if I'm gonna tell my mom."

Nate lifted his arm so I could lay against him again, "I mean, I'd say fuck 'em but maybe you should talk to Con about that. Y'know, daddy issues and all."

The room felt awkward when neither of us laughed.

"So," Nate was running his hand over my back, I couldn't tell if it was to comfort me or if it was just something for him to do, "Do you like... Wanna talk about Travis?" I felt like I could hear him cringe.

"I don't know," I sighed, "He broke things so bad I kinda figured maybe he could fix 'em, you know?"

"Hmm."

Nate spoke again, "You slept with him, huh?"

"Yeah..." My voice was flat, no emotion, just an answer.

I couldn't tell what he was getting at, but he didn't seem upset by it, he didn't really have a reaction at all, but his hand was still on my back, and I was just glad things were okay.

When nothing else was said I figured I should say what I was thinking, "You were right, I should've let him go a lot sooner."

Nate got the biggest smirk, "Sorry, what?"

"I said you were right."

"Didn't catch that."

I punched him in his side, but he just laughed it off.

"So, how's the sex?"

I laughed back, "Why you wanna know so bad?"

He shrugged, I took that as an invitation and sat up right to meet his face.

In a split second we were making out and I was ignoring that little bit of instinct that said "*hey, maybe this isn't a healthy coping mechanism.*"

After a minute Nate stopped, he laughed realizing what we were doing.

"The fuck is wrong with you?"

"What?" I rested my head on his shoulder trying to bat my eyes all innocently.

He just rolled his eyes with another laugh, "Seriously, how're you even horny right now? I knew a guy back home that went through opioid withdrawal and chewed a hole through his fucking mattress."

"Sounds like a good excuse for bad behavior on that mattress."

"Oh, my God, you're so stupid."

"No, you're fucking stupid." I mocked until we were laughing like idiots and making out again.

He rolled over on top of me, and I pulled his pants off, but we didn't get very far.

There was a loud thud followed by Conner screaming, by the time I realized it was him falling through the door he was running out of the room like a startled newborn deer.

I was laughing my ass off, but Nate didn't think it was funny yet, he actually looked a little like he was gonna throw up.

I didn't feel like I did anything wrong, but I also had the default feeling that I need to fix it...

Especially since Nate was looking at me like I needed to fix it.

"Con," I followed him to the living room, "Conner! Stop yelling!"

Aaron took out his headphones and looked between us like we were crazy, "What's going on?"

"Did you know they were a thing?!" Conner kept shouting.

"Sh! Shush! We're not a thing."

"That wasn't a thing?!"

"No, we weren't even doing anything!"

"What?" Poor Air was just so confused.

Conner sighed, his hands on his hips, "I just walked in on Nate and Parker having sex."

"Okay, worried about you and Drew's sex life."

"No, no, no," Con's hands were off his hips and he was gesturing wildly now, "You don't get to turn this around, not now. Do you even know how incredibly unhealthy this is?"

I crossed my arms, "It's not like it's anything new."

Nate picked a great time to walk out, and I could feel his glare.

"What the hell does that mean?" Conner looked between us.

Neither of us answered.

Con rubbed his temples, "So this has been going on for a while? And yesterday, when everyone was spilling their guts, you failed to mention this?!"

"Didn't think it was important."

"How did you figure it wasn't important?"

“Well," Nate got defensive, "It wasn't talkin' to the dearly departed or attempted suicide! So nah, wasn't fuckin' important."

"Hang on, hang on," Aaron tried to wrap his head around it, "So you guys are hooking up?" He wasn't as mad but just as confused as Conner.

Nate stayed quiet; arms crossed like he was gonna beat the shit out of me.

"I dunno... " I sighed, so unsure of what I could say, or even why Conner was mad.

But everything I did just made things worse.

"It's not like you're thinkin'." Nate said

"It wasn't even really sex," I added.

“Right.”

"Mostly just making out and hand stuff… Mouth stuff…"

"Stop talking." Nate growled.

"Yes, God, please do." Conner shook his head.

"I just, that's surprising, but I guess that's why you guys have been so weird!" Aaron connected.

"I mean, is it that surprising? I'm kinda the bisexual gateway and he's just a guy, I mean, *can I make it any more obvious?"*

"Shut. Up."

"Wait, so Nate, you're…"

Nate didn't even let Aaron get the question out, "Nah, nope, not nothing." He opened the cabinet before slamming it shut, "Where's my tequila?"

"Gone," Con raised his eyebrows, clearly proud of himself, "So are your cigarettes, and your weed, Parker's pills and his coke, and Aaron's energy drinks."

"What did I do?!" Aaron piped up.

"You drank three in a half hour last night; your heart is going to explode."

"Is the coffee still there?" Air mumbled.

"What's your fuckin' problem?"

"Um, hello?! Have you not been paying attention to anything going on around here for the past week?" I got the feeling Con laughed 'cause he didn't wanna scream, "I couldn't care less about the fact that both of you are men, I'd hope you'd think more than that of me, this is all about honesty and transparency. And if you guys have been hiding this from us, what else have you been hiding? How are we supposed to have any trust or know we all have each other's backs when we don't even know what's going on in each other's lives? How are we supposed to hunt like that? Parker, how are you ever going to get sober when you can't be honest with us?"

I crossed my arms, I didn't know where that was coming from and I didn't like where it was going, "Who said anything about getting sober?"

The three of them looked at me like it was obvious.

"What?" I snapped.

"I get it," Aaron slid off his glasses to tuck his hair behind his ears and then replaced them, "Both of you, I really really understand what both of you are going through and yeah you probably need some time to sit with it and adjust to it but you can't run from it. Trust me, that's when bad shit happens."

I looked over at Nate and he gave me the same judge-y look.

"You're bisexual."

"You're a junkie."

"Hey, not necessary," Conner intervened, "And neither of those are a bad thing. One just means you need some help and the other is just who you are."

"I'm not fuckin' bisexual!"

"It's not something you have to come to terms with right..."

He cut off Aaron again, "Fuck off, I'm done."

He stomped off, slamming the front door on his way out.

"Hey, look at that," I carefully pulled myself up onto the back of the couch, "That's my move."

This seemed like a lot of work for a guy that wouldn't even plow me.

I figured things would've been easier if I were less of a mess and he wasn't ashamed of being caught with me.

Hell, maybe Con was onto something with the whole sober thing...

Nah.

Nate showed up later that night, after Aaron and Conner fell asleep, I figured he was waiting 'cause he was wasted. And I thought he'd be mad and want nothing to do with me still.

So, I was totally off guard when he grabbed me and kissed me.

Okay, not mad, and definitely not drunk.

I tried to laugh off the shock, "What was that?"

"Shut up. I don't wanna talk about it, I don't wanna think about it. I just wanna figure it out, okay?"

A massive shit eating grin broke across my face, "You have no idea what you just signed up for," I wrapped my arms around his neck to pull him into another kiss, "You got a safe word?"

He slapped me on the ass on our way to the bathroom.

03:30

Aaron

I couldn't tell you what was happening with absolute certainty, especially since I didn't want to think about the moans coming from the bathroom, so I opted to ignore it and sleep through it.

But I was woken up when Conner finally broke and started pounding on the door, howling "WE CANNOT LIVE LIKE THIS!!!" and I just felt like it needed to be noted.

November 29 2007
18:45

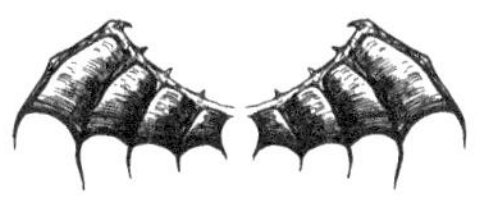

Parker

Nate wasn't talking to me today, at first, I thought it was about last night, and that he didn't wanna talk about finally closing that gap... No pun intended... Okay, some pun intended.

But then I realized he was refusing to deal with anyone, and it wasn't anything personal, he was just greeting everyone with "shut up" today.

And based on how quiet my phone had been, Caitlin wasn't talking to me either.

"This is... Odd." Conner said what I was thinking as he clicked around on his computer.

I connected the dots myself and jumped at the thought of a hunt, God I would've killed for one, or absolutely any other kind of normalcy.

"You got something?"

"No, that's what's weird. Turn on the news."

He glared at me when I refused to dig myself out of the comforter I drug out to the couch, but he eventually got up to change the TV.

"I was watching that!" I whined.

"I'll give you twenty bucks if you can tell me what show was on."

"... One Tree Hill."

"Not even close, It's Always Sunny In Philadelphia."

"We live in Washington," I scoffed.

"Jesus Christ," he mumbled, turning up the TV to drown me out.

He watched it for a half hour, looking more confused as the segments changed, "This is so weird. It's been a week, and in seven days, not one person has died strangely. Nothing, and no new missing persons? That's, look," He grabbed his laptop and scrolled through The Seattle Times website, "Every obit is a grandparent or someone who was terminally ill..." He looked up from the screen, "You're looking at me like you don't think that's weird. Okay, well, last year King County estimated that we had around 4.10 homicides per 100,000 deaths, from that Aaron was able to estimate that about an eighth of those were vampiric in nature. Again, those were all just in Seattle alone, don't you think that's weird?"

"Con, you know I haven't said anything, right? Wait, how exactly did you get rid of my coke?"

He rolled his eyes and went back to his desk.

He was right, though.

I figured by now Donnie knew I screwed him over, and every day that passed without revenge only meant something bigger was coming.

And clearly, I wasn't the only one who saw it that way.

"Stop that." I didn't even notice I was doing anything until Con spoke. I'd been anxiously snapping the rubber band on my wrist. Drew made me wear it when she made me swear, I would stop cutting... And then she apologized for an hour when she realized it said, "Thank You For Giving Blood!"

I honestly couldn't tell if this was irony or if the universe was just laughing in my face at this point.

To be fair, all of this was getting too creepy.

All of it, everything was so convenient.

It was like the moment in a horror film where the bad guys down and everything seems like it's going to be okay...

Too okay...

I haven't smoked in days, why the hell am I so paranoid?

Unironically, at the same time there was a loud knock on the door that scared the shit outta me.

Conner glared at me when I screamed and I realized I was just being overly paranoid, but nothing could've prepared me for what was on the other side of the door.

Caitlin stood there, arms crossed, a bitchy glare but still looking like a smoke show.

Her hair was curled and twisted up, her makeup was done, she was wearing all gold jewelry, a skintight red dress, a push up bra, and a fur coat I really, really wanted to touch.

"What the hell are you doing here?"

"You owe me an apology, and a dinner."

I laughed but it only pissed her off more.

"Come on, you're kidding, right? What did you really come here for? Slash my tires? kick me in the nuts?" Courtney had me well versed in crazy ex-girlfriend, "Well, jokes on you I don't have a car, and I'm kinda into that."

Caitlin looked at me like I was the crazy one, "No, gross. I'm serious, you moron. So go in there and try to look a little less… I-violate-people's-cars-until-they-pay-me-to-stop."

I laughed.

"What?" She snapped, she wasn't joking.

"You've got no idea how spot on you are."

"Gross," She rolled her eyes, "I'll be in the car."

I literally just pulled a sweatshirt over my head, assuming we were just going somewhere with witnesses so she could feel better about yelling at me.

If that was the case, Con would've loved to piggyback that.

Caitlin glared at what I was wearing when I got in the car, "I thought I said something less methadone?"

"Well, benzies are just so last season."

She kept glaring, but didn't say anything else. It was all rage.

Bored, and a little afraid she might snap at any moment, I looked for anything to do.

Then I noticed buttons on the door next to me.

Immediately deciding I had to know what they did, I hit them both.

No frickin' way, automatic windows!

I kept messing with them.

Up, down, up, down, down some more, up a little

and just a little…

"Stop it!" Caitlin finally snapped.

Oh, I'd be dead in 15.

"Jesus Christ. Is there something actually wrong with you?! Or are you just a particularly sick sadist that gets off to driving people fucking crazy?! Seriously! I can't decide if you should be medicated or studied. You are the single most self-centered, manipulative person I've ever met, and I work in real estate!"

By the time she finally stopped for air I wondered how she hadn't passed out.

I let her drive through a few intersections.

"Well, you're not going to say anything?" She snarked.

I shrugged, "What do you want me to say, that I think you're right? That, I mean really, I wouldn't have given myself three second chances."

She shook her head, "Don't do that, don't pull that shit, you don't get to make me pity you!"

"I don't want your pity."

She looked like I said the sun set in the west or something fucking stupid.

“Honestly, I don't even know what you still want with me."

Her grip tightened on the wheel, "Just, stop. Stop talking. Stop being so… Parker and just have dinner with me. That's it. Sit there and be quiet.”

I was kind of weirded out by the request, but I figured I owed her at this point.

When I didn't say anything for a while she reached over and put her free hand in mine, "That's perfect… That's all I need.”

Caitlin pulled up to the fancy valet of the fancy restaurant with a fancy French name even Conner would've rolled his eyes at.

"We have an hour wait." The host tried to blow us off the second we walked in.

"Try again, and check your book,” It was nice to see her bitchiness aimed somewhere else for once, "G-a-r-c-i-a." She clacked her perfectly manicured nails against the reservation desk.

His glare turned to the fake smile when he realized she was right, “Yes, right this way. Mrs. Garcia."

"Better, but it's Miss.” She corrected him.

I waited for him to leave before I purred in her ear, "That was so hot.”

"Not now." She rolled her eyes and then cleared her throat loudly when I sat down.

And then she crossed her arms when I didn't get it, which in that dress left me drooling.

“Parker!” She snapped me out of my trance, “Get my chair.”

I only did it because I thought she was joking at first.

“Yes, mistress.”

She rolled her eyes again, "Is that being quiet, pet?" She played along, I'm assuming to get me to shut up.

Nothing was said after that, even when the waitress came by to ask if we wanted drinks, Caitlin waved her off.

"Okay, look, I'm not just giving you another chance outta the goodness of my… Shit."

I raised an eyebrow and decided it would be funnier to make fun of her than follow her gaze over my shoulder, “I think you mean out of your ass.”

“Not a word!” She demanded in a hushed tone as she stood to greet someone.

“Well, well, well, if it is not my favorite agent, fancy seeing you here.”

I practically snapped my neck to turn towards the familiar voice.

“Mr. Sotos!” Caitlin was somehow just as surprised as I was, but instead of wanting to shank him with a steak knife she hurried to get up, rearranged her coat, and shook his hand, "So funny to see you here this evening. Parker, this is Mr. Sotos..."

"Ah, Caitlin," he stopped her, "That is Donnie, to you." He joked in a way that wasn't overly flirtatious but enough that pissed me off.

Caitlin ate it up, she giggled, tucked her hair behind her ear and fidgeted with the buttons on her coat, "Mr, I mean, Donnie just acquired my real-estate firm in quite the merger." After that I was practically invisible to her, but Donnie made it obvious he wasn't forgetting about me that easily.

"So, date night with the Missus?" Caitlin asked in a way that made me wonder if she was testing the waters to see if he was married or not.

I snorted at the thought, "You mean Mister?"

Caitlin shot me a glare and Donnie went on like he didn't notice.

"I am afraid my visit here tonight is one of business," he let out a casual laugh with a glance in my direction.

"That doesn't surprise me, you might as well own the city at this point, what's another five percent?"

Another laugh.

"What about you? This is such a lovely place for a date."

"Oh, this isn't a date." She said quickly.

I gave her a look, and she returned it.

"Well, it isn't." She kicked me under the table.

There was an awkward pause that ended with Caitlin clearing her throat, "Mister, er, Donnie, would you care to join us? I mean, I'd love a chance to chat business."

Donnie hemmed and hawed for her sake, "No, no, I would hate to infringe on your night..."

"You're right, you're really crossing a line." I crossed my arms and leaned back in my chair.

Caitlin glared at me again, "He's joking, of course. It's not a bother at all, please join us."

"If you insist..."

"I do." She got the attention of the waitress who brought over another chair and table set.

I made a move for the steak knife that Donnie "accidentally" swatted off the table.

"Oh, pardon me, I can be a bit gawky at times." he smirked.

"Anyway," Caitlin twirled her hair around her finger as she started a ramble that put me to shame, "You know we've been in business close to sixty years now… Of course you did, you just bought us," She let out a little laugh, "Well, I just meant, my grandpa came to this country with the clothes on his back and a business idea, and so having an opportunity like this is everything, and I just know that we're going to shatter the glass ceiling."

Donnie chuckled, taking a sip from a whiskey glass that seemed to just appear, "I must say, I do like hearing that. As you know, I do make a habit of offering these life altering opportunities where I have the chance, but I cannot tell you how many pass for one reason or another," He paused to make sure he really hit me over the head with the point, "It does break my heart, so to hear you speak like this, to hear you so excited, yes, it thrills me."

"They're idiots," Caitlin caught herself only after it came out, so she tried to laugh it off, "I mean, they just don't have a head for business like us. And yeah, I know my father was ecstatic to hear your name come up in our little firm. I have to admit, I was a little… Unsure, you're just so young, but to be fair, you've done a lot with so little." She laughed again, this time it was more of a giggle, and she had that flirty pitch she usually got right before she'd started barking orders at me.

"Well, I may be young, but being an immigrant myself, I have lived a lot of different lives. You pick up a thing or two." He winked at her, and I could've ripped his head off.

Caitlin beamed, "I didn't realize you were an immigrant, too."

"I sure am," His normal accent, which was usually barely noticeable, was suddenly way thicker and less European, "Venezuela, my parents sent me up when I was just fifteen."

She asked him something in Spanish and the second he answered her back I became completely invisible.

I couldn't understand a word, but it was obvious he was trying to close the deal with her, and she was all over it.

He finished his drink with a sigh and switched back to English, "Darling, I hate to be a bother, but I am absolutely parched," He reached into the pocket of his suit jacket and slid his black Amex card over to Caitlin, "Be a doll, and get yourselves something, no, never mind that. In fact, your entire evening is on me."

He gave her that perfect Prince Charming smile, and I don't know how he did it but everything about his eyes changed, they were bigger, browner, more inviting, and completely innocent.

Like a puppy that just crapped on the carpet and didn't wanna get yelled at, he managed to take all the threateningness out of his eyes and it made it weirdly predatory.

Caitlin didn't even think about questioning it, she was up and away from the table without giving it a second thought.

And the second she was gone; I flew across the table.

Donnie just laughed at my lame attempt and brushed my hands away from him, "Now, now, wouldn't want to cause a scene now, would we?"

"I'll fucking kill you!"

He made an over exaggerated bored expression, "So you keep saying, and yet..."

I grabbed him by his tie, pulling him closer to the table where I white knuckled the steak knife that he thought he got away from me.

The entire time, he wouldn't wipe that smug smile off his face, "Go ahead, but think this through, Parker. All you're really going to accomplish is angering me, and your little girlfriend is right over there, among many other witnesses."

"Leave her out of this." I growled.

"Oh, don't be that way, *love*," He thought this was funny, wrapping his hands around my waist in a way that if he hadn't pissed me off so bad, probably would've gotten my pants off by now.

"Relax, take a breath for God's sake," He talked to me like I was a dog with a tight grip, "I have no interest in harming her, in fact, I only benefit from her safety."

I glared at him, trying to decipher what that meant.

"Both her physical and employment safety are secure, you have my word," He nodded towards the bar.

Taking my eyes off him felt like an obvious trap, but I had to check on Caitlin, I couldn't let anything happen to her.

She was sitting at the bar, chatting with a blonde, one of Donnie's girls I guessed.

Donnie raised one of his eyebrows, "A man's word is all he has these days, wouldn't you say?"

"Nice try, I'm guilt proof."

When I wouldn't ease up and he was done playing with me he decided to physically remove me himself, easily picking me up and placing me back on my chair like a defiant toddler.

He was very clearly waiting for me to address the problem, so I ignored it.

"You're Venezuelan now, huh?"

He chuckled, "Well, the poor little farm boy thrust into a world war story can only get me so far with a certain crowd."

"So did you learn Spanish before or after bottoming for Hitler."

He laughed again but it didn't reach his eyes, “After, that was how I learned German.”

“Of course, you know German.”

“German, Spanish, Romanian, Romani, Latin, Mandarin, Japanese, Dutch...”

"I got it," I had to stop him before he continued, "Did you have a point to coming out here to piss me off, or was that just for fun?"

"I believe there is pleasure in business, heads and tails of the same coin..."

"I'm not gonna answer your fucking riddles three so what do you want?"

"Maybe your girlfriend would be more willing to call this a date if you were more willing with foreplay," He chuckled to himself, taking a cigarette out of his pocket and lighting it in the same fluid motion.

I rolled my eyes, "Are you trying to say you bought a real estate firm to fuck me?"

"Don't flatter yourself, Parker, I once bought a quarantine wing in a hospital because I needed a cigarette."

I scoffed, when I realized we weren't really gonna get anywhere I decided to bite, "How the hell did you get so rich?"

“That's the fun part,” he blew out the smoke in his mouth, “I'm not, when you have what everyone else thinks is “a certain je ne se quoi”, they are willing to bargain with you, and the world is yours for the taking. That's only the main point I've been trying to hammer through that thick skull of yours. I thought with your savvy thinking, you would have gotten the point by now. It only took three years to get you to sign the damn papers, then what? What in the hell is it that you pulled exactly? Explain it to me."

"What do you want from me? You got your deal, get outta my fucking face."

He lowered his voice until it was just a low growl, "Did you not read it? Your life is mine until the end of it. Did you forget that part?"

I shrugged, "That's where we're fucked, technically, I died."

He searched my face, waiting for a punchline or a laugh.

"I died three years ago, everything since then has been..." I shrugged, "Divine intervention, it's a whole Frankenstein theory I'm working on but I'm gonna need a bottle of Jack, a cigarette, and a corkboard to explain, but basically, I don't have a life to sell you."

He let out a dry, coarse laugh that was like nails on a chalkboard, "You are the proverbial thorn in my side. Your thinking is what I admire most about you, Parker. It is also what bugs the hell out of me the most, I can never guess what you're going to pull next."

"Then why do you want me so bad?"

"*That* is why I want you. You are just like me; I am just like you."

He shifted his head to the left, letting the candlelight on the table reflect off his eyes as he did that weird shifty thing where they went from brown to a glowing red.

He tried to lock in on me, but nothing happened.

I crossed my arms, "You almost done?"

"What is it?" *Oh, he was pissed,* "How are you blocking me?!"

"What are you talking about?"

I blinked and he was on his feet pulling me up.

In an effortless but violating move, he shoved his hand in my hoodie pocket, pulling out a little velvet bag I didn't even know was in there.

He stood over me, bent so there he was only a few inches above my face, "This game that you think you're so good at, remember that I'm the one that invented it decades before you came around. What is it you think I'm going to do to you? What are you so scared of? I took you out of the gutter, I gave you life, I held your little hand, and walked you through a second chance, and this?" He held the bag up in my face, "This is how I'm rewarded for my efforts? I treated you far better than anyone I ever have before. I gave you everything. I gave you every opportunity,"

Donnie laughed again, like a fork on porcelain, "Oh, ah, but no, no. You voided our deal, and trust I am well with in my mind to go back on my side also," he shoved me hard, and I fell back into my chair, "Know that if you decide to wage this war, there is no telling what could happen to your friends." He warned.

My body ached from where his hands had been, then where the chair hit me, I let my head fall forward and my hair cover my face.

I wasn't sure exactly what set him off, but I tried not to let the amusement show on my face.

"I'm tired,"

God, that was so true. These past months had dragged on like decades but also came at us like milliseconds.

I continued, "And I'm sick of being scared of you,"

I thought about the last few days, the love and support and protection that the guys refused to let waiver once, I could've cried just thinking about it but at the same time it made me feel so powerful, like something other than this parasite was swimming in my veins.

I cleared my throat to make sure my next words were clear, "So you want a war? You got fucking a war. I'm done taking your shit, and I'm done holding back."

Donnie had both of his hands pressed against the table so he could tower directly over me.

He moved his hand off the table so fast and angry that I thought he might've slapped me and the pain just hadn't registered in my brain yet.

He buttoned his coat, "Enjoy your night, Parker. It may very well be the last one that you see."

As soon as he was gone, I reached for the bag.

It was just a little velvet sachet with a swirly tree in a circle branded on the center.

I knew the design I saw somewhere but I had to rack my brain to remember.

Aaron, I knew it had something to do with him.

I pulled the string holding the back together and dumped the contents onto the table, but the just left me more confused.

It was a bunch of different colored leaves, a couple twigs, and a handful of sparkly rocks.

I didn't have time to figure it out though, 'cause Caitlin was on me as fast as Donnie had left.

Her hands were a flurry of slaps, "What the hell did you say to him?!"

"Ow, ow!"

"If I get fired I’m going to kill you!"

Everyone in the restaurant was staring at us now, and Caitlin started to turn red from her chest up, "Get up," she grabbed her things off the table and then grabbed me by the back of my arm, "Get up, Parker, I'm not fucking playing around with you."

She drug me through the restaurant and tightened her grip while we waited for the valet, all without a word.

Then she waited until we were in the car to start hitting me with her purse, "I asked you for one thing! One thing!" After a few more good hits she got her rage enough under control to pull the car into traffic.

At the first stop light she put her hand up in front of her, exasperated, "I don't have any words, I'm so pissed off, I literally do not have a single word to say to your right now." I could tell that wasn't gonna be true, "Everything just has to be about you all the time, doesn't it? You always have to be having a good time either popping pills or liquored up, or stirring the pot you..."

I zoned out most of her rant, it all started to sound the same anyway.

Besides, from what I could tell I may have just gotten the US into an international incident with Romania. Donnie's metaphors were so mixed I couldn't tell for sure; she was asking a lot from me.

I did get a little nervous though when I realized she hadn't said anything in a while and was now driving through a closed park.

She pulled into the abandoned parking lot that looked more like an abyss at this hour.

"If you're gonna kill me..." the air was quickly taken out of my sails when I realized I didn't really have a great argument here, so I let my train of thought wander, "Wouldja at least do something kinky like choke me? Stab me?"

Caitlin rolled her eyes so hard I thought she might've fallen over if she wasn't sitting down, "We need to talk." And then she didn't say anything else.

"... Like about anything? 'Cause I'd like to circle back to the choking thing."

"Jesus Christ," she muttered, "Parker, look, I've tried a million ways to make this easy on you and you've dodged me every way but straight on so," she shrugged, then straightened out her shoulders to prove she was better than me, then she hit me in a total blind spot, "I'm pregnant."

Suddenly everything that happened tonight was outta my head, hell everything was out of my head! You could've asked my name and I would've stuttered.

My brain was just overloaded.

I sat there for a second, trying to decide what to do with the information, then I realized she wanted a response right now.

"Okay?"

"*Okay?*" She repeated.

I shrugged, "What do you want me to do about it?"

Then the hitting started again.

"Ow! What do you want from me? Like a congrats? Jesus, I'll send you and the dad a card, okay?"

"Oh, my fucking God," she put her hands on the sides of her head, "You're the dad, you braindead jackass!"

Before I even had time to laugh at that idea, she blurted out, "I wanna get an abortion."

"Okay? Good for you? Why do I care?"

There was a pause, she sighed, and I could tell I was finally going to get the truth.

"I can't tell my parents, and my insurance doesn't cover it."

"Wow, wooow."

"Oh, stop whining! It's just a thousand dollars!"

"Oh, my God!"

"Look, you're the one that couldn't wear a condom, so," she shrugged, "You should be the one to deal with it."

"I don't, I," I scoffed, "What makes you think it's mine?"

"You're a piece of shit."

"Well, you're a whore,"

She slapped me so hard my ears rang, and my face burned in the shape of her hand.

"Jesus, fuck!" I pressed against the car door to get away from her, "I didn't mean it like that! Fuck, a city councilmen had me on his payroll for shit's sake. It was just a fucking question!"

She settled down just slightly, but her arms were still crossed, "I'm almost positive it's you."

"I'm positive it's not."

Her back straightened, her jaw clenched, "Why?"

"I'm pretty sure I'm sterile,"

She laughed, "Right, I'm sure that works on all the other sluts you try to trick into..."

"Wow! You hateful bitch! And for your information I'm serious, I'm dead!" That just kinda slipped out.

"What?"

I shook my head, "I meant I'm dead serious."

"Well, you're a known liar, so sorry if I don't just take your word for it."

"What's your problem?"

"You've got a lot of fucking nerve, you know that? Since the nineth grade all you've done is cause problems and, God! You're like this *vacuum* dragging everyone else around you down to just make yourself feel better, you're an emotional vampire!"

I put my hands up.

I had nothing else, and I know it sounded awful, but I just didn't care anymore.

"Fine, whatever. I hope you and that baby have a nice life 'cause I don't have a thousand bucks." I felt around for the handle on the door and slammed it when I got out.

"Where the hell are you going?" She rolled down the window.

"Anywhere away from you."

I started to walk off and she yelled after me, "You're a real son of bitch, Parker Winston!"

(＼(•̀w•́)／)

20:50

Conner

At some point during the night, while I was keeping watchful eye on the Seattle Times, Parker decided to bust through the front door like the goddamn Kool-Aid man taking out practical everything on the kitchen island and one of the stools.

I let out a heavy sigh, "Are you drunk?"

It was my fault, really, what else was I expecting him to go do?

"No, just Parker-isms." He picked up the stool he slammed into, "Where's Aaron?"

He clearly didn't realize he was yelling until Aaron opened the bathroom door with his hands up, "I just had to pee."

Parker fumbled with something in his pocket "What is this?"

"Oh, you took my hoodie? I've been looking for it all night..."

"Aaron!" He cut him off in a squeaky tone that would only be rivaled by Aaron, "What's in the bag?!"

Nate laughed from the couch, "Calm down, coked up Brad Pitt." He thought he was funny.

"Oh, sorry," Aaron took the velvet bag, and undid the tie, smoothing out the fabric on the counter so all the stuff sat in the middle of the pentagram that was painted on the inside, "It's just some cinnamon, white sage, juniper..." He continued to rattle off a bunch of other things that just sounded like a bizarre grocery list.

"Curandero," Nate muttered.

"I'm not a witch," Air crossed his arms, "It's just a simple... Warding, you know, for protection. You can never be too careful, it's mostly for energy, ghosts... Magic..." he mumbled.

"Does it work on vampires?" Parker asked?

"Hmm? Maybe you should tell me?" He sprinkled a few of the leaves and twigs in my hand.

Parker was clearly at a loss as to what to do with it so by default, he threw the handful into his mouth.

"What are you doing?!" Aaron cried.

"Well, I don't know what I'm supposed to do with it!" Parker crunched.

"You're not supposed to eat magic!"

"I thought it wasn't magic." Nate popped off.

I laughed, "I think the answer is it does nothing to vampires."

Park shrugged, "Smells good, tastes weird."

"Of course it does! You're not supposed to eat it!" Aaron cautiously put two of the rocks in his hands, "Don't put these in your mouth, please I like these."

I got up and started to poke around at the bag's contents with my pen, "Where's the interest in witchcraft coming from?"

"It's not witchcraft." Aaron stated as he waved something over my head that sure felt like witchcraft.

"I had a run in with our not-so-friendly neighborhood vampire,"

My eyebrows raised but my words contradicted it, "That doesn't surprise me, I'm actually surprised it took him this long."

"Yeah, me too. Anyway, this pissed him off royally and then things got a little gang war-y after that, so whatever it is we should bottle it."

"Why would he care about a warding spell?" Air asked.

"Aha!" Nate shot up off of the couch, "Curandero! Quemar a el brujo!"

"Hang on, hang on, hang on!" Air clearly had an idea, "How much do you think Donnie knows about magic?"

I crossed his arms, putting my hand under my chin to think, "You think he's using magic?" I sounded more skeptical than I meant to. In all fairness, I was about to blow a gasket trying to process the thought of ghosts.

"I think at least the hypnosis might could be magic, maybe even the telepathy? That's all shadow work. Hell, they're vampires so it could possibly even be blood magic, I'm not sure, my grandma was a big believer that "the goddess' gifts" should be used for good, so I don't know much about that side of things, but," He shrugged taking a second to catch his breath, "It would make sense, basic binding spells would be consistent with a lot of the stuff he's been able to pull off, sprinkle in some blood and a little human sacrifice. Who knows what he could pull off."

"Hang on, hang on again!" Aaron sprinted the few steps to my desk and started shuffling pages until he found the picture of Donnie as Jamias clearly in a concentration camp.

I could tell by his face, the picture made Parker sick, and he really couldn't make himself look at it.

"Look," Aaron traced his finger over the darker one of the triangles pinned to Jamias' chest, "This is either black or brown, which meant "asocial" which was really anything from prostitutes to pacifists, but a large part of the Holocaust was also against the Roma people."

Parker had to shove his hand away and flip the picture over, "Air, what are you getting at?"

"On the magical side of things," He lowered his voice for a second, "When it comes to the Celts, we're more powerful when we come from our homelands, when we're born from the correct bloodline blend,"

"... You're starting to sound a little master race-y,"

Aaron smirked, "I'm telling my Jewish dad you said that."

"Sorry!"

"Anyway, if Romani magic is anything like Celtic, then a lot of magic you have to be born with. And based on what we know about him; I think Donnie just might be. That could be the added layer to this vampiric parasite or bug or whatever we think it is now?" He looked up to me for confirmation.

"... Do you think that's why I'm not zombie brained?"

Air tilted his head and squinted around Parker, "You know, I don't really know. You've always had a strange aura, but I just had kinda assumed it was the whole undead thing. Could be something to look into."

Nate smirked with a laugh, "A'ight, what's my aura, then?" He tested.

"Oh, orange," Air said like it was obvious, "Sometimes a little rosy, I'm assuming because you love us."

Nate blushed a little, it was actually strangely adorable. He then mumbled something in Spanish and did the sign of the cross.

Now that there was a quiet moment it seemed like things were starting to settle in Parker's head.

He let his head lull back to stare off into space for a second, before something caught his eye, he was pulling himself up onto the counter against the fridge.

He could just barely reach the cabinet above the fridge, and was trying to feel for something in there

"You're gonna break your neck up there." I warned him.

"Ah ha!" He laughed, pulling a tiny baggie of pills and threw them in his mouth before I could get to him.

"Are you serious?" My hands flew to my hips when I realized I couldn't get to him in time.

"I've had a weird night, okay?!"

I crossed my arms while I glared at him, "We need to talk about you getting sober,"

He rolled his eyes as he hopped off the counter.

"And your cutting, and your purging,"

"Yeah, yeah, yeah, I get it!" He snapped, but then quickly deflated when he had to look at me, "I'm working on it, right? I'm not cutting,"

He pulled up his sleeves to prove his point, "And I haven't made myself puke, on purpose, in weeks."

"You haven't eaten in weeks, either."

"I'm not snorting coke, I'm not snorting meth, or crushing up Ambien, okay? I had a really stupid fucking day and if I wanna take two Xanax, smoke a blunt, and let Nate blow my back out in the shower, I'm still doing a Hell of a lot better than I was three days ago."

I took a second and realized I wasn't being completely fair, "You're right," I softened with a sigh, "I'm sorry I haven't acknowledged that, and I'm sorry I'm being overbearing but you scared the hell out of me, and I just can't let you get there again."

He stared at me, unblinking, for a solid minute.

I don't think he knew what to do with the positive reinforcement.

So, he decided to race around the island and tackle me onto the couch like a rational person that knows how to express love and affection.

"Parker!" I huffed when he knocked the wind out of me, "Okay! I can't breathe."

"C'mon," Nate tried to coax Parker off me like a cat, "Let the little guy breathe."

"Don't get jealous," I teased him back for the little guy remark.

Nate glared at me, but his face was reddening to my level of blush, so his threats fell empty.

"Can I ask about that?" Aaron asked, moving from his stool in the kitchen to the chair in the corner of the living room.

"No," Nate answered flippantly, trying to pretend he wasn't embarrassed.

"Okay, never mind." Air shrugged it off.

I, however, wasn't nearly as respectful.

I rolled my eyes, "Fine, I'll ask. I know it's none of my business, and please spare me the nitty gritty, but you two are screwing around, but you're still seeing Caitlin? By the way, she has a helluva way of asking people out on dates."

"Nah, he's into that." Nate was more than happy to joke now that the pressure wasn't on him.

Parker scoffed as he crawled off of me, "No, that wasn't a date, she made that very obvious and did everything short of giving Donnie a handy under the table to make sure I knew it."

I cringed at his choice of words, but tried to move past it, "Then what was that all about?"

He shrugged, adding a few weird gestures for emphasis, "She's pregnant, and for whatever reason decided that was my problem."

He got up and investigated the fridge to see if I was serious about pouring out all our booze.

I was, and our fridge was entirely empty without it.

When he turned around and gave us a weird look when he realized we were all staring at him.

"What?"

"What do you mean 'she's making it your problem'?" I air quoted.

Parker laughed like it was the most asinine statement in the world "She thinks it's mine."

Maybe I was just uncreative and couldn't see the humor?

"What part of this is funny?!" I yelled.

"Pendejo." Nate rolled his eyes.

"... So, your girlfriend is pregnant," Aaron said slowly like he was trying to get me to break the news slowly to Parker.

"She's not my girlfriend."

"Yeah, that's what the problem is right now." I waved my hands around; Parker's ridiculous gestures were rubbing off on me

"How the fuck are you so calm? My ass'd be on the next plane to Guatemala and lookin' up vasectomy clinics." Nate was more stressed than Parker was.

He shrugged with another laugh, "Even if this isn't just more attention seeking bullshit, it obviously wouldn't be mine."

"... Okay, explain it to me?" I asked.

"For us non-methheads." Nate crossed his arms.

Parker was getting annoyed with us; *how dare we use logic!*

"Hello! I'm dead! Dead body, dead heart, dead swimmers!"

I scratched my forehead and tried to understand his logic, "Right, but you do have a heartbeat, so that's not the case entirely, but... God, help me, I don't want to have to ask this. Can you get it up?"

“Obviously!” He crossed his arms, exasperated, “That’s never been a problem.”

"Right, so don't you think, with that, theoretically, you could..." I struggled to find words I wanted to use.

But Nate quickly stepped in, "Dumbass, you think you got enough blood to get a boner but not knock her up?!"

"I don't know! You're making my head hurt!" Parker yelled back as he sunk into the couch, "Talk about something else. Please?" He tried to tack that please on in attempt to be less demanding... It didn't work.

I blew out a breath and tried to remind myself that all of this didn't need to be my problem right now.

"Oh," I did remember what I needed to tell him finally, "I spoke to Drew's professor and she thought that maybe we could try a strong anti-parasite now that we know that's what it is. But the doctor seemed worried that your immune system would remain compromised and..."

Parker was very obviously not hearing a word I was saying, I'm used to it, but he stood up in the middle of my sentence, mumbled a quick "I'll be right back." and just walked out of the door.

"I wasn't done talking, but I guess we can take a break." I said mostly to myself.

(＼(•̀w•́)／)

22:00

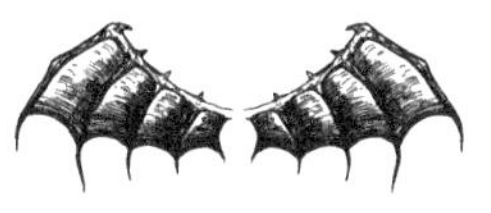

PARKER

Shit started hitting me all at once, I felt like I was going to puke, pass out, have a seizure, and probably puke again.

And like a normal person, I was taking it out on the buzzer of Caitlin's building.

I must've pressed it a gazillion times in the few seconds it took her to answer.

"What?!" She snapped, annoyed as hell.

"It's me, can we talk?"

She groaned, "Go away, jackass, I don't want to see you."

"I don't wanna see you either but we gotta talk."

"Goodbye!"

"Wait, wait!"

The intercom clicked so I buzzed it another billion times.

"Stop it!" She yelled loud enough for the front door guy to poke his head out of the door.

"Is everything okay out here?" He asked.

I heard Caitlin sigh over the intercom, "Hi Jack,"

"Is this guy bothering you?"

"I'm her boyfriend," I answered.

"He's not my boyfriend, and yeah, he's bothering me. Go home, Parker."

"You need to leave." Jack stood between me and the intercom.

"I just wanna talk. Just give me a minute?"

"Why should I?"

I finally snapped, "Cause if you don't I'm gonna start buzzing your neighbors!" I glanced over the list of names on the side of the intercom, "You get along with Casey Klerich?"

"Stop!" She demanded.

"Are you serious about being pregnant?!"

Suddenly Jack didn't wanna be a part of our bullshit anymore.

"Keep your voice down!"

I buzzed the button next to the name Casey twice, it took another two buzzes until someone answered.

"Hello?"

"Hey, hi. My name's Parker, I'm screwing your neighbor Caitlin, and she..."

"Oh, my God! Enough!" Caitlin screamed over me, "Ugh! Jack, is he drunk?"

"I'm not drunk!"

"Okay, so you're high?"

"No! I'm not!"

"Jesus. Fine,"

She didn't say anything else for a few seconds.

Bzzztt.

"I'm coming down there, you idiot! Stop with the buzzer!"

Caitlin took her sweet ass time coming downstairs.

"Why'd you come down?"

"'Cause the last time I let you up you swiped twenty dollars, a necklace my sister bought me, and a yogurt bar from my freezer, you freak!"

"... Oh, right. That bar was disgusting, by the way."

She crossed her arms, she tried to look annoyed, but it was obvious she was just trying to keep warm.

"So?" I awkwardly said when I realized there was nothing good to say.

"*So,* I'd like the twenty dollars and necklace back."

"No! I mean, like, about being pregnant! Are you serious?"

"Why would I lie about this?"

"Don't act like that wasn't just a Friday night for us in high school."

"Wow, look, I don't have time for your games, okay? You said you wanted to talk, so either talk or I'm going back upstairs and unplugging my buzzer."

I took a deep breath and tried to figure out where to start, "You're sure?"

She nodded, "Yeah, I've taken like six of the home tests, I even freaked out and had my doctor do a blood test, so I'd know what else you gave me."

"Other than a great night," I smirked.

"Right, sure, whatever." She didn't think I was funny.

She fished her keys out of her coat and unlocked her car and slid into the driver's seat.

I half expected her to back over me.

When I didn't move, she rolled down the window, "Are you going to get in, or are you hoping to get turned into an idiot'sicle?"

"Will you take another one? In front of me?" I asked, getting into the passenger seat.

"What?"

"A pregnancy test."

"I'm not peeing in front of you, freak." She scoffed as she clicked on the cab light, then started digging around the console between us before tossing a stapled stack of papers in my lap.

I scanned them as closely as my amphetamine riddled brain would allow.

King Clinic Hospital headed the corner of the paperwork, with address, phone number, doctor name...

Okay, that would be a lot of effort to go through, fair enough.

But I still pulled out my phone and punched in the number.

"Are you serious?!"

It was a real clinic, or so the answering machine claimed.

I clapped my phone closed, "How? *How?* How is this possible?"

She crossed her arms, "You tell me, you're the one that wouldn't use a condom." She tried to throw that back at me again.

"Because you told me you had it!"

"Oh," She dropped her arms into her lap, "I forgot about that."

"Obviously not the only thing you forgot."

"Hey! My mornings are busy! I live a very active lifestyle! It's ridiculous, okay?! I can't be expected to remember everything! I'm just one woman!"

I don't think she was expecting me to laugh 'cause she looked at me like the sound was totally foreign.

"This is so fucked up!" I kept laughing like I was having a psychotic break. To be fair, I felt like I was.

For the love of Christ, not even a full week ago I was a quarter inch from death and now... My head couldn't catch up. It wasn't something I even knew I should be worried about.

My stomach felt like it was going to fall out of my asshole, but at the same time the feeling was being taken over by a warmth in my chest.

It was weird, like relief or comfort? Or maybe the pills were just now kicking in.

"And you're sure it's..."

She gave me a look like she was waiting for me to snap at any second, but nodded, "There's been no one else, it's just you."

"How long have you known?"

Caitlin immediately lost any bark she had, and stared straight forward out of the windshield, "Three weeks."

And we were back to fighting.

"Are you fucking serious?!"

"Hey, you haven't exactly been easy to get ahold of! Plus, every time I tried to tell you you'd either stand me up or show up plastered!"

"Yeah, whatever! That's a solid argument, but! How many times have we fucked since then?!"

"I don't know!" She shrugged, "I was just going to keep you out of it and handle it myself until I realized my insurance wouldn't cover it."

I tried to breath out my anger.

It didn't work.

"How much do you need?"

"Six hundred, fifty-nine."

"I thought you said a thousand."

"I did, I thought it would make your head explode."

"Jesus, thanks."

"In full transparency, I only need one fifty. I get paid on Wednesday."

I shook my head, "Don't worry about it, I can get the whole amount, it's not a problem."

It really wouldn't be, I knew I had two options; I could kill Donnie and take all his money, or I could go grovel to my parents... Killing Donnie would be the easiest, least painful choice.

She didn't say anything for a really long time.

"... That's what you want, right?"

"This is so fucked up," she pulled her hair back and twisted it a couple of times before she dropped it and let it fall over her shoulders, "I should know, right? I should know what I want to do? I did all the research; I called the clinics..."

Out of nowhere she started sobbing, and I started to feel like Ashton Kutcher was going to pop up with a camera at any moment.

"Cat, if you don't want an abortion, I'm not going to make you get one."

"I know, but I don't know!" She did that awful scream/cry thing.

I gave it my best effort to rub her back and try to sooth her, "Calm down before your door guy calls the cops on me."

She kept wailing, and I started to panic 'cause I had absolutely zero idea what to do.

"Caitlin, please! I'm not used to being the non-hysterical one! It makes me uncomfortable!"

She let her hands fall from her face to her lap, taking a few deep breaths, she sat back in her seat, "I thought I knew what I was doing, but I don't!"

"I never know what I'm doing."

"No! I mean!" She took a few more deep breaths until she could talk without screaming, "I'm doing the career thing right now, and it's going good..." She sat back in the driver's seat with a hard exhale, "I don't know. Yeah, I want a family, and yeah, I want babies, but now? God, it's just awful timing, and with the wrong person."

"*Thanks,*"

"Well, it's true! I don't want to start my family with the guy I've been revenge banging every other week!"

I crossed my arms, sitting against the door, "I get it, I'm not most people's first choice."

"Parker, can this not be about you for one goddamn minute?!"

"Hey, you think this is any better timed for me?! I almost died seven fucking days ago!"

She scoffed, "You always have an excuse for..."

"I tried to kill myself, you heartless bitch!"

Caitlin looked at me like I slapped her, I kinda felt bad for yelling, "What are you talking about?"

I couldn't rehash this anymore, but I'd already dug my hole, and it was too deep to get out now.

I filled her in, in the last horrific way I could manage, minus the fangs and the blood parasite (by which I obviously mean Donnie).

She just kept blinking at me like she was dizzy or something.

"That bullshit happened, my friend was murdered, and another OD'd and died in my arms, all things considered I have a new treatment option, but that's probably just going to make me sicker like all the other ones, plus I'm trying to get sober. So yeah, not like it's good timing for me either."

"You're getting sober?"

I hadn't noticed it until she sounded shocked.

"Uh, I'm gonna be honest, that part just kinda slipped out, haven't really thought it all the way through yet, but I know it's, like, the right thing to do..." I shrugged, "And I haven't done any like big boy drugs in a week, and I mean, other than a few Xanax which y'know the only reason I'm not currently curled up in a ball on the street. But yeah, no coke, no meth, no alcohol, that's a huge one for me."

Her eyebrows raised, "You smoke meth?"

"Snort," I corrected her, "Oh, come on, don't act like you don't love railing and rails."

"You're an idiot..." She paused, "But see? That's why I didn't want to tell you."

"Cat," I tested the waters by touching her hand, when she didn't scream or slap me, I slid her hand into mine, "Everyone's got shit, you shouldn't have to go through this alone, I'm not your first choice but hey I'm all you got and whatever you decide, I'll be there... Don't know if that's a promise or a threat."

"I don't either, but thanks." She offered a phony half smile.

"For what it's worth, you'd be like, eh, second, third on my list."

"Oh, gee thanks."

"Not for lack of hotness, though. Different situation and I'd be begging you to shoot tequila off your stomach. Oh, God, or your tits. Jesus Christ, your tits are amazing,"

She rolled her eyes, but I could tell she appreciated it, "I feel like we're off topic."

"And you have the most beautiful labia I've ever seen."

I don't know if she was laughing out of shock or not but at least I got her to laugh, "You're so fucking bizarre."

"Thanks,"

"Come over tomorrow, seven thirty, if you blow me off again... I don't know what I'll do, that labia thing threw me off."

I smirked, "That's my line."

She shook her head, "Go home, Parker."

"You're not gonna take me home?" I semi joked.

She gave me a look.

"What? I thought we were good, and it's cold!"

"Fine, just stop being gross."

"Uh,"

"How 'bout you just don't talk?"

"Fair."

As the car lurched forward, I reached over to turn on the radio.

Semi-Charmed Life played through the car.

Fitting. But it did remind me of something.

"Were you really gonna fuck Donnie?"

Caitlin's head snapped around to look at me like it was the last thing she thought I'd say, "What? No! Why? Were you?"

I scoffed, "He wishes."

"How in the hell do you even know him?"

It took the liar part of my brain a second to warm up, "He's an ex, it's touchy."

She laughed, "Fine, don't tell me."

"What? You can pull him, but I can't?"

"He's a twenty-one-year-old billionaire, Parker, he's six two and he looks *like that*. How do you top that?"

"Don't have to," I smirked, "I'd bottom, that's kinda my thing."

She put on the brake, "Get out of my car."

We were in front of the building, though, so the threat was empty.

As I walked around the car, she rolled down the window to yell at me, "Tomorrow, 7:30, don't be late."

I crouched down to be level with the window, "No good-night kiss?"

She rolled up the window and revved the engine.

Nate was chilling on the front steps smoking a cigarette when I walked up.

He acknowledged me with a nod and a grunt.

"Can I get a hit of that?"

He lazily held it up for me to take, "How are you not a fucking puddle right now?"

I took a few quick puffs, "Xannies are a helluva drug. I probably will be later, though, I don't think it's taken yet." I gave him back the cigarette.

"Word." He mocked me.

"Wanna go make out?"

He stubbed it out on the concrete step then got up, "Idiota."

He unlocked the door and let it slam behind him.

"Wait! Let me in!"

He just flashed me a shit eating smirk on his way up the stairs.

Asshole.

November 30 2007
15:15

Aaron

My recent layoff left me with a lot of idle time, which was both okay and just plain awful. I've never been one to just sit with my own thoughts, I think that's probably why I drank, but now that everybody knew the situation, I felt a strange new security or I guess accountability.

Granted, yeah, I knew my parents would be disappointed in me if I slipped up, but knowing the guys were actively making sure I didn't slip up took a massive load off my shoulders.

I was even occasionally getting texts from Drew, either a casual "Just checking in! :)" or hilariously "The dog has been standing in the living room for a half hour straight! Ghosts???"

I did have more time for various mechanical experiments, as well as strangely deep conversations with Conner about things that truly didn't matter.

Conner would try to confirm a headline he breezed past earlier, "So I guess Kid Rock punched Tommy Lee at the VMAs?"

"Oh!" I would remember something that had nothing to do with the initial comment, "But did you see Stephen Colbert officially dropped out of the '08 election?"

"Was he ever officially in it?"

"I don't think so?"

Conner would say something profound, typically in a monotone without even looking up from whatever he was doing, "What a polarizing caricature of American politics."

"Well, it couldn't get any worse than W. Bush... Right?"

As quickly as we were down the rabbit hole, we'd lose interest in it and go back to whatever we were doing, and I'd put my headphones back in.

Nate waved his hand in front of my face before he tugged out my earbud, "Got a sec?"

"Sure,"

I went to put down my project, but he stopped me.

"Ain't a put down the screwdriver situation," He joked, pulling the other stool over to sit across from me, "What ya working on?"

"A more streamlined, or *steam* lined holy water bomb." I beamed at my own pun, then held up the components of what I was working on, "I took the heat coil from the toaster, put it into this cylinder, water goes into this part, and boom, holy vapor."

It was more of a ball shape than a cylinder, about the size of an apple. I hadn't realized how close it was to being done until Nate asked.

He picked up the bottom half of the ball and weighed it in his hands, "Could get good curve with this. How do ya come up with this shit?"

I shrugged, "Kinda got the idea while I was watching Parker the other night."

Nate raised an eyebrow, asking without having to say words.

I sighed, "Okay, I was watching Pokémon reruns, alright?"

He chuckled and set my prototype back down.

After a few seconds without saying anything, he bent at the waist, using the counter to hold himself up.

"What did you want to talk about?" I asked.

Next he was fidgeting with my Walkman, trying to look at the tape without taking it out, "What've you been listening to? I wore out my mixes and everything on the radio's shit..."

It took me a second, but I caught on to what was happening.

"Nate, it's okay,"

He didn't want to look at me, but after a few seconds he could stand the eye contact.

"Sexuality doesn't always make sense. God, gender *never* makes sense either!"

He sighed, "That's it, though. I never thought about... Dudes like that. So, what the fuck?"

I shrugged, "And I never thought I was a dude until I was. Not everything is linear, a lot of things are fluid, and your journey isn't going to be the same as mine or as Parker's, but I'm here to help wherever I can just let me know when I can."

He squeezed my shoulder, "Y'know I like you better than my real brother, right?"

I laughed, "Thanks."

After a few seconds of silence I asked, "You want to talk about it?"

"Nah, we ain't got time for my character development." He joked nodding to Conner who looked like he had something to say but was trying really hard to seem like he wasn't listening.

"I swear I'm not listening," Conner spoke up now that there was a lull, "But do you have a second? I want to go over some stuff with everyone."

"Sure,"

Parker had asked to borrow Conner's laptop earlier this morning and was engrossed in whatever he was doing. So much so that Conner had to hit his knee to get his attention.

"Huh? Sorry,"

As I stood, I caught a glimpse of the homepage of three Betty Ford clinic of Bellevue before Parker closed it.

A wave of pride washed over me, but I tried to curb enthusiasm before I scared him off the

idea.

"So, Dr. Sneek said…"

"Doctor Snake? "Parker asked.

"Sneek, Drew's professor," Conner clarified.

"Drew's veterinary professor's name is Dr. Snake?!"

"Sneek! E-E-K!" Conner rolled his eyes, "Anyway, she said the parasite responded well to the anti-malaria drug,"

Parker's excitement cut him off. "That's awesome!"

"It is, but she said there was a… Rejuvenation period, basically the parasite, in an attempt to save itself, split. The main one died, ultimately, they both died, I'm guessing because it didn't have access to a blood supply, but the important thing is that the main one died first. I'm a little worried about what it would do with a blood supply in your body, but if were just left with the adolescent, then…" Con hesitated for a second before he backtracked, "It would put you through the first stages of infection again, but if the parasite were back in its earlier stages, then we could nuke it."

Parker's eyebrows knit, "I would have to die, again…" He mumbled, "How do we nuke it?"

"Drugs, there are a lot of different ones to try. I won't lie to you, though chemotherapy and radiation are the most effective for things like regular parasites, malaria, and even HIV."

"Like... For cancer, right?" Parker was understandably concerned, but I was used to his "Just do it" mentality so I found it surprising.

"It's one of many treatments. And yeah, of course, there's no guarantee it would work. It's extremely aggressive, this would just be the place to start."

Parker was quiet for a long time.

In the meantime, I felt a presence over my shoulder.

I think his name was Robbie, took a few steps over and put a hand on Parker's shoulder.

Parker seemed to react to the touch, I wondered if he even noticed.

"Don't be stupid, bro, get treated. It ain't worth it."

Parker took a deep breath, "What does it matter? We have to get rid of it. How do we make sure I don't turn in the process? What if I lose too much blood or whatever or it just decides to kick-in instead of killing me?" He laughed even though he didn't find it funny, "What if I eat my baby?!

Nate, however, found humor in it for the both of them.

Conner shot him a glare before moving to answer Parker's question, "We'll have to stay on top of it and make sure everything is... Properly satiated."

"Don't say it like that."

"Okay, well, if you drink the blood, it helps heal you, but if we do a transfusion, it feeds the beast. Either way it buys us some time. We're going to figure this out."

Parker chewed on his nails, motionless, while Conner bounced anxiously on the balls of his feet.

For a split second, I wondered if they swapped bodies.

After nothing was said for a while Con cleared his throat, "I'm going to do everything, absolutely anything, to make sure you're okay."

Parker relaxed with an exhale, "I know."

"I'm sorry to interrupt," I spoke up, "But now that we know Donatello has been fighting with all of the Goddess' gifts, well, I can too."

Parker's attention snapped to me.

"This whole time you've had a spell or a little magic trick?!"

"No, well, I don't really know. I'm honestly behind and then rusty on my teachings, but according to Celeste, my grandma has been chomping at the bit to Obi-Wan me since she passed.

Conner chuckled. "Only you could turn Obi-Wan Kenobi into a verb."

"It was your mom's verb actually."

"Of course it was." He smirked.

(＼(•̀w•́)／)

18:50

“Parker,” I tapped his shoulder so he would take out his headphones, and hoped Nate would pick up on the proper etiquette to get someone's attention, "You asked me to remind you when it was seven.”

"Oh, Shit." He popped up and rushed into the bedroom.

“And where are you off to, young man?” Conner joked watching as I pulled on my coat.

I hesitated at first, but then laughed when I realized I didn't have to, “You know, last week I would've lied to you and said I picked up a shift, but now I'm unemployed and you know I'm an alcoholic. So, I'm going to an AA meeting." I put my fists on my hips and attempted what I thought a prideful smile would look like, but since Conner and Nate were looking at me like a newborn kitten, I had to assume it wasn't very successful.

Nate chuckled, "Want me to come? Moral support or whatever gay shit?”

“That's okay,” I pulled my hair out of my coat, "Parker asked me to drop him off at Caitlin's. Plus, it's been a while since I've been to a meeting… It'd be embarrassing to talk shit about you to your face.”

Nate raised an eyebrow with a half snort, “He's talkin' ‘bout you.” He told Con.

"You mind if I ask how long it's been?"

I ran a strand of my hair between my fingers, "Um, a year, maybe two?" I mumbled.

Conner's eyes widened while Nate just stared at me.

"Okay, should I be worried that you feel the need to go right now?"

"No, honestly." That answer I was positive on, "I've just been neglecting this side of things and," I shrugged, "It feels hypocritical to tell Parker what to do when I don't do everything I *should* be doing either."

Con nodded while he processed, "Would you tell us if things weren’t okay?"

"Of course... I know I lied, and I really shouldn't have, but this isn't something I'm willing to fuck around with, not again, that's the whole reason I'm going today, that's the whole reason I told you guys."

Conner sighed, "I hope you know that it's not because I don't trust you, it's just... Unfortunately, you aren't the only person I've experienced having substance issues," He nodded towards the bedroom door where I could hear Parker shuffling around in a hurry, "And I'm easily anxious and a natural worrier." He tried to joke.

I smiled, “I get it, I really do and I appreciate the support. I promise I'll be okay!”

To be fair, I thought I would be.

(＼(•̀ᴡ•́)／)

19:15

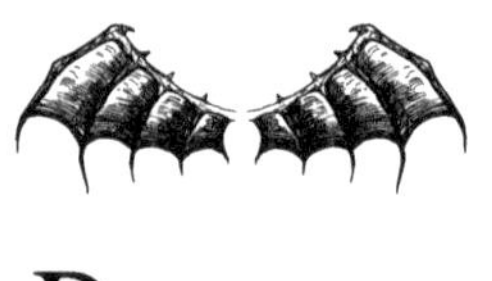

Parker

I asked Aaron to drop me off way earlier than I needed because I know I'm always late but Goddamn it I was trying desperately to prove a point.

Aaron gave me my space, slipping in a Paramore tape and casually singing along trying to politely ignore my struggle to get a grip on my reality.

A lot was going through my head at once, but the one thing that crept into my head was *how the hell did I not notice this bitch lived in uptown Bellevue? Good God, this is exactly what Billy Joel meant.*

Caitlin looked at me in complete shock when she answered the door.

I waved my hand in front of her face, "Hi?"

"Sorry, I just really didn't think you'd come,"

"You buzzed me in."

She looked at the clock behind her on the wall before giving me a suspicious look, "You're even early."

I crossed my arms, "I told you I'm working on it."

"Who are you and what did you do with A-hole Elm?" She half joked stepping out of the door to let me in.

"Mm, so glad that nickname stuck."

"You should've heard what the cheerleaders called you,"

I rolled my eyes, "Itsy Bitsy Peter, Parker? Trench Coat Mafia? Fag Brag? Most Likely To Jump Off A Bridge?"

She snorted, "Takes It In The Elm."

"Mean, but accurate," I shrugged, "Itsy Bitsy Peter, Parker followed me to art school, though."

She laughed.

"Thanks,"

"Oh, get over yourself, they called me Easy Pussy Cat."

I sprawled out on her couch and sucked a sharp breath between my teeth, "I kinda started that one."

"I know, and it was Itsy *Bitchy* Peter, Parker, by the way."

"You're so hot right now."

She rolled her eyes, "I'm gonna order a pizza. Hawaiian okay?"

"I'm vegan and only murderers put pineapples on pizza."

"I'll see if they can put extra ham and pineapple."

"Wanna make out?" I half joked.

Nothing else was said until the pizza came.

Caitlin sat at the counter, tearing off little bites of her slice while looking over different pamphlets.

I stood across from her, picking pineapples off the pizza. She compromised by not getting ham but made a point of ordering extra pineapples on it. If my stomach wasn't in such a wild knot, I would've tried to eat more than just the pineapples.

"So... Who knows?"

"What?"

"About the baby?"

She looked up at me, the silence was more awkward than the question.

"You, my doctor, that's it."

"*That's it*?" I repeated.

She shrugged.

"Aren't you and your sister pretty close?"

"Parker," She shook her head, "Stop... Please."

"Sorry."

I was quiet for a while, but it just made me want to claw out of my skin, so naturally I started going through her cabinets.

"What are you looking for?"

"I dunno," I closed the door with my shoe, "Booze, Diet Coke, Narnia, I haven't decided yet."

She let out a small chuckle, "What's the matter with you?"

"Mm, I think sobriety's killing me more than the drugs were."

"God, this is you sober?"

"Tell me about it. This is like that time I ate a crack rock all over again."

Caitlin just sighed real heavy and put the pamphlet she was looking through, "I can't do this, Parker."

"I was kidding... Partly."

"No, I mean, this!" She held up the pamphlet before throwing it on the counter, "This! This, this is just all way too much!"

I went to put my arm around her and finally saw the pamphlet now that she wasn't waving it around. It was a detailed step-by-step guide to an abortion, and I didn't blame her, it looked scary.

I held her and gave her a few minutes before I pushed.

"So, what do you want to do?"

There was a long pause before she shrugged off my arm and sat up straight, "I want to have it... I want to have the baby."

She looked at me like she was waiting for a huge freak out, so I swallowed my panic.

"Are you sure?"

"I don't think I could be more sure about this."

"That's good enough for me, let's do it," There was a small part of me that was almost relieved? "Let's have a baby."

She was laughing but sobbing at the same time, "Okay, okay, okay, okay." She grabbed my face and kissed me, "I guess we're having a baby."

19:30

Aaron

I decided to stay close by where I dropped off Parker, mostly in case he needed to leave, but partly because I needed to know that if I went to this AA meeting and something terrible happened, I would never have to see these people ever again...

I should've known how this night was going to go when the one church I decided to walk into was in the middle of bible study.

Everyone's heads snapped and stared at me when I walked through the doors, I tried to tell myself it was just because I was a new person and not because they knew all of my sins.

"Hi, I'm Aaron..." I mumbled and immediately wondered why I felt that was necessary, "Sorry, sorry, I was just looking for an AA meeting?" I gestured towards the bulletin board outside since I could feel my anxiety shutting down my vocal cords.

"Oh, they only hold them on Wednesday and Friday." The pastor spoke up over the giggles of judgy teens.

I gave an awkward nod and ran for my car before my knees buckled.

What's wrong with you? This is not a fight or flight necessary ordeal! I lectured my racing heart.

I thought I would hang out at a coffee shop until Parker was ready to go home... But every café I drove by closed at 5 and I had to wonder how that was good business sense in a place like Seattle.

Instead, I just stopped at the first restaurant I saw.

"Welcome, welcome," The host smiled, "Just one?"

I nodded.

She grabbed a menu and led me into a packed dining room, "We're a little full tonight, is it okay if I put you at the bar?" It was a question, but she had already put the menu on the counter and was rushing to get back to her station to greet the other people that walked in.

"It's... Fitting." I mumbled.

It was only as I was trying desperately to not make eye contact with the bartender by hiding behind a menu that I questioned what the hell I was doing here. I tried to reason that I've done this a million times with the guys, and I was just fine, "You're just over thinking." I told myself.

"What can I get you?" The bartender interrupted my inner argument.

"Diet coke and, um..." I hesitated, why would I hesitate?!

The bartender leaned over the counter like he thought he just couldn't hear me.

"And, um, with lime, please?"

He gave me a weird look before turning around and walking off with a nod.

"You okay, kid?" The man in the seat next to me held himself against the bar.

I offered an awkward chuckle, "I'm not much of a drinker."

He didn't say much, he just looked at me waiting for me to say more.

"I'm sober." I said tentatively and hoped he wasn't hitting on me.

He laughed, "Then what are you doing in a bar? Shouldn't you be at like AA or something like that?"

"Mm, I don't usually go to meetings. I've been doing fine on my own."

I sighed when I realized I sounded like Parker, "I know how that sounds, and I don't mean it like that. I'm fine. I am."

His silence felt like an interrogation tactic. It reminded me of that time in high school I got drunk and some "friends" decided it would be a great idea to break into a 7-11.

I had more confidence then... Granted, I was blasted out of my skull at the time.

"Really," I added, feeling the pressure, "I've been fine for six years, it's just lately life has been... Life-ing, I guess." I realized any true answer would've only brought my sobriety further into question than it already was so I just left it there.

The bartender dropped off my soda on his way down the bar.

I took a long drink like it was going to solve all of my problems, but it burned my throat and warmed my chest.

Rum, I guessed.

The world around me felt like it crumbled when I realized the mistake.

God, what was I thinking? I was just asking for this to happen.

The guy on the stool next to me, it felt like his eyes cut through me, and I forced myself to look him in the face.

He was a lot closer to my age than I was expecting, well I was guessing, it was hard to tell exactly since he had his Mariners cap pulled down so low.

He was wearing jeans and a tee shirt and for all intents and purposes seemed normal, but he had a strange aura to him.

My spine steeled.

"Are you okay? You look like you've just seen a ghost." He asked, sitting back he flashed a smile, "Do you plan on exorcising me?"

Donatello's pictures were a only a mere fragment of him, while Parker's caricature painted a far closer expectation.

I sat up straight, and ignored the pounding in my chest, "I'm not afraid of you."

"I don't want you to fear me, Aaron, not yet anyway. I just had to meet you," He moved his hat back and leaned on his elbow on the bar in one fluid motion, "The man, the myth, the mage. I have done my reading on you, I must say, very impressive,"

My head was swirling, but he kept talking.

"The alcoholic, high school drop out that got a full ride engineer scholarship, and threw it all way in the name of vampire hunting,"

"... I was valedictorian."

"Oh, good, I was starting to think you weren't listening." He reached over and took my glass, "I do apologize about your drink, to be fair you have a stronger willpower than I was anticipating," he took a sip, "Though, it is a shame to waste good rum." Another sip, "So, Celtic, is it? Your linage goes back a long while, I'm guessing even longer than you could know.

Funny, some of my people, the lucky ones, settled in Ireland between the wars. I bet we aren't too far removed, you and I.

Perhaps our great-grandmothers shared goulash recipes, or traded secrets, maybe they took care of each other. Perhaps we're meant to carry on the tradition."

I heard a loud boisterous laugh; it took a moment for it to register that it was me.

But Donatello looked at me as if I had started screaming just the same.

"Sorry, it's just..."

He held up his hand to stop me, "Loyalty is such a useless emotion, especially for someone like Parker, he doesn't deserve it. It's just a good excuse to hold yourself back from your true potential. Besides, every talent has a price."

"I'm sorry to be the first person to tell you this, but my "talents" aren't for sale. Neither are my grandmother's."

I twirled the string to the tiny satchel I had in my pocket.

Donnie's ears seemed to perk up instantly.

"So that's what you're looking for?" I asked.

His eyes instantly turned to a bright red, "Give it to me."

"No,"

His face twisted in shock, the color dropped from his eyes, and he immediately started looking at me as if I was something under a microscope, "What do you mean no? You don't get to say no."

"Well, I said no."

"How? No one can ever say no to me." He chuckled like he was impressed, "How did you do that?"

When I didn't respond he probed, “What is it you think I'm after, young Aaron?”

I wasn't completely sure, so I turned it around on him, “If you're looking to play games, I think you should find them somewhere else.”

He glared at me, waiting for me to change my mind, “Fine, you show me yours and I'll show you mine, fair is fair? What's in your pocket?”

“It's a protection spell. What does it do to you?”

“Seems that it's blocking me, however that could be you. I'm mostly having a headache, and I feel like I shouldn't be near you."

"Interesting, maybe you should listen to it.”

“Aren't you just adorable?”

“What you do with your eyes, is that magic or vampiric?”

“Magic, simple *shared mind's eye* spell, really. What's in the bag?”

I skipped over his question, “Do you have a grimoire?”

“Ah ah ah, not so fast.” A smile spread over his face like a crack in glass, “What's in the bag?”

“Herbs, wood, crystals,”

“Blood?” He tipped his head.

“I don't deal in the shadows.”

“Ooh, a pure soul, how sweet. Let me guess, someone sold you the whole “white witch” thing.” He got the bartender's attention and held up two fingers, “Yes, to answer your question, it was my mother's, and it went back eight generations before her. Unfortunately, it burned with my village, my farm, and all our sheep.”

“... Sorry about your sheep.”

He nodded dismissively, "Do you?"

"Yeah, my grandmother's, but your guess is as good as mine as to where it is now. Do you keep a personal spell book?"

"Perhaps I can ask your mother about it myself." He tested.

"Go ahead, she'll suss you out before you step a foot in Oregon."

"Ah, I thought your mother wasn't a believer, that's what you told Parker, no?"

"She isn't, but she's a superstitious businesswoman that thinks all men in suits are liars."

He pressed his hand to his chest and pretend to gasp, "Well, I am more than just a salesman, something tells me your mother might be able to see through the facade." He winked.

I was so used to Nate and Parker that I rolled my eyes without thinking at all, but the more I thought about it the more impatient I was getting, "Do you have a spell book or not?"

"Less a spell book, more a hodgepodge of things I've acquired through the decades," He smoothed out his vintage Pearl Jam tee shirt with his hands making me think he was uncomfortable in it, "I would be willing to let you study it, should you come to my way of thinking." He raised one eyebrow to prompt me and looked through me like a cat observing a mouse before pouncing.

But I saw an opportunity to be the one who pounced first, "I think you'd find me more cooperative than Parker is."

He scoffed into his whiskey, "I have found rabid animals more cooperative."

I tried my best just to shrug and act casual, "I might be more willing to change my way of thinking should you."

"Christ almighty," He blew out a breath, "Is this all you people do? Speak in circles? You are aware English isn't my first language, correct?

"I'm willing to hear you out, but no tricks, magical, spiking drinks, or otherwise." I crossed my arms and narrowed my eyes at him, "Did you really expect that to work?

"No, I expected it to cost me,"

"Oh, it will."

"Aaron, I fear you may be dangerously close to earning my affection and not just my interest. " He chuckled, a phone appearing in his hand, "Come to my hotel, let's talk business."

I slightly hesitated.

He raised his eyebrows, "That sounded far more sexual than I intended."

I pretended to mull it over while I really slipped my hands into my pockets, luckily my coat was big and bulky enough to slide open my phone and feel over the keys without being too obvious.

"Am okay, just track." I hopefully typed and sent it to Conner before muting the ringer completely.

Donnie drummed his fingers against the bar, "What do you say, we continue this *tit-for-tat*? I might be willing to show you a few things in my book, should you be willing to show me a thing or two."

There was a pause before he sighed for show, "I understand the apprehension, I am just a stranger asking you to get into my car and all. But, I promise, I'm not as bad of a guy as Parker tells," He held his hands up with what I'm sure others would've called a charming smile, "And I won't bite."

I pushed down the anxiety that was shredding up my insides and nodded.

"You are more agreeable." He chuckled to himself as he tossed a hundred-dollar bill on the counter and stood.

He led me outside to an all-black car that thirteen-year-old Aaron would've lost his mind over if he saw it in my uncle's garage.

Donnie walked me down the length of the car to the passenger side and I couldn't deny the little part of me that was ecstatic that I got to sit in it.

I listened for a second as he turned the keys, and the engine roared.

"V12, I'm guessing?" I asked.

"I'm sorry?" He answered as he carefully pulled out of the parking spot.

"The engine, 12 cylinder?"

"Exactly," He sounded surprised, "I didn't take you for a car man."

"I get that a lot. My uncle," I caught myself, and then felt more awkward for not finishing the thought, "He loved working on cars. What's the horsepower like?"

"453," Donnie seemed eager to brag, then added, "Zero to sixty in five point seven. She also tops out at 155."

"Hmm, so does my Chevy."

"Hard to impress," He clicked his tongue, "I like that."

He made a point of driving way over the speed limit after that.

Not much else was said during the drive, and I had to wonder if I was in way over my head.

He started to slow down once we crossed the bridge and there was a derelict building on the horizon, which he drove around and pulled into the alley where a man stood, seemingly waiting for us.

For half a second I considered that we were being mugged until Donnie tossed him the keys without another acknowledgement.

"Hold on just a moment," Donnie floated around the car to stand in front of me, "Leave your phone here."

I waited for further elaboration that never came so I shrugged and handed it to him, he tossed it into the back seat of the car before turning to the door in the side of the building.

He unlocked it and held it open for me.

Stepping through the threshold was like stepping into another dimension entirely, it was something between a library and office with a flair from the Victorian era that would've made Edgar Allan Poe jealous. To be fair, the walls of books made *me* jealous.

"Forgive me for keeping you to my office, but... Well, it would be asinine to walk a human through a den of hungry vampires, like throwing a steak to a bunch of lions, wouldn't it?" He waved his hand as he scrutinized the papers on his desk, "Please, make yourself comfortable."

In that split second, I was analyzing the spines of books across the walls.

There wasn't anything in particular that stood out.

It was a mix of classic literature, philosophy, different kinds of medicines as well as sciences, there were seemingly books on almost any religion I could think of, or any war I could remember the names of.

Then there were business and politics, both of which had their own shelves, but nothing on magic of any kind.

"Not a fan of fiction, I guess?" I asked.

Practically without moving, Donnie was by my side, he pointed over my shoulder, "Behind the desk, though to be fair, I have yet to find anything better than Lord Of The Rings,"

"The Fellowship Of The Ring is probably my favorite book." I nodded along scanning more of the shelves, "This place has a... Strange aura."

"The room or the building?" He asked as if what I said was normal.

"Both, but in here specifically, I'd have to survey the whole building to tell you that, though." I ran hand across the spines until my fingers found a certain book and the energy reverberated through me, there was something truly wicked in this book, and I wanted far away from it.

I tossed it on the desk, it didn't have a title or cover, just bound in plain leather.

Donnie examined it, "Is this the culprit?"

"One of them,"

He watched me, studying me as I searched more of the books.

"What Should I do with it?" He tested.

"Burn it," I pulled another book and handed it to him, "This one doesn't want to be around that one. This one needs to be cleansed, that one needs to be charged."

"How do I do that?"

"Full moon," I shrugged, "The room could use a good sage-ing. You also do have a major ghost problem. Nothing I can't solve for you."

He nodded. Impressed.

"I can assume that will cost me?"

"Yep, I want to see your book, I know it's not in here, I also know those were all plants. Next time, you can just ask me what you want to know."

He was amazed now. "Aren't you just something? I'm starting to think I was wrong about Parker all along and it should be you I'm after."

I crossed my arms.

I was starting to have enough of his games, especially since I was still empty handed.

"Okay, I'll ask plain, what are you?"

I stared at him blankly, "What? Am I supposed to say the devil or something?"

I wasn't expecting him to laugh, so the sound startled me.

"No, but I like the answer. I mean it, seriously, you aren't a dhampir or a strigoi."

I didn't have an answer, I mean who would? What else do you say when someone is questioning your humanity?

"Human." I didn't waiver.

He laughed again, "You aren't, but I guess I shouldn't expect you to know when I can't pinpoint it myself."

The room was completely silent for a moment, yet his attention snapped to the door opposite to the one we came through and said "Come in."

A man far more easy-going than Donnie stepped through with a few books stacked to his chest.

A woman also came into the room.

Nobody acknowledged each other and I started to wonder If I was the only one who saw the two of them.

The books made a loud *thunk* when he dropped them on the desk, and I had my answer.

"These are the hodge-podge of everything I've picked up over the years." Donnie plucked one of the books off the pile and thumbed through it absent-mindedly, "What would you like to know?"

"Sir," The other gentleman said, "I'm sorry to interrupt. but the maintenance man for the, um, basement door is here he has questions for you."

"Now?" Donnie frowned.

"If not now, then he won't be able to make the repairs until after Christmas."

Still frowning, Donnie turned to me, "Excuse me for a moment, I'll be quick. Do me a favor, don't break any windows." He made a big show of turning the doorknob so I'd know it was unlocked, "You can let yourself out at any time."

He closed the door behind them.

I couldn't help feeling like this was an exercise in trust especially since the woman was still staring at me.

"Hi." I felt awkward…

"You can see me? Oh, thank God!" She appeared right in front of me. "You have to get out of here! It's not safe here."

"Don't worry, I know..."

"Shush!" She stopped me, "They're listening,"

"Of course they are," I whispered, "Okay,"

I looked over the desk for a piece of scratch paper, so I didn't blow my own cover, "What's your name?"

"Alice," She answered as I continued to write, "You have to get out of here! I don't know what he's going to do to you but he has the entire building blocked off so it can't be good."

She looked at the paper when she realized I was done writing.

"Do they know you're here?"

She shook her head, "No, you're the first person that's ever been able to see me."

I picked up the book on the top of the pile, I figured he was expecting me to look at it at least.

"Don't," Alice warned, "It's cursed, I saw him do it this morning."

I tilted my head and squinted, trying to take a peek at the energy surrounding it, "It's not cursed, it's warded." I mumbled.

"Is there a difference?"

I grabbed the pen, "A ward can be broken, but I don't have time. There's a loophole, though, go through it and tell me what's in it?"

She blinked at me a few times.

"I can help you. I promise."

She hesitated.

"He can't hurt you anymore." I whispered softly.

She set her shoulders and straightened her back, "Are you going to kill him?"

"I'm working on something..."

She nodded, "I'll help."

She disappeared for about fifteen minutes; I used the time to write down a spell of my own. I figured I could use it as a wager against Donnie that way if Alice was able to get something for me it didn't seem like I suddenly lost interest in his books.

Alice was back, she looked more scared and crestfallen than before.

"Could you..."

She nodded again, before I could finish asking.

I got a feeling deep in the pit of my stomach, "How bad is it?"

"There's pages and pages on necromancy, reanimating corpses, ritualistic cannibalism, demon sacrifices," Her eyes were wide, snapping towards the door as Donnie walked through.

He gave me a look like he was surprised that his books and I were still there.

I used the toe of my sneakers to swivel the desk chair from side to side and crossed my arms pretending that I was bored.

You weren't doing anything. He doesn't know, you weren't doing anything. I had to remind myself.

Alice's silence and nervousness scared me more than anything, all of her anxiety stifled me, and the room felt like it dropped fifteen degrees in a manner of seconds.

"Pardon the interruption," Donnie placed a hand on the desk in an effort to not be displaced by my claiming of his seat.

I folded the paper I wrote my spell on and slid it towards him, "Spell for spell?"

Curiously, he went for the paper, but I pulled it back.

"Make it worth my while."

He chuckled, "You are a man after my own heart," he chose a book, said something in Romanian, and took his time paging through it, weighing his options, "Is there something in particular you're hoping for?"

"What's your trade?"

He paused what he was doing, I must've finally caught him off guard, "Pardon?"

"Your magic," I clarified, "What do you trade in? My grandma was a psychic, I'm a medium, I come from a long line rooted in divination."

"I see," He returned to the book, "I fear Roma isn't as straight forward."

"Try me,"

There was the very essence of a hesitation that I wouldn't have caught if I was dealing with anybody else, "I suppose you could call what I do a form of Arcane Shamanism, my goal, after all, is to harness the very thing that wishes to kill me, whether genetic, energy, infection, parasitic, or a damn worm, that's for science to decide, I can only manage to the best of my gifts and abilities." He stopped on a page halfway through the book, "Can I interest you in body, illness, and toxin cleanse spell?"

I kept playing it like I was bored, turning my focus onto folding my spell into one of those paper cranes, "You can do better."

"Fair enough... Can I expect you to read Latin?"

"Quid: num difficilest?"

He laughed, "Far be it for me to question."

I wrote on my scrap paper, "Is there anything good in that book?"

Alice leaned over my shoulder and then popped up behind Donnie, "No, stuff about scrying? Am I saying that right? Anyway, it looks like "glimpse into the future", past, some herbs... I think he's lowballing you."

"Is there anything in any of these?"

"No, there's another book, though. He keeps it in his room in a safe under his bed, but he seems like he knows when it's touched."

I shook my head, so my hair fell over my shoulders, and ran my hand over the stack of books until I found the one that felt like it was made out of electricity.

It definitely got his attention when I picked it up, "What's in this one?"

"Demonology," Alice shrugged, "Seems a little preachy."

"Can you get into the safe?" I wrote and then quickly drew a cat over the letters.

Alice got a devious smile and then disappeared again.

"What's in that book," He paused, hoping I would think it was a genuine hesitation, "I'm willing to perform those spells for you, but I won't give them away."

"Deal," I stood up and stretched my arms over my head, "Do you want your ghosts gone?"

"No, I want to see what you're really capable of, summon someone for me. In return, I'll tell you how to cure Parker."

I knew he was bluffing. All that about the devil in the details and what have you.

I crackled my knuckles, "Who, when, where?"

His smile turned to a chuckle, and he carefully patted me on the back, "Aren't you just precious? How about we put a pin in this? Give me a few days to pool my resources and find something truly worth your time?" He slung his arm across my shoulders and led me towards the door, "We should get you home before your little friends notice you've strayed too far, you know how Parker gets with his lack of impulse control."

(＼(•̀ω•́)／)

CONNER

Nate told me he wanted some "alcoholic time", not wanting to look too deeply into that I went over to Drew's when he left.

We had dinner and a movie, but Drew's apartment parking lot was full, so I had to walk down the street and through an alley back to my car.

I should've known better by now.

My phone buzzed in my pocket.

I didn't bother to break my stride, plucked it out of my pocket and read Aaron's text, *"Zed ok trac pone."*

I was a little confused, but tried desperately to ignore the pit in my stomach, "What? Are you okay?"

No response.

I stopped dead in my tracks and called his phone.

No answer.

By the time I looked up from the screen I was at my car, a small shadowy figure leaned against the passenger side door.

A chill ran through me.

"Mr. Stephens?" She asked stepping into the light.

Before I could respond something hard, cold and metal sent a pain shooting through the side of my head.

(＼(•̀ᴡ•́)／)

NATE

I didn't wanna think, I didn't wanna talk, and goddamn it, I was sick of feeling my fucking feelings.

I just wanted to drink without anyone pouring my tequila down the sink, smoke without anyone asking me when I was gonna quit and get lucky without anyone asking what it meant.

Walking down Roosevelt and 12th and chain smoking, I was on my second pack of cigarettes, my second beer, and the first bar full of women hating me.

Fair.

Part of me wanted to try a gay bar, part of me was scared shitless so I stuck to what I knew; shamelessly coming on to girls that want nothing to do with me.

So much for not thinking, I guess. How does Parker do it? Go days without having an actual thought? Maybe it's the pills. God, I wish I was a junkie.

I stopped at a crosswalk and lit another cigarette.

I was the only person on the street, only a few cars whizzed through the light.

It was weirdly quiet 'til I heard a loud yell.

"¡Ayúdeme!" Down the sidewalk a girl staggered forward without seeing me, "¡Ayuda! ¿Alguien? ¡Por favor! ¡Ayuda!"

I got her attention, and hollared towards her, "¿Qué necessitas?"

She started running when she saw me, "Tienes que ayudarme! Por favor, Dios, ayúdame!"

"Puedo ayudarte, qué pasa?"

She slammed into me, as I tried to steady something else slammed into the back of my head.

(＼(•̀ᴡ•́)／)

Aaron

It's ridiculous how quickly things can shift.

Like how the sunny weather can turn into a thunderstorm, a cigarette butt in a patch of grass turns into a raging forest fire, your diet coke has rum in it, or the person you've been cleverly stalling decides to take you as a prisoner of war randomly.

We had barely got down the street when Donnie's phone rang, he picked it up and listened to it without saying a word.

He turned around and led me back into the building.

"Perfect timing," He opened the other door which led into a long hallway, "I had them clear out the building for a few minutes, I wanted to show you my study,"

I could tell something wasn't right, "Isn't that where we were?"

"That's more of an office,"

But I couldn't tell what kind of turn this was going to take, even if I could I didn't know how to get out of it.

Donnie stopped at a golden caged elevator door.

He yanked the door open with a fluid motion, gesturing for me to get in.

When I hesitated, he chuckled, "Oh, sweet Aaron, don't you think if I wished to hurt you I would've by now?"

Before I had time to respond he reached out and gently pulled me into the cart, careful not to hurt me.

I glanced between him and the switchboard.

"Sub-basement, this is starting to feel a little Stephen King-y,"

"Hmm, worse news for my wife than for you," He joked, "No, you'll notice the building is on a corner street. Back when it was built that street was a crossroad, a beautiful metaphor for transformation and change. My mother once told me a crossroad is a somewhat portal between realms, forming an epicenter of magic. Slavic magic is different to Roma, but when you live in Slavic countries for a few generations, you pick up a superstition or two; doors, windows, other entree points can also work as a crossroads and should be protected as such."

"The two doors in your office," I nodded.

"Yes, exactly. There's a window right behind the desk, and behind a curtain, of course. But it forms a perfect triangle."

"What's the significance of it being underground?" I tested.

"It's directly under the street, then you bring in the earth magic element."

The elevator stopped.

A dim hallway ushered us to a giant industrial metal door, which Donnie unlocked and opened with ease.

The room on the other side was like a vacuum, allowing no light to penetrate the void.

He guided me through the room to a wall and felt around for the switch.

When he flipped it, nothing happened.

He swore under his breath and tried again.

Nothing.

"Are you serious?" Pulling his phone out of the pocket in his jacket he used the light to get us to the next door and unlocked it while dialing a number at the same time.

He gestured for me to come into the room anyway

"Yes, the power in the lower quadrant is out, I..." He tapped his fingers to the bridge of his nose, and took one step out of the doorway, "Is that better?"

He sighed and hung up, "Change of plans, dear Aaron."

The massive iron door screeched across the floor and slammed shut.

There was the sound of metal on metal, like a slot on the door being slid open, "Sit tight, one of my girls will be in shortly."

He laughed menacingly.

What exactly did I expect?

(＼(•̀w•́)／)

21:00

Parker

Caitlin didn't want to talk about the baby anymore, she seemed really overwhelmed by it, I couldn't blame her, I was too.

She wanted to go to bed early, I offered to stay but she said it was fine and tried to find a non-bitchy way to ask me to leave. So, I told her to call me in the morning, and gave her Conner's number in case she couldn't get ahold of me.

I felt like everything went great, I felt like Caitlin, and I were on great terms... I was a little bummed she didn't want me to stay the night, but I got it. And I'd be lying if I didn't feel entirely overwhelmed, too.

I tried to call Aaron to get a ride back home, but he didn't pick up.

I didn't think anything about it, and thought I felt well enough, so I ran home.

The living room of our apartment was entirely empty, which was bizarre.

I knocked on the bedroom door and when there was no response I tried to call Conner, which went straight to voicemail.

My stomach dropped and twisted into a figure eight.

As soon as I hung up my phone rang, a number that started with +40 blinked back at me.

I answered, but refused to wait for a response on the other line, "Where are they?"

"I have no idea what you're talking about, Parker. Did you take too many pills?" I could hear the smirk in Donnie's words.

"I'll rip your fucking building down to the sub-basement, do you fucking hear me?"

He laughed, "Oh, calm down, that's really no way for a father to speak, mind you. Besides, I think we can come to a reasonable agreement on this."

"I'm going to kill you," I said through clenched teeth.

"Promises, promises."

"Where are they?"

"Be at my hotel in forty-five, we can talk about this."
"Talk ab...!"
He hung up on me.
MOTHERFUCKER.

(＼(•̀ω•́)／)

Aaron

Two figures entered the dark with me, neither of them said a word, but had clear intentions of subduing me.

I tried to fight back but they were both so much stronger than me that all I accomplished was tiring myself out.

By the time they had me tightly secured to a chair a seam of light broke through the darkness.

A vaguely Donnie shaped shadow stepped in and flicked on the lights, a blinding florescent light flooded the room with a dull buzz.

"Did he give you much trouble?" He asked the two women standing over me.

"Nope," She bent down to pinch my cheek and then pat my face, "Didn't even need the cattle prod,"

"Well, keep it handy, I can't be certain how well behaved the other two will be."

Donnie went to undo the rag that gagged me, but stopped just short, "Don't bother screaming, even if someone could hear you down here, everything's been cleared out for a three-block radius, understand me?"

I nodded and he untied the gag.

"What do you want from me? I was pretty clear that I didn't have anything for you."

"Don't be so sure, you've got a wealth of knowledge, my friend. And I intend on tapping it."

"By torturing me?" I didn't mean to laugh but it just came out of me, "I was a queer kid that went to high school in the 90's, there's nothing you can do to me that hasn't been done already, I'm a steel trap."

He chuckled to himself, "Hit him."

A current of electricity crackled through my body, and I floundered against my restraints.

A scream lifted from my chest but twisted into a hysterical laugh in my throat.

"Great," Donnie sighed, "Another bloody masochist."

I was grasping at straws, I knew that, but I still had one last ace up my sleeve.

"Who's Charles?"

He was caught off guard, he tried to quickly hide it, but I could read it all over him, "I'm sorry?"

"Oh, sorry Charlie," I cast a glance over his shoulder purely for effect, "He says it's Charlie."

Donnie's shoulders seemed to turn to stone, but he remained emotionless.

"He's mad," I continued the bluff, "He says he should've left you in the hell he found you in if he knew the monster you'd turn into."

He back handed me, and I laughed again.

"You're all fucking nuts."

"Go fuck yourself!" I yelled as loudly as I could.

He turned to the girls now, "Have your fun with him, but write down what he has to say before you kill him this time," He wrapped his hand around the doorknob, "Unlike that druggie, he is no good to me silent."

The metal door slammed shut on his disappearance.

The blonde one walked behind me, trailing her fingers up my torso while she pulled off my shirt, "Your shot."

The brunette jabbed something into my side, sending another electric shock.

She pat my face when I gasped.

"Let's have some fun, little boy."

(＼(•̀w•́)／)

Nate

"I'll kill you, you motherfucker!"

I shook my head, I was still seeing stars, but that voice sounded familiar.

"Get your bitch ass back in here!"

I tried to look around, but it was too dark to see anything.

"HEY!"

"Conner?" I tried to move towards his voice, but I was stuck to or against something.

"Nate?" There was something that sounded maybe like chains rattling, "Nate, you're here?"

"I guess, where's here?"

An industrial light loudly clicked on and overwhelmingly lit up the room.

Con was on the other side of the huge concrete room, chained to a chair, a stream of blood trailing from his hairline.

"Evening gentlemen," A suit stepped between me and Con, "How are we feeling? Can I get you anything? Some water perhaps?" He joked.

"Eat me." Conner spat.

I couldn't help laughing, never heard Con talk like that before.

"Tempting." He walked over towards me, he crouched down to be at eye level, "A true pleasure, Nathaniel. Glad to see you've decided to check into this meeting." He flashed a demonic smile, "Ladies?"

Two chicks walked in; their heels clicked against the concrete floor. One hovered over Conner, she stuck her tongue out, licking the blood from the side of his face, he winced and tried to pull away.

The other walked behind me and played with my hair.

"Ain't seein' a problem here."

She swung her leg over and sat on my lap.

"These are my girls, Laurie and Clarice," Donnie spoke but I barely heard him.

"Hey gorgeous." I didn't know where this was going, but I was definitely into whatever torture Donnie-boy thought he was unleashing.

"Howdy," She smiled, pulling a cigarette from her pocket, she lit it, blew out the smoke and put it in my mouth.

If Conner wasn't staring at me, I could've written this off as just another Friday night.

I took a few hits before Donnie cleared his throat, "Here's the deal, as you know, there's only three things I can use as leverage on our dear friend Parker. So, I figured why not hedge all my bets and get you thinking on what your little friend will bite at. You go quiet, decide to lie, or otherwise step out of line, well," He raised an eyebrow, "Clarice?"

She took the cigarette out of my mouth, tapped the ash on the floor, and then put it out on the back of my hand.

I bit at the inside of my cheek and scoffed at the pain, "That's it?"

"That's barely an appetizer, go ahead, hit him."

The little skank tased me.

I grit my teeth, being too much of a bitch to give him the satisfaction of a yelp.

"Oh, come on, honey. A quiet boy doesn't really do it for me, give me a good scream, wontcha?"

She hit me across the face.

"Son of a bitch!"

"Better,"

The other girl wailed on Conner pretty good before Donnie decided to get involved.

"So, what do you think, we got a deal?"

"Shove it up your James Dean, pretty boy, puta ass." I offered.

"Conner? No takers? I figured as much, but I have something I think will..." He made a gesture, "Give you some motivation. Marion, Samara, bring him in."

Two other girls came in carrying a chair, someone was sitting in it, they were chained up too, but their head was covered.

They ripped the black fabric off his head and Aaron slumped forward.

"Aaron?!" Con yelled.

"I'm okay," He answered, everything else said otherwise, he looked like he was drug through hell. Wet, shivering, bruised and bleeding.

"You son of a bitch!" I fought against the chains.

"You have ten minutes to make a decision, you can help me, or I kill the boy. Girls," He raised a hand dismissing them, "I will be back."

He disappeared.

"What the fuck?!"

"Are you okay?"

"What happened?"

"What did they do to you?" Con and I went back and forth.

"Is he gone?" Aaron deviated from the questions.

"Yeah, are you..."

"Fine. Are either of you wearing a watch?"

"What?"

"Watch, do either of you have a watch?"

"Yeah?" Con answered

"Can you get it off?"

Con nodded.

"Kick it over here."

Conner did as he was told.

Aaron moved it closer using his foot, he positioned it and smashed it with his boot. He was able to slide his arm back far enough to feel through the debris of Conner's smashed watch and pulled out a pin, he managed to pick the lock with.

"Perrito, te amo."

"Don't say that just yet, we still need a plan."

Like he expected it, the door slowly cracked open and one of the girls slipped through.

I looked for something, anything I could turn against her.

But she acted like she wasn't even surprised we weren't tied down.

"Down, boy," She kept her voice low, "I'm not gonna hurt you, look." She dropped a key to the floor and slid it towards me, "Follow the hall to two sets of doors, go past there all the way through to the end, the lights go out and it looks like a dead end, but feel for a ladder, there's a hatch you'll need the key,"

"We're two floors down," Aaron thought out loud.

Crossing her arms she said, "Wasn't done. It'll spit you out into the sewer, first manhole three hundred feet east puts you behind the fence, another three hundred puts you in the middle of the road." She turned on the flashlight in her hand, shined it in Aaron's face and threw it to him, "Try not to become a traffic pancake."

Conner was the idiot that had to ask, "Why are you helping us?"

"We don't answer to him, we're... *Freelance,* and what can I say, I'm a sucker for an underdog." She said sarcastically taking a step closer to me, a smile stretched across her face and flashed a row of fangs, "Hit me,"

I didn't get what she meant right away.

She rolled her eyes when I still didn't do anything.

"There's six of us down here, bitch. He's not gonna think you just got outta here. So come the fuck on and make it believable!"

It felt... Weird, so I hit her with a quick jab from my left hand.

"Hit me, you faggot!" Her voice bounced around the concrete walls.

I wound my arm back and threw a right hook to her nose.

She laughed, black sludge dripped from her nose spreading across her teeth, "I knew I liked you."

(＼(•̀w•́)／)

Conner

Blindly feeling around a damp, humid, sewer, bumping into each other a dozen times per second while our flashlight flickered was about as glamourous as it sounds. I had to assume we looked like The Scooby gang.

"That's three hundred feet," Aaron announced, I had been fumbling by, more focused on getting away than truly where we were going so his statement felt random.

"It's not even been three minutes," Nate argued.

Aaron searched the ceiling with the flashlight, sure enough finding a manhole cover just a little bit further than we were.

The cover was heavier than I was expecting, and the sun was blazing.

"Conner?!"

I blinked a few times before I could see Parker mid-dismount atop the chain link fence a few feet in front of me.

"What are you doing?" I hushed my response as I pulled myself up onto the concrete.

"What do you mean what am I doing? You guys were fucking kidnapped."

"Yeah, and you took your sweet ass time! Where the fuck was your ass while I was getting fuckin' electrocuted?" Nate popped up behind me.

"Shh!" Aaron followed.

Parker tried to jump, landed flat on his ass, scrambled to get up, and ended up in an awkward spider-like squat that was long reminiscent of Tobey Maguire.

I fought the urge to slap my forehead, "Are you okay?"

"Fine, just shattered my ankle a little."

"Well, get up! It'll heal in five minutes." Nate mocked him.

Aaron hit Nate's shoulder, "Stop yelling."

"Yeah, what? You've never been taken hostage before?" Parker half whispered half yelled, and I had to think if there was a way for Aaron and I to sacrifice the dumbasses without being recaptured.

In the meantime, Parker wrapped his arms around my waist and bent to press his ear to my chest, "Today's been a lot."

"Not great for us, pendejo!" Nate continued, "Did you even bring anything or just your bitchy personality?"

"No, *bitch*, I brought all that." He gestured over his shoulder, a pile of our second-string weapons among the leaves on the ground.

Nate started hitting him, "Are you fucking serious?"

"Well! I saw Conner and I kinda focused on getting over the fence!"

"Jesus fucking Christ, it's like a six-foot fence!" Nate hopped over it without even a second thought, grabbed everything Parker dropped and jumped it again while refusing to break eye contact with him.

"Okay?! I'm like two feet tall, what do you want from me?"

Aaron peered down the manhole then weighed it against what he saw down the street, "I think if we go east for another mile, we would be in a better position to be talking, don't you think?"

"We're not going anywhere," Parker's face hardened, "Not with this prick still alive!"

"We were beaten,you bitch ass, hasta fucking luego, puta. I'm out."

"You don't get to be out!" Parker argued.

"We're kinda knee deep in shit together," Aaron reasoned.

"Cállate," Nate reprimanded him, "Do you even have a plan? You thought that far yet? What? It's fucking Die Hard? Or you just all the way in, y todo, and whatever's whatever?"

Parker crossed his arms with a sarcastic smirk, "Hey, you were all the way in without a plan last night, and *I* trusted *you*."

Nate groaned, turned around and kicked the fence, "I should beat the shit outta you!"

"Ooh, make it hurt, Daddy."

"Christ," I muttered to myself as I weighed my weapon choices, "Not to agree with Parker, *yikes*, but Donnie's just going to corner us again, who knows if we'll ever be able to plan this properly. At least now we have an opportunity and he's not expecting it."

My words sounded so uncharacteristic.

Actively ignoring the growing pit of anxiety in my stomach, I half wondered if this was a side effect of my possible concussion, like how victims of traumatic brain injuries awaken from a coma understanding Einstein's equations or playing Mozart.

"And it sounds like we got some support on the inside." Aaron added.

"I hate all of you." Nate crossed his arms.

"Put up or shut up, baby." Parker kissed him on the cheek and then hopped down the manhole.

"If we don't get killed, I'm killing you." Nate yelled down at him.

(＼(•̀ω•́)／)

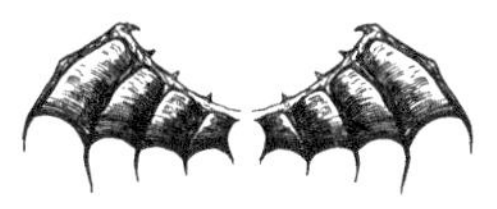

PARKER

This was it, my pulse pounded in my ears, my hands sweat and shook.

Conner's "half assed" plan washed over me in between waves of fear, rage, and paranoia as I forced myself to hyperfocus on his every word.

"You'll go in first, act like you don't know anything. We'll be close behind..."

He was still talking but I was overtaken by a flash of their bodies broken and bloodied in my head.

I gritted my teeth until the pain passed and grabbed them all as tightly as I could, "If it starts going bad..."

Conner's fingertips dug into my arms, I could barely see him in the darkness, but I could feel his seriousness, "It won't. We don't have any other option; it has to go well."

I swallowed the lump in my throat with a nod.

Aaron helped me find the hatch in the floor, and I tried to fall through as softly as my clumsiness would allow.

As soon as I landed, two women appeared from the shadows.

"Stupid, really stupid." One of them sighed while the other pulled me to my feet and slammed me into the wall to pat me down.

A light finally clicked on.

The tall, muscular blonde looking me over like I was mud her leather boot, "Parker?"

"Uh..." I struggled for a response, especially since her friend was getting awfully handsy, "Yeah?"

She sighed again, "Really? This scrawny bastard?"

The other woman stopped but still held me against the wall, she said something to her in a language I couldn't place.

"Hivno," She rolled her eyes, and handed me the knife her friend confiscated off of me, "Down the hall, elevator is through the first door, first floor. *He* wants you in his office. Do me a favor, huh? Don't miss." She bent to whisper, "Heroiam slava." In my ear, then pat me on the back with enough force to make me stumble.

The long walk and even longer elevator ride felt like the finally lap around death row after a long stay.

Through I found a weird comfort in grimness, it's the freeing thought after a near-death experience where you tell yourself "Well, I almost died, what worse could happen?", or maybe it was the freedom that Death promised me years ago.

But all those thoughts came to a grinding halt when I glimpsed at the other side of the coin for once; Conner, Nate, Aaron, Drew, Caitlin...

Hell, Life was offering me a second chance. Literally, Life was putting an unborn, brand-new life in my hands if I was just willing to stick it out and fight.

God, how could I be so blind? Barely a week ago I was more than willing to give it all up in exchange for a bleak, vast nothingness.

I couldn't make sense of any of it, but it didn't matter anymore, I was standing in front of Donnie's office door.

The door jerked open, and I had zero time to prepare, Donnie stood clean across the room, looming like a Bond villain.

"Ah, the father to be!" He clapped his hands together making me jump, "I was just about to have my assistant send you and your girlfriend a basket."

I couldn't think of a way to respond and all that fell out was, "She's not my girlfriend."

"Mm, a baby with no relationship, isn't that so... American?" He waved me into the room.

I fidgeted with the knife in my pocket while I found my feet, "Where are they?"

"Hmm?" He twisted the stopper off the crystal decanter and poured to glasses of whiskey, then in a bored monotone said, "Oh, I suppose this is about your friends, they're fine... For now,"

"What do you want?!" My yell echoed off the walls.

"Don't get so emotional, dear," He swirled the amber around the glass before taking a drink, "I'm not stupid, I can see their purpose, a talented bunch, really. You want your friends, I need the talent, I think we can broker a deal here, don't you?"

I gritted my teeth and reluctantly brought my voice down, "What do you want?"

"Your friends' freedom for yours, it's that simple." He moved smoothly in front of the desk, leaning down to be level with me he dropped his voice to a whisper, "Come on, Parker. Let's leave everybody out of this," A smirk stretched across his face like the sewn-on smile of a corpse, "Let's me and you run away together." He laughed.

"Don't touch me, you fucking monster!" I shoved him back.

"Oh, darling, you don't know how monstrous I can be. Take the deal, boy, it's a good one."

"I don't negotiate with demons."

"Very well," He set down the crystal glass, "Since you're so holy… '*Wherefore, redemption cometh in and through the Holy Messiah; for he is full of grace and truth. Behold he offereth himself a sacrifice for sin, to answer the ends of the law, unto all those who have a broken heart and a contrite spirit; and unto none else can the ends of the law be answered. Wherefore, how great the importance to make these things known unto the inhabitants of the earth, that they may know that there is no flesh that can dwell in the presence of God, save it be through the merits, and mercy, and grace of the Holy Messiah, who layeth down his life according to the flesh, and taketh it again by the power of the Spirit, that he may bring to pass the resurrection of the dead, being the first that should rise. Wherefore, he is the first fruits unto God, in as much as he shall make intercession for all the children of men; and they that believe in him shall be saved*'."

He cocked a dark eyebrow at me, "Or maybe you'd prefer *2 Nephi 31:19-21*? '*And now, my beloved brethren, after ye have gotten into this straight and narrow path, I would ask if all is done? Behold, I say unto you, Nay; for ye have not come thus far save it were by the word of Christ with unshaken faith in him, relying wholly upon the merits of him who is mighty to save. Wherefore, ye must press forward with a steadfastness in Christ, having a perfect brightness of hope, and a love of God and of all men. Wherefore, if ye shall press forward, feasting upon the word of Christ, and endure to the end, behold thus saith the Father: Ye shall have eternal life. And now, behold, my beloved brethren, this is the way; and there is none other way nor name given under heaven whereby man can be saved in the kingdom of God...*'."

"Good for you, you read an old book. But I serve no God, and yours would be ashamed of you."

He laughed again, this time loud and over the top, "And you? The yard stick of morality? You have the moral backbone of a gin-soaked olive. Do not speak to me about morals. Besides morals are for mortals," he sang, "You and I have been handpicked by something so much higher; you are my Jesus Christ, can't you see that?"

This must be how Clarice felt with Hannibal.

"Do you think it was just good luck I found you that night? Do you think it was just good luck you possess the talents you do? The genes you have? Is it all a big coincidence? It's divine intervention."

"You're fucking crazy, and whatever God you're talking about was dead wrong," I laughed, I couldn't hold it in anymore, rage poured out of me in waves, "I'm no one's savior! *Copy?!*"

Before Donnie's eyes could narrow, before he could call anyone, before he could even figure out what was happening, the outside door slammed open, the guys poured in, and I dropped my knife from my sleeve.

Donnie laughed; the motherfucker laughed.

In a blind rage, I had to use the only advantage I had, surprise. And I took the opportunity to jump across the desk like I'd been dreaming of for months, I pinned him to the floor, "Still wanna make a deal?"

He didn't struggle at all; he didn't even put up a fight.

This was the moment, I was finally going to kill the bastard, my heart pounded, and my mouth ran dry...

But he didn't react at all, I sat on his chest, and he did absolutely nothing about it.

We just stared at each other, unblinking.

"What're you waiting for?!" Nate yelled, fighting to keep the door on its hinges.

"What are you waiting for, Parker?" Donnie added, "Do it. Go ahead, kill me."

"...You're not gonna try and fight?"

"Why? I know when I have been bested." He raised his eyebrows, "Go ahead, end it for all of us. Once and for all, finish this."

I got that feeling again, the overwhelming eeriness like I'd been here before, done the same thing, and I hesitated.

I don't know why, but I fucking hesitated for two seconds, and that's all he needed.

He grabbed my wrist, overpowering me and stabbing the knife into Aaron's thigh, Conner and Nate's guard dropped to help Aaron who was understandably yelling words I felt were illegal for him to know.

The door slammed open, the girls and about two dozen others flooded the room and swirled around us, they added to the scene but didn't really help anyone.

In the chaos Donnie yelled from under me, "Putares vellem uti a reali carmine!"

"What the fuck did he just do?!" Nate's hand shot to his head.

Conner's nose started to bleed, "Kill him!"

"Scio Latinum malum esse de me scribere debes," A wicked smile on Donnie's face when Nate dropped to the floor.

I slammed his head into the hardwood floor and tightened my grip on the knife, "What did you do?"

"A test in morals, it seems. I nicked the little blond one's artery, and the spell will kill the other two in less time than it'll take for him to bleed out. So now you have quite the pressing decision; do you want to save your little friends, or do you want to kill me?"

The smell of blood filled the room, it was so overpowering I could hardly think straight.

My brain felt like a TV with a bad signal occasionally blipping out to static, I had to fight just as hard as I was fighting Donnie.

"Tick, tick, tick..." Donnie baited me, Aaron screamed; "Fucking kill him!" Conner was coughing up blood, and Nate had stopped moving all together, while everyone else in the room stirred around us.

It was all happening too fast, but I felt like I was in slow motion.

I pressed the knife closer and harder to his throat, before I sighed, "Fix it." I dropped the knife by his head.

He smirked and dusted himself off, then raised his hand waving it flippantly over Conner and Nate, "They'll be fine, but you should get him to a hospital." He gestured to Aaron with my knife before handing it back to me.

Hesitantly, I took it, unsure of what he was doing.

"This isn't the end of this."

"Oh, sweet Parker, it's only just begun." He put his hand to his forehead in a sort of salute, "Ai grijă."

I was too busy trying to help the guys that I didn't have time to piece together his disappearing act, but as soon as he was out of the room, I felt a heavy weight leave with him.

This wasn't how I wanted things to end, but I think a part of me knew it would. Donnie was right, the deck was stacked against me, it always had been.

But I didn't really have the time to wallow in self-pity, Aaron was fading fast.

I couldn't even tell you how we got him to the hospital if you asked.

Nurses swarmed us like wolves on a wounded animal.

Based on how one of the nurses looked at Conner when he tried to explain plus the nagging feeling in my gut, I got the feeling a millisecond longer would've been too long.

In a flash, Aaron and Nate were both out of my sight and I was sitting behind the curtain of an emergency room cubical watching Conner argue with a male nurse.

A lot was being said to me and around me but only every third word wasn't completely gibberish.

My hands shook, cold and caked in Aaron's coagulated blood, and then it was gone.

As quickly as I blinked, I was cleaned off, there was a cordless phone in my hand, and a doctor was talking to Conner, who looked more bruised and bloodied than a remembered a few seconds ago.

"Please," Conner's voice and words sounded regular again as he pleaded, "I'm not asking to call the president here! I just need to call my girlfriend."

"You can call your girlfriend or the president, or, for all I care, you can call a hit in *on* the president in a minute, for now stop moving and try to follow my pen with your eyes."

"That's not nice," I crossed my arms, "Don't tempt him like that, that's rude."

"Fine," Con grit his teeth and let her poke around his head.

I managed to pull Drew's number out of the fogginess in my head, dialed and handed it to Conner which just screwed up the doctor's test.

"Drew, it's me, hi." Conner all but shoved the nurse away from him.

He paused, and sat up straight like something was wrong.

The growing knot in my stomach twisted.

"Okay, okay," He spoke fast, "Don't say anything, I'll be right there." He hung up and tossed me the phone, "We gotta go,"

"Excuse me," The doctor tried to get Con back on the bed, "You have a concussion, he just had a seizure and a very probable mini stroke, your friend needs staples in the back of his head, and the other one is in surgery. I have no ID's, no phone numbers, no insurance, no idea how this happened to any of you and you're the only emergency contact I have for anyone, I can't let you leave."

"Who had a seizure?" I asked and the doctor's eyes widened.

Conner clarified, "He didn't have a mini stroke, he's just like that,"

"Thanks," I added.

He ignored me as he kept reasoning, "I'll give you whatever phone numbers you want, I'll even sign something! But we... We just gotta go."

December 1 2007

01:35

Conner

"Are you going to tell me what's going on or are you gonna keep acting like me?" Parker asked on the cab ride back to the apartment.

"I don't know, Drew just told me she was questioned by police,"

"What? Why?"

The side of my head throbbed as he spoke and I wondered if there was a correlation, "She didn't want to say over the phone."

"What about Aaron? What happened? Is he okay?"

I nodded, "They thought he'd be okay, but the stab wound was a lot deeper than they had thought."

"And Nate?"

I pressed my fingers to the sides of my temples hoping to alleviate some of the pressure, "I don't know, I guess he split his head open. What happened to you?"

Parker shook his head, "Nothing, nothing, I'm fine... Was it like a real seizure?"

"You barely even blacked out; I have no idea why the hospital was so touchy about it."

The cab rolled to a stop in front of our building, right behind a white van labeled SPD.

When I got out in front of it, I saw nearly three dozen cops and countless crime scene techs swirling around the building, in and out, like bees through a hive.

Parker's brown eyes widened, "Please tell me you flushed all of my stashes."

I shushed him and tried to get the attention of a cop carrying a box out of the building, but she ignored me.

I glanced around, most of our neighbors were standing around in their pajamas looking just as confused as we did, but luckily that ruled out the nagging, anxious, voice in my head that said our entire building had just been slaughtered.

I tried to go up the steps to the front door, but was stopped by a massive cop.

"What's going on?"

He looked over my shoulder with a nod, "Conner Stephens?"

I shook my head, "What the hell is happening right now?"

"You're being placed under arrest," He answered, quickly grabbing me and pulling my hands behind me.

"What?!" Parker yelled over me, "For what?"

Without thinking, I whirled around out of his grip to ask again, it wasn't until he went for the gun on his belt that I realized how stupid that was and the full weight of the situation dawned on me.

I interlaced my fingers behind my head, "Jesus, okay, look I'm cooperating."

They seemed laser focused on me even though Parker was the one putting up a fight and making a much smaller cop chase him around.

(＼(•̀w•́)／)

PARKER

They handcuffed me to a table in the smallest coat closet they could find in the station.

I was standing on top of the table trying to use my body weight against the restraints while also trying to remember how to dislocate my thumbs when the door opened, and an older lady walked in.

"Elmer Winston, correct?" She asked, like I wasn't standing on the goddamn table like a goat.

"It's Parker, what do you want?" I pulled as hard as I could and when it didn't work, I reluctantly crawled back down, "Is anyone ever going to tell me what the fuck is happening?!"

"Settle down,"

"Am I being charged?"

"Yes,"

"With? Is this about that rioting thing from like '02?"

"Well," She turned a few pages in her folder before sliding it in front of me, "Three pages, front and back, of charges, I guess you can pick your favorite."

There were a lot of lawyer-y words like "Aggravated assault, breaking and entering, conspiracy to commit murder", when I saw murder, I nearly spat.

"This, this... What? What is this?"

She put a photo of Donnie's hotel on the table in a very X-Files manner, "This building, you didn't break into it this evening?"

"Uhh, I mean..."

"Right, let me guess, you also didn't hold the owner of the property at knife point, and you definitely didn't tell him," She squinted at the paper as she read, "I'll cut your motherfucking throat out, you motherfucker. Die, motherfucker, die, die, die"?"

I shot up out of annoyance, the handcuffs clanked against the metal of the table, "That never even happened! He's a fucking liar!"

"I'm sorry, do you know Mr. Sotos personally?"

"Yeah,"

"How so?"

"He's been stalking me for the last year! He kidnapped my friends, and he killed my best friend!"

"Hold on, do you understand the weight of the allegation you're making?"

"WHAT ABOUT HIS ALLEGATIONS?!" I screamed.

There was a knock on the door, the other cop poked his head in and just said, "Detective?"

They were gone forever, but the clock said it'd only been a half hour. I never calmed down though; I sat on edge the entire time.

When the detective came back, she unlocked my handcuffs.

I pulled my hands away from her as fast as I could, "What, is this like the nice cop thing now?"

"You're free to go, your charges are being dropped."

"What?"

She looked at me like I was an alien.

"So... What?" I crossed my arms, "Just like that? It's over? Donnie waves his hand again and, boom, magic?"

She shrugged, "I could find something to book you with, if you'd like."

"I can just... Leave?"

"Well," She sat back down in her chair, "I'd like to ask you some questions about your 'firecracker' friend, but I can't hold you for that."

"What? You mean Conner? Why? Wait, why didn't his charges get dropped?"

"They did, but there's a warrant out for his arrest."

I laughed so hard I had to actually catch my breath, "I don't think you know who you're talking about."

"He kicked out one of the windows in the back of the squad car, I know exactly who I'm talking about."

I laughed again and she scrutinized me.

"Would you say that's usual behavior for him?"

"Conner?" I held my hand out a few inches shorter than me, "Tiny, chubby, looks a little like a cinnamon gummy bear? He and his girlfriend look like teacup Chihuahua trying to fuck a German Shepard?"

She didn't find me nearly as amusing.

I crossed my arms, "No, I don't know shit about shit and if you wanna ask me anything else you can ask it to a lawyer."

As soon as I was out of there, I ran my fucking ass off to the hospital.

Nate ripped into me for "abandoning him" with "hella" cops around.

They wouldn't let us back to see Aaron since it was so late but I made them promise me up down left and right that he was going to be okay before I would leave, then I had to awkwardly go back in and ask to use the phone.

Drew came and picked us up, I tried to explain everything that happened, but she was just as freaked out as I was, and I think our panic attacks synced up and formed one massive hysteria.

I don't know if any of it made any sense, but Mrs. Hart felt bad enough that the cops had closed our building, so she insisted on us staying the night.

"Are you sure I can't make you boys something to eat?" Mrs. Hart asked, handing me blankets and pillows for the couch.

"It's fine, it's late. Besides, I don't really eat, plus I'm vegan..."

"He doesn't speak for both of us." Nate added on.

She waved for him to follow and led him into the kitchen, where she also barricaded the dog, so he'd stop barking at me.

"Are you doing okay?" Drew made me jump; I forgot she was there.

I chewed my nails, "I don't know how to answer that."

"That's," Drew nodded, "Yeah, I don't know what I expected you to say. But they said Aaron was doing good and he's in the best place for him, and we'll be able to talk to Conner in the morning and hopefully we can post bail."

I took a deep breath, but nothing would've made me feel any better.

"Parker," Drew put her hand over mine, which was anxiously snapping the rubber band on my wrist, "Are you not telling me something?"

"No..."

"*Parker*?"

I sighed, "Fine! I really wanna go to your mom's incredibly fancy beach bathroom and crush up six Xanax, and do a line as long as the counter will let me,"

She shook her head.

"Then I want Nate to throw me against that counter at least twice,"

"I, um,"

"And I wanna find whatever fucking portal that little bitch disappeared into and cut his heart out! And then!" I shrugged and let my hands fall in my lap, "Figure out a way to break Conner out of prison, maybe like a One Flew Over The Cuckoo's Nest thing? I don't know, I haven't thought that far yet, I also didn't finish that movie."

"Well, he died at the end, maybe let's pick a different movie?"

"Huh? Where they tunnel out to the sewer?"

"That's Shawshank."

"What is?"

"Don't worry about it." She pat my arm, "Okay, I know your anxiety's understandably super high right now, but the guy I let cheat off of me in biology, he works at the Block Buster down the road. I got 96% on our last final, trust me, he owes me."

"A 3 AM Block Buster run sober?" I whimpered and let my head fall against her shoulder, "God, being up this late without coke is just not worth it."

She chuckled and rubbed my arm, "You'll be fine."

Drew's friend brought over But I'm A Cheerleader, Mrs. Hart went back to bed, and Drew and Nate fell asleep halfway through the movie.

I waited about a half hour to make sure everyone was asleep before I snuck out and retraced every single step we made in Donnie's little hotel of horrors.

When I walked in, I half expected but mostly hoped to see his smirking face on the other side of the door, but no one was around for blocks, every light was off, and the inside of the building finally matched the outside. The entire place was ransacked, turned upside down, or broken, and I wished I was the one that finally destroyed the place.

God, why did I hesitate? This isn't the way this was supposed to end. Part of me was pissed I didn't kill him, but the rest of me raged like a wildfire that Donnie just *vanished.*

This was all so convenient, and it was bugging the hell out of me.

I stayed, scoping out the entire building floor by floor and brick by brick, until mid-morning.

But I couldn't find fuck all, it was like the place never existed.

(＼(•̀ᴡ•́)／)

07:02

CONNER

Six hours.

Six hours stuck in a holding cell with two drunks who really couldn't hold their liquor, and another guy who was violently coming off something much harder, all while everyone else refused to tell me why I was really in here.

I had to assume Donatello had blown the whistle on us but I had no way to be sure, especially since I had no idea if Parker was in adjacent cell.

"Stephens!"

Defensively, I jolted up right at the sound of one of the officer's voice, no one had settled down all night so when I finally did nod off it felt like it could be a fatal mistake.

He laughed at me and then gestured for me to get up, "There's an agent here, wants to talk to you."

He took me to another interview room, and I was just glad to get away from that damn cell.

"Hello," It took me far too long to register the figure of a woman sitting in the chair opposite to the table in front of me, "You must be Conner?"

She was wearing a nice skirt suit which made the police uniform pale in comparison.

"Please God, tell me you're a lawyer,"

"No, sorry," She offered me a particular warm smile, "I'm here to talk to you about your charges."

"Fantastic," I sat down at the table, "Can you tell me what they are?" I asked matter of factly, which seemed to take her off guard.

She tilted her head at me, "You don't know why you're here?"

"I know you expect to hear someone where I'm sitting say no but trust me when I say I have no idea."

"Well, I'm going to have to write someone up for that," She offered me a warm smile and extended her hand, "You can call me Sasha."

I went to shake her hand, but the cuffs stopped me.

"For God's sake, uncuff the boy." Sasha shot a glare at the guard that just did as she said.

I couldn't help chuckling to myself, she kind of reminded me of Drew's mom.

"Anyway," She sat back down, "Someone had called Seattle PD making claims you and three others broke in and assaulted him, but I'm assuming that was a misunderstanding since I see he dropped the charges. Well, I'm here to talk to you about the warrant we had out for your arrest,"

"We?"

She took something out of her pocket, a badge, and slid across the table, "Special Agent Angelica Sasha, Federal Bureau of Investigation" read the card.

Every word I wanted to say caught in my throat and produced an audible gulp.

"To give you a short summary, you're being held for multiple counts of hacking government records as well as a few other fun legal terms the bureau came up with that they don't pay me enough to memorize,"

"... When you say multiple...?" I trailed off, worried it might come back to bite me on the ass.

She glanced at the paper in front of her, "Twenty-seven,"

And there's the bite.

"Hang on, am I going to need a lawyer for this?"

"I mean you can if you want to, but on the record, this isn't an interrogation,"

I raised an eyebrow at her.

"It's more of a job interview."

I searched her face, desperately searching for any clue because I had none.

"This isn't a joke," She clarified, "We've been watching you for some time, Conner, you're good at what you do."

"Obviously not or I wouldn't be here." I muttered before I realized how guilty that sounded.

But she chuckled and tried hard to keep a friendly demeanor, "Don't be so modest, you're only suspected of twenty-seven, we can only prove one."

I wasn't going to admit it, but twenty-seven out of possible a hundred thousand wasn't too bad.

"And the only reason we have that one is because you logged onto MySpace after you scrubbed everything, and it set off a kind of mousetrap."

I groaned, knowing that had to be Parker, "So what am I up against?"

"Hold your horses, like I said, I'm here to offer you a job. I'm not sending you to prison. Basically, with the rate the internet and cybercrime is picking up, we need people like you."

I wiped the sweat off my forehead, "I'm sorry, what?"

"Here's the deal, you can come work for me in a cyber crime unit, doing what you do *legally*, or you can go to prison."

I was quiet for a second.

My thoughts were racing, mix in the concussion migraine that was settling in, and add the unwavering smell of vomit for added effort and I couldn't make sense of anything.

"It's a good deal, at least I think it is," she put a paper with an FBI seal stamped in the corner in front of me, "It pays well, 401k, PTO... Do you have a wife?"

I blinked a few times before I realized she asked me a question, "Um, a girlfriend."

"Well, should you decide to marry her there's insurance for both of you, paternity leave even, but it sounds like that's further down the path for you now." She offered a smile.

I had an infinite wealth of questions, and whichever one came to me first was the one I asked, "... How long do I have to work for you?"

"Fifteen years,"

"And prison?"

"Mm," She wrinkled her nose as she thought, "Let's say you have an awful attorney and the judge nails you with every charge, a possible fifty years with about a minimum of twenty."

"Deal." I blurted.

She laughed at me, "Yeah, I would say the same, but I have some paperwork for you to read before you jump the gun. I'm assuming you don't have a lawyer, so I'll go ahead and call one for you, then we can go over everything together that way if you or they have any questions I'm right here to answer. Sounds good?"

I nodded.

(＼(•̀w•́)／)

09:00

I considered it, I truly did.

I weighed my options, and talked to the lawyer, Sasha even let me talk to a few people on the team that was trying to recruit me.

It didn't sound so bad, it's better than being unemployed, and a million times better than prison time, plus the lawyer seemed to like the deal and Sasha was very open to his negations, so I signed it.

Not even fifteen minutes later they let me leave without another word about it.

Drew ran to hug and kiss me the very second she could see me walking through the door.

"Are you okay?" We asked each other at the same time, then started laughing.

Parker ran over, shoving Drew over so he could jump on me like an overly excited dog, "Oh, my God, I missed you so much!"

I awkwardly pat his back, "It wasn't even twelve hours."

"I thought we'd never see you again!"

"That's... Thanks." I shooed him off.

Aaron was trying to hobble over on a crutch, he looked like hell, a black eye and several bandages dotted his face, and he looked like he was in a lot of pain just standing there.

I tried to help him, but he stopped me, "Are you okay?"

"Yeah, why?" He still joked with a big grin, "Just a couple hundred stitches, a little surgery and a few bruised ribs, it's all good."

I gave him as gentle of a hug as I could, "I'm so sorry, I'm glad you're okay."

"They put him on Percocet," Parker crossed his arms, "He's great! Hell, I'd chop off my left nut for a bottle of those."

Nate chuckled, "Based on your batting average, you should consider it."

"Huh?"

"Caitlin's pregnant!"

"Yeah? I know that. I don't get it."

Nate opened the driver's door of Drew's car and pointed at me, "Don't fucking leave me with that pendejo anymore. ¡Chingao!"

Once we got Aaron situated in the backseat Drew gave me another quick kiss.

"Okay," She wiped her lip gloss off my lip, "Can you please explain to me what happened? I tried to bail you out and they said you had no bail, but no one could tell me why."

"Yeah, all of our charges got dropped, even Aaron's, I mean! Imagine fucking stabbing someone and pressing charges on us?!" Parker was still very agitated; I couldn't blame him.

"Apparently I had a warrant for hacking."

Aaron looked surprised, "*You* did? How? I thought you said that was only for morons and a rookie mistake?"

Subconsciously, I shot Parker a glare.

"So, why'd they let you out?" Nate asked, glancing at me in the rearview mirror.

"Well, I kinda work for the FBI now."

"Que mierda?!"

Parker had to grab the wheel from him before he drove us into the building.

Aaron

Conner tried to casually explain everything to us, but between Nate's random bouts of yelling "Fuckin Feds", Parker having an off-topic question every five seconds, and then with the amount of pain I was in, not a lot was making sense.

"Hang on," Parker whipped around to look at us, "Did you really kick out a squad car window?"

Conner turned bright red but shrugged, "They said I wasn't a threat."

Drew kissed his nose, "Court would be so proud."

They started another conversation, but my pain quickly overwhelmed it.

"Sweetie," Drew leaned over Conner to get my attention, "I really think you should take one of your pills."

I shook my head, "I took some Tylenol."

"Aaron," She said softly even though she wanted to smack me, "You had a ligation of the femoral artery and vein, a fasciotomy, laceration repair, a skin graft, and a blood transfusion, Tylenol isn't going to help with that. They gave you pain killers for a reason."

Parker clicked his tongue, "They're not even good pain killers, you couldn't even get high if you wanted to."

"I know, but it's a slippery slope and that's why I gave them to Drew in the first place."

"And you trusted me to keep you on a schedule, right? I'm telling you need a pill." She took my hand, put a pill in it, and gave me a serious look, "The teach us how to administrate pills on particular tricky cats, so you better take it."

"Ooh, so there's an anal option?" Parker joked.

The pain also overwhelmed the little voice that said this was a bad idea, so I took it and tried my hardest not to think about it too much.

Which was easy, since Nate had just pulled up to our building and having to climb the four flights of stairs suddenly felt like a cruel test of faith from a power-hungry god.

Nate helped me stand while Parker fumbled with the key.

Parker's hand dropped off the door handle as soon as he opened it, I couldn't see around him, but I could tell something wasn't right by his posture.

"What the fuck?"

He took a few steps forward and we finally saw what he was reacting to.

Nothing.

Literally nothing, there was nothing in the entire apartment, our couch was gone, Conner's desk, our bookshelf and all the books on it, not even our fridge made it out unscathed.

Drew gasped, Nate swore, but Conner stayed completely silent as he walked through the empty space.

"Guys," Nate called us into the equally empty bedroom, "Mira," He pointed at the window.

A piece of paper was taped to it with a single word scrawled, "Checkmate"

Parker snatched it down, tore it up in a fit of rage, and then punched a hole in the wall.

I waited for Conner to reprimand him, but it never came.

Conner knelt; he practically sank into himself.

Drew rubbed his back, "Are you okay?"

"It was all of my mom's stuff, my dad's stuff... It's all gone."

"But it's just evidence, they'll give it back, right?"

"It's not coming back, Andrew." Conner straightened out but he looked like he wanted to fall over, "The cops don't have it, Donatello does, and I'm never seeing any of it again."

"GOD FUCKING DAMN IT!!!" Parker screamed loud enough to make the neighbor's dog down the hall start barking, "I should've killed him! I should've fucking killed him! Why?! Why didn't I?!"

"Reign it in," Conner snapped.

"Hang on now," Drew commanded our attention, "We're not giving up so easily. Let's go back to my mom's, get Aaron off that leg, call Agent Sasha. Even if there's nothing, she can do we need to report this and see where we go from here.

"But"

She stopped Conner by wagging her finger, "You're big, bad Mr. FBI now, even if we have to rewrite it all ourselves, no one is cheap shotting us into giving up."

(＼(•̀w•́)／)

09:50

Aaron

While Conner called his new boss, Drew bullied me until I agreed to sit down then threatened Parker with the TV remote if he tried to take it from me again.

Nate came back from the kitchen with a bag of chips and his phone in his other hand.

He hit me on the arm, and held his phone up in front of me so I could hear his mom yelling at him in a Spanish rage.

"Thanksgiving," Nate mouthed covering the mouthpiece, "This shit ain't even on speaker!"

I groaned, "I was able to convince my mom I was "working" on Thanksgiving but I'm going to have to tell her eventually, and if I show up on crutches, she may never let me leave her sight again."

Nate snorted, "I don't even remember when Thanksgiving happened, like I know it was a Thursday, but... Yeah, I'm still here." He rolled his eyes at his phone, "No, 'cause you were yelling at me, Ma! Mom? Mom... There's a fire, gotta go, love you, bye!" He hung up and blew out his breath.

"That's great, you should call my mom next." Parker said flatly.

Conner was back and Drew's ears perked up.

"What did she say?"

Conner sighed, "She said most of it had been turned over to them since they took over my case, but she didn't want to promise me anything."

"Baby, that's great, why are you upset?"

He shrugged, "It's a stupid mistake and too close of a call, this wouldn't have happened if everything was still in Byre with my grandma."

Conner's father's laugh echoed in my ears before he appeared next to his son, "As if we haven't lost those damned books a hundred times ourselves."

"C'est comme ça, c'est stupide." Celeste shrugged in response.

"It's okay," Drew assured him before I could relay the message, "There's no way you could've known this would happen."

"Hang on," I tried to readjust how I was sitting so I could turn to look at him, "Drew said something earlier that I've been thinking about; between, well, all of us and probably your grandma, what if we did rewrite it just to compile it all together?"

Drew was enthusiastic, "I've read most of it too, and I'm sure my mom would have some stuff to add."

Parker crossed his arms, "You've been making me keep a journal for the past year, you better do something with it."

Conner nodded as he thought it through, "That would be pretty cool, I mean, then the Stephens legacy is broader than just me. Is that really something you guys would want to..."

Parker's attention span had weaned and so he started turning up the TV over us.

Conner rolled his eyes, "Really? It wouldn't kill you to listen to me, you know that, right?"

"Sh sh, shush, shut up, look." Parker waved his hands around, so we'd look at the TV.

Donnie sat on the colorful sofa of the morning talk show, the smile on his face easily led you to believe this was an entirely different person than the one we dealt with last night. He looked his age, young and naive, as if the deepest secret he harbored lied between him and his college roommate.

Parker unwaveringly watched the TV, visibly trembling with rage

"Good morning, Emerald City!" The host on the other side of the couch greeted the camera, "It's the top of the hour and the top of our morning! Grab your coffee and settle in 'cause we've got a high of 38° and an exclusive interview right here after the title." The screen darkened and played an intro.

Parker was inconsolable, Conner had to grab him before he broke the TV.

"Calm down,"

"Nuh-uh!" Parker tried to wiggle away from him, "I'll kill him from The Today Show to fucking TRL! I don't fucking care!"

"I do! If you break Mrs. Hart's TV, you're gonna have to replace it, do you have 900 bucks?"

Parker only calmed down because Conner pinned his arms above his head, "No,"

"Are you going to behave?"

"Probably not."

Conner shot him a look and Parker sighed.

"Fine! Yeah, I'll calm down!"

By the time Conner let him go the show was back on.

"So, Donnie," The host started, "As you know, we've been trying to interview you for years. What's changed?"

"Well, I've never really had much to say before."

"Oh, come on, now that can't be true! What about all your charity work? Or the obvious fact that you're one of the youngest billionaires in the world?"

Parker had a hard time sitting still, but he stayed quiet.

"A man can do a lot of things, but that doesn't make him interesting, and money hardly makes someone interesting, I've just made a few lucky investments,"

"You own a corporation and eight... Right? You own eight small businesses here in Seattle? I would say that's far more than a few lucky investments!"

He waved the comment off with his hand, "Owner has such a harsh implication especially since I do none of the work. I love this city and the people in it,"

Parker rolled his eyes.

"Both have done so much for me, and I jump at every chance I get to give back. I know what it was like, my father and I would sheer sheep and go sell the wool, and maybe then, on a lucky day, we could afford bread for our dinner. Back then someone saw something special in me, I took that opportunity and look where I am, now it's my turn to find that something special in others."

"And that's what your hotel is, right?"

"It's more of a hostel that I'm working on, but yes, I want to help those who can't help themselves. And well, that's part of the reason I decided to finally do a proper interview, I wanted to speak about the future of the hostel,"

"Please, yes, tell us everything."

"Construction has taken much longer than I had expected but I do believe we're getting close!" His excitement seemed so out of place, "But it's a big project and, unfortunately, not something I can do alone. So, as part of other revelations I've had recently, I've decided to donate the building to the city with, of course, the money to continue the renovations and to also run it as I intended."

"Wow, that is..." The host shook her head, "I'm speechless, that's just so generous! What made you decide to do that?"

"Well, I've thought on it a lot and as I'm recently married..."

There was a pause full of gasps from the host and the in-studio audience alike.

"Congratulations! When did that happen?" Asked the host excitedly.

"It's been a few months now, she's..." He laughed, "What can I say? She's a firecracker, but we *are* very private, so we weren't too keen on making much of a fuss about it. But as I was saying, we want to settle down and start a family soon,"

"Bullshit!" Parker yelled at the TV with his arms crossed.

"And so, I believe the Seattle chapter of my life is over. I've been away from home for far too long now..." He paused for a second, like he said something he didn't mean to.

The host pounced on it immediately, "Where is home for you?"

He paused for a minute longer, I would've sworn I saw his facade slip and a glimpse of genuine emotion appear on his face, but it could have been my pain meds, "I couldn't tell you where "home" is, if I'm being quite honest, I think I lost that years ago... But to answer your question, I've done a lot of work here and I think it's time to turn that success onto the village in Romania that grew me into the person I am now."

"When you say that you think your Seattle chapter is over..."

"It's for the time being," Donnie clarified, "I don't expect this to be a proper move but perhaps more of a pivot. All though Seattle has become my home, I feel as though I've lost something here, I'm hoping to find more easily in Romania, though should that search not be as fruitful I know I can return to the particular gem that I've found here." He smiled at the camera, "Or I should say I *will* return for that."

Parker shot to his feet, his knuckles clenched so tightly they turned white, but he didn't continue to move or say anything.

"So that's it? You're really going to leave Seattle?" The host seemed genuinely saddened by the news.

"Only for a few years, don't worry, I never leave anything unfinished."

With that, Parker tried to hurdle the back of the couch, but Conner caught him by his belt.

"Where are you going?"

"I'm!!!" Parker growled loudly, "Ugh! I don't know! I'm gonna go find him! This isn't the end! It doesn't end like this! He doesn't get to win!"

"No one's won." I shook my head and mostly mumbled to myself as I thought of all the lives that had been lost in the past few months.

"Exactly!" Conner's voice brought me back down, "He's running, can't you see that? We did the impossible, we've shaken him. We just have to give it a minute, he's going to slip up again, and this time we'll be ready."

Parker wasn't convinced, swaying back and forth on his heels he made it obvious he was ready to bolt.

"Give me a week," Conner spoke fast trying to reason with Parker, "Give me a week, let me see what I can dredge up, okay? I just need some time... And a computer."

"Fine, do whatever you want, I'm going back out there, I'm finding this motherfucker."

"Parker, you know that's not a good idea."

"What the fuck else am I supposed to do? Why not?!"

Conner's eyes widened to indicate the massive elephant in the room Parker was missing, "Because this time last week you were shivering in a puddle of your own blood! Yesterday you found out you're having a baby, and then you came narrowly close to killing your stalker! Sorry, but yeah! I'm worried about you."

Parker stared at him for a long minute, then quickly pulled his hand away and zipped down the hall and slammed the door instead of running out of the house.

Conner and Nate both got up to go try and talk him down, but Drew stopped them.

"It's okay, let him have a minute," She sighed, "There's not a window or anything in there anyway, it's a linen closet."

(＼(•̀w•́)／)

10:15

Nate

I think we were all suspicious that Parker was about to suffer some kinda psychotic break, so we tried to give him some space, which was ironic since he locked himself in a closet.

When it was obvious he wasn't coming out anytime soon, Drew stretched, "Well, I'm going to go make breakfast."

"I can help," Conner followed her into the kitchen.

Aaron hit me with his big ol' puppy eyes.

"Que paso, perrito?"

"Will you go check on Parker?"

I made a show outta sighing, "When'd I become the bitch wrangler?" I joked.

"Do I really gotta say it?" He asked making a move like he was gonna get up.

I put my hand on his forehead and pushed him back down onto the couch, "Cochino, fine, I'm goin'."

Parker did that thing where he tried to be quiet, so I didn't think he was in there when I knocked on the door.

"Park, it's a fuckin' closet."

"Go away, I'm brooding!"

I opened the door anyway, "Man, you really gotta work on your storm offs."

"I thought this was a bathroom," He crossed his arms over the pillow he was clutching to his chest, "And what're you doing, I told you to go away!"

"Yeah, so?" I reached over him and grabbed a comforter down from the top shelf and threw it at him. He'd already made himself a bed out of pillows and towels, so I considered it a contribution.

"Move," I tapped him with my shoe.

"Get out!"

I kicked him lightly now, "Shut up, my head hurts, jackass." I sat on floor and moved the comforter around 'til I was comfortable.

"Sorry, how's your head?"

"One girl said sloppy but enthusiastic."

He snorted, "Don't make me laugh, I'm mad!"

"Get over it."

He glared at me.

"What? Not like you're the only one being fucked with. Air's got a bigger axe to grind than you do for Christ's sake, he got stabbed and I got whatever's Latin for a concussion."

"That's what pisses me off! You guys shouldn't be involved! Neither should Drew or Caitlin, or the greater Seattle area!"

I grabbed him by the face and shook, "I'm only gonna say this one more time, puta. He fucks with you he fucks with all of us, we signed up for this shit."

"Fuck, you're hot when you're mad."

"Shut up, *cállate*."

He cackled, "You just blushed! Holy shit, that's adorable."

I pulled him in by his shirt and kissed him just to get him to shut the fuck up.

He did this thing with his tongue, and I had to push him off of me.

Parker gave me a weird look, "What? I thought you liked that?"

"I'm not fucking you in a fucking closet, fucker."

He gave me a weirder look and then he got that little bitch smirk that made me wanna slap him, "Ohh, you gotta stop before you can't kinda thing, huh?"

He bit his lip and got closer to my face, "So you'll only let me blow you in the car, and you'll fuck me in the shower, but not in a closet?"

He laughed to himself while he kissed my neck.

"Don't you got a girl?" I asked, but didn't push him off.

"No, if anything I got a baby mama." He pulled away, annoyed, blowing his hair out of his face, "What's that have to do with anything?"

I scoffed, "If a girl told me that I'd might as well join a monastery 'cause my dick'd never talk to me again."

He shrugged, "What do you want from me? I'm self-destructive! And instead of feeling fucking anything I just wanna fuck and do drugs and kill someone! But no one will fucking let me!"

"So this is you processing?"

He put his head on my chest with a whimper, "Will you get me some pills?"

"Nah,"

"Coke?" "No," "LSD?" "No," "MDMA" "No," "GHB?" "No," "Special K?" "No," "Meth?" "No," "Weed?" "No," "Bath salts?" "No," "Crack?"

"Fuck's wrong with you?"

"I ate a crack rock once! What do you want?! What about heroin? I won't even bitch about the needles!"

"Nope,"

"C'mon, booze?! A fucking cigarette?! I need anything! Aaah!" He screamed, got hella tweaky for a second, flailed around, and outta nowhere, just sat on the floor completely silent.

This was, no doubt, the psychotic break.

"I don't know, I don't know, I don't know! I mean yeah, like this is fucked up and weird but like... I don't know, I'm kinda... Glad?"

No *this* was the break.

"Que mierda, you're glad?!"

"I don't know!" He threw his arms out, "Like yeah, I think having a kid's gonna be cool, but it still scares me shitless. I just, I don't know..." He mumbled again, "I always kinda thought I'd be a dad." He said real quiet.

I straight up didn't know what to say to that.

"God, it sounds crazy, but I've... Fantasized about it, getting cleaned up or whatever, meeting someone who'd, y'know, not kick my ribs in."

It was weird to hear this from him of all people, but I was surprised he'd never mentioned it before, "You never told me that."

"But yeah right, what kind of dad could I ever be? How the fuck could I ever get clean? Fuck, vampire disease aside, who wants a literal junkie whore? It's stupid."

"It ain't stupid, you could do whatever the fuck you wanted to. Hey, you're already doing better than my asshole dad he took off when my mom told him she was pregnant. And hey it's pretty obvious you know what not to do. 'Sides," I cleared my throat, "Who doesn't wanna meet the perfect girl and have it all?"

He put his hand on my face, and gave me that feral street puppy look, "It doesn't have to be a girl."

"But it should be, that's what'cha got, it's what you want, you should take it. You've gotten a lotta second chances, I'd hate for this to be the one you walk away from."

He pressed his lips flat like he was unimpressed, "You really think I could be a dad?"

"Hell, if not you got another junkie in there and two whores to help you out." I shrugged, throwing my hand over my shoulder towards the living room, "Same thing with the vamp-ness, same thing with Donnie, and with Court, we don't got the answers now but we're working on it, not a lot of people can say that."

His eyes watered, but he laughed and wrapped himself around me, "I still wanna plow you so bad right now, but like *I love you.*"

"Yeah, sure," I pat the top of his head, "That's enough." I stood up but he still clung on.

The door opened a crack, and Drew weaseled her head in with her hand over her eyes, "When you guys get a sec, I made breakfast."

She quickly shut the door, and I pried Parker off of me.

Conner

I helped Aaron get comfortable while Drew handed Nate and Parker their plates.

"Eggs and potatoes," She looked at Parker's plate with a shrug, "I'm still kinda unclear about what you eat, but Conner said you don't like fruit or oatmeal so... Extra potatoes."

"Don't let him bullshit you, he drinks whole milk." Nate was already on his second bite before Drew had even let go.

"And cheesecake." Aaron piled on.

"And bacon." I added.

"Hey, who asked you?!" Parker stuck his tongue out and then kissed Drew on the cheek, "It's great, thanks Mom!"

I rolled my eyes and gave Aaron his plate.

In the brief second my eyes were off him, Parker's plate and fork crashed against the hardwood floor.

I expect him to be screwing around, but when I glanced over, he was cringing in pain.

"Are you okay?" I went to help him while Drew got a broom.

The doorbell rang and Parker stumbled to his feet even though he was unsteady.

"Don't get that!" Parker yelled at Drew who was peeking out of the window in the door.

"It's just some girl? Oh shoot, she saw me." She looked at us with wide eyes.

I made him sit back on the couch and went to stand by Drew as she opened the door.

"Hi, can I help you?" She was her usual sweet self while I was probably painfully obvious about being on the defensive.

"Hi, good morning. I'm sorry to intrude," The girl on the other side of the door matched Drew's niceties, but I was still taken off guard since she looked more like Courtney than I was expecting, "I was actually hoping to talk to Parker."

Parker moved his body in a strangely exorcist way in an attempt to see her from the couch but ultimately gave up and ran over to the door.

He clearly didn't like who he saw, he moved in front of me and Drew, "Do I know you?"

"We met once," She answered, "Well, technically twice, but you wouldn't recognize me from that. I gave you Donnie's immigration records, that ring a bell?"

"Right, you're one of Donnie's girls."

"I'm nobody's girl," She clearly didn't like the suggestion, "Look, I could easily rip out your throats and have a nice little mid-morning snack, but instead I'm standing out here in the cold with the sun burning a frickin' hole into the back of my neck just to give you good news."

Parker crossed his arms, "And what's that?"

"Donnie's officially throwing in the towel."

Park held his defensive stance, "So I've heard. What do you really want?"

"Enemy of my enemy and all that. If you brought me the same news I'd kiss you."

"I'm supposed to just trust you, then?"

"Nope, any relationship needs a healthy dose of skepticism, but why would I, one singular vampire in a tiny mortal vessel, walk into the house of a hunter, with three other hunters, a witch and a strigoi that could scramble my brains with one look, all staring me down, and try to cause problems? Not in my best interest and also, hey; *fucking stupid!*"

Drew turned her head to make it less obvious that she was whispering to me, "Do you have your gun?"

I nodded.

"Hey, if you wanna bring guns to the table, I've got no problem with that so long as I get a seat at the table."

Parker and I exchanged a look.

Park probed, "Why do you hate Donatello so much?"

"Uh, how long you got?" She blew out a breath, "The cliff notes, let's see; owes me money like a lot of money, destroyed my nest, stiffed me on this whole vampire deal, let my girlfriend die, killed most of my employees and friends, ate my familiar, he just won't fucking die, gave me a Pepsi instead of Coke, air pollution, global warming, natural disasters, my favorite show was cancelled, that thing where you're just starting to fall asleep and you jerk yourself awake, and he was a selfish lover. Want me to keep going? I blame him for everything, I could literally do this all day."

Parker fought to hide his smirk, "Fine, we can talk."

She waited for Drew to nod before she stepped into the house.

Now that I could see her without the sun behind her, I realized she didn't look as much like Courtney, yes, she was small, and her hair was a shade of blonde that only happened seconds before a severe chemical burn, but that was where the similarities stopped. Her skin was more golden, her face was tiny, and her eyes were a dark brown.

"I remember you," Aaron watched her close.

"Hi, doll." She raised her hand in a gentle wave, her smile quickly turned to gritted teeth, "My girls really did a number on you, you poor thing. I really am sorry."

Parker squinted at her, "Harley, right?"

"Hayley," She corrected him, "But it's fake, it's actually Valentine... Well, for now, at least."

"What do you mean by 'your girls'?"

"What? Don's the only one allowed to have a vampire refuge?" She shrugged, "I have a cute little Charlie's Angels situation going for me. It's mostly for rapists and child abusers, basically we offer our services to women who are put in a tough spot. But *ironically,* Donnie's been taking advantage of us for years."

"So, all the people he's killed? That's you?"

She crossed her arms, "I'll admit I handled a few, yeah. But once I realized we were going after innocents, then my girls and I started pulling our punches."

"That's not what I felt yesterday." Nate scoffed.

"Sorry, my girls got a little sweet on ya. Must be the blue eyes," She winked at him, "For what it's worth, I'm sorry. You guys look like hell, but it would have been dangerous for Donnie to know we were shifting our stance on him."

"Okay?" Parker crossed his arms, annoyed, "Doesn't help me at all, so dish, sis."

"Hang on, before you think I'm just as ill-mannered," She dropped her canvas bag down from her shoulder to her hand, "I don't come empty handed, where can I put this?"

Drew pointed to the kitchen, and she followed, giving Drew a glance over as she did.

"Oh, you're human. How cute."

"So, what are you?" Parker retorted.

Valentine raised an eyebrow, but decided to make a joke instead, "Vietnamese, Japanese, and one sixteenth Dutch."

I stayed close behind as did Parker while Nate helped Aaron along.

I watched Valentine closely as she dumped her bag on the table and took a seat. She was playing nice, but it would be stupid for any of us to buy it.

"So," She drummed her fingers against the table, "I'm here to offer you a deal."

There was a long pause.

"Oh, c'mon! It's a joke, remember those? God, you guys are too serious. Anyway, I'm supposed to just come down here and give you guys the message that Donnie's done chasing his tail with you guys, but then I figured, hey why not cash in on his little fuck up."

Parker shook his head, "Six months he put us through hell, and I'm just supposed to believe some girl he screwed over that he's done?"

"You don't have to believe me, but I'm serious, he's found love or Jesus, or something gross like that." She shrugged, "To be fair, I think you guys got dangerously close to ending him finally! He genuinely doesn't know what to do with that. He's scared" she thought for a moment "and he's running." She said almost in awe.

"What are we supposed to do with that?" Parker asked.

"Whatever you want, doesn't matter to me. I happen to know he left the country, scrubbed every trace of himself there is in the US database, so he doesn't really have much to comeback to, I mean other than you me and the 99,998 others he's fucked over."

"So... That's it? That's... This is just how it ends?" Parker was up and pacing, "No, no, this can't be, this *isn't* how it ends."

"I really wish I had something better to tell you. God knows the only thing I want from that man is to use his head as a pen holder on my desk. But the good news in the bad news is that he has a habit of giving people the silent treatment when he's pissed, which means we've got plenty of time to pool our resources and *actually* end this when he does come back."

"That's what you want, then? I'm supposed to join your team instead of his?"

"Nope, I don't want you guys anywhere near my team, no offense. I just wanna hedge my bets and make sure that when the asshat does come back, I'm not the only one trying to end this."

Parker crossed his arms, and gave her a suspect look, "Obviously."

"Good, good."

"That's it?"

She shrugged again, "I did swipe a few of Donnie's things before he sanitized the place. Consider it an olive branch,"

Nate finally spoke up, and wanted to know the important things, "Who's the wife? Some A-lister?"

She dug through her bag, "Chloe? Claire? Britney? Who knows, it's like spouse number twelve, and at this point I don't keep up anymore. Here," She took a laptop out of her bag and slid it across the table in my direction.

It felt like a weird double handed trick, so I tried to seem as uninterested as I truly was, "My laptop? You can't be serious."

"Why not? I'm not an asshole and I don't really have a use for any of it." She handed a sketchpad to Parker, Aaron his walk-man, and Nate a giant Ziploc of weed I was disappointed to see again.

She hesitated then she looked at Drew, she was holding a slip of paper she went to hand it to Drew, not quite being able to give it to her she ended up leaving it on the table, "I also pulled some strings, paid off some friends in high places Donnie kept around, asked them to do a proper search..." Her pause wouldn't have been apparent, but since it felt like she was watching us for a reaction it was glaringly obvious.

Valentine gave the paper, a business card for a detective with Seattle Police, to me instead of Drew, but still addressed her, "I'm sorry, doll, but they did find something... I'm sure you'll be called down to the police station sometime later to identify the body. I don't recommend you go alone."

I could feel Drew's hand start to shake as she took the card from me, but she didn't let it show on her face, "And this is...?"

"Donnie's connection, if you guys need anything, well, she's a cop so that's a strike against her, but she's a damn fine detective. I'm sure you'll speak with her sooner or later but if not, I wanted you to have that ace up your sleeve, too."

Drew only nodded the once and squeezed my hand under the table.

"So, now what?" Parker asked.

"Dunno, besides aren't you the psychic?" She joked, "Right, you don't take to jokes so well. I'm sure in a few weeks, months, years, decades, whatever, Donnie'll get bored and decide he wants to play with his favorite toy again."

"And?"

"*And?*" She echoed back in surprise, "And we'll be ready to cut that little fucker from throat to scrote, huh? So, you do your hunter thing, I'll do my vampire mistress thing, and we can call each other if the other gets any leads, cool?" Valentine stood, pushing herself off the table, "Cool, babies."

She held up her hand and wiggled her fingers, "Toodles."

As soon as I blinked, she disappeared from the room.

Parker let his hands slam down against the table, "What the fuck just happened?!"

"She didn't even leave a phone number." Aaron had the audacity to find this slightly funnier (which it was) than Parker deemed acceptable, which resulted in a third-degree glare.

(＼(•̀ᴡ•́)／)

19:50

Conner

I spent most of the day scouring through my laptop, I was amazed that everything was still on it and untouched, which made me more skeptical than relieved, so I spent the rest of my time scrubbing absolutely everything off it and scanning it for spyware before I felt comfortable using it for anything.

Then came the call from the police.

It came later, after Mrs. Hart had insisted on making us dinner, as Drew and I were washing dishes.

Mrs. Hart didn't need to say a single word, her expression made it crystal clear what was happening.

I felt dizzy, and anything that was said after that I couldn't hear.

I had thought that Valentine was just preying on our easily exposed nerves.

And part of me, the part that knew now there was no way I could deny that Courtney was gone, the part that knew I couldn't keep pretending that she was just in New Jersey, the part that would have to tell the guys, the part of me that now knew I would have to bury my best friend, as terrible as it sounded, all those of those parts had wished that this day would never come.

Drew begged me to go with them, I agreed and did my best to tell her everything would be okay, but I wasn't sure anything after this would ever be okay again.

The cops wouldn't let me in the room with them since I wasn't immediate family, but they let me sit in the blank and morbidly gray hallway to wait for them.

No one had to tell me, I could hear Drew scream from down the hall.

Then it all came rushing back, holding her in my arms.

The warmth of her blood pooling around me.

The sound of her laugh being drowned out by the rattle in her chest.

I wanted to scream, too.

December 10 2007

17:00

PARKER

All of us took a pretty hard hit after Conner told us they'd found Courtney.

I wished I hadn't asked so many questions, more than anything I'd wished that Mrs. Hart hadn't told us that she had to sign a paper agreeing to release Courtney's dental records because everything else was too badly decomposed to identify her any other way.

Everything seemed to get worse after that; Aaron complained about his pain a lot more, Conner really threw himself into trying to find Donatello without remembering to sleep or eat, and I don't think Nate said more than a hundred words in a week. And I kept slipping up, sneaking out in the middle of the night to go drink or do drugs like I was in high school again.

I was embarrassed, Hell I knew the guys could tell I was tweaking out of my skull, but the emotional pain was way too much for me to even know how to deal with it properly.

Then Caitlin called a few days ago and asked if I could go with her to the doctor, suddenly, I had a whole new thing to cry over.

It's... Funny, really. How fast things can change.

I tried to think about it one of the nights that I couldn't sleep, I tried to compare the person I was when Courtney first met me verses who I was a few days before we lost her, then to who I felt like I was now...

If I'm completely honest, at first, I didn't think there was really much of a difference, but the more I thought about it the more I realized that, for the first time in my life I felt hopeful, and I was excited about my future.

But at the same time, I felt like I was at one of the lowest points of my life.

I was both the saddest and happiest I'd ever been and I wished I could pin point literally anything that I was feeling but it all just came at me like a tsunami, and it wasn't just one thing, it wasn't looking at the guys and realizing I wasn't as alone as I thought I was, it wasn't even getting to hear the heartbeat of my unborn baby, it wasn't losing a friend or the love of my life, it was everything but it was nothing at the same time.

Nothing was different, but everything was changing, and it changed so fucking fast.

No one is the same person they used to be, even from five minutes ago, and maybe that's the good thing.

Maybe that's what keeps us alive.

Maybe that's what keeps us human...

Maybe that's what kept *me* human?

All I know is sometimes duality is a cruel bitch.

I brought Caitlin back to the house with me and everyone flocked us, the second we walked through the door.

Caitlin looked at me with wide eyes and tried to hide the fear in her voice, "I take it you told everyone...?"

Drew gave me a sharp look, "Only a little bit."

"Sorry," Mrs. Hart giggled to herself while she shooed everyone away from Caitlin, "We're a little baby crazy in this family."

Caitlin laughed while I took her coat and told her to go sit down, "You're fine, but here I was thinking Parker was being overzealous."

"Do you mind if I ask how far along you are?" Mrs. Hart asked.

"Um," Caitlin squinted while she thought, "Five weeks, right?"

"Seven," I corrected her, "We got to hear the heartbeat! And we saw him!"

"Wait for me!" Aaron screamed from the kitchen.

Mrs. Hart laughed at him, "Are you having morning sickness yet?"

"Mm, you know, the morning sickness hasn't been too bad, but the afternoon and evening sickness, however..."

"But! She's starting to get a bump. Look," I pulled her shirt up and put my hands on her belly.

"Parker!" She batted my hands away and tugged her shirt back down, "I'm glad you're excited, but your hands are cold, and I'd rather not show everyone in the room my bra!"

"It's fine, it's your cute bra, anyway."

Aaron awkwardly staggered in as fast as he could while Conner followed close behind making sure he didn't fall over.

"Pictures?"

I pulled the ultrasound out of my pocket and Aaron snatched it, "You can't really see him, but he's the size of a raspberry!"

"Oh, my God, I love raspberries." Air pushed up his glasses and squinted at the image, then a light bulb went off and he got excited again, "I'm gonna send this to my mom!"

Con's eyes widened, "AARON WAIT!"

He didn't even slow down.

"Well, his mom's gonna have a nice panic attack." Con pressed his lips into a line.

Nate laughed, "She's gonna kill him."

Mrs. Hart just shook her head and asked, "When are you due?"

"He's coming late June," I answered, "Maybe July."

"We don't know it's a boy." Caitlin nudged me, "We're not gonna know for a few months."

"I'm the only boy of six! It'd just be weird if it wasn't a boy."

"No, you're not." Con crossed his arms.

"Huh?"

"You have a brother?" He reminded me.

"Oh, shit, right."

Cat's phone started to ring, and she sighed, "Great, I should probably go before someone realizes I'm not in my office."

"I'll walk you out." I offered.

She thanked Mrs. Hart on our way out and then we didn't say anything for the half a block to her car.

If it was a lot for me to process, I couldn't imagine what she was feeling, so I tried my best to just keep my dumbassery to myself.

"Thanks for coming with me." She finally broke the silence.

I nodded, "Yeah, it was cool, I'm glad I did... Sorry I blabbed to everyone."

She gave me a half smile as she opened her car door, "Don't worry about it, I'm really glad you're excited."

"Really? It's not too much?"

She shrugged, "Maybe, but I kinda like that you're too much."

I didn't know what to say so I just nodded, "Call me later? I'll bring over dinner, or ice cream, or something, anything you want."

She nodded back, "That sounds nice."

There was an awkward minute where we just stared at each other.

"Parker,"

"Yeah, I know... I'm going."

"No," She rolled her eyes, "Come on, I'm the mother of your child, you're not gonna make me ask for a kiss, are you?"

"Hell no, actually don't think about it anymore."

She laughed as I kissed her and it made me laugh, too.

It was probably the worst kiss ever, but it was weirdly sweet.

She moved the hair out of my eyes, "I'll call you after work."

"Awesome."

I waited for her to pull out of the street before I went back to the house.

Conner was on the couch laying across Drew's lap while she combed her fingers through his hair, "Don't think I'm pushing you guys because I know my mom loves having you all here, but I was kinda wondering what you're going to do? I mean, apartment wise?"

I decided to give them a sec before I interrupted.

Con sighed heavily, "I really have no idea, none of us really have the money to replace our furniture..."

She stopped him, "Well, I kinda had an idea. I'm pretty set on staying here with Mom, but my apartment still has a few months on the lease, and my roommate just left so you guys would have both rooms, plus furniture. Although, I really think we should talk about getting you and Nate separate beds though."

"He'll miss me." Nate only answered 'cause Aaron was kicking his ass in whatever card game they were playing.

Con ignored him anyway, "Really? We can do that?"

"Of course, I mean you guys can't be too loud and if anything breaks, you'll have to call me and I'll call the landlord, but hey the kitchen tap isn't rusted, and you won't have to rat check the shower."

Conner sat up just to grab her and kiss her, "God, I love you."

Drew giggled, "I love you, too."

"Puke!" I joked and made a point of squeezing between them.

"Two words *pregnant girlfriend,* I don't wanna hear it." Con rolled his eyes.

"She's not my girlfriend." I booped his nose.

"Seriously?" Drew added, "She's pregnant."

I shrugged.

"That reminds me," Conner sat up right, "I think we need to talk about something,"

I chewed on the inside of my cheek, "Yeah..."

"You know what about?"

"Well, I'm guessing this isn't the 'how babies are made' talk."

"This isn't a joke,"

I sighed and squirmed once everyone started staring at me, "Yeah, I know... I know you guys know I'm using again, and I know I'm a fucking mess, God, I have been for a long fucking time. I wanna stop... I'm gonna stop."

"Parker, I'm not judging you, none of us are. I just need you to know this is serious and you've told us that a lot."

"I know... This week got away from me and I-I fucked up, I get that. But this time's different, and I really mean it. Seriously. I do."

"Good, because we're out of options after this. If it keeps happening, we're going to have to talk about more extreme boundaries."

I had to just talk fast before I lost my nerve, "I thought about asking my parents for the money to go to rehab."

Con tried really hard not to look surprised, but he couldn't control Nate and Aaron's heads snapping to look at me.

"Why didn't you?"

I chewed on my nails and shrugged, "I don't know how to tell them how fucked up I really am, and I don't know how to tell you guys I'm fucking terrified of getting sober."

"Anything worth doing is going to be terrifying," Aaron offered, "But come on, we hunt vampires, if we can do that, we can do anything."

"It's just, I don't think I even know who I am without drugs or self-loathing. Like, I've been doing this shit since I was fifteen, eleven if you count cutting."

"Don't you think it's time to find that out?" He asked.

Nate tried his best to help, "It's kinda, I dunno, exciting, right? Finding something out 'bout yourself," He shrugged, then winked at me when he knew I was looking at him, "Pretty gratifying."

I didn't really know how to respond so I just nudged him with my shoe, "But what about Caitlin? She needs me and I wanna be there for her... And I can't leave you guys... I need you, too."

Air leaned as far forward as he could to grab my hand, "There are plenty of rehabs that you can do as an outpatient, that's how I finished high school."

I nodded while I thought, then realized thinking's never been good for me and I knew I had to do all of this before the self-doubt crept back in, "Okay, I want to. I wanna do it."

"I'll make some calls later," Air squeezed my hand and looked at me with his big puppy eyes, "This is huge, and I'm really proud of you."

And that was my third reason to cry today.

Con hugged me and held onto me while I cried, "This is going to be great; I swear to you."

"He's right," Drew rubbed my back, "They both are."

Nate half-heartedly patted my leg, "You'll be fine."

Conner must've shot him a look 'cause then he added, "Jesus, what? It's not like he's gonna die in detox. He'll be fine!"

It took me a solid minute to get it together, I wiped my face on my shirt, "Okay, I said I'll do it. Now can we talk about something else? What are we gonna do about Donnie? Jesus, how am I gonna have a baby, hunt this prick, get sober, and hold down a job?"

Con tilted his head at me like Aaron usually does, "You're... Getting a job?"

"Well!" I shrugged, "Caitlin's gonna have to go on maternity leave eventually, and I don't have to eat but I'm sure her and the baby would like to."

Con laughed, "Definitely, I just didn't realize you had thought that far ahead."

"... I guess I didn't either."

"Anyway," Conner quickly changed the subject before I could fully freak out, "I've been trying to track him, well, as limited as I can without tipping off the FBI, and for all intents and purposes it really does seem like he's off the grid."

I couldn't believe it, "Seriously?"

I could tell he couldn't either, "Yeah, plus the city's crime rate has dropped down almost five percent, it's flat out bizarre."

"So... That's really it?"

"The words stick in my throat, but like Valentine said *for now.*"

I blew out a breath, I could be comfortable with "for now", Hell I could even be happy with "for now"

I chewed on my nails while I tried to think through everything that just happened, things seemed to be coming in waves, and I wondered if I really could time this right...

Then, as usual, I lost my train of thought.

"I know this is out of nowhere, but can I get your guys' thoughts on something?" I got up and flipped though my sketchbook, "I want another tattoo, and I guess now would be as good a time as any, right?"

I'd been working on it for a while, long before Donnie made everything disappear, it was a bat with its wings stretched out and a wooden stake in its claws, if you looked close enough the stake had our initials carved into it CAPN, with a little heart around it for Courtney and Drew.

"What do you guys think?"

"Dude," Nate took it from me, and held it over his ribs, "I been thinking of something for a flank piece."

Nate handed it to Aaron who laughed, "I think it'd be big enough to cover the stab wound scar, don't you?"

"You guys really piggy backing my tattoo right now?" I joked.

Air shrugged, "It would be a cool matching set, right?"

We all looked at Conner, probably all remembering the same memory of him insisting that tattoos just "wouldn't look right" on him.

He just chuckled, shaking his head, "What the hell? You know I'd do anything for my brothers."

"That's it! I'm getting the camera." Drew threatened us.

But then again maybe some things don't ever change.

There's a strange kind of life after death, and when I first heard that I thought it meant the people we leave behind when we die, but now that I've actually died, I realize now that's literal. And that's where I am.

I'm back from the dead, and no one can ever fucking take that from me.

My name's Parker Winston, and I've been alive for eighteen days.

Nate got the tattoo as soon as his next paycheck cleared.

Aaron's leg healed beautifully, and he decided to participate in an outpatient rehab with Parker, which both completed successfully.

Conner is thriving in his new job, he even published his first manuscript,

Drew graduated and started a residency at a local animal hospital, she also proposed to Conner later in the year. (He said yes!)

Parker and Caitlin are now officially dating, they welcomed a healthy baby boy, Jeremy Journey Winston, in the summer.

And Parker's vampiric treatment seems to be going well, but he still hasn't learned how to shape-shift.

Courtney was peacefully laid to rest, and her ashes were scattered around Barnegat Lighthouse State Park in New Jersey.

And Donatello wasn't heard from, not for a long time, at least.

But that's a story for another day...

After Word

There's no easy way to end a story, there's no good way to say goodbye, and there's no promised futures.

I don't know what the future holds, and Hell, I'm starting to think maybe I don't know what the past holds anymore.

I've always lived my life as fast and as ambitious as possible, but recently I've found myself looking in the review mirror more and more. The problem, though, is it's blurry.

I try to squint and adjust my eyes so much that by the time I look back to the road ahead of me that that's blurry now, too.

I've never been one for the phrase "lose the battle win the war" because I want a future that's certain, and I want it now. But more than anything, I want a past that's solid. One that's not fogged by others' lies, one that's true.

Hell or high water, I'm going to take that for myself, no matter how bloody or dirty it gets.

You can only try waking the dead or spend your time chasing ghosts for so long. Besides, Frida Kahlo put it best, "I wasn't ever fragile like a flower, I was fragile like a bomb."

And maybe I don't remember how it truly used to be or who we were without the rosy haze of these glasses, but if nothing else, know that I'm grateful for the time we had together.

I'll see you soon.

Xo xo Courtney ♡

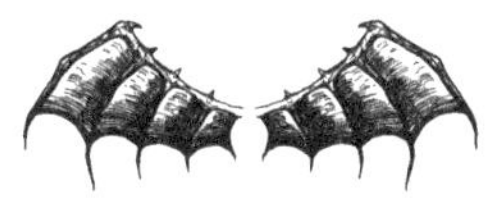

About the Author

Photo courtesy of Kara Cooper Photography

Gabrýel is a 22-year old author, artist, and musician based in Portland, Oregon, whose work dances between the realms of gothic allure and post-punk energy. A former high school valedictorian and poetry prodigy, she claimed nearly every accolade her high school had to offer, yet it's her unflinching exploration of identity and cultural intersections that defines her true voice. With a mixed-racial and queer upbringing steeped in religious paradox, Gabrýel's work is raw, evocative reflection of her experiences.

Her debut novel, *Holy Water Hurts: A Vampire's Guide to Vampire Hunting* (coming summer 2025), was penned while she was still in high school, offering a glimpse into a mind that's always been ahead of its time. As she blends gothic classics with her unique perspective, Gabrýel proves to be an exciting new voice in literature—one to watch as she continues to carve her own path in the shadows of both the literary and music worlds.

Bio courtesy of Mark Goretez, President of BBD (Board of Best Dads)
I love you, Dad.

www.ingramcontent.com/pod-product-compliance
Lightning Source LLC
Chambersburg PA
CBHW070646310726
48982CB00001B/440

* 9 7 9 8 2 1 8 6 6 3 9 1 9 *